The Horse

the Red Umbrella

By

Hugh Thomas

www.publishnation.co.uk

Acknowledgements

I would like to acknowledge and thank my first readers;

Dr Simon Cave, Andrew Rowles, Lady Rachael Billington, Jade, Penny, Kim and my sister, Christine, both for their time and their comment.

A big thank you goes to the town of Dorchester for its hospitality, which I extend to its townsfolk. In particular to John Fiori, owner of the cafe 'The Horse with the Red Umbrella' for the use of the title and front cover image.

I would also like to thank all the idiosyncratic, mad, unhinged, mean, generous, horrid, caring and thoughtful people who I have encountered throughout my life who have unknowingly contributed to the many and varied characters in this book, which is a work of fiction, other than when recalling historical events.

For,   Kim, KC, Skegs & Maisie

'All that glisters is not gold'

William Shakespeare (1564-1616)

'All that is gold does not glitter'

J R R Tolkien (1892-1973)

This book has been self-published and has therefore not had the benefit of a professional editor. Thus giving you the opportunity and experience to read it 'straight from the author'.

Please forgive any repetition or typos that have slipped through my net.

Hugh

PROLOGUE

DISTRACTIONS

In hindsight I believe it happened because I was distracted.

It was five am. The all encompassing darkness of the night had steadfastly refused to give way to the first timid hint of dawn. The rain was atrocious and the double speed windshield wipers were an irritant. I was tired, it had been a long and difficult night.

The phone call had not been unexpected, but it had still altered my mental equilibrium.

My thoughts had been lingering on the scene I'd left behind me, in the dressing rooms of one of London's most famous and gargantuan, internationally recognised arenas, it was a scene that reflected immoral and depraved behaviour. Post-concert the dressing room of one of our country's most idolised boy bands was outrageous, without doubt there was vomit, blood, urine, semen and the torn and discarded, flimsy underwear of young female fans who were the chosen ones, those who had been gifted entry into the dressing room to enjoy the after show drink and drug fuelled debauchery that was all too often the norm. I wondered, would a minority of these young girls live to have regrets and would the band members be facing prosecutions in middle age? A few moments of salacious pleasure exchanged for a life of angst and lament.

When the phone rang to interrupt my thoughts, it was my older sister Anne calling me to inform me that our father had died.

These elements, combined with an excess of recent rain in the southwest caused me not to see the vehicle whose engine and lights had failed moment's prior to my approach. A desperate swerve to the right, resulted in me crossing the road and hitting deep water at sixty-five miles an hour. I aquaplaned up onto a shallow but wide verge, destroying the low growth of plants in

1

its path, I then continued to drift to the right and into a deep water-filled ditch. The noise of the water hitting the windshield was shocking, the breaking of branches, the removal of the driver's wing mirror and the smashing of the windshield, traumatic.

The phone call had been deeply wounding.

The crescendo of crashing, breaking and smashing sounds lasted just eight seconds. It felt much longer. Those few seconds seemed to be in slow motion, did my past flash before his eyes? No. Did I believe my life would end in the next second? Yes. I expected the next tree, or significant branch to come through the front window and impale me. Once the eight seconds were over the van came to rest on its side, my side, in a deep, water filled ditch. I had no time to relish surviving the accident, thanks to my seatbelt and airbag. Water, black and very cold rapidly began to fill the vehicle, the night was very dark, the thick moisture laden cloud had completely obscured the moon and a plethora of stars. The vehicles engine and electrics had failed, I was cold, wet and in fear of my life, I released the seatbelt, the right half of my body now submerged in foul, almost freezing water. I used the centrally located fire extinguisher to break the passenger window, and I was free. Free to enjoy the dark, the cold, the wet and the shock that was gaining a hold on me. Clearly the vehicle was a right off. I checked my pockets, I had my wallet, mobile phone, though not working, and the keys which I had instinctively took from the ignition, I then walked away from the vehicle and began the process of disassociation with what had been a very comfortable and pleasant drive.

He was eighty-six, he had had a good innings.

The eighth vehicle to pass by my stricken van stopped to picked me up, the driver both had a waterproof coat to protect his passenger seat from contamination and he was travelling in the optimum direction. I was dropped at my home a half hour later, foolishly I believed that I had dealt with the accident and the loss of my vehicle, there followed a quick explanation of my very recent past to my wife Liz and my two daughters, and I was in a hot bath in reflective mood.

My father's death is not a surprise, he had been ill for almost a year, but it is a fundamental jolt to lose a first parent.
Amongst my jumbled thoughts were that I would now step back from my part time work in the events industry and stick with what I do best. I had only filled in for others over the past two summer seasons, and being honest with myself, in the thirty or forty days that I had, I had seen a little more than was good for me. The dressing room I had left during the night appeared to contain sufficient DNA to reconstruct an additional band member! I can add to that scene a five thousand pound food fight which was drug and alcohol prompted, that I had witnessed the aftermath of at a major sports stadium last time out, it is easy to understand my own reticence.

The stage crew and all the behind scenes production staff, thought appearing to be the oddballs of life with their tattoo's, body piercing, pony tails and outlandish dress which is the norm, are the most helpful and sympathetic of people. Though always busy, always under pressure, they have their own tight schedule of work, but if any one sees you struggling, an extra pair of hands appears to lighten the load. Whereas the festival goers who wallow in mud, alcohol and body fluids can appear to be the detritus of humanity. They leave an uncountable number of tents, sleeping bags, seats and empties behind. On every occasion they abandon a mountain of waste, much of it newly bought for the event, to be bulldozed into a landfill site. It is affluent arrogance beyond the average person to comprehend, and to miss-quote the BBC's Michael Burke, 'It is waste on a biblical scale.'

He was eighty six and had been suffering from either pancreatitis or pancreatic cancer, the family never did get a definitive answer as to which, but as the symptoms were the same, as was the eventual result at his age, it mattered little to my Dad.
It is an industry of contrast and waste, at festivals the public enjoy such 'privileges' as queuing on grid locked roads, queuing again to enter the site, paying hundreds of pounds for tickets, up to seven pounds for a poor quality burger in a dry bun, and up to

3

five pounds for a half litre of water, a price which seems to rise with the temperature. They get to stand, sometimes in the rain and watch their idols, then queue again to leave, suppressing the urge to defecate for several days due to the inadequacy of the latrines. I suspect that even the troops on the western front had a better place to shit. For proof of this one merely has to visit any motorway service station within fifty miles of any festival on exit day, the queue for the toilets goes right through the building, as does the stench.

Behind the stage it is a different world, the stars are pampered with individually tailored dressing rooms, beautifully prepared food, individual toilets and artist liaison personnel and transportation. At one festival an American artist claimed to have been allergic to the colour of the twelve red sofas in his dressing room suite, a truck was dispatched urgently to rectify the situation, but it is the sheer waste that affects me the most.

He had achieved a good age, despite being crippled for the last sixty years, and bitterly resentful of it. Apparently he died in his sleep in the end, aided by a morphine drip, his last ten months had been a continual battle against pain, sickness and diarrhoea. I imagine that he won't miss tomorrow. He died at ten minutes passed midnight, but the best of him died along with many, many others on D-Day, on those Normandy beaches on the 6th of June 1944.

Liz came up to the bathroom with two mugs of tea, sat on the toilet seat next to me and listened to my rantings and grumblings, she exorcised my anger and frustration with her usual patience and skill.

I was soon in bed catching up on a missed night's sleep, having decided that my career in events was now history, as was my father.

ANY POST?

"Any post?" This was my usual way of greeting my wife Liz on my return from a day or more away. I had just walked through the door of the family home, on returning from a long day. I'd left our Dorset home at around 05.30am to attend yet another day at College in Liskeard, Cornwall, part of my retraining. This is something that my twin daughters find highly amusing. 'Old man goes back to school' had spewed from them more than once. Others may say Hello darling, or Hi is the kettle on? Or maybe whose car is that in my space? Or next door's dog has shit in the drive again or, very rarely, how was your day? But with me, it's any post? Being self-employed everything comes in the post, work to price, orders of work secured, payments and of course, bills. I've always had that boyish optimism that some kind of pleasant surprise will turn up in the post.

"Yes." Liz, my wife, replies. "There's a nasty one for you and yes I had a crap day, thanks for asking!" Now when Liz says a nasty one she means OHMS, On Her Majesty's Service. I wonder does the Queen really know the severity of the demands that are made of us on her behalf? Perhaps she does, and is it comforting to us that we pay to keep her in the splendour to which she has become accustomed? Perhaps a portion would agree but I don't think many under fifty would. As for supporting the wider Royal Family, public opinion seems to have turned against them and will the public embrace Charles as King? I have grave doubts, the death of Diana, though ten years ago in August of '97 is still a cancer to the Royal family. I step over the sleeping dogs to pick up the envelope, it feels heavy, that's a good sign, probably a form to fill in. Tax demands are usually single sheets, it's amazing how big a number they can get on a single sheet.

"Are we driving tonight? It's my turn and I'm going to work at seven so I've only got an hour." Says Claire, the eldest of my two girls. She was born just before midnight on 20th January 1990, Emma was born just half an hour later on the 21st.

"Umm, yeah, OK, why not? 5.30 in the drive and change your feet, you're not driving in those again. Last time you drove in flip-flops, the car was flipping and flopping all over the road."

"OK, I'll drive barefoot. How was your day at schooooool, old man?"

"Not easy today, it was all about self projection, writing your own witness statement, mythology of Method Statements and Risk Assessments. It might as well have been in Cornish or Welsh .Where's Emma?"

"She's doing two hours in the kitchen at the pub 'cause one of the others has called in sick."

Both girls have got part-time jobs which we encouraged when they ganged up on me to ask for a monthly allowance, which it seems most of the other girls at College were getting, according to Claire and Emma. I responded with a fairly quick no, but then added, if you get a job, I will double whatever you earn. So Emma's waiting on tables at a local pub/restaurant for five pounds an hour and Claire's egg picking at Jackson's Chicken Farm for the same minimum wage and with my bonus, both of them are picking up £10 an hour – not bad at 17. Liz quickly chipped in that if I'm paying them that much then they could buy all their own toiletries and clothes so we got our daughters working at no extra cost to us, to quote a much loved famous TV character 'everyone's a winner'. I took my tea from Liz, she knew that I'd prefer a glass of red but as I'm taking Claire out in the car there was no chance.

"Thanks for the tea," and, retrospectively I add, "Your day?"

"It was fine, I finished early so did the shopping. Don't be too long out with Claire, you've got drawings to price tonight which they want back asap and Emma's working down the Green Man and needs a lift back at seven."

"Why do they . . . . . . ? "

"It's not their fault, it was posted five days ago. Actually it's your fault, if you'd accepted their proposal to e-mail all drawings you would have had them days ago, both you and the postal service are stuck in the past, wake up and smell the coffee, it's late September 2007." I hear Rod Stewart singing 'it's late September and I really should be back at school', which feels odd as I am back at school. She's right of course, I'm a bugger for resisting new technology. I don't have an ipod, I don't have a web-site and

I've never hotmailed or emailed and wouldn't know a blog from a tweet if one was on my dinner plate. My flip-up mobile phone is a step that's far enough for me at present. I often wonder what my grandparents would make of today's way of life. My grandmother never had indoor plumbing, the cold water tap was at the end of the lane in which they lived and she never had an electric cooker. She wouldn't trust electric things, fancy tackle she used to call them, always cooked on a wood or coal burning range and never had a fridge or a freezer. She kept the butter and milk in a bucket down the well.

The drawings are of proposed new school buildings. They are from a Main Contractor in the Midlands who use me for all their roofing requirements. That's me, that's what I am, a roof builder and tiler, for the present, but I'm now retraining to be an Energy Surveyor for the Labour Government's new HIP packs, compulsory for all future house sales. Depending on which national paper you read, I might be wasting my time and money. In fact, it's only The Guardian and a couple of the gutter press that suggest I'm following a wise course, which makes me feel very unsure. I go into my office and open the drawings, it's a large two storey building at a Secondary School in Cheltenham. A school in which I've already built two large roofs, that's a good sign, there is a very good chance this one will become an order, so on goes an additional ten percent.

I open the OHMS, its jury service, my first time. I experience gut reactions, crap that's two weeks unpaid and second, shit what if it's a big nasty trial. It could be armed robbers or immigrant workers' evil gang masters, if the jury find them guilty I could be pursued by petrol bomb wielding maniacs? My bowels feel uncomfortable. No, surely not in Dorchester, it's more likely to be burglary, buggery or car theft, I reassure myself. But then we do have a number of immigrant agricultural labourers in the South West, mainly Polish, Lithuanian and Latvian, so it could be, but we don't get armed robbery down this end of the Country, not west of Bristol. Oh Christ, it could be a rape or a child sex case, no, not that, I couldn't handle that.

"Liz, it's jury service, how do I get out of it?"

"You can't, it came through first time three months ago, I deferred it for you because you had that huge job in Newcastle and

I knew your college course was due to start. This one you have to do, I knew you'd get funny about it so I kept quiet. You've already told me that you're short of work in October so I kept stum, but you have to do it or you're in contempt of court."

"Crap, when does it start?"

"Have a look, I think it will be the 8th to the 19th."

"But I was hoping to catch a couple of World Cup games in France, Christ it's the Rugby Union World Cup."

"Nothing you can do about it unless you want a month in the cells."

As usual she was right, there would always be another World Cup and we, England, are playing the worst rugby I could remember despite being world champions. So I just have to accept it, but before I capitulate completely I read the small print. Apparently if I get a doctor's note to the effect that I'm terminally ill then I'm excused. Now I'm a friend and an admirer of my GP and when it's required of me, I repair and patch up the roof of his crumbling listed farmhouse, for which I refuse financial reimbursement and instead receive absolutely first class Bordeaux reds. But I believe that would be asking too much of him, I won't go there.

"Come on old man." Claire is banging on the office window from the outside with her car keys dangling. When I say her car keys, I mean the keys to my old diesel estate that we recently gave her. Not a cool car for a teenager but it was free and given the chance between it and buying her own, she showed remarkable common sense for a teen' and went for it. No such luck with Emma, never did two children come out of the same gene pool less alike. For Emma I managed to obtain, for fifty quid, a Renault Clio from a friend. It's older than she is but it did have three months MOT and tax. It's a horrible little thing with a vicious clutch but she's OK with it. I finish my tea and take Claire out for an hour, just time to get to Yeovil and back with only one major involving a fox and a couple of minors with a cyclist and a lunatic on a motorcycle.

Back home this jury service thing is bugging me. I've never objected to doing my bit for Queen and Country but two weeks and no pay! By way of attempting to come to terms with the idea, I telephone a couple of friends whom I know have done it.

8

"Totally boring, suggest you take a good book." Says Alan. "I loved it, really interesting." Is my reply from Michael. So I'm still on the fence but I will dig out an easy reading novel and perhaps something a bit more challenging. What the hell, I'll just have to get used to the idea, in for a penny . . . . . . All the rugby is on the box in the evenings, so I'll be better off financially. A couple of trips to France were going to cost me a thousand and England's chances of reaching the latter stages of the tournament appear to be very limited. I ring Richard my most likely travelling companion. We had left it to the last minute, he being a self-employed joiner and never quite sure how busy he'll be or how profitable the next job is going to be. If we're both on high profit jobs we would have gone, if not we would have still probably gone. Richard takes it well, says he's on a very good earner at the moment working for a famous actor near Oxford and all for cash, he says that in another month he could buy himself a world cup.

So in two weeks I'm in the jury box, there was a film wasn't there with Gregory Peck or Kirk Douglas, Twelve Good Men, must get one of the girls to find it on the internet, the internet that I so disapprove of.

The two weeks leading up to my jury service are not the easiest, they conclude with my father's funeral in Oxfordshire which coincides with a very cold, wet, windy day and some very difficult personnel memories. There is also a protracted argument with my insurance company over their derisory offer for my total loss van, and a trip to Cardiff to pick up a replacement for it. Add to that a broken finger whilst working on site in Bristol and several driving lessons for both the girls, including one major with Emma into a hedge and some kind of airlock problem with the old Clio, causing the engine to overheat spasmodically. Also I get confirmation of the large two-storey project in Cheltenham that means good paying work through November into December and turkey on the table for Christmas. With the price I put in and the monies saved from not visiting France for the rugby there could be a week's skiing the first week in January, before the girls return to college, for all of us. I'll have to get Liz onto that, see what she can find. Her natural sense of caution, what happened to the girl I met twenty years ago? Means she likes to wait until the money is in. But for me, it's enough that the order is in, it's a good price and the Company I sub to are good payers, so long as the job is finished and finished well. So I wind the girls up and ask them if they fancy a week skiing and can they find a rich friend to come with them. That gets them jumping up and down a gets me that look from Liz. That, how can you promise them the earth when you're not sure look, and she adds,

"And we still haven't sorted out my new car."

I'll borrow it, go overdrawn if we have to. Don't know how many more times the girls will want to come with us, serious boyfriends are probably just round the corner. That'll change things, up to now Claire always seems to have a good friend who is male, but no-one special, whereas Emma seems to regard boys as foreign objects, not to be trusted, not clean, not very bright and a nuisance. She calls Claire's male friends fuck buddies, what charming things today's teenagers are.

The major event in the first two weeks leading up to my jury service was my father's funeral, he died of cancer of the pancreas, well that was what was on his death certificate but we never knew if it was that or pancreatitis. He'd been very ill for almost a year, it was hard on Claire and Emma as he was their first known grandparent to die. They only saw him perhaps two or three times a year, he living with my mother near Oxford and ourselves living in West Dorset, but he being the first to go it was an untimely reminder of our mortality. The girls said very little. Claire asked a few questions but Emma never spoke of it. During the following few weeks I received a lot more hugs and physical contact than had become the norm. It was a temporary regression for them, they would sit closer to me than usual or sit against the side of me whilst viewing television. I know subconsciously they were imagining for the first time a future without a dad.

What did the future mean to me without a dad? I'll miss him of course but he had been ill for so long I think I had adjusted to his death before it happened. My one sadness was that he had been a fan of the Reading Football team since the Second World War when he was demobbed and had married a farm labourer's daughter in North Berkshire. Sometime after his death Reading won promotion for the first time to the top football league. Often on visits to him in the Royal Berks Hospital he would ask me how they were doing. I was proud to write and read the eulogy as neither of my sisters was feeling up to it. Even the Vicar mentioned Dad's love of the round ball game. He missed out on his favourite team's promotion, but then he also missed out on their subsequent relegation two seasons later, every cloud has a silver lining. What I miss of my Dad is what I've missed since I was around five to ten years old, his knowledge of nature. I grew up to realise that his knowledge of any subject was limited but when I was a boy, he was a fountain of knowledge. He could name all the trees, birds and butterflies that I could see. He gave me an interest in nature and wildlife that will never leave me, he made the world interesting to be in and gave everything a name. He, along with my mother, made sure we three kids were warm, dry and well fed, not an easy task on a very limited income just after the Second World War, I am, and always will be, eternally grateful to them.

Having got my father underground it was time to look forward and stop looking back. I never understood as a child or as young man the purpose of a funeral, it seemed to me to be piling misery on top of misery, but a funeral does bring closure, it does give an opportunity to people close to the deceased to celebrate their life and then to move on. Odd that Dad should end up underground, that's where all his family spent their lives, they had been tin miners in the extreme south west of Cornwall. For hundreds of years all the men in the family had worked in extremely difficult conditions both underground and under the ocean. He had been born into one of the most arduous professions on earth. His only chance to escape was to put on the uniform of a soldier and face the might of the Third Reich. He was shot in both knees on D-Day, June 6th 1944, on Juno Beach, his injuries kept him in a wheelchair for the rest of his life. The average soldier who enlisted for the Second World War had a longer life expectancy than those who mined tin in Cornwall, good for you Dad.

England opened their 2007 Rugby World Cup campaign with a poor win against the USA and a thrashing from South Africa like I have never seen before, thank goodness for jury service. Tomorrow, Monday 8th October, I have to be at the Crown Court, Dorchester for 09.30am.

DAY ONE

THOMAS HARDY & ROADKILL

I'm up at six for breakfast with the papers, I take two daily papers since my Dad died, I've always read The Times because I'm comfortable with it and the rugby coverage is to my liking and since losing Dad I also have The Mirror delivered. Not because I like it, I think it stinks, but I've added The Mirror to my order just to give myself a chance to share something of his day. For a few moments at the start of each day I try to find something that would have interested or amused him. He bought The Mirror all his life, I think if he'd realised how much it had altered from a working man's down to earth labour paper to an over sensationalised and frivolous piece of nonsense he wouldn't have wiped his arse with it. But that's exactly what we used to do as children, cut it into squares, punch a hole through it with a meat skewer, thread a piece of string through the hole and hang it on the wall in the outside lav', to wipe our arses with.

One strong coffee and a piece of toast and I'm at the table and into the papers,

In the Daily Mirror today:

On the front page there is reference to the tragic disappearance of the toddler Madeleine McCann, her parents Kate and Gerry fear that they will be suspects forever, if the child is not found. Other items include a warning to vicars by safety experts not to wear their dog-collars when off-duty to make them less vulnerable to attacks and that a twenty million pound Monet titled 'Pont d'Argenteuil has indeed itself suffered an attack, it appears that a yob has punched a hole through its middle. Further news informs that a Magistrate in an Exeter court has informed a defendant that he was in 'deep shit', I wonder will such colourful language be broadcast in court today? There is also strong comment on the cost of the inquest into the death of Princess Diana, the comment being that £10 million of our money is to be spent to find out that 'being ferried around at high speed by a drunken driver whilst not wearing a seatbelt can result in accidental death'. A final offering is from today's problem page, 'Dear Agony Aunt, I have had m/s for some years and have a problem with incontinence. I've met someone who would like our relationship to become sexual but I'm afraid I might have a leakage during sex. How can I avoid this?' Is this really the stuff my father digested on a daily basis for over 40 years?

The Times is sure that Gordon Brown bottled it when he didn't call a snap autumn election. Brown it seems wants to get on with all the good things he has in mind for us. Also, technology experts have devised an intelligent shopping trolley that will alert shoppers when junk food items are dropped in, giving us all the ability to blame our weight gains on a trolley malfunction, not our fault at all! And, very sadly, a ten-year-old girl has been found hanged when her pyjama cord got caught on a door handle. I presume Health and Safety will now ban both pyjamas and door handles. This one item alone should give the European Union Ministers six more months on the Gravy Train. A final offering from today's curiosities is that the sloth has been declared an approved pet for the nation, I sympathise with one contribution on today's letters page, 'Who would need to adopt a sloth as a pet if they already have a teenager living in their house'?

The drive over the hills to Dorchester is an uneventful one, with Claire driving her old diesel estate. She schools in Dorchester at the Thomas Hardye School. It's actually college now for her as she is doing her A's. Her driving test is on Friday, she's driving me back and forth this week for additional practice. Emma attends school in Sherborne. Being modern, individual, non-identical twins, they were both determined to express their individuality and attend different colleges. They refuse to be called twins or wear anything alike, because they have separate birthdays they have to have separate everything. I think it might have been easier for us to lie about the times of birth. Or had they been born on the night that the clocks went back, Claire would've been born first at a quarter to twelve, and Emma second at a quarter past eleven, so then which one would be the oldest?

On the drive we see in excess of a dozen wild deer on the hills south of Buckland Newton. The very name Buckland Newton makes me think of Hobbits, The Brandywine Bridge and The Prancing Pony Inn at Bree, images from 'The Hobbit' and 'The Lord of the Rings'; comfortable, homely, fireside images, long before things turned threatening and dark in 'Middle Earth'.

There is a mild frost and just two notable items of road kill, both badgers. I have an interest in road kill. I keep an annual record in my head of how many of which animals are most commonly put to death by BMWs, Range Rovers and the like. This year, as is usual of late, the badger is out on its own, with over a hundred victims. Just a decade ago the rabbit was the most predominant animal to adorn our roads. I do pick up certain items, usually to take back home to tie to a twenty foot pole, which I've erected at the bottom of my garden to encourage buzzards, red kites and owls to feed locally. I like to think I'm repairing just a little of the damage caused to these species by modern farming methods, in their never-ending pursuit of maximum yield and profit. I do pick up slightly damaged fresh items for consumption at home, rabbits, pheasants, pigeons and occasionally a duck or a deer will find its way into the pot.

Approaching Dorchester from the North East is a pleasant experience. As you crest each gentle rise the spread of the town opens up before you, as if to welcome you with open arms, though I submit that the prison to the east is not the most aesthetic of buildings. Perhaps it would not be out of place next to its illustrious cousin on Dartmoor. The rest of the town seems to both say 'Good Morning' and to mean it.

Claire drops herself at the college. I congratulate her on her driving and park at the top of town, near the famous and striking Military Keep. I cross the traffic directly to the foot of the Hardy statue. I stop for a moment and gaze at the effigy cast in what I assume is bronze, 'Thomas Hardy 1840 – 1928', and ask myself, what do I know of him? The answer is, very little. Almost forty years ago at secondary school we were all given two of his books to study for GSE. I remember reading 'The Woodlanders', fantastically descriptive, yet fantastically boring to a sport-

14

obsessed fifteen year old. We were given another Hardy, the title of which escapes me. What else do I know of him? I think the sum total of my knowledge is that he renamed all of the local villages in his novels, he lived and died nearby and that his heart is buried locally but his ashes are interred in Westminster Abbey's Poet's Corner, not sure why I know that.

The information supplied with the jury service compulsory request, now that is an oxymoron, suggested we bring along a book, crossword, mental puzzle or some other such occupational literature to fill in times of low demand. Directly behind the statue is the library, and as I have failed to bring any such literature with me I decide to call in, join and look for the lost Hardy from my school days. As I approach the library, I am taken back twenty years to the last time I walked through its doors. It was my first ever visit to the town. I had arrived on a one-way rail ticket for no good reason I could think of, other than to leave the place I had come from. I called into the library for a town guide and had hoped to walk to the seafront. I was then a single man, running away from many things, love and loss amongst them.

In the library, the joining process is quick and simple, and the book in question was not hard to locate as it had an odd title, 'Far from the Madding Crowd'. I'm a sucker for an odd title. Amongst the last dozen novels I've read were 'The Shipping News', something about 'Tractors in the Ukraine', 'The Curious Incident of the Dog in the Night', 'Salmon Fishing in the Yemen' and 'Back When We Were Grown-Ups', all very odd titles and all very good reads. If I add to those, 'The Woman Who Walked into Doors', 'A Short History of Nearly Everything' and 'The Death of Common Sense', I realise that I do not judge a book by its cover, but by its title. The more quirky the title, the quicker my hand reaches out to the book. In addition to the novel, I pick up an autobiography of Thomas Hardy by Michael Millgate. If these two weeks are to give me periods of low demand I am now determined to make some use of this time and learn something of Dorset's most famous citizen. With the two books tucked under my arm, I present myself, dressed tidily for me in my fawn suit trousers, black t-shirt and black short-sleeved shirt. It's a

15

comfort to see that I'm not too casual or too smart, thank you Liz.

A court security officer in uniform with a uniform sprinkling of dandruff shows me into a room with some twenty or so seats, a coffee vending machine and a flat-screen TV. The rest of the room has a decidedly tired, Victorian feel. Peeling cream paintwork, which in places had turned yellow/brown, and an enormous, heavy radiator that would look at home in the Victoria and Albert Museum. The security officer has a commanding voice, and a body odour problem,

"Hi. I'm Andy. I'll be your guide around this place for the next two weeks."

I'm the seventh of the jurors to arrive, apparently there are to be fifteen of us from which twelve will be chosen. I quickly calculate my odds of a free day, four to one against.

I catch the eye of one of my fellow female jurors. Her 'Good Morning' is both friendly and genuine. Her raised eyebrow and fleeting glance towards the odorous Andy is easy to read. She is forty-ish and a women who goes to extraordinary lengths to make everything match and has the figure to carry it off. Blouse, skirt, leggings, handbag, shoes, earrings, necklace and lipstick all very carefully put together, and all very soft on the eye. She is, I imagine, the sort of woman who would check her make-up and image in the mirror before allowing a fireman to lift her from a burning building.

"Hi, I'm Joyce, Joyce Ashworth from Portland."

"Hi, Jude Saunders from Hazelbury Bryan, that's up in the North of the county."

Dawn arrives and introduces herself. She is a court usher, smartly turned out in her black court gown, although it is full length it fails to conceal her delightful contours. She speaks to the now ten of us and informs us that two have had to withdraw last minute due to personal problems and have been excused their duty. Maybe they know their doctor better than I know mine. So now the odds of a free day are down to twelve to one against. I look around at my fellow jurors and note that a just six feet one I am the tallest amongst them, I serve myself an indigestible coffee and sit down. Now we are thirteen, a lucky number for one of us, but, being honest with myself, having written off the next two weeks I will be disappointed if I'm not called onto the jury. I have become interested in seeing today's justice in action.

There's a chap in a blazer who has a military looking tie on, he looks around seventy years old and also looks like a prime candidate to be jury foreman. He's holding a folded newspaper, The Telegraph, with the crossword visible and it is all but complete. He also has a novel that I recognise, 'The Smoke Jumpers'. One that I had read earlier in the year, because of the odd title I imagine. I recall that it was a good read, the cover is very familiar but to recall the content is elusive. I am sometimes very frustrated with myself that for a day or two I will be completely engrossed in a novel, but just a month or two later, on seeing the cover I struggle to remember even the rudimentary basics of the narrative. I am always able to glean from the cover the degree to which I enjoyed the book, but little else. The flip side of this lack of recall is that after a period of perhaps two or three years, I can enjoy rereading the novel, as I have recently done with 'The Shipping News'. Mr 'Foreman' catches my eye and introduces himself,

"Good Morning. John Foreman." What sort of luck is that? Perhaps it would have been prudent to purchase a lottery ticket on route to Dorchester this morning. I reciprocate,

"Jude Saunders."

"First time for you?"

"Yes," I reply, "I'm quite looking forward to it now I'm here. Yourself?"

"I did it once before, twenty years ago in Bristol. With a name like mine I was Foreman then."

"And somehow, I think you will be again." I reply.

"What's that? Who wants to be foreman?" says a stout-looking fellow, quite short, around sixty. The three of us do the introductions. He is Terry Johnson, who owns and runs a rope and sail accessory store in Weymouth. He is a decent looking fellow who declares himself a very keen rugby fan, with faith in the current England team, despite our sound thrashing by South Africa at the weekend. This declaration brings an immediate response from another juror who introduces himself as Tim Partner. Similar age to Terry but not so well dressed and not in possession of Terry's all too obvious wandering eyes toward the fairer sex. Tim interrupts with,

"You rugby boys have had it. Once we qualify for the European Championships next weekend, there will be no stopping us. The press have got it in for the manager McClaren, but he's no idiot."

I leave the two of them to discuss the pros and cons of team sports with different shaped balls. I am going through the rudiments of introduction to a middle-aged woman called Lynda Short, strangely dressed in what looks like a man's grey trouser suit, no make-up, lipstick or ear rings and the shoes are definitely male. She is possible fifty-five, forty-five to fifty if she is unlucky in her looks.

The thirteen of us are addressed by the court usher Dawn, who when she sweeps past me in her elegant court gown, for just a brief moment transforms the fragrance of the room from Andy's body odour to Estee Lauder White Linen, but all too soon the aroma assaulting our senses reverts to the former. Dawn instructs us whilst holding aloft a court floor plan of our immediate whereabouts and which parts of the court are green for our use, and those areas which are red and strictly prohibited. Apparently the Jury, the Defence, the Prosecution and the Witnesses all benefit from designated areas of use and are strictly forbidden to mingle, for obvious reasons. We are then told we will be called in for selection as soon as the Court Preliminaries are completed, in around thirty minutes. I follow the lovely Dawn out of the room until she takes a left turn toward the main entrance, or rather my eyes do. Immediately interrupting my line of vision is a browned, sun-wrinkled, leathery face,

"Morning. I'm David, David Kingston. This is my third time. Is it your first, as it seems to be for most people here, or are you an old hat like myself?"

"Yes, first time for me." I reply, "You just come back from abroad? You didn't get that tan in Dorset, I know."

"I did actually, I'm a keen sailor. Go out whenever I can from Poole, I am really looking forward to the Olympics down at Weymouth. My son is a great sailor and has a fifty-fifty chance of getting on the GB team for twenty twelve." He then goes into an incredibly detailed analogy of our weather and tidal variations, wind speeds, prevailing winds, barometric pressure, and tidal extremes. I reach the point where I'm looking for any type of distraction to escape the meteorological onslaught which seems to have no end. This man could bore for Britain.

Eventually we are interrupted, at first by a very strong, inexpensive perfume and then by its wearer, a woman in her fifties wearing a full length fake-fur, her hair is dyed as black as a witch's hat. Her huge chrome looking earrings and necklace would look at home as free gifts on a hoopla stall, or rifle range at a funfair. She introduces herself as Alice Black, and just as quickly excuses herself to go in search of the smoking room. I notice as she walks away, one of the heels of her black patent shoes is split, as is the heel of her tights, allowing a glimpse of extremely pale flesh to be exposed each time she puts her foot to the floor, in stark contrast to the shiny black shoe. Here is a lady who clearly dresses from the charity shops, a today's woman, she believes in recycling. The fake-fur and the perfume are overpowering. I try to imagine what type of living creature the fur is failing to represent. An image of a compilation of a ferret and a domestic cat comes to mind, with a touch of giraffe on the collar and cuffs. The lasting impression of Alice Black as she disappears from view is both the coat and her shocking choice of Barbie pink lipstick on her lips, and around her mouth, which is also indelibly ingrained into the fissures of her teeth, like pink silicone.

Talking of silicone, two very well presented handfuls come into the jury room immediately after Alice, (fake-fur), leaves. The two handfuls, and I mean handfuls for a large hand, are neatly tucked behind a black lace-edged bra, and a short apricot t-shirt dress, the sharp contrast of the black and apricot guaranteed to draw attention. I lift my gaze above the two hemispheres to the face of Hanna Preston, forty eight going on twenty eight, a little too much make-up, applied perhaps with a paintbrush and a little too much jewellery, insufficient material at the hem of the dress and not enough flesh on the over-exposed legs. A classic case, I fear, of mutton dressed as lamb. Hanna (implants), goes in search of coffee and I wrap up my conversation with David, (the weather man), I sit down between Joyce (matching accessories), and a very dull and ill at ease

19

looking balding chap, much like myself in that regard. He is wearing a beige cardigan, dark brown corduroy trousers with a fairly even covering of white dog hair and old fashioned round spectacles. This man also exudes a rather unpleasant tang, not one of stale perspiration but more of a stale life. His odour conjures an image of a man who has lived alone for many years, apart from the dog, a man who lives in a house where little, or perhaps nothing, has changed in a generation. I envisage a 1960s television drama being filmed around him, whilst he treats himself to a weekend luxury of Welsh rarebit, Bassett's Liquorice Allsorts and a mug of cocoa for supper. My character assassination of him is interrupted as he introduces himself,

"Hello there, I'm Barry Reeves. I'm a prison chaplain in Dorchester. I've held that position for twelve years now, thought I'd be exempt from this sort of thing as I have to deal with the boys this court sends down to us, but no, apparently I have to do it. Not looking forward to it at all." All I can say to him of comfort is, "You might be fortunate and not be chosen." He replies,

"I shouldn't be here. If we give some poor bugger two years I'll have to meet him on a regular basis. I don't think I could do that. I'll have to pack in my job. My job is my life, it's what I do, and it's who I am." At this juncture, Barry becomes visibly upset and is fighting back tears. He apologises and composes himself. Quite a show of emotion for a man of his age – I would guess between sixty-five and seventy.

General conversation floods the room. Once the ushers have left us, three of the four women adjourn to the smoking room. Barry (chaplain) notices that I am carrying 'From the Madding Crowd', which is, by coincidence, also his selection for today. I experience a wave of dread that this man will become like a great uncle to me, sending me long, hand-written letters, in fountain pen of course, engaging me in decade long postal debates on the finer and not so finer points of English literature.

"Oh, that's interesting. We've chosen the same book. My wife and I usually read the same book at the same time so we can discuss it as we go along." A satisfying wave of relief courses through my veins, destroying my projected image, there is a wife to shoulder my imagined burden.

"It used to get me some funny looks in the library as I often take out two identical books, but they are used to me now and they are kind enough to let me know which books they have in duplicate."

"Really? That's interesting" is all I can manage for the moment. Joyce (matching accessories) bless her, the only non-smoker amongst the women, has taken note of the one-way conversation and asks me what it is I do, as Barry is slowly filling his lungs for another long sentence.

"I run my own roof tiling company. Schools mainly, some universities and hospitals, I build pitched roofs." To demonstrate this my hands come together to form an apex, just in case she cannot imagine what a roof looks like. "It's all mud in the winter and dust in the summer." I add.

"And what, may I ask keeps you occupied?" She starts to reply,

"Oh I have a part-time job at Laura Ashley, Bournemouth." But she is interrupted firstly by the odour of Andy, the court security officer, and then by his voice. He goes through a Health and Safety talk on exits, behaviour, no smoking, no running, whereabouts of fire extinguishers, etc., etc. He then puts on a five-minute video of who's who and who sits where in court. It is impossible to decide which is more mind-numbing, the video or talking to Barry, the prison chaplain on his vocation and how he befriends some of the least dangerous prison inmates and invites them to his home after their release. I believe I would take the option of an additional month's incarceration to avoid an afternoon with Barry. Why is it that some people, so genuine and caring, can be so tedious?

Soon we are required to file into the back of the courtroom to await selection. I'm the second name called, so there is to be no day off this week. The large willow that is leaning precariously towards my homemade pergola has a week's reprieve. One juror is temporarily held back before being released whilst we are then informed of all the names of all the persons involved in the case, including the accused, witnesses and all police officers. If we, the jury, know any of these people we must leave the court now. No one takes this option, so we move to our benches. We are sworn in. Curiously I am the only one to take the alternative to the Bible, not because of the possible bonus that it might put some mental space between Barry (chaplain), and myself, but because it would be hypocritical of me to do so .

The ageing judge asks us if we have chosen a foreman. John (foreman), stands up, declares himself the foreman and is instructed to move to the end of the lower bench nearest the judge. This is my first ever non-televised view of an English court of law. It is extremely humbling and intimidating. It occurs to me that it would perhaps be a useful and constructive idea to allow all students, of perhaps my daughters' age, to visit, albeit for a brief period, to educate and inform the population at large as to what to expect if they are called as jurors, witnesses or in any other capacity. Maybe, I think, playing Devil's Advocate with myself, that this initial humbling experience produces the required degree of respect, in the building and, consequently, in the legal process. There is a great deal of polished wood and various wooden platforms at various heights, a representation of the English Class System, lower, middle and upper, but for this purpose the class levels are legal and not social or financial. The one, over-powering surprise is the elevated glass cage in the centre of the room directly facing the judge, it is empty at present but is surely for the accused. This we all find disturbing, as we have seen toppled dictators, ethnic cleansers and terrorists in these cages on our television news. We, the Jury, as members of the general public are unaware that this is now common practice for all accused, minor criminals or otherwise, and we now, each and every one of us, anticipate the emergence of a dangerous felon. So dangerous, in fact, that he or she must be restrained behind reinforced glass to protect us all.

The judge introduces us to the legal teams for the defence and for the prosecution, and then calls for the accused to be presented to court. Inside the glass box there are a number of seats and a hole in the floor through which, ascending a staircase, appears the accused flanked by two prison officers, one of which gives a discrete nod of recognition to Barry. The accused comes into view, he is a tall, thin, shaven-headed, tattooed lad of around twenty years old, he is dressed in a black t-shirt with a skull and crossed bones on its front and torn jeans. He is obviously guilty of whatever crime he is about to be accused of, and your Honour,

I believe that is the unanimous opinion of the Jury, the entire Jury and nothing but the Jury.

The charges are read out. I'm already thinking why bother, let's just send this vile individual to be incarcerated with Barry for all eternity. The charges are that on the date of the second of May in the year of our Lord two thousand and seven, the accused, Arran Spelling of Briar Lea Close, Poole in Dorset, did cause grievous bodily harm to one Barry Read of Briar Lea Court, Poole in Dorset, with a baseball bat and that the aforementioned Arran Spelling did also cause criminal damage to a vehicle belonging to the aforementioned Barry Read, also on the date of the second of May two thousand and seven. At this point I strongly believe that all members of the jury, with the exception of Barry, were ready to give the guilty verdict, go home and set about some useful task. Unfortunately, the appearance of the accused has created such a negative aura surrounding him that he has destroyed his own defence, but this being an English Court of Law, he was entitled to a fair hearing and a defence, and he would get it, Hurrah for the system.

After a few court preliminaries, the Judge informed us that we, the Jury, could ask a question if we wished, by writing it down on the pad provided and attracting the attention of Dawn, the court usher, which she would then pass on to him, he would assess its merits and forward it to the defence or prosecution if he felt it raised a valid point. If I were a single man I might take advantage of this facility and inform the lovely Dawn of my telephone number and my dishonest intentions toward her.

During the rest of the day, I am quite sure that I have never heard so many people tell so many lies. Every witness, be they friend or foe, of one side or the other, told one version when questioned by the defence and a differing version when questioned very subtly and suggestively by the prosecution, all were under oath. I quickly became aware that the prosecution and defence barristers could not be under oath, as they both had the freedom to give completely opposing views of everyone's testimony and each piece of evidence or police reports. So at best at least one of these teams was also lying, or perhaps both.

It was with this realisation that the value of the Jury first came home to me. We were twelve independent people, who knew no-

23

one in court and had no prior knowledge of the preceding events and it is only we who could cut through the lies, counter claims and falsehoods of every person giving evidence in the court room, and ultimately give a fair and honest opinion. It occurred to me that I am taking part in one of the most democratic and fundamental practices enshrined in English law. The importance of our considered decision hit home, just like the proverbial ton of bricks, an overwhelming realisation that we were the only twelve people who had an opportunity to judge this event in a careful and considered way came to us all. If we got it wrong, mucked it up, somebody else would pay the price. In an instant the appearance of the accused vanished, it was irrelevant. What was required here was attention to detail not to the fashion of the day. Lip rings, nose studs and tattoos became invisible. This realisation hit all of us during the first day, at different times. It was possible to feel the moment that it hit. Each jury member would take a deep breath, lean forward, pay extra attention, alter their body language and become Judge, Jury and Executioner in their minds, and this for a case of minor thuggery. What must it be like for the twelve who are sitting on the Princess Diana inquest case as we sit here? The eyes and ears of the World's press were awaiting their decision. The obligation each jury member would feel to get it right must be all compelling and overwhelming.

We reach lunch and are warned again to discuss today's proceedings with no one. I go into Dorchester and buy myself a small Cornish pasty, something I can never do without thinking of my father. He would claim that his mother made the best pasties West of Penzance, I never knew if this was a joke or a boast. The weather today is warm and dry, I sit in the Borough Gardens Recreation Ground, eat my lunch and commence reading 'The Madding Crowd'. I read around fifty pages before I stop and attempt to recall what I have just read. I can remember very little.

I release the book from my grasp and begin to people watch. There is a pair to my right, mid-twenties office types, who are somehow managing to keep their hands off each other. The strain of what they are not doing is plain for all to see. She is wearing a provocatively split skirt, it is open to the top of the thigh and is holding it closed as many women do. I wonder, is she holding it closed to prevent public gaze or his hand from slipping inside? To the far side of the park opposite me is Barry (chaplain), engrossed in his copy of one of Hardy's most famous titles. Obviously this is one he is not sharing with his wife, I recall that he believes he is sharing the book with me. I quickly exit the park.

I leave the gentle ambiance of the autumnal park and wander into town. It quickly becomes clear to me that I have not spent sufficient time in this pleasant county town during the twenty years I have lived in North Dorset. The town is very pleasing architecturally, and some of the townsfolk are also pleasant on the eye. I stroll down the high street and am tempted to call into the curiously named café, 'The Horse with the Red Umbrella', which exudes an air of agreeable welcome. So welcoming is it in fact that there appears to be not one seat unused. I later learn that the cafe used to be a modest theatre, its name coming from the last play to be performed within its walls. Opposite the café I walk up a narrow lane, Grey School Passage and into a small lavender garden behind the Holy Trinity Catholic Church and park myself temporarily on a bench that occupies its spot in memory of a Mr McLuckie. I notice on the church there is a plaque celebrating the fact that Benjamin Ferry 1810 – 1880 was hereby a Dorset architect in 1875 – 1876; a man who, by the nature of his employment, would unquestionably have been known to Hardy. (I later glean from Hardy's biography that it is the very same Benjamin Ferry who not only designed the present Town Hall, but who also gave Hardy a letter of introduction to take with him to London in 1862, upon his move to the capital at the tender age of twenty-one years, to seek employment as an Architect's clerk). I am in the immediate vicinity of the Holy Trinity Church, the Town Hall with its splendid clock tower, St Peters Church next door and the Corn Exchange, a series of well designed, stone-built, superb structures, believed locally to be the longest run of listed buildings in the county.

Moving on, I pause outside St Peter's church to view the statue of one William Barnes 1801 – 1886, again a man whose lifespan coincided with Hardy's. On the plinth of Barnes' statue is the inscription, "Zoo now I hope this kindly feace is gone to vind a better pleace, but still wi'vo'k-a- left behind he'll always be a kept in mind". How much a language can change in one hundred and twenty years, Hardy himself being one person responsible for a degree of that change. Crossing the road and walking a little into Cornhill, a small plaque in a modern shop window catches my eye, it reads: 'This building was the home and workplace of Thomas Smith Pouncy 1802 – 1871 and his son Thomas Crook Pouncy 1828 – 1902 saddlers and collectors of tax for Dorchester'. It is surprising how readily it is possible to observe the recorded lives of people who lived at the same time as Thomas Hardy and must have been known to him and his family. Mr Pouncy and his son would surely have been avoided as much as was possible.

I wander into the area known as Antelope Walk, which consist of a Victorian pitched roof over a glazed and ventilated arcade, the aroma of recent baking and freshly ground coffee assaults my nostrils. I enter an establishment whose sole purpose is to purvey Cornish pasties. Whilst waiting to be served a second small pasty I lean against an aged mantelpiece beneath which harbours a quite splendid original black range, flanked with pictures of Cornish mining and pilchard netting, screens of a bygone age. I am temporarily transported to a time when the world was a different place. I am brought back to the twenty first century on the third occasion I am asked, "Can I help?"

Finishing my impromptu second lunch whilst walking back up the high street, I arrive at the courthouse fifteen minutes early. A discussion is going on between the merits of our national football and rugby teams. When asked to become involved I come down firmly on the rugby side, which pleases Terry (rugby) and disappoints Tim (football). Tim is a burger seller at all manner of events and car boot sales on weekends. When I ask how his wife puts up with that he goes into a well-rehearsed line about being three times married and being halfway along the route of Henry the Eighth – divorced, beheaded, deceased. There follows a few seconds of total silence, as the five of us who have returned early are dumbstruck. He fills the gap with a brief explanation, he divorced his first wife, his second was beheaded in a rail accident some twenty years ago and his third wife died of lung cancer last year. He then adds that a couple of his mates call him Henry the Fourth because he's half way to being Henry the Eighth. He says all of this without emotion to a mute audience.

John (foreman) then arrives in the Jury room and asks if we are up to a challenge. Several of us ask him to quantify his remark. He explains,

"Well last time I was up for Jury service we had a chap called Jerry Relton, a really sharp fellow, he knew his English like nobody I've ever met. Each day he would challenge us to ask a question that contained a predisposed word. It had to be a question of merit and relevant to the case. Asking for a toilet break or why the walls are painted pink has no merit, are you with me?"

"Yes." Says David (the weather man) and Thomas who has yet to be introduced to me, with an immediate positive response, which also included a nod from myself, Tim, Terry and Lynda (menswear), she being particularly enthusiastic, so John was onto a winner. He gave us our first word for the day, which was indent, not in its more common usage that was to notch, score or mark, but in its less common form to mean request, order or ask for. John's dare soon infiltrated the entire room. Most persons were up for the challenge, it was only Joyce (accessories) and Barry (chaplain) who voiced mild opposition. They felt that such a diversion might introduce an element of flippancy into an otherwise sombre occasion. John had won the day, most of those present endorsed John's challenge with buoyant enthusiasm, the rest with reluctant acceptance. Either way, John had struck a chord with a significant number of his fellow men and women, sufficient to elicit a noteworthy response. More than half attempted to construct a retort containing John's dare immediately in our minds.

Soon we are up to our full count of twelve again and back on our uncomfortable benches. The four women and John all pick up cushions from the jury room to take into court. This afternoon session carries on much as the morning left off. More lies from all concerned, but a general picture is building up. Also it is becoming clear that the prosecution barrister is worth his weight in a bright coloured and heavy, yellow substance, and the defence barrister is worth his weight in a less dense, brown substance.

It was Lynda (menswear) who interrupted proceedings mid way through the prosecution's questioning of the defendant by attracting the attention of the court usher and passing a note to the Judge via the usher. The Judge, who seemed ill amused at the interjection, read the note to the barrister,

"A member of the jury wishes to know, 'could you please indent clarification on the question of whether the witness did or did not speak to his alleged assailant immediately prior to the alleged attack?" Lynda received both a satisfactory answer to her question and an acknowledgement from John.

We are dismissed for the day at four pm. We all linger in the jury room very briefly, just allowing John significant time to set our word task for tomorrow, which is to be tautology. He was, I believe, the only person in the room who was confident of its meaning.

I drive to the Thomas Hardye School, Claire comfortable negotiates the afternoon traffic, we arrive home in one piece without incident. Claire walks in the door in front of me and shouts,

"Any post?" She turns to give me a grin and runs out of my reach to play with the dogs. Liz replies,

"No post to worry about. Are we still OK to go looking for my new car on Saturday?"

"Yes," I say, "no problem." Emma pipes up,

"Talking of cars, can we go out in a minute for a lesson? I've got minging homework to do later, so the sooner the better."

"OK, give me ten minutes for a drink and get over the shock of Claire's minging driving." For which I receive a very un-ladylike hand gesture from Claire. Liz asks,

"How'd it go in court today?"

"You know I can't give details, but the oath clearly counts for nothing. Everybody swears to tell the truth, the whole truth blah, blah, blah, and everybody lies their arse off."

"So if everybody's lying, how do you know who's telling the truth?" She replies.

"That's easy," I say, "Nobody is." Emma and Claire both butt in, in a request for more information,

"But Dad." My raised hand and eyebrows kill the conversation.

"Five minutes Emma."

"OK, I'm nearly ready."

Only one minor with Emma's driving in that we add one rabbit to today's road kill tally, which quite upsets her, not nearly as much as the Clio overheating upsets me. Honestly, you pay fifty quid in good faith, and from a friend! Actually two of my friends have used this car to get their four sons through the driving test, so it owes nothing to anyone. At least the rabbit is in good enough condition to go home and go in the pot. I also pick up a pheasant for the buzzard pole. I love to watch them descend on to my feeder. They try to take the meal with them, but as I've cable tied the carcass to the cross bar at the top of the pole, they have to remain in full view of my monoscope.

Later in the evening, I hear some of Liz's day, standard stuff, some housework, a routine mammogram at Poole hospital, shopping on the way back, a walk with the dogs and two hours spent in her dark room developing. She has resisted the modern trend to go digital up to now as she still enjoys using her single lens reflex Cannon A1, but she feels she will finally succumb, she says she feels a bit like King Canute and the tide is up to her neck. I remark to her of my frustration on reading the first three chapters of the Hardy novel and being unable to recall any details, unusual for me. I also tell her I have an hour plus for lunch and would love to find something absorbing to read to make the time fly. Dorchester is a pleasant town but for an hour and a half a day for two weeks I will run out of places to walk and things to see within half an hour of the courts, and I'll be lucky to experience the weather of today regularly. Liz takes a deep breath and says,

"Well, I may have the very thing for you that will keep you riveted to the page."

"I'm all ears."

"It's Jayne's book." I tense up, and the hairs to the back of my neck bristle.

"Now please wait before you say anything. The girls found it in the loft a few months back when they were looking for costume clothes for school. They asked what it was and could they read it," she continued, "I told them it was your ex-wife's, I didn't mention your part in it and told them that both I and you would want to read it first to check the content was suitable for them. That was just stalling them I know." I pour myself a glass of good red, which is actually a Saint-Emillion Grand Cru, one I'd been looking forward to. A friend gave it to me along with two others for fixing his roof. The wine is superb and settles the hairs back into place on my neck.

"Over the last few months while you've been away roofing, I've read it more than once. I've retyped it, spell-checked it on the computer and re-tensed it into the past tense so that it now makes sense to read. It's taken me around a hundred hours. I think it would do you good to re-read it. You've neglected it for over twenty years and, after re-reading it myself, I'm sure it has value to you, emotional value, and who knows, it might have some commercial value and you could finally give it a title." I finish my wine and search for an answer. Nothing comes to mind. I pour Liz a glass of red and top up my own. I tell Liz of my new friend' Barry (Chaplin) and how disappointed he'll be if we're not reading our Hardy novels together, and how normally he and his wife read a novel simultaneously so they can discuss it at length. I hear from behind me a simultaneous,

"Boring." From both Claire and Emma. When your offspring reach a certain level of satire and cynicism, you begin to realise that not only have you done a decent job with their upbringing and preparing them for the adult world, but also that the job is all but done, and perhaps soon they will fly the coop and take their highly tuned sharp tongues elsewhere. Not a day to look forward to. Do any parents, I wonder?

I tell Liz I want to consider whether or not to go back into my past and read the old manuscript, and meanwhile I think I owe it to Barry to read and digest a little more of the Thomas Hardy novel. So I settle down with the Saint-Emillion on the sofa next to Liz and do exactly that. The first few chapters grip my imagination on the second attempt. I was, on this second reading, able to enter the beguiling world of Hardy's accurate reflections of life in rural Dorset in the mid to late nineteenth century. After a pause for an hour to share a meal with Liz and the girls, and a cursory glance at BBC News of the Day, I slipped back into the past, this time into 'Thomas Hardy, A Biography' by Michael Millgate, a university professor of English, whose biography of Hardy is quoted as 'by far the most detailed and comprehensive account of Hardy's personal and literary life available'. He claims;

Hardy is said to have been almost unique in his intense, paradoxical preoccupation with the personal, local and national past.

He was born to very humble parents, in a remote corner of the English South West. Nothing in his ancestry or early upbringing offered the remotest hint that he would live to become the most famous writer of his day. His name, which he did not enjoy because of its commonness at the time, was not unique even among the noted and famous of his small corner of England. Another similarly named Thomas Hardye of nearby Frampton was to endow and lend his name to the Dorchester Grammar School in 1579; it still bears that name today and is attended by my eldest twin. And, of course, it was another Thomas Hardy of Portisham who was Nelson's Flag Captain at Trafalgar, he of the 'kiss me Hardy' fame. It is this Thomas Hardy whose monument on the South Dorset Downs has led to much embarrassed confusion by visitors from both near and afar. I continued my reading of Hardy's excellently informative biography.

DAY TWO

MORE LIES

Tuesday the ninth of October was a colder morning than its predecessor, with a strong westerly wind. Liz was out on her early morning walk with the dogs and I, who in truth had barely spoken to her since she had presented me with the prospect of rereading Jayne's book, now had to overcome a knot in my stomach as I recognise the manuscript sitting on the dining room table with my mobile phone and car keys on top of it, lest I forget. Twenty years has passed since I completed the manuscript, is it time to reread it? I am undecided. I drink two coffees, as is my norm, and peruse the papers whilst eating my toast.

In Today's Mirror, the revelations of top jockey Frankie Dettori catch my eye. Apparently the famous jockey has confessed that he likes to eat horse meat and that he has never had sex in a stable. Presumably this means with a horse, a woman or a fellow jockey. Also, the Jury on the Princess Diana inquest, which I sympathised with just yesterday, were driven to Paris by coach to view for themselves the location of the accident. Firstly the coach knocked a police outrider off of his motorbike, then mounted a pavement hitting a pillar and bursting a tyre, all of this happened directly outside the Paris Ritz. More shocking was a ten minute delay caused by a cameo walk past by Victoria Beckham and speculation that she may have believed the zealous press attention had all been meant for her, the paper speculates as to whether it was a coincidence that she was there?

The Times leads with all British troops to leave Iraq in 2008 and that Britain is now the favourite destination for asylum seekers, overtaking and putting France into second place. Hopefully the French will remember this and sympathise with us if we should meet in next weekend's rugby world cup semi-final. Also Ian Hislop has revealed that after a recording of the popular show 'Have I got news for you' the guest panellist Boris Johnson was heading off to a party meeting when he turned to Hislop and asked him if he knew the Tory policy on immigration. Hislop replied 'no', Johnson replied 'damb'. More seriously a council accountant has been jailed for five years for siphoning off £870,000 of public funds, Leeds Crown Court was told that the father of six had a grudge against his employers because they demanded his wife return maternity pay after the death of their child. There are two curious items from Italy, firstly anti-mafia police are investigating eight people for the illegal trafficking in nuclear waste and clandestine production of plutonium, and more frivolously that dormouse has returned to restaurant menus in Calabria, as it once was in ancient Rome. Finally from The Times, A 32 year old German man in Berlin was killed by a 10,000-volt electric shock when he tried to steal a live copper cable, so swift justice there and no need for an expensive trial and jury.

The journey south to Dorchester today is an eventful one. My learner driver daughter, Claire has forgotten how wide her car is and is using far more of the road then she is entitled to. There are fifteen deer to the East side of the road past Buckland Newton. One dead deer and a fox cub is today's road kill tally, but alarmingly there is a tractor with a burst tyre on a tight bend. I make Claire stop the car, to her great annoyance, while I get out and direct traffic until Claire is safely past the obstruction. This is the exact scenario which lost me my first wife twenty-five years ago in Oxfordshire and I've no intention of losing a daughter the same way. It was both frustrating and embarrassing for Claire, who calls me stupid one too many times. My loud reaction results in a silent second half of the journey.

After parking the car, my nod of recognition to the Thomas Hardy statue is not returned. His statue is beginning to glisten with the onset of a fine early morning drizzle now that the wind has abated. In passing the sculpture I recollect further excerpts from the great man's biography and with that memory comes a general recognition of just how hard it was to live in the mid 1840's.

Leaving Hardy behind I reach the jury room and am greeted by John (foreman), who has today finished the Telegraph crossword in twenty minutes, eighteen seconds, his time being recorded in the margin of his newspaper. He is now working on a limerick to best summarise yesterday's events in court. I sit in the only gap between Tim (football), and Terry (rugby), and immediately regret my choice of seat. Two minutes of competitive sports banter is sufficient for me.

I cross the floor to serve myself an indigestible coffee, which I have no intention of drinking. I am acknowledged by Joyce (matching accessories) who has today chosen a main theme of black with an underlying theme of Barbie pink in her choice of lipstick, earrings, necklace, scarf, wide belt and heels, somehow the whole ensemble reminds me of liquorice and candy floss brought together in just a tad too much haste. While she is talking to me of the weather, the awful coffee and Andy's bouquet of the day, I imagine her without the outer cladding of black and pink. These thoughts are both appealing and distracting, so much so, that by the look on her face my answer to her last question is clearly amiss. She repeats the previous question, this time with exaggerated intonation. I quickly redress her and respond with,

"No, sorry, yes. I mean no, and really." This seems to leave her equally confused as I am. I need to talk to Lynda, (men's wear) much easier to concentrate. I am re-adjusting to give the now fully dressed Joyce my full attention when I am sidelined by Barry (chaplain),

"How did you get on with 'The Madding Crowd' yesterday?" I respond to him with admiration of Hardy's penmanship and our general conversation advances my knowledge of the novel. Eventually I break free from Barry and engage David (the weather man), a retired pasty seller,

"I spent forty years bringing 'em up from Cornwall to sell in industrial estates, cafés and garages along the south coast. I made a good living. Now I can devote all my time to sailing. My son and I have got a smashing forty footer in Poole harbour." Which I later realise is just about all there is to know about this pleasant, fellow juror. After a brief chat, whose main subject was also the weather, with Thomas Cobble, a fifty two year old farmer from west of Dorchester who seemed to be obsessed with numbers, temperature, wind speed, barometric pressure etc. I think had the conversation not been stopped by Dawn the court usher and a quite delightful whiff of White Linen, I would have learnt his date of birth, his inside leg measurement and how far he could throw a sheep, both wind assisted and otherwise.

Soon we are all ushered into our seats in court, all of us now taking a cushion with us from the jury room, for another day of claims and counter claims, lies and counter lies. At lunch time the weather is that unpleasant combination of cool, wet and windy. I buy myself a takeaway lunch and return to Claire's car as I am aware that Tim (football), Thomas (numbers) and Terry (rugby) all bring their lunch with them and stay in the jury room for the duration.

Once I'm inside with the car door shut and the food consumed, I pull out both 'The Madding Crowd' and the as yet unnamed manuscript that was a collaboration between my first wife, Jayne, and myself, although at no point did we work on it together. I consider both. The Hardy book swiftly brings images of Barry and his wife sitting either side of an electric log fire, dual-foot single slippers on, complete with dog and after-eight mints, both clock watching because there's an hour to go before they can open the box. Fighting a wave of nausea I drop the novel on the driver's seat and consider the alternative. Should I read this piece of work that so tormented and tested me? Should I go back there? And revisit so many painful memories.

A realisation hits me that I am within sight of the park where, over twenty years ago, Liz rescued the book from a rubbish bin that a despairing and drunken version of myself had cast it. This memory does bring home to me some of the effort that went into the book, not only Jayne's and mine, but also Liz's. If my girls are going to read it and bombard me with questions, I ought to get it fresh in my head. Where is that glass of red when you need it? I open the ring binder which begins with two chapters of my work, the writing of which proved to be greatly therapeutic at the time, which has now been rewritten by Liz to read retrospectively.

JAYNE

FEB' 1987

As Jayne's coffin was lowered into the ground, Jude could only think of how cold she must be. He knew she would never be warm again. Jayne often woke in the night and moved toward him to draw from his warmth. Jude's memories were disturbing him. He felt sure if he could know that she was warm, then coping with her loss would be easier. He questioned himself. Why did it have to be such a cold day? He had attended few funerals, it seemed to Jude that they had always been on unpleasant days. Perhaps the coldness came from within?

A handful of soil and a handful of words and it was all too quickly over. He hoped with every ounce of his soul, that his wife, Jayne, could not feel as he did the absolute finality of their separation. Jude had been told by family and doctors that it was perhaps a blessing Jayne had not survived the accident considering her injuries. He felt he wanted to receive those injuries. Surely nothing could be worse than his loss. Jude felt an arm to his left side. It was his mother Faye, time had come for them to move off. He felt numb toward the people standing at Jayne's graveside, they could not share the love he had felt for her, he could not now share his grief. They moved off at a pace set by the pallbearers who felt it to be apt. Jude focussed towards the paving stones, on one, a small brown and white stripped snail had spent the afternoon gaining half a yard, only to be crushed by a careless foot.

On reaching the cars, many people took their leave of Jude, with either a shake of his hand or a pat to his arm. Noticeably, Jayne's brother, James, had stayed close by throughout. As Jude entered the car, he felt its luxuriousness and warmth, in stark contrast to the solid coldness of the earth. He felt guilt in its comfort. He was sure he would never lose the feeling of guilt, in whatever pleasures or comforts that may follow Jayne's death.

At home with Jayne, all pleasures had been doubled if they had been shared, without her he had no reason to look for them.

The car pulled away. Jude's mind went back to a Wednesday morning, just seven days previous. It had been a crisp, frosty February day. Jude had driven into the company's yard at Newbury after a pleasant drive south from Oxford. On leaving the car he noticed a strained look on the face of Martin, one of the fitters who services the tractors and combines. What Jude did not know, and Martin did, was that the police had tried to contact Jude there earlier, the lads in the yard had been asked to say nothing, and send Jude to the office as soon as he arrived. After trying unsuccessfully to read Martin's face, Jude strode to the nearest doorway. Colin, the work's manager, told him that his wife, Jayne, had been involved in an accident, she was taken to Oxford by ambulance, he added that he was sorry, but he knew no more.   A disgusting feeling of nausea flowed from his stomach to every cell in his body. A high pitched noise developed in his ears, which grew to an alarming crescendo, as a police car siren wailing drew into the yard.

In just a few moments, Jude was in the rear of the car which was leaving for Oxford at a tremendous speed. Jude was beginning to feel numb with dread. The sergeant travelling as a passenger told Jude that Jayne was alive, but apart from that he had no more information. Jude's instincts told him that because of the speed they were travelling, he should doubt one or other of the sergeant's statements. He could recall little of the conversation that passed between them in the short time before arriving at the hospital. He did remember telling them wrongly that Jayne would be thirty in two weeks. She was, he said, not looking forward to reaching that milestone because they had no yet had a child. Jayne had assumed this would happen long before reaching her thirtieth year. Jude explained that this had not been the case for them.

The car slowed at the hospital and something inside Jude altered radically, a feeling of panic set in, his bowels felt weak, his stomach heaved over. The crisp February air failed to cool his panic. He was not taken to a ward as he had expected, but instead was shown to a side room, this increased his feeling of dread. The room was sparsely furnished, curiously the window was adorned with only one curtain, and the room gave off a clinical air. It was in that emotionless room that a senior doctor told Jude that his wife, Jayne, had died of injuries received in an automobile accident earlier that day. Jude sank to his knees, and struggled to control his bowels. He demanded to see Jayne, assured that the doctor, senior neurological surgeon Peter Dean, had made a mistake. Dean was doing his best to persuade Jude not to see his wife, saying that he should remember her as he last saw her. Oh, how Jude wished he had listened.

Hospital personnel took him to the mortuary. He could not remember their faces, voices or any other detail about them, except one, a female had a finger missing on her left hand. He wished that she and Jayne could change places, they could cope with a finger missing.

The mortuary was both barren and cold. A curtain was drawn back from one small section of the building and the object that occupied the centre of the room resembled a piece of furniture which had been covered with a dust sheet, as it might be in a disused house. Jude knew that the doctor had made no mistake. He was led to one side. He braced himself and indicated that he still wanted to see Jayne. The nurse partially exposed the body of his wife. He gasped, releasing a peculiar sound. How could this be Jayne? She is at his mothers, having judgement passed on the first chapters of her book, he told himself desperately. Jayne always had Faye, his mother, give an opinion of her work before anyone else saw it, even Jude. He took one pace forward, his eyes focussed more acutely on her face. It was, he thought, too pale to be his Jayne. Once again he said that there had been a mistake, but he delivered his words without conviction. The two members of hospital staff standing by did not react to his comment, they had stood there many times before. Indeed they had been chosen for their remarkable ability to handle this particular situation well. They had immediately noted that Jude Saunders was the type of person who choked on his grief and not the type to display it verbally.

Jude wanted to brush Jayne's hair from her damaged brow, as he had so often done in the past. He lowered his face to touch hers and moved his hand to her far side to draw her to him. It was a combination of the coldness of her face and the alien feel of her skin, which caused in Jude a build up of shock induced chemicals. He felt his legs weaken for a second time, he fainted. Falling backwards, he struck his head on a hand basin and fell to the floor, passing into sweet unconsciousness.

He later discovered that he had been treated for the cut and concussion, cleaned up and put to bed in a side ward to await his return to awareness. He has wished many times that he had never regained his senses. He felt that the horror of touching Jayne's lifeless body would remain with him until he too lay cold in the earth.

The journey home from the funeral was a short one. Jayne had been buried in the local village of Swinford, a little under four miles from Oxford. They reached Jude's parents' home in the town in just ten minutes. Jude could sense James' presence beside him. He was deep in thought and very hurt by the loss of his only sibling, but to his credit Jude felt sure that James' first concern was that of Jude's own welfare. In the ten years they had known each other they had become great friends. Jude had often wondered if it could have been possible to have a better relationship if he had had a brother. James, who stands six feet three and weighs one hundred and seventy pounds, has the looks to match his stylish sense of dress. He worked for some years as a solicitor's clerk before qualifying in his own right at the age of twenty-six. From that moment on things fell into place for this blonde haired gentle man, whom Jude had come to know very well, particularly during their spare time on the golf course.

On arrival at Jude's parents' home, the number of mourners had been reduced to his mother and sisters, complete with offspring and of course James. Jayne's father John had not been well enough to attend the funeral and his second wife Kate had as always stayed by his side. Bob Saunders, Jude's father, was in a wheelchair, as he had been since the much-celebrated D-Day of 6 June 1944. He greeted them with as much sympathy as he could muster.

"Jude." He shouted, "Get some of this tea inside you, you look frozen." Which was typical of his father, he would keep things simple, there was to be no emotion or tears. He had been hardened to the ways of the world by the endeavours of the Third Reich, forty years before on a Normandy beach. Anne, Jude's eldest sister, was busy as usual herding her four kids. Her voice could clearly be heard,

"Mark, serve the teas and be careful mind. Sally, let Granny sit there. Karen take Paul with you and sit in that corner and tell him to put that damn cat down." Anne was capable of a constant flow of such dialogue.

Barbara who at twenty-eight is two years younger than Jude and four years younger than Anne and is Jude's only other sibling. She has only to see Anne's kids occasionally to remind herself that she is content to remain childless, living in France, as she has done for the past twelve years since her marriage to Jean Pierre, she sees them less than once a year. Jude has always felt closer to Barbara than Anne, despite seeing her so seldom, because Anne, a full-time mother gives herself one hundred percent to the rearing of her offspring, she has retained little identity. Jude feels that Anne does not have a serious opinion to voice since she is far too busy enjoying the muddle of growing up four times over. When he asks Anne how she is, she replies, 'Oh, the kids are fine'. Her husband Derek is as content as she with his role in life, a corner stone for them all to lean on.

Tea was taken. Jude shared conversation with Derek and James. As the afternoon drew on, Jude explained that he must return home to feed the animals, as he needed to escape the conversation of weather and the children's progress at school. James immediately offered to drive Jude home. They were soon travelling toward Swinford. The car passed the spot where Jude's beautiful young wife had been fatally injured whilst attempting to pass a ditched tractor on a bend. The driver of the milk tanker coming against her knew the road so well he did not need to slow down. He had not had an accident in thirty years of driving on the Oxfordshire roads. After the accident, he was able to drive on with his day's work, as Jayne had been on the wrong side of the road, there would be no case to answer. James apologised for using that particular section of road, but both of them knew it was the only road connecting Swinford and Oxford.

On reaching the village they turned left at the Pig & Whistle, drove over the railway crossing, turned left again at the Fox & Hounds and the cottage appeared a mile out from the village on the right hand side. They had chosen the small, detached whitewashed cottage for many reasons, one of which was the distance it sat back from the road. This was all of two hundred feet, with a similar garden at the rear. James offered as they both knew he must to stay, but now was the time for Jude to spend his first night in the cottage alone. He felt he had to regain at least some sense of normality to his shattered life. James drove off.

Jude turned to walk the driveway. He felt odd not passing the car as he neared the house, but then he knew where the car was and the condition it was in. He opened the door, immediately he could hear the two cats, Whiskey and Scrumpy, scratching at the kitchen door to be allowed in. They too had missed their share of love from Jayne. They stepped over each other to reach Jude first, he did not know whether to fuss them or feed them. He took the easy way out and gave them a large enough meal to require at least four hours sleeping off.

Jude drifted into the back garden to feed the half dozen chickens that had supplied them and the cats, with as many eggs as they could eat. Immediately he was accosted by Campbell, the large white gander that owns the back garden. The first action one must take on entry into his territory is to seek his permission to move freely. This is always granted after a loud hiss and a long upward shake of his head and neck. After receiving his freedom, Jude fed the birds and returned to the house to the sound of Campbell insisting that the chickens had eaten their share and they should go to roost.

The house, which Jude could no longer look upon as his home, was exactly as it had been the last time Jayne had moved things around. Each item upon which he looked now meant so much less, each article of furniture or patch of décor had been carefully picked by Jayne. Before purchasing she would seek his approval, but Jude could not recall a time when her choice of colour or style had not been ideal for the situation she had had in mind. Looking around, Jude realised that Jayne had spent more time than he had ever appreciated transforming the cottage into a comfortable home. A home in which there seemed to be a room to match whichever mood he might be in. All this she has achieved in a moderate three-bedroom cottage. At the time they bought Blenheim Cottage nine years previous, it had looked very sad indeed. He paced to and fro in the house, the only sound he could hear was that of Campbell ordering his troops to roost.

He shut out the cold February evening. The all consuming feeling of guilt returned as he sat on the warm and comfortable sofa in the lounge. Immediately Scrumpy saw an empty lap and was on him. The following ten hours were spent in that position, Jude would sometimes stroke or talk to the cat, he would sometimes talk to Jayne. A tear would occasionally land on the cat, which was in such a deep sleep it would go unnoticed. Jude's sleep, when it came, was alcohol induced and very unsatisfying. When finally he gave up all hope of further sleep at around five o'clock in the morning, he ate the meal that should have been yesterday's lunch. He then fed the birds, which was much to Campbell's annoyance, it was three hours early.

He paused to take in the damp, early morning air. Jude realised that surviving through one day, as he had just done, only brought him into another and this new day would be as challenging as the last to complete. This was the first time in his life that Jude considered ending his own life. It was not to be the last time that the easy escape would appeal to him.

A LONG WALK

Jude turned his back on Blenheim and took an early morning walk. When at first he lost Jayne he thought to preserve everything around him, just as she had left it, surrounding himself in her memory. Walking away from the house he found it less painful not having her memories smothering him. As he walked the country lanes, he realised he was taking little or no interest in his surroundings, quite unlike their walks together when they would point out to each other all the tiny features of the countryside. Jude knew that if he was to conquer his loss he must begin something new. He made himself a promise that before he returned to the house from his walk, he would have some project in mind, something constructive and mentally taxing. He somehow knew that if he failed to find an absorbing task to pitch his mind against, the easy escape would appeal to him more and more.

His work came to mind. As a salesman for a manufacturer of heavy agricultural implements, he travelled the counties trying to persuade the farmers who say that they cannot afford a new tractor, combine or baler, that they could not afford to be without one. He enjoyed his work, especially the down to earth attitude of the farmers. The sons and work hands would show great interest in the advances made in mechanical engineering, but the farmers would often tell him to 'Bugger off and take you fancy tackle with you,' or 'Stop putting daft ideas in that boy's 'ead, anythin' to save 'ard work's good by 'im no matter the cost,' but to be fair there was always a drink on offer at the end of a long drive.

He thought that perhaps he could change his work, but what could he do? He could not work indoors again as he had done in the past. His first job came to mind. He was employed as a trainee accountant. He completed three years of intense deskwork, it seemed to Jude that he was still at school. Had he qualified as an accountant, he would now be enjoying James' social circle, but this was not something he longed for. He left his first employer on impulse and fortunately fate smiled on him, he joined a small independent forestry company as a labourer. The work, although very hard and contradictory to his previous employment, he found satisfying and enjoyable. Amongst a team of six, he travelled a great deal. Both the work and the locations varied tremendously. As he had been the only labourer who had been interested in staying on through the winter, he began in the spring of his second year as foreman at only 22 years old. It had taken until this time for his father to begin speaking to him again. His father Bob had been very upset at Jude throwing away a good career and wasting his exam results. Jude questioned his decision to drop out a great deal in the first year, but as the months went by he knew he had found the kind of work that returned variety and a host of ever changing characters to keep his interest keen, and of course there was his boss's daughter. He had quickly noticed that the owner of the company, John Marshall, had a very attractive daughter, Jayne. He soon began to look for ways to talk to John when he knew Jayne would be close by. She was twenty years old, slim, five feet six with deep brown hair and eyes to match. He thought her so beautiful, she had only to smile in Jude's direction to put him on a high for the remainder of the day.

John took Jude more and more into his confidence. Jude would occasionally spend an hour or two in the family home discussing contracts, work rotas or wages. Was it Jude's imagination or did Jayne make sure she was always nearby whenever he was in the house? He struggled with the shy nervousness of a teenager for many months before making his move. When finally he did ask if Jayne would accompany him to the local cinema the following weekend he both kicked and congratulated himself, for her answer was, "I thought you were never going to ask."

They had often looked back on that first nervous night out when Jude had been in two minds whether to kiss Jayne or not. He did many times and was overwhelmed with her response. With other girls he has always felt that it had been he who had been giving the kiss and the girl had been receiving, but with Jayne it was quite different. She was by comparison, so much more alive, so positive. Jude found her welcoming response breathtaking and her smile enchanting, but it was her eyes that

Jude could not forget. Each time they parted he would allow his eyes to linger on hers, Jayne's eyes were quite simply magical to Jude. They soon became great friends, Jude still enjoyed his work but he looked forward to the weekends with wonder, as their relationship developed both as friends and as lovers.

Jayne was employed by a hotel in Oxford. During her third year she was sent to the companies head office in London to complete a course so that she might achieve an upgrading. It was during the weekend between those two weeks in her hotel room they first made love. Their movements were very nervous, they were all too obviously afraid of offending or hurting each other, both physically and emotionally. The whole weekend had been wonderful, discovering London by day and each other by night. It was during the fortnight away that Jayne first developed an interest in writing. Her words were of her love for Jude and her admiration for him as a lively, determined and humorous young man, and as a gentle and considerate lover. Their lovemaking became exploratory and passionate. They would spend many hours discovering the physical and mental limits to which they could take their intimacies. Jude could never tire of Jayne's body. The soft texture of her skin, the warm fullness of her breast and her intense response to the touch of his hands and tongue made each session of their lovemaking a new page in a favourite book, a book without end, or so he had thought.

He told himself that on his return to the house he would seek out something of Jayne's written work. He continued his walk, his thoughts were some ten years behind him on the day they announced they wished to marry, hopefully with their parents' blessing. Jude's father agreed at once. Jude felt sure the reason for Bob's uncharacteristically quick decision was that Bob saw a future for Jude as a partner in John's business. This was a strong possibility, but not one of Jude's motives. His mother Faye warmed to Jayne the first time they met. They were married in the spring of seventy-three, Jayne was twenty two and Jude twenty four. They honeymooned for two weeks in the south of Ireland. After an awful crossing of the Irish Sea which had them both suffering from nausea the entire trip, they sped away from the ferry, very relieved to be on Irish soil.

They toured, making use of farm cottages for bed and breakfast, and took great delight in the mountains of Cork and Kerry. The farmer's wives were very hospitable, treating Jayne like a daughter. The countryside and people they found enchanting, from that day Jude had always felt it a great pity that such a beautiful and welcoming place should be viewed in the eyes of the world for its infamy and problems.

They were able to rent a small cottage from a landowner who was well known to John. The rent was low, which gave them room financially to save toward a place of their own. Fortunately, there was sufficient room in the rear garden for Jayne's pet goose, the ever bossy Campbell.

Jude put no pressure on Jayne to stay at work, although he did agree with her that it was a good idea for her to stay until they had put down a deposit on their own home. Jayne's interest in writing quickly developed. She managed to get into the local newspaper with a once a week column, thanks to Faye, who knew all the right people and how to influence them. The aim of the column was to point out to the locals the attraction of their own area as an area of natural beauty. Jayne accomplished this well, for she loved the area deeply. The affection she had for the Chilterns she shared with her readers through her written word, but if Jayne was not writing or with Jude then she was reading. Jayne could absorb books at an astonishing rate. Jude would dither over the first twenty pages, but not Jayne. She had that enviable ability to be completely engrossed in a book. Jude loved to watch her reading, she would often smile or hold back tears as the character she had become experienced ecstasy or agony.

From the age of two Jayne was raised by a succession of nannies after her mother's death from an unforeseen brain haemorrhage , she showed no outward sign as having missed out as a child and Jude never detected any inward suffering. If she was affected at all by the loss of her own true mother, then Jude believed the scars were so well hidden that Jayne had herself misplaced them.

The next few years seems to speed by. John encouraged Jude to become more involved in the running of the company. He would often be asked to tender for work, review contract prices and accompany John whenever a landowner or estate manager

46

sought his advice as a forestry consultant. This side of John's work brought out the very best in him. After a day with John the customer would be convinced that he was talking to the man who could foresee the timber needs of the country thirty to forty years hence. Each year brought a new gang of labourers, a host of differing characters, their names Jude had forgotten, but to recall their faces would bring a flood of humorous memories. The seasonal workers brought with them a carefree attitude. They worked hard when supervised, but it was their sense of fun and their practical joking that made hard work a genuine pleasure. Jude continued his walk into the past. He found the thought of doing this type of work again stimulating. This was the first time since Jayne's death that anything had appealed. The appeal was the pattern of work, early starts, late finishes, seven days a week, he knew it would leave him exhausted at the end of the day, with little time to dwell in self-pity. He walked still further from Blenheim. He had, at this point, decided that this day was to be very important to him. He would allow himself to look back as much as he dared today, but tomorrow he would move forward.

He and Jayne had been married four years when they first saw Blenheim. Instantly they prayed they were the first to see it for sale. Taking the agents sign with them into Oxford, they offered the asking price and began what was then the long and difficult process of buying a house. They experienced many problems in gaining a mortgage. Jayne was very anxious during this period, for the cottage which stood alone on a small hillock looking south for many miles was in their opinion the perfect spot at which to bring up children. They were also pleased with its closeness to a local reservoir, making it a great spot from which to observe the many and varied migrating water birds, an interest they shared. They subsequently spent many days wandering the local countryside, and many more weeks knocking Blenheim's damp, decaying walls into shape, or out altogether. It had been soon after they moved in that Jayne came home one day carrying two black kittens, subsequently named Whisky and Scrumpy, two very innocent-looking balls of chaos.

Jayne's written word was yielding enough cash for her to leave her full-time employment. This concentrated her efforts on her writing, Blenheim and becoming pregnant. The latter being the only one of the three subjects that failed to produce any immediate result. Blenheim was fast becoming a reflection of Jayne's character and her writing was now to be found in two national magazines. She spent many hours with Faye, and it was from her that she obtained many ideas to develop on paper. They had, between them hatched an idea that was to become Jayne's first book, on the question of its theme they were keeping very quiet. Jude could only speculate on its background from the type of books Jayne had borrowed from Oxford's vast library for reference. They were of such mixed subjects that Jayne had him completely foxed. The first chapters of the book had been amongst Jayne's belongings returned to Jude by the local police after the accident. He remembered seeing her name on the cover page of the notepad, Jayne Marshall. She preferred to write under her maiden name of Marshall, saying this gave her a second option of their name of Saunders should she fail. The both knew in truth she liked her father, John, to see her using his family name.

The demise of John's business came as a great shock and as a result of John, at fifty-eight, suffering a quite severe stroke, which left him both physically and mentally affected. On the physical side they all thought at first that he would never recover sufficient movement to continue working at all, but to everyone's pleasant surprise his physical condition improved greatly, he regained almost full use of his once paralysed left side. It was his mental condition that at first appeared to be only slightly affected, which did not improve at all. This progressively worsened, leaving John unable to cope with any problems which required judgement or concentration, in every day matters he continued to function, but word spread among the landowners that his expertise could no longer be relied upon. The order book soon dried up. Jude pressed on trying to broaden his scope and diversify, but he was always battling uphill and finally, eighteen months after John's stroke he was forced to admit defeat. This was a very unhappy time, witnessing the break-up of a man's life achievement. When finally it was over John took a long overdue holiday with Kate.

Kate was the last of five nannies, she stayed on as housekeeper after James and Jayne had grown independent.

Their holiday was on the Canberra, cruising the oceans of the world for five months, which did little to improve John's condition, but gladly he did return married to Kate, much to everyone's surprise and to Jayne's obvious delight. Kate was an ideal partner for John. She always kept one step ahead of him, coping ably without dominating him, this allowed John the dignity of feeling that he was master of his own affairs. After leaving John and Kate on board the Canberra, Jude was now free of employment, he spent the next four months at Blenheim putting the finishing touches to modernising the cottage and landscaping the gardens. During this time Jayne purchased half a dozen chickens from a local farm. These were soon housed in the rear garden much to Campbell's pleasure. He soon found he could boss the new arrivals, this gave him the authority he had always longed for.

They took a holiday in Greece, their first since Ireland. On their return James breezed in one day saying he had a couple weeks to kill and that he would help Jude with his slicing problem on the golf course. James had just qualified as a solicitor and was looking for a company to join, but he was in no hurry. James' couple of weeks grew into a couple of months. On reflection Jude felt this summer of 1979 had been the most relaxed and enjoyable time of his life. The three of them complete with James' fiancée, Sue, also holidayed in France, staying with Jude's sister Barbara and her husband Jean Pierre. Toward the end of the summer, Jayne was showing great disappointment at not having become pregnant. The one reason they could rule out for sure was that it could not be through lack of trying. Jayne fixed both her and Jude appointments to have medicals and blood tests, Jayne also had a smear test and Jude a sperm count. There was no problem. The doctor hinted that perhaps they should try more often or take a holiday!

The holidays were over. James was fixed up with and established company in Oxford and Jude applied for two posts, one as manager for an egg packing station at Swindon, for this he never saw the first interview, the second was for the position of sales representative for a large manufacturer of heavy farm equipment, ten miles north of Oxford. The second application was successful. Jude was given a fair salary, a car and an area to work, which covered four counties. He was also given a list of established clients and a much longer list of cold call clients. Jude felt he needed to work again. Financially he was required to work to maintain his standard of living, because what little cash they had saved and the settlement money John had paid him was all but used up. Apart from the money, Jude felt that he wanted to work. He knew he had been fortunate in that he had enjoyed a marvellously relaxed summer, now he felt like a school boy returning after the summer break, knowing that if he did not return the resulting problems would become insurmountable.

Jude quickly fell into a routine. His area, which extended from the South West to the Midlands, he split into three. He would spend a week in each section and follow this with a week in the office at Oxford. Jayne, with Campbell's approval would sometimes accompany him, for she enjoyed the scenery of the four counties that Jude had to canvas. Custom was at first very slow, so much so that Jude felt his employment would be terminated once he had completed his six month trial. However, in the nick of time, and after much market research, he produced his one great success. This came as a result of Jude persuading his company directors that leasing their equipment was a sound alternative if a sale could not be agreed. Jude was able to place over forty combine harvesters and an even greater number of tractors and silage cutters under leasing agreements. Forty percent of these machines went to one man, Jack Mortimer.

Jack had made Jude's spell as a company representative successful. His company contracted under fierce competition to cut crops on any farms in the West Country and the Midlands. He would send his clients a crew of machines and drivers, these men would cut from dawn until dusk seven days a week and quickly move on to the next job. The drivers would stay with the machinery over night, sleeping wherever they could. Jack had twice tempted Jude to work for him as a contracts manager. On both occasions, Jude had turned down the offer, he now felt differently. Jude decided his first action on reaching Blenheim, would be to telephone George Harris his employer, to resign. He would of course say that it is too soon after the funeral to think clearly. Perhaps thought Jude he would be right, but the decision had been made and it would stick.

Blenheim was his immediate problem, Jude knew he had to spend time away from the cottage. The whole place was Jayne. He felt that somehow, sometime in the future, he would be able to live there again, but for the present he knew that if he was to overcome the despondency of Jayne's loss, he must seek new ground. A decision was made, now he felt he could turn and walk back in the direction of the cottage, knowing he had, for the present at least, some sense of direction for his immediate future.

Once Jude had telephoned his employer, events moved swiftly. George came to see him at Blenheim just hours after receiving his call. Jude convinced him of how he felt and George reluctantly accepted his notice, which he said he would not be required to work. Jude then contacted Jack Mortimer and asked him not for the post he had previously been offered as a contracts manager, but for a job as a driver with one of his cutting crews. Jack was puzzled at Jude's request, but gave him a starting date in mid-April. This was, said Jack as close as he could guess to the date of the first silage cut in the West Country. He added that he was genuinely distressed to hear of Jude's bereavement. Jude now knew that he had a definite date to work towards. This gave him six weeks during which time he had to find a live-in minder for the cottage and the animals. After speaking to Jack he was looking forward to some hard work.

Within a few days the telephone rang bringing Jude a stroke of luck. It was George. Jude felt sure on hearing his voice that he was going to try to persuade him to accept his old job back, but to his surprise the purpose of the call was to ascertain if he would consider renting Blenheim to the chap who had filled the vacancy. Jude had already told him of his summer intentions, so in Jude's mind George had the simplest of motives, which were purely to do him a favour in finding him a rent paying minder for the cottage. George's motives in offering the new chap six months rent free accommodation whilst he served his trial period were to leave the back door open for Jude. George felt sure that six months would be sufficient for Jude to realise the error of his decision and as he had been the most successful salesman he has ever had, George had been hoping to groom him to take over his own job as company sales manager, to enable himself to take the next step up the ladder of management.

Peter Jackson, the new man, was transferring within the company down from the Manchester area with his daughter and housekeeper. With George offering to provide accommodation he readily accepted. A rate was soon agreed and Jude informed him that he could move into the cottage in mid-April. Jude knew that he would have to look for digs for himself around late September or early October, once the cutting season was over.

During the hours of daylight Jude managed to keep busy, family visits, James and the animals drew on his time, but the evenings and nights were becoming increasingly difficult to spend. They were no easier than the first terrible night he had spent at Blenheim alone. He used up the early hours of darkness wallowing in Jayne's writing. Whilst reading her words he felt that she was all around him. He could sense her presence, hear her soft but distinctive voice, but most of all he could smell her perfume. This was one of the many reasons why Jude loved to be close to Jayne, for he adored the many and varied liquid fragrances, which she applied to her skin. Jayne knew just how much perfume to use and where to use it. Her neck and shoulders often reminded Jude of wild roses and honeysuckles in their early evening flush of scent. On her back he loved to detect the very subtle fragrance of her natural musk as he kissed his way down her spine to the smooth and downy cleft in her buttocks. Sitting alone reading he could visualise her as though she were with him. He pictured her hair, her beautiful mid-length, brunette hair was in his mind as it had always been, a credit to her, though she was constantly trying to improve its style and texture. He allowed himself only moments of this intimate reminiscing for he knew it was not the answer to his loneliness, though he had become absorbed in Jayne's writing. He was finding almost as much pleasure in exploring her neatly written lines as he had in the past exploring her body. He read the first chapters of her book over and over again. He began creating events in his mind for the many and varied characters after Jayne's words had ceased. He began to wonder how anyone, particularly Jayne approached the idea of writing a book. He attempted to analyse how Jayne's mind worked whilst she was alone writing.

Many of his evening sessions ended with the same two questions. Did authors write from off the top of their heads, allowing their own passion to sway the events, or did they write to a formula, listing all the characters, major and minor events, a beginning and an ending, and then write them to fit each other? Jude searched all the literature in the house for clues to Jayne's method of writing. The more he searched the more curious he became and the more he realised he knew very little of how Jayne approached the subject of her writing. Half his days and all his evenings were spent in this pursuit, often until very late in the night. Eventually alcohol would overcome his active mind and he would pass into sleep wherever he sat.

Jude had not once slept in their bed alone because of his fear of the shock of waking, which he knew would be worse if he awoke in completely normal surroundings. The moment of waking was the very worst moment of the whole day for Jude, because Jayne was with him in his dreams. She was very much alive, smiling and loving, the moment of waking he dreaded as he had to accept afresh, every day that she was gone. This daily instant of realisation was so painful that even knowing sleep would bring Jayne back to him, he hated the very thought of sleep. There was a short time at the start of each day that suicide seemed to Jude to be the most effective painkiller of all.

Jayne's book played on his mind. He became possessive with it. For a reason he did not know he lied to his mother when she rang to ask if he had found anything which could be the start of Jayne's book. His thoughts had become jumbled. Why did I lie? Why was I protecting the book for myself? Surely I should be looking for someone to continue and perhaps finish it? No. I could never give it to anyone else. If anyone is going to finish it it's got to be me, ridiculous? But why not? How can I?

Ridiculous as it seemed Jude knew it had to be the answer. The more he thought of it, the more he knew it to be so. He who had always struggled to complete reading a book now wanted to complete writing one. How was this idea borne inside him? On reflection, Jude thought it to be a challenge, a battle of wits Jayne's and his own. Yes, that's it Jude thought, I must try to finish the book. This was how Jude talked himself into the mammoth task that was to bring him both satisfaction and despair. Jude filled his last month at Blenheim reading paperbacks. He purchased and read all the top ten best sellers. He

53

now found it possible to read them, as he was not reading them purely for their storyline, but instead to take note of the author's style of writing and the method which had been used to write them. He was never sure if he imagined all works fitted into his two categories, or if indeed they actually did. It appeared to Jude's untrained mind that each book he read had been written along what he determined to be either the mood or the formula method.

Firstly, those works which fitted into his mood category, which included Jayne's, he believed began with an idea or character, the story line would be built up around this basic idea on the whim of the author, the plot would develop to a certain stage and then be thrown into chaos by a character's death, or a sudden discovery. Jude felt that these sudden changes reflected the author's mental attitude or mood at the time of writing. These books he found changed in tempo many times, often shocking tragedies shattered a calm and pleasant period. He found these novels contained great passion and romance, with the inner emotions of the author surfacing often.

The alternative, as Jude saw it, was the formula method. He was convinced that with this style of writing the author listed a beginning, all the characters, complete with lifestyles and backgrounds. These characters would be chosen carefully to appeal to certain age groups or social classes of reader, also listed would be all the major and minor events and finally the chosen conclusion. He felt sure that everything would then be placed in its desired order to form the skeleton of the book. Individual sections would be written and finally each section, or chapter, would be written into each other. Jude thought these novels benefited from the very complex and intriguing plots. He convinced himself that all great thrillers and crime novels were written this way. The more he read the more difficult it appeared to him to write as Jayne had, from the heart with natural talent, and the easier it seems to Jude to follow an already laid path. This he knew was the only way conceivable he could approach such a project. He wondered to what degree his input would have on Jayne's book, would it leave it with the perceptible characteristics of two differing styles? Would an astute reader quickly discern the variation, he dismissed the ramifications of his thoughts. He knew the whole idea of his involvement with the book was quite contrary to his mainstream thoughts, which were to leave Blenheim for the summer throwing himself into hard, physical graft designed to keep him fully occupied. The book could only take him back and remind him of Jayne. One thing he knew, more than anything, was that he could not forget or leave behind her book. He had read it over and over. When the time came to pack what little he needed for the summer, he knew that it would not be overlooked.

This time was soon to come. Peter Jackson came to Blenheim on April the 8th to spend the afternoon. He had travelled down from Manchester early in the morning to see George Harris. Peter was obviously pleased with the cottage and thankfully Campbell gave his approval of Peter, his daughter and his housekeeper. His daughter Wendy would, he said, be sure to love the animals. Wendy a sufferer of Down's Syndrome had led to the breakup of his marriage. Peter insisted that she remain at home, his wife insisted that she live away, or indeed it would be she who left. Obviously Wendy had won Peter's heart.

The housemaid, Bridgette did not fit the pre-conceived image Jude had constructed for her. He had expected somebody who would remind him of Kate, Jayne's ex-nanny, someone very homely and seemingly domesticated, someone who would know nothing of dance floors or fashionable clothing, but this was not the impression he got from Bridgette. She was a tall, slim blonde no older than thirty. Jude felt sure that this very attractive and carefully dressed young woman made more than just financial demands on her keeper. They all seemed to love Blenheim, the cats and the poultry. The matter was swiftly settled. Jude gave Peter a set of keys before he left. The next day Jude placed all his personal belongings in the third bedroom, he felt sure they would only require two bedrooms. He now had just forty-eight hours before his employment with Jack Mortimer began. This left time for a few short family calls, an evening with James and Sue and on his last day at Blenheim, which was a warm April Sunday, he walked to Swinford churchyard intending to tell Jayne of his decisions.

The churchyard was a little over two miles from the cottage. Jude walked toward the tall, grey spire of St Mary's, his mind was producing vivid memories of the last time he had seen his wife alive. It had been a Wednesday, Jude needed an early start as he was travelling to Bristol for the day, but before he could aim for Bristol, he had three customers to see and he needed to call into the servicing yard in Newbury. Jude had been first out of bed as usual. He fed the cats and the birds and made tea for them both as he had always done. Jayne liked a single piece of toast in the morning so Jude had prepared this for her. He often said to her that she need not get up so early in the morning, but Jayne insisted on seeing him leave the house every day, for which Jude was appreciative.

This particular Wednesday Jayne wanted to visit Faye, for she was troubled over a part of her book. Jayne knew Faye would be going into Oxford shopping as she had always done on mid-week. She thought she might go with her and discuss the decisions she needed to make concerning her central character over lunch. Jayne was in the kitchen buttering her toast when Jude returned to the house after feeding the birds,

"Tell me, am I allowed to know anything about this book which is giving you so many problems?" Jude said.

"You can read all I have written just as soon as I have decided one or two more things."

"Which are?"

"Well, they are to do with the main character. I can't decide which country she is taken to."

"What do you mean, taken to?"

"Oh, never mind, your trying to pry details out of me. Drink your tea it's getting cold."

"Which particular countries is the decision between?"

"Well, it's either Mexico or Colombia."

Jude drank his tea, replaced him cup in the saucer and said,
"Mexico."

"Why Mexico?"

"Well, George went there once and had the time of his life, so send your character there for a holiday."

"Jude nobody gets taken by force to a holiday, they go of their own free choice."

"Oh so your character is kidnapped then?" Jayne had been tricked into saying enough.

"Listen, you will have to wait and see. Perhaps you can read the first two chapters later, if you're good."

"Oh," said Jude slowly and seductively, "I promise to be very, very good." With that he picked up his keys, gave Scrumpy a gentle pat and left the house. Just before he closed the door he clenched his teeth, pulled his lips tight and said, in his best Humphrey Bogart voice,

"See you later kid." He could see Jayne laughing through the glass door as he turned toward the car.

On reaching the cemetery, Jude leant his hand against the stone wall to push open the wrought iron gateway. The coldness of the stonework pierced him. Memories of that cold February day flooded his mind. He paused at the gateway but did not enter. As his bare hand rested against the cold granite, the memory of Jayne's lifeless body hit him.

He reached Blenheim breathless and drank himself into oblivion. He could not get warm. That night, his last in the cottage, he slept fitfully under heavy covers. He saw Jayne in his sleep. She was set in ice. Each time he attempted to touch her the cold burned his skin. He awoke in shock, his skin wet with perspiration and his inner self frozen. On coming to his senses he reminded himself that these were his last few hours at Blenheim. He packed a sleeping bag, some clothes and some cash. He added several note pads and some pencils, for he expected at least some time to himself in his sleeping bag at night. During this time, he hoped to add to Jayne's book. With his last two hours he sat down and read the first few chapters of a book that would take him literally across the world.

JAQUELINE

By Jayne Marshall

This was her last chance. With three in the jump off against the clock she simply had to beat Jonathan if she was to gain the final place in the British Olympic team for the Summer Games. Three of the team places had been settled in the autumn, but for that final place their two names had been like equally balanced weights on a scale. Was it to be Jonathan Roberts of Jacqueline Forbes-Brewer?

This meeting, the first major outing of 1984 had produced a cliff-hanger finish. Due to the press coverage it had become common knowledge that one of the two of them would make the team and the other would be reserve. As this was the last major outing before the games selectors must separate them on today's performance. With the cross-country and the dressage behind them they were neck and neck, both were desperate to represent Great Britain as a three day eventer. Jackie was last but one to jump and Jonathan would follow her. Whilst watching Anne's round, Jackie knew that she had only two minutes to wait. She had never suffered from nerves like this before. Her mount, the wonderful Nelson was alert, ears pricked, he knew he had to perform and perform well. Jackie found her legs were so weak she could barely grip with her knees. Richard was by her side as always.

"Now then Jackie, we know how important this one is. Look at that, Anne has screwed up that second double, that's the only real fence out there and that's the one to look out for. All the rest, Nelson can handle. For that double pull him up early for the first part and then very early for the second."

Richard was shouting to be heard over the crowd. Anne had completed her round, twelve faults in all. She rode passed Jackie and breathlessly wished her luck. Anne knew the importance of the next two minutes. She had been there, she had scaled great heights, her Olympic silver was her most prized medal. Jackie nudged Nelson forward with Richard still shouting behind her,

"Remember to get him up early." Anne's score was announced and Jackie heard her own name loud and clear over the sound system. Her throat dried up. She could not remember being so terrified of a round of fences. She took Nelson once around the arena to relax them both. He was a little tight. He needed his bowels open, again around the arena. Nelson was now relaxed and she too felt as ready as she would ever be.

"Come on Nelson, we owe this one to Richard." She shouted and playfully clipped his ear.

The first six single fences were no problem. He took the water well in his stride and the first double. Nelson clipped the first wall turned and took the white gates comfortable within his stride. Now for the triple, one, two, her left foot slipped from the stirrup, she yelled,

"Jump, Nelson!" He did. She slowed him, corrected her position and put Nelson back in his stride. They had lost valuable seconds. Jonathan would have seen that, he now knew that he would have seconds to spare. Jackie was furious with herself. Now for the parallels and the double,

"Go Nelson, up, and again." Yes, he was over. Onto the wall, and they were clear. The cheers surprised both Nelson and Jackie. She turned her mount the leave the arena, as Jonathan rode in their mounts brush together. He gave Jackie a nod of respect. He knew he had to go clear, and that he had a couple of seconds to ease the tight turns. Jackie dismounted and fell into Richard's arms.

"That was terrific." He said. He could not help but add, "It might have been easier with both feet in." He kissed her cheek, the type of kiss one receives from Great Aunts.

"Come on Richard. I must watch Jonathan." He had already cleared the first four fences. He rode so masterfully, she envied him his male strength. His mount, Apollo, would seldom be allowed to put a stride wrong. His round continued, clear at the water and the first double, he was fast too. He had her beaten for speed. The triple and parallels were taken well in his stride. Jackie was desperate for him to fault. He approached the double looking great. He took the first part neatly and pulled up very early for the second part – it was a fraction too early. Apollo's hind legs came crashing down onto the top rail. It flew into the air bounced back on its mounts and almost in slow-motion out again onto the floor. As Apollo cleared the wall Jackie's head was dizzy with joy. This time Richard kissed her full on the lips, "Terrific, we're going to the States and we're riding." He said. Richard was elated. She threw her arms around him – all her suppressed adrenaline and emotion surfaced in a flood. Tears were flowing down her cheeks, friends and fellow competitors were congratulating and applauding her from all sides. She had done it. Her sense of achievement was paramount. She had to go to Nelson. He was standing quite alone in the practice ring and she remounted him for the prize giving.

Jonathan approached them. He was still astride Apollo. He shook Jackie's hand saying,

"Well done, Jacqueline. I'll help you celebrate in Los Angeles."

"Thank you Jonathan, now can we please stop competing against each other and become members of the same team." She replied. "I'm sure after battling against you, the Olympics will be easy." She jokingly added.

They rode into the arena for the ceremonies – Jackie on Cloud Nine, Jonathan devastated. Jackie looked left towards the selectors, some had already left. She felt proud that they had left with the name Forbes-Brewer on their minds. Nelson received his rosette with his usual head nodding, much to the crowd's delight. Jackie didn't try to stop him, she felt he had earned a little showing off. She too revelled in the spotlight of attention. All those heads turned towards her made her feel quite naked. Several thousand pairs of eyes beamed to her, she shifted uncomfortably in the saddle. The attention she was receiving and the emotion she felt within was creating an ache, it was an ache that only Richard could satisfy. She received the trophy and the applause, completed one circuit of the arena and dismounted. She handed Nelson to Simon, her groom, who she knew would treat him well. The next time she saw Nelson he would be bedded down in the stables at home. Simon was a very capable young groom and a good friend. Jackie knew that Simon had an even greater understanding with Nelson than she, although she would never admit that to anyone but herself.

Now she had to find Richard. She spotted him engaged in conversation with Julia Summerford, among others. Jackie's opinion of Julia was low. She had often described her as 'that horny cow that by all accounts rode as badly in bed as she did on horseback'. Jackie knew Julie would love to be able to claim Richard as one of her successes.

"Richard, we simply must leave soon, it would be unforgivable to be late for tonight's party." Julia flashed Jackie her best 'why the hell did you have to come along' look and said,

"Well done Jacqueline that was a marvellous ride. I really thought Jonathan would make the team. He must be feeling terrible about that mistake. It could so easily have been the other way round."

"Thank you, Julia. I do feel sorry for Jonathan, he's an excellent rider."

"Yes." She said and with raised intonation added "I can confirm that he's a very good rider." The stupid bitch thought Jackie, if she knew Jonathan well enough she would know that he was gay. If he wasn't, she felt sure that Julia's weight problem would prevent him from becoming her next victim. Jackie turned to Richard, ignoring Julia's last remark,

"Richard, we really must leave soon."

"Okay, but let's check Nelson first and then we can go. I have already confirmed with George Hamilton that the fourth team place is ours." George is the Chairman of the selectors. If he had told Richard that they had made the team, then it was official.

"Nelson's fine. Simon's taking care of him. Let's go."

"My," said Richard, "You really are in a hurry to leave." After speaking to Julia, her desires were turning to anger. She was not about to allow Julia to spoil her day. She turned to the small crowd that Richard had been talking to,

"Goodbye all we have to dash." She slipped her arm around Richard's waist to encourage him to move off. Julia cut her one of her devil looks. Serves the cow right, thought Jackie, I'm not surprised her mount refused, who wouldn't with her on their back. They made slow progress through the throng of well wishers, having to halt many times to make light conversation of the accident she'd had with the stirrup. Finally, they broke free of the crowd. It was always the same after a major event. There were more people behind the scenes than in the arena. Jackie noticed two men with a German shepherd dog and mirrors on long poles, they seemed to be checking over their Range Rover.

"Richard, what the hell are they doing?"

"It's alright, they are part of the security cover. All cars in the same compound as the Princess's have to be checked for suspect devices." As they approached, their vehicle was pronounced clear and they were soon inside and travelling toward the family home near Aylesbury. During the first half hour, amongst slow traffic, they spoke very little. But once on the open road it was Jackie who began conversation.

"You know Julia wants you, don't you?"

"Whether she wants me or not, she's not hanging my head on her wall. Besides, you are all I can cope with."

"Pull over and stop. You know I want you."

"Christ no, I'm not having my name in the papers because big events make you horny." He continued, "I know why we had to leave so early. It's only five o'clock now, we need not show our faces until at least nine tonight. Your father and Louise can begin their first anniversary celebrations without us."

"Why did you have to mention Louise? I was just beginning to feel good."

"Now come on Jackie, Louise is not all bad. I know she puts you down in front of your father, but she is his wife and you do live in their home."

"I do yes, but not for much longer. When we are married in the autumn she can go to hell. I really can't see what Daddy sees in her. She's not a patch on Mama and it would not surprise me if she were a flirt behind his back."

"Steady Jackie."

"No, I'm serious, when Humphrey the US Ambassador was over for dinner last month, her eyes never left him for a moment."

"Be fair Jacks. She was there for him to lean on after your mother's death. We knew Emily was going for a long time with that damn illness, when she did finally go Louise suffered your father in a very depressed way for two, or perhaps three years."

"I know all that Richard, but why does she have to be so distant with me?"

"Well that's because you have such a strong bond with your father and when you are all together she sees his affection going your way. She's plain jealous of you."

"Well, she won't have to be jealous much longer. In just four short months we will be installed at Coombe Park. It really was nice of your father to pass on the family home so early."

"It really was a question of health and no more. Both he and mother feel they cannot take another English winter, so in September they are off to enjoy the Italian sunshine. Although, to be honest, I would rather the English weather than be surrounded by Italians, they talk too loud and too fast for my liking. But as for their food, wine and scenery, well that's a different matter."

They soon came to the huge stone pillars of St George's Hall, home to the Forbes-Brewer family for many years. Richard steered the car to the rear of the house. Just in case he had forgotten how she felt she gently squeezed his groin before leaving the car. They were met at the rear door by Roddy, the butler, who politely congratulated them on today's win. He had, he said, been watching it on television.

"We are all so proud of you Miss Jacqueline. They seem to think on the television that you will now be in the British team for the Olympic Games. That's splendid."

"Yes Roddy, I believe I shall."

"Shall I have Margaret run a bath for you, Miss Jacqueline?"

"Yes, definitely for me Roddy and you Richard?" Richard nodded his agreement. "You carry on, Roddy. I'll find the port. I think we need a drink."

"Thank you Miss Jacqueline."

"Come on let's have a drink Richard." They toasted Jackie's medal chances at the Games and joked about bringing home gold. Very soon Roddy informed them their baths were ready. They slowly climbed the wide marble staircase. Jackie's room was the first on the left and Richard's the first on the right.

"See you soon." She said.

She entered her room. As usual Margaret had laid out both towel and robe, she undressed quickly, it was always such a pleasure to shed the jodhpurs. She lay naked across her bed allowing her hands to roam freely over her body, enjoying the fresh tingle of sensation they left behind. She gently brushed her nipples, all the desire she had felt earlier returned in an instant. She moved her left hand, allowing her fingertips to slide across her abdomen, over her modest, blonde pubic hair, gently parting her lips. She closed her eyes and began to indulgently stimulate her clitoris, her mind took her back to her college days with her friends Caroline and Franny. Abruptly she stopped herself, she knew that this would not satisfy her, she needed Richard. Putting on her robe she crossed the landing into Richards's room. She knew Louise would be in the kitchen giving the staff hell and ensuring that all is as she desires it to be for her fathers return. She preferred that Louise did not see her enter Richard's room, feeling sure that if she did, she would be sure to put it into the conversation in front of her father.

She could hear Richard in his bath, muttering to himself. Quickly and silently she moved into his bathroom, as she did she allowed the rope to fall to the floor. Richard turned towards her and widened his pupils, first focusing on her small breast, which were for their twenty seven years as firm as they have ever been, his gaze then moved to her slight natural blond tuft of hair, the look in his eyes told her that she had not made a wasted journey across the landing. She loosened her hair allowing her blonde curls to fall onto her shoulders, without speaking she stepped into the bath and astride Richard, their arms and legs entwined in a long slow embrace. She could feel his hardness rising beneath her. She shifted her position to allow him to enter her, closed her eyes and nibbled on his shoulder as he gently thrust to and fro. He was good, he never withdrew too far or thrust too deep, his breathing kept pace with his movements, the warm water lapped her thighs as his hands caressed her back. They maintained a gentle motion for several minutes, until eventually Richard's movements became more positive, his hands slid down her back, across her waist and came to rest on her hips, he was now drawing her towards him as his thrust became stronger. This brought her to the verge of orgasm, Richard aware of her state of arousal sought to slow things a little, to prolong the pleasure.

"No Richard, don't tease me, not this time." She took the lead, trusting herself upon him, he responded cupping her breast in his hands, allowing her nipples to be squeezed between his fingers, this was the spark she needed. Her abdomen and thighs went into spasm, her head began to swim and she came with a shuddering of emotion and splashing of water that might have been heard on the landing. Richard's tongue forced its way between her lips, it took all her self control not to bite into its soft warm flesh. As her breathing began to calm, she felt his hot seed released inside her, this caused a second climax almost as intense as the first to tremble through her body. They recovered their breath in the warm sudsy water, washed each other and Jackie stepped from the bath, she dried herself and returned to her room, they had barely spoken a word.

The next time she saw Richard he was immaculately dressed, talking to her father, Sir John, in the study. Jackie compared the two men, both of whom meant so much to her. Richard Brewer, a well proportioned six feet two towered over her father, they both smiled as she approached. Jackie thought how old her father looked. At sixty-four he was twenty-five years Richard's senior, and he looked every year of it. He had never credited sufficient importance on his health. He had been around three stones over weight for as long as Jackie could remember, causing him heart trouble, which culminated in open-heart surgery five years ago. Richard's light ginger hair and high cheek boned face was in strong contrast to her father's grey haired rounded features. She joined the two men,

"Hello Daddy, nice trip?" She kissed him on the cheek, adding, "I must say, you two are looking rather dapper tonight."

"Actually, the trip did not go as planned, but we can talk about that tomorrow. Talking of looking smart, I think you take the biscuit tonight Jacqueline. Don't you think so Richard?" Before Richard could reply, Sir John added, "But don't tell Louise I said so."

"Yes", said Richard, "She looks stunning now in quite a different way to that of this afternoon."

"I hear from Richard you stole the show today my girl. Damn well done."

"Thank you Daddy."

65

"I hope Sir John, that you will be able to escape the business world for long enough to see her ride in the Games."

"My boy I would not miss it for the world, even though Los Angeles is my least favourite city."

"Come on you two, Los Angeles is a long way off. I think it's time we all had a drink. What keeps you in this stuffy old study anyway?"

"I was discussing with Richard his father's intentions for the autumn. I am surprised he has chosen Italy for a spell of peace and quiet. I know the region Richard speaks of. It is quite a busy tourist area, not my idea of tranquillity at all."

"My mother has a passion for the area and the estate she has inherited, it was there she spent her childhood."

"Well that's a great help, but I am sure she will see many changes."

"Come on you two, what about that drink? I think we should toast your anniversary Daddy."

"Yes let's do just that." Said Sir John, they moved into the great hall to join the thirty or so guests who had already arrived.

Louise was in conversation with the Matterson's, even Jackie felt a little sorry for her. The Matterson's had recently befallen two tragedies, which Louise must be trying desperately to avoid in conversation. Firstly, their eldest son had publicly been declared a heroin addict and secondly, the family had encumbered a huge debt through no fault of their own. Jackie thought that they must be simply impossible to talk to. Sir John joined in the conversation whilst Richard and Jackie steered around them to be met by Roddy with a tray of champagne. They left his tray lighter by two glasses and were soon joined by Charles Robinson, the local Hunt Master, who demanded to be talked through Jackie's final round of fences earlier in the day, fence by fence. During the evening she completed that final round, in all, a dozen times. Each time a little more was left out. By midnight, the tale of her afternoon was beginning to sounds quite uneventful.

When finally an hour later Sir John and Louise approached them, they had to renew their glasses once more to toast their anniversary. The toast over, Louise began to search Jackie out for a weakness. Jackie was determined that she would not succeed this time.

"John, wouldn't you say that Jacqueline is looking splendid tonight. That was true to form, thought Jackie, open with bullshit to draw me off guard. She replied,

"Why thank you, Louise, it's so nice of you to say so." She knew this was a game of mental chess, she knew also that Louise was an expert, she responded with nothing sharp, just a straightforward answer, something to give Jackie time to think.

"After such a hard day it must be difficult to appear so bright and fresh." Said Louise. Jackie could not tell where she was trying to lead the conversation.

"Ah," said Jackie, "The pleasures of a long, hot soak in the bath. It softens the bruises."

"Oh but Margaret said you had not used your bath. She had been quite surprised. And Richard, you must have had a whale of a time, water everywhere."

Fuck that bitch, thought Jackie, why did she have to be so petty? And why did she always fall for her silly little traps? Louise, she thought, acts as though she has never had sex in her life. Jackie was quite sure, that Louise felt that if her father knew she and Richard were intimate, then it may weaken the bond of closeness between her and her father. Jackie realised that although her father was years ahead of her with his business sense he was also very old fashioned in his relationships and of course, would like to think of her going to the altar as a virgin. Sir John realised that this was unlikely. He knew also that it was unlikely that Richard was Jackie's first lover, but to hear it spoken of as Louise had just done embarrassed him. Jackie knew this. Why does Louise have to be such a cow? She made her feel that she was betraying her father having sex in her own home. Soon she thought, she would have her own home and if she wished to she would make love on the lawns. Jackie felt her reply should be addressed to her father,

"Well, you know what they say, save water. Anyway, I twisted my neck earlier when my foot came free of the stirrup and I needed a massage." Once again Louise had made her feel uncomfortable in front of her father. Richard broke in,

"That careless mistake with the stirrup could have cost you your team place. You will have to look out for it. A small mistake like that could cost the whole team a medal at the Games."

"Yes, I know. I think Jonathan must have thought the place was his at that moment. From the far side of the hall she saw Jonathan making his way towards them. She turned to her father saying, "Oh, there is Jonathan now. Do forgive me, I must have a word." With that, she glared at Louise, she then moved with Richard towards Jonathan to prevent him from joining them. They met part way across the hall, sufficient distance to be out of earshot of Louise and Sir John. As Jonathan began to greet them, Jackie exclaimed,

"Damn that woman."

"Hello," said Jonathan, laughing as he did, "Having stepmother problems?"

"I swear one day I'll make that woman look so small she will never challenge me again."

"What's the problem?"

"We had it off in the bath earlier on and she just had to let Father know." Jackie felt her answer was a little blunt and possibly embarrassing to Richard who was looking at her with obvious disapproval. She added, "Well you know how it is Jonathan, after an important ride I get all screwed up and it has to be the best way of unwinding."

"I deal with it in my own way, as you know."

"I tell you what. If Julia had a say she would deal with you her way." Jonathan burst into laughter. When he had calmed down he replied to Jackie,

"Julia approached me some time ago. I told her straight, I'm gay. She laughed at first, then when she realised she was laughing alone she dried up."

"I wish I'd seen it." Richard excused himself, leaving Jackie and Jonathan to gossip. Jackie felt that Richard found it hard to accept Jonathan's homosexuality out in the open. He would discuss it when they were alone, but here, in the great hall, she was sure that he felt uncomfortable. Jackie discussed with Jonathan the forthcoming games. Richard circled the great hall basking in congratulations for training an Olympic qualifier. Sir John and Louise were toasted by all present at around one o'clock. Sir John said a few words with Louise hanging on his arm. Jackie thought that this could only be in the vain hope that some of his respect and success might rub off. She knew this evening was Louise's idea entirely and that she intended that her Father's social circle should see them together as often as possible. She knew her father had shortened his latest trip to arrive back in time to pamper to her whims. Jackie was certain that her Father could do much better than Louise, if only he saw her as she really is – a jealous social climber. The guests, some two hundred in all began to shy away at around two o'clock. Very soon the great hall was all but empty. The half dozen who were staying, those who had too far to drive were shown by the ever present Roddy to their rooms. Jackie found Richard again and they bid goodnight to her father. Once up the staircase, a quick goodnight kiss and they were in their separate rooms. Within two minutes being so tired and slightly drunk, Jackie fell into a deep and satisfying sleep.

"There you are Jackie, been looking all over for you." Said Richard.

"You should've known I would be with Nelson. I have given Simon a break and I'm grooming him myself. He really is in good shape, isn't he?"

"Yes. I don't think he has been this fit for a couple of seasons. Where is Simon, by the way?"

"Oh he's gone into the village, taken the mail with him."

"Damn I wanted Troy to have a really hard run this morning. I felt the leg yesterday and I think he is fully recovered."

"Take him yourself."

"He may be ready to carry Simon's nine stone, but my fourteen could set him back for weeks and before you volunteer yourself your father wants to see us both in his study as soon as, something to do with his last American trip."

"Well you're in luck, here is Simon now." The three of them chatted for several minutes about the horses. Simon had been waiting for Richard to rise to find out if he could push Troy with his next run. The matter was settled and Nelson groomed, Jackie and Richard returned to the house to meet with Sir John. They were met in the hallway by Louise, whose opening gambit was,

"Good morning, did you both sleep well?"

"Thank you yes, very comfortable." Richard replied. Jackie made straight for her fathers study, glancing back to Richard as she reached the door to say,

"Shut the door after you Richard. We don't want the staff to hear." With that she entered the room feeling pleased with her last comment, but disappointed that she had lowered herself to playing silly games.

Louise hated the fact that Sir John only discussed the family's financial background with Jackie and in recent months he had included Richard. His answer to her was always the same whenever she questioned him – 'Running St George's is difficult enough. I would hate to burden you further with finance, my dear'. What that amounted to, which they were all aware of, was that Jackie, his only child, was his next of kin and the estate would be willed to her and Richard once they were married. Louise no doubt, would be well catered for in his will, but she knew she would never take precedence over Jackie. It is this that would always prevent them from having a genuine relationship of any kind. Jackie walked across the study feeling a little uncomfortable in her riding gear. It was the only room in the house that could make her feel this way, for this room symbolised Sir John's strong character and the Forbes-Brewers long ancestral background. Jackie reclined into a chair,

"Hello Daddy."

"Ah, there you are. Have you found Richard this morning?"

"It was more a case of the reverse Sir John. She was out in the stables as usual." Said Richard as he entered the room.

"Well sit down lad, this is for both of you to hear." As Sir John began to speak he assumed his board meeting tone of voice, which was quite unusual in the house.

"Now then, we are here to discuss my death."

"Father what on earth do you mean?"

"Easy Jacqueline these things need to be discussed in a businesslike manner before they happen. It can be a hell of a problem leaving them until after." Richard and Jackie looked at each other in great surprise. "I was told to expect no more than five years after the operation. Well five years is almost up, although to be honest I feel healthier now than at any time during the past twenty years." They were both silent, suppressing the urge to speak. It was clear that Sir John had much to say.

"We will assume for convenience sake that I live to see you both married. I see no problem in the four short months to pass." Jackie was stunned by the seemingly emotionless way her father delivered his words.

"Richard you have already agreed to take on the name Forbes-Brewer. I thank you for that. Now assuming you are married and I am no more, you will both become full voting directors of the group Forbes-Brewer Industries. My Chairmanship will go to Arnold Elliot, his judgement is as sound today as it has always been. In the event of his death the Chairmanship falls to you Richard, by which time I hope that you will have learnt enough about the Group to fill in this position. Of course if you two do not remain married then Jacqueline you will hold both votes and become Chairwoman, should Arnold not be around fall back on Peter Gould for guidance. Hopefully, this situation will never arise."

"As a rule you need not attend the Annual General Meetings, although this would be desirable. But your presence will be required at the extraordinary meeting following my death. All the businesses are soundly run, we have teams of advisors and consultants who all report to myself, Arnold or Peter constantly. They also keep a check on individual company boards so you should have ample time to both train and ride. I hope you continue your excellent standard, I hope also that you produce at least one Forbes-Brewer to keep an old man happy. We, as a family, have certain financial commitments to societies, charities and trusts, which I hope you will continue to support. Although these are quite a large drain on the domestic budget, I would hate to see them axed."

Jackie and Richard sat in silence greatly surprised by Sir John's openness. He had always kept Jackie reasonably well informed, but this was something quite different. Jackie was sure that Richard was as shocked as she at her father's frankness. He continued,

"On the home front, St George's will go to you Jackie, as well as all other properties and land."

Jackie could not quite believe this. Her father was dealing Louise a completely blank hand. Sir John saw her puzzled expression and dealt with it immediately,

"Louise will be welcome to live here until her death, although I think she will probably wish to move on. If that is the case a proviso has been put in my will to provide her with a home equal to that of her former custom, with a settlement figure of a quarter of a million pounds. In the event of either one of your deaths, the other shall control all, unless, of course, you have any children. This then becomes quite complicated and will be explained by Mister Rowles, our family lawyer. All this takes effect from the day of your marriage. Of course once you are married and I am no more than a photograph on the mantelpiece the destiny of the Forbes-Brewer Estate and Industries will be determined by your own wills, which you must draw up as soon as possible after the wedding." Jackie immediately realised that her wedding day was indeed a very important day. Not just for her and Richard, but also for hundreds of people who depend on the Forbes-Brewers for a living. Sir John drew his revelations to a close,

"Well I have some papers here for you both to sign. If we can get this out of the way I'll ring for Roddy for a glass of port. I know it's a little early but I think it's called for."

"Daddy, it's all those glasses of port that were responsible for your heart trouble."

"I know, I really must cut down." Sir John replied, smiling. Very soon they were raising glasses, with Sir John wishing them a long and fruitful marriage. The three of them spent the next half hour in conversation. Sir John told them all about his latest trip to the States and how he narrowly missed out on a bid which, had it been successful, would have secured a near perfect monopoly on one of his best selling products across America. After they had watched on video Jackie's final round of competition the previous day Sir John wished them well for the Olympics. He also said that he would be around very little during the next three months as he needed to make trips to France, Singapore, Hong Kong, Australia and the United States, but he guaranteed them that he would not miss a single performance of Jackie's at the Games.

They strolled to the Morning Room for breakfast joining Louise and the guest who had stayed over from last evening. Everything her father had said was running through Jackie's mind. Louise was to have just two hundred and fifty thousand and a modest home, and both Richard and she would become directors in one of the country's largest industrial groups. She would have to try to make her father slow down. She knew that she had little chance of success, but she would try. She promised herself that after the Games she would insist that her father spend more time at home. What she, or no-one could know, was that after the Games, Sir John would come home to St George's permanently.

Breakfast was taken with Louise looking rather upset at being left out of their earlier conversation. Though as always, she acted the perfect hostess. After breakfast Jackie took Nelson for a short run and Richard drove off to see his father for two days. Jackie left him with a kiss and a promise to bathe alone until his return. Richard told her that as soon as he returned they would begin their very rigorous Olympic preparation.

The next two days Jackie spent close to her father. The way he had spoken reminded her of how precious he was. For they are living reminders to each other of the love they shared for his dear Emily, Jackie's mother.

EAVESDROPPING

The two days were all too quickly over. Sir John flew to Nice from Heathrow and from there to Singapore. Richard returned to St George's and they very quickly moved into a breathtaking pace of training. They made several long journeys to training grounds as part of their preparation. On these occasions, the complete Olympic team would be present. Richard would hand over control to Francis Moore, the British team coach. Francis had the ability to leave them all totally exhausted after each day of training. Twice they moved the horses' short distances by air to get them accustomed to flying. All but one was relaxed; the troublesome mount was the reserve, Apollo. On the second occasion Apollo had to be knocked out to prevent him damaging himself. The whole team especially Francis was becoming quite anxious.

When shortly after the second flight Apollo cracked a shin, Francis was distraught. They must have a reserve that was as able as any member of the team. Any mishap to a team member would be a complete catastrophe, if they did not have a first rate reserve they could not compete. They were faced with just six short weeks in which to find Jonathan a suitable mount and to get the two of them accustomed to each other. After much deliberation it was decided that the most suitable mount was Jackie's reserve mount, Troy, who is half brother to Apollo. Richard had no objections and Jonathan said that 'one Greek god should carry him as well as another'. As so little time was left for man and mount to become familiar it was decided that Jonathan would move into St George's, by living in he could spend up to sixteen hours a day with the horse.

This was a very worrying and exhausting time. Jackie had ridden and trained with horses since she was four, but nothing in her experience could compare with the gruelling routine she was now being put through. From dawn until dusk, everything they did was aimed at a top medal place in Los Angeles. The team had very little time to relax. Jackie found that she and Richard had little or no physical contact. They were so exhausted that they were often asleep as their heads were on their pillows. She became increasingly anxious due to her lack of intimate contact with Richard, a feeling which was intensified by his apparent indifference to her unease. She felt that Richard had enough problems with the horses so did not voice her frustrations.

With just two weeks left to departure date the pace began to slacken. Francis had included spare afternoons and evenings as part of the final weeks of practice. He knew that to keep up the pace he had set would leave him with five stale riders and five worn out mounts. It was during these free afternoons that Jackie found herself on three occasions, in the right place at the right time, or from the point of view of others, it was the wrong place at the wrong time.

On each occasion Richard was away in London at the Olympic Conference Centre making arrangements for their stay or watching on video their competitors. On the first occasion Jackie had driven back to St George's alone from a dressage practice. Simon was with Nelson and the horsebox some two hours behind her. Sir John had left for Hong Kong just two days before and Jackie knew the only person at home was Louise. She felt sure that she could avoid her, as she wanted nothing more than to pick up a good book from the library and take it with her into the bath to soak away her soreness whilst getting into a good thriller. She parked the car, walked to the front door and kicked off her riding boots as she entered. She stepped silently across the hall, but her thoughts were interrupted by a loud shout from her fathers study. It was obvious that it was a curse and it had clearly been issued by Louise. Jackie opened the study door, she was shocked by the sight in front of her. The safe was open, her father's desk was littered with papers, his share certificates and will were openly placed on the desk. Louise's eyes were buried in her husband's will. She was about to thump her hands on the desk when she saw the door open, she looked up to tell one of the staff to clear off. When her disbelieving eyes recognised who was standing in front of her she clasped her outstretched hands around her head in a child like attempt to hide herself. In all her forty-five years she had never been so compromised, this very situation would be eclipsed a thousand fold at St George's in the future. Jackie was gathering her senses to verbally attack Louise, whom she expected to back into submission, but it was she who attacked first,

"You smug little bitch! You have known about this for a long time haven't you, pay me off with a pittance whilst you who act like a whore in this house gets everything." She yelled. Before Jackie could reply, Louise had thrown the nearest book at her, which struck her on the side of the face and within a few seconds Louise was out of the study.

Jackie's first reaction was to chase after her using all the obscenities she could think of and to tell her that she would be thrown out of St George's on her father's return. With the study door half open Jackie stopped herself, she went back inside and seated herself at her father's desk and considered her next move. She decided to keep the knowledge of this to herself, at least for a while. She made tidy the room, leaving it just as it would normally be. She now knew that Louise was capable of far greater harm than she had suspected. After tending to the graze on the side of her face Jackie had her bath, dressed and went in search of Louise. She found her in her room looking very angry and rather drunk. This time it was Jackie who opened the conversation,

"Shut it Louise before you even think of starting. I've been able to see through you since the day we met. You are nothing but a cheap social climber and I fail to see how you have fooled someone as intelligent as my father. You have never fooled me. For the moment I will not speak of this to father, but once Richard and I are married I shall come to you with a list of do's and don'ts. If you step out of line just once, I shall see to it that you are discarded penniless, thrown from this house. Now give me the safe key." Louise opened her mouth to speak. "Shut it Louise and hand me the key." With that Louise threw the key over Jackie's head onto the landing and returned to her bottle. As Jackie left she added,

"Remember, I will see you after the wedding. Until then you are to be the perfect wife."

Jackie mistakenly thought she had handled the affair well. She did not want a major upset for her father or the whole family prior to the games and the wedding. She knew she would have to keep an eye on Louise, and felt rather smug holding Louise's fate in her hand. The truth was that it was Louise who derived the most satisfaction from the exchange. She had discovered all she had hoped for and more from Sir John's papers. She had expected to find that once married Jackie's position would be unassailable. What she had been pleasantly surprised by was Sir John's legal contingency plan should the wedding not take place. This was altogether another matter and one that fell wholly into Louise's lap. It had been unfortunate being discovered by Jacqueline, but Louise had been pleased by her own reactions in allowing Jacqueline to feel that she had the upper hand. The stupid girl had given her the one thing she could have denied her, which was to Louise imperative, her freedom to move as she pleased until the wedding.

The second occasion on which Jackie found herself in a surprising situation involved Jonathan and Simon, she herself played no part. She had returned Nelson to the stable mid-afternoon, it being such a hot June day she thought to give him a little shade. Richard had been away in London for the whole day. Simon was out with Jonathan and Troy who were making great progress and getting along fine. After settling Nelson down Jackie was leaving the otherwise deserted stable block when she heard some kittens in the hayloft. She decided to go up and see them. She had to climb both sets of well-worn wooden stairs into the very attic above the hayloft. It was quite dark at the top of the building, though there was one small skylight which allowed a patch of sunlight to fall on the dusty floor. In this tiny, bright square of light three kittens played, but on Jackie's approach they scuttled into the darkness. Jackie sat for a while on the warm, dusty boards, content that this part of the stable was free from vermin, Molly the cat would have seen to that. After just a few moments the inquisitive kittens began to explore her. They decided she was harmless and returned to biting each other's ears and tails, they were a pleasure to watch. The warmth of the sunlight and the comfort of the hay on her back, along with the riding fatigue combined to send her into a pleasantly dreamy sleep. She dreamed of Olympic Gold. She was on Nelson reaching forward to receive her medal, when suddenly Louise appeared and snatched the golden prize from her hand. She awoke with a start. She heard voices below her, not on the ground floor, but on the landing below where she lay. They were male voices and one of them, Jonathan's, was quite loud.

"Come on Simon, I have to ride in the Games. She will never know it was you."

"Jackie is no fool and she trusts me. My answer is no." Simon replied.

On hearing her name Jackie prevented herself from speaking. What on earth she thought, could they be talking about? She decided to stay quite still and listen, feeling suddenly like a young girl eavesdropping on grown-ups. The two men were talking whilst tossing bales to the ground for bedding. Jackie synchronised her movements with the landing of the bales so as to turn sideways, lie on her stomach and peer through the well worn boards on which she was now laying. The ability to see and not be seen increased her feelings of secrecy. When first she saw Simon he was sitting on a bale looking very anxious for his twenty-four years. He appeared to have the troubles of the world on his shoulders. Jonathan was out of her sight.

"Careful," said Simon, "You could hit Nelson with one of those."

"If I did it might solve my problem. You seem to be of little help."

"Look, even if I did prevent Nelson from riding, Jackie would only take over Troy. You would gain nothing."

"Not if you go to work after we land in the States. By that time each rider has to be registered to his or her mount, so if Troy was to come in at a very late stage, I would have to ride him."

Jackie could not believe her ears. Her own groom and a good friend were plotting to prevent her from achieving a once in a lifetime ambition. She felt tremendous anger and wanted to jump down and throw them to the floor. She envied them their male strength. She was fighting with herself to remain in hiding. She decided to stay put. It was something in Jonathans' voice that prevented her from involving herself in their nasty conversation. He was speaking with a tone she had never heard before. It made him sound quite menacing, perhaps even capable of throwing her to the floor.

"Well, Simon do I have to spell it out for you. I'll tell them at St George's and every one else about you if you don't help me. I'm not ashamed of myself, but you obviously are."

"You wouldn't dare, you bastard."

"Oh but I will if I don't get a ride in the Games."

"You really are a bastard. Have you any idea what it would do to my father?"

"How you and your military father cope with the public knowledge of your sexuality concerns me not. I will ride in the Games and nothing will stop me."

At this point, one of Jackie's booted feet became cramped and she was forced to move it. At the sound of her sharp movement both men ceased talking. She could see Simon looking directly into her eye. Fortunately for Jackie her boot came to rest on the tail of one of the kittens. The poor little creature gave a yell and scuttled across the floor. It was Jonathan, who re-opened the conversation,

"It's only a bloody cat. Just look at the worry on your face. It's you who are as nervous as a kitten not that mangy old cat up there. Well, let's see just how nervous you can be shall we."

The voices stopped and a rustle of material was now the only sound to be heard, it was Simon, who next spoke,

"For God's sake Jonathan, what the hell are you doing? Not here, not now, no!"

Simon's voice was so troubled Jackie pressed her face harder to the boards in an attempt to see Jonathan. She need not have, Jonathan stepped forward into her line of vision, he was now standing less than a yard from Simon. When Jackie first saw him she almost gasped. He was completely naked, erect and facing Simon. Jackie could see only his back view. Once over the shock, Jackie found the sight of his naked body arousing. Form his slim white legs to his tight muscular buttocks and back, she could not look away. She hated him for what he was saying, but envied Simon for his closeness to Jonathan's naked body.

"Get up." At this command Jackie thought that Simon would strike out or leave the stable. His response was to do neither and was just as shocking to her as Jonathans' nakedness. Simon slowly and passively stood up and embraced Jonathan. They kissed. Had Jackie been asked how she would react in the situation in which she found herself her answer would have been quite positive. She would have been repulsed by the actions of these two grown men, but this was not her reaction. She found she could not look away. She knew she was looking through a forbidden window, a window rarely opened to an onlooker in a lifetime. Jackie surprised herself in that she never once tried to turn her gaze away from the now two naked bodies before her. They sank to the floor embracing each other. Jackie would never have thought it possible for these two men who were just moments before on the verge of a quarrel to be so considerate of each other. She could only look on as an outsider, in jealous disbelief at their actions.

Several minutes later when it was clear that both men had ejaculated, Jonathan snapped back into his former self. He was up and quickly dressed. He left just as quickly, his parting comment of,

"Remember Simon, our little secret is safe as long as I ride in the Games." Finally, and completely shattered the gentle atmosphere that had developed between them. Jackie found that after watching completely spellbound the physical pleasures her groom and friend had experienced with each other, she had became aroused. She wanted Richard, Simon, Jonathan, anyone who could release the ache in her loins. As she watched Simon dress she allowed her fingers to search out and stimulate her clitoris. A few moments after Simon left the stable she reached a very unsatisfying and empty climax, almost an anticlimax. Her jumbled emotions of hate, love, anger and lust were capable of so much more.

She left the stable for the house. She was alone again and in a bath of hot water considering her newfound knowledge. Not only had she Louise to protect her father from, she had seen a nasty streak in Jonathan that appeared to be capable of almost anything. How far would he go? And could Simon stand up to him? She doubted that. This time she could not contain herself, she knew when Richard arrived home later she would tell him everything. Concerning Louise she thought he would believe her, but of Jonathan and Simon she felt it would take some time to sink in.

She felt at first that she had predicted his reactions well, when later in the evening she revealed her full story. Firstly, concerning the catching out of Louise, he reacted almost casually, but to her saga of Jonathan and Simon he exploded, not in disbelief but anger. His blood boiled to think that Jonathan, whom they had taken in and allowed to ride their reserve mount was plotting against them. Jackie thought that Richard's reaction to her second piece of news was extreme. She herself felt angry but Richard sounded as though he could kill them both. When later she brought the conversation back to Louise he showed no emotion. He had no time to think of it. He appeared possessed with the downfall of her fellow rider and groom. He became very positive, almost frightening, she had never seen such a show of emotion from him. He suggested Jackie retire to bed to allow him to consider his move.

He had become so changed by her revelations she wished she had not told him but she felt she simply had to. The burden of keeping so much to herself was too great and she had felt threatened by Jonathan.

Jackie was awoken the next morning very early by a single loud gunshot which had been fired close to the house. She quickly dressed and descended the staircase. She met a very troubled looking Richard in the hallway. He had a revolver in his right hand.

"Richard, for God's sake, what has happened?"

"It's Troy. I was going to take him for a run. We were less than a quarter mile from the house when he caught his front right in a rabbit hole. I have never seen such a bad break. Christ I need a drink. That was one of the worst things I have ever had to do."

"Richard it's not yet six o'clock, what the hell were you doing out so early?" She screamed.

"I needed to think. What you told me last night shook me up. I must have been riding carelessly, pushing him too hard. Damn it, the matter is settled now, like it or not." Jackie passed Richard and ran out to the stricken horse. He was led some two hundred yards from the stables. As she approached she could see blood still pouring from the gunshot wound to the side of his head. On seeing his damaged foreleg she vomited. It was in a terrible state. Poor Troy must have suffered agony. She knew that Richard had done the right thing. Thank God she thought, that it had been him and not she who had had to pull the trigger. Within moments she was joined at the side of Troy by Jonathan. She was so shocked, she had no emotion for him, no hate, no friendship, nothing.

"What the hell has happened here?" he said, "Jesus Christ who was stupid enough to ride this close to the house? And who was riding my mount anyway?" Jackie answered simply,

"Richard." without looking at Jonathan who yelled his answer,

"Richard! For fuck's sake he of all people should know better. He told me never to ride the back lanes from the stables. He knows the verges are sand and full of rabbit holes." Jackie knew that what he was saying was right. He had known about the lanes and he had only been with them a few weeks but then Richard had not been thinking right. Jackie had seen his mood of the night before which had been caused by her revelations of Jonathan's evilness. She felt that they were all to blame, she turned to look him in the eye,

"Jonathan if I were you I would be very careful how you challenge Richard. At the moment you and your scheme to ride in the Games by blackmailing Simon over his sexual preferences are at the fore front of his mind." She could tell from his eyes she had shot a bolt right through him. She delivered her sentence with such neutrality it must have given the impression that she had known of it for some time. This was not deliberate, she was so shocked by the death of Troy that her speech had become emotionless. Jonathan quickly regrouped his thoughts, finding an outlet for his anger,

"I don't know what that little bastard Simon has told you but it is obviously lies. Where is the little runt? I'll make him squeak."

"Simon told me nothing. Indeed no one has. Yesterday when you and he were talking in the hayloft it was not a cat above you, it was me. I heard and saw everything, and I do mean everything."

He quickly realised the full implication of her words. His face and throat coloured and he gave Jackie one last glare and he was gone. He packed and left St George's without a word to anyone.

Fortunately for Jonathan, Richard was busy on the telephone in the study, finding someone to dispose of Troy.

Jackie found Richard striding across the hallway the revolver still in his right hand.

"Where the hell is Jonathan?" He shouted.

"He's left. We will not be seeing him again." Jackie replied.

"What the hell do you mean, he's left?"

"Richard, for Christ's sake calm down and stop shouting at me. I told him how I came to know of his plans and his threat to blackmail Simon, with that he up and left."

"I bet he did. I would have liked to have been there to see his face."

"Richard, I think I would have felt quite smug about it if it were not for my feelings for Troy. How long does he have to lie out there?"

"I have just telephoned the kna…, the necessary people. They will be here shortly. This really is a great loss." He said.

"Richard, what made you ride him on those sandy verges? We have always avoided them." He looked troubled by her question, which she had not planned to ask him. Indeed, she was surprised to hear the words herself.

"I never slept at all last night. I was thinking of how much time, work and expense we have combined into your Olympic effort and that those two were plotting to put an end to our endeavours. I don't think I have ever felt quite so angry. I could have killed the pair of them halfway through the night. At first light I had to get out and do some clear thinking. Was it to be the police? You know what would happen once the papers got hold of it." She nodded her agreement. Richard continued, "Or should we withdraw Troy and dismiss Simon, leaving Jonathan no option but to withdraw himself. I am sure now that would have been the best thing to do. I had not intended to ride Troy in particular. He was the first mount I came to; it could have been Nelson. I was soon out of the stable and on his back, paying no attention to anything. I needed to gallop. I'm afraid Troy was injured almost as we set off." Richard's last words tailed off and his mood changed, easing from aggression to regret.

"How will you ever forgive me, Jacqueline? I was so blinded by the thought of those two plotting against you, I…"

83

"It's ok Richard, I understand. When at first I heard Jonathan yesterday I wanted to give him a bloody nose myself. If I were a man I believe I would have. But he is gone now and we must forget him. I know I shall never forget Troy but I do not blame you alone. We are all to blame, except I think Simon. You need show no malice against him for he was resisting Jonathan's threats. He could not resist his advances but I feel he would not have bowed to his blackmail. I want Simon to stay on as Nelson's groom, he handles him so well." At this, Richard was unsure. It took Jackie some time to convince him of how determined she was to retain Simon. After a few minutes Richard accepted Jackie's view. He released his grip on the revolver and left the house to deal with Troy.

It took several days before Jackie was able to ride flat out again. Each time Nelson landed heavily she was afraid for him. Francis saw to it that the fault was quickly ironed out. With the saga of Jonathan behind her and Louise keeping well out of her way, Jackie's final preparations were going according to plan. Sir John had telephoned to wish her well, saying he would see her next in Los Angeles. He had been upset by the news of Troy.

Jackie had just two days left in England. The whole Olympic team had been booked on a flight from Heathrow on Friday, 12 July. It was on the Thursday, Jackie's very last day in the country, when for the third time in two weeks she chanced upon a situation that left her much to consider.

On this occasion it was a fine warm July day. The wet weather of the past two days had ceased and Richard was away sorting final details. Jackie had spent all morning on the telephone calling friends and replying to any mail which could not wait a month for her return. After a light lunch, which Roddy served to her in the library, she decided to take one of the young mares out for a run on the farm to the south, which occupies a third of the estate. She felt sure that old Mable, the farmer's wife would want to see her before she left for the States. Maggie, the young mare was keep to gallop. They quickly covered the three miles to the farmhouse. Mable was a charming old woman. She had been like a grandmother to Jackie when she was a child; even now Jackie thought of her in that vein.

At ninety years of age Mable had seen all the changes she was prepared to accept and quite a number she would not. Jackie spent a pleasant hour talking with her. Mable insisted that Jackie eat at least three scones to help her put some meat on her bones. Jackie tried to tell her being five feet six and weighing eight and a three-quarter stones was fine in today's world. Mable's solution to her trouble, as she put it, would be to fatten her up, or she should have a child, 'that would stop her gallivanting around the world chasing rainbows'. Mable was the only person who could talk to Jackie in this way for they both felt a strong bond between them, which need not be spoken of. Jackie loved this small, frail, determined old woman and Mable always referred to Jackie as 'our Jackie', as though she were of her own flesh and blood.

After leaving Yew cottage Jackie did not turn back to the house, but instead rode further south to the borders of the Forbes-Brewer estate, passing through one of the loveliest beech woods for miles around. She enjoyed the sight of so many deer which were little disturbed by the horse. On reaching a steep chalky slope she dismounted and walked Maggie to the top. The track was still slippery from the recent rain. Near the summit she halted and dipped into the saddlebag for the extra scones Mable had given her, which she fed to the young mare. In the bag she also found Simon's binoculars. She took them out and offered them to her eyes, hoping she might see a fawn, as it was the right time of year for them to be nosing around during the day.

She sat astride the stile whilst Maggie enjoyed the scones. She gazed all around, halting whenever a small point of colour attracted her attention. She was constantly focussing and refocusing from near to far. With such a marvellous view to the south and west she tended to keep the lenses pointed in that direction. Whilst viewing to the south outside of the estate she picked out two cars parked very close together and some ten yards off the road into a copse. Although the vehicles were some half-mile distant it was clear to Jackie that the nearest one was Louise's. Jackie began asking herself questions. Why was Louise there? What business could she have here and with whom? She knew the car was at the hall when she had left. She tethered Maggie to the stile and walked some distance to the furthest point of the hillock, keeping to the north side of the ridge. The chalky soil was quite wet, for, being north-facing the day's sun had not yet dried its surface. On reaching the furthest point at which she could remain hidden from view she took a few paces forward to the top of the ridge. As the southern view became visible she sank to her knees. She had come closer to the cars than she expected. They were now no more than one hundred yards away from her and fifty feet below her position. This gave her a commanding view. She saw two heads in an open-top Rolls-Royce, one of them she knew to be Louise. The two people in the car were looking directly towards her. Fortunately she was amongst some blackthorn bushes that offered good cover. She brought the glasses to her eyes, resting her elbows on the sticky soil. By this time the wet had penetrated her clothing, her thighs and knees were both cold and uncomfortable. Once the binoculars were focused the two occupants of the car became very clear.

Louise was wearing a button-fronted, white cotton dress, she looked very relaxed and smiled often. The gentleman in the driver's seat whom Jackie estimated to be aged fifty to fifty-five she felt she recognised, but no name came to mind. After a few minutes they kissed. Not a peck but quite a passionate kiss and the gentleman's right hand cupped Louise's left breast, she then moved to her own car and drove off. Jackie could hear the car ever more quietly as she drove back into the estate towards St George's. She turned her gaze once again to the Rolls. Its registration plate was just one digit different to her father's, she knew that to be too much of a coincidence. This car, she thought, must be owned by the Forbes group. She knew her father had ordered three last year for delivery on the same day. This had to be one of them. She challenged herself that before the day was out she would discover the identity of the driver and apparently Louise's lover. Jackie felt nothing but contempt for Louise. She thought her an arrogant cow, for she judged Jackie in front of her father by her high and mighty standards yet behind his back it is she who is acting like a whore.

Jackie returned to the stile and quickly rode back to the stables. There she met Simon to whom she handed Maggie. She spoke to Simon for a couple of minutes about the forthcoming

Games. Simon had been very upset at the loss of Troy and visibly relieved by the subsequent disappearance of Jonathan. He spoke very little but he sang and whistled far more often. Each time she saw Simon Jackie could not prevent her mind from recalling the sexual experience that he had had with Jonathan. She looked into his eyes, he seemed to her to be relaxed and untroubled. She was glad that she had not told him of her eavesdropping in the hayloft and glad too that she had resisted Richards wish to have him replaced.

Jackie never did reveal her knowledge of the matter to Simon. It was to be a very desperate Richard who would recall to Simon, amongst other startling and shocking revelations the afternoon that he had spent with Jonathan in the hay-loft. Jackie walked to the house preoccupied with the name that belonged to the face in the Rolls. As she entered St George's the telephone was ringing. It was Louise who answered the call. She listened for a moment and handed the telephone to Jackie.

"It's Richard for you." She looked Jackie up and down, noticing all the chalk on her clothes. She added, "Did we have a fall today? No broken bones I hope." Jackie felt that Louise handled sarcasm as badly as she did loyalty. She lifted the receiver.

"Hello where are you Richard?"

"I'm just about the leave the centre. We have not come up with a reserve, I'm afraid we shall be the only team without one. The Germans have also had a serious blow, their number two has had to change his mount and the Americans have tried to pull a fast one by altering dimensions on almost half the fences. A protest by the Europeans and, surprisingly the South Americans has put a stop to that. We shall have to watch out for them, they love to change the rules at the last minute."

"You seem to have it all under control. Will you be back here today?"

"No that's why I'm ringing. I shall meet you at the airport tomorrow at two o'clock. Don't concern yourself with Nelson. I have already spoken to Simon and everything has been arranged. Just make sure you are ready when the car arrives to collect you at twelve noon tomorrow. Don't worry yourself to sleep tonight and remember I love you Jacks."

"If you were here I would not have time to worry. Can't you make it, for me? I'll show you how much I love you."

"Sounds great but really I must see my father before I go to the States. To come from there to you would leave me too worn out to be of any use. Keep it on ice, and I'll see you tomorrow. Bye Jackie."

"Oh Richard please…" He could not hear her. He had closed the conversation.

After cleaning herself up and dining alone Jackie went into the study and scanned through all the papers she could find, but there was nothing relating to company transport holdings. She would have to make a telephone call. She thought about this for some time and eventually telephoned Sandra Tomkins, her father's secretary. It was she who answered the phone.

"Oh hello Sandra it's Jacqueline here. I have had an odd call from the police. They rang to say that a Ford car used in a crime was bearing father's number plate and would I check that the vehicle had not been stolen". Jackie gave Sandra the registration number." Could you just check to see if that is indeed the right number? I believe the car is at the airport awaiting Daddy's return."

Jackie felt quite pleased. She felt that she had said just enough. Sandra returned a moment later.

"Well Jacqueline this is a mix up for sure. I agree Sir John's car is at the airport but the number you have given me is not Sir John's. Could you check it?"

"Oh that's odd. I'm sure that's the number they gave me. If it's not my father's I wonder why they telephoned here. They must have made a mistake."

"Well it's not much of an error. You see the car which bears that number is registered to Forbes-Brewer Industries but it's not Sir John's its Peter Gould's and I'm sure that his car is not stolen."

"Oh well that was the main point, to establish that the car has not been stolen. We have accomplished that. Thank you Sandra."

"Before you go Jacqueline we would all like to wish you well for the Games. I believe you leave soon."

"Yes tomorrow, thanks again Sandra, bye now."

So it was Peter Gould who was with Louise. What on earth would those two have to discuss that could not be said over the telephone? From the relaxed manner with which they touched Jackie felt sure they were more than just familiar with each other. Jackie pondered the possible results of a well-developed relationship between Peter Gould and Louise, assuming of course that it was Gould in the car. She knew he was in a very elevated position within the group and her father apart, he was second only to the ever-reliable Arnold Elliot. Peter she knew to be highly trusted by her father. If Arnold were to leave the scene his most reliable and highly paid director would be Peter. He and Louise were both in privileged positions of trust and access to her father. If they were lovers she knew it would hurt him very much but if they were plotting against him she knew it could hurt them all.

She told herself that when she saw her father next, which she knew would be in Los Angeles quite soon, she would take the first opportunity to warn him. He would never trust Louise again. She hoped her father would not think she was trying to get back at Louise, for, if he did, she was afraid he would not treat the matter with the seriousness that she felt it deserved.

LOS ANGELES

The following morning found Jackie in a panic. There were forgotten phone calls to make and last minute local purchases. Simon and her mount Nelson had disappeared mid-morning and were not her concern. She spoke to several of the staff before she left, all wished her well. Louise was conspicuous in her absence. As her car slowed to pass between the stone pillars she glanced back. St George's looked marvellous with the early summer sun across her stonework. In the heart of winter the house could appear impenetrable and forbidding, but with the rhododendrons and azaleas in full bloom and the lawns mown, her family home was at its best. Jackie knew there would be changes on her return. Richard and she would be married just two months after the Games and she felt that Louise's days at the Hall were surely numbered. She was not to know that more than a year would pass and that she herself would bear the mental scars of horrendous ordeals before she would once again pass through the stone pillars of her family home.

On arrival at Heathrow Jackie joined Richard, Francis and the rest of the British team. There were no more than a handful of the press there to greet them. They do not flock to show jumpers in such numbers as they do for star athletes, although Jackie being the glamour puss of British show jumping as she has been labelled by the tabloids always received more than her share of attention.

The flight was smooth and without problem, other than William, a fellow member of the team taking on rather too much gin. Lunch came and went in a half-dozen or so plastic containers, one extra was required for William. They landed in Los Angeles roughly the same time of day they had left Heathrow. This was to be a very long day. The American press and administration made a fuss of the visiting teams. They were escorted into a private lounge, issued with various tags and passes, photographs were taken for the FBI and they were then escorted onto waiting coaches to be driven to the Olympic Village. All this had been handed with precision, efficiency and a degree of vigilance and suspicion. Once in the Village there were more forms to sign, another photograph and finally keys were handed out to their rooms.

Richard and Jackie would spend the next month living some distance apart. He had been booked into the coaching centre and she in the huge competitors block two miles distant. The many sections of the village were serviced for transport by free ride trams. These were to become an essential part of their lives during their stay. Jackie being the only female in the British Equestrian Team was given one of the few single rooms. It was a pleasant room apart from the bold colour scheme. There is a lot to be said for English pastel shades, thought Jackie.

Richard had said he would meet her for dinner in three hours. She showered, changed and had time to unpack. She crossed the lounge to her bedroom, which had been more tastefully decorated. The room was twelve foot square, had a generous single bed, a chair, dresser and a whole wall of built-in wardrobe. She spent a full hour unpacking. It was clear to her that some of her clothes were too dressy. Once unpacked, she took a look around. There was a small kitchen annexed to the lounge and a bathroom with a shower. The windows in both rooms overlooked the park area towards the south side of the Olympic complex. Beyond the park and its border of trees she could see only the highest peaks of the main stadium, the Los Angeles Memorial Coliseum, it was decorated by flags of many nations, except of course those of the Soviet and Eastern block Europeans who predictably had stayed at home to diminish these games as the Americans had done to their own.

One hundred and fifty nations were to take part, a record, despite sixteen countries boycotting the Games of the twenty-third Olympiad of the modern era. The entire Soviet block had declared in a joint statement on May 8th that they would not participate due to security concerns, chauvinistic sentiments and an anti-Soviet hysteria being whipped up by the United States. The exception was Romania (who subsequently finished second on the medal table). The Soviet-bloc boycott was a predictable response to the United States boycotting the last Olympic Games in Moscow, a time when the United States had whipped up anti Soviet sentiments and hysteria in protest of the Soviet invasion of Afghanistan. A country that the United States would themselves eventually invade with a great deal of help from the British, or more specifically Tony Blair. Iran and Libya also had declared they would boycott the Games for political reasons, Iran being singled out as the only country that had failed to attend both the Moscow and the Los Angeles Games. Curiously Iran's capital Tehran was the only other registered bid opposing that of the Californian city of Los Angeles. When Tehran declined to make its final bid the Games were awarded to Los Angeles by default, it was to be the only city that has hosted the summer Games twice, oddly in 1952 the previous time that the city had held the Games their bid then was also unopposed.

The park was busy with athletes and journalists. Jackie turned her gaze away from the early evening activity and fell back onto the bed. This had indeed been a long day and tiredness had closed her eyes. She jumped to her feet, she knew Richard would not be pleased if he found her asleep in an hour or so. She undressed for a shower, picked up a towel and crossed the lounge to snap shut the lock on the door. They had been warned to lock doors at all times to reduce thefts to a minimum. As she reached for the door it was thrown open. In the doorway, indeed blocking the entire doorway was Wayne, a six-foot plus African-American wearing only Bermuda shorts. Jackie stared open mouthed at this black giant for an instant before covering herself with the towel.

"Do you mind? Is it not customary to knock before entering in this country?" Her voice sounded frail, even to her own ears. When her intruder spoke it was with a deep heavy southern accented boom.

"Sorry lady. I dun got the wrong room."

"Yes you dun have. Now please close the door."

"I said I was sorry lady. Boy you're really som'in, English too." She slammed the door. She worked out that his last comment had been a compliment, for as it was delivered he looked her up and down, reliving the momentary glance he had had of her naked.

She had her shower trying to imaging having sex with him but somehow it seemed impossible. He was almost as wide as he was tall. There was simply too much of him. After her shower she made friends with her hair and face, took a call from a miserable Richard and dressed casually. The teams were free to choose their own garb, being required to don the red, white and blue jacket, blouse and slacks at official functions only. This was something Jackie was particularly pleased with for on past representative trips things had become very stuffy. Tonight, she could relax in a loose grey, cotton jumpsuit.

In just a few days her attitude towards her clothing had become complacent, for in summer in Los Angeles nothing looks good. The atmosphere of this wretched city as described by her father is so badly polluted from cars and industry it is not fit to breath. This was something for which the British team, even though warned, were quite unprepared. The real shock came on the first day of practise, before they could begin to ride in the stifling 104 degrees Fahrenheit, they were all shown how to operate oxygen masks and cylinders, not just for themselves but also for the horses. Poor Simon, wherever Jackie and Nelson went he had to be there with an enormous amount of survival gear for them all. It was easy to appreciate why Sir John thought so little of this city, the combination of the heat and the LA smog were getting everyone down. Getting through each day was becoming increasingly difficult. Jackie often had to rest Nelson, in specially provided areas of shade. She and Nelson were competing well in dressage and jumping, but the cross-country was causing concern. Nelson was tiring too quickly and Jackie was loathe to push him too hard. It was at this particular discipline she knew poor Troy would have surpassed, for he had true stamina. Stamina that Nelson sadly lacked, after their first two attempts at cross country, Jackie had led Nelson home in need of both shade and oxygen. Ironically if Jonathan and Troy had been at the Games, a very difficult decision would have been faced at this point. Simon was all for pulling Nelson and subsequently the whole British team out of the Games. Francis kept a level head and took an overall view, all the other teams were having problems and Nelson was improving.

In contrast to the problems of the days the evenings were a joy, competitors, athletes and coaches from all over the globe came together to dine in the huge Olympic complex. There were tongues of every language and bodies of every colour, shape and size and no shortage of entente cordiale. It became a game guessing which country one individual was representing and in what sport. With six thousand eight hundred and twenty nine competitors and just over twenty percent being female there was an extensive diversity of mankind to choose from, even though almost a third of the expected total had stayed at home.

By the middle of the second week all the hard work was reaping rewards. All four horses were acclimatised and performing well, though Nelson was still the slowest at cross-country, Francis as usual had done his homework and judged things well.

Jackie received a telex from her father to say he was flying in the following Monday, the very day before competition began proper. They were all rested over the weekend; it was when free from riding that Jackie's mind began to wander. She spoke concerning Louise to Richard who seemed troubled but not by Louise, telling her to put it out of her mind until after the wedding. If Jackie was honest with herself, it was telling her father of her suspicions that was causing her the most concern.

The night before Sir John arrived she was very anxious. She knew that once she had spoken to her father his shrewd mind would examine every possibility and form all manner of contingency plans. Jackie went to bed that night but slept not at all. She felt ever-growing unease that she and Richard had not made love since some time before they had left home. She felt that he was avoiding close contact with her. Some distance had developed between them which Richard put down to pressure and competition. She tried to make herself dream of their wedding day but sleep eluded her. It was a very confused and unhappy Jacqueline who was walking the park at around 5.30 am.

By seven she received a call from her father at the Los Angeles International terminal. She remarked that he sounded tired. Sir John replied that he had slept little during the flight from Singapore and suggested they meet for breakfast. Jackie gave her father directions to her favourite breakfast diner outside the village, knowing that he would have a self drive Rolls-Royce waiting for him at the terminal, Sandra Tompkins would have seen to that. Although Sir John always used a chauffeur at home he never did abroad, supporting his claim that he was the only

Englishman who always drove on the right hand side of the road. Jackie telephoned Richard and arranged to take the free bus with him to the diner. She then telephoned Simon to check that he would be with Nelson for the full day as she wished to show her father around the village if she could stay awake, she wanted to spend as much time with him as was possible before she dropped her bombshell.

Jackie showered and dressed, met Richard at 8.15, they boarded the free bus together. Richard was ill at ease, obviously so. He explained it away as concern over tomorrows' competition. Jackie felt his answers to her questions were inadequate. It was plain to see that he was tenser than she. She tried to discuss Nelson's fitness which succeeded in giving rise to an even greater sense of anxiety within her. As she talked to Richard she felt she was talking to a stranger or member of the press. Shortly before they disembarked Jackie had had enough.

"Richard, what the hells got into you this morning? You're talking like we are no more than trainer and rider, and if we're honest that's all we have been since we left home." "I told you I'm worried about Nelson and that cross country in the morning, that's all." "Rubbish, there's something on your mind and before the day is done I'll know of it." "Okay. Have it your way. Here's our stop. Let's have breakfast." They joined Sir John in the diner.

"Hello daddy. You look well. Not half so tired as you sounded just an hour ago." "Ah, I'm one coffee ahead of you. Good stuff too." "Well if it's that good let's order, just coffee for me Richard." Sir John leaned close to Jackie and surprised her. "Things aren't going so well are they girl." "The teams in pretty good shape, it all starts tomorrow."

"I'm not talking team, I'm talking you." Jackie choked on her words, she didn't know what to say first. What does he know? Does he mean Richard and her or Louise and him? Can he read her mind? She reflected of course he can, he's my father.

He squeezed her hand saying,

"Richard's coming with the coffees. We'll talk later." That worried her even more, what does he know that he can't discuss with them both present and why is Richard so damn strange? They breakfasted talking at length of LA and its unique air. Sir John gave a brief resume of his Far East trip and the three of them

95

were soon in the Rolls. Richard, seated in the passenger seat was the only one who noticed the black Ford Sedan, which pulled out from the diner directly behind them. The Sedan followed closely. Sir John put the Rolls into the mainstream of traffic heading towards the stadium. Neither driver could see or hear the helicopter above.

"Daddy where are you staying for the next two weeks?" "I managed to get in at the Ramada, but I had to pull a few expensive strings" "I think I got one of the rooms vacated by the Presidents security staff. Apparently they had the whole hotel last week for the opening of the Games. Really, was three hundred rooms absolutely necessary to guard one ex-cowboy, I know Ronald Reagan is solidly with Mrs Thatcher, thank god we've got her, the only politician in Europe with a spine but Reagan had a total of six hundred staff here. I would suggest that was a tad excessive."

"Yes he did have a huge back up team. We were hoping to get a glimpse of him last week but all we saw was a group of well dressed men in dark suits each with one hand inside their jackets, didn't we Richard?" She turned to look at him but never received a reply. Richard had heard the Sedan accelerate.

As Sir John turned the Rolls into a slow 90 degree right along-side open parkland the black Sedan drew alongside and forced them off the road. Jackie looked to her left. She was shocked at the closeness of the driver in the Ford. He was inches from her. Richard urinated. The two cars quickly halted. Sir John was overcome with anger. The two occupants of the Sedan were quickly out of the car. The driver, a weasely built Philippine pointed a pistol at the Rolls. Jackie relaxed. They were detectives, it was a mistake.

Sir John never heard the first shot. It came via the windshield and entered his forehead – he died instantly. The force of the 38mm bullet whiplashed his head back breaking his neck. Jackie went into shock, numbed with terror. Her door was thrown open. She turned in time to receive a blow to the jaw. She passed out. Wayne, the huge Negro she had met once before pulled her from the car, he lifted her onto his shoulder as a man might a bag or sack, the Philippine fired at Richard. The first shot tore open the flesh to the left side of his neck, the second hit and smashed his collar bone, the third lodged deep into his shoulder blade.

Few people had even heard the sound of gunfire due to the landing helicopter, less than sixty seconds from the first gunshot, Wayne, his baggage and the Philippine were airborne and swinging eastward at full tilt. Jackie was injected in her arm with a minimum of 12 hours sleep.

From the moment Richard had been hit with the first bullet his sense of fear was transformed to terror. His neck was on fire, his left arm and shoulder immobile. He had never imagined such pain. The fire high to his left shoulder spread to his face and down to his waist, its flames licked through the nerve cells of his body. He checked again and again that his left arm was still attached. All feeling had been removed from his hand and the blood from his neck had run down his shirt, as it slowed to congeal it was thinned by the urine he was sitting in. His mind raced and raged,

"What the hell is....?" "Christ this is the US, won't somebody please...." "I can't stand...." "Don't pass out, don't pass out, you'll bleed to death." "No not me, where the hell is...." He noticed more blood on his legs, it was Sir John's. He looked at Sir John and finally passed out. Within seconds he came to. It was then that help arrived. He was quickly relieved of his pain and his consciousness and removed from the car.

Sixteen hours had passed before Richard regained consciousness in a dimly lit hospital room, with one nurse in attendance and both police and press impatient in the adjoining corridor, waiting to gain access to the room to speak with him. The press had been evicted repeatedly but returned with the welcoming regularity of an incoming tide of sewage. The hospital corridor more resembled the backstage area of a theatre on opening night, since the shooting of the day before all hell had broken loose.

A nurse indicated to the senior police official from the L.A.P.D. that the patient is awake with a tap on the smoke glass window that separates silence from chaos.

Richard is quickly subjected to a barrage of questions, questions he ignores and he then asks,

"How is Jackie and Sir John, how is Sir John." "He's dead and she's gone what can you tell us?" replies Detective John Faulkner.

"Jesus Christ John there's no need for that." Injects Detective Inspector Brian Howard

"Sorry Brian but this guy just doesn't seem to hear." "And how would you be with half you god dam body shot away, go get some coffee." "Look I said I was sorry can we move on." "You'll be writing tickets if you don't get that coffee, now go." Added Howard, he continued,

"Now then you are Richard Brewer correct?" "Yes Sergeant." "That's Inspector, I am sorry but your future father-in-law was killed yesterday and your finance appears to have been kidnapped." "Kidnapped, Christ by whom?" "We don't know that's where maybe you can help us. Can you describe who you saw, how many, what Caucasian?" "Slow down Sergeant." "That's Inspector." "Look this might seem selfish to you but where am I, how am I, and who are you and where's Jackie?" "Coffee boss?" Injected Faulkner.

"Christ you're right John this guy doesn't hear so well, find him his doctor, we'll send the day crew in later, come on." Richard was left to gain his senses, he later talked with his surgeon who explained that the minor wounds to his neck and collar bone had been treated and stitched and that he was on a drip of antibiotic to help him resist infection and morphine to help with the pain. There was however still bullet fragments lodged in his left shoulder blade that would require surgery in a few days. He'd lost a lot of blood but the incident had occurred just two miles from the hospital, he was fortunate to be alive. Richard felt many emotions but he did not feel fortunate. He needed to make an urgent phone call to England, he wanted to be out of the hospital but thought that until he understood better what had gone wrong the previous day he was perhaps safer where he was.

Sir John's body was being crated for flight back to England.

Jacqueline Forbes-Brewer was more than a thousand miles south of Los Angeles.

The British Equestrian team withdrew from the Games of the twenty-third Olympiad.

It had been announced in England that Louise was under sedation.

Richard recovered slowly, eventually he told the police what he could about the enormous black man and the shorter Philipino who had attacked them. The local police were working along the lines that he had been shot in mistake for Sir John as Sir John always drove with a chauffeur in England and Sir John was shot because most chauffeurs in the US were armed. Richard could not follow their line of thinking, he was twenty-five years younger and almost a foot taller than Sir John and not to be mistaken for him by any sighted person, and furthermore if Jackie had been kidnapped surely her father was both the wealthiest and most likely person to come up with a huge ransom. After four days a ten million dollar ransom demand was made through the London Times and Reuters of New York, the most public blackmail demand ever made, if we overlook Khrushchev's Twisting of Kennedy's arm almost to snapping over the 'Bay of Pigs' affair.

The police and the press had a field day on both sides of the Atlantic. The Forbes-Brewer affair was on the front page for two weeks, the Los Angeles general hospital was encamped with press from dawn till dusk.

Richard had still not made his urgent call to Louise, the Games of the twenty-third Olympiad continued as planned.

After a three AM shoot out in the hospital corridor on the fourth night of Richard's incarceration which resulted in the death of the nameless Philipino and the courageous Sergeant John Faulkner, the American law enforcement agencies were completely out foxed. Why had this guy risked all to come back and finish off the guy who was most likely to pay the ransom? By this point Richard is senseless with fear, in his mind he has managed to fill in the missing pieces of the puzzle and now Louise is the last person he wants to communicate with. He asks to see Simon who visits him later the same day, for just ten minutes they are alone, it's the first time since the sound of gunfire was heard in the corridor that Richard has not had an officer in his room, for the officer it's the first time in three hours he can have a fresh coffee and relieve himself of the last one.

Richard gains no knowledge of use to him from Simon who is due to fly back to St Georges the next day with the horses; he takes with him a letter from Richard addressed to Collins and May of Westminster, Richard's family solicitors. Richard has had time to reflect on how he had arrived at his current situation. He delved into his past, how had he allowed himself to be part of such a conspiracy? It was all down to Louise, she could sell sand to the Middle East. As a young man he had been desperately shy and inhibited. Girls never came his way, he would fumble conversation like a one arm juggler. He put this down to being brought up on a large estate with a private tutor, he had few contemporaries, few peers, he just had the horses, which became his life. That was until Sally arrived, Sally was assistant to the local farrier, she came into his life like a hurricane, she turned him upside down and left him transformed. He was a twenty-seven year old virgin when they met, nine months later when she finished with him because he had become too possessive he had had sex in more places and in more positions than most people achieve in a lifetime. For Sally it was a bit of fun, Richard fell in love. For years after Sally's disappearance Richard worked hard to build a reputation as one of the country's leading young trainers, there was nothing he could not achieve with a horse but he was a damaged man, always he burnt a candle for Sally. He began to see Jackie regularly which turned eventually into a physical relationship but it was not like the one he had known, he felt inhibited, he was not someone who could take the lead, he never felt comfortable in pursuit, he preferred to be pursued. Then he met Louise, she had the look of Sally in her eyes and so it proved. Louise was so poised in public and devastatingly uninhibited in private, her repertoire was more extensive than Sally's, she understood S and M and how and when to use it. Richard was putty in her hands.

How had she come by this knowledge?

Louise was a war baby, she was the result of a one-week liaison between her mother and an American serviceman in December 1944. He was on a short stopover returning home from newly liberated northern France, she had lost her husband two years before in North Africa and was in need of comfort. The American G I's were striking, their haircuts, their uniforms, their

100

accents and their swagger, all of this greatly impressed young broken-hearted British women. Regardless of their attachments back at home, many of the G I's found solace in the arms and in the beds of lonely widows, and married woman. Louise was abandoned by her mother at the tender age of just one year, she grew up in a Barnardo's children's home. By the time she was sixteen she had learnt that men would go to extraordinary lengths to share her uninhibited attitude to sex. She decided to use it to fleece them, this she did with panache. On reaching twenty she was no longer capable of love but she could feign the emotion, which she used devastatingly as a tool. She had to scheme and fight for her success and success itself became an obsession. Everyone who became a target was blinded by her control in public and total lack of inhibition in private, Sir John, Richard and Gould had all been swept away by her skill and many before them. It was with other women that she struggled to feel confident, she felt that she had little to offer them. This made her distrustful and suspicious of women, she knew men were puppets, stupid pliable pawns but women she judged by her own standards, she was ever cautious should she encounter an equal. Jackie had interpreted this as hostility. It was hostility that was easily nurtured within her as she felt Louise was a poor replacement for her mother Emily.

In the hospital Richard is guarded around the clock, his parents and Simon are his only visitors, he lays for hour after hour running everything over in his mind. The truth was when Jackie told him her stories concerning Louise and Jonathan, Richard was horrified both at Louise for being so clumsy and at Jonathan for threatening their plans. Jackie was to him a very pretty, unintelligent rich girl, a good rider of horses but not a companion to satisfy him mentally or physically, but Louise, now there was a formidable woman.

Louise had captivated Richard with a fatal combination. She projected herself with elegant poise in public and had the energy and skills of a whore in private, specialising in fellatio perfectly accompanied to 'un bel di vedremo', from Puccini's Madame butterfly, this was a combination she was able to call upon and direct to whom so ever she chose, with powerful results.

Louise being five years older, very cunning and a quick thinker had seduced Richard with a five year plan to replace Sir John and his wife eventually with herself and Peter Gould, a man with similar ambitions to her own. Being Sir Johns PA she had been able to help his wife Emily on her way with small but persistent overdoses of her medication. Gould had surprised her, in that in his company she felt fulfilled, his ambition knew no bounds. The zenith of their plan would be achieved at the Los Angeles games, much easier to hire a lunatic with a gun in the US than in England, she felt that the distance between her and the incident and the bumbling American police who she thought would not see the wood for the trees, would prevent suspicion from being directed her way.

With Sir John, Jackie and Richard killed, a false and very public ransom demand (Gould's work), which of course the police on both side of the Atlantic would advise against paying, at least until proof that the dumb blonde was still alive, she would be free to live as she had long planned. Free of the ageing unexciting Sir John Forbes–Brewer, free of his darling, irksome, stupid daughter and free of the clumsy and disgustingly vexatious Richard, who was for some unknown reason still alive. Richard in pain, angry and confused had by now realised he had been totally duped by Louise, their plan or so he had thought was for him to be injured and to return to England to pick up where had had left off with her, he had wanted all this to happen soon after his wedding to Jackie by which time he would be next of kin to Sir John, Louise had argued against this for Jackie and Sir John both needed to be out of the way, the Games were the ideal opportunity and in the event of both deaths she was already Sir Johns next of kin. Richard was of course essential for being one of the finest Equestrian coaches in the country his role was to make sure that Jackie was on the team, this done he was superfluous.

Had Louise allowed the wedding to go ahead a whole new set of yet unknown wills would come into force a chance she was not prepared to take. The day that Jackie had caught her in the study was fundamental for her, she had that day found out to her satisfaction that all was as it should be. She had allowed the girl to believe she had the upper hand and had also that very evening

102

confirmed to her accomplice and lover that they had a green light for their plans.

On hearing from Jackie of Jonathan's attempts to interfere with their plans at the Games Richard decided he could take no chances, he stayed awake most of the night and thought carefully of what he should do. The right outcome came to him in the early hours, he knew he needed to act fast and decisively, he came up with a simple solution. At first light he went to the stables, saddled Troy, walked him two hundred yards and shot him through the head, then smashed his fore leg with a mallet, swiftly dealing with any problems Jonathan might cause him. Where Richard had made his mistake was with Louise, for he meant to her no more than Jackie had to him, but after a session of fellatio with her he was no more able to resist her mentally than a puppet could resist the pull of its strings. She had through Gould arranged not only the destruction of Sir John and his daughter but also Richard Brewer, who had not been shot by mistake, Gould was withholding the second payment until the job was completed.

It was to be three weeks after the original shooting whilst undergoing surgery to remove bullet fragments from his shoulder blade that Richard was given a lethal dose of anaesthetic through no fault of the hospital staff but by the premeditation of the contractors awaiting payment from Gould in the form of a further transfer from one numbered account to another, of five million U S dollars.

Richard's body arrived home the same day as Sir John Forbes-Brewer was laid to rest in the family mausoleum at St Georges Hall in Aylesbury Buckinghamshire, it was a fine August day just one month after his death, and just three months away from the wedding date set for Richard and his daughter Jacqueline.

It would have taken a person of quite extraordinary persuasion to convince Jackie of just one ounce of the truth regarding the part played by Richard Brewer in her present situation, for she both loved and admired him, she was now ready to believe anything of Louise. Louise had played her extremely well that day in the study, so well in fact she had left Jackie feeling in control when in truth Louise had discovered all she needed to convince her that the timing was right to go for the Los Angeles Games.

The ransom demands ceased after one month as arranged by Gould, just as Louise had with the help of many of Sir Johns contacts including Elliot and Gould raised the sum of money demanded. The Forbes-Brewer affair continued to be high profile news until a plane from Frankfurt on route to New York via London Heathrow crashed into the Irish Sea killing over three hundred German, British and Americans, it had been bombed out of the sky, a devastating and tragic incident for which no organisation or individual ever claimed responsibility or was punished.

The Forbes-Brewer affair was moved to the gossip columns and in time it simply ceased to be of interest.

On its six month anniversary Louise Forbes-Brewer Co Chair of Forbes-Brewer Industries made an impassioned plea on television for any news of Jackie, she even put up a reward of one million sterling for news of the whereabouts of the missing heir to Sir Johns empire, which she was required to do by the family lawyers, it being an essential step required by them if Louise was to inherit after three hundred and sixty five days of Jackie's absence. Jackie was classified as missing presumed dead.

DAY TWO

(CONTINUED)

I leave the deeply troubled Jacqueline Forbes-Brewer, officially missing presumed dead, on the passenger seat of Claire's car and quickly return to the jury room with just two minutes to spare. A quick coffee and I was back on the hard bench of the courtroom for the summing up of the Prosecution's case. By the second afternoon all the jury members were using cushions from the jury room and experiencing pain in the coccyx area, which Dawn informed us was the norm.

There was just one interruption in the proceedings in the afternoon when Lynda (menswear) again scored a point by passing a note to the Judge requesting, 'Without meaning to cause the court to suffer a degree of tautology, could we for the purposes of clarification have the question again as to whether the victim did or did not have a penetrative sexual relationship with the defendants girlfriends during the week prior to the attack?' The judge positively revelled in the detail of the question and Lynda's reputation amongst us was elevated. The summing up of the defence case followed, where it became abundantly clear that the two sides could agree only on the time of day and the date. The judge dismissed them telling all who had the stamina to listen that he would give his summing up in the morning and we, the jury, could then retire to consider our verdict. There was just time for John (foreman) to set our word challenge for tomorrow, and we were away.

Claire was full of beans on the journey home. She had received a far higher mark than expected for some coursework and, more importantly, one of the in-crowd boys had asked her to help him with his overdue coursework. Her driving was a little erratic as was her mood. We stopped just once on the twenty-mile journey to move a dead badger from the centre to the verge.

She is, I think, now as ready as she can be for her test in just three days time on Friday.

"No," says Liz, "there isn't any post and Emma is ready for her driving lesson." Claire walked into the house as I walked back out, Emma had turned me around saying,

"Say Hello, say Goodbye."

I got into the passenger seat of her Renault Clio and we sped off, a little too fast for my liking for Sherborne and Yeovil, as this was the area she knew and had requested to do her test. Both girls were having professional driving lessons at lunchtime from their respective schools but were desperately keen for extra practice in the evenings and both were also very eager to be the first to pass. Should Claire not pass on Friday Emma's chance would be on the following Tuesday. This had built up a competitive atmosphere between them. I didn't think it was the healthiest situation considering the care and attention required to drive in today's world. We made it back home none the worse for the experience. I gave Liz a long overdue hug and thanked her for the cup of tea, I was disappointed that it wasn't a glass of red wine. As she prepared dinner, I went to swot up for an energy assessment exam in two weeks time. Liz asked, "How'd you get on with the book?"

"Okay. It was a bit weird to be sat in sight of the park and all its memories."

"Yeah I guess so, but I think it's something you need to do." She added, "and don't spread that paperwork across the table dinner's nearly ready," and "How'd it go in court today?"

"Okay. We've just got the judge's summing up tomorrow morning and then it's down to us."

We all dined together, which is becoming less frequent. It's often the case that I'm away or one of the girls is either at a friend's or at work. After dinner Claire and Emma disappeared to their rooms to do their 'mining' homework. Liz went into town to take her photography class and I studied best practice and efficiency under the guidelines of the 2004 Housing Act. Later by way of relaxation I had a large glass of red, a long soak in a hot bath and I picked up where I left off last night with Thomas Hardy.

Toward the end of the day, I put down the biography and chatted to Liz briefly regarding her day and looked up the full meaning of John's challenge, which was for tomorrow garner. This one, I am fairly confident with, is to collect, amass or accumulate. With Lynda, two points to the good, I'll have to get a question in early tomorrow if I am to have a chance of competing.

I experience a nonsensical dream, transporting the dilemma of Jacqueline Forbes-Brewer back in time to Hardy's period of hardship and malnutrition for all but the ruling class and the clergy, with horses being the only common denominator linking the two eras.

SUMMER 1987

Jude closed the book. It had taken him longer to read than he had expected. He glanced at the clock. It was six fifteen. He had no more than a few minutes before his taxi would arrive from Oxford. He quickly scribbled notes for Peter Jackson concerning the feeding of the animals. He then drank a carton of fresh orange juice as his throat was dry and stale from the previous night's alcohol. After a scrambled wash and shave he fed the cats and birds and completed his packing. At the very moment he chose to stand in the lounge and say to himself, that's it, nothing else to do, he heard a car horn outside. He closed his mind to the wrench of leaving Blenheim and its furnishings. He locked the door and put the keys back through the letterbox.

"Oxford Station isn't it?" The taxi driver said. Jude nodded and sat in the back of the car, his backpack next to him. It was early morning. The sunlight was already quite strong, its reflection from the whitewashed walls of the cottage caused Blenheim to interrupt in sharp contrast the otherwise green landscape. Jude was made aware of the cottage in the driver's rear view mirror several times during the first mile of their journey. Eventually the car swung a ninety-degree right at the Fox and Hounds and Blenheim was out of view and out of mind.

Jude pictured Jack Mortimer's face, he was a large, jolly man. Overweight by four or five stones, his large red face framed by wisps of ginger. When he smiled, which he did often, his body seemed to join in as his hands would come together with a great slap at around waist height and they would then be rubbed together violently whilst being lifted to head height. This would raise his huge stomach a few inches making him seem even larger than he really was, it was like some kind of mating display ritual to dominate opponents. Jack had been puzzled when Jude rang asking him for a start on one of his cutting gangs and he believed that Jack was genuinely sorry for his loss. He gave Jude the start he asked for right away, but also bet Jude a hundred pounds that he would ask for the Contract Manager's job that Jack wanted him for within ten weeks. He appeared very confident, saying that the sheer number of hours which he would be expected to work and the hard nature of the work would quickly wear him down. Jude could not tell whether this was throwing him a challenge, perhaps giving him something to fight against to prove himself, or if indeed Jack genuinely thought he would quickly buckle and opt out.

Jude stepped out of the taxi and bought himself a one-way ticket for the train journey ahead, which felt to him very strange. This was something he had never done before, it made him pause and consider his position for a moment whilst he drank a hot coffee on the near deserted station platform. Jude began to feel like he was now an industrial nomad, he was carrying with him his few essential possessions, he knew that he had no address to return to if things went badly wrong for him over the next few weeks. His future living accommodation could not be vaguer, all the information that Jack had given him was that he would be one of a gang of three and their first job was silage cutting in West Somerset. The job should take just two days and that one of the other lads would meet him at Taunton Station. How they would recognise each other he had no idea. Of his two companions for the summer season Jude knew nothing at all. Jack had told him in the past that the majority of his seasonal workers were of a hardy breed, mainly ex-lorry drivers, ex-soldiers or ex-cons. He remembered him saying that this was a job that men usually take to escape from something or other.

The train journey from Oxford, through Wiltshire into Somerset was a pleasant one, through the Vale of the White Horse, passed Swindon and on through Salisbury Plain. Jude was both skipping through The Times and gazing into the fields to take note of any agricultural activity. There were few distractions in his compartment, very little to prevent his mind wandering back to the hospital scene at Oxford and that very cold afternoon a week later at Swinford. Any benefit he had received from the hot coffee quickly evaporated. He scanned the railway carriage, his gaze halted on a rail poster advertising European Rail Travel, France caught his eye in particular. Yes France, he thought that he would like to visit his sister. He knew there was much unsaid between them but what exactly? He now felt that she would find him awkward to converse with, as so many others had since Jayne's death.

He knew that most people found it very difficult to use her name and few looked him in the eye as they spoke but he appreciated that he had been enveloped with everyone's best wishes and that his true friends encouraged him to talk about Jayne. Thank goodness for James, he admired James greatly and knew him to be a very solid and reliable character. He wished he were with him now. James had a sense of order and correctness about him, not a man to take short cuts, Jude felt that his long and disciplined training to become a Solicitor had brought out the best in him. It had taught him to think in neat lines, no grey areas, for James everything was either black or white.

Jude's own mind was in tatters, he felt that he had never been disciplined in thought, he always questioned every decision he made and each and every action he took. He had always felt that he was never really sure of anything, excepting his feelings for Jayne, he was never confident of how people would receive him. At this very moment he was aware that he knew nothing of his two summer companions, of their backgrounds or motivations, or indeed if they knew of his situation. So very soon he would have to begin again his mental struggle to exclude Jayne from conversation, but he knew also that he could never exclude her from his mind. He realised that Jayne had much of James about her, she was both organised and disciplined, and her confidence had been growing by the day.

The train slowed as it approached his destination, his thoughts became jumbled and began to race, he felt a sudden surge of unanswered questions. Had he made the right decision? Was Jack right? Would he fold after a few weeks and what the hell would he do with his life if he did? And why did that God-forsaken tractor get a puncture on that bend? He felt his eyes flooding and his throat became hot and dry. Swallowing became impossible and breathing almost as difficult. His mind raced on into anger, had some bastard penny pinching farmer allowed that tractor to run on worn tyres? Tractors don't get punctures like cars. His thoughts became more intense and detached from the norm as he struggled to suppress a panic attack. Yes he thought, that was the trouble with the Country's farmers, they would not spend a penny unless they absolutely had to and they didn't give a shit about anybody but themselves. They were always complaining about being short, needing subsidies for just about everything, the bastards were holding the Country to ransom. Jude was prevented from mentally slating any further the very people whose company he had enjoyed immensely, by the sudden and final jolt of the train as it halted against the barrier.

He gazed out of his window to read a sign that was unmistakeable in its clarity, Taunton, his destination. He cleared his mind of his jumbled thoughts opened the door and stepped from the train. Two minutes later he was standing outside the station on the pavement watching the Town's people and the traffic gathering momentum towards their moderate version of the morning rush hour. Quite soon a small white van pulled up beside him, the driver was both younger and more smartly dressed than Jude has expected - this fellow could be no more than twenty. He wound down the window of the van and shouted to Jude,

"'Ere mate, where's the Police Station?" Jude heard the words but asked the chap to repeat the question to allow himself time to recover from his mistake.

"I said, where's the Police Station to?" Jude said that he was sorry but he did not know. As the van drove away it was immediately replaced by a well-worn Land Rover. The driver's window of this vehicle was already open, indeed it appeared to not have any side windows at all. The driver's head and right arm were out of the window before Jude has focused on the vehicle.

"You Jude?"

"Yes."

"Got no bags?"

"Yes." Said Jude again, looking at his bare hands in disbelief. Jude quite calmly said, "It's on the train."

"That's a good start." Replied the driver, he was unable to resist a boyish grin from advancing across his face, his hand came out of the window for Jude to shake.

"Kristen."

Jude shook the hand, turned and ran. He ran past the ticket office without a word of explanation and he ran as fast as he could along the platform with little or no regard for other travellers. He could think of only one thing, the book, the book, the book, these two words repeated themselves in his mind until he reached the empty platform five and then the words changed to, the train, the train, the train, where's the fucking train? The train had left the station and with it Jude's most precious possession, Jayne's unfinished novel. He turned to the station porter and yelled,

"Where's that bloody train gone?"

"Back to Oxford pal," was his reply "I reckon either you missed it or you left this on it." He held out Jude's backpack with sleeping bag attached and smiled. Jude took a deep breath, calmed himself, took charge of his possessions and slowly walked once again from the station. He could feel his pulse racing and hear his heart pounding in his ears. So swift is the human body to recover from minor shock he was breathing quite normally again when he opened the door to the Land Rover and climbed in beside Kristen Anders who is, as the name suggests, of Scandinavian origin.

"Sorry about that, now where were we? Yes, I am Jude, Jude Saunders and sometimes I forget things."

"And I'm Kristen Anders, but please call me Kris and I forget things to."

He spoke with only a very slight accent, which gave little of his original place of birth away, but just one glance at this man and one would quickly guess at his Northern European origins. He was born in Finland in 1953, almost a decade after the Second World War and raised in a rural region of his country. A country that bore its share of terrible scars of that cataclysmic event that desecrated the greater part of Europe. He had been coming to England for his summer wages for four years. This was to be his third with Jack Mortimer and his second year with Nick, the only other permanent member of their crew. Kris was keen to appraise Jude. His very first impression was that Jack had sent them another duff, for during the previous season he and Nick had got through four partners. Two had tired of the work, the best of them had been tracked down by the police and arrested. The other had left behind no clue as to his permanent absence but having gone through his backpack after his disappearance, it was clear he had a cross-dressing problem, so it had been a relief that he never returned.

The lack of a third settled member of their crew had spoiled last summer. Both Kris and Nick, who was at present on the first farm coupling up and checking over the machinery, had told Jack that the first man they were given had to be hard working and reliable, or the threat was that they would move on. This showed how much faith Jack had in Jude for he valued Kris and Nick highly. Kris for his hard work and organisation and Nick again for hardwork and also he was one of the most resourceful mechanics he had known, an essential element in every crew.

Jack had wound Jude up by throwing him a challenge with a hundred pound bet that he would cave in within ten weeks as a little insurance, he felt sure that Jude was the type of man who would rise to a challenge and as he was paying Jude a little less than his two colleagues for the first month, the hundred pounds was his due wage for that period anyway, so Jack felt that he couldn't lose.

As Kris steered the battered Land Rover through the town Jude felt an obligation to strike up a conversation. Kris appeared to him to be the silent, confident type.

"This your first year with Jack?"

"No, I've done the last two seasons and last year with Nick, that's the other guy you'll be working with. You won't like Nick, nobody does but we get along, he works hard and he can drive and fix anything."

"Your accent sounds what, Swedish? Norwegian?"

"Close Finland, but we won't go there just now. There will be time for that after twelve hours driving. Tell me how familiar are you with the machinery and its handling?"

It quickly became obvious to Jude that Kris would not talk openly with him until he had proved himself worthy. That was OK by Jude, he could play this man's game and Jude's first challenge was to prove his worth to himself by burying himself in hard work, if he could carry Mr Cool and silent type from Finland with him he could kill two birds with one stone.

"How familiar am I with the machinery?" Said Jude almost cockily whilst he considered his answer, "Well I'm fairly sure that every piece of equipment that you used last year and will be using this year I sold to Jack. And I mean everything, the silage cutters, carrier bins, tractors – that's the D90's, D101's and D120's - the combines, balers and maize cutters, the lot. As for handling, I demonstrated everything to Jack before he parted with a penny. So I had to know how to drive it and drive it well. I know you'll probably think that demonstrating is one thing and working it is quite another thing. Well in previous employment I've driven tractors from dawn to dusk up to seven days a week which I believe is the base requirement for this job." It felt good to Jude to parry with a stranger, to fight his corner.

"Tell me what you were cutting."

"I wasn't cutting, I was hauling, hauling felled timber to a cable hoist."

Kris was very familiar with these terms, he had done this work himself in his native Finland. He knew it to be very arduous and dangerous work, which required extreme concentration and a strong body, for if when driving you allowed the tractor, which would usually be the largest and most powerful on the market, to lift over one stump wrongly you could be pulled over backwards by the weight of the following timber. Kris was pleased that Jude had experienced this type of work and knew he would suffer nothing so difficult this summer, his problem would be fatigue.

"Now you're talking my language, it won't be stumps you'll be going stare crazy looking out the windshield for 'til your eyes feel like they're bleeding, it will be boulders, deer, kids and each other." Jude looked at Kris in surprise.

"Yes believe it or not, we have managed to hit each other." He added that item to show a flaw in himself for he felt Jude had met steel with steel and he could relax conversation just a little. Jude smiled and Kris added,

"I put the blame squarely on Nick's shoulders and his drinking habits. We were in combines and Nick was trying to make the gate first. It must have looked like two tanks playing chess, each way I turned Nick had me beat. If there's one thing Nick can do apart from fix things and drink, he can drive anything and anyone into submission." Kris felt that he had said enough. The rest of their conversation before they pulled into the farm was of the weather and the immediate job they had in front of them, which was an isolated spot between Wellington and Tiverton.

As Kris slowed and then stopped the Land Rover, Jude saw the three gleaming new tractors, each one had a bright red silage cutter attached. Two of them appeared to be ready for use and the third had half the casing removed from the cutter. Jude's eyes focused more sharply, he could not believe what he was seeing. The blades were whirling noisily but sticking out of the cutter was half a man! He could see only a pair of trousered legs and boots, Jude knew from the position of them that the rest of the body must have been cut to pieces by the blades. He looked at the grass chute, where was the blood, he looked at Kris who couldn't contain his smile, Kris held out one hand in the direction of the legs.

"Meet Nick, well at least meet the half of him that's easiest to get on with, it's the other half that can be a pain in the neck." A closer inspection of the legs showed them to be a straw stuffed boiler suit with a pair of boots tied to the ankles. Jude breathed a huge sigh of relief and for the second time today the drum beat in his ears calmed. From behind the cutter came the owner of the legs, a man no more than five feet four inches tall, 38 years old, stocky built with a broad grin on his face, he was somehow managing to keep a half burnt, self rolled cigarette between his lips as he smiled, he was of course not wearing boots. Nick dismembered his dummy and recovered his feet. Jude thought that Kris had been wrong when he said he would not like Nick, he reminded Jude already of characters he had enjoyed working with at the time he was employed by Jayne's father, John Marshall.

"Well you'll know by now that I'm Nick, Kris here is the moody one but watch him, he's a dark horse and you?"

"Jude, Jude Saunders." They shook hands, Jude's right hand was now heavily soiled with grease. He had learned one thing about Nick already, his hands were never clean.

Jack Mortimer employed many crews of cutter/drivers, in each crew one man was responsible for the running repairs of the equipment, and Nick was their man. He was the only seasonal employee who stayed on the payroll through the winter, he serviced and maintained all Jack's machinery. Nick was Jack's

115

ideal type of man, he was single, rough and ready, worked hard and did his job well. When he wasn't driving, tools and oily rags surrounded him, but he was OK, if you put up with his constant cursing and clowning.

Kris left Jude and Nick and went in search of the farmer who's Land Rover he had borrowed. Jude donned a boiler suit and helped Nick to close up the third cutter ready for use. The two men shared a straw bale for a seat and the last two cups of tea from Nick's flask, on what was for mid April, a pleasant warm morning. It was by now almost ten am, not a late start as often the moisture level of the crop was too high at this time of day and cutting would not commence until ten thirty or eleven am, but once it had started they both knew it would not stop until after dark, depending on the weather.

They talked of the recent weather and growing conditions and how the grass in the West Country was around a week to ten days ahead of the Midlands. This particular spring of 1987 had been ideal for rapid growth, it had been both warm and wet, coupled with the use of today's nitrogen fertilizer the grass had been forced quickly upwards toward the spring sunshine. They knew that the day after they had finished cutting the land would be re-fertilized and they would be back in six or seven weeks to repeat the whole process, weather permitting.

This particular farm is typical of Jack's clients, it is a mid-range farm with two main concerns, beef and cereals. The largest estates have enough financial muscle to purchase and maintain their own equipment, they are loathed to use outside contractors, for them, profit margin is everything. The small family concerns are financially unable to use outside help for they simply cannot afford to pay. If they are unable to harvest a crop of maize in a wet October because their limited equipment will bog down then the crop is lost, because the cost of hiring in state of the art specialist equipment is prohibitive. These farms bumble through the year with all the voluntary help they can pull in, family members and schoolboys assist, the only reward here at the end of a long hot summers day will be a pint of ale and a good night's sleep.

It is the mid range farms that know the advantage of contractors, with efficiency and careful management they can

116

reduce staff and equipment to an absolute minimum. An owner, two tractors and one more pair of hands, often an unpaid son will take feed to the cattle in the winter, muck spread and odd job. They may plough, seed and fertilise but when it came to cutting a thousand or even two thousand acres quickly, in come the Contractors and Jack Mortimer is one of the largest and most reliable of these. These farms pay on tonnage produced in the barn, this makes good business sense. There is no fortune to be made by the likes of Jack as competition has cut rates. The farmers get a good deal as the equipment used is always new or as new, so days lost due to breakdowns at prime harvesting time is rare. Many of Jack's clients had nursed their own combines or balers for eleven months only to be let down by them when they were most needed. These are the ones whom once they have sold off their own machinery are committed to Contractors, they never have a good word for the Contractors and they take as long as possible to pay their bills, but at the end of each year, they know it makes good business sense.

"Where the hell's Kris got to? It'll be lunchtime before we start." Nick was keen to get on. Kris was discussing with the farmer, Frank Butler, the order of works for the day.

"Jude, I don't know if Kris told you but if you get any problems with the owners or their blokes, take it to him and he'll deal with it. If you get any problems with the kit, bring it to me and I'll deal with that if I can and of course, if you get any personal problems of your own bloody well keep 'em to yourself." With that he gave Jude a wink and a nudge, "Here they come, now we can get on."

Frank and Kris joined them, Kris passed on the farmers' instructions word perfect. This was to become a ritual at the beginning of each day. Soon they were following the Land Rover in the gleaming new tractors.

Jude at the rear turned into the first field on his right as instructed, he lowered his cutting blades and set himself into a rhythm which was to last him several hours. A dozen or so times during the morning he returned to the yard to tip the cut grass, which was quickly heaped up behind him by the farmer's son. For the entire time he was concentrating on keeping his line, checking for obstacles and keeping an eye on the catch bin. He was so engrossed he needed to be called in for lunch around one thirty. They had just one break a day for around half an hour, during this time they would check the blades for problems. Jude slowed into the yard, the others were already into the basic food supplied by the farmer's wife. This was the custom at lunchtime but at night they would find their own food.

Jude was soon teased by Nick for being the slowest of the three of them, they had each brought in two more loads than he, Frank Butler did not give voice to his feelings, but he was mightily impressed with them all. It seemed to Jude that all too soon he was back in the tractor. He was very grateful for the modern tractor with its soundproof, tinted glass, air-conditioned cab and the sprung seat and radio made his life unrecognisable from the life of a farm worker just twenty years previous. In the second session Jude again managed two loads less than his companions before the fading evening light and rising moisture content forced them out of their machines. They had gathered a mountain of silage, Kris was sure they would finish tomorrow so he rang Jack to let him know that they needed a new client for Wednesday and to organise low loader transportation for them and the equipment at approximately six pm the next day, if the next client was a distance away. This was Kris's job at the end of each day's work, to report into Jack's office.

Nick's responsibility was the machinery, check for leaks, and top up with water, oil and diesel. Jude's job was their domestic arrangements, could they stay somewhere on the farm? Where was the nearest Inn or hostel? Where could they eat and shower? If, as on some farms they could stay overnight and the family would feed them for a consideration on the final bill then Jude's job was all but done for him and he would help Nick. All Jude was required to do today was roll out their three sleeping bags in the warmest and driest barn as sleeping on site was no problem. On this occasion the three men washed in an outhouse, changed clothing and once again borrowed the farmer's Land Rover to set off for the local Pub. The three of them squeezing into the small cab, Kris driving, which was to be the norm and Jude, being the 'boy' was in the middle.

Jude was made to feel like a novice by his two well-organised and well-disciplined colleagues. They knew their routine and did

118

not question or complain, they simply got on with the job. He admired them both and felt that the three of them would get along just fine. Jude could feel his back and legs aching terribly, his eyes were sore from staring ahead and his neck was aching from looking behind him. He knew the other two were feeling just the same but not a word of complaint. Yes he thought again, the three of them would be ok.

They drove to The White Hart in silence. Once inside the door it was Nick who broke the silence,

"Well Jude how you feeling?"

"Okay."

"Shit, you're knackered. I know I am and I know Kris is."

"Okay, I'm knackered. Have you used this pub before?"

"Yep, they do a good bit of grub here."

"You remember the pub from last year?" asked Jude.

"Yes," said Kris "we remember the pub but let's hope they don't remember us. Nick had us thrown out on our second visit last year."

"What the hell was that for?" Jude asked

"Tell him Nick."

"Well I took a fancy to the Landlords missus but he didn't take a fancy to me."

Kris added, "I don't blame him, can we at least have something to eat tonight before you take a fancy to anyone? I'm starving."

"Me too." Added Jude. They ordered three pints of bitter and three meals. Kris paid the bill and said it would be Jude's turn tomorrow. Nick put up one thumb and quietly mouthed to Jude,

"New landlord". The meals, when they arrived consisted of three large plates of steak & ale pies with plenty of chips and were eaten in almost silence, as all three were ravenous. The farmers were rarely generous with their lunchtime food. After the meal and another pint of beer the three men began to relax. This for Nick meant rolling himself a scruffy little cigarette and giving any woman who happened to glance his way the eye. He joined in a game of darts with three locals purely because he fancied one or all of their girlfriends. Kris and Jude sat on their bar stools and talked for the rest of the evening, Nick joined them only when his glass was empty which happened on six or seven occasions. Kris had had his two pints and would drink no more as he was driving. Jude offered to drive but Kris was firm,

"Another time perhaps." He added "You have no idea how bad things can get when Nick has had too many, so I'll stop at two thanks."

Jude described in detail the work he had done for John Marshall, being careful to leave out any mention of Jayne. Kris was a good listener, several times he drew comparisons for Jude on how the particular task he was describing would be carried out in his home Country. Kris painted a very hard picture of Finland, the weather and the terrain were extreme and the work both arduous and unending. He worked in England for he preferred a greater variety of work and the money was far better, often in Finland he would be on the same felling site all year round and it was dangerous work. They talked until closing time. Jude had wanted to ask him of his personal circumstances, did he have a wife or family in Finland? But he held back feeling the more he knew of Kris's life the more he would be obliged to give away of his own and in that department he had no wish to be forthcoming. They left the pub at around eleven and walked to the Land Rover. Nick was well on his way to being drunk and was playing at being a soldier, he was stamping out his drill. Although lack of practise and a great deal of alcohol was making a mockery of his attempts, it was still obvious to Jude that he had once been able to do it to a high standard.

Back at the farm they stumbled through the dark barn climbed into the hayloft and dropped into their bedrolls. All three were soon asleep, had it not been for Nick's snoring they would have shared an unbroken night. Here Jude overcame another hurdle, for it was the first time since losing Jayne that he went almost immediately into a comfortable sleep, for every muscle ached and he could not recall the last time he had felt so physically tired. Only once briefly did Jude dream of Jayne, it was when they first met, he lingered on her eyes.

It was Nick who woke them, he appeared to have an inbuilt clock that would wake him around six thirty, and Jude soon learnt that if Nick was awake everyone was awake. Jude raised himself, washed and reported to the kitchen door for what was to become their regular breakfast, toast, eggs and bacon and as much hot tea or coffee as they could drink. The second days' work progressed better than expected. They had shaken off the stiffness of the previous day and quickly swung into rhythm, Jude found he could allow his mind to wander. His thoughts were of Jacqueline Forbes-Brewer, Jayne had certainly left him with a conundrum, he had found no notes in the cottage referring to any future passage of the book for guidance. Jayne, he thought, had been remarkable for she must have stored all the details and plot twist and turns for the books conclusion in her mind. It was these thoughts that caused Jude to almost hit a deer, he chastened himself and brought his concentration back in line.

At around six pm transportation arrived for the three men and their machinery. This consisted of two HGV's with long low loader trailers to load and drive them the thirty miles to the next job and unload. This took them all but three hours, they thanked the drivers and were able to walk to the nearest pub just in time to be the last food order for the night. The evening passed without incident, even Nick was uncharacteristically subdued but it was Nick who once the meal was finished fired the conversation.

"Well Jude that's one job under your belt, how safe is Jack's bet?"

"So he told you about that, I think it's looking good from my side."

"Good on you, you haven't complained yet so I figure you won't duck out and we can all enjoy a good evening when the cash is in your pocket." Jude changed the subject,

"Tell me what you fellas do when the weather is against you." Nick replied,

"Me, I'll spend a day or two servicing the kit, but if the holdup goes on more than two days I'll ship back to Jack's, he's always got something for me. Now Kris here will curl up in a dry corner and bury his head in a book if he can't do other casual work for the farm 'cause Jack won't pay you, eh Kris?" Kris did not reply, he was engrossed in a paperback.

"Your job is gofer Jude"

"Gofer?"

"Yep, rainy days for us are washing days, number three man goes to town to do the laundry and buys in what we're short of, food, shirts, boots, tools and all that stuff."

"And something else to read after this." Said Kris holding his book aloft.

"You and your bloody books, come on Jude let's have a game of pool and somebody fill the glasses."

"You set the balls up, it's my night to fill the glasses." Said Jude.

"Oh crap" said Nick, "that means it's my turn tomorrow."

A routine was quickly established between them. Jude's responsibilities were their creature comforts, washing, organising what food was or wasn't on hand at the farm and picking the best available sleeping site. He usually came up trumps, in all the time that the three of them worked together the worst night they ever had was mid-summer, high up in a Dutch barn full of hay with a noisy family of owls. Even on that occasion they would have had a good nights' sleep had one end of the barn not caught fire due to Nick's earlier neglect with a cigarette end. The fire was quickly contained and no real harm done.

Days soon became weeks, the jobs lasted between two and six days. At first all the work was silage cutting, Jude was always amazed at the sheer mass of tonnage that the three of them could produce in a day, many of the land owners would stare in disbelief at the volume of feed they had cut once they had departed. If they moved more than twenty miles between jobs, Jack would arrange transportation for them and their equipment but more often than not they would drive their kit to the next job. Fuel was obtained from the farms and contra charged against Jack's invoice. By the time of the second silage cut, some seven weeks into the season the three men had slipped into a well-disciplined routine and had each learnt something of each other's backgrounds. Jude had opened up to the loss of Jayne and his reasons and motivation for joining them for the summer.

Nick had spent a twenty-year stretch in the British Army, he went in as a trainee mechanic at the age of sixteen and had served in Germany, Malta and twice in Northern Ireland before Civvy Street beckoned. The army life had suited him, responsibility and forming a close relationship with a partner were not his forte. It wasn't until he left the army after his second and very difficult stint in Northern Ireland that Nick had ever really lived with his wife properly and it was then that he found he could not live with her anymore than he could go back to Belfast. The bulk of his wages were now being paid directly to his ex-wife Carol and their three children. It was only at the very rare mention of a problem with one or other of his children that Nick would go into himself for a period.

From the first day of his new life Jude knew he had made the right decision. He had little or no time to dwell on the wrong things. Of each twenty-four hour day he would spend perhaps a half hour at dawn and an hour at dusk with their comforts, laundry etc and around two or three hours in the pub at night, what was left was for sleeping and working. Jude felt he would recommend his new lifestyle to anyone seeking mental rehabilitation. Whilst he was driving Jude allowed himself some time to wander into Jayne's book.

He felt he had come to know the characters well, he played them against each other in his mind, looking into their strengths and weaknesses. With Sir John dead and Jackie removed who would be Louise's partner? Gould? Or did Louise need a partner? What was Gould's history? He thought that originally Richard had been shot, mistaken for Sir John. As Sir John never drove in England it would be fair to assume he was the passenger. The assailants' instructions may have been to shoot the driver and male passenger. The car had been following them for some time, the occupants must have known their intended victim. The age difference between Sir John and Richard was too vast for it to have been an error. Jude wondered why Richard had been killed and then foolishly realised that the reason for Richard's eventual murder was his decision. Jude could debate with himself for hours on just one such point. Where had Jackie been taken and why? These and many other questions could occupy Jude's mind for a major part of a working day. Several times on wet days during the summer Jude tried unsuccessfully to put pen to paper. This would be on the occasions when they had been rained off for more than one day. Jude would use the first day as an opportunity to take their serviceable clothing into the nearest town for laundering and do whatever shopping was required for the three of them. It was always new shirts for Nick, who would use them for rags and paperbacks for Kris.

Whilst Nick took things apart and put them back together again, Kris would keep Jack informed of the acreage and tonnage and try to keep up with weather forecasting or just sit and read. If the stoppage went into a second day it was Nick that became their problem, his lunchtime drinking and womanising was destined to cause upsets.

They had been working together no more than six weeks when on a second wet day near Bristol the three of them went into town for what Nick often called a wet lunch. A wet lunch was only ever an option on a wet day. They were in the village of Stratfield Mortimer, Nick wasn't comfortable in the Railway Hotel so they decamped to the Fox and Horn, Nick had apparently been in there the day before whilst the others had stayed at the farm. It was Nick who strode in and loudly ordered,

"Three pints of that Tanglyfoot tackle please. Come on you two they've got beer in 'ere that'll make your hair stand on end. Game of pool Jude?"

"OK, why not?" Nick continued,

"Kris grab the beers, we're on the table and let me tell you three pints of this stuff and you won't be on the table, you'll be on the floor!" The two men began their game of pool. Kris collected the drinks and ordered lunch, it was his turn to pay. Two hours and two pints later the two men were still on the table. Nick was as high as a kite,

"Jude you bloody cheat that was my shot. Now piss off out of the way you shit, make room for the Master. Kris sort him out will you and these empty glasses?" Jude turned to the bar with the empties intending to hand them in and not get refills. Behind him one of six local lads had picked up the ball from in front of Nick's cue saying,

"We've waited long enough for you muck spreaders to clear off, now you can both make way for the Masters." Nick's cue caught him under the nose, splitting it wide open,

"Look out Kris." Nick shouted. Kris's reaction was too slow, he buckled under a blow to the side of the head. Nick hit his victim once more with his cue before succumbing to a hail of blows. Jude emptied his hands of glasses and turned to help his mates, but with Kris and Nick on their knees the odds were so firmly stacked against Jude he took on the roll of peacemaker and eventually helped his colleagues into the street. This was the very worst side of Nick and what Kris had in mind the first day he met Jude and warned him he would not get on with him. It was usual to learn a day or two later that he had been in touch with his ex-wife and one or other of his three children was having problems with their stepfather. He was also an army man and a man who, by all accounts, had a more volatile temper than Nick.

As the summer months passed the three men came to rely on each other for their individual responsibilities and learned much about each other. In such close proximity it was virtually impossible to hide any facets of their character. Nick was doing this work because apart from his army experience it was all he knew and he wasn't going back to the Army. His second stint in Northern Ireland had taken him to the brink of a breakdown. The twenty-four hour nature of the threat caused many men who had previously believed themselves indestructible to suffer prolonged bouts of doubt, anguish and depression.

Kris was treading water for a few years, building up his accumulation of cash until he could return to his native Finland permanently with enough of an asset to purchase sufficient land and a timber lodge outright and fund his desired business of hiring out and giving guided tours on quad motorbikes in the summer and snow ski-doo's in the winter. He would return home to Finland as usual in late October early November to drive a huge snow packer up and down the ski runs in the North, near to his birthplace.

As for Jude the summer work had been for two reasons, firstly to occupy him both physically and mentally and to keep him from looking back and feeling sorry for himself. In this respect the work had more than achieved its goal, for if he wasn't working or sleeping he was looking after their needs. It was in the second of Jude's ambitions with regard Jayne's book that he had failed utterly. His mind had often listed for him the problems to be solved but he had not ticked a single item on the list. As mid-summer approached Jude would only allow himself a short period at the end of the day, just prior to sleep, to chastise himself. Often his last thought was that there were a great many days ahead. He passed the ten-week bet period with no significant problems, certainly none that would make him pack the job in, he now knew that he was not only earning a little more per hour, but there was also a bonus waiting to be collected, at the end of the season.

The work which they had started in West Somerset took them both eastward and northward through Gloucestershire, into Hereford and Worcestershire on some six occasions. In April and May and into early June for the two silage cuts and June into July for barley and oil seed rape. July into August it was wheat. September bought the last silage cut and October was the last harvest which was maize. On the last time that Jude found himself at Frank Butler's farm, west of Taunton for his first experience of maize harvesting he began to feel unease in himself, as he had developed a dread of the five months' winter break. He needed to form a cohesive plan.

Late summer turning into autumn had been kind to them as regards weather and Nick had not provided any further upsets worth a page. He had got lucky on two occasions with local lasses and on the second occasion in a very pleasant Inn near Tewkesbury he had attempted to involve Jude with the friend of his companion for the night. Jude had refused immediately and automatically as an instinctive response. Later that night and for the following few nights the thought of a physical liaison with the woman in question was occupying his mind for longer than he would have liked. His sleep was becoming troubled, for the end of the season was in sight, they had perhaps just a month or no more than five weeks left if the pleasant and dry weather held. The last few weeks of the harvesting work was interrupted by eight days of poor weather. During the last two working weeks, Jude's unease at the impending winter break was without him realising it changing his character outwardly. He was withdrawing into himself, he was avoiding asking himself the obvious questions for which he had no answers. If Nick or Kris raised the subject of his winter plans he would reply using the minimum of words possible, not sure or I'm undecided was his standard response. Jude felt that metaphorically he was accelerating towards a brick wall. Each day only hastened him to his crisis. Eventually the day came, their last working day for the season of 1987. It ended at around five pm near the city of Worcester on one of the largest farms that the three of them had regularly worked on just outside the small town of Bromyard. Transportation was waiting to load their machinery even before they returned to the yard for the last time. They said their goodbyes to Nick who returned with the equipment to Jack's yard near Trowbridge, east of Bristol. Kris and Jude stayed at the farm overnight where once again Kris plied Jude for his winter plans. Jude replied,

"I don't know, I just don't know. I've not been looking forward to this day but now it's here I'll deal with it somehow. First I must catch up with my family back in Oxfordshire and then I think I've decided to go south to either the coast or to France. I have a sister there and we have a long overdue conversation but that's it, that's all there is for now." They were in the local Inn and made a commitment to each other that they would do it all again next year, also with Nick if he was up for it.

The following morning the farmer's son dropped them and their belongings at Worcester Station. Jude said his goodbyes to Kris and boarded a train heading east to Oxford. Kris went southwest to Bristol and on to the airport, he was in Northern Finland before it was dark in England. Jude had felt all summer that once this day arrived he would have a sense of direction, that some external force would guide him. Taking the train to Oxford was for no other reason that it would take him back to his life, to Jayne? He felt a sense of misplacement, comparable to a last day of school term, stepping into the unknown with eyes closed. The summer's hard work had been exactly what he had needed. He could feel a tightness and keenness in his muscles, his arms, back and neck were taut and glistening from the summer sun. He felt ravaged by the combination of exposure to the sun and physical effort, but in truth he had never looked better. Were he now laid on a Mediterranean beach amongst Europe's affluent and bronzed holiday makers he would not look out of place.

These thoughts are far from Jude's mind. It is his mental attitude that is making him feel fatigued. He is disappointed in himself that he has achieved nothing during the summer other than spend seven months hiding, gaining cash and an incidental tan. He is dismissive of the progress he has made in distancing himself from his grief. He now feels as though he is on the same train that took him from Oxford in mid-April and that he had merely fallen asleep and the train has turned to commence its return journey. He has with him a backpack full of well-worn clothes and he is aware that the clothes he is wearing need repairing or replacing. His great disappointment is that he has not added one word to Jayne's book. He checks his bag to make sure he still has it, something he has done countless times throughout the summer.

WINTER 1987

DORCHESTER

Jude spent three days at his parents' home in conversation with his mother Faye and his sister Anne. He found the experience claustrophobic, they were both very concerned and supportive, but Jude heard himself lying unconvincingly once again to his mother with regard the whereabouts of Jayne's book. Also the updates of his sisters' children's progress at their various schools and their various abilities and ailments, which should have been, and would normally have been of interest to him, were going in one ear and out the other.

He lied again and said that he had to meet someone on the south coast who may have some winter work for him. When pushed as to where this was he replied Dorchester for no other reason that it was the furthest place away from Oxford on the south coast that he could think of, other than Penzance, which seemed too far even for a lie. Had he taken a little longer to reply, Plymouth would have been his destination and the rest of his life would have taken a very different course.

The following day Jude checked his latest bank statement, which he was impressed with, as not only had seven months' wages accumulated but also the rent from Blenheim had been added. He also confirmed with George Harris that the status quo regarding Blenheim could be maintained as he would not need the cottage for the foreseeable future. George was happy with his new man Peter Jackson, so instead of giving him a pay rise George would continue to pay the rent. Jude took the news of the death of what had been his and Jayne's pet goose Campbell and tucked it away in that part of his mind that was out of bounds, even to himself. His last phone call was to Jack Mortimer to thank him for the summers' work, to pledge himself to Jack again for the next year and to inform him that the first thing he would do was to spend his hard earned £100 bonus on some new clothes. Jack's reply was,

"Enjoy spending it you earned every penny." He thanked Jude for his hard work.

That done Jude was free to go, he actually gave his mother the £100 to spend on his sister's children for Christmas should he not return by then and to 'treat yourself and dad to a damn good bottle of Brandy', which was their favourite drink at Christmas time. His mother was very anxious for him and seemed to realise that he had to escape his old family home. Jude packed some winter clothes that had been moved over to his parent's house from Blenheim during the summer by James and departed for Dorchester, or wherever. Once at the railway station he relaxed took a deep breath and looked about himself. It was noon on a dreary Wednesday in the first week of November and he had no idea of what he was doing or where he would go. After two cups of coffee and a stale sandwich at the station he found himself once again buying a one-way ticket to a place he had never been to before. When Jude asked for a ticket he was asked the question,

"Where to?" He replied,

"Dorchester." For no other reason that it was the town's name he had used when he lied to his mother the previous day. The train journey from Oxford through Reading and on to Southampton was incident free. A change at Southampton and along the south coast to Dorchester and finally Jude departed the train and the station platform, just as the light began to fail at around four thirty pm. Jude's thoughts drifted to Kris, he was a man Jude admired, he would by now not only have arrived in the northern Finnish town of Oulu but he would most probably be working already. With endless trips up and down the ski slopes, he would be compacting the relentless falls of autumnal snow for the winter visitors, to the backdrop of unceasing twilight and the northern lights. Jude envied the structure that Kris had in his life. He was a man who Jude thought was sure to succeed, he would realise his dream, he wished him good fortune and looked forward to working with him again next season.

He wandered but not at an aimless pace from the station through the deserted cattle market, along Cornwall Road to the top of the High Street and then followed signs to the library. The very same library he walked into over twenty years later to find a copy of Hardy's 'Far from the Madding Crowd'. Just before reaching the library he passed the Hardy statue and, on this occasion, he passed by without pause or recognition. He bought a local map and guide at the library and quickly left. He had asked and received instruction as to his best chance of finding lodgings. He was advised that at this time of year he would be spoilt for choice.

Jude ambled down the High Street and considered what he knew of Dorchester and the sum total of his knowledge came to him. That it was or had been the County Town of Dorset and it had a very obliging library assistant. The nose stud he had found an unwarranted distraction on an otherwise attractive face. From the High Street he turned right or left on a whim and found himself ambling along West Walks, the Borough Garden's Park was to his right and there were many properties to his left, where there were several vacancies signs. He climbed half a dozen steps and rung a doorbell as it began to rain softly. An elderly white haired woman whose broad Scottish accent was both surprising and welcoming opened the door, Jude remarked,

"You're a long way from home!"

"Aye and that's the way it's going to stay. Come in young man out of the cold and wet. It'll be lodgings you'll be after is it?"

"Yes," said Jude "what have you got and what's the going rate?"

"Well that depends on how long you're staying." Jude heard himself say,

"One week, perhaps two." He could not give himself a full answer as to why.

"Well yee can 'ave one of the big double rooms in this hoose or yee can have one of the three stable conversions out back, at this time of year the rates are the same but most prefer the stables. The bedrooms are smaller but it's got its own wee kitchen and shower, a bit more private. Yee can let yourself in and 'oot as you please."

Jude took the latter option, a rate was agreed and he paid for one week in advance with cash, which was much to Mrs

131

Nayland's liking. He entered his stable and was struck by the coldness of rooms that had not been heated for several weeks. He dropped his backpack, turned on the heating and walked back to the High Street in what was now a wintery drizzle, in search of a pint and a hot meal. On his return to West Walks at around eight pm his rooms were comfortably warm. He took a shower, lay on his bed and began to ask himself a series of difficult questions. Why was he here? What did he hope to achieve here? How long would he be here? Where would he move on to and why?

He knew he was there to escape his old life, to escape the constant reminders of Jayne and the constant questions of 'how are you?' from his well wishing family, but to be here in South Dorset he knew to be random at best, he could be in any street in any town. He was here also to take on the challenge of Jayne's book, he lifted it out of his backpack and dropped it beside him on the bed. How long would he be here? He had no idea and where would he move on to? His questions were too much for him. He picked up the un-finished book which would be a distraction from his thoughts and read it through once more. Around midnight he turned out his light and slept a warm, deep, comfortable sleep, unusual for Jude.

On waking he went out for breakfast, the rain had passed through in the night and it was now a clear, bright and chilly November morning. After breakfast he bought some provisions for his tiny kitchen so that he could snack at home. On returning to the house he met Mrs Nayland and assured her in reply to her enquiry that,

"Everything was fine in his rooms". Jude also asked her, "Which direction do I take for the seafront or beach?" She replied,

"There's nay beach here laddie we're miles away, you've got to take the train to Weymouth or gee along the coast to Bridport or Lyme Regis. Obviously I'm nay the only one who's a long way from home."

Jude thanked her and laughed at his mistake. He un-burdened himself of his shopping, picked up a notepad and pen and did exactly as his landlady suggested. He took the ten-minute train journey to Weymouth, it felt good to walk the seafront and to be amongst the fishing boats along the harbour. He had lunch along

Hope Street, but increasingly he began to run out of hope as his efforts of writing were no more than jumbled notes discarded at the end of the day. He spent his evenings consuming ever increasing quantities of wine or beer and always by reading Jayne's book, which was beginning to torment him.

As Jude moved into his second week, other than write to his sister Barbara in France and to telephone his mother he had little or no personal contact. His thoughts were becoming further and further away from his norm. He experienced two more days when he felt that he was going through the motions of his journey to Weymouth and back and two very drunken nights when he could not face to read his torment again. His sleep when it came was disturbed and unsatisfying, his dreams were of Jayne but she would never look at him. She was forever walking away from him, he was forever pursuing her without conclusion.

On his tenth night in his rooms at West Walks he hit the buffers. He consumed three bottles of wine and barely slept at all, he had not picked up the book for several days and he had not showered or shaved for three. He had been violently sick during the night. In the morning without having had any food other than coffee he walked across the road into the park carrying Jayne's book. He had come to a decision, the only way he could move on was to say goodbye to Jayne, go back to Oxford, pack his bags and find work abroad, voluntary work or paying work but he knew he needed to be working and he needed to be away.

His physical appearance matched his mental state. His clothes were creased and stale, what little hair he had was unwashed and flattened to his head, he was unshowered, unshaven and unaware that he was wearing odd socks. His eyes were dilated and lacked focus. His outward demeanour exactly corresponded with his deranged thoughts. He knew he had been both drinking too much and thinking too much, he knew too that he was missing the discipline of the summer work, but could not and would not admit to himself that it was Jayne that he was missing, beyond calculation. To admit that was to admit defeat, he knew too that he was unstable and at a precipice.

Jude entered the park with Jayne's book under his arm, he was walking in a clockwise direction taking in nothing of his surroundings and noticing nothing of the other park users on what was a very pleasant and warm November morning. He was so absorbed in his hung-over, tormented thoughts that he never heard the shutter clicks from the single lens reflex Canon camera which was coupled to a telephoto lens that was focused in tight on his face, he was oblivious to both the camera and its operator. Jude continued on a clockwise walk of the park and on reaching the next wire waste bin he dropped his vexation into it. The owner of the camera is more than just curious and walks to the waste bin. By the time she has closed the forty yards to the bin Jude is hidden from view by a stand of ornate conifers. She lifts the object from the bin, its weight does not surprise her as she noticed through the lens the degree to which the discarded object compressed the junk food wrappers that had already been deposited. She took the carrier bag, heavy with pages and left the park to sit at a nearby street cafe to investigate.

Jude's thoughts were jumbled, perhaps even crazy, he told himself he could at least give the book to Faye, his mother, she could pass it onto the right source to complete it. Jude's tour of the park brings him into sight of his waste bin. He's heart rate quickens instinctively as he knows he can recover from his mistake in just another sixty or so steps, he is now striding and not ambling reluctantly. He reaches the bin and attempts to retrieve that which is his. The realisation of its absence takes a full minute, by which time Jude is standing dejected next to an empty bin, rubbish all around him. Jude slides to the ground and begins to sob, he sobs for the loss of the book, he sobs for the loss of Jayne, and he sobs for the loss of his life. Eventually he is wrung out and sits leaning against the bin, a light drizzle commences, he is an abject sight. The dampness of the ground penetrates to the skin of his legs and buttocks. He focus's onto a pound note that lands on his lap. A passerby has mistaken him for a gentleman of the road and tells him to,

"Clear up that bloody mess and get yourself a sandwich and a cuppa tea, you're a bloody disgrace." Jude's sobs turn to mild amusement. He forces himself onto his feet and does exactly as the stranger had commanded. Once the bin is refilled, he looks around for anyone who might be the thief but to no avail. He leaves the park in search of a liquid tonic. His loss is now total and his only consolation is to be alcohol.

The owner of the camera notices Jude enter the bar and watches him leave some three hours later, by which time she has read the material she reclaimed from the waste bin. She then takes notice of Jude's next destination, his lodgings. She spends the evening and half the night, typing and photocopying Jayne's book. By three am it is well presented in a binder and at nine am she is up again showered and in the park.

Jude spends the rest of the day in an alcoholic haze, he eats nothing at all but consumes a vast amount of wine, which eventually overpowers his consciousness around late afternoon, he then slides into oblivion. His last desperate thoughts were of his own limitations and abject failure. He feels wretched and miserable and looks pitiful and pathetic. His early dreams are again of Jayne, she is forever walking away from him, he is never able to successfully pursue her, but later in the early hours of the morning his mind plays a trick on him and gives him almost exactly what he needs. Jayne is some distance from him, he as always is giving chase, she is walking slowly across a meadow of buttercups, she is in silhouette. The sun is ahead of her and he's unable even to reach her shadow, she pauses and slowly turns to him, her face is bewitchingly illuminated. Her half smile stops Jude in his tracks, he is able to read her expression, it is one of calm tranquillity. He can see into her eyes, they are full of love, full of love for him. The sun is shining through her hair, she has never appeared so beautiful to Jude. Slowly she raises a hand to blow a kiss to her pursuer and then still half smiling she waves to him, he begins to recede, to draw back from her. He, in his sleep, shouts out,

"No, no, don't go", but Jayne is standing still, it is Jude who is forsaking her. He thrust his arms forward throwing the covers off of the bed waking himself up, he is badly disorientated. He looks to his left for Jayne for he believes himself to be at Blenheim, he shouts for her, there is no reply, he is crushed.

On realising his true position he re-orientates himself and dwells for a moment on the vision he had of Jayne, was she telling him to let go? Was she encouraging him to move on mentally? Whatever the hidden message if there was one, he was eternally grateful for the experience, he had been almost within touching distance of her and he had perhaps for the last time

135

looked into her eyes. He knew it was time to look forward and stop looking back, he glanced at the clock, it was five-thirty, he felt like shit. Over the next few hours he drank three pints of water and put his life back on track.

The next day she barely recognises Jude when he appears late morning. He is showered, shaved and wearing a change of clothes, he has transformed himself. Jude walks to the corner street cafe, sits and orders coffee. This for Jude is his last morning in Dorchester. As he sits and drinks his coffee and prepares to move on his gaze falls upon a young woman walking along the street. She is tall, dark haired and slim. He admires her appearance, her sense of dress, her long legs, her stride, he admires everything about her. As the young woman approaches his table Jude looks away to his coffee, realising that he has gazed too long in her direction. As the slim figure drawers level with Jude she drops a heavy package on the table making both the coffee cup and Jude jump, saying,

"That's good stuff, can't believe you dumped it." Jude looks into her face and his hands reach out and pick up what he knows to be that which he stupidly discarded. Jude stands and puts out his other hand,

"Jude Saunders." She responds,

"Liz Reese, may I sit down?"

"Please do, how did you come by this?" He says holding aloft the weighty pages.

Liz explains and says she has several dozen close ups of a very disturbed looking man in her camera. Conversation develops between them, Jude who is now recovered from the shock of Liz's interruption opens up to her. Every time he looks into her eyes he sees deeper and deeper into her, her eyes are mesmerising deep pools of brown. Jude orders coffee for them both and finds himself talking more freely than it would be possible to imagine with a total stranger. Liz had spent the previous afternoon and evening reading and re-photocopying the tattered pages and putting them into a presentable binder. She has added several pages of questions and thoughts. This she explains to him, which draws him out more and more with regard the origin of the book and its author. Jude reaches the point where he feels his is laid bare before her on the subject of the book and what his intentions were up to the point where he dropped it into the waste bin, and what his intentions had been on discovering its absence and that she had put her hand into his mind and re-scrambled his thoughts.

"I'm glad I've made an impression on you." She said.

Jude asked if she lived in the town and what did she do? It was Liz's turn to open up a little. She said she was mainly a freelance photographer but that she had one or two contracted assignments annually, which would take her abroad very soon. She much preferred to do her own work but the one contract was a very good payer which gave her the freedom to do as she wished for the bulk of the year. She was currently staying with her grandmother in the centre of town but that she was not brought up locally. In fact, she had been born in Cambridge, which was as far as she was prepared to go down the family route. Conversation moved in more general reflection on how they both happened to be in Dorchester at that particular time, a chance in a million.

He is comforted to have the book back at his side. He is also comforted to a greater degree by the closeness of this attractive, well presented young woman, whose engaging perfume he is struggling to identify. He allows his gaze to linger a little too long into her eyes. He breaks the spell and goes to refresh their coffees. On his return conversation is more general. It is of the area, what they've been doing for the past few days and eventually the weather. At this point they both realise that they have opened up as far as they are prepared to for the moment and a silence falls between them. Jude is thinking, what next, how do I end this meeting of strangers that has been shockingly intimate? I owe this girl so much, how do we part? Liz is thinking more boldly and says,

"We seem to have exhausted conversation, what now? Do we step back or forward?"

Jude looks deep into her enchanting brown eyes, only to feel that she is gazing through his eyes into his past. Then there is silence, a deep profound and intimate silence and a mutual stare. Jude cannot believe what his eyes can feel, this girl is laying herself bare, mentally and physically. Still the stare is unbroken. This is the chess game from the 'Thomas Crown Affair'. This is raw sex without physical contact. After two incredible long, silent minutes Jude stands and puts out his hand, Liz responds. That first contact is electrifying. Jude leads her away from the tables and towards his lodgings. Their silence prevails, Jude unlocks the door and follows Liz inside.

They had been in the room no more than five minutes before he ejaculates deep into her naked body with a force neither of them had experienced before. Momentarily they cling to each other as might two survivors after a terrible storm. Eventually it was Liz who broke the intense and passionate silence between them.

"Wow, no-one would describe you as Casanova. Can we do that again and can you take me with you this time?" They do and he does. 'This time' Jude is considerate of his companion, he takes time and care to satisfy her. They then lie spent in silence, a quite different silence to that of a short while before. Now that they are physically and mentally relaxed it is an easy silence. It is the silence that can usually only be enjoyed by people who have been together for many years, when to be silent together is to know the thoughts of the other, so much so that words are superfluous. They are both surprised to feel their own ease with this silence. It is at this moment that they both allow a weakness in the wall that is their mutual, mental defence against all comers. It is a wall that was put in place to defend them against emotional strife and disappointment. It is far too early for them to admit this even to themselves let alone to an almost complete stranger, but none the less the first signs of a crack in the wall are there.

They dress and Jude opens a good bottle of Spanish red, the only bottle he has left. The degree of their passion and intimacy that has passed between them has surprised them both. Now dressed and further relaxed by the wine conversation moves on to their respective immediate plans. Jude confesses that he has none, he has work in April of next year but nothing in mind for the immediate future.

"No, that can't be," says Liz "what had you in mind for tomorrow?"

"When I thought I'd lost the book, I was perhaps going to look for voluntary work abroad. Maybe look for an Agency that could place me."

"But now you've found it again?"

"Well now I don't know again. It was my intention to carry on with it but I've found it impossible."

"How can you sit here in dark, damp Dorset and write of events abroad? Surely you must be there to be able to experience it?"

"Maybe you're right, I don't know."

"Look your book or rather your wife's book is taking you where? America? Colombia?" Jude had forgotten that Liz had read the book and already seemed to have a good understanding of it.

"Yes, that's where I've got to pick the thread up from, but what you're suggesting is crazy."

"Why?"

"Well because, because it's mad isn't it, to go to America or wherever on a whim? What would I do when I got there?"

"Smell it, taste it, feel it, live it and then write about it."

Such was the simple persuasiveness of her argument that Jude found it hard to contradict. He changed the subject but found once again that his female companion was a step or two ahead of him.

"So we do know that I don't know what I'm doing this week or next, what are you up to?"

"Me, that's simple. Tomorrow I fly from Heathrow to Iceland for a couple of weeks and then on to Canada to photograph the ski slopes, the Hotels, the restaurants, the sunsets and the tourists for what I believe is the best known package holiday company in Britain. Every three years they upgrade their brochures, last winter it was Italy, France and the Balkan region. The year before all of Scandinavia, next year I'll be back there again, it's the same in the summer, it can be between eight and twenty weeks depending on which region needs covering."

"Nice work, how'd you come by it?"

"My ex was very senior in the editing side of the Company and got me the job. To be honest it's a bit of a bind because the subject matter is dead boring, I prefer to catch people in unusual situations or in difficult circumstances, you were a good subject yesterday, clearly not a man at ease with himself, but the brochure work pays fantastically well, any monies I can pull in for my own work is a bonus."

"And when do you leave?"

"Tomorrow at four in the afternoon I leave from Heathrow. You got your passport with you?"

"I have yes. Thought I might go to France to visit my sister, she lives there."

"So it's drinking wine and cosy family chats in France, or you can test yourself and get a flight to the US and come up to Heathrow with me tomorrow then?"

"You're breathtaking, you know that? I met you just a few hours ago, you've put me back on track with the book, you look terrific dressed, flawless naked and you're a great in bed, and now you're proposing I go to Heathrow tomorrow and fly where exactly?"

"L.A for starters, that's where the games were and then on to wherever you need to go and who knows, after Iceland and Canada we might catch up with each other again and tongue in cheek, I wouldn't say you're great in bed, there's room for improvement! Perhaps we could try again in ten weeks' or in ten minutes?" She glares into Jude's eyes with an expression that says I dare you. Jude finishes his glass of wine and kisses her softly and passionately. They undress each other, make love, shower, drink the rest of the wine, make love again and fall asleep together until mid afternoon. They awaken famished and go out for dinner, eventually parting company mid evening. Liz tells Jude that she will be on the eleven am train from town and that if he's not going to be on it, it would be nice if he came to see her off.

Jude returns to his stable and cannot remember the person he had been just twelve hours previous.

It is so good for Jude that he fails to re-conjure his former mood and so it is that after several telephone calls, one to his Oxford family, another long call to Barbara in France and another still to British Airways booking desk at Heathrow, that he is walking to the railway station in the morning, bag in hand, having paid Mrs Nayland to the end of the week. He doesn't see Liz in the station doorway but this time he does hear the shutter of her camera as he passes. On the train through Southampton, on to Central London and out to the airport they talk mainly of Liz's assignment for the next ten weeks, she gives Jude a copy of the travel brochure which is the most recent of the regions she will be visiting and which contains her camera work of three years' previous. She tells him 'that if he turns a page a day, he can follow her progress.'

In the last hour they have together at the airport Jude begins to go into himself, he is quiet and he follows Liz as she airport shops, something she is familiar with. She buys perfume, socks and paperbacks, her last purchase is a T-shirt in Jude's size with the slogan 'Forget me not" on it which she wraps up and as she passes through her gate to board she tosses it to Jude and with a broad smile she is gone.

Jude has four hours to kill after Liz's departure and often during this time whilst he does his own airport shopping he hears her last words to him 'don't doubt or question what you're doing, just do it and don't doubt me, I'm for real and I will meet you after my work is done. Take care.' He opens the gift and smiles to himself, he wishes so much that he had given her something to remember him that he aches with guilt and thoughtlessness. At just after eight pm his plane takes off for Los Angeles but his mind is flying north to Iceland. He sleeps for much of the flight, which leaves him disorientated when he arrives at his destination at midnight, local time, after almost eight hours' sleep.

He spends his first night and day in an airport hotel, several times he reads the notes and questions that Liz added to the binder she dropped onto the cafe' table back in Dorchester. On the inside cover he writes Liz's last sentence to him at the airport 'don't doubt or question what you're doing, just do it and don't doubt me, I'm for real and I will meet you after my work is done. Take care.'

On the morning of his second day Jude ventured into Los Angeles. He spent just one day doing touristy stuff, he visited an enormous film studio, took a taxi ride up and down 'the strip' and visited the site of the Olympic Stadium, now put to use as a sports stadium for one of the local franchised football teams. He finds none of what he has seen inspiring, he is adrift.

He admits to himself that he is missing Liz, her broad smile, her bottomless eyes, which bewilders him as he is now missing

Jayne to a lesser degree. The intensity of missing a living person he finds so fundamentally incompatible to that of his all too familiar longing for his deceased partner that he is a little nonplussed. His dream of Jayne on his last drunken night back in Dorchester is beginning to take on a new relevance. Was it Jayne's way of saying goodbye and letting him go, or was it his way of doing the same? He knew that meeting Liz had softened the blow of losing Jayne, whom he now felt further away from, but refreshingly this feeling did not come loaded with extra guilt. That was it, he told himself, the guilt had lessened, both the survivor guilt and the guilt he experienced in pleasures. He knew that his love for Jayne was impervious to erosion, but what he didn't know was exactly how Liz would fit into his life and how much significance his meeting her would have. He suspected and hoped it would have a great deal of bearing on his short term future but could no guess or suppose beyond that. She was such a different character to Jayne, she was spontaneous and clearly very intelligent, could he be a satisfying partner? He closed his mind to such irrelevant speculation and brought his thoughts back to the present.

Jude was disappointed with the degree of corporate domination assaulting his eyes, there were signs everywhere. He attempts to imagine the town without advertising and conjures up an image of the colonial Wild West. But even this vision is impregnated with iconic manufacturing representations, cowboys wearing Levi 501 jeans, firing Winchester rifles and Smith and Weston handguns and using the Wells Fargo stagecoaches and the Pony Express to travel and communicate. It occurred to him that perhaps the United States had always been portrayed with a corporate twist, he dragged his thoughts back into the late 20th Century and looked around him. Omnipresent were bill boards with huge seductive depictions of products and foods, trying their utmost to convince Jude and all passersby that they could not and should not go through the day without their indulgence. It was a hot, dry, dusty day, the six metre high Coca Cola can was depicted with ice cool liquid condensating on its exterior. The McDonald's burger, again, several metres across, was both over stuffed with crisp wet lettuce and oozing with tempting BBQ sauce. The Taco Bell Mexican style food was again a hundred times larger than life and overflowing with its deep red coloured filling, and the building sized image of the latest four wheel drive offering from Ford Motors was shimmering with wet metallic paint and had the most delightful wet bikini clad young lady leaning across its bonnet, sponge in hand. Jude pondered, how many men had been so impressed by this girls' firm arse and erect nipples to book a test drive? The overall impression of the billboards was one of cool, moisture, the coke, the Budweiser, the lettuce, the car and even the girl were both cool and wet, all in stark contrast to the stifling dry and dusty atmosphere of what was becoming Jude's least favourite place. He recalled Sir John Forbes-Brewer's impression of the city, how had Jayne known so much about a place she had never visited? The distant high ground was calling to Jude with a much stronger pull than any corporate image could, he knew it was the time to leave the city of angels.

He chose to dine at Taco Bell, it was his way of resisting the cool, wet propaganda, as the four metre wide meal portrayed was the only product not shimmering with condensation. It was his protest, his minor rebellion, though he conceded that the splayed legs and taut arse of the smiling, wet, busty blonde, who might wash his new Ford Tahoe four-wheel drive, did have its appeal.

His taco, when it arrived wasn't even half a metre wide, his cynical comment regarding its lack of size was misunderstood. His food was immediately taken away and came back with everything on his plate doubled. Such was the nervousness of staff that obviously fear a possible lawsuit from an unsatisfied customer. Jude looked at the mountain of food which confronted him, he knew that had there been another person with him and that both he and his imaginary friend, who he thought of as the immensely rotund Billy Bunter, a childhood British comic book character of insatiable appetite, there would still be surplus food.

He took in the clientele of the diner, there were several families of Billy Bunters, with stupefaction and awe he realised that the bulk of the restaurant's customers were of billboard proportion. Both parents and the two point four children were enormous. He looked back at his family meal on the plate, if it was possible to consume that amount of food for as little as eight dollars, it was also possible to put two and two together and realise the cause of one of America's growing problems. The country was now rich beyond its own realisation, rich beyond reason. The adults were killing themselves with greed and they are killing their children with kindness. Jude felt obliged to eat half of his food, the rest he was given in a doggy bag. With disgust he deposited the uneaten portion of his giant meal in a waste bin. He took his overfilled stomach back to his hotel and requested the Receptionist book him a flight to Colombia on the first available plane, he needed to get back to reality. Several aspects of American life had surprised him, but none more so than the high quality of service and the genuine warmth of the often expressed phrase, 'have a nice day', he felt for sure that when they said it, they meant it.

The following morning he took a taxi to Los Angeles International Airport, bought a Spanish language book, a comprehensive guide and history of Colombia and flew to Palmira, a city he had never heard of.

WINTER 1987

COLOMBIA

He had imagined he would arrive in either Bogota or Medellin, the only two cities he had limited knowledge of. Palmira, he discovered after landing, was to the south west of Colombia. Before departing the airport, he purchased a national and a local map, a guidebook which was surprisingly in English and a phrase book. He then had to decide where to stay for the night. On the flight he was outnumbered by more than forty-to one by Hispanic peoples, their colourful clothing and language was a sign of things to come. The plane landed late afternoon, local time, it was the humidity that Jude found extraordinary, he had not foreseen its severity. It was both unexpected and stifling, as he walked from the airport building, aimless and directionless he knew he was overdressed and unprepared for such weather. It felt to Jude as though it was forty degrees centigrade and the heavens were about to open. His instincts were right on both counts and open they did. He experienced a forty-minute downpour which passed over as swiftly as it arrived, leaving pavements, vehicles and rooftops steaming in the late afternoon sun. He had never imagined such a high degree of humidity. He took a taxi to the town square and paused to take in that which confronted him. As he scanned his surroundings it occurred to Jude that he had never felt so alone.

Across the street from where he stood was the Ayuntamiento (town hall), he realised he would need to absorb a degree of local language. He felt foolish for not being better prepared and he also felt at a great disadvantage, but now that he had arrived, he was determined to make the most of it. The plaza he occupied had a centuries old atmosphere. Its three and four storey buildings were of stone and coloured render, sporting wrought iron balconies of diminishing size the higher they rose above the street. The highest row of windows underneath the broad

145

overhanging terracotta tiled roofs were, in almost every building, smaller and less cared for than their counterparts on the lower levels. Many of the shutters to these half-sized windows were ill maintained, hanging lose or absent, a number of the smaller openings were just that, an open square of stonework without glass, frame or any form of adornment. He wondered what activity took place in such a crudely finished building.

He ate a rice-based meal in a cafeteria and drank two glasses of the local beer that he found pleasingly palatable. He casually studied his Colombian map and tour guide. He knew he was in the south of the country but still a considerable distance north of the border with Ecuador, he was surprised to discover how far west he was from the capital, Bogota. He had assumed for no sound reason that he would visit the capital but on further study of the map he decided to head further west to the town of Cali, which proved to be a two-hour bus ride to travel just ninety kilometres. Both the mountainous terrain and the necessity to follow extremely slow, overloaded and underpowered vehicles resulted in an average speed just a little superior to that which a man could casually run.

On this first bus journey Jude experienced several aspects of local Colombian life that were to become the norm. A greater proportion of the passengers were female, many of which were extremely verbose, they combined loquaciousness and a volume which was new to Jude. The bulk of the women were colourfully dressed and carried an excess of weight, but they were generally either remarkable cheerful or intensely argumentative, rendering them difficult to ignore. Whereas the few male passengers were, as a rule, solitary, quiet and almost always smoking, it became a rare feature if one or more of them did not carry about his person, in a crate or above the seat, a live chicken. Jude surmised at first that these chickens were a gift to perhaps the man's mother or a friend or a relative. As he travelled more extensively, he accepted what he first conceded to be a surprising phenomenon, was the norm and although it amused him to regularly observe such an occurrence, it eventually failed to raise an eyebrow. Also the men, excepting the young, were dressed more sombre than their female companions. Usually in shades of brown or black, whereas a large proportion of the women wore spectacularly bright dresses, scarves and shawls which somehow always managed to look clean and freshly laundered in spite of the high humidity.

Through the bus window, despite the cigarette smoke, Jude was able to glimpse extraordinary views as the vehicle manoeuvred the many twists and turns in the road. As the driver guided them through the mountainous terrain, vistas would appear and disappear to both left and right. Panoramic scenes of tumbling hillside waterfalls, vast landscapes of lush green forested hills and wide outcrops of barren rock were visible. Jude had never seen such spectacular scenery. He had already gleaned from his brief perusal of his Colombian map that the bulk of the occupied portion of the country was similarly disposed.

There was a relatively narrow strip of land to the west known as Choco, bordering the Pacific Ocean which was sparsely populated and a vast tree covered completely unpopulated region to the east bordering the Amazon Basin, known as The Lands of Orinoco. Thus leaving the central and most populated districts of Colombia to be dominated by three massive north-south aspect mountain ranges known as, from west to east, The Cordillera Occidental, The Cordillera Central and the Cordillera Oriental.

Jude's bus was ascending the first of these ranges, The Occidental toward the elevated city of Cali. The outskirts of the city were industrial, smoke laden and unpleasant. The air on the bus was hot, muggy and stifling, but the air entering the bus through the few open windows was decidedly less pleasant.

For a moment, Jude took stock of his situation. He was the only westerner on a busload of loud colourful Colombians entering a city he knew nothing of, he was hot, sweaty and felt extremely uncomfortable. Add to that a growing feeling of insecurity and his anxiety level was at an all time peak. Eventually the bus halted as it reached the old colonial centre of Cali known as San Antonio. Jude seized the opportunity to leave the debilitating atmosphere of the vehicle, only he and two other passengers left the bus, the rest went on to the final terminus known as Centeriario, Jude had had enough. The style of the old colonial buildings was to his liking, they were a tremendous relief after the expansive industrial region. He was content to be out of the suffocating environment of the slow moving vehicle in which he had just spent almost two hours.

He looked around, he guessed he was in the expensive part of the city but cared not. He demanded of himself that for one night at least he cast aside his predisposition of roughing it, or living like a local and entered the nearest and possibly the most expensive Hotel. He booked a single room for a single night at the Hotel Del Molino la Mesó. After a shower and a brief look at his already worn map he dedicated the evening to learning fundamental Spanish, feeling that the difficulty he had experienced booking the Hotel room had been completely unnecessary.

He imagined that if he could acquire a vocabulary of perhaps two or three hundred words to begin with, he could alienate his complete inadequacy in dealing with local people. He stuck to his task, booked a second and third night at the Hotel and apart from leaving the Hotel twice for meals at lunch times, he spent forty-eight hours either cramming his head with his host country's language or sleeping. His first lunchtime trip was unadventurous, he merely walked to the top of the local park and ordered, in Spanish, at the San Antonio Pizza. The menu boasted several creative variations, including fruit pizza's bearing cherries, peach and pineapple. Jude was conservative and ordered 'tradicion'.

On his second excursion he was more adventurous, his ambition took him on a half hour walk to the Granada District. He entered a restaurant known as 'Barra de Mayolo' and ordered, in Spanish, a combination of fried calamari, Spanish ham, (jamón) and chorizo sausage. He felt pleased with his performance with the language, but got horribly confused over payment as he misheard the waiters' request, that small embarrassment aside, he knew he was making progress. Much of the Spanish he was learning was similar to the French he already knew, he was encouraged enough to move on. He had decided to head further west towards the coast, a little over a hundred kilometres to the town of Buenaventura for three reasons. He knew he needed to be in a more rural position, also he wanted to be nearer to the coast, he felt the air would be easier to tolerate and he was attracted to the name Buenaventura. Had it been the title of a novel on a bookshelf he felt his hand would reach out to it.

He left the comfort of his Hotel in the old quarter of Cali and after two mistakes he eventually boarded the correct bus for his choice of destination. He had seen little of the city, a city founded in 1536 by Sebastian de Belalcázar, a Spaniard who fresh from conquering the Incas' to the south had moved north after quarrelling with his former masters to go it alone. Arriving in the Vale del Cauca in 1536 he named the new settlement Santiago de Cali, today known simply as Cali.

Over hundreds of years the Spanish shipped in many thousands of African slaves to provide labour in the newly established sugar and cotton plantations. Giving this region of the country both a radical diversity and an incredible concentration of beauty amongst its women, the style and beauty of Cali women is renowned nationally. Jude discovered that the vale is still a huge producer of agricultural products, but added to sugar and cotton is vast amounts of coffee, coca leaf and some grapes. What Jude did not realise was that more than half of Colombian exports including a vast amount of coca leaf refined into cocaine passed through Cali by rail and road on its way to Buenaventura and on from there around the world. Subsequently this route was guarded and watched by a vast army of ordinary people, farmers, taxi drivers, railway workers, corrupt government officials and police, all in the pay of the cartel barons. There were other attractions and dangers that Jude had avoided by staying put in his Hotel to increase his knowledge of the local language. Such as an area between the district known as Sexta and its neighbouring quarter that housed many Guest Houses and Hostels, this zone is the main locality frequented by putos, transsexual prostitutes, displaying alarming surgical alterations and if the night had not been a profitable one, it is a vicinity in which a tourist or passerby could well be robbed at the point of a knife or gun.

Jude left Cali intact, mainly due to his naivety and ignorance. He was pleased to be leaving a city of over three million people but knew little or nothing of his chosen destination. His tour guide informed him, curiously, that Buenaventura with a population of approximately 200,000 was the largest and only city on the pacific coast. His map confirmed this, he was surprised to see almost a thousand kilometres of uninhabited pacific coastline, Buenaventura being the exception that proved the rule. To his knowledge, in places as vast and different as Europe and Australia the bulk of the occupational settlements had occurred at the coastline and in particular at the mouth of major rivers, but here was a vast area of undeveloped shore, the reason for which was obscure.

His guidebook also informed him that more than sixty percent of Colombia's legal exports passed through the city's docks and much of its illegal exports. This began to ring alarm bells in Jude's mind, his naivety did not disconnect vast quantities of illegal trade with huge numbers of villainous operatives. He reminded himself that he would have to be careful and stick to safe parts of the city.

On the bus journey that took him from Cali to Buenaventura, Jude read extensively on the past and present history of the area and the country. As he travelled through breathtaking scenery, which resulted in him transferring from the right side of the bus to the left to enjoy the finest vista's he had observed since arriving in the mountainous, panoramic country, he realised he was a tourist in a country that was in violent political and economic turmoil. He was planning to walk freely in a land that many could not. He was beginning to comprehend that it was a time in Colombia when the drug cartels were the leaders and rulers of ordinary people. His guide book contained a forty page recently added appendage which was basically a warning to all visitors to be aware that operating in Colombia at the present time were dangerous and ruthless men such as Pablo Escobar who had become legend. Not by way of fifteen minutes of fame on a TV show, but by the same way that men like Al Capone, Billy the Kid and Ned Kelly had, the hard way. Through indiscriminate use of violence designed to silence and remove opposition and competition, with the use of both firearms and explosives.

Pablo Escobar had become the most infamous, prosperous and well known of the Colombian drug barons at this time. Though he was without doubt a ruthless man and destroyer of lives, he was also a multi billionaire who was idolised by the many thousands of people who were his greater family. He and his enormous team of aids were always looking for new ways to flood cocaine into the United States to satisfy the ever increasing demand. He and his minions had transported thousands of tons that had made him one of the ten wealthiest people on the planet. He used a portion of his money to support many of the poorest people in Colombian society, building dwellings and schools, paying for tuition, medicine and food. Acquiring legend along the way similar to that of Robin Hood, he had become the people's hero.

However there was a very dark side to the drug trade. In 1983 in the city of Medellin alone, almost 1700 people were murdered. More recently Jude read that the Cali cartel had declared war on the Medellin cartel. The killings had increased, cities such as Cali and Medellin were deserted at night due to widespread fear. Jude could not believe what he was reading, the cartels had apparently taken on the government by destroying the Headquarters of the Colombian FBI, blowing up an airliner and killing Government officials and policemen on a daily basis, the country was at war with itself. He read on, Colombia had signed an agreement with the US to allow Special Forces operation teams to enter the country, to pursue and kill the drug barons. This was backed up with an extradition treaty to allow the United States to bring the traffickers to justice in the US. The all too regular killing of Government officials and police took its toll. Colombia did an about turn and cancelled its extradition treaty. Escobar then built, maintained and administered a prison to house himself and other wanted men in comfort. He later became suspicious of his own governments dealings with the United States. Fearing extradition once again, he fled into the jungle evading capture for almost two years, but eventually time and the US Special Forces caught up with him. He died a day after his forty-forth birthday, gunned down on a rooftop. He had been negotiating to have his family freed from house arrest and to be allowed to leave the country. He had become a man of legend, at one time 'Here Lies the King' was inscribed on his tombstone. He was a man of contradiction. He controlled governments, built submarines to transport cocaine, he raised an army to wage war, but he also set up a Social Security system for the poor people of his country. Violence was no stranger to people like Escobar, he had grown up during a period known as 'La Violencia'. From the mid 1940's to the mid 1950's, in excess of three hundred thousand innocent people were murdered by guerrilla armies in Colombia, many of them mutilated by the use of machetes.

This was a period of fear and mistrust in an otherwise extremely beautiful country, a country rich in nature and rife with corruption. It was a country that had been for millennia ruled by wealthy and powerful families, whose wealth was kept within, little or none of it filtering down to the very poor in society. A country in which bribery and illegal payments to government officials and policemen was the easiest and sometimes only way to succeed, to progress, or to lift your family from a life of poverty. So, when the growing drug trafficking business offered an opportunity to young men such as Pablo Escobar to earn as much as ten years' wages driving a truck carrying hundreds of kilo's of raw cocaine from Peru to his own country for refinement, the temptation to elevate himself and his wider family from perpetual impoverishment was a temptation of unimagined proportion. Instantly a man could be propelled from pauperism to prosperity. Escobar himself when still a young man was known to sometimes fill a truck with provisions, drive to an extremely poor district of Medellin and hand out free, literally tons of food. The people adored him for such gestures. Yes he committed terrible crimes but the ordinary people of Colombia loved him for his generosity and kindness.

Within a few short years the cocaine trafficking business and in particular Escobar's part in it was described by Virgil Barco the Colombian President as a 'great and powerful organisation, the likes of which has never before existed in the world.' Escobar was soon earning more than two million dollars a week, smuggling cocaine in to the US on planes. Paying off officials along the way to prevent discovery and ensure a smooth trouble free operation. Some of the most dangerous people in Colombia at this time were the guerrilla groups operating in the jungles. Their co-operation was ensured with massive bribes that eventually saw them become armed guards to the jungle laboratories producing the valuable white powder. At one of these laboratories as many as two thousand people would work and earn a reasonable living, all faithful employees of the top boss's, men such as Pablo Escobar, their workers loyalty was assured. He not only provided them with a fair wage but he would pay for a school to be built and he would hire teachers, build a hospital and hire competent staff to provide medical care and medicinal drugs. He cared for and looked after his employees. Ordinary people were better provided for working for a notorious drug baron that in a city doing legitimate work. It was this devoted loyalty that law enforcement was at first unable to succeed against.

The ingenuity of men such as Pablo Escobar was fully realised when it came to developing new ways to smuggle their precious cargo into the United States and Europe. They employed chemists with tremendous imagination and skill. Not only was cocaine hidden in such places as aircraft tyres, huge electrical transformers and purpose built and operated submarines, it was also transformed into liquid form and chemically blended into plastic, timber, wine, beer, soft drinks and clothing amongst many other varied and diverse products. At its destination it would be recovered by reversing the process to retrieve the valuable white powder. The drug barons even employed their own sniffer dogs to confirm a new products satisfaction. The whole operation depended on saturation corruption along every route. Through Panama, the Bahamas, Mexico, and Central America and throughout the United States, all officials and those holding positions of power and influence were on the payroll of the cartels. The sums of money paid to these people would transform their lives instantly, but the sums of money travelling back along the same route were both phenomenal and unprecedented. Eventually billions upon billions of dollars found their way by many diverse routes back to Medellin and Cali. Some of this money fed the hungry, gave shelter to the homeless, employment to the unemployed and provided medical care and education to those who could not afford it. Pablo Escobar looked after his people and removed those who stood in his way or displayed a lack of trust.

This was the Colombia that Jude entered as a tourist, a country torn apart by violence, distrust, suspicion and disloyalty. Family members and neighbours could become sceptical of each other and as for foreigners, especially Americans, many people were either apprehensive of them or were blatantly fearful or hateful of them. They believed them to be connected to one of the various law enforcement agencies, attempting to discover knowledge of the whereabouts of the cartels operation.

Jude's greatest disadvantage was that he could be and would be mistaken for an American. He had learned enough from his guidebook, which he now viewed as a volume of doom. He asked himself why had Jayne brought her character Jacqueline to such a country and how did she aim to complete this section of her book without personal knowledge of the country? He had mixed emotions, the guidebooks recently added warnings to foreign visitors had spooked him. He was torn between leaving the country by the quickest possible means or staying and finding a quiet, rural location in which to further his knowledge of his adopted country's ways. He decided he would look for work, rural work and that he was a traveller by nature working his way around South America. This would be his story, simple and easy to defend.

As the bus stopped to allow a similar vehicle coming in the opposite direction to negotiate a particularly difficult bend Jude looked to his left out of the window and observed a scene which had not altered in the countryside of this huge rural country in hundreds of years. Two elderly women, he estimated that they were in their eighty's were bent double picking grapes by hand into wicker baskets. They had barely half a dozen rows of vines to pick that were no more than thirty metres long. Jude assumed that the tiny area of vines were sufficient for one family's use. He had seen similar small family crops in rural France. At the end of the short row of vines there was an elderly man of similar age to that of the two women who stood upon a crude, wheeled and unsophisticated wooden platform connected by a harness to two muscular but aged looking mules. The elderly women were dressed in what appeared to be rag covered feet and pinafore dresses that were all the rage with kitchen maids in service in Britain in the 1920's and 1930's and tightly wound headscarves allowing just a hint of their aged white hair to escape, hair which had clung to their damp perspiring foreheads. All of their clothing had been harshly hand washed for so many years that their original colours could only be guessed at. On receiving the baskets of lustrous looking fruit the old man tipped them into an aged looking iron mangle with a large open throat. He was turning a wooden handle, which drove an immense geared wheel which in turn crushed the grapes. The result was a semi liquid, attractive red mash that was spewing from the ancient contraption into wooden barrels. Jude assumed these would later be transported by mule power home to be fermented into next years' family wine. Jude was daydreaming into the past, a sudden forward jolt of the ageing bus brought him back to the present.

His scenic journey was later interrupted by a police roadblock. Initially when Jude looked forward through the windscreen he felt alarmed, but on seeing that the impediment to further travel was manned by police he relaxed. Immediately the bus halted two armed officers boarded. There were approximately thirty passengers on the bus, a Dutch couple in their late twenty's or early thirty's and two Americans both male in their early twenty's, Jude, two dozen locals and of course a chicken. The two American lads were agitated. The two uniformed officers first approached the Dutch couple demanding to see identification. All the locals on board and the middle-aged bus driver were nonchalant, they had witnessed this performance many times before. Once the police were satisfied with the Dutch couples' ID they asked for wallets and purses, these they emptied of cash and then politely handed them back. As Jude was at the back of the bus, he was both able to witness all that transpired and gain an ever-increasing sense of alarm. Ignoring all locals the police next moved on to the Americans who not only had passports ready for inspection but also held out their wallets, obviously seasoned travellers. Once the wallets were emptied the officers insisted the two American's take off their shoes, which they did under a degree of protest. Sufficient protest to result in one of the two being pistol-whipped to the side of his head, which split the top of his left ear causing obvious severe pain. At this point Jude was mentally booking the first flight out of Colombia. Once the two solidly built officers had emptied more cash in the form of US dollars from both men's shoes they threw them from the bus through an open window.

They then continued down the bus and stopped at Jude, first demanding 'pasaporte' which Jude, now terrified, held out. This soon landed back in his lap, next the single word command was 'dinero'. Jude understood this command and handed over his wallet, which was rapidly relieved of its cash content and dropped back to him as had been the passport. The officers then left the bus, dismantled their crude roadblock and drove off. The bus driver was kind enough to give the two American boys sufficient time to retrieve their shoes before continuing on his journey as if nothing had happened. For it was the case, that for himself and all the Colombian nationals, nothing had happened.

Soon after their journey recommenced Jude moved forward to sit to the right of the American lads. Introduced himself and asked,

"What the hell was that all about?" The one with the badly cut ear introduced himself as Gary and replied,

"Oh that's pretty normal down here, that's why we keep ten percent of our cash in our wallets, ten percent more in our shoes and the rest in our jockey shorts, you should try it."

"But how did they know to take your trainers off?"

"Oh it's been an old habit with us from the good old US of A to keep cash in our shoes. They know it so it's not good policy to let them down. If they don't find it there they might take you off of the bus and strip search you, leaving you with nothing but your birthday suit. So we leave a few bucks for them to find and away they go."

"But what about your ear, is that normal?"

"No, no it's not. I guess I said a bit too much, my fault I should have said nothing." The other guy introduced himself as Kieffer, and he had the Californian tan, perfect white teeth and blonde hair to go with the wacky name, he asked,

"Hey, you're a Brit right, what brings you here?"

"A long story, I'm doing a bit of research, if you two expect that sort of treatment, why are you here?"

"Simple, to buy a few kilos of the local white powder and get it back home somehow and make enough money to set up our own surf shack on the west coast and never seriously work again."

"Sure thing." Added Gary.

156

"You're kidding me." Was my immediate response, but the matter of fact manner and the fact they didn't even lower their voices made them convincing.

"Not one little bit, there's enough coke down here to cover the States and inch deep. We just need to move a few kilos and we're sorted for life." Jude eventually asked,

"How are you going to get it back home?" As he asked the question a shocking image of the two American's dismembered bodies dumped to the side of a country road flashed across his consciousness. He dismissed the image as quickly as it had arrived, in time to hear Gary's reply

"Can't give that away and it's not going back home which is Portland, Oregon. It's going to San Francisco but that's enough of our plans. Did you get cleaned out by those bastards?"

"Yep, all the cash I had."

"Right, well you got to wise up. Like I said, 10% in your wallet, 10% in your shoes and the rest where even your mother wouldn't find it, but you being a Brit will probably only lose what's in your wallet. It's us from the States that they are really out to get, they just got lucky with you."

"Ok, if I'm staying in this bloody country, I'll wise up, thanks."

Most of the conservation was overheard by the Dutch couple who joined them after a few minutes. The conversation broadened but all generally agreed that the police were totally out of order. The Dutchman, Dirk, said he believed that the local rural police were paid so little it was just a way to subsidise their meagre salary, it was he said a sign that those particular police were more honest than those who were controlled by the drug cartels, who were paid so well they need not bother with fleecing tourist. He explained in a reply to Jude, who questioned him as to his reasons for being in such an insecure place that he and his wife, Anna, were perpetual travellers. They had left their native Holland at 18 and they were now both 29 and had not yet been back home, it was a plan to return one day but there was always somewhere else to see. They had worked their way across Europe, India, the Far East, Australia, New Zealand and Africa. They were now on a working tour of South America. Jude was very interested to hear their tales. When serious work was

157

mentioned both Gary and Kieffer switched off. It was left to Jude to delve deeper into the methods of obtaining work with Dirk and Anna. They said they were looking for work in the vineyards, they would not work in the coca fields or laboratories and preferred not to work in the coffee plantations which, they told Jude, were now becoming increasingly mechanised.

Jude asked, "What type of work are you expecting to find in the vineyards?"

Dirk replied, "Cutting back the vines, the humidity here is so high that the vines produce far too much growth. So two maybe three times in the growing season the vines have to be cut back to encourage the grapes to put on weight."

"And have you found a contact for this work?"

"We believe so, we have to get ourselves about twenty kilometres north of Buenaventura to a small place called San Isidro and there we have a good chance of work."

Jude replies "Mind if I ask you two a question or two?"

"Go ahead."

"How did you get to speak English so well? And do you mind if I tag along with you? After that episode with law enforcement I'm feeling very vulnerable on my own."

"Sure, that's no problem. As for the English it's simple, we are Dutch. We speak many languages in our country. Everyone does and around the world yours is the most useful."

"OK thanks. Are you stopping over in Buenaventura?"

"Yes for sure, we always use back packer Hostels. You're welcome to, how did you say, tag along."

They reached their destination without further adventure, Jude mainly listening to tales from the road from Dirk and Anna. Anna was quiet at first but came more and more into the conversation as time passed. Anna looked typically Northern European, her skin pale and her blonde hair tied at the back revealing unusually pale, beautiful blue eyes. Dirk had a little of the Viking in him, he was a tall man with a large head. His hair too was tied in a ponytail with the slightest hint of grey at his temples and in his considerable beard, but his face had a lined, ruddy complexion, it was the face of a seafarer. Jude looked at him and saw his ancestors rowing to Britannia to conquer and pillage.

158

As if to order, as they stepped from the bus mid-afternoon the rain began to fall. Not cold English drizzle that Jude was familiar with, but warm, heavy tropical rain that ran off roofs, off vehicles and quickly built up to a small river of water washing clean the streets of this new town, which would both surprise and delight Jude as well as shock and dismay.

Gary and Kieffer soon disappeared into the deluge of falling water, Jude never saw them again. He did however stick close to Dirk and Anna. They led him to a two storey food market called Le Garelia, after passing the surprisingly named Hotel Titanic, Jude speculated, wrongly as it later turned out that with such a name he was one foreigner who was never going to set foot in that hotel.

Before they entered the market, Dirk warned Jude to keep a close watch on his valuables as the place was likely to be cruised by cutpurses or what he might know in England as pickpockets. Jude shrugged and said, "I have no money". On entering the market Jude senses are assaulted by aromas, flavours and colours beyond his experience. There were many elderly women preparing dishes for sale exactly as their foremothers had done for generations before them. The market was a busy, crowded, bustling, chaotic place. Most of the beautiful fruit on sale Jude could recognise, but the bulk of the vegetables on offer from the greengrocers were new to him. There were both root and leafed vegetables outside of his knowledge. He knew he would not know how to cut them or how to cook them. He was prevented from attempting to imagine cooking up a concoction of veg' by a pull to his arm from Dirk

"Here Jude, this is what we're looking for."

Jude pushed through a small throng of people to experience a wonderful smell. Dirk explained,

"Here, we'll get you a bowl of this stuff, it's simply the best street meal you will get anywhere. You can pay us back later at the Hostel."

"OK, I'm game, what is it?"

"The locals call it 'Sancocho de Pescado', its fish. Don't ask me what sort, it's cooked in coconut milk. It is what I think you English say, to die for." They took three steaming bowls of the mixture into the street and under the protection of a huge

159

Avocado tree ate what Jude later agreed was one of the best meals he had ever had.

"Absolutely." Said Dirk "And for just cop$ 1000". Jude exclaimed loudly,

"It was how much?"

"Relax, it's about half a US dollar."

They stayed the night in a low-grade hostel in a mixed room containing a dozen people. Jude felt very aware of the lack of security for himself and his backpack that contained just about everything that was important to him at the moment. It was when alone at night that he allowed himself to think of Liz. Where was she exactly and what was her situation? He guessed she was in far more luxurious surroundings than he was. Sleep, when it came was intermittent. He dreamt that the two American lads he had met on the bus from Cali had robbed him and left him naked in the jungle, to suffer a terrible fate. Awakening from this dream he moved his backpack for its safety and used it as a very uncomfortable pillow.

In the morning, after a brief look around the city centre and areas of the docks that were not off limits to visitors, Jude, Dirk and Anna found themselves once again on a poorly maintained bus, outnumbered by locals and chickens and heading through thick forest. Jude's impression of Buenaventura was not as grim as his tourist guide had portrayed, though he did find the ever-present site of so many armed military personnel unsettling. Both due to their number and the degree to which they carried weapons and ammunition, they tended to create the opposite effect to their purpose.

The coast line both north and south of the town had been for decades a favourite spot for both national and international visitors, but in recent years a sporadic outbreak of Colombia's curse 'La Violencia'; murderous, irrepressible and erratic violence which breaks out without warning had drastically altered the status quo. This violence was usually fuelled by uncontrolled rage on the part of the Guerrillas, who would strike from deep in the jungle and had all but destroyed the tourist trade. Hotels were empty and beaches were strewn with both flotsam and jetsam. The presence of so many soldiers was twofold, to reassure the local and visiting populations with a feeling of security and to guard both the vast amounts of legal and illegal exports.

Many of the buildings, especially the Hotels were a physical representation of the glory days of the 1920's, which had been a time of affluence and stylish growth. Many of the three, four and five storey buildings had been refurbished to best display this style and sported decorative wrap around veranda's, but all were now looking tired and in need of care. What Jude did not witness was the vast amount of road and rail traffic that enters and leaves one of the busiest legal and illegal trade ports in the world. Buenaventura is a transport city for timber, coffee and cocaine, fortunes change hands daily. Under the sweltering, humid conditions, few people are visible because of the heat and the almost daily rain, but the lack of detectable human activity mask a colossal movement of material.

Jude had managed for the second time in two days, to pass through a City learning more from his limited tour guide than from actual experience. The bus ride to San Isidro was no more than an hour. Jude had hidden away ninety percent of his newly acquired cash, but it proved unnecessary on this occasion.

Jude knew instinctively as he descended the three steps from the ageing bus that he had arrived at the right place. The town of San Isidro did not merit a mention in his guidebook, it was in fact a tiny town, population approximately five hundred. It stood between the Pacific Ocean and the Cordillera Occidental mountain range, the area for miles around the small town in all directions was hilly, green and wet. Its west facing slopes were so wet that only native rain forest loving plants and trees would grow, but the east facing slopes, those with their backs to the gigantic Pacific Ocean were with a great deal of toil able to be farmed and in this region newly planted moisture resistant vines were proving to be viable. A little coffee was grown in pockets in this district, which was known as Choco and some coca leaf, but this was a crop visitors were never permitted to see.

Jude took his direction from Dirk, a formidably seasoned and experienced traveller. With Dirks' international fluency the three of them were the next day, after a poor nights' sleep in what could only be described as a hovel, set to work for COP $30,000 a day, which translated to eleven and a half US dollars. A

161

pittance in the United States but sufficient to sustain life for two weeks in southwest rural Colombia. In hindsight Jude realised he agreed to do the arduous work for little reward because it gave him a purpose, it gave a definition to his day and because he liked Dirk and Anna. They all lived in what amounted to a bunk-house, which was a mice infested wooden building with no privacy afforded. Yet it did at least have three enormous ceiling fans that slowly counted by the days and nights with their four huge wooden blades, one of which would pass by every second.

Apart from Jude and his newly acquired Dutch friends there were four young Spanish men and two girls and a dozen local people of mixed age. Work started at six in the morning when it was relatively cool. This first session was bearable, but after lunch, which was usually eaten cold and consisted of left over's from the night before, the temperature and humidity would increased to a level which drastically reduced productivity amongst the twenty or so people who were struggling to achieve a days' work.

On the many days when the late afternoon rain came it was welcome. It both washed away fatigue and perspiration and heralded an end to the day's work. The work involved cutting back new growth from the vines. The humidity would cause an explosion of secondary shoots to quickly reach several metres in length. The vines had to be cut back exactly to the point that they had been cut earlier in the season and all cuttings removed from the rows, as moist cuttings would encourage mould which would quickly spread to the grapes and destroy the years' crop. Jude was competent at the arduous job of cutting back the new growth even though for the bulk of the time he was working, he was standing with one foot considerably higher than the other due to the steep slopes they were all working on. It was the job of going back over his last row and dragging the pale green material to the end of the row that he and the others found particularly onerous. It was extremely punishing work, which required a herculean effort. It was only the immensely strong Dirk who did not visibly display discomfort at this task. Indeed he would leave Anna to cut all day and clear both his rows and hers. Thought there were some evenings when even he was quiet and did very little due to fatigue.

It was the evenings that Jude enjoyed. His muscles were tight, his body ached and the food which was supplied by the estate owner Juan Javier Hernandez was good. It was usually a rice based meal which they all took turns to cook. Sometimes paella, other times arroz con coco, a delicious dish of white rice cooked in coconut milk served with patacones, green plantains, which were a banana type fruit squashed into thick pancakes and deep-fried until golden brown. A favourite of Jude's was pandebono, a bread made from corn flour, cheese and eggs, which was quickly consumed by everyone warm from the ovens and would accompany many different meals. If not rice based, then fritanca was a regular alternative. This was a plate of grilled beef, chicken, ribs and sausage, which included chunchullo, cow intestines, served with small potatoes and fried bananas, which were not at all sweet.

Friday evening was a celebration of a weeks' hard work completed, it would always be bandeja paisa, arguably Colombia's national dish. This was a huge mixture of food on a platter. It was both traditional not to use a standard plate for this meal and sensible as it amounted to a mound of grilled steak, fried pork rind and chorizo sausage on a bed of rice and red beans, topped with a fried egg, a slice of avocado and sweet banana chips, it was a favourite with everyone. All the meals were washed down with costeña, a locally brewed beer. The locals would then go on to drink rum or lulada, a speciality to the Cali area, which was a potent local cocktail made with pulped lulo fruit, water, sugar, ice and a generous addition of vodka. Jude and the other non-Colombians wisely drank this heady mix only occasionally. It was a pleasure to sit on the wooden veranda protected from above by the huge overhanging roof, listening to the endless reverberation that came from the forest. One sound would compete with another for supremacy amongst the near constant rapport. With local help they were able to distinguish both the incessant red howler monkeys and their marginally quieter cousins, the spider monkeys. Pride of place amongst the clamour was always reserved for the unremitting and colourful toucans, parrots and macaws. Each time one of these large fruit eating birds released a volley of sound it would leave the listener in no doubt that for just a few seconds, it was King of the Jungle.

In addition to the near unbroken din from the trees, the sight of spectacularly colourful kingfishers, fruit bats, butterflies and numerous different species of hummingbird, some of which were quite tame was an absolute delight for Jude. His full admiration and wonder was reserved for the high flying, majestically awesome condors. The Andean Condors with their largest mean wingspan of any bird on the planet were mesmeric to watch, their effortless climbing and descending on the days' thermals were both enthralling and to be envied.

The combination of the fine views from the veranda east toward the Occidental mountain range and west toward the Pacific and enjoying fine food and not such fine local wine and good company was a true delight. Often in late evening long after the rain had passed the skies would clear, it was during this time that Jude would share with Anna her love for the stars. She was able to point out many celestial bodies to Jude, he at first recognised nothing, he being near the equator for the first time, everything was either new to him or, as he put it to Anna "it's all arse about face, and upside-down". Her knowledge of this subject was deep, so to was her passion. Jude was forever able to identify a number of constellations in the southern hemisphere and was eternally grateful to the beautiful Dutch lady with a pale complexion and blue eyes that he was fortunate to meet in San Isidro.

Often late in the evening when weariness had eventually overcome the irreducible Dirk, Anna would share her thoughts with Jude. She was a very philosophical individual and would become almost meditative under a blanket of stars, she was also a very perceptive individual, she seemed to know what was in Jude's mind and his heart. Jude would listen, entranced by her reasoning and values until he too would succumb to physical exhaustion. He remembered few dreams from the first four weeks of his physical work but those he could recall, invariably involved Liz.

Several times during the first month, the estate owner Juan Javier would fly in, in his sleek, shiny helicopter to hand out wages, praise, encourage, scorn or disparage the workforce as was his mood of the day. Jude's Spanish had improved to the point where he was able to glean the overall message of the day, even if he could not decipher every word. Dirk, who had command of five languages, was always able to fill in the spaces. Jude was able to garner from general conversation amongst the locals that the boss was well respected and also feared. He was held in similar regard to that of a godfather figure, a man whose compassion was genuine when it was expressed, as was his anger, which surfaced less often.

They discovered from the local people that he was a man determined to produce a quality wine, although his family history and fortune was one of long established coffee production. Many generations of Colombians had laboured in the humid conditions of the western region of Choco to establish the Hernandez family as a powerful player in the area. The locals also admitted to something that Juan Javier never would, that he like most powerful, rich men in the rural areas surrounding the City of Cali was also a producer of coca leaf, and a major producer. Not a trafficker in cocaine but still a vital link in the perpetual multi-billion dollar industry that had been created by the insatiable desire of the United States in particular and Europe to a lesser degree to experience the temporary high of the refined product.

Jude felt he was learning much with regard the structure of local society and its economy. The difficult working conditions and the remoteness of their location along with the weather, fauna and flora were all aspects of Colombia he could not have imagined back in wet, cold Dorchester. He was grateful to Liz for pushing him into the experience but was always nagged by a sense of insecurity. He was paid COP $150,000 a week which meant he now had COP $600,000 which he kept strapped to his body in a sweat proof, rain proof polythene bag. He joked to Dirk that he felt like a drug baron himself with half a million units of the local currency, though in truth they both knew that it amounted to little more than two hundred US dollars.

After four weeks Dirk and Anna left to go south into Ecuador. Jude knew this parting of the ways was coming but it hit him badly. He became more and more insecure and took to hiding some of his wages in odd places, a little of which was gone when he went to retrieve it. He became insular and isolated himself by his actions. He usually ate alone and allowed himself to become segregated, almost detached from the locals, which he hated himself for but seemed unable to prevent. It was during this period he realised he was only a day away from Christmas. With no means of contacting the person he most wanted to be with. It was for Jude the longest and loneliest Christmas he had ever had. He was beginning to feel wretched and loathed himself. Once again, as in the past, his sleep became fitful and unsatisfying. His dreams became disturbing and he knew he too must leave. He had been shown kindness and companionship by those around him but felt increasingly unable to respond. He missed English conversation more then he could ever have imagined. He still experienced some interaction with the local people but felt himself to be less than genuine. He felt also that he had learned all he could of the area to help him with Jayne's book and as he had made copious notes, it was time to move on, but where too?

On an exceptionally hot day, three weeks after the departure of Dirk and Anna, Jude made his decision. He informed the owner that he would end his work with him as soon as he could be paid off. Juan Javier's' response was,

"Jump in the helicopter, I take you to my home and pay you today." His command of English surprised Jude. Whilst on the short flight, which he did not pilot, he told Jude "I am told that you and the Dutch man are two of the best men who ever work on the grapes. I am happy to give a ride in my blackbird to such a man". He asked Jude,

"Where do you go next?" Jude replied,

"Canada, I have a friend I want to visit."

"Ok, I can help. It is a long, hard journey from here to Bogota, which is the only airport that will fly you where you want to go. Sergio here will drop you at Jean Javier's runway, we have planes everyday fly to Miami, it will save you time and monies."

Jude, aghast at his generosity accepted his offer with thanks. The thought that he could leave the humidity behind so quickly made him extremely grateful.

"It is no problem to help someone who has work hard for me."

The helicopter landed on the flat central roof of a large compound, a vast hacienda. Jude stayed in the blackbird and within minutes he had another COP $450,000 in his pocket. He now had COP $1,000,000, 300 US dollars. Juan Javier gave some quick instructions to Sergio the pilot and they were airborne once again. Jude now in the window seat was able to view better his surroundings. Juan Javier's home was magnificent indeed. It occupied a high spot amongst many other buildings. As they rose higher and swung away to the east Jude was able to see the extent of the family's compound, which he guessed to be a two-hectare site. Fenced all around and surrounded by a vast and impenetrable jungle, oddly with no visible roads in or out. He guessed that the access roads must be hidden by the interwoven jungle canopy.

Twenty minutes later Sergio dropped Jude at a runway cleared from the jungle. Jude boarded one of the two waiting piper Navajo planes which was quickly airborne. The coolness of the air at two thousand feet was a tremendous relief from the humidity at ground level. Apart from the pilot, there were two other passengers who were both Colombian. Jude managed brief exchanges with them before settling into his seat to enjoy a refreshing and scenic flight. It took four hours for the small plane to make the trip to a small airport juxtaposition to a large industrial estate outside of Miami. It was approximately half way into the flight that a small bomb went off inside Jude's head.

Having read some of the recent history of Colombia, he now realised that he was on one of the many daily flights taking illegal drugs onto the United States. He started looking around the plane and imagined the many places where cocaine could be or was stored, under the floor, in the wings or even perhaps as he had read in the tyres? The plane landed smoothly and after passing through passport control, where he was required to declare himself as a transitory alien and guarantee his departure within 48 hours or he would then be declared an illegal immigrant. He took a taxi to Miami Airport and caught a regular shuttle plane to J.F.K New York. From there, after a nights' sleep in the extraordinary comfort of an air-conditioned room, he flew on to Toronto.

He had studied the winter ski brochure that Liz had given him, he knew she had two weeks in Iceland and that she would then fly to Newfoundland in the east of Canada and work her way westward. He estimated she would be in or near Toronto by now. His plan was to telephone the seven Toronto based Hotels in the ski region to catch up with her. He hoped he had not assumed too much.

Prior to landing at Toronto the pilot thanked the passengers for flying Air Canada, he expressed that he hoped they would fly with the Company again and reminded those on board who were new to Toronto in early January that it was minus twenty outside with a minus twenty wind chill, he warned them to dress appropriately and to take care. Jude's naiveté was beginning to feel like a disability. He chastised himself, minus forty and he was dressed for an autumnal day in Dorset. He cleared customs and walked to the airport terminal doors. As they opened automatically for him his body experienced a drop from twenty degrees centigrade indoors to minus forty degrees centigrade outdoors. He is dressed in an open fronted jacket, cotton shirt and jeans, he has never encountered such an enormous fall in temperature and never would again. The occurrence leaves him shocked, his face feels as though it is burned with cold, his nipples feel like they are frozen and so brittle they could snap off. His genitalia instantly assume child-like proportions and attempts to hide in his abdomen. He does an about turn and looks for an internal telephone booth. He is happy to be back inside, back on the planet he knows. He is able to breathe normally again, standing outside for just half a minute, his breath hurt his lungs, he was having to breathe with his teeth closed to warm up the air before allowing it into his shocked system.

With Liz's winter brochure in his hand and a recently purchased phone card for twenty Canadian dollars, he ducks to put his head in a modern phone hood. As he does this, a tall beautiful young Englishwoman, dark haired, brown eyed, carrying a Canon A1 single lens reflex camera walks unnoticed behind him, towards a flight confirmation desk. By the time the first Hotel has confirmed Liz has checked out, she has her boarding pass and has unburdened herself of her luggage. By the time the third Hotel has confirmed that a Miss Reese has departed, she has completed her airport shopping. Jude visits the toilet and purchases another twenty-dollar phone card. Almost an hour later after he has had a snack, the fifth Hotel follows suit with the first four and authenticated Liz's arrival and departure.

She was now in the Toronto Departure Lounge.

The sixth Hotel endorsed the information of the others. When finally Jude was informed by the seventh and last Hotel, after a long debate regarding data protection issues that Liz had in fact booked out of the Hotel that very morning bound for the airport his level of excitement and anticipation was at fever pitch. He picked up his backpack and quickly moved to the flight information desk as Liz passed through Departure Gate 17. Another long discussion regarding data protection occurred. The Airport's female representative was sticking solidly to Company Policy and refusing to admit to any passenger's name that was on a flight, which was still in the airport. Jude was ever persistent and a little more frantic on each attempt to extract the information he wanted. After twenty minutes of such debate, the woman in her forties glanced up at a screen, relaxed and said,

"I'm sorry for the delay Sir, I can now confirm a Miss E Reese is on Air Canada flight 365 for Vancouver."

Jude, in exasperation said,

"Why suddenly can you admit to what I've been asking you for ages?"

"Like I said Sir, we cannot give out any passenger names on flights that are still in the airport."

"Meaning?"

"Flight 365 for Vancouver just became airborne."

For just a few seconds Jude held both his breath and the assistants gaze. She then said to him,

"Have a nice day, Sir." A little nervously she adjusted her corporate badge that wrongly gave her name as 'Carol / Air Canada'.

Jude thought it should be 'Cold hearted bitch / Ice Maiden'. He then saw himself for just an instant in an interview room with local police officers questioning him,

'Look we've got CCTV of you strangling the girl. All we want from you before we lock you up and throw away the key is the whereabouts of her body.' He sees an image of the mildly overweight, forty something year old strapped to an aircraft wing, frozen solid and hears his reply,

'I'm sorry, I can't admit to a murder whilst the corpse is still in the airport.' What he actually says is "Thank you, I will."

He then moves to his left and looks out toward the midday sun. Flying across the low red winter sun is a black spec, Air Canada flight 365 to Vancouver.

The brochure Jude was holding was full of the wondrous things to see and visit in and around Toronto. Jude's only experience in his entire life of the beautiful modern city is frozen nipples and shrinking genitalia. Four hours later he boards a late afternoon plane, Air Canada flight 366 to Vancouver. The sun is below the horizon whilst they are on the runway but soon after takeoff he is treated to a spectacular and prolonged sunset as he is heading west with the sun at seven hundred miles an hour at thirty three thousand feet. To his mental comfort there are no frozen bodies strapped to the wing.

He lands in Vancouver early evening having gained time in the air. He takes a taxi to the first hotel on Liz's agenda, she having numbered them in order of her trip. As he walks into the foyer he sees one of the best views in the world, Liz's rear, she is dressed in heeled boots, blue jeans and a red blouse. As Jude approaches her she is standing waiting to be seated in the restaurant. He overhears her say,

"A table for one please." He leans over her shoulder and says,

"She means a table for two." Liz spins around totally shocked, mouth wide open and he adds, "If that's alright with the lady?" She exclaims,

"Wow, how did you? When did you? Where did you come from?" They embrace and kiss, he is so thrilled to see that wonderful sparkle in her eye and he knows that it's unquestionable for him. Eventually they are seated and enjoy both an excellent meal and a non-stop catching up session which continues in a physical sense in Liz's Hotel room well into the early hours. They sleep entwined, Jude is as happy as his recent memory will allow him to be.

At breakfast Liz explains that she is absolutely delighted to see him but that she cannot interrupt her programme or have him with her all day. She needs to be alone to be able to work. He is fine with that as long as he can meet her in the evenings.

She asks, "What are you going to do all day?"

"Well first I need some warm clothes, I almost became a eunuch at Toronto."

"I can't believe we passed somehow in the airport."

"Me neither, when I've got myself togged out I'll see a bit of Vancouver or if it's just too cold I'll doss about the hotel writing. I've got tons of notes that need to be put in some kind of order."

"OK that's good, you can use my hotel rooms, I usually get a double but we'll have to pay separately for your food, is that OK?"

"Sure that's no problem, look I'm a millionaire." He dropped COP$1,000,000 on the table. She picked it up in amazement instinctively shielding it from the view of others. She counted it out on to the table.

"Christ Jude, there is a million of these COP$ here. What the hell did you do to get this?"

"Well I could say I sold fifty kilo's of raw cocaine, but to be truthful I worked my arse off cutting back grape vines for eight weeks. That lot is only worth about three hundred US dollars."

"Is that all?" she smiled "for fifty kilo's I think you got stuffed."

They laughed. He said "I'll change this for Canadian Dollars and spend it on properly insulated clothing. I bet my COP$1,000,000 won't go far."

The next week flew by, with Liz working and Jude being a day time tourist and writing many memories from Cali and San Isidro. In hindsight he realised that it was stupid of him to accept the flight to Miami in the small Piper Navajo plane, for had it been full of packages of white powder, he could have been detained for a very long time in the US.

They flew back to England together in early February after many long pleasant evenings in various Hotels. Jude was unable to exchange his Colombian currency so he remained a millionaire for the immediate future. Two days before they arrived back at Dorchester, Liz's Gran succumbed to a bout of pneumonia. Liz was overcome with sadness to lose her last relative. The house in a row known as Victoria Buildings and its entire contents were left to Liz, who quickly decided that she did not want to live in it. They booked into Mrs Nayland's stable and with Jude's help they emptied her Gran's house, storing a few pieces that Liz wanted to keep. It then needed modernising if it was to be sold. They both worked on re-decorating every room and installing a new kitchen and bathroom with the aid of a plumber and electrician. In six weeks the house was unrecognisable and was put up for sale. Liz's reason for selling it with such haste was 'If I move in there I'll never leave, because of Gran. I don't want to live my whole life in one small house in Dorchester'. Jude felt she would have loved to live there for a while but Liz feared herself becoming too attached. The house sold quickly, Jude never asked Liz what she did with the money. Soon after the sale of Liz's Gran's house, Jude sold Blenheim to Peter Jackson, the guy who had taken over his old job. He sold it without ever going back, complete with its furnishings, which again Liz understood.

Jude was preparing mentally to carry out his commitment with Jack Mortimer for the summer. He visited his family in Oxfordshire briefly and he visited Barbara in France, alone because Liz had an assignment in Italy for ten days.

All too soon it was time to pack his bags, which he did reluctantly to join Kris and Nick. He told Liz and Jack Mortimer his summer boss, that this second summer would be his last. He did not know what else he was going to do other than finish the book but he knew he wanted to do it with Liz and all indications were that she was increasingly happy with regular involvement with him.

She moved to Weymouth renting a small two-bedroom town house near the boat yard. The second bedroom rapidly became her dark room.

DAY THREE

BARRY (CHAPLAIN)

6:30 in the morning of Wednesday October the tenth found me in a familiar position, a hot coffee in one hand, a piece of toast in the other and two papers in the other!

The Mirror: An unsuccessful conman who tried to get a supermarket cashier to change a fake one million dollar note was arrested in Pittsburgh, USA. Also, a cow has been arrested over the deaths of six people in road crashes after they swerved to avoid it in Phnom Penh, Cambodia. A little worryingly for me is an article written by someone who has recently qualified as a domestic energy assessor to provide energy-performance certificates for domestic homes, as part of the 'home information packs' or Hip's, the writer claims that he or she is struggling to pick up any work. What hope I wonder is there for me?

And so to The Times: In its lead – Chancellor Alistair Darling is in trouble for raiding the conservative election locker of ideas and stealing proposals to exempt families from inheritance tax. More seriously, a charity campaign that claimed to have raised £750,000 from Premier League Footballers to help nurses has collected less than a quarter of that amount, suggesting that many players have gone back on their word. We have dishonest footballers, surely not? And 28 swans have been found shot and buried in a pit in Radwell. The swan it claims is a protected bird. Killing one can result in a £5,000 fine and six months in jail. Let's hope someone gets a £140,000 fine and 14 years in jail. I'd like to be on that jury. Finally a primary school teaching assistant who did not want her children getting mixed up with drug dealers solved the problem by supplying them herself. She commented 'some people give their children alcohol and cigarettes at an early age but I gave mine cannabis'. She described herself as a 'liberal parent'.

Today's proceedings came to mind. I wonder how the other eleven will vote. My view was cast in stone. I could not imagine any, or all, of the jury being able to persuade me otherwise. Claire seemed to have readjusted to the correct proportions of the estate car and the journey was notable only in the fact that nothing of note occurred, with two pigeons and a squirrel to add to this year's road kill tally.

Thomas Hardy was like the weather, dull and overcast this morning. I was beginning to have a brief, imaginary conversation with him each morning. Perusing his biography which I had collected from the library along with his novel, I had learnt much of his early life and works, much of which has been a revelation.

The jury room was half full, it was a relief to see David (the weather man) and Thomas (the numbers man), engaged in a fact swapping, and I don't hesitate to imagine a numerically competitive conversation. I engage John (foreman), and Joyce (accessories) She is unusually turned out today in black fishnet tights under yellow shorts and a black blouse with yellow accessories. This woman's wardrobe must rival that of Demelza Marcos. John is sharing yesterday's poem / limerick with Joyce as I interrupt. John is a wordsmith, not by profession, he is actually a pharmacist and has been handing out, out-of-date drugs, painkillers and flu remedies mainly, to all who will have them. Alice (fake fur) has unashamedly taken advantage of this. Once his crossword is complete John pens a short poem or limerick relating to the previous day's court procedure, he has a vitriolic wit. More and more often jury members are asking his opinion on drugs and remedies, he seems to both enjoy and court the attention. He has lived alone for the past nine years since the death of his wife and obviously enjoys company, although he is a little aloof and judgemental. Judgemental, who am I to use such a term to describe another?

When asked by two of the women, Lynda (men's wear) and Elizabeth (chain smoker) of his opinion on homoeopathic medicines, he replies that he refers to them as 'go home and don't be so pathetic' remedies. He firmly believes that if a medicine does not have an active chemical ingredient then it has no value, other than its possible placebo effect. I've not had the opportunity to put a name to the face of Elizabeth Foster (chain smoker) before, as she seems to be a permanent fixture in the smoking room. She is always the first in there and the last out. Whether this is nerves or addiction it's not possible to tell, perhaps it is a combination of both. She is unusual in that she is the only woman among us who is modestly dressed. The cut of her clothes suits the shape of her body. I guess she is around forty-five years old and therefore one of the younger members of the jury, the exception being the thirty-ish year old male who was not selected for the first case and, curiously, never appeared again. The little conversation I have heard from Elizabeth suggest that she will be easily led during our debate to achieve a verdict, as she seems not to have a fixed opinion on any subject and is able to agree with almost everyone on every issue. In short she is able to run with the fox and chase with the hounds.

We are informed by Dawn (White Linen) that there will be a delay before proceedings can commence. Apparently one of the main protagonists has had an incident prior to arriving at the courthouse. Andy (body odour) later tells us that it was the barrister for the prosecution who was pelted with eggs walking from the car park to the court building, presumably by supporters of the accused.

I have been standing for far too long and take the nearest available seat, which unfortunately is between Terry (rugby), and Tim (football), but I immediately note that conversation is unusually subdued between these two, who are becoming a double act.

"Okay you two? How's things?" Tim replies,

"Okay, I've got a nice earner booked in for Sunday with the burger van, big car boot sale just off the dual carriageway. Things are looking a little less optimistic for us football fans and a sight better for you rugby boys, with your wins over Tonga and Samoa, but I think Australia in the last eight will be the end of the road for you and France too, they've got New Zealand." I nudge Terry to bring him into the conversation,

"Hey Terry, we can turn Australia over, what do you think?"

"Yeah sure, s'cuse me, I'm in need of one of those shitty coffees." I look to Tim with a raised eyebrow. He explains,

"Terry had a bad night. His eighteen year old paralysed son had a seizure during the night. He's now just half a mile up the

175

road in Dorchester County Hospital. Thank Christ for the air ambulance. It brought him in just before midnight. He was choking on food. Fortunately for Terry's family they live next to school playing fields, somewhere easy for the helicopter to land, otherwise who knows?"

"Bloody hell, should he be here?"

"He's told Dawn of the situation and that he may have to leave at short notice, but the lad's stable now. Anyway, Dawn has said that judge will accept a verdict from eleven, apparently even ten in extraordinary circumstance."

"How'd the boy come to be paralysed?"

"Broke his neck playing rugby for Sherborne, apparently the same club Terry played for. It was his first game in the seniors. Terry says he shouldn't have played. He was only eighteen, he thinks that he wasn't strong enough, not ready to take the enormous pressures of senior rugby. The boy was keen, he saw it as an opportunity to impress the coaches, as a number of the senior players were unavailable due to injury, now the poor bugger can't wipe his own arse." Terry returns with his coffee and sits to my left hand side. I feel embarrassed by my good fortune, almost guilty. I engage him,

"Hey, look, I'm really sorry to hear about your son. Will he be in hospital long do you know?"

"Hopefully not, we've had this sort of thing before. He's usually back home in a couple of days. I think he does it to get a free ride in the air ambulance."

He's already putting on the good old British brave face. I think we do this better than any other part of the world and it's something we have in common throughout the union. Scotland, Wales, Ireland and ourselves, we are consummate when it comes to dealing with adversity. Humour can disguise everything if you don't look too deep. He continues, addressing Tim,

"Just wait 'til your boys go out against Russia at the weekend. You'll need a dozen ambulances." Tim lets him have that one. Barry (chaplain) is opposite me waving his copy of 'The Madding Crowd'. I acknowledge him and mouth the word later, hoping he can lip-read and that he will stay put.

Eventually we are called into court to hear the judge's summing up. The judge looks like a kindly, old gent, with a frail

176

body and shaky hands, in stark contrast he has steely, piercing eyes that give the impression of a coiled, venomous creature lurking and biding its time, concealed in a crumbling shell. He chooses his words very carefully and refers, at great length, to the claims and counter claims we have had to endure. He tells us that perhaps it is possible that we have not heard the definitive truth in this case, but that we must not lose sight of the original charges and that someone did cause grievous bodily harm to Barry Read. We have heard the medical report, these injuries could not have been self-inflicted and that criminal damage was caused to his car, and that the accused, Arran Spelling, had claimed to be at his home engaged in the past time of computer games all evening. Further to that, his father, mother and younger brother had all corroborated this fact. Further still, that this corroboration had been proven to be false by a number of reliable eyewitnesses, including two police officers. He then instructed us to adjourn to the deliberation room and come back with a verdict to which we were all agreed.

We are shown into a room, at its rear was a kitchenette area where we were welcomed to help ourselves to tea, coffee and court supplied biscuits. There was a buzzer to press on the door if we needed help, or to press when we had reached a verdict. Most of us sat down. Two of the women went to make tea.

Terry said, "Shall I press the button now or do we need to talk about it?" John, responded with,

"Well let's all get around the table and see if anybody has a point they wish to make."

After teas and coffees were dispensed, John brought the table to order and asked if anyone had something to say before we took a vote and would they do it in an orderly fashion, beginning with Joyce (matching accessories) on his left hand side and continuing around the table in a clockwise manner. He added,

"For the moment please hold back your opinion of guilt or innocence." Joyce took the opportunity to say, "I don't think I've heard such a pack of lies in all my life. I thought everybody would, like us, uphold and respect the court, and conduct themselves with dignity and honour. Frankly I am for the moment appalled by human nature." Many of us agreed and voiced our support for her statement. Tim (football), was next,

"I have to agree with Joyce and in my simple mind this case is cut and dry."

Then myself, "I've been surprised by the degree of flippancy and freedom allowed to the barristers, it is quite clear they are free to disparage, disregard or blatantly disagree with true or false statements as they see fit. What has happened to honesty and integrity?"

Lynda (men's wear), and Terry (rugby), voice their opinions in agreement with Joyce and myself. Alice (fake fur), mutters under her breath,

"I don't care what he's done, I'm not having it on my conscience that that lad goes to jail." I didn't think John had heard her but obviously his sixty nine year old ears are in good order. He asked Alice to repeat what she had said for the benefit of us all. She sheepishly repeated her sentence, adding, "I'm not laying awake at night with that hanging over me."

John asked Terry who was sitting nearest the door to ring the buzzer. This immediately gained the attention of all present. Dawn opened the door so quickly she must have been standing on duty on the other side. John went to the door and spoke very softly to Dawn, who then asked him and the rest of us to remain seated for a few minutes, we sat in silence. Just two minutes later, Dawn returned and asked Alice to leave the room, collect anything she had left in the jury room and leave the building, and that she would not be required to serve on the next case. She then followed Alice's fake fur and third-rate scent out of the room and closed the door. We never saw her again.

John addressed us saying that in his opinion Alice Black had compromised herself and shown herself to be unfit to sit on a jury. He had informed Dawn of his opinion and asked for clarification from the judge, who had not hesitated to evict Alice from the building. The judge had also informed us through John that a verdict of eleven jurors was not a problem and quite common. John had wisely held back a further comment from the judge until later.

Next to speak was Barry (chaplain) he started by choosing his words carefully in the light of the previous occurrence. His delivery was both bumbling and emotional. Three times during his offering he had to pause to compose himself. The essence of what he was saying was that he had begged not to be here. He had to work in the local prison for twelve years and he would have to engage with the accused if he was found guilty. He said that he wasn't stupid, all the evidence was against the lad and that he would do what he had to do as a member of the public, but it would be at great personal cost. I believe we all sympathised. Here was a gentle, elderly, caring man who did not have the courage of his own convictions, who, given the age old choice between fight and flight would always chose the latter. I believe we all recognised his decency and his cowardice. We swiftly completed our circumnavigation of the table with James (yet to be introduced to me), Elizabeth, Thomas and David all agreed with the statements made by Joyce (matching accessories) and myself (road kill obsessive, smart arse?) John then asked for a show of hands for guilty. To our surprise all eleven of us raised our hands, even Barry, who was at this point, openly crying, but had found some inner resolve. John wrapped it up by saying,

"That's good a unanimous decision, although the judge did say he would accept a ten-to-one. Just one formality this form in front of me requires of me that I ask for any persons undecided, thank you none, and any not guilty, thank you none." Barry, now a little more composed, raised his hand, saying,

"You did say the judge would accept a ten-to-one? Would any of you mind if I changed my vote? It's me who's got to live with it, not you." I don't know if I was more appalled by his spineless display of retreat, or impressed by his courageous ability to make a complete arse of himself. Barry added, "I don't mind you all thinking I'm a complete idiot, but can some of you try a little harder to hide it?" The perception of this comment surprised most of the jury to a similar degree to that of his change of heart. John accepted his about turn, certainly Bob my father would not have, I think he'd have had him shot for desertion. John then asked Terry to ring the buzzer. Our verdict was delivered and we were on our way home with almost indecent haste. The guilty young man would be remanded in custody pending psychological profiling, before the judge could pass sentence. So we the jury would never know whether Arran Spelling was to be incarcerated or released on probation. I

179

imagine two years in her Majesty's pleasure would be a fair result.

We were informed just before we left that the case starting tomorrow was expected to run until the end of next week and that our number for tomorrow's selection process would be fourteen. Also that those not selected would no longer be required and could return to work or domesticity. The judge thanked us for our diligence, wished us well for the next case, which he would not be presiding over and said goodbye.

There had not been an opportunity to engage in word play today. John set us the word maladroit for tomorrow. I'm not sure that any of us, with the exemption of our task master, had a clear understanding of its meaning, but most of us would return with its definition on the tip of our tongues in the morning.

I collected Claire at four thirty from college and we were soon on our way across the downs toward Buckland Newton. I picked up a rabbit for the buzzard feeder and remarked to Claire,

"Well I've done all I can with you, now it's up to you. Be careful and take your time on Friday and remember, you won't fail if you drive under the speed limit, but you will fail if you drive above it."

"Thanks Dad. I need to pass – I've told three friends I'll take them down to Studland Bay on Sunday to walk the dogs."

"Hi, any post?"

"Yes, they messed up my mammogram and I've got to go back on Monday for another one and there's some info for you on your exams for the week after next."

"Okay I'll just have a cuppa, put this rabbit up for the buzzards and take Emma out." I shout, "Emma, where are you?"

Emma comes running with her car keys aloft and almost runs into the dangling deceased rabbit, saying, "I'm here Old Man. Argh! That's totally disgusting! Why is it that my dad is like the weirdo? None of my friends' dads are anything like as mad as you."

"No but I bet they are happy to buy and eat meat that someone else has ill treated, badly fed and badly housed, mass murdered, injected with drugs, water, colouring and flavouring, stuck in a plastic bag and left in a shop for a week. This is free-range, fresh, healthy meat. So wise up, and to use one of your phrases, get real."

"Mum tell him not to bring his dead, furry friends into the house again. It makes me want to throw up. I don't think I want my dinner tonight and I think I'm going to be veggie from now on. I can't stand the thought of eating anything that Dad's run over."

I get a 'well done' and some raised eyebrows from Liz. In contrast, Claire says,

"Give me your furry friend. I'll put it up for you so you can take Little Miss Perfect out of the house and give us some peace."

I hand Claire the rabbit, say thanks, turn to talk to Liz and fail to see the two girls connect with well-aimed kicks at each other. I say to Liz,

"Are you sure one of those two wasn't swapped at the hospital? Someone out there has a sweet, quiet and polite little girl in their house and we've got their problem child."

"No-one's got a sweet little child, this is the age of the teenagers of the village of the damned."

"Oh yes I remember that film. Didn't the children end up eating all the grownups?" Emma is pulling me out of the house, saying,

"I suppose I could hold off becoming a veggie for a while, just until we've got rid of you. Come on."

I lean forward to kiss Liz but Emma's tug on the back of my jacket is just sufficient to ensure that we do not make contact. In truth my girls are so different, but in so many ways like Liz and I. They both have Liz's good looks and slim figure and although they are blonde by manufacture, their natural hair colour is brunette, as is Liz's. They have her eyes and lips. Emma has her character nose and unfortunately my temperament. Claire has my flatter nose, but they both have a tremendous sense of humour, so I guess we've got the right two.

Emma's driving is a bit off. She gets frustrated at the number of tractors hauling maize in catch bins back to farmyards. I lose concentration for a while and imagine myself back in one of the tractors with Nick and Kris twenty years previous. My mind wanders back to Kris's accident and in the nick of time I grab the handbrake and prevent Emma from conducting a risky manoeuvre around one of the tractors. This alienates her from me and destroys the fun atmosphere that had developed between us today. The rest of the lesson is conducted in silence.

On my return to the house I pour a glass of red and ask Liz about her hospital appointment,

"So, what's up with the mammogram?"

"Oh they say the machine was giving faulty readings, so I need to go in on Monday to re-do it that's all."

"You okay with that?" "Yeah it's no problem. I can do it Monday afternoon after my morning class." Liz takes photography classes three days a week at Kingston Maurward College down at Dorchester. The college is an impressive building and is mentioned many times in Hardy's biography, his family being masons for generations doubtless worked on the main building and its many outbuildings. She continues, "So, what happened in court today, guilty, not guilty?"

"Oh defiantly guilty, guilty as hell. Some thug took a baseball bat to his girlfriend's ex and his car. He'll probably get a couple of years and be let out after six months. The next case is a bigger one it's expected to run until next Friday, but we've no idea what it's about yet. We will hear the charges tomorrow morning. If I'm lucky I won't be involved, two of us will get the week off."

"Good. You can sort that dangerous tree out the back and maybe we can go look for my new car."

"Okay but don't bank on it."

After dinner which was just the two of us with Claire at the chicken farm and Emma at the Green Man, I spend some time in both Thomas Hardy's biography and his novel. Later after two glasses of wine Liz comes to bed with all the energy of a teenager. A deep and satisfying sleep follows for us both.

DAY FOUR

CLARE

I awake at 6-30, Liz is already out with the dogs, I go down to the kitchen and slip into my familiar routine. Today's Mirror is very concerned about the sum of money Sir Paul McCartney will have to part with to gag his second wife Heather Mills once the divorce is settled. It also seems to be a day for underwear. A woman's male gardener has been jailed for entering her house and dressing up in her skimpy pink vest and thong, which was quite a surprise for her on her unexpected return home. And a lesbian tennis coach has admitted wearing her 13 year old student's knickers by mistake, even though they were name-tagged and half her size. This was at first denied but expensive testing found the coaches DNA in the girl's underwear. What a sound use of public funds. More public funds have been spent by the New Mexico University to reach the conclusion that lap dancers collect higher tips at their most fertile time of the month, it is evidence the university says of women having days 'on heat'.

On a more serious note, The Times is claiming that last week's non-election fiasco is the beginning of the end for new Labour, and that Nobel Peace Prize winner Al Gore's award winning climate change documentary titled 'Inconvenient Truth' is littered with nine convenient untruths. Also the Tate Modern's latest art installation which is a 167 meter crack in the floor has caught out three admirers who have fallen into the exhibit. Staff are now handing out leaflets warning of the dangers of modern art. On a predictable note the bill for the Olympic stadium has doubled from its original price, and disgustingly the newspaper reports that the jury in the Princess Diana inquest have been told that photographers scrambled over the Mercedes to get clear pictures as Diana lay dying, making no effort to assist those in the vehicle, the hearing continues.

Claire's driving on her last day before her test is okay and three badgers were added to my annual tally. There is an argument nationally regarding the gassing or shooting of badgers to limit the spread of Bovine Tuberculosis. I think if we just continue to construct roads eventually the badger will become extinct. I drop off Claire and park. Leaving the car park for the courthouse, I note that today Thomas Hardy is glistening in the early morning sun up on his plinth.

Today I am one of the last to arrive in the jury room. I try to time my arrival to avoid some of the inane conversations that automatically ensue, but today there's a long delay before we are required in court, so inanity it is. John (foreman) is on top form today. He's finished his Telegraph crossword, amused us all with his limerick of yesterday's court procedure and is busy handing out, out of date painkillers. Terry (rugby) is back to his best today. His son will be returning home in the afternoon and he is engaged in a conversation on the pros and cons of sail rope, which he sells for a living from his Chandlery in Weymouth Old Town, with the sailing enthusiast David (the weather man). Although for how long he can keep conversation on rope is anyone's guess.

Thomas (the numbers man) has borrowed John's Telegraph and is trying to concentrate on a Sudoku challenge and trying not to concentrate on the one sided conversation in his left ear from Tim (football), the conversation being of a predictable nature. Elizabeth (chain smoker) has left the room, with Lynda (menswear), again for predictable reasons. Barry (chaplain) is engaged in conversation with Joyce (accessories) who looks to me with a desperate hope that I will interrupt their conversation. I turn away from Joyce's magnetic ensemble of jade and grey. With jade creased leather boots, grey woven leggings, a knee length corduroy dress finished off with a wide leather belt and grey woven scarf, it all works very well. She stands out as the only person who made a tremendous effort and got it right earlier in the day.

I make the mistake of turning to my right and engage Hanna, with her silicone valley on display for all comers to peruse. She is talking to Richard Barnett, who it turns out is a self-taught DIY builder from Blandford, who was excused from the jury for the first case due to personal reasons. No other explanation was ever forthcoming. He quickly hands me one of his cards, which informs me no job is too small or too big and that I can call him 24/7. Apparently he's already got a bathroom to re-tile for Joyce and a gutter to repair on Barry's bungalow. I warn him that a trip to Barry's house could take longer than expected, but as he's paid by the hour he rubs his hands together and does a fair 'Del Boy' impression with a loud 'lovely jubbly'. Richard (I can do that) the spiv builder moves off to spread the word that DIY salvation is at hand, and I am left with Hanna (silicone valley) who is today dressed both tragically and comically. As always the skirt is too short and the silicone is in full bloom. Add to that, high heeled patent black boots, sufficient make-up to qualify as war paint and what can only be described as too many false hair pieces and extensive eye lashes that presumably keep the inside of her car windscreen mist free when she blinks, the result is a combination guaranteed to turn away most males, with perhaps the exception of those afflicted as per our last home secretary, David Blunkett. The only other persons present are James Lynton, a sixty six year old retired engineer from Wimborne whose hobby is the breeding of rare butterflies, and Anthony Woodcock, a twenty eight year old car salesman from Poole. These two are not selected to serve on the second jury.

I find a seat and am rapidly joined by Barry (chaplain) and after polite preliminaries we are into 'The madding Crowd'. Clearly Barry is enjoying the book but is feeling a little disjointed because his wife is taking the opportunity to read a Jackie Collins, something that would never get on to Barry's approved list, he expresses disappointment in his wife's choice of reading. My remark of 'live and let live' is lost in the many furrows of his brow. Barry also expresses his hopes and fears for the next case. I believe we all share his emotions.

Eventually we are called into court by the delightful Dawn (White Linen). James Lynton and Anthony Woodcock are dismissed. The remaining twelve of us are sworn in. Again I am the only one who takes the option of not swearing on the bible. John is again chosen as foreman and we are dismissed for lunch. An entire morning has gone without any significant court procedure other than to choose the jury.

The weather is fair. I walk with Thomas (numbers man) into town for a pasty, during which time I learn that one hundred and eighty two of his two hundred and twenty one ewes gave birth to twins last year, and twelve had triplets, leaving a disappointing twenty seven who had just one lamb. So last year's total of four hundred and twenty seven lambs is the target he hopes to beat in the coming spring and, as he has added thirty new ewes he is fairly confident. Thursday the eleventh of October 2007 is a pleasant, sunny day in Dorchester, with just a hint of winter breeze. I am naturally drawn to the park. I consume my pasty and stroll, deliberately discarding the wrapping in one of the personally historic waste bins provided. I then return to the car and today continue where I left off with my Hardy novel.

With a half hour left of our lunch, I wander along west walk, under the first of many avenues of plane trees. Glorious in what appears to be full leaf, despite evidence to the contrary, a carpet of yellowing to brown buckled and twisted leaves. Each leaf holding its body away from the damp grass or road on its stem and two or more points in an attempt to prolong its autumnal beauty for a day or two, or perhaps no more than a few hours. I pass by the building that was owned by the cheerful Mrs Nayland, the Scottish woman who was my landlady for a time in the late Eighties. She, now long since passed on. I recall her good-humoured disposition. She was ever obliging, though elderly in her years and increasingly less mobile. The converted stable block to the rear of number eight that was my temporary home now appears to be permanently occupied.

I turn left continuing along west walk. The splendour of the plane trees now gives way to the might of horse chestnuts, squirrels abound. People are photographing the boulevards of trees now resplendent in their autumn costume. The various walks and pathways are overlaid by their untidy, yet bewitching, disburden. Another left turn and I am heading back towards the courthouse through Salisbury field, an area of open parkland with both a children's play area and a replica ancient beacon post. How often I wonder is this one ever ignited, and I imagine that when it is, it is always in celebration, never in alarm. The far side of the park is shielded by a terraced row of ten comfortable looking homes, known as Victoria buildings. One of which was owned and occupied by Liz's Gran, Tryphena, she was an independent woman who bore her problems and worries with great fortitude, but who had by the time I'd made her acquaintance succumbed to Parkinson's disease to the extent that she had lost all of her fiercely defended self-reliance and not surprisingly, almost all of her wicked sense of humour.

The agreeable row of red brick homes, each with identical arched doorways is separated from another indistinguishable terraced row by a narrow alleyway. Each house is defiantly pushing a row of four ornate chimneys into the sky, in all there are eighty becoming decorative chimneys, all but redundant. To the front of the houses is an extended line of black iron railings which protects the passerby from an increasingly high drop to the road as the pedestrian gradient diversifies from the vehicular. These buildings in the Fordington district of Dorchester were built long before today's reliance on the motor car. It rapidly became apparent that to live here and own a car would be problematic, not a concern for Liz's Gran during her tenure. Walking back across Salisbury Field it is possible to view the huge spire of All Saints and the large square tower of St Peters. Behind them only visible to the residents of Victoria buildings during winter once the horse chestnuts are fully disrobed, is a vast collection of enormous brick chimneys. I promise myself on another day during a period of low demand that I will wander in their direction to discover their purpose.

Now walking up the high street I realise the town has an abundance of archways and alleyways. One such arch leads me into Greening Court and into a flagstone paved terrace of stone, flint and brick houses, each with its own style of doorways and windows, one is red brick, another white-painted brick, another still stone. It is an attractive terrace that few passers-by will ever glimpse. Some of its attraction is lost to me as I imagine the colossal effort required to move one's own possessions either in or out through the limited access, directly onto the high street.

As I stroll back to the courthouse I become conscious of the fact that it is difficult to lose track of time in Dorchester, the town goes to considerable length to remind its residents and visitors or the hour. Several shop windows, the Town Hall and the Borough gardens are amongst the many who take on the task of punctuality. I arrive back at the jury room and am immediately brought into a conversation between Lynda (menswear) whom I can only assume has run out of cigarettes and Richard (I can do that) the DIY builder. Lynda is shockingly dressed today in brogue shoes, what has to be her father's or grandfather's moleskin trousers, checked shirt and waistcoat, requires my opinion on a matter of home improvement. She has asked Richard how to strip off washable, waterproof wallpaper, a long inconclusive conversation ensues during which Richard three times uses his now given nickname, I can do that. I think in Lynda he has met his match, she only wants to pick his brain and not employ him, the former objective being a relatively simple task for a woman of her calibre.

I inform Barry of my progress with the Hardy novel, which I see gives him a target for tonight and then foolishly, albeit absentmindedly, engage in a conversation regarding the weather with none other than David (the weather man) and I am informed, to my eternal delight, that the average temperature for South Dorset last month was the warmest on record in a hundred and forty years. Somebody help me. I have a vision of David and myself marooned on a tiny tropical island, and every hour on the hour I receive a report that it is hot, dry and sunny, but that later in the day it will be dark, and again tomorrow it will be........David has unfortunately fallen into a carelessly placed mantrap and has been impaled on spikes, the diet of fish had become as predictable as the weather!

Joyce (accessories) comes into my view. I ask her if she is aware of this new found startling information. She replies that she is and glares at David who leaves us in pursuit of a beverage. I confess my vision to her, she then looks me in the eyes and asks me if I am aware of the fact that at fifty-ish as she calls me, and very close to the truth she is in her estimation, I am probably the only male on the jury whom the females would take with them if allowed to on their desert island, referring to the Rory Plumley creation 'desert island disc' on Radio Four, as their selection of a luxury item. Any embarrassment on my part is soon absorbed and I offer Richard as a more suitable subject, due to his ability to do almost anything. The moment passed between us with a degree of levity but we both know that she has thrown down a gauntlet, all I have to do is pick it up and my life could change in an instant. I smile at her by way of accepting the compliment. I then step over the gauntlet and engage Terry (rugby) on our National team's prospects, with a semi-final against France at the weekend, having seen off Australia in the week.

Andy (body odour) calls us into the court. We are soon seated in our familiar positions, with the only changes being Richard (I can do that) replacing Alice (fake fur), and Hannah (Silicone Valley) replacing James.

The judge, who on this occasion is a little older, perhaps seventy plus, then he of the last case, again gives the impression of a steely-eyed viper cosseted in an ageing carcass, calls the court to order. He explains that as a circuit judge the nature of his work is peripatetic and that it is some years since he presided at Dorchester and that he is not familiar with any persons present, be they ushers, court officials, barristers, solicitors or witnesses for either the prosecution or for the defence. He then calls for the accused to be brought into court. Up to this point a degree of relaxation had spread like flu symptoms throughout the jury. We were comfortable with our last decision and quite ready to start the process again. I believe as a group of trusted, responsible adults we were relaxed in our anticipation.

We watched as Michael Merryweather ascends the stairs into the glass cage that dominates the centre of the court, he was flanked by two uniformed police officers. I think all of us lost a degree of comfort at the sight of Michael. He was perhaps twenty eight to thirty years old, badly shaven and badly dressed. He was not tall, perhaps five feet seven and medium build. He was dressed in a suit, which looked like it had been scraped off a road kill victim. It was 'Norman Wisdom' like in that it was a size too small for him. It was dark brown, too tight, too short in the leg and a single button was fastened in the centre, stretched to near breaking point. His thin tie was knotted so tight I can only imagine it would have to be cut from him. That and the grubbiness of the collar were, to me, signs of discomfort and nerves, clearly he had been frequently tugging at and fingering this area. His dark, cropped hair, dark complexion and half shaven face and small tattoo on his neck did him no favours. He confirmed his name and at the same time confirmed that he had

189

never visited a dentist, his teeth were the colour of his complexion. He then sat, causing his trouser legs to rise up his shins revealing unclean grey socks and worn, distressed shoes. His legal team had presented him very poorly indeed.

The judge then asked the Clerk of the court to read out the charges, which he did without delay,

"The charges are; Charge one, that the accused Michael Merryweather, of 22 Harbour Side Terrace, Poole, did cause an actual sexual assault on the sixteenth of February 2007, in that he did put his erect penis into the vagina of a minor. Charge two, that the accused Michael Merryweather, did cause an actual sexual assault in that he put his erect penis in the mouth of a minor, also on the sixteenth of February 2007. Charge three, that the accused Michael Merryweather, did cause an actual sexual assault in that he used his tongue bar to stimulate the clitoris of a minor."

The shock and awe that went through each member of the Jury was palpable. We experienced much perturbation. Everyone else in the room had some kind of prior knowledge of the nature of this case. To us, the Jury, it was like a kick in the guts. Two of the women, Joyce and Elizabeth were visibly shocked and were in tears. Hannah was struggling to hold back tears, as was Barry. The last of the women, Lynda, had a stern, resolute look about her, she appeared ready to crucify the accused. There was a small degree of physical movement amongst us as we took in the nature of the charges. What was the age of the victim, four, eight, ten? It was an appalling realisation that this animal in front of us may have done these things to a child. Joyce left the court to throw up. I wiped the sweat from my hands onto my trouser legs. All of us made mental and physical adjustments to brace ourselves for what was to follow.

There was a few moments pause whilst we waited for Joyce to return, which she did looking very pale and shaken. The judge asked her if she was able to continue, she nodded and he then stated that as there had been a measure of disruption among the jury whilst the charges were being read out, to make matters clear as day, the charges should be read out once more. This received an audible gasp from Joyce and Elizabeth. There had been little or no disruption of note from the Jury. We were to a man, or woman, dumbstruck by the serious and repellent nature of the charges. Nevertheless we had to sit through them again, for I believe the perverted satisfaction of a strange old man who seemed to get off on hearing naughty words in a public arena. Our judge was clearly gratified to re-hear such words as penis, vagina, and clitoris, as each of these were delivered he gave a firm and satisfying nod of his head.

Then we had to go through the judge's insistence that the tongue bar should be shown, in case any members of the jury not be familiar with its existence or method of use. So the defendant Michael was asked to stand, face the jury, and walk to the edge of his cage and poke out his tongue, it was quite bizarre.

All the players were then introduced from both sides of the case. The prosecuting barrister explained to us at length that in no uncertain terms he would convince us that the accused was guilty of all charges and that we would all feel relieved to find Michael Merryweather guilty and that to remove him from society was both our duty and our obligation. Even though we had to a man or a woman pre-judged the first defendant, Arran Spelling, I'm sure that at least eleven of us were in agreement with the prosecution barrister at this point. This animal in front of us needed to be excluded from society for crimes that were abhorrent to us all, we had learnt nothing from the first case.

The council for the defence, a little surprisingly is a female barrister, fortyish with a large crop of auburn hair splaying out from under her court wig. She informs us of Michael's innocence and that she would leave us feeling assured of the fact. We would, she said, leave the court having acquitted Michael Merryweather of all charges with a clear conscience. We were left feeling that it was ourselves whom were to be the victims of abuse.

The judge very sensibly and observantly said that he felt the jury had absorbed sufficient information for the day and he deemed that we needed a period of time to process the sensitive nature of the case and opening statements. He then dismissed the jury for the day, it was just after three pm. I then felt I'd been a little harsh on labelling him Judge Tourettes for his love of dirty words, for clearly there was behind the nonsense, a man of long experience and great wisdom. I would have to think again. I

191

reminded myself that those suffering from tourettes did not have a love for shocking words, they were compelled to use them against their will.

All twelve of us returned in a very subdued and sombre manner to the jury room, no one quite knowing how to commence a conversation. Clearly to discuss the weather, the process of our national sporting teams or how many sheep you can fit in an average family saloon was inappropriate. It was Richard Barnett who broke the silence,

"Look I've got to go. I've got a job to price on the way home. I've given some of you my card. I'll leave a few on the table. Take a couple each if you like. Hand them out to neighbours and friends. I'll see you tomorrow."

With that inanimate sentence the dour atmosphere among us was broken. Two went to the smoking room. Two more left without a word, which left a handful of us who sat quietly and deliberately recaptured our prior mood. I felt as others did I'm sure that the gravity and nature of the charges we had just heard needed to be absorbed and reflected upon as a body, not just individually. It was John who used his sagacity and perception and spoke for a moment. He spoke for all of us that were present when he said we had heard some disturbing accusations and that the case in front of us would be traumatic and challenging, but that we should attempt to compartmentalise or pigeon hole the information to allow ourselves to function as normal, leave the horrors in this room and go about our normal lives. He added that perhaps the dreadful anticipation we were experiencing would be a degree worse than the actual experience and that some of our fears would be groundless. It was David (the weather man) who thanked him for his words, told us all not to let it get the better of us and sleep well tonight, he then added that it was too fine of an afternoon to be hanging around indoors, and he left. I thanked John, patted his arm in a comradely gesture and I too left the room. I could hear that conversation was reverting to more usual, daily topics behind me. I had an hour to kill prior to collecting Claire from college and as David had pointed out it was a fine, dry, warm afternoon, so I decided on a whim to find a local churchyard in which to catch up with my Hardy novel.

192

I walked East down the high street in search of a tall, pointed, decorative building, a place of worship no less. I carry no religious beliefs or paraphernalia inside me or with me, but like many people I gain a degree of solace and comfort pursuing a well-kept graveyard, which almost without exception, is juxtaposition to the aforementioned place of worship. I adore the architecture, the stone vaulting, the doors, the clever use of buttresses and particularly the flying buttresses that allow so much extra light to penetrate an otherwise sombre building, and the intricate use of stone and timber inside the building. I also revel in the crowning glory of the stained glass windows. Though I find it a perversion that at a time when the average family would so often go hungry, shoeless and know nothing of medical help for simple ailments that could and would degenerate into fatal conditions, robbing them of their children, that the Church of England could spend unimaginable sums of money building massive stone structures to the glory of God. Is it not possible to pray in humble surroundings, it seems to me that it was necessary that the flock should not only respect God but should also fear God. These huge structures in which all were encouraged to kneel and pray were effectively a men's club, magnificent buildings in which women could kneel to pray and kneel to scrub the floor but could never affiliate. John Lennon was right when he coined the phrase 'woman is the nigger of the world'. How good it is that finally women can now take their rightful place at the altar, pulpit and font. Will they ever absolve us for closing the door on them for so long? 'Forgive me father for I have sinned, I have treated half the population of the world unjustly and unfairly for two thousand years'.

I stroll into the churchyard and allow my attention to wander. It quickly dawns on me that the central churches of Dorchester have no significant graveyard of merit, have they been moved? Clearly I must delve deeper and look further afield to discover the resting place of the town's past residents. I return to the secluded bench that celebrates the life of Mr McLuckie and pick up the hugely impressive Hardy biography that is becoming an equally valuable insight into the plight of the nineteenth century common man, as is 'The Madding Crowd'.

193

Soon it was time to collect Clare for her last parental driving lesson. The lessons have, I'm sure, been of benefit to her and have conveniently fitted with my jury service. From the outset Liz was not interested in teaching the girls to drive. She's been great with them from Day One, but she perhaps wisely said that as she felt I would make sure that somehow I would put in my six penny worth, she would step back.

'It's no good us both teaching them because we drive quite differently'. She has wisdom, good looks and skill with the camera that I can only envy, but it is her perception that sets her apart from everyone I've ever met. She can read me like a book, like no one else ever has, not even Jayne. If I make a bold or careless statement she will instantly filter out the bravado and the disingenuousness and expose the crux of my intentions, or in reverse if I have attempted an innocent criticism of someone but have cloaked a degree of malevolent or maliciousness she will again expose this. This singles her out above all others and constantly makes me aware of any thoughtlessness or carelessness in my approach, which I wouldn't swap for anything. The insincerity of a relationship with a trophy wife or a busty bimbo must surely have appeal only to the very selfish and self-centred.

Clare is in a great mood when I pick her up. She is positively buoyant, her face effervescent.

"Well tell me then. I know you haven't won the lottery you're not old enough to buy a ticket."

"I've been asked to fill in for a friend of Kate's. She's going to Cuba next week. Everything is paid for, the flight, the hotel, the food, everything. Kate's best friend Laura has broken her wrist playing hockey so she's asked me! Can you believe it?"

"Not at the moment no, I can't quite believe it." I reply in a dull, monotone voice, Jack Dee-like.

"I've only got to pay one hundred pounds towards the activities. It's going to be great."

"What activities?"

"Sky diving, parasailing, scuba diving, bungee jumping, jet skiing and swimming with dolphins, which is all booked up and paid for, same as the hotel and food. I can't believe it's happening to me."

"No, me neither", I continue in a droll tone, "So who's going with you and Kate if you go on this trip of a lifetime?"

"Kate's mum and George, her lezzie friend." I'm playing catch up here as quick as I can,

"How can someone with a name like George be a lesbian?"

"Her real name's Georgina. She's Kate's mum's friend, has been for four years since she kicked Kate's dad out. George is good fun, she's dropped me back home a couple of times after I've stayed at Kate's."

"How come I've never seen her?"

"Oh she drops me at the gate, she doesn't come in. Probably thinks you won't approve of her appearance."

"Come on, I'm pretty broad-minded."

"Dad you haven't seen anything like George close up."

"Go on then, fill in the details."

"Tell me I can go first."

"Fill in the details."

"Okay I will but let's get driving, I've got work tonight. I need the money more than ever, can I borrow about sixty pounds from you for Cuba? You know I'll pay it back."

"You're not driving tonight you'll be seeing dolphins on the road instead of rabbits. You stay in that seat, I'll drive. Anyway I think you're ready for your test tomorrow." I thought she'd protest more but clearly she has bigger fish to fry and can't afford to fall out with Dad tonight. I pull into the late afternoon traffic and settle behind a Chelsea tractor on the school run and aim for the familiar downs to the North East of Dorchester.

"Come on then, give me the low down on George."

"She's twenty nine works in graphic design and is a bit of a Goth."

"A bit of a Goth, Which bit?"

"Well most bits really. She dresses in black men's clothes, uses enough black eye shadow for about ten people and has some body piercings and tattoos."

"Some?"

"OK a lot. Most of the tattoos are hidden away but there's a lot of piercings on display. But she's really lovely and good fun."

"Okay George looks weird but is good fun, now tell me about Kate's mum."

"Kate's mum looks pretty normal but she is weird. When she kicked Kate's dad out she changed her name from Carol to Page and put in a couple of nose studs and spent a fortune on implants, and Kate says she drinks too much."

"So what chance do you think there is of me and your mum agreeing to this trip, with the tattooed lady and an alcoholic?" As I say this there is an explosive impact on the windscreen. I had just opened up the throttle now that we are free of other vehicles and out on clear road. For a split second we were looking toward each other in conversation and in that split second whilst travelling at around seventy miles an hour, a pigeon flying against us must have impacted on the windscreen in excess of a hundred miles an hour. I jumped and put my hands in front of my face instinctively, Clare screamed and the pigeon disgorged its contents across the surprisingly not broken glass. I slow down and attempt to clear the windscreen with the washers but this only spreads the multi coloured discharge wider and I can see nothing. I stop, put on my hazard lights and get out of the car to clear the now opaque window. Clare opens the passenger door and vomits. I've been driving for over thirty years and have rarely experienced anything quite so violent.

Once back on the road Clare recovers quickly, she even manages a joke about the pigeon only being good for soup. I tell her that it is the sort of thing that can and clearly does happen to anyone, any when, so she must always stay alert when she's driving.

"So, where did we get to Dad?"

"If I recall I said, what chance do you think there is of me and Mum okay-ing this trip?"

"I text Mum earlier, she's okay with it. I would have text you but you said you leave your phone in the car on court days."

"Your Mum's okay with it? What about the George element and Kate's mum's drinking?"

"Oh Mum knows George. She attends Mum's evening class. George is into graphic design and wants to add an element of photography to her CV."

"Mum knows George? How come I've never heard a mention of someone so interesting?"

"Because mainly you're always going on about what you're interested in and what you're doing."

"That's a bit unfair."

"Is it? I don't think so, neither does Mum or Emma." "Come off it, I'm always asking you what you're up to at school and at home."

"Yes, you do, but I bet I know more about the latest book you're reading or how many buzzards have visited the garden this week or how many badgers are victims of road kill this year." Jude the numbers man? A wave of thoughtlessness and selfishness washes over me, in a matter of seconds I question my entire existence.

"Okay then, tell me about Kate's mum, the drunk."

"She's okay when George is around. They spend half their time in bed and George will be with us the whole week. Come on it's only one week, it's when George has to spend time away for work that Kate's mum gets wrecked."

"And what's this thing about changing her name?"

"She saw a film once where the character she identified with was called Page, so when Kate's dad left she saw it as a new start. It's only a name after all."

"When her dad left?"

"Okay when he was kicked out. Kate said he was a bit of a weirdo anyway. He used to stay up all night listening to jazz and surfing the net for porn. Christ who listens to jazz, except you?"

Clearly my daughters have been exposed to aspects of human nature that I had not considered. When I was around fifteen to eighteen years old I felt that I was at the coal face of experience. We had stuff that our parents didn't understand and couldn't share. We had Woodstock, Frank Zappa and the Mothers of Invention and their 'Help I'm a Rock' and 'Susie Cream Cheese', we had Kraftwerk, Monty Pythons Flying Circus, Tonto's expanding headband and if you were Simon Tong in our sixth form, oral sex, if you were really lucky. We felt we had left our parents behind, they were wooden tops, what did they know? Clare was now making me feel decidedly wooden in her open and honest observations. I was pleased that she could be so candid with me but didn't scratch my head, in case of the risk of splinters.

"So come on Dad, please let me go, please, please, please? And can I borrow some money?"

I take a long, slow, deep breath through my teeth, pause, exhale slowly and say,

"Okay, but there's one condition, that you text me every day."

"Yes, yes, yes, yes, yes, yes, yes! But I can't afford to text you every day, it'll cost loads from Cuba won't it?"

"I'll give you an extra tenner for your phone if you promise you'll text every day, just once a day or you're going nowhere."

"Okay you got it! Thank you, thank you, thank you!" She adds, "I can't believe I'm going to sky dive and do a bungee jump and go scuba diving!" Shaking my head I say softly,

"No, me neither."

We arrive home in twenty minutes and apart from the exploding pigeon, I have no recollection of any road kill for my tally. Claire runs into the house to share her good news with her mother and Emma is already sat in the Clio with the engine running so I join her and we are off to Sherborne. Thankfully incident free on the outward journey but the overheating problem reoccurs on the inward stretch. She nurses the car back home and I have a decision to make.

Liz says, "No, there isn't any." As I walk up into the house. Good, I didn't feel up to pricing drawings tonight. I go in search of a large glass of quality red,

"Pour me one as well please," she adds, "and are we still okay to go looking at cars on Saturday? I'd like to start with the Audi A3 and then look at the Golf and the hatchback Volvo. So far I've booked test drives with the Audi and the Golf."

"Yes no problem, are you really okay with this Cuba trip?"

"Not completely but it is a fantastic opportunity at very little cost. George is okay and I trust her to keep an eye on Kate's mum, whatever her name is. And Kate's like Clare she's a sensible kid. So we'll have to trust to luck. She's only got about six hours coursework left to do, she's done really well, so I see this as a reward for her good effort."

"Has she told you of the activities she's hoping to do?"

"Yes it sounds fantastic. We can't wrap her up in cotton wool all her life."

"I know but sky diving and bungee jumping? Christ, you'll be having kittens."

"She didn't mention the bungee jump… Give me that wine."

Both girls go out to work, we dine in peace and catch up with each other's day. I finish the evening by picking up Hardy's novel but something in me rejects it. I go in search of another glass and return to a task that I've neglected for two days. Liz is in her dark room preparing work for her classes so I pick up once again the untitled manuscript written by my first wife Jayne, and a very different sort of self, not Jude road kill, more Jude lost soul and I catch up with the very troubled Jacqueline Forbes-Brewer.

A NATURAL BLONDE

Missing she was and would continue to be, but dead she was not. Jackie awoke in a rough wooden crate with no natural light, the crate was moving, swaying slightly from side to side, she thought that perhaps she was on a large boat. She vomited, she assumed this was due to the motion, it was the after-effects of the strong shot of anaesthetic she had received in her arm the previous day.

She measured the crate to be approximately two meters by one, it was damp and stinking, so too where her clothes, she had been laying in her own urine. She began to gather her thoughts, she remembered her father's head whiplashing backwards and the blood, she vomited again. She panicked and hit out at the crate, she tried to shout out but all sound was swallowed by the sound proof nature of the container she was confined in. She somehow managed to stifle a panic attack, she urinated. She could hear a dull mechanical sound, she thought that it was not a train or a truck, she felt that she might be on a plane. She gathers herself to the dryer end of the crate in which she is imprisoned. She wipes her mouth on her blouse, brings her knees up to her chin and stays in that position for almost two hours.

Her rough wooden box seems to be dropping, her ears begin to hurt, this always happens to her on the descent whilst flying. She is at least now aware of her mode of transport, she over balances and puts a hand down to her right side, it comes to rest on a small length of hose pipe through which cool air is coming into the crate, she now knows how she has stayed alive in her sound proof, sealed box.

The plane lands on a small private airstrip ten kilometres to the east of Doe Quebradas in the Colombian mountains, some two hundred kilometres west of the capital, Bogota.

Had Gould known of this the second payment of five million US dollars would not have been paid, he had been assured the girl was dead, as were the people who had passed the information on to him.

It had been in Northern Mexico whilst Jackie was unconscious that she had been crated and flown south instead of killed as planned. She was worth double to the men who had been paid to dispose of her. If kept alive, a blonde English woman could fetch a good price among the cocaine barons in the South. To add the sale money to the price they had been paid to drop her over the vast rain forest in the North of the country, the three men involved will have had a very good day. She had been spared for the price of a second hand Cadillac.

She had been reloaded onto a return flight back to Colombia from Mexico on one of the regular cocaine runs. The bonus the pilot had paid for her would buy someone the afore-mentioned second-hand American car, the pilot was hoping for ten times this amount when she next changed hands. This was less than a drop in the ocean of the vast annual sum the US pays for its unquenchable desire for cocaine.

Jackie was thrown around in her crate as the single engine six seater plane made a crude landing on the grass air strip, the engine was silenced and the crate hand lifted onto the back of a two seater pickup truck.

Her hand came to rest once more on the short length of pipe keeping her alive, the incoming air was now hot and moist, which added to her sense of claustrophobia and panic. With a roaring and tearing sound, the outer layer of sound proofing was removed from her crate. Dazzling strips of sunlight pierced through the roughly hewn wooden container and with the light came heat, moist tropical heat, again she panicked, she shouted and hit out at the wooden walls, the resulting loud laughter silenced her. She listened to the voices of the men who held her destiny in their hands. Where was she? Who were her captors? What was expected of her? Her container was secured with rope in the pickup truck, she could not identify the language, she was aware only of the sounds of their voices and the overbearing odour of herself.

She was extremely disorientated by not knowing the time of day, or indeed what day it was, or which direction she had travelled in, she could not guess at the native tongue of the four men haggling over the price on her head. She could feel the heat of the midday sun on her stifling wooden prison, it was incredibly humid. She guessed that she had travelled south and thought of the Caribbean islands but quickly moved away from that notion as the voices she could hear were not West Indian, they were Hispanic, she felt that Mexico was the most likely answer to one of her most pressing questions. The four way conversation reached a peak and abruptly stopped, just as suddenly one plank was prised open to allow the purchaser a first hand view of the cargo. An impasse had been reached in negotiations, the pilot was being forced into too low a price for his comfort, he was attempting to raise the stakes but needed to prove that his captive was a natural blonde.

Jackie saw blinding sunlight and clear blue sky's through this temporary window, then a face, a poorly tended half shaven sunburnt face, its eyes were fixed in a permanent squint from gazing ever long in competition with the fierce Colombian sun. The face shouted at her making her jump with surprise, she remained quiet, she was shouted at again, she replied,

"Let me out of this stinking box you pig." Carlos Cordova the pilot reached into the box and tore a small clump of hair from the right side of Jackie's head, she screamed and the plank was replaced, she was back in semi-darkness. The pilot handed the hair to Miguel Garcia the spokesman for the three brothers with whom he was attempting to get the best possible price, he put his hand to his crutch to indicate that his cargo was a true natural blonde. This excited the three men and they wanted proof of this, but the pilot added that if he did not take off soon he would be suspected of making an unscheduled private stop to sell cocaine and he would loose his job and maybe his legs. Miguel looked at the blond roots of the hair and was satisfied that he was bidding for an English speaking blonde. He paid the pilot his bonus and the plane quickly took off to get back on schedule. His boss, the plane owner would not stand for any off route collections or drops, he must waste no more time in making his next pick up one hundred and fifty kilometres to the south. Jackie knew now that she was in even worse company than before, she had no idea what took place at the airstrip but her instincts told her that things had gone from bad to worse.

She was hungry and thirsty like she had never known, like she had never thought possible. She had of course seen hunger before at home on the television, but surely she thought nobody had experienced the gnawing cramping pains that she now had in her stomach and abdomen. Her upbringing had not prepared her for an experience that was commonplace to one third of the worlds population. She was bumped along dirt tracks for twenty kilometres, it was no consolation to her that one of the three brothers was also travelling in the back of the steel bodied, poorly suspended pickup.

She knew that she must be a kidnap victim, but could not fathom why her father had been killed. She knew in her heart that there was little or no chance that he could have survived, assuming her father was dead who would pay for her release? Richard? Louise? And how quickly would it be sorted out? She doubted she could stand one more day of such treatment. She felt utterly wretched, filthy and hungry. To compound matters her abdominal pains were not solely those of hunger, her period had come on making her feel even more miserable and squalid. When a few moments later a large knot was knocked out of the side of one of the planks of her crate and a foul smelling penis was poked into the hole by Jorge, the youngest of the three brothers travelling in the rear of the truck accompanied by much laughter, her sense of fear and dread reached a new and altogether all consuming level. After half an hour her journey ended and she was evicted from the crate into what is unimaginable high humidity by the brothers. These men were all native Colombians, rough in dress and rough in manner, they each had large families to feed and no regular income. They survived from one deal to the next, this bonus cargo would provide something extra, perhaps a new truck, new weapons or schooling for several offspring.

Jackie stood in the bright sunlight in dirty, stale clothes, stained with her own urine, vomit and blood. She knew her hatred for these people was misplaced and misdirected, she knew also that she must keep her venom for the perpetrators of this terrible crime against her family and that these people in front of her were no more than hired thugs. But at the moment these people were all she had to hate and she hated them with every cell in her body.

She crumpled to the ground and took in her surroundings. The truck had stopped at what looked to her to be farm buildings and one small wooden house, all were single storey. Beyond the dry dirt road and the various buildings were tall trees, thousands of trees all of the same variety which were unknown to her, two half starved dogs sat nearby looking at her and many birds and insects were airborne and inordinately vocal. She cowered against the side of the pickup truck but was for the moment being ignored by the brothers, all of whom were drinking beers and discussing their next move, Jackie stood up thinking that she might be able to reach the nearest clump of trees before she was missed, both dogs stood to attention bared their teeth and growled, she sat down again, the three men laughed.

The instincts of the two younger men was to pleasure themselves with the blond English woman, it would be a first for them, but the older brother Miguel knew that to get the best price for her she would need to be in better condition than she was. He told his younger brothers this and that once they had collected they could have any woman they wanted for one hundred kilometres. Miguel went into the house to use their two way radio to fix up a meeting later with Diego Perez, a powerful fixer who would buy and sell anything except cocaine, instructing his brothers to hose down the girl and leave her to dry in the sun and find some food and drink for her.

Having fixed the meeting for eight o'clock in the evening and feeling that she would look better in evening light, he returned outside with a clean white blouse that belonged to Liliana his wife who was working in the local town making bread. He knew he would need to hide the girl in the barn later or he would get no peace from his wife, she would always give him hell about his money making schemes but she would later enjoy the benefits of the money.

When he returned outside, Jackie is naked to the waist, screaming and struggling with all her might to keep her jeans on. He roars and fires a shot in the air, his brothers' protest but they know he is the boss and they leave their prey and go into the house in search of more beer. Jackie stands up covering her small breasts and looks to the ground for her clothes, they are ruined and no more than rags, Miguel throws the white blouse to her which she rapidly puts on. He takes her out of the bright sunlight into a barn and tethers her by a long length of thin chain to the heavy timber door frame. He returns to the house, where she can clearly hear an argument has started, she hopes that the older and stronger of the men is able to maintain his domination of the others.

He is soon back with a jug of water, some stale bread and some foul tasting cheese, which Jackie is left alone to eat. It is the first comfort she has had since she was pulled from her father's car in Los Angeles thirty six hours before. She sits down on the straw covered dirt floor and eats the food, the bread is palatable if dipped in water, the cheese is vile, she thinks that it is stale goat cheese but the water is divine, it is fresh and cool, she drinks plenty and cleans her face and hands. The power of fresh water to aid recovery amazes her, she looks around and takes stock of her surroundings and situation.

She is in a poorly preserved, once sound barn. Its solid stone walls and main roof timbers are still in good order but its roof coverings are not. There are numerous shafts and sparkles of daylight showing through the tiles, many of the smaller timbers supporting the tiles are decaying and some have fallen inwards, dislodging or bringing tiles with them. Hanging around the once white painted stone walls now sepia with age are many tools, some wooden handled, some iron, all of them rusted, decades have passed since they were last sharp and in the hands of honest hardworking men. Some of the longer scythe like tools Jackie recognises from her childhood, similar implements were hanging in her grandfather's old work shed. But there were others that she could not guess at their purpose.

How long would she be left in this place alone? But for her two attentive guard dogs, she could only speculate. She could see huge spider's webs everywhere, larger than she had ever seen at home, she did not want to stay long enough to see their creators. If the barn housed spiders what else might it be home to, she speculated, snakes, scorpions?

To one side of the rectangular building was a small stack of firewood, which she supposed there was little demand for in such a humid climate and a small area of the floor had been cleared and was being used to dry what she guessed to be tobacco leaves. Next to the leaves was a collection of tired and disused machinery, she attempted to discern its use, wine or beer making? Or grinding and mashing animal feed were her best guess but like the tools this machinery was long past use, it stood idle, a monument to an industrious age long since passed. Opposite on the other long side of the barn were a row of upright timbers with wide enough gaps between them for the heads of cattle to come through in search of food from the now ruined feed trough. All the timbers had been worn thin and smooth by the necks of generation after generation of hungry animals. She could imagine the cattle rubbing their necks for comfort against the aged timbers and butting their heads together, the building and its use were very familiar to her, similar buildings still existed back at home and one of them was a favourite of hers to play in as a child. At the end of the row of timbers there was a scaled down version for the calves, each space had it own small rusted drinking bowl connected by iron pipe supplying water from outside the barn, this brought back vivid memories of her childhood, she used to love to stroke the calves as they drank. An old and damaged wooden ladder led up to the mezzanine floor, she knew that many years ago animal feed would have been stored to protect it from the weather and vermin, sadly this building and all its memories had perhaps no more than a decade left to stand, unless someone caring and industrious came to is rescue.

She brought her thoughts back to her current situation, where exactly she was and why was she here? She could make no progress with the first question other than a Spanish speaking country and could only speculate on the second, a botched kidnap? Was she wanted as a sex slave, or a brood mare? Her frightening speculations were interrupted by an extremely loud high pitched call from a Howler Monkey, which had momentarily silenced the backdrop of tropical bird sounds, the moments silence passed as soon as it had arrived.

She was feeling extremely uncomfortable in that she needed to defecate, the more she tried to suppress the urge the more the force from within her body let her know it would not be denied. With the dogs disapproval she moved to one corner of the barn and relieved herself, cleaning herself up with semi dry tobacco leaves. The dogs squandered no time and quickly ate her waste. It was late afternoon, perhaps early evening but even in the relative cool of the barn the humidity was very high and the effort of her bowel motion had made her sweat profusely. She was hot, tired, hungry and frightened, she sat back down on her spot and to her surprise, she slept.

She is awoken twenty minutes later by three children who despite being told not to have come to satisfy their curiosity. The two pretty young girls perhaps four and six years old take their lead from their only slightly older brother. The girls who are barefoot and wearing brightly coloured short dresses, timidly reach forward to touch Jackie's hair, she does nothing to alarm them, allowing them to run their grubby fingers through her blonde locks. They talked to her in their native Spanish. She asks them where she is, what country she is in, what is the nearest town, they step away from her laughing, her tongue is alien to them.

The boy steely eyed full of hate unzips himself and begins pissing on her legs, she is shocked by his action. Before he is able to fully empty his bladder a woman Jackie assumes to be his mother approaches from behind him, the thick wasted woman clouts the boy to the side of his head and pulls the children away from the alien. Before she leaves the barn with the children she spits at Jackie, whom the boy and the older girl emulate. The young girl merely mimics the motion, Jackie is paralysed with revulsion at their actions which are beyond her comprehension.

To understand their motivation for such horrific treatment towards her, she needs to know that they believe she is American. Earlier in the year American Delta Force law enforcement troops shot and killed both the woman's brothers in an anti-drugs raid. The boy is one of their sons, as far as her captors are concerned Jackie represents the ultimate enemy. The woman comes back alone and whilst screaming at Jackie she tries violently to retrieve her blouse. She would have been successful in destroying the blouse had she not been halted abruptly by her husband, Miguel, the oldest of the three brothers. A violent argument breaks out between them, they are yelling at each other, the woman pointing out of the barn doors often. She is a Colombian woman and used to having things her own way around the house. It is normal for such women to rule the roost at home, away from the house the men can play at being boss, but here on her doorstep she is the boss. The argument only subsides when the strong thickset man offers physical violence upon his wife. Before leaving the barn defeated the woman suddenly grabs Jackie by the hair screaming at her and rubs her head in the dirt floor, she then spits again at Jackie and is gone.

Miguel now has an expression of exasperation on his face as he looks Jackie directly in the eye, she can see he is making a decision. She has recovered some degree of composure but greatly fears the outcome of her captor's deliberation. She speculates on her fate; will he surrender her to the younger men? Kill her? Or simply abandon her?

She cannot in her mind find the lesser of those evils. She then thinks a little more clearly, she believes that this foul smelling, evil man has paid money for her and he would want a return on his investment, she shudders at what that might be. Clearly a decision has been made, her enslaver strides from the barn purposefully, returning within two minutes with a huge metal bucket filled with water, drawn from the well outside. He places the bucket a metre in front of Jackie, she is petrified and watches his every movement vigilantly. He forces her to kneel in front of the huge bucket. She now believes she is more trouble than she is worth and she is to be drowned like an unwanted farm animal. She fights back with all her might tearing at his clothes and scratching at the skin on his huge muscular arms. She is powerless to prevent her head going below the surface of the water. Once her head is submerged with a huge hand gripping the back of her neck, she closes her eyes, she knows it is futile to resist the enormous power in the arms of her executioner. She thinks of her home, St George's Hall, the rhododendrons, her father in his study and her mother walking the white rose garden, which was her favourite place to be in the early evening, these thoughts are a comfort to her as she relaxes her body and accepts her imminent death. Were it not for the pain in her lungs she could leave this world agreeably. Whilst she is consuming what she believes is her last breath and both her pain and consciousness are fading, Miguel is tousling her hair, now that he has a free hand he is rubbing her filthy hair against her head. To her great surprise, relief and a little disappointment she is pulled back from her watery death, she is left gasping frantically on the floor of the barn, the bucket of cold water is then thrown over her. As she recovers to a state that is part way to normality she is thrown a worn and tattered towel to dry herself. When she is fully recovered from the shock of her brush with death she realises she has just had her hair washed local style, she is then left alone.

Once she is dry she is put into the passenger seat of Miguel's pick up truck and driven away along rough roads, under a near continuous canopy of tall broad leafed trees. After an hour of uncomfortable travelling they reach a small town, the central street is dirt, the buildings to either side are wooden, many with rusting tin roofs, they are obviously commercial properties, Jackie recognises the signs Tabac and Bar.

Just past the small collection of buildings on the main street they stop at a wooden building surrounded by a veranda. Sitting on an old wicker chair is a weasely built man with greased back, jet black hair and a face like a dried olive, one Diego Perez, he is smoking a hand rolled cigarette and drinking what even he would describe as shit, local rum. Jackie's heart jumps in positive anticipation for sat next to the slight man is a much larger uniformed law enforcement officer, she hopes that her captor is handing her to the police. As she is lead up the four uneven wooden steps to join the men her hopes are vanquished. The large man wearing the uniform steps up to her, he moves both his hands in a mock movement as if to grasp her breasts and laughs. Jackie steps away from him and he is gone, down the steps and across the street to one of the many bars that are the high street of the tiny town of La Poyata, population 300, elevation 1410 meters.

Jackie is looked over as one might a pony that is being considered before being purchased for a child.

The slimy looking dealer in whatever product is in demand, be it vehicles, animals, weapons or humans, but never drugs, that is someone else's domain, nods to Miguel and the three of them move indoors. Jackie looks around before entering the building, she considered screaming with all her might for help, but then remembered that even the local law enforcement will not lift a finger in her favour, she saves her breath. The dealer more closely examines her, Miguel holds her arms behind her whilst her jeans are opened and her bloody knickers are lowered to confirm what is needed to be known. Perez is satisfied, money changes hands, Miguel is happy to be unburdened, his wife will be very happy.

Jackie is locked in a back room, given clean clothes and ordered in Spanish to shower, which she both understands and finds agreeable but is uncomfortable that she is unable to secure the door to her room from the inside. The water is warm and wonderfully invigorating. When just half dry she dresses and is then given a plate of fried chicken and rice and a hairbrush. The food is good, she is grateful for the hairbrush but asks herself, what is this fascination with her hair? She is left in the locked room to sleep.

SOLITUDE, SUBORDINATION?

In the morning Jackie is given bread and coffee for breakfast. Her white blouse and jeans have been washed, dried and pressed and are given back to her with clear instruction by hand signals that they are to be worn. Whatever the next step along her strange and frightening journey is, clearly this foul little man was leaving nothing to chance, she must look her best. This makes her fear the worst. She is shackled at her ankles and wrist and put into a car whose rank odour makes her wonder why it was imperative that she had to be presentable. She tried several times to converse with the driver, who has clearly invested a great deal of money in her and is anxious to see a quick profit. A long journey ensues, not into a large town or city as she expected but deep into the rain forest, which for Jackie feels even more sinister and threatening, but looking for something positive she reminds herself that nothing could feel more threatening than having her hair washed by Miguel, who would now be able to buy a new vehicle and send his two deceased brothers in-laws five children to school.

After more than four hours travelling they arrive at a road check manned by four men, who were sufficiently armed to win a small war, the driver reaches over to Jackie and brushes her hair. He also speaks quickly to the armed men and they are allowed to continue their journey. After another mile or so under a complete canopy of trees the vehicle reaches the gates of a huge compound. This is the second level of security, there are more to follow. The car is left behind, Jackie's feet are unbound and the local people around the fringe of the compound are curious and well armed. As they penetrate further into the collection of buildings, past a laundry, a small medical centre, a school house and amongst others a bake house, people become more relaxed and few weapons are visible, as Jackie and her warder pass between two buildings she is awestruck by what she sees ahead of her. She stops walking to take in the vista. Sitting above all other structures is a four storey flat roofed building. It is large by

211

any standards, each storey has what appears to be a wrap around veranda. The walls are almost fully glazed.

Mr Slimy tugs at her "sí sí, sí su nuevo hogar." (Your new home) On the roof of the four-storey palace is a sleek black helicopter. Jackie doesn't know it yet but it is the home of Jhiro de Montaya de Vale de Cabrerra, the man who calls the tune for more than one hundred miles in all directions and is the patron of over two thousand local people.

She feels she is in an oasis, she conjures all that words many connotations, retreat, hideaway, haven and sanctuary they are all relevant. She is surrounded by exotic tropical trees and palms, pineapples and mangoes, the backdrop to which is howling monkeys, screeching parrots, toucans and massive security.

Jackie is instantly aware that whoever owns this compound, the main house and helicopter is a very wealthy and powerful man. They walk amongst many children, chickens and women going about their daily task, all of whom with the exception of the chickens pause to view the new arrival.

After passing through a low barrier designed to keep out everything undesirable, children and chickens included, they are now walking in ornate gardens that border the main house on all four sides, up three terraces of six steps, the gardens become more and more ornamental and decorative until they are on the ostentatious paved terrace that immediately encircles the edifice that dominates the entire enclosure. Before they walk into an office on the ground floor Jackie pauses to look up, she is aware of two figures on the second floor observing her, she is unable to focus on faces but she is able to determine two male figures, one hopelessly obese, the other slim, she knows that both are looking down on her.

Outwardly she is looking the most presentable that she has since she sat in her father's hired Rolls-Royce in Los Angeles, inwardly she is feeling like a second hand car that has been given a superficial lick of paint to gain a better price. She is so bewildered and traumatised by recent events that she calmly sits on a chair in the corner of the office to await her fate. The giant man who had watched them enter the building comes into the room, a few guarantees are sought in Spanish from the dealer and after satisfactory replies are received a bargain is struck. The

212

dealer Diego Perez leaves and collects a large sum of money, which is on his car seat when he reaches his vehicle, there will be no more shit rum for him, it will be imported whisky and clean whores for the next two years, Jackie never sees him again.

She is left in the Spartan office with the enormous Colombian. She stands up and says,

"Ok fat man, just you try it on and I'll kick your balls until they're black." He politely nods to Jackie unties her hands and knocks twice on the door behind him. Two beautiful young women come into the room, they are dressed in pretty floral dresses and each has a flower in their hair to match those in the material, they lead Jackie back through the door from which they came. Jackie estimated the two girls to be around twenty years old, they are a breath of fresh air after her last wardens. The girls give Jackie their names Natalia Nadia and Fernanda Catalina, Jackie responses by given her name, which comes back to her as 'Jzzaki'. They lead her up one flight of internal stairs to a room that contains a small kitchen and dining area, food is laid out for her and she is able to serve herself lunch, a glass of white wine was offered but she refused, she was going to keep a clear head for when Mr Big tried it on. She tried repeatedly to question the two girls as to her whereabouts and what was expected of her. They did not understand a word of English. After lunch the two girls bathed her as though she were a princess, whilst washing her they would occasionally touch her blonde pubic hair and grin sheepishly, once clean she was given modern western style tampons for her period and she was dressed in a thin cotton dress which was much more comfortable than denim jeans in the high humidity that she was assuming was the norm, the girls sat her down and spent an hour drying, brushing and making a fuss of her hair, which was now beautiful.

She was now comfortable, clean, fed and well clothed, but she was braced for the battle ahead. Each time she had changed hands it had been for roughly ten times the previous value and each time her sense of dread had increased, she felt that this last exchange was final. Conditions for her were now finer than they had been previously but somehow it felt fouler. The food, the bathing, the clothes and the attention were not she knew purely for her well being, she felt like a birthday cake, put together with loving care, but she was planning to spoil someone's party.

The two girls stay with her all afternoon and evening, they cook for her, fuss over her, and prevented her from leaving the house. Eventually after a long confusing day in which she has only understood the words 'sí' and 'ninguno' she is shown to her bedroom, but throughout the later part of the day anxiety has built up in her. She begins to panic and is overcome by fear, shouting 'no, no, no', she grips onto one of the girls, they try to calm her but she is inconsolable and after a distressful period she has a full blown panic attack.

She is screaming for her father and suffers a breakdown, the girls stay with her, applying cool rags to her brow and are constantly reassuring her, each time she wakes in the night she goes into panic, the girls who are sleeping in the room next to her respond immediately and each time she is calmed by their close and sympathetic attention.

This becomes a pattern for her next ten days, calm orderly days in which she is allowed to walk in the upper tier of the gardens, which she takes a degree of comfort from with its backdrop of jungle sounds, and beautiful visiting butterflies and hummingbirds, but as the day turns into night she suffers repeated bouts of anxiety and panic attacks, her sleep is broken by frightening nightmares of being in a small dark place with no exit, she is surrounded by animals and people who are baying for her blood.

On the tenth night she wakes only twice and her bed is not wet, in the morning the two girls who have been in constant attention know she has made progress and that she is exorcising her demons. During this ten-day period she sees few people other than Natalia and Fernanda, those who see her during the day are always fascinated by her hair, in the compound she is the object of much excitement. She tries to talk to everyone she sees but apart from a smile and "sí, sí " she gets no response, other than the desire to touch her hair. Many of the women who work in the compound bring their small children to see her believing it is good luck if their young infants touch her hair. For many of the peasants in this wild part of Colombia she is the first or in some cases only the second person they have ever seen with blonde hair. The two girls that bathe her every day spend a great deal of time brushing and handling her hair, this is part of her afternoon routine which she has grown to find both comforting and therapeutic, it is part of the reason that she eventually is able to face the dark and the loneliness of going to bed. She is in her third week before she sleeps through and by this time the wet beds are no longer a thing of the night.

Often during the day a black helicopter takes off or lands on the roof above, the girls usually point and say Jefe, meaning boss or chief but Jackie assumed the man's name is Jefe and when Jefe comes for her she will be ready, she is surprised the helicopter can carry his bulk.

Her one overriding frustration is the fact that she is unable to communicate with her girl wardens. That no one can or will speak English to her is a constant vexation, this is enough sometimes to bring on a feeling of such isolation that she can feel a panic attack rising in her chest, her throat is dry and tight, she learns to control her breathing, not to hyperventilate, to breath slowly and rhythmically, she is then able to suppress the rising storm within her.

Her routine continued until after her next period, she is then moved up to a bedroom on the next floor, the third, just one level down from the floor whose flat roof supports the helicopter. Her last room was plain and sparsely furnished, this new room is gargantuan, its furnishings luxurious, its enormous window looks over the not distant jungle and has doors that open onto its own veranda, two large ceiling fans and every comfort a paying guest at a luxury hotel could expect including a huge comfortable bed.

Her panic re-visits her for the first two nights in her new room, she wedges a chair against the inside door handle to provide herself with a little false security, knowing deep down if Mr Big wants to enter the room he has only to lean on the door and it will fold under his bulk. She is surprised that she has not suffered any indignities since her arrival at the jungle compound. Always when she is alone her thoughts are of her father, Richard and the situation now at St Georges, she has become ever more

215

suspicious of Richards role in her current position, but always reserves her venom for Louise, who she now thinks of as the evil stepmother but is loath to use the word mother in connection with Louise, preferring the word witch. She is often overcome with sadness for her own mother and cries privately for her loss, but not to be able to attend her father's funeral and to be so remote from his and her home is beginning to draw from her another emotion, anger. It is this anger that she will nurture and hold onto that will ultimately sustain her and see her through her anxiety and panics, it is her anger that will give her something of herself to grasp on to, to use to fight back.

Her new room, which has its own beautiful well equipped en-suite, has no lock on either side of its door, she continues to jamb a chair against the door knob at night but recognises its futility, outside her bedroom is a well equipped lounge with its own kitchen area, each morning a maid, another pleasant young girl provides bread and coffee, both are delicious. She continues to try to communicate with her new maid, she talks to her in English at all times, after another week of solitude she shouts and screams at her maid and breaks down in tears, begging to be told where she is, what country she is in and why. She cannot accept that no one speaks any English. Her maid Catalina gazes around furtively to make sure she is not overlooked or overheard, she draws a finger across her lips in an internationally recognised symbol for silence, she then writes on a small piece of paper. 'Colombia, new wife for boss man' Jackie starts to speak but it silenced by the hand of Catalina, she whispers,

"You do speak English." The maid shakes her head and again puts her finger to her lips, she then screws up the note, which she puts in her skirt pocket.

After one more day the maid is changed for a young girl of no more than sixteen, she doesn't see Catalina again for a long time. Now at least she knows she is in the Colombian rain forest, she ask herself what does she know of Colombia, she believes it is neighbours with Brazil and Venezuela and perhaps Peru and Ecuador but she is not sure. The country was named after Christopher Columbus and is known for its production of coffee and cocaine. This is the sum total of her knowledge, she is a little surprised that she cannot name a single person from Colombia.

She knows also that she is 'new wife to boss man', the enormous and obese Jefe.

She tells herself that if some evil, sweaty, fat, Hispanic thinks I'm his wife, well he's in for a shock, I'll kill him, I'll kill myself, but then she realises that if he's paid for her in his eyes she is technically his. A few minutes after seeing the note she ran from the house, through the tiered garden, through the lower compound past many people, mainly women and children but also some men. They all watch her bemused, no one attempts to stop her, she eventually leaves behind the last of the wooden buildings and runs into the jungle. Her legs are quickly tangled in vines, it is difficult to make progress, she is no more than sixty meters into the thick lush undergrowth when she is brought to a halt by a raucous call from a red howler monkey, followed by an ear splitting shriek from a macaw. She stops and looks around her, the canopy above is almost totally blocking out the hot morning sun, the humidity under the trees is 100% and above her is a yellow tree frog which she focus's on for a moment until it is devoured by a large green tree snake. She knows she has made a huge mistake. There are airborne insects of size and colour beyond her experience, she runs as best she can back to the edge of the compound.

She knows she is defeated, the dense green under growth of the rain forest is totally impenetrable and filled with hazards beyond her knowledge. She returns to the house, her retreat is watched by many people, as she make her way back everyone smiles at her, some laugh and make gestures with their hands like spiders and snakes. Everyone understands her position, she is stuck in the compound unless the boss man, the Jefe releases her. She goes back to her room barricades herself in and cries for her murdered father, her mother, St Georges and her normal life. The maid tries the door to her room, but cannot enter, she feels she has won a small victory.

The maid leaves her, everyone leaves her, after twenty-four hours, desperately hungry she moves her barricade of furniture to one side and comes out for coffee and bread. Once again watched by many she walks to the edge of the jungle and stands alone and considers her options, she has none. She tries to walk toward the only exit road which is completely concealed from above by the tree canopy. This road is heavily guarded by armed men and dogs, the men smile at her and wave their guns in the air. Once again she returns to her room and builds a hindrance of furniture across her door, but then knocks down the obstruction in self-mocking defeat, she sobs for her old life and cries at her new predicament.

On regaining her composure she decides that she has cried her last tears, she will fight back, she will work out a strategy. She will not be defeated. She is in a beautiful house, her bedroom wardrobes are full of beautiful clothes, her bathroom is well equipped with toiletries, her food is prepared for her, she wants for nothing but freedom, she decides to use whatever she can in whatever way possible to release herself from what is in effect house arrest.

The next day she is having her evening meal alone in her modest kitchen-dinning room when a door opens she has never seen used. A slim attractive man of around forty years enters the room, she has never seen this man before, she is surprised by his appearance, he is clean shaven, has clean hands and is well dressed, he speaks to her in Spanish, she picks up her knife and holds it up in preparation to strike. He smiles at her, his teeth are pure white and straight, he introduces himself at Jhiro de Montaya De Val De Cabrerra, she notices just the first hint of grey at his temples. His plain white shirt is in contrast to all the other men she has seen within the compound and it fits him perfectly, as do his tan coloured trousers, they could have been made to measure, his shoes look to be very expensive perhaps Italian leather, his abdomen is flat and firm, this is a man who has looked after himself. He is softly spoken, he serves himself a plate of fish and rice from the kitchen area and brings it to the table, as he puts it down he asks Jackie in Spanish if it is ok with her if he joins her to eat. She just stares at him, her arms now folded in defence. She half understands his gestures and merely shrugs to him in reply. He eats his meal not more than a meter from her, she recommences eating her meal with her fork only, the knife is locked into her right hand. This close to her the man's personal hygiene is evident. He has a freshly washed appearance and his cologne is a fragrance she knows but cannot recall its name. The man is very well presented and does not wear a ring

218

on any finger but has two rings, one a man's and one a woman's hanging on a thin gold chain around his neck. He has no tattoo's she can see, but she notices that many years ago he wore an earring in his left ear. Jackie's body language continues to be totally negative, even when her mealtime companion offers her a glass of wine from a bottle he opens. She shakes her head. He talks to her intermittently, he ask about her day, is her room OK, does she like the clothes in her room, if not he can have them changed, and would she like to share his bed for the night. As every word is spoken in Spanish she understands nothing of it. After an hour of silence on her part and occasional burst of speech on his part, his is an eloquence that says very little, hers if a silence that says much, he picks up his wine glass bids her politely goodnight and leaves through the same door with which he entered, leaving the door open.

Jackie still silent, finally releases the knife from her right hand, her hand is so stiff and cramped she would have not been able to mount any kind of effective defence. On taking her plate back to the small kitchen area she passes the open door and is unable to stop herself glancing through the opening. It is a bedroom three times the size of hers, as is the enormous bed that occupies a large portion of the room. The man she ignored at the table is nowhere to be seen, but she can hear him talking in the room. A telephone is put down, as he moves into her view Jackie steps out of his.

She sits awake in bed for many hours digesting this new experience before sleep finally overcomes her.

The next morning she attempts in gestures and signs to find out from the young maid who he was, each time she points at his bedroom door the maid replies sí, sí, Jefe. Her mistake begins to dawn on her that this word everyone uses is not the man's name but it confirms his status. He is the boss, not the grossly obese monster she had assumed. She asks herself if this well groomed, almost polished individual is the top man of this entire operation, why has he not forced himself upon her? She has been under no duress, she has experienced no coercion from him or those who do his bidding.

She spends most of the long uneventful day outside the main house on the shaded veranda, the daily novelty that is the multitudinous and colourful humming birds that visit the extensively flowered terrace are only eclipsed by the myriad species of kaleidoscopic butterflies, there is so much to hold her attention. Added to which is the sound of the rain forest, the many types of fruit eating birds and monkeys compete day long for the ears of those who will listen, but she is today pacing the wooden deck almost blind and deaf, Who is he? What does he expect of her? Why does he hold back? She has been here six weeks and last evening was the first time since the day she arrived that she had been in a room with a male, he is the first man to have spoken to her. She is confused, is she an ornament, or a toy, a possession or a pleasure yet to be sampled? Clearly someone here, it must be this Jefe, has a keen interest in her, so why the suspense? Why the waiting game? She decided that she too can procrastinate. She is feeling mentally stronger of late, her nights are now infrequently disturbed, now that she has a focus for her anger, she feels that she too can play the long game.

Her evenings are now the business end of the day, she is joined in her dinning area each evening at eight o'clock by Jefe, he serves himself food from that which is prepared by the staff and brings it with him to the table, he politely ask Jackie if she would like wine, she always declines, despite her desire to do the opposite. He speaks often in his now familiar deep but softly spoken way, she imagines he would suit the role of a narrator, he appears to both choose his words thoughtfully and deliver them with care. She considers taking her food into her room to dine alone, but rejects the idea as a backward and defensive move. She is beginning to feel she has nothing to fear from this well presented and uncommonly hygienic man. She decides to stay and deal with him face to face.

She remains silent, each evening as he leaves the table he picks up his unfinished wine and departs, always leaving the door open through which he leaves. On the sixth such evening as he prepares to depart he slowly and carefully reaches his right hand toward her face, she grips her knife tightly in her right hand. His hand which is moving ever more slowly towards her neck gently lifts her blonde hair away from her shoulder and allows it to

220

slowly sift through his fingers, as a child might release sand from its hand whilst dreamily preoccupied on a beach. Satisfied he has crossed a new threshold he withdraws into his open room for the night. The next morning the black Sikorsky helicopter lifts off from the roof and he is gone for four days.

She is still expecting him to appear each evening, and knowing that she is making a small degree of extra effort with her appearance, which is causing her perplexity. Each evening she chooses clothes from her extensive wardrobe with a little more care, she repeatedly tells herself that she can play this man's game.

On the fifth night he reappears, immaculately dressed as always, toward the end of their evening during which he has told her as always in completely incomprehensible Spanish, the details of his last four days, he steps forward and allows her hair to run through his fingers. As he does this she allows her focus to fix on his eyes for the first time. His clear dark brown eyes are full of sadness, his face still smoothly skinned for a man of perhaps forty only gives away its age around the periphery of his eyes, there is evidence of a lifetime of squinting against the fierce Colombian sun. For a fleeting moment they share each other's sadness, Jackie breaks the spell by lifting her head up and sharply to the left, shaking her hair from his fingers. He withdraws to his room, as he leaves he makes an open hand gesture towards her to encourage her to follow him, she is unmoved.

During the night she wakes several times and relives the compassion and sadness of the man's eyes, but it is her anger that rises to the surface. At a little after three am she leaves her room, stands in the doorway of his room and screams a volley of abuse at him, she rants on the subjects of her fathers murder and her nightmare journey that has brought her to her current impasse, she slams the door and returns to her room. He is unmoved, he views her outburst as a positive sign, a progression, now they are communicating.

Three more days go by much as before, he talks, she remains silent, after touching her hair he invites her by gestures into his room, she remains stoic and outwardly unemotional, but longs for human companionship and intelligent conversation.

221

In the next six weeks the template of behaviour established to date is consolidated into a predictable pattern. For several days Jefe is away in his helicopter then for several days he returns. She often visits the edge of the rain forest during the day, or wanders a short tolerable distance down the exit road toward the manned obstacle, but knows that both options are closed to her. Always she returns to the huge opulent house which she views as both her prison and her refuge. On the nights she is alone she often sits on the veranda if it is a cloudless night, the beauty of the stars is beyond her previous experience and is only bettered by those who know long sea voyages where light pollution is unknown. On the nights he is present she plays the game and sits opposite him in silence. Her frustration at not being able to speak to anyone is building within her, she feels she is experiencing the most vexing form of social solitude.

She endures another week of his absence during which she manages by sign language to obtain pens and copious quantities of A4 paper, she has decided to record everything she can remember of her life, from as far back as her memory will allow. This new occupation is both refreshingly time consuming and hugely therapeutic. Starting with her grandparents and on to her earliest school friends, nanny's and pony's, she fills tomes of pages and relives every incident that is in her sphere of recollection. She regrets not beginning this work earlier, but is satisfied that she has begun a task that is proving to be restorative, almost medicinal to her. Her days are consumed in this way and her evenings are either solitary, which she shares with the stars and the jungle noises and fruit bats, or they are social but companionless, spent opposite Jefe at the dinner table. Increasingly she feels that the enmity between them is from her part, there appears to be no measurable hostility from across the table.

If the helicopter is absent she allows herself to drink wine, sometimes a bottle in an evening, the quality of which astounds her, but if the sleek black machine is on the roof she will not allow herself even a glass, for she knows its power to affect human judgement. Her self-disciplined, self appointed day time curative task of recording the details of her known life, is giving her both purpose and inner strength, so mentally recuperative is her mission proving that she surprises herself after Jefe's latest absence. Toward the end of the evening as he moves to touch her hair she verbally and physically attacks him.

She stands to face him and harangues him with a verbal rant that covers all of her frustrations fears and desires and as she spouts forth her tirade she hits him time and time again, to his chest his shoulders and his face, in all she hits him more than a hundred times. He does not defend himself, he is motionless, by the time she has run out of words to scream and energy to swing her arms he is left with blood trickling from his right eye and his bottom lip, his crisp, cleanly laundered white shirt is both blood spotted and torn beyond use. She is exhausted and sits down and is disappointed with herself that he is still standing and that she is in tears. He is experiencing more pain and soreness to his previously unblemished face than he will ever admit to anyone. He stands in silence looking down at her, blood dripping onto his shirt. He is debating with himself if the time is now right to make a huge concession, a revelation to the tearful but far from pitiful woman who sits in front of him, he holds back, something prevents him. He feels immense admiration for Jackie and he has respect for her fortitude, but still judges that this is not the time for a dramatic expose'. He steps back from her, holds his right hand out toward his bedroom door and calmly says through bloodied lips in Spanish, "Te gustaria venir a mi cama" (Would you care to come to my bed). She is bowed but far from defeated, she looks him in his slightly bruised and bloodied eyes and replies quietly,

"If you ask me nicely in English to come to your bed, you may be pleasantly surprised." Now his instinct tells him the time is perfect. He replies in near perfect English,

"OK. Jhiro will be very happy if you accept the offer of his bed for the night." She is stunned by his reply, she sits for a moment stupefied, open mouthed, she recovers from the revelation, takes several calming deep breathes and responds saying,

"Why didn't you tell me you could speak English before and how did you learn to speak it so well?"

"Jhiro learn to speak it in London and in Bath, in the West of England." "You have been to England, to Bath?"

223

SUMMER 1988

KRIS

Taking his book notes with him Jude boards a train with a single ticket to Taunton, in a repeat of his actions of a year ago. He was looking forward to the discipline of hard work, long days, short evenings and sleeping like the dead. Unsuccessfully he was attempting to conceal from himself the degree to which he would miss Liz. He had not expected anyone to make such a dent in his mental wall so soon. He felt that this was the case for both of them, that Liz, like himself had been burnt and was not looking for any kind of emotional tie.

His meeting with Kris was a genuine pleasure, albeit that the weather had turned to rain and their first day together was a non-productive one. After catching up on each other's winter experiences, Kris spent the afternoon reading and Jude scribbling, which is how he describes his attempts at writing. Nick joined them the next morning, which was a bright, dry, windy morning, the three of them swung back into their last year's routine on the season's first silage cut, like the old hands they were.

Kris had spent his winter snow-compacting on the ski slopes of his native Finland and confessed to Jude that he had taken an option on an 80,000 hectare parcel of tundra which he believed was perfect for his future plans. Which were to set up a snow-mobile and cross-country ski training and trekking area in the winter, and a camping, fishing, walking and quad biking area in the summer. He hinted that this summer was possibly his last in England. This depended on his selling the idea to his father, he had encouraged him to come in as a financial partner, otherwise he would need two more summers of driving. Now that he had a purchase option on a suitable parcel of land, he was keen to put his plans into practice.

On their third evening together Jude opened up regarding his previous trip to Colombia and the reason for it. Kris joked that he would look out for Jayne's and Jude's book if it ever got onto the shelves. Nick's exasperated comment to Jude is,

"You're as bad as 'im. One writing and the other always reading, don't know what you see in them books. Now give me a manual on a British tank, a Hurricane or Spitfire and I'll show you a book worthy of killing an evening."

The three men swiftly fell back into their familiar duties. Kris would call the tune as to their start time, breaks and finishing time, he would record all work done regarding acreage and tonnage and liaised with the boss Jack Mortimer concerning their hours worked, general progress and transportation needs. Nick was as always the spanner man, he would set up the machinery, service, lubricate and maintain all mechanical equipment as required, which would often entail him disappearing on wet days for lubricants, filters and parts.

Jude was as before, responsible for all their domestic needs, sleeping arrangements, food, laundry and shopping. It was a sharing of labour that worked handsomely. All three men took their own responsibilities seriously and did not begrudge the other two their duties. Kris would have loathed the obligations of the domestic chores as much as Nick would have found Kris's tasks both onerous and tedious, and Jude would have recoiled from Nick's mechanical burden. As abhorrent as they felt each others' assignments were, if any one of the three of them was overburdened, help was swiftly to hand.

The first two weeks of the season were hit and miss due to the vagaries of English weather, almost alternating a fine day with a damp one, which was a blow to productivity, as even on the dry days it would often be late morning before the crop was sufficiently dry to cut. By mid-April a high-pressure system settled over the United Kingdom and showed no signs of shifting. The fine weather persisted for almost twelve weeks, making the spring and summer of that year a most memorable one.

Nick had to leave for several days in late May to put one of his kids back on the straight and narrow. His temporary replacement was a young man of twenty-eight, he was single, strong and fit, in spite of his enthusiastic consumption of alcohol.

His name was Dennis Rothwell, his regular employment was that of a JCB digger driver. Jack Mortimer had pulled him in from an agency, it was Kris and Jude's task to knock him into shape quickly, his driving and concentration levels were quickly up to scratch, but on a personal level he was a handful. When not driving he was constantly grumbling, complaining and moaning, and where ever he went he was accompanied by a small radio playing shit music, he snored like a buffalo and he would consume more food and drink than Jude and Kris combined, for a tall leanly built young man, his appetite was staggering.

On his fourth and last day as Nick's stand-in, he left Nick an additional task, he caught the right hand edge of a silage cutter on a heavy oak gate post whilst leaving the yard to commence the last shift of the day. Such was the force of the collision the entire assembly was twisted, all its mounting brackets either broken or contorted beyond use, Kris's reaction was uncharacteristically aggressive. Jude later put his extreme response down to the fact that they were on their last session at a farm which was far from their favourite. The farmer was a particularly tight-fisted man, bordering on genuinely mean, their sleeping arrangements left a lot to be desired, their breakfast was meagre, offers of tea or other refreshments were infrequent, and transportation to a local hostelry was sporadic at best.

The damage to the machine could result in their remaining on the farm for an additional day, if Kris and Jude could not cover the supplementary work by driving well into the evening. These thoughts and Dennis's under reaction, his almost casual response to the incident, brought out a singularly harsh backlash from Kris. Had Jude not been there to witness it, he would not have believed it. Under personnel verbal attack Dennis's adrenalin and testosterone levels soon matched that of Kris, the two men were remonstrating, which soon escalated to the physical, they were grappling with each other which inevitably due to the intensity of the exchange resulted in angry blows aimed at each others heads. Jude quickly intervened, catching a fist square to his nose for his trouble, from which man the punch was delivered he was unsure, but he did get between them, his eyes watering, his nose blooded. He pulled Dennis away from Kris, shouting 'leave it' many times. He escorted the younger man back to the farmyard, waited whilst he stowed his few possessions in his backpack and drove him to the nearest railway station. Not even bothering to request the loan of the landowner's Land Rover, the keys for which were permanently in the ignition. They spoke little during the eight-minute journey, Jude gave Dennis twenty pounds for his train fare and was glad to see the back of him. He never imagined a replacement for Nick could be more difficult than him to live with.

When he returned to the farm, the farmer was standing hands on hips in an arrogant pose, waiting to tear a strip from Jude, whose nose had by now swollen and coloured up considerably, the stinging sensation had undergone a metamorphosis into a deep throbbing and spreading pain. Jude anticipated a negative exchange with farmer Wiseman, knowing that attack was the best form of defence, he delivered his riposte prematurely. Pointing at farmer Wiseman's face he said,

"Don't say a word, I took the Land Rover to get rid of the bastard who did this to me." Now pointing to his own swollen nose and rapidly closing eyes. "He wanted to do it to you, claimed he'd never seen so much space on a breakfast plate, or been so thirsty and hungry in his life, so I did you a favour, your Land Rover is still in one piece and I've got work to do." He turned and walked to his tractor, fired it up and joined Kris in the forty acre field, which was now to be their afternoons and evenings work, he sported a wry smile, he was at ease with his exchange with Mr Wiseman, if not with his own face. A warm south-easterly drying wind aided the efforts of the two men, by holding back the onset of the evening dew until almost midnight, they completed their task shortly after ten pm, tired and very hungry, with no idea where the next meal was coming from. They need not have been concerned, it was not only the nature of the pain to Jude's face that had undergone a metamorphosis but also the attitude of farmer Wiseman. A generous evening meal awaited them and the accompanying half pint of beer each resulted in a sardonic smile between the two men. This was their first exchange since Jude's intervention between Kris and his protagonist. After the meal they thanked Mr Wiseman, who in turn thanked Jude for his earlier intrusion between himself and Dennis. Kris drew a breath to question the exchange but was rapidly shoved through the farmhouse kitchen door towards their crude lodgings by Jude, who later explained his less than tactful, one-way conversation with the farmer, Kris smiled and replied,

"I couldn't work out why all of a sudden he'd become charitable, well done, he thought that little shit was gunning for him."

"He wasn't a little shit Kris, he was a big stack of shit."

"Wasn't he just."

"What the hell was all that about this afternoon?"

"Look I'm sorry."

"You don't have to apologise to me."

"I do, it's my fault your face looks like its been hit by a tree."

"Feels like it too, that little shit as you called him, packed a big punch."

"It wasn't him, it was me, I'm sorry."

"You, you did this?" Jude laughed, "I should have taken you to the station, why did you explode?"

"It was his attitude, he was a thoughtless, selfish bugger. The three of us put up with long hard days, we don't complain we just get on with it, we all know its tough, and we suffer in silence. That's what makes it work, you Nick and me we just do what we have to do. I know at the end of a fifteen hour day you're done in, because I am. That shit never let up, his shoulders ached, his neck ached, he was hungry - greedy bastard ate everything in sight, he snored like a pregnant pig, the final straw was when he mangled that cutter. I said to him 'how the fuck did you manage that?' he looked at me smiled and said 'chill out, shit happens', I wanted to rip his head off." Jude replied in a very calm and posh voice,

"And please inform me, how frequently has this psychopathic tendency towards decapitation surfaced? I only request this information because I suffer from selfish, survival tendencies myself." They laughed the episode into diminishment, Jude took four painkillers and slept like a baby.

The next day was not a productive one, other than a fine breakfast, courtesy of farmer Wiseman, the rest of the day was not one to be proud of. Nick arrived around lunchtime with the necessary mounting brackets to repair the damaged machine, which took him the rest of the day to effect. Jude had left soon after breakfast to track the fifteen miles to their next contract, Kris joined him early afternoon after hanging back to assist Nick with the heavy lifting. Nick finally joined them a little after eight pm in time to adjourn the days work and drive the short distance to the Horse and Groom public house, for sausage, mash and several pints of London Pride all round. Even Kris broke his rule of only drinking two pints, as Jude had said that the Land Rover knew its own way home.

Nick found the tale of the previous days pantomime highly amusing, he said that had it not been for the multi-coloured bruising, which had now spread across Jude's face, he would have doubted the whole story. The following day, normality was restored, the grass was dry enough to cut by ten am, and productivity was back to its usual high level. Over the following six weeks the heat of the day combined with a mild, warm breeze, reduced the level of night dews to a bare minimum. They were often able to commence cutting by nine am, a rare treat, giving them more time at the end of the day, when it was best appreciated. In the early evenings Nick would tinker with their machinery, Kris would read, and Jude scribble and all of them would consume various quantities of local bitter in the nearby public houses' at their leisure.

On a warm June day, a half hour before lunch, Nick ran his machine into an obstruction. They had been warned by the land owner, William Orr, that the recent phenomenon and annual pestilence that was the crop circle makers, had been seen locally and that both he and the neighbouring farm had been targeted. He remarked that they needed to be particularly careful to avoid any paraphernalia which may have been left behind. The object that Nick's machine tried to devour was not crop circle maker's paraphernalia, but a crop circle maker.

At first Nick did not recognise what he had hit, he thought it to be an old deer carcass or a large bundle of rags. He stopped his combine, which had been harvesting malting barley as soon as his reflexes would allow. Climbing down to ground level he walked to the front of the broad header which scooped into its throat everything that was in its path, he was greatly surprised by the scene that confronted him. Not shocked as this was a man who had served two terms with the British army in Northern

230

Ireland, a man who had collected limbs of fellow service men and friends post incident in Newry, Armagh and Belfast. Had it been either of the other two members of their crew that had made the discovery they would have suffered a great deal of revulsion, for it was indeed a grisly unearthing. Nick immediately recognised the object for what it was, a corpse not recently deceased. The blades that cut the stalks of barley had dislodged chunks of flesh, the lack of blood being evident to the bodies past demise. He spoke to Kris and Jude neither of whom had a desire to view the obstacle, they were openly grateful that it had been Nick who had made the discovery, as they both knew that they would not have coped anything like as well as he had. They knew nick to be the most problematic of the three of them, but he gained enormous respect from them both by the dignified way he dealt with the problem. They carried on with their work knowing that Nick's machine would now be down for the rest of the day. They now had extra acreage to cut and knew that it would result in another very late finish. They were happy to be enclosed in their machines. Nick did what he knew he must, he locked his combine and walked back to Mr Orr's farmhouse to call the police.

Two officers arrived by car an hour later, the elder of the two Sergeant Wilson took the incident in his long and experienced stride, the much younger P C Brett was affected by what he saw and subsequently slept badly for the next two weeks due to nightmares which he never admitted to anyone, least it be a sign of weakness. But with patience and understanding from his young wife the flaw was ironed out of his sub-consciousness, though she felt that from that moment on he was akin to a little boy who had lost his belief in Father Christmas. Sergeant Wilson called in forensic assistance, a team of three pathologists arrived mid-afternoon and Nick was resigned to not completing his acreage from the moment that he had recognised exactly what it was that he had scooped into the header of his machine. It took the two men and one woman a further three hours to free the body, pausing often to photograph the operation. Their final report would take two weeks to complete and it would then be the task of the police to decide a course of action.

231

What the police would discover in time from the two usable fingerprints and dental records and Jude, Kris and Nick would never know, was that the body, which had been deceased six days prior to its discovery, had once been a certain Adrian Needham. Mr Needham had changed his name on two occasions, firstly to Mark Ryder and later to Sean Lawson, which hampered the efforts of identification by the law enforcement team assigned to the case. The pathologist were able to establish cause of death to be a broken neck attributed to a possible blow from behind to the base of the skull, but as Nick's combine harvester had removed sufficient chunks of flesh from the neck, thereby removing all surface bruising, the exact cause of Mr Needham's broken neck would never be discovered. At the inquest which was held in September, the Coroner recorded on open verdict. Nobody ever came forward to formally identify the corpse. It took local police four and a half months to link the disappearance of Bristol betting shop owner Sean Lawson, with the body of Adrian Needham found in the barley field in North Somerset. It would eventually be almost three decades later that the local force would receive a letter from a recently deceased Mr Robert Telford of Limassol, Cyprus, that would close the dormant case.

The officers assigned to the case never discovered Mr Needham or Mr Lawson's exact cause of death, had Jude or his companions known Mr Needham, or Mr Lawson as he was currently identified by his driving licence, they would have been acutely begrudging with their sympathies, for he was not a pleasant person. He owned and ran a betting shop in the outskirts of Bristol, which he used to supply himself with sufficient cash to feed his dual habits of illegal drugs and gullible, beautiful, young women. The thirty-six year old had left a trail of destruction in his wake. He was an extremely calculating and callous individual, with his hand consistently in the till. He would without fail take just one percent of his turnover in cash, so as not to attract the attention of revenue inspectors, his tax returns were consistent in that they showed a profit slightly below the eleven percent national average. This would have eventually flagged up an extra-ordinary inspection, which he did not live to witness. His best days were the class-one races, the annual horse racing events that captured the imagination of the general public -The Derby, The Grand National, The Cheltenham Gold Cup, and The Queen Elizabeth Diamond Stakes at Ascot to name the most popular. On these occasions he would receive so many bets that he could and would put between twelve and twenty betting slips through his official recording machine, without the horses name or the odds recorded on them. They were just blank timed slips, after the premises was closed he would write the victorious horses name on them and take his considerable winnings from the days takings, he believed wrongly that he had a foolproof tax avoidance system.

He both loved to have cash in his pocket and to demonstrate the fact in the company of what he deemed to be suitable young women. His unquenchable attraction to slim, teenage girls and young women would eventually cause his downfall, but not until he had left behind him a trail of misery. Once he had identified a new victim he was relentless with his considerable charm and expensive gifts. He would take his latest girl out, pay for first class meals, buy clothes and pay for entertainment. There would appear to be no end to his generosity, but from the very start he would be calculating the exact cost of his courteousness, this sum total would be remembered and ultimately retrieved.

He was able to achieve a high degree of trust with his victims, due to his natural good looks, his manipulative nature and his scheming use of his financial superiority. Girls fell under his spell, once they had accepted his introduction to ecstasy and later cocaine, which was a passion of his own they were as a paralysed insect in a spider's web. Not all his prey took this final and decisive step, but for those that did they were on the cusp of a very steep and slippery slope. He would be devious beyond their comprehension, administering an increasing level of intoxication to debilitate the girl in question. He would then have sex with his victim in all its forms, abhorrent or other wise, at will. Once satisfied he then reached a point in the relationship when he would switch off his involvement with the girl. He loved the chase, the pursuit, the reeling in and entrapment of his quarry. This for Adrian Needham was the game, once the girl had become compliant beyond her own resistance he would disassociate himself with her on a personal level, he would never touch her again. At this point he would recoup his initial outlay by both introducing Rohypnol into her diet and introducing sufficient of his low life betting clients to her prostrate form, so that they might abuse her for a fee. Once he had recompensed himself for his earlier outlay he vanished from the girl's life. He had left six of his victims to suffer drug addiction and his latest but one, a beautiful twenty-six year old, Melanie Telford, was the second to die by self-administration of an overdose of cocaine.

It was events of this magnitude that had prompted him to twice change his name. From his first identifying a new girl to their eventual abandonment would usually take between six months and a year, he would sometimes begin work on his next target before the previous one had fully recompensed him for his former generosity. This was to be the occasion prior to the death of Melanie Telford, for he had seen her younger sister Meredith on two occasions whilst he had been observing Melanie to ensure that she was exactly where she said she would be at a given time. The twenty-three year old Meredith was a straightforward and simple fish to reel in. So upset was she by the tragic and untimely death of her only sibling that the sympathetic kindness showered onto her by Needham was readily absorbed.

The distraught parents of Melanie were shattered by her death, her mother, Dorothy, a wheelchair bound alcoholic simply hit the bottle harder than usual, but her father Robert reacted very differently. He never touched alcohol as he was witness on a daily bases to its damaging and debilitating powers. He had been deeply suspicious that all was not well in Melanie's life, the new clothes and assorted gifts that often accompanied her on the occasions she returned to the family home were very sudden and unexplained. Melanie rented a flat with a friend, unlike Meredith who still lived at home helping her father to cope with her mother, so Robert never got to see Adrian Needham. Even before his eldest daughter's death he noticed that his youngest, Meredith, was bringing home expensive items, clothing, handbags and perfume, he questioned her as to their origin, she was unusually reticent to answer, it was unlike her to be so taciturn. On the day that she arrived with a particularly noteworthy, red, expensive, designer handbag his suspicions were elevated to a new and menacing level. He searched through

Melanie's possessions that he had recovered from her apartment, which confirmed his suspicions, he found an exact matching bag, and went on to find matching perfume and items of clothing, he quelled the rising panic attack within himself. He knew that he couldn't follow Meredith, he neither had the skill at deception or disguise, he hired a private detective to do his bidding for him.

The private detective spoke to many people who had known Melanie, some of whom had seen her together with Needham, their description of him was sufficient to identify Meredith's new boyfriend Sean Lawson as one and the same man. After he had plied two of Lawson's bitter and resentful clients with alcohol to confessing a love-hate relationship with him, he reported back to Robert Telford. He confirmed that the man who now called himself Sean Lawson was the man that had seduced Melanie with attention, gifts and drugs. And that two customers of his had confessed that they hated him because they were always in his debt either at the betting shop or for out of hours favours, but they confessed also that they were like moths to a light with regard Lawson because he periodically found them compliant beautiful young girls, who would do anything. The fact that two of these young girls had deliberately overdosed due to recurring, flashback nightmares caused by their Rohypnol ingestion seemed to be of little concern to them.

On having his suspicions confirmed, Robert Telford was determined to act and act decisively. The private detective, a Mr Andrew Langford, had been thorough. He had also discovered that Sean Lawson had ready access to cash and drugs and that for further amusement he belonged to a team of crop circle makers. Apparently he couldn't resist making a mockery of so many stupid people who were fooled by the mysterious modern phenomena. He had also established that the group meet once a week in the spring, at The Turks Head public house on the Gloucester Road, north of Bristol. Robert was happy to hand over five thousand pounds for Mr Langford's knowledge and future silence. It was in fact Langford who sowed the seed of revenge into Robert, so disgusted was he with what he had learnt about Lawson.

Robert Telford was an engineer with Rolls-Royce aviation division near Bristol. His modest salary did not permit such expense often but on this occasion he felt he had spent his money well and also that Mr Langford was a man he could rely on. He knew he had little time to waste, he visited The Turks Head every night for two weeks, feeling sure that he had identified the crop circle makers and Lawson. The first week he saw them he made a point of engaging some of them in conversation, the second time they met he took the bold step of saying that he had overheard them on a previous occasion and that he would very much like to join them. After a short debate he was welcomed into the fold, mainly due to their designs becoming increasingly sophisticated and requiring additional people to carry out the work. They said that it would be another two weeks before the crops were ready to work with. This being because they only used crops that had been tractor sprayed, like barley and wheat because these fields contained the tractor tyre footpath with which they could enter and leave the crop. They laughed that no-one ever questioned why such crops as potatoes, beans and peas never had visitations from outer space, these fields not having tractor footpaths would have resulted in them leaving tell-tail entry and exit tramplings. They called themselves the Celestial Creators and were all rather smug. Robert was introduced to them one by one, shaking the hand of Sean Lawson was the most difficult thing he ever did.

Robert was unable to act on their first two excursions, which occurred in early June. They had all approved Celia's latest design and been issued with centre stakes and pre-cut lengths of rope to establish the circle diameters, and finally on the night in question, their wooden paddles, a six foot long pole with a flat six foot head, which they screwed into place in turn using a fully charged cord-less screwdriver, creating something that looked like a massive broom without the bristles. It was to be this night that Robert's opportunity would present itself.

On their third trip southwest into Somerset he was alone in a field of malting barley with Lawson, at approximately two am. Whilst Lawson was busy creating his nominated portion of their latest design,   which was a scaled down representation of the universe, Celia was particularly proud of this one as it was a step up for the whole team. Robert made his move. He had just completed the small body of Titan, one of Jupiter's moons, when an opportunity offered itself. By the light of the moon he moved away from the small body of Titan into the huge circle of Jupiter, as he approached Lawson he was calm, much calmer than he had been each time he had imagined this moment, calmer in fact than when he had shaken Lawson's hand. His target was so busy destroying a farmer's crop for his own amusement he did not hear Roberts approach. When he was within range, Robert swung his blunt ended wooden paddle with all his might. It struck Lawson at the base of the skull, instantly and audibly snapping his neck, the whiplash from the blow momentarily leaving Lawson's body leaning forward with his head facing skyward, some ninety degrees askew from the norm, he collapsed silently, he was brain dead before he hit the ground. Robert starred at the prostrate figure and said softly,

"That was for Melanie, you sick bastard." He then dragged the body, its heart still beating, some fifty yards into a neighbouring crop, dumped his and Lawson's paddles into a copse and walked to the nearest town, awaiting daylight and public transportation back to Bristol. He was confident that none of the Celestial Creators knew his real name or address, he felt safe, only Langford the private detective could have exposed him but a second five thousand pounds secured his silence.

Within eighteen months Robert's wife had succumbed to liver failure, his daughter Meredith had married a Cypriote tour guide and the three of them moved to Cyprus. Robert occupied the annex of Meredith and Dimitri's house, which was close to the ocean, he supplemented his pension by given walking tours of historic sites to groups of British tourist, a task he took to readily. But every night before he fell asleep he saw both his beautiful daughter Melanie and his act of violent revenge on the man who destroyed her life.

He confessed in a letter to Bristol and Avon Police which he had left with his will, posthumously he was assumed to be guilty of murder. Throughout his twenty-nine years in Cyprus he kept his silence, he knew he was very fortunate to watch his grandchildren grow and to see his great-grandchildren to school age. He would though always sub-consciously favour his daughter Meredith's third child, her only daughter, his only granddaughter, Melanie.

The weather continued to be perfect for cropping, the three men had long since moved from silage into barley, which was mature a full ten days earlier than was the norm. At the very end of June, Kris's emotional outburst towards their temporary agency replacement for Nick was matched emotionally but not aggressively by an out pouring of a very different nature. After a particularly long, hot, dry day, harvesting barley Kris had borrowed transportation to visit the nearby town of Wotton-Under-Edge to speak to his father by telephone. He had not contacted his father as promised for three months since leaving Finland, which was an agreed period to allow the patriarch of the family time to consider his son's proposal. This was that of a sleeping partnership in Kris's ambitious plans for the future. His father had put the time to good use, when Kris returned from town he was a changed man. In fact he lived the rest of his life in a hiatus or suspension of normality. So effervescent was he with his news, that his every day reserved nature was temporarily arrested. Had he known exactly how brief the rest of his life was going to be, he would have been overcome in a very different way.

On his return from town he brought with him fish and chips, a crate of quality bottled ale and a bottle of champagne, for the three of them. He handed the hot food to Jude and Nick and opened the bottle saying,

"I know this is what you do in your country when you feel the need to celebrate." He poured the cool, sparkling liquid into three porcelain cups belonging to the proprietor of the farm whose barn they currently occupied. Jude, who was taking great pleasure in observing every detail of Kris's out of character behaviour, asked,

"What do you do in your country when you need to celebrate?"

"There is a lot of hugging, back slapping and drinking of Russian vodka." Nick interjected, half speaking, half mumbling, his mouth full of hot food,

"What are we celebrating?" It was the spark of ignition and invitation Kris needed and brought from him an outpouring of emotion unparalleled in his thirty-two years.

"I've just spoken to my father to find out if he is interested in investing in my Summer- Winter tourist and educational activities centre, he has just overwhelmed me. I thought he needed the three months...argh, what is your word, grace, yes grace, I thought he needed the three months grace to give him time to decide, but he used the time to talk to his two brothers and now all three of them are wanting to be involved." Kris is pacing backwards and forwards in front of his two friends whilst he is talking, he has a cup of fine quality champagne in his right hand and is gesticulating with his left to emphasize each and every word he is saying, his food is ignored.

"I can hardly believe it, my father has done so much for me in my life and now he has brought the family together to honour my grandfather and support me, this is the best day of my life." Jude was smiling, he was observing Kris's body language, his friend was barely able to contain himself, he was unable to stand still, he was pointing, waving and spinning around like a whirling dervish, he was gripping his fist one moment, and spreading his fingers the next.

"I'm sorry I'm talking in riddles. My grandfather owned a huge chunk of land in the west of Finland, near Vaasa, it was a perfect site for the development of skiing, which became popular after the war, my grandfather was a visionary. He saw the future, he saw the possibilities, he understood people and money. He applied for a licence to open up a vast area for skiing, he saw the potential for tourism way way before others. A bastard government official who saw my grandfather's application, tipped off and joined forces with his wealthy brother who had made a fortune buying and selling weapons during the war. The government bought the land by compulsory purchase, I think you have the same facility here. The reason given was that the steep terrain would make it suitable for the provision of hydro-electric power, but just a year later the government declared that a survey had contradicted their opinion and the now worthless land was sold for a pittance to the brother of the Minister. My grandfather fought it every step of the way, but with only right on his side and not enough power, he was defeated. The area is now one of the principle ski resorts in Finland, our family has been angry for two generations, my grandfather died consumed by bitterness. So

239

all their lives my father and his two brothers have lived with their fathers' regrets and sourness, my ambition has rekindled in their minds his ambition. All three of them want to help, they want to invest in my dream, I cannot believe it. My father's younger brother Peetu who has no children, I mean he has no children now, he had two sons, Aleski was killed in a motorcycle accident whilst he was racing to become the Scandinavian ice motocross champion and his brother Luka was lost at sea fishing for cod in the Icelandic waters. He apparently was leaving half of his worth to me on his death, so he is investing expecting nothing in return, that one piece of news is beyond my dreams. I have talked to the Banks, they would equal the money I have, so I always knew I had to borrow half the money to start up, but now with money from my father and his brothers, I won't need to borrow at all, the entire enterprise will be funded by the family, it is unbelievable." Jude butted in,

"And the other brother?"

"Yes yes, my other uncle, uncle Roope has two daughters. He wants to put in a twenty-five percent stake in the idea, his money is not going to be a loan, he is giving me the money and I will pay his daughters, my cousins, a return of future profits for the rest of their lives. He trust me and sees it as a better prospect than putting money in the bank, I am so happy to be giving my cousins Aada and Oona an annual share in the project rather than pay huge interest to the banks. I thought I needed to work two more years to have enough money to convince the banks to back me, but now I can put my plans into operation this winter, I can't believe my luck." Jude and Nick looked at each other, nodded, put down their cups and food, and stood up. Kris said,

"What are you doing?" Nick replied,

"Giving you hugs and slapping your back, we will pretend the champagne is vodka." The three men embraced, both Jude and Nick wished him well and promised to visit his winter wonderland in the future.

"So," Nick said, "This is your last season living like a tramp in the West of England."

"Yes I am afraid so, no that is wrong, I am glad so." Jude added,

"Come on lets raise our glasses, or rather cups to your dream." The three men chink cups and emptied them. Jude continues, "This is probably as good a time as any to tell you that I don't think I'll be back next year, I've met someone who has, to put it simply, taken my breath away. I don't want to spend another summer away from her."

"Her name?" Nick asks

"Liz, she's a photographer, no she's more than that, and she's unbelievable." Kris raises his now refilled cup.

"To Liz." They replicate his action and a general chorus of to Liz reverberates amongst the exposed wooden rafters of the barn.

The rest of the evening was spent in the consumption of beer and expressions of congratulation, all three of them snored loudly oblivious of each other well into the early hours of the next day. They were a little sluggish first thing the following morning, but after a hearty breakfast, which included the mysteriously recuperative power of smoked bacon they were soon back in their machines and as productive as ever. The barley season was to be the hottest, driest and dustiest any of them would ever know, memories would have to go back to the long, hot, dry spring and summer of 1976 to equal their current endurance. Kris continued to act out of character, he was more buoyant and jovial, and he would whistle often, it was as though all his birds had come home to roost. His deepest satisfaction was reserved for the feeling that he was rectifying a long standing injury to his entire family, he was walking taller than at any time in his life, with his families support he was a man bursting with a toxic mixture of ambition and satisfaction.

It is often said that a disaster needs a combination of factors in its favour, if it is to succeed.

This was the case for our crew one day in early July. It was, to date, the hottest day of a very hot year, the crop was the last of this years malting barley, it was as dry as it could be. The all enveloping dust from the crop was debilitating. In the morning session Kris's door handle had come away in his hand and he had to be let out of his machine by Nick who promised him that he would sort it at lunchtime. He knew the crop was far too dusty to work with the door open and they all knew it was dangerous to work locked in. This was factor number one.

They were operating as usual in a staggered line but in an unusually large field. Jude had had to stop and fall back from the other two as his on board grain store was full and his following tractor was delayed in returning to him because of problems with visiting cars being inconsiderately parked in the farmyard. This was factor number two. Kris's machine had developed a pinprick leak in one of its pressurised hydraulic hoses, the high pressure caused a mist of oil to gradually coat the underside of his machine, this was factor number three. By the time this had registered as a low oil warning light, Kris was on his last line before lunch, he ignored the early warning light knowing Nick would soon be under his machine, factor number four. The all enveloping and unusually dense column of dust coming from the crop was factor number five. From Jude's distance of a quarter mile he could not see either combine, just a huge pall of dust. For these unconnected elements to come together into a catastrophe, a spark of ignition was needed. Factor number six. It came from Nick's machine, one of the bearings on his combine that drove the high-speed mini-prop shaft that operated the seed conveyor, seized up. The high pitched screaming noise it made went unheard by all of them, the bearing overheated, became red hot and shattered, falling to the ground and into a combination of bone dry, dust, chaff and stubble, which ignited instantly. Nick was oblivious to the problem as the conveyor was still operating efficiently on the remaining nine bearings, so no warning lights came on. The fire couldn't wait to get at Kris's machine, the fine mist of hydraulic oil literally sucked the flames from the burning stubble, instantly the whole of the underside of his combine was engulfed in burning vapour and oil, which for the moment went unnoticed by all of them.

Jude was the first to register that a possible disaster was imminent, he saw that the huge cloud of dust which was obscuring his colleagues machines had a darker element to it, too dark to be dust alone, he knew it could only be smoke. He ran from his combine towards the quickly darkening cloud, the flames under Kris burnt numerous rubber seals and hoses, causing more and more oil and fuel to escape, feeding the rapidly

242

developing fire. By the time Kris had several warning lights on his screen in front of him his machine was engulfed in flames. He stopped abruptly, the pressure of his foot on the break pedal forced another huge jet of hydraulic oil into the flames, taking the intensity of the fire onto the next level. As he stopped the smoke and flames replaced the dust, his vision was obscured in all directions. He could smell burning rubber and feel the additional heat, he realised at this juncture, no more than a minute after Nick's bearing had shattered, that he was in danger of losing his life, which was still his to command until he reached for the missing door handle.

All the aforementioned elements now amalgamated to rob him of choice, of decision, and of his existence. Both Jude and Nick received burns requiring hospital treatment to their legs and arms as they braved the intense pall of black smoke and ever increasing wall of flames attempting to open the now welded door to Kris's combine. They assumed Kris burnt to death, but unseen to them in their increasingly desperate and frantic attempts to free their colleague, Kris was overcome and killed by a lack of oxygen and smoke inhalation in just forty seconds from the realisation that the minor factor of the missing door handle had assumed much greater significance.

Jude never worked again for Jack Mortimer after that day. He had three weeks of hospital treatment for his burns, during which he flew to Finland to attend Kris's funeral and after which he went to the place where he felt most comfortable to recover both physically and mentally. This was not to his family in Oxfordshire, or to his sister Barbara in France. It was to his adopted home of Dorchester and to Mrs Nayland, the Scottish landlady of his lodgings to await the return of Liz from her summer vacillations with her camera. He then moved into her rented Weymouth property in Hope Street near the harbour.

He was gratified to meet Kris's father and his two brothers at the funeral, it was fulfilling to express to them just how much it meant to Kris to receive their backing with his plans, but with Kris being the only grandson left, it became clear to Jude that the whole family had pinned its future aspirations on Kris's broad shoulders. His untimely and devastating death had been both calamitous and ruinous to their ambitions. Jude spent just one day with the bereaved, it was evident to him that Kris had been a beacon to his immediate and wider family, all of their hopes and aspirations had been heaped onto him, they now felt rudderless and without a future, they were a family defeated beyond their own imagination.

WINTER 1988

SAN ISIDRO

Jude jokingly says to Liz one day whilst he's working on Jayne's book in the Weymouth house,

"What's missing from my memory of Colombia are pictures, your pictures." Liz responds,

"Well you know my feelings, even though you've described it as a dangerous country, I'd love to see it. Your description is of a raw country full of colour, life and vitality, you know I'd love to photograph it."

"Well yes it does have a huge appeal, despite its troubled history of drug trafficking, it was a fascinating place."

"Well ok, why don't you go back, do a bit more research for the book, I've only got around eight weeks this winter in Scandinavia, so I could join you for a month, say, in January, you know I'd really like to see the place."

"Make it the last week in December and you've got a deal, last Christmas alone in the rain forest was as bad as it gets, but there's one more condition."

"Go on."

"You cut your hair short and dress as male."

"What?"

"It's a dodgy country, I have enough problems looking out for myself, it would be much easier if everybody thought we were just two mates."

"Jude, are you serious?"

"Yes, cut your hair short, rough it up, wear no makeup, not that you wear much anyway, dress down and always wear a baseball cap to hide your gorgeous eyes."

"Suppose it could be fun."

"It would only be for what, a month?"

"OK I'd love to be let loose in Colombia with my camera and don't forget you're still a millionaire out there."

"For sure, and I would love to see your resulting pictures and have them here with me to refer back to."

"OK then, now that your burns are healed, when do you want to go?"

"If I go I'll go the same time as you, how long do we have?"

"I've got to be in Helsinki by the first of November, so we've got a month. You build your strength back up, your last trip below the equator sounded pretty strenuous, I've got plenty to do in my dark room and I've still got four private commissions to complete."

"OK I'll go out to Barbara in France first, but this time when I get to Colombia I'll start much farther north. I'd really love you to see and photograph the beauty of San Isidro and the boss's compound, it looked to me like utter luxury in the jungle, and it's something I want to use."

"OK it's a deal, but if I have to go in drag, shall I take a dress for you?"

"Make it a long one to cover my horrible knees."

During the next month Jude did an increasing amount of running and cycling and visited his mother and his sister Anne in Oxford. He was satisfied with his writing, and found pleasure in building the characters that Jayne had left him to work with. As she had left no notes for guidance he was free to develop the story line, a freedom he was finding enjoyable, but he was frustrated by his slow progress. All too soon it was once again departure day, Liz left Heathrow for Helsinki, and Jude went via Portsmouth for France, their goodbyes were becoming increasingly difficult, but they both understood and respected the nature of each others tasks.

Jude arrived in mid-France for what was to be a week's visit, but as was the norm, his sister Barbara and her husband Jean Pierre made him overtly welcome. In all he enjoyed a month in their company, it was to be a November of very agreeable weather. The month ended as it had begun, with glorious bright, uninterrupted blue skies, sunny days and chill nights, many with a sharp frost. The radiant weather conditions produced a resplendent display of autumnal colour. Barbara and Jean

Pierre's farmhouse was covered from ground to roof in handsome Virginia creeper, to walk out from the house and to look back to its ever changing colour was a daily revelation. At this time in the autumn of each year as the temperature drops rapidly in northern Europe, a week-long extravaganza of bird migration takes place. Countless giant, grey cranes from all the Scandinavian countries, Holland, Belgium, Russia and beyond, head south for warmer climes. They come together to fly a narrow corridor west of the Massive Central, and east of the Atlantic Ocean. Directly below this confined channel is the two hundred and fifty year old farmhouse that is Jude's temporary home. During the rapidly shortening days, to be able to both see and hear the continuous mass migration of such huge elegant birds was for Jude a unique and spectacular pleasure. Skein after skein, some of them measuring many hundreds of birds would congregate whilst resting on thermals directly above and in all directions of the comfortable old farmhouse, which was for four weeks Jude's transient domicile. The beautiful, sleek, long legged creatures were constantly calling to each other, whether this was for recognition, comfort or guidance was impossible to know, the resulting concordant sound was enthralling to witness. The exodus south lasted five full days and nights, Jude spent much of that time walking the country lanes with Barbara, collecting wild mushrooms, walnuts and chestnuts, or just sitting with one or both of his hosts with a glass of wine on their rustique oak decked veranda, with the constant backdrop of the grey cranes migratory, melodic resonance.

Chez Thoma is a small hamlet of just eight houses and twelve barns, all were built within a twenty year period in the mid to late seventeenth century, resulting in every building displaying the same style of workmanship and uniform appearance. All of the attractive, multi coloured, exterior stonework had been quarried locally and erected in a relatively short time by the same craftsmen. Each roof was adorned with aged and faded, handmade, terracotta, roman style tiles. It was not difficult to understand how Barbara had fallen in love with both Jean Pierre and Chez Thoma. The tiny village had a bewitching ability to captivate all who were fortunate to visit, they would quickly fall dreamily into its tranquil spell. Jean Pierre too in his manner, was alluring, he betrayed an eminence with his intelligent and thought provoking conversation, which along with its revealing intimacy added further to the agreeable nature of Jude's visit.

Jude consumed a number of days working on the book when both Barbara and John Pierre were at work, but increasingly the evenings were spent in conversation of a more and more intimate nature, during which he progressively revealed his true situation. His first confession was that of Jayne's book and his inability to be truthful with their mother when questioned regarding its whereabouts, and also his entanglement with it at the present time. He also talked of his plans to re-visit Colombia and of his many impressions of his previous journey there.

As he became progressively more comfortable in their presence and under the seductive beguilement of Chez Thoma, he opened his soul fully. He spoke fluently with intimate revelations of both his grief for the loss of Jayne and his newfound and breathtakingly swift attachment to what he described as the phenomena that was Liz Reese. It was his divulgence of his feelings for Liz that surprised and delighted Barbara and Jean Pierre. Barbara could feel a resurrection of passion in Jude that excited her too when he spoke, that her older and only brother had taken this gargantuan step was a joy to her which she did not conceal. She was so pleased that he had from somewhere recovered the enthusiasm to look forward, little did she know that she too would be ultimately tested and would require the very same fortitude in the future. At the end of the month Jude acknowledged with reluctance that his stay in Chez Thoma must end. He openly declared himself in love with the place and he conceded too that if he did not make himself leave soon there was a danger that Liz would be in South America before him. A last evening meal with the few residents who occupied the village was a perfect send off.

Barbara dropped him at Angoulême railway station the next morning, the combination of the super fast T.G.V. train and a French airways jumbo jet saw Jude land in the capitol of Colombia at midnight local time, equipped much as before, including Cops $1,000,000.

Bogotá is a sprawling city of over eight million, it sits at a dizzy two thousand six hundred meters above sea level, but is still only the third highest capital in South America, after La Paz, Bolivia and Quito in Ecuador. Jude suffered forty eight hours of mild altitude sickness and he was surprised that he had arrived at the start of the dry season, he was also a little disconcerted with regard the temperatures. With day time highs of around sixteen Celsius and night time lows of six to eight he was left feeling inadequately dressed, once again this rugged mountainous country had surprised him. Dressed in a t-shirt and two top shirts he was barely comfortable, he stayed for two nights in the hotel Dorantes, a mid-price range hotel that offered a degree of colonial grandeur, or more so a hint of its colonial past. Its chipped paintwork, tired façade and well worn wooden floors demonstrated that the hotel was in the autumn of its existence, its spring had been in the roaring twenties, a time when the capital city had been a true revelation to its visitors.

Jude visited La Candelaria, the bustling, busy central region, which contained a mixture of both attractively restored and sadly dilapidated centuries old buildings. These were blended clumsily with a range of both architecturally impressive and disappointing modern structures. He ate pizza in the Plaza de Bolivia, a colourful and hectic area that was dominated by the arresting, neoclassical Catedral Primada, which his trusty and well thumbed tourist guide claimed to be the largest Church in all Colombia. He decided to view the interior, and he was again surprised. There was relatively little ornamentation, its one dominating feature being the tomb of Bogotá's founder, Jimenez de Quesada.

Although Jude enjoyed the central city area during daylight hours, common sense prevailed and he made himself scarce after eight pm. He would return to his hotel to swot up on his Spanish and he would also, each night, look at the European winter holiday brochure to keep track of Liz's progress, which in turn helped him feel a connection. He knew that it was a good idea to visit Colombia again and he knew too that he was looking forward to having Liz with him in a few weeks, but now that he was in Bogotá alone, he felt very flat and began to question his motives. He was missing the intensity of the evenings in France, and he knew too that he was missing Liz. She had become very important to him in a short space of time. He did not believe that this was because she had cushioned the blow of his previous loss, but it was because of her vibrant and spontaneous personality and of course, her looks. In truth it was a combination of both, Barbara could see it, Liz could feel it, Jude deigned it.

Jude's third day in the city saw him wandering in places he should not have. Just a few streets from the touristy city centre he was constantly stepping to avoid dog faeces and missing drain covers. The air soon became rancid with the smell of sewage and each time he attempted a double left turn to return to La Candelaria, the colonial centre, the road would wander downhill and drift to the right. In a short space of time he found himself in a very unsavoury district where he was forced at the point of a long sharp knife to part company with the contents of his wallet to three youths no older than fifteen. Humiliated he berated himself for allowing the situation to develop, but also on retracing his footsteps he congratulated himself on taking on board the advice of two foolish Americans he had met on his last trip, he had left only ten percent of his money in his wallet. The experience had unnerved him, he decided to leave the capital the next day, but he knew in truth that the incident that had unsettled him could just as easily happened in London, Paris, New York or Rome. He had strayed too far from the central area, but at no point did he feel his life was in danger, they were just boys flexing their new found muscle. Had he decided to take them on or remonstrate with them he felt that they would have backed off, but for Cops$90,000 (twenty eight US dollars) it was a chance he wasn't prepared to take. He hoped that they would spend the money on much needed shoes, and not drugs. If Jude had known the truth, that the money had been given to their mother for food, he would have viewed the incident less seriously than he did.

That night in his hotel room he studied both map and guide book for inspiration. He then fully realised the vastness of his host country, there was a huge area to the north that boarded the Caribbean Sea and another even larger region known as Llanos Del Orinoco, a part of the Amazonian basin, both of these regions were way beyond his reach. He wanted to be out of the country but he had made a pact with Liz and would stick to it, it would be great to have her photograph the San Isidro area. He decided to take a nine hour bus ride to the town of Pereira, mainly because it is a step closer to his eventual meeting place with Liz. The cost of the bus ride is Cops$42,000, similar to the cost for each night in a hotel, and the cost of a meal, Jude is realising that it is far easier to spend a million Colombian Cops$ than it is to earn. Another attraction to Jude apart from the spectacular bus ride itself, is its close proximity to a National Park

He remembered the booming, roaring and raucous sounds from the rainforest that he had enjoyed from the veranda at San Isidro, it was an experience he very much wished to repeat. His trusted guidebook informed him that for as little as Cops$29,000 a day (eleven US dollars) he could hire a local part English speaking guide at the five thousand hectare Santuario Otun Quimbaya, National Nature Reserve, which it boasted was set between 1800 and 2400 meters above sea level. Its high biodiversity claimed to support more than five hundred species of birds, butterflies, bats and monkeys, and it claimed that it is also possible to see the giant anteater. The guidebook had sold the excursion to Jude, it had achieved at least one of its goals its creator had aimed for at its conception.

After a long, tiring but extraordinarily scenic bus ride, which oddly had no chickens on board for the duration, Jude arrived at the vibrant, vivacious city that is Pereira, population 440,000 elevation 1400 meters. Being tired and hungry he walked into the first hotel that caught his eye. It was the Castilla R'eal, a small but clean and attractive looking hotel. Once seated at his restaurant table, he realised that the hotel catered exclusively for businessmen. He ordered a bottle of Malbec wine, which was to his liking and debated, for just a short time, on whether to order the parrilla de carnes, a mixed grill by another name, or the robalo, which he knew to be sea bass. He looked to his left and saw two huge men tucking into the former and subsequently ordered the latter. The fish and the wine were soon consumed, as a result Jude slept soundly in what was a sparsely furnished but very comfortable room, despite some persistent and pulsating, distant music.

In the morning he decided that he was comfortable with his choice of hotel and subsequently booked a further two nights. After breakfast he took the short bus ride to the nature reserve. He was not disappointed, the numerous species of exotic birds and butterflies were extraordinary, he also saw six species of monkey, he was able to identify the red howler and the spider monkeys but no other. His only disappointment was the English speaking tour guide, which, because Jude was the only person requesting such a service had cost him Cops$58,000- twice the suggested amount in his guide. His disappointment related to the extent of his guide's English vocabulary, which when fully expanded consisted of, 'Hallo, bird, butfly, monkey and bye bye'. Fortunately Jude's Spanish was able to fill most of the gaps. He imagined wrongly that the actual bilingual guide was unavailable and he had sent his brother or cousin to fill in. It did not detract from his day, it had been a marvellous experience and his one regret was that Liz had not been on hand with her camera.

Later that evening in the restaurant of the hotel Castilla R'eal he ploughed through the enormous meal that was parrilla de carnes and another bottle of Malbec, again he slept well but was aware of throbbing distant music. The following day after a late breakfast he people watched in the central Plaza of the town, under the watchful gaze of a giant statue of the celebrated liberator, Bolivar. The eight-meter high plus, eleven-ton bronze of a naked figure impelling his stallion onward with fanatical fervour dominated the square. He viewed a range of museums and churches, the museums for their myriad of exceptional golden articles and the churches for their architecture.

After a light lunch of bunuelos, small deep fried doughy balls of curd cheese and flour, a firm favourite for locals, Jude spent the afternoon jotting down notes for future reference. Mid-afternoon a Spanish couple of his own age joined him at his table, they were holidaying in Colombia for three weeks as a joint thirtieth birthday celebration. His new found companions Pepe and Salsi spoke very good English and had both spent time in London studying art. The three of them wiled away a dry but increasingly humid afternoon drinking a little too much chicha, an indigenous corn beer, than was good for them. Jude happened to mention the pulsating music he had heard from his hotel for the past two nights, his recent acquaintances were both keen to track down the source of the midnight rhythms. Fuelled by too much chicha and a desire not to be alone for the evening, Jude agreed that the three of them would meet again at eight o'clock, post showers and a change of clothes, to pursue the nocturnal music. Immediately on meeting again with the plainly dressed couple he had met earlier he felt inadequate, Jude was wearing a self- coloured pastel shirt and jeans. Pepe was wearing more colours than Jude had adjectives to describe, Salsi was dressed to thrill, her red heeled shoes and very short, red, pleated skirt showed off most of her long bronzed legs, both her midriff and half of her small pushed up tanned breast were also on display, it required discipline from Jude to keep his gaze onto her pretty face as she greeted him. After a meal of momposino, thinly cut flank of beef dressed with onion and tomato sauce during which Jude imagined Pepe kidnapped by aliens and Salsi naked in various compromising positions, they walked together to the north of the city centre in search of entertainment.

They did not have to walk far, just four streets from the famous statue of Bolivar they found the nightclubs, it was ten pm and most clubs had only been open for an hour, but already they were throbbing. At the first club they entered, Chango's there was insufficient action for Salsi, they hit the jackpot at their second port of call. At the bar La Iguana Jude felt that he had entered a discothèque-cum-circus, it was exactly what his Spanish companions were looking for, the music was extremely loud, the drinks were cheap and the decoration was extraordinary. There were all kinds of stuffed animals in cages hanging from the ceiling and enormous, live snakes in glass cages, also live toucans and macaws were hanging in wicker baskets, suspended around the massive room at random. How the birds survived the flashing lights and thumping music was impossible to comprehend. In one corner Colombians were throwing horseshoes onto a steel floor liberally sprinkled with gunpowder, the winner appeared to be the one who achieved the most satisfying explosion.

Salsi immediately took to the dance floor, followed quickly by Pepe, her rhythmic gyrations increased her sex appeal tenfold. Jude was watching from nearby, he felt too self conscious to join in, but he was unable to prevent his gaze from following the ever shortening hemline of Salsi's skirt, which would soon reveal her underwear. As he was not dancing, standing alone and male, he quickly became a target for local girls asking him if he wanted to buy them a drink, which was how the local prostitutes had been taught to approach Americans and Europeans, with the local men they took a far more direct approach. After being targeted by a range of wig wearing girls, blonde, redhead and brunette, he was about to be targeted by a tall, slim, dark haired stunning looking lady boy. He then decided to join Pepe and Salsi, he had become more self-conscious standing alone than in the throng on the dazzlingly lit, glass, dance floor. No sooner had he got into his rather stiff rhythm when he was the object of Salsi's attention. She put her arms around his neck and pulled him in close, the heat, lights, music and drink, combined with Salsi's ever shortening skirt, was having an effect on him. They were being constantly buffeted by other dancers, several of the men close by and two of the women disturbed them to congratulate Salsi, she beamed a huge smile back in return. Jude was a little bemused, he knew her dancing was good, but not so exceptional as to warrant such attention. Looking around the glass dance floor other women too were achieving the same level of recognition. He withdrew his arms from his dance partner and gave her an open handed shrug, coupled with a left and right sideways glance to question exactly what was going on. The gesture was necessary as conversation was impossible due to the base volume of the music, that was not only shaking the building and slowly killing the live birds, but it also felt to Jude that his fillings were loosening.

It was the cue Salsi had been waiting for, in response she took a half step back, stood with her feet apart and pointed to the floor. Jude looked down automatically, instantly recognising three things, firstly that the floor was not plain glass, it was mirrored glass and with so many lights aimed at it, he was both able to see that his dance partner was not only not wearing knickers but that she also sported a perfectly shaven vagina. He was struck dumb, which due to the terrific volume of the music was not a disadvantage, to give himself a little time to react appropriately, whatever appropriately was, this was still a consideration in his mind, he kept his gaze to the floor, looking further afield in all directions, he now understood the congratulations Salsi and others had received. She was not alone in her sense of undress .Jude looked into Salsi's eyes, instantly he knew that this beautiful, rhythmic, perspiring, sensual woman in his gaze was available to him, he looked to his right on Pepe's approach and received from him a smile and a nod. As he looked back to Salsi she took his right hand and put it between her legs, under her skirt. Even with his brain dulled by alcohol he realised now that he had been targeted earlier in the day. One of his trademark visions flashed across his consciousness, he was naked, drugged, trussed and bound, and appearing in a b class pornographic movie, his first and last ever staring role, his fifteen minutes of fame. He allowed his hand to linger at the moist portal to his temptress's channel of desire for a fraction longer than was decent, he then caught a taxi back to his hotel.

As he left the nightclub he was aware that the cages containing live, dying and preserved animals were receding into the dark area of the roof space, above the plethora of multi-coloured lights. Replacing them in a downward direction were a small number of larger cages, which contained naked couples performing a variety of sex acts. This new exposé was received with tumultuous applause, for the patrons of the club it was the signal that it was midnight and previous restrictions no longer applied. Whilst in the rear of the taxi Jude's last semi-drunken image of the nightclub is of it being raised to the ground by exocet missiles, and in its place a remembrance garden of erotic plants. He corrected himself, he now realised that even visions can have senior moments or more accurately Freudian slips, exotic plants.

Unable to sleep, he was tormented by whether or not he was a fool to have walked away from what may have been the ultimate sexual experience, or had he saved himself from a spider's web? He replaced the image of Salsi with that of Liz and of their first sexual encounter back in Dorchester, this pushed all other thoughts from his mind, he concluded that if he was a fool, then he was a fool in love, he masturbated himself to sleep with a naked image of Liz on his mind, he slept long into the morning.

The next three weeks he spent backpacking amongst an ever-changing group of mixed Europeans, Aussie's and Kiwi's, he was made aware of this possibility by his trusty travel guide. It had in its content all backpacker hostels and routes listed, once he had found the first, he could not imagine any other way of travelling in a country as unknown to him as Colombia. There were many benefits and almost no disadvantages. The structure and organisation built around the backpacker dogma was both impressive and reliable, and now made Jude, in hindsight feel foolish in going it alone. Their maxim was one of safety first and a fundamental part of their doctrine was safety in numbers. Backpackers did not wander alone in questionable parts of cities, they did not get targeted to appear in S and M pornography films, and they did not get robbed at knife point, but did sporadically get ripped off by armed police on buses. Jude travelled from Pereira south to Palmira, almost entirely on foot, through breathtaking landscapes, with never less than a dozen companions. His only concerns were mild blistering to his feet and the humidity, though their daily targets were realistic and everyone did their bit in the evenings to prepare food and to clear away. There were perhaps one or two individuals whom he met that he would prefer not to meet again, but on the whole the three-week experience had been a positive one. He found it refreshing to be amongst a group of people who shared a common goal and who were helpful and sympathetic towards each other. He would have liked an off switch or at the very least a dimmer switch, to reduce a degree of the night time snoring, flatulence and love making. But to be fair, his guidebook did declare that the communal sleeping arrangements at many of the makeshift hostels would not suit all, rarely had so few words described so much.

He arrived at Palmira just two days short of his planned rendezvous with Liz. As they had no reliable way of contacting each other their understanding was that if she did not arrive on either the 22nd or 23rd of December, she would not be coming for a reason to be explained later and he would fly home as soon as he could, hopefully in time for Christmas. He spent the two days keeping much to his own company, topping up on his Spanish which he was becoming satisfied with and making notes for future reference for the book. He enjoyed the local food and wine but not so much the climate, which had been bearable, but was once again becoming extremely humid. He was also reading more of the country's history and culture, much of what he was learning was either surprising or shocking to him. It seemed to

Jude that the purpose of life for men in Colombia was not to get rich but to live and get drunk, and that remarkably the woman are the bosses in the home, their men folk can display as much bravado and machismo as they like away from the home, but in the house the women are in charge, without question. A further revelation that Jude discovers is that despite the countries infamous reputation for the production, refinement and trafficking of illegal drugs, few Colombians use these drugs themselves. Reading into the countries current problems in the late 1980's it is apparent to Jude that the real war is between the cities and the country. It is clear that the wealthy city politicians have little or no compassion with the many families whose very existence is the coca leaf. The reasons they grow it are simple, it is well suited to the area where it is grown, it is in huge demand, it is very profitable and they are poor, which is a simple equation to comprehend. The government's attempts to destroy the coca leaf production, with American encouragement and backing, is simply alienating themselves from their own people. Massive resources and manpower are being used to destroy crops, jungle laboratories, transport links, and in attempts to sever the contacts between corrupt officials, police and the all powerful drug cartels. These resources are so immense Jude speculates that they could be used to give all Colombians a better way of life, with improved subsistence, health, and education, if the money were used to pay farmers to grow such crops as coffee, grapes and timber, topping up their wage to coca leaf levels then everyone is working together. The real root of the problem is clearly to halt demand, a solution which lays way beyond the country's borders. Jude reads on and is staggered to read that by 1983, the most powerful of the drug traffickers, Pablo Escobar, had an estimated personal fortune amounting to US $20 billion dollars. He was able to form and fund his own political party, establish two newspapers, bankroll huge housing schemes for the country's poor, and fund massive public works projects. In the next paragraph of Colombia's recent history Jude reads the most amazing fact of his entire life.

The Colombian government, with the assistance of the United States had in the recent past launched a campaign to go after the drug cartels, by both allowing US delta force troops into the

257

country to pursue them and allowing for the first time, the US to extradite the leaders of the cartels back to the US to face American justice, despite the fact that many of these men had never set foot on American soil. This was totally unacceptable to the men who ran the illegal drug trade, they preferred a grave in Colombia to a jail cell in the US. In an attempt to reverse their governments' new policy with the United States and have themselves declared immune from both prosecution and extradition, Pablo Escobar and his associates offered to invest their capital in national development programmes. The point that made Jude audibly gasp is that they offered to benefit every Colombian by paying off the country's national debt, some thirteen billion US dollars! After the government refused the offer, the violence which has over the years become sadly symptomatic with Colombia, erupted once more, this time on a scale not witnessed before. The cartels were blamed for bomb attacks on an airliner, homes, banks and the government itself. The government responded by confiscating almost a thousand cartel owned properties, it was the beginning of the end of the all-powerful cartels. Several years after Jude would depart the country for the second and last time, it would take a special US led task force of over one thousand five hundred men a total of four hundred and ninth nine days to track down the infamous Pablo Escobar, a truly remarkable feat for one man against so many.

The next day Jude arrived at Palmira airport at eight am to check the incoming flights, there were none from Europe, but four from the US. He spent the day in great anticipation only to be disappointed, after the last American flight from Washington had cleared, he left for his hotel. The taxi ride from the airport was a gloomy one, he had spent ten hours at the terminal building, and several times he had had to explain himself to armed soldiers, who eventually left him in peace. The following morning he arrived at eleven, having checked the previous day of the arrival time of the first plane in from Europe, it was an Air-France flight from Paris, in Jude's mind it was the most likely of today's arrivals to have Liz on board, it did not. Two US flights arrived either side of lunchtime, Jude watched every passenger clear the arrivals area, almost without exception they were

Colombians returning home for Christmas. Looking at the arrivals scheduled the most likely and last flight she could be on was from Madrid, arriving at eight pm local time, other flights were coming in from Johannesburg, Barbados and Nairobi, these he dismissed. He had already checked his best bet of flying out the next day, his only realistic option of reaching Dorchester for Christmas was to take the return flight to Madrid, Spain, leaving at midnight. He was glad that he had booked out of his hotel and had his backpack with him. From Madrid he could get a connecting flight with a seven-hour delay to Charles de Gaulle, Paris, and a further flight on to London, Heathrow, landing at nine am Christmas morning, he was hoping Liz would be in the mood for an early morning drive. The two flights from Africa cleared, as did the one from Barbados. He had just over two hours to wait for Liz's last chance of joining him, before he booked his flight out. He checked, and there were five seats available, but as many people were arriving at the airport he was becoming nervous that he would miss out, he had tried to reserve a seat, but this was unacceptable, he had to pay in full on his credit card as it was the day of departure. After a huge through flow of Spanish speaking peoples he checked again on the availability of a seat, and was disappointed to learn that the plane was now oversubscribed by two, he could if he wished add his name to the list of those anticipating a cancellation. He sat down head resting on his hands, exuding negative body language. Either Liz was on the flight from Madrid, or he was stuck here on his own for Christmas, his mood was slipping toward despondency by the minute. He noticed that he was now one of just four people waiting in the arrivals lounge and there was another two hours to wait for the Madrid flight. There was an elderly, poorly dressed, over weight Colombian couple full of anticipation, Jude imagined their grandchildren were flying in for Christmas and a thin gangly looking European type, in army fatigue trousers, a camouflage jacket and baseball cap, partially covering unkempt hair, the peak of which was low over his eyes. Jude was trying to gauge his age, the poor attempt to grow a moustache put the lanky youth at around eighteen. Jude looked again at the baseball cap, on its front it had the insignia of the Cornish Pirates Rugby team, his heart leapt from around seventy to one hundred and sixty beats a minute, it was his own cap. He somehow managed to contain his reaction, picking up his backpack he sat down next to the gangly youth. After a brief silence he said,

"You should have bought a Yankee Dodgers cap." Liz threw her arms around him, they laughed, they embraced, they laughed, they kissed, they embraced and they laughed some more. It was Jude who spoke first.

"How long have you been here and what's that on your top lip?"

"I've been here long enough to watch you put yourself through the emotional mangle, you and your mood swings, you are so transparent and that is a little waterproof eye shadow, what do you think?"

"You look great, I mean you look weird, but you still look great, I can't believe your actually here, I almost booked a flight back to Madrid tonight."

"I don't think so, I watched Mr Grumpy come back from the flight desk."

"It's so good to have you here."

"It's so good to be here."

"How did you get in, in disguise? You look nothing like you passport picture."

"Just goes to show how secure the airways are, I think I could have had bomb written on my rucksack and I'd have got in, perhaps it's the Christmas effect."

"Its backpack, rucksack went out with Parker coats, flat top and page boy haircuts." Liz took off her baseball cap, and said,

"That's two things you've got wrong already."

"I can't believe how raunchy you look dressed as a boy."

"Careful Casanova, there are still some countries where you can be arrested for what you're thinking."

"Come on let's get out of here."

"OK take me to your posh hotel."

"Actually I booked out, half thinking I wouldn't be coming back."

"Oh ye of little faith, I didn't want to spend another Christmas on my own either." They took a taxi back into town, whilst Liz explained she had to stop over for twenty four hours in Barbados, having flown from London the day before. It was, she said, impossible to get a ticket for a direct flight so close to Christmas. They did not return to Jude's previous hotel, instead they went up market, staying for three nights at the hotel, San Pedro de Managua, which felt a little like staying in a pet shop, as the hotels stunning, old colonial courtyard had many flying residents in the shape of parrots and parakeets to liven up the atmosphere. With an abundance of flowering vines adorning the walls, it was a restful and beautiful place to spend Christmas. The hotel staff made a fuss of them as Liz had 'accidentally' spilt confetti as they booked in. She had by this time, taken off the camouflage jacket, the cap and wiped clean her top lip. As newly-weds they were given the best of treatment, for which Jude tipped very generously.

They saw little of the city in their stay, but a great deal of their hotel bed, the restaurant and the colourful hotel courtyard, greatly enjoying the quarrelsome parrots, the hummingbirds and the butterflies who were frequent visitors to the many flowers that emblazoned the old stone walls. Having caught up with each other's past and spent a few days relaxing and making love, they were ready to move on two days after Christmas. Liz became a boy again and they caught a bus to Cali mid morning on December 28th. The short, uneventful, one-hour bus ride was followed by a four hour ride, complete with several chickens, and an enforced stop to pay a bonus to the local 'non-corrupt' police force, they then travelled on to the town of Buenaventura.

This time Jude did stay in the Hotel Titanic, it being a four story hotel, it had a roof top bar-restaurant terrace with superb views across the estuary that leads on to the Pacific Ocean. From their commanding outlook they were able to identify many different species of water birds in the early evenings and view a multitude of stars late evening and into the night. On their first night they ate a plate of mixed fish with rice and they drank two bottles of local wine, after which Jude confessed that he had now spent one million cops$, to which Liz replied,

"C'est la vie," she corrected herself "or should I say Eso es' vida?" Jude replied,

"That's close enough."

So enchanted were they with the hotel named after Britain's worst ever maritime disaster they stayed for two more nights, walking before breakfast along the waterfront whilst it was still relatively cool and again in the early evening whilst it was not. Each night they tried something different from the restaurant and each night they drank a little too much wine. Liz was fascinated by the appearance of the customary late afternoon downpour, Jude passed on an explanation he had been given, which was that the hot sun of the day evaporated a huge quantity of liquid from the humid rain forest and that eventually so much moisture built up in the atmosphere that there was only one possible result, it fell back from whence it came and so began the cycle again. Liz dressed down again which she was having fun doing, they left the Hotel Titanic and took the short bus ride to San Isidro. She had at this point taken over two hundred pictures, but that figure would soon be eclipsed.

On arrival at the Juan Javier Hernandez estate, Jude was remembered from last year and was immediately taken on again to do the same work, he explained in understandable Spanish that his companion Les was a photographer and he asked would it be ok for him to stay also. He volunteered Les as an unpaid cook to influence the decision, as Jude was remembered as one of their best foreign workers, his request was swiftly granted and Jude offered to pay for Les's meals.

As it was only ten am, Jude was put to work immediately and once he had walked the half mile to the vines carrying his cutting tools accompanied by Les and 'his' camera, he was delighted to discover that his previous years companions, the indomitable travelling Dutch couple Dirk and Anna were working the vines. There was much hugging and kissing all round, but a little confusion over the appearance of Liz, which Jude explained very briefly. Dirk and Anna had spent the entire year in South America, reaching the very southern tip, Tierra del Fuego in mid-summer. They were on their way back up the country toward Central America and they had stopped where they knew they could find work. They had been working for Juan Javier for just one week, so had three weeks left there. Jude remembered that they never stayed anywhere longer than a month, according to both of them, life was too short. Jude had spent a day doing arduous but satisfying work, with Liz wandering nearby capturing on film the lush landscape, the rain forest and some of its inhabitants. She had been delighted to achieve close ups of huge kingfishers and several large exotic butterflies, but she was disappointed in the shyness of both the red howler monkeys and their smaller but equally verbose cousins, the spider monkeys. After being shown the ropes by two of the estate's female workers she took over the role of assistant cook for twelve locals, two Spanish backpacking couples, Dirk and Anna, who she quickly came to be very fond of and herself and Jude. She often ribbed Jude for volunteering her for the role but enjoyed it from the start, for it both integrated her quickly with everyone present and taught her culinary skills she would never forget. The local girls were amused to be served food prepared by a male, it was a novelty for them and gave them a boost.

As before the evenings were spent on the long veranda that protected the bunk house from the worst of the penetrating sun, they would either sit exhausted and watch the rain, or listen to the reverberating racket that emanated from the tree canopy an hour before darkness. Anna was impressed by the number of constellations Jude could recall, Liz observed that immediately a very comfortable bond had been re-established between Jude and both the very amiable and approachable Dutch travellers. She was pleased that he had found such kind people on his previous visit, she would have hated him to have been companionless. Once Jude had fully explained Liz's appearance and that it had become something of a game, the four of them struck up a true friendship. Liz (Les) eventually worked half day with Jude and spent the afternoon, which she simply found too humid to work in, trying to capture on film the ever illusive monkeys. She came to believe that they were both deliberately hiding from her and also targeting her with fruit and nuts from the canopy, which was their domain. They were more successful hitting her than she was capturing them on film. She was extremely careful not to follow them into their comfort zone, she skirted around the perimeter of the hazardous jungle. She felt vulnerable as she knew it was perilous to go more than a few meters under the canopy. They had all been warned about snakes, spiders and scorpions that could make a person very sick or even kill if hospital treatment was not readily available. She wore thick leather gaiters tied around her lower limbs, these were given to her by one of the local boys who seemed to have developed a crush on her/him, whether this was because he thought she was male or female was unclear.

Jude watched her move confidently among all those who were on the veranda, he preferred her with short hair, the moustache he could forgo, she reminded him of the impish Aubrey Hepburn in a number of films with Cary Grant, or was it Gregory Peck? Or was his memory playing tricks on him? He wasn't sure. What he was sure of was that Liz was becoming increasingly significant to him. His thoughts of his association with her were developing a far reaching element. He was now able to look into the future with pleasant anticipation, just two years after losing the love of his life. He could still remember how he felt after losing Jayne, but he could no longer turn on at will that desperate degree of panic and despair that had been festering just below the surface. He used to be able to switch on despondency and melancholy so that he could wallow in self pity. He would still try sometimes to recall the last dream he had had of Jayne the night before he met Liz, but he was no longer able to recall with clarity her expression. Perhaps his mother had been right, memories do fade and time is a great healer. Watching Liz move assuredly amongst the locals and backpackers he felt proud to be her companion, her confidant and lover, he was in danger of telling her he loved her for the first time. She could feel his gaze but misunderstood it to be sensuous, she walked behind his chair, leant close to his left ear and whispered,

"Hey Casanova you need a cold shower." As she walked away from him she caught his eye, she was wearing her impish grin, even with her darkened top lip and her Cornish Pirates baseball cap she had never looked so gorgeous, so desirable and so flirtatious, there was a risk of Jude making the ultimate grand gesture. He controlled his emotions, mouthed silently 'I love you' and smiled a wry smile back to her, holding her gaze long enough to convey a deep message, her smile broadened and she mouthed, 'I love me, too.'

Clearly the time was right for Jude to take a giant leap for mankind but not for Liz, he chose a clean page on his ever-present note pad and penned a verse that would always remain private;

I never knew I could feel such rich love, I will never forget our first kiss,
You came into my life with the key to my heart, you say with your eyes more than most when lips part.
To steal a kiss, or to steal an embrace, to share a glance across a crowded room,
To share a smile, a scene or a scent, to share the lyrics to a beautiful tune.
These moments are crumbs to a hungry man, they are the moments by which I mark time,
Time,
It's the only measure of love, and in time may you one day be mine.

He dismissed such thoughts and returned to his page and to more constructive thoughts. Liz was enjoying a portion of Anna's celestial knowledge, Dirk was sharpening all their tools for the next day. When he had finished the tools and a little too much local wine he sat next to Jude, saying in unusually imperfect English,

"I understand exactly why you ask-ked Liz to dress as you did, it is huge extra responsibility travelling with attractive woman, even more so with Anna because of her blond-ed hair, it is a magnet in this part of the world for weirdo's and forever Dirk has one eye's on Anna and one eye's on life."

"I'm glad you understand, I think Liz sees it as a bit of fun, but it's good that someone else appreciates my point of view."

"Oh I speaks to Liz, I explain it is a good fing for her protection, but she still looks wonderful, I do not fink Anna will do such a fing."

"Dirk, I don't think I have ever met a couple so well suited, don't try to change Anna."

"Thank you. You two also seem to have a good understanding."

"I think so and I hope so, do you have anything planned for the weekend?"

"Oh yes, I want to tell you we have meet someone who is with a boat, not far from here at the harbour at Ladrilleros. He is good man I believe, for small money he will take us for the day on

Saturday, if you two come it will be more fun and less monies for us all, what you fink?"

"Dirk I think it's a good idea, I'll talk to Liz, but I also think that you have drunk enough wine tonight. Your English is not perfect for the first time since I have known you."

"Oh is it, what did I say?"

"Its nothing really, let's speak tomorrow."

"OK I sleep." Within sixty seconds he did just that.

Later Jude joined Anna and Liz stargazing and they all agreed that if the weather was ok they would all go out to sea together on Saturday, Anna joked,

"Did you manage to understand Dirk? When he drinks he gets a little muddled."

"Oh he was OK, not bad at all."

"Sometimes when he feels we are in a safe place he drinks a little too much, it is to relax, to forget his responsibilities and then he sometimes mixes Dutch and German in with his English, I think then I am the only person who can understand him."

"Does he drink a lot often?" Liz asks.

"Oh no, only when he feels we are very safe, or more so when he feels he doesn't have to be responsible for me. I know how safe or unsafe he feels by his drinking, if he refuses all drink I know we will be moving on quite quickly. Here things are good, but when you two arrive it became much better. Dirk knows that with you two here I have all the help I need if I have a problem, so he can relax sometimes and enjoy a drink." Liz replies,

"Do you mind?"

"No no, not at all, he is a beautiful man to be with in every way, he works hard and cares for me deeply. I know that but we all need to relax and forget our responsibilities, its Dirk's way, on the unusual occasion when he drinks more than just a glass with his meal, I know it is my turn not to drink and not to relax, for then I become our eyes and our ears, it is a temporary role reversal. I have no problem with it, he only leaves me to be responsible at the very best of places, once we have been there for a week or more, he is thoughtful, kind and protective." Liz gives Anna a hug, and replies,

"You too are very thoughtful, kind and protective, the two of you seem to have a great understanding."

"Thank you, it works well for us." After stargazing for another half an hour and listening to the night sounds from the rain forest they all retire to bed.

After two more days, when on each rain thankfully halted work late afternoon, it was Saturday. The four of them and one of the Spanish couples took the short but bumpy bus ride to the coastal town of Ladrilleros, which was one of two small towns either side of a narrow stretch of sea water. On the opposite side of the peninsular was the town of Jaunchaco, whose beaches sat in the leeward side of the prevailing winds and were consequently littered with the flotsam and jetsam that the Pacific Ocean brought its way. Whereas the side the visitors were on was buffeted daily by large waves and strong winds, resulting in clean, pristine beaches. They met Dirk's acquaintance, Enrique, a Colombian that he had met at Tumaco, close to the border with Ecuador. He had told Dirk that every Saturday from November to April he was for hire at the small town of Ladrilleros, he was as good as his word. They shared the surprisingly large boat, which was a twenty metre homemade combination of a pleasure cruiser front half and a fishing vessel to the rear, with four Colombian tourists and a Spanish couple from the estate.

The engaging but untrustworthy looking captain was eager to collect the money and as was usual, which was becoming a yardstick to measure the Colombian way of life the price was different to that quoted to Dirk just a month ago, they thought that it was odd that it was never lower on arrival. Dirk's irritation and embarrassment were soon dismissed. It was a fine, but hot and humid day, everybody was looking forward to a day of refreshing sea breezes. As the boat gathered impetus and left behind the humid, tree canopied shoreline, everyone relaxed, the Pacific Ocean was calmer than usual and the sky was clear. Above the noise of the engine Dirk was able to converse with the slightly built but rugged looking skipper, he was a man in his sixties, with a badly deformed left hand. After an extensive conversation with him, Dirk came to the comparative quiet of the fore of the boat to share his new-found knowledge with his companions. Having made sure that all three of them could hear him, he started by saying,

"There is something I must share with you," he continued, "I asked the Captain, or do you say Skipper?" Jude interjected,

"For us it is usually Skipper."

"OK, so I ask the Skipper if we will be doing any fishing today as I see the boat is full of equipment, he replied proudly no, because this whole area has been declared a Santuario de Flora Y Fauna Malpelo, which I'm sure you understand makes this area a marine sanctuary. He went on to say that we are very fortunate people, this is why the price is more than he had said it would be, we are extremely lucky to be in a no fishing area that has many different and huge species of fish and shark. Apparently some of the sharks are amongst the rarest in the world, there are silky sharks, hammerhead sharks, and short nosed, ragged tooth sharks, to name only the ones I was able to translate, but there are many others and several species of dolphin and porpoise. He added and now this is the interesting bit, that on Saturdays the whole world can pay him to see all the wonderful big fish in this special area. I asked is it only on Saturdays that people are allowed on the water, thinking that no boats no disturbance the rest of the week is a further precautionary measure to protect the area, his reply is I think you English will say priceless. He says no, my boat is only available on Saturdays, I fish with it Monday to Friday and I do not work Sunday, I ask him where he fishes, he replied, 'Here, it is only a Santuario de Flora y Fauna Malpelo at the weekend.' He believes it is a clever solution, the world is demanding that Colombia declare it a sanctuary and the many hundreds of local fishermen and their families will starve if they cannot fish, so they work out a clever solution. The world gets its marine sanctuary and the locals get to carry on fishing, and we have to pay extra to be here today because it is a special no fishing day, can you believe it?" Everyone is aghast, Jude in response then tells the full story of his discothèque-cum-circus experience, leaving out nothing. Liz jokingly says that she is proud of him, but adds that she hopes that he washed his hands. They all laugh, Dirk says,

"This was the kind of thing we had trouble with in the first year or two of our travels, but we got wise, we know where not to go, every country is different in the cities at night. Our own city of Amsterdam is one of the worst in the world, you have to be careful and be wise and then it is no problem." Anna adds that she cannot dance anyhow, Liz chips in with a humorous comment, which brings them all to loud laughter, she says,

"They wouldn't think much of me there at that night club, you can tell by my top lip that I don't have a razor."

The boat cruises around a number of very small islands for an hour and eventually anchors in calm, shallow water. As it is a flat bottomed vessel, the Skipper then removes four large wooden panels from the floor of the deck, exposing a glass bottom. All the passengers are thrilled to see the diversity of plant, fish and mammal life under the boat. They witness several species of shark and Jude guesses that leopard spot dolphin are also visible, the smaller fish and plant varieties are too numerous to count, it is easy to see why the conservation organisations of the world are determined to preserve such a place of beauty.

The skipper hands out wine and asks for volunteers to prepare food whilst he cast out four lines. Dirk says to him that he was under the impression that it was a no fishing day, the Skipper tells him that everyone must eat and that we are only eleven persons, we cannot eat all the fish in the ocean. Soon fresh fish are on the boat's Bar-b-que, it is only the four Europeans who eat with a guilty conscience. After lunch, which included copious quantities of extremely cheap local wine, the wind picks up and the skipper quickly heads for shore, not quick enough to prevent half of those on board from ejecting their lunch back into the ocean from whence it came. By the time the boat begins to enjoy sheltered conditions close to port everyone has had sufficient buffeting. As the vessel is tied to the dock the afternoon rain begins, this time it does not cease until after midnight, the day trippers are soaked by the time they reach the bunkhouse.

A lazy Sunday is spent by all, Dirk and Anna read, Jude writes and Liz flirts between a novel and her camera, should something unusual catch her eye. The following week, which is the last week working on the vines for all of them, dawns all too quickly. As they are the only Europeans ever to visit the estate twice the owner Juan Javier Hernandez makes a rare exception and invites them to dine with him at his home. He announces this invitation a week before they are due to complete their stint with him on the occasion of his paying their wages. After the boss man, the

'Jefe' leaves in his flying machine, a Sikorsky helicopter, the other local workers drop to their knees in mock adulation, the moment of levity passes quickly. This announcement suits Jude perfectly as he wants Liz to photograph the owner's home, he was working his way towards asking when the invite was divulged. Their last week goes by with one notable incident, two of the local Colombian workers have a physical dispute over a pretty young girl who had been flirting in an exaggerated manner with both of them. All who were present could have predicted the confrontation once the boys had started drinking, as the protagonist had clumsily brought the situation to a head. To be fair to the middle aged local man who was manager of the vineyard he did court opinion from all who were in the group. Everyone had been honest with him and his decision which could not be described as arbitrary was that the two young men should lose a week's wages and that the beautiful but hazardous young girl should have her buttocks thrashed in front of everyone and be put to work in the laundry of the bosses compound, this was always the least popular job due to the heat and humidity. None of the European contingent stayed to see the punishment administered and all of them thought it extreme, but this was the local way, local problems were resolved locally.

During their last week Liz, Jude, Dirk and Anna stayed ever closer together. They had become good friends and did not look forward to their parting of the ways. In the evenings, whether stargazing, or listening to the jungle sounds or the rain, they were all but inseparable. Their friendship was more than two girls getting on and two guys finding common ground, they had quickly developed a genuine affection for each other. Every one of them knew that soon they would be continents apart and were uncomfortable with the knowledge that it was highly unlikely that they would ever meet again. They could not give each other telephone numbers or addresses, as Dirk and Anna had neither and Liz would be renting a temporary house on her return. Jude gave them a ray of hope when he said that,

"If you are ever in the west of England, look up the electoral register, which is supposed to have everyone's name and address on it." That tiny glimmer of light on a dark situation was accepted publicly, but dismissed privately as a forlorn hope.

On their last night they were all whisked away to the Jefe's compound in his sleek blackbird, which was his preferred term for his helicopter. Liz was nonplussed by the scale of Juan Javier's compound, Dirk and Anna were speechless, the Sikorsky landed on the roof of the main house, a staircase to the side of the roof led them down to a wrap around veranda that was approximately thirty meters on all sides. The Jefe believed he had brought two men, one straight, one gay, an awkward looking young man and a beautiful blonde woman with him when he showed them into his home. They were all astounded that the entire top floor, all thirty meters square was one room. It was vast, spacious, light and absolutely stunningly furnished. It contained a huge dinning table that could seat twenty, a grand piano, a harp, an original Wurlitzer juke box, a billiard table and a dance area, add to all of that a compendium of exotic plants and fine furnishings, the four visitors had never seen or envisaged such a space.

They were allowed to gaze open mouthed for only a short time and then brought down one floor and showed to their rooms to prepare for dinner, though the owner, Juan Javier was a little uncomfortable having two males in the same room. They were given their final wages and one hour to prepare for dinner. Jude and Liz's bedroom was astonishing, it was not only colossal, it was beautifully furnished, it had its own well stocked bar, the en-suite was the height of luxury and the view over the rain forest was magnificent. They were on the third floor, the sleeping floor, below them was the kitchens and a breakfast area, below that was the cellars and stores. Liz was the first to speak,

"Did you see the disapproving way he looked at us?"

"Yep, we go'nna show him?"

"You bet and can you believe this place?" Jude savoured every moment as Liz removed her male attire, showered, fluffed up her hair, applied a little lip shadow to her eye lids, put on black, lacy underwear, unrolled and slipped over her head a silk, semi-see through, low cut, backless, black, leaf motif dress, it was a dress that showed off most of her long smooth legs, she added a pair of three inch black heels. The heels, dress and underwear had been rolled up and had taken up very little room in her rucksack and were now put to devastating effect. Even Jude, who knew her well, was astonished by her metamorphosis from gangly male teenager

271

to ravishing man eater, she recognised the look in his eyes and commented,

"Slow down Casanova, not to be touched by human hand until after midnight, go and have a shower, preferably a cold one, you won't believe the size of that bath room," she continued, "how does a coffee and wine grower get a state of the art helicopter and a fabulous home like this?"

"Simple he grows coca leaf."

"What?"

"For sure he has to be a coca leaf grower."

"You brought me into the home of a drug dealer."

"No no, he is a coca grower, he grows the leaf and sells it for a lot of money, it becomes a dangerous drug way down the line, this guy is doing nothing illegal."

"Oh what the hell, I'm too wound up now not to see tonight through, in for a penny in for a pound." She makes use of the well stocked bar.

"That's my girl."

"Go have that shower, you've spent three-quarters of an hour watching me, you've only got fifteen minutes left."

"Five is enough, why don't you come and play with me for ten?" He replies patting the bed next to him.

"By the look of you, if I came to play we would have nine minutes to spare, get in the shower." Reluctantly Jude obeys orders.

Fifteen minutes later, suitably attired but not one percent in competition with Liz, Jude ascends the stairs in front of her to the grand room above. Dirk and Anna, semi-smartly dressed are there before them, they too are astounded at Liz's transformation, Anna keeps touching her to continually reaffirm that she is for real. Liz says to Anna,

"Do you think I've gone a bit over the top."

"Way way over the top, but don't change back now, I want to see the look in everyone's eyes as they enter the room."

"Everyone's?"

"Yes look the table is set for twelve."

"Oh Christ what have I done, quick help me change back."

"Too late here comes our host." Juan Javier Hernandez enters the room and whistles loudly, he goes into a harangue in Spanish whilst circling Liz, she blushes red which only encourages him, eventually when his oration subsides into profound laughter he slaps Jude hard on the back and shakes his hand vigorously. Dirk attempts to translate,

"There was a lot of local expression in that bluster, which I'm not sure I understood, but in essence he is saying, you are an extraordinary revolution, or it might have been revelation, but he whole heartedly welcomes you both, no, all of us to his table, but he reserves particular praise for you Jude, for keeping this princess hidden from view, he says that there would be no work on the vines if the princess is there, only love sick men, as he is now, I think that's how most of it came out." Juan Javier shouts out,

"Si, si, si princess, princess." They are then introduced to Juan Javier's wife and his two sisters in their forties and four cousins, two male and two female all of similar age to their visitors. All the women are beautifully and colourfully dressed, the men in self-coloured shirts and black trousers, all their clothing appears to have been tailor-made, as the fit is exceptional. Poor Dirk is required to do the bulk of the talking, eventually most of the Colombian contingent admits to a bare rudiment of English and Anna, Jude and Liz chip in with a little Spanish, but the two dominant voices at the table are those of Juan Javier and Dirk.

The meal commences with champagne and fresh lobster and moves on to red wine and Argentine fillet of beef. All are of a standard way in excess of any of their experience, excepting those who have been seated at the table previously. The fillet melts in the mouth like pate, the red wine is Chateau Latour '82, one of the finest wines in the world, the champagne is of a similar standard, both the food and the drinks are of such quality they would not be out of place at the table of nobility.

Through Dirk, Liz asks Juan Javier, 'How is it possible to have such fine wines here in Colombia?' The answer to her rather naive question is that her host has a collection, which was started by his father, who was an enthusiast and that she is welcome to see the cellar in the morning. She also asks Dirk to convey to Juan Javier, that his home, his food and his wine are the finest she has ever experienced and might she be permitted to photograph his home tomorrow. He replies that she can go where ever she wishes with her camera if he can have the first dance with her after the meal.

273

She defers to Jude, which he finds both revealing and surprising, he smiles and nods so she too smiles, nods and says,

"Si si," to her host. The meal, the company and the surroundings are altogether sumptuous.

The table is cleared by staff and four piece band appears as if by magic, they play local music and Juan Javier gets his dance with Liz, as the dance commences his left hand is around her waist, at its conclusion it is gently supporting her right buttock. The music goes on long into the night, the opportunity is afforded for most people to dance with each other. There is no misbehaviour, excepting that at the stroke of midnight unseen by anyone a hand slides up inside Liz's dress to caress her bottom, Jude whispers to her that she did say she was not to be touched until after midnight. It was another two hours before they were naked in each other's arms and Jude is teasing Liz with his skilled coitus reservatus, she eventually takes the lead, which brings them both to a shuddering orgasm. Their post-coital glow is a short one as they are both asleep quickly, once their breathing has returned to its norm.

In the morning Jude wakes a little after nine am, Liz is standing naked looking from the window into the rain forest, on noticing that he is awake, she says softly,

"This place is unbelievable, I am so glad we came here."

"You mean the house or the country?"

"All of it, come on sleepy head I can't wait to get at it with my camera." Once outside accompanied by a member of staff who apologises that the Jefe has had to leave early in his helicopter, they realise just how commanding a view the main building has. There are many other surrounding buildings and each has its purpose. Liz fires her shutter like a person possessed, both inside and outside the main building. She is fascinated by the huge natural rock cavern utilised as a wine cellar. The only floor she is denied access to is the ground floor, she questions this and is told that it is not possible to see inside. She replies that,

"Juan Javier, the Jefe, gave his permission for us to go anywhere we chose." Her guide says,

"Si si, it is so." He opens a wooden door, punches a code into an electronic control and a huge, thick, steel plated door automatically slides to the right, as the door opens the vast room that confronts them is lit with self-activating lights, Jude is stood beside Liz. The look on their faces would not be dissimilar had they seen themselves dead. The large steel lined room is stacked full of munitions. Numerous rifles, grenades, mortar bombs and rockets are among those items Liz and Jude recognise from the many times they have seen them on their television screens at home. Liz says,

"Please close the door."

"Si si si" is her reply, they now want to leave the compound as soon as is practicable. Jude does ask Felipe their guide, in Spanish,

"Is it not very dangerous to have this material under the house?" His reply is brief,

"No, no detonators here." The four of them meet up again in the main room for breakfast of fresh coffee and bread, accompanied by a range of cold meats and local cheeses. Dirk says that they have been offered a free flight to Miami in the U S, but he feels he is being cautious not to accept, Jude agrees and the four of them do accept a ride in a huge four-by-four truck to the town of Buenaventura. As they leave they all thank the staff for looking after them, Felipe, their guide holds one finger across his mouth in the internationally recognised signal for silence, Liz nods her agreement.

The four of them part company at Buenaventura bus station, Dirk and Anna take the bus to Cali, where they join in with a backpacking crowd heading north. Their eventual targets are the west coast of the United States, west to east across Canada, Iceland and home, in perhaps eighteen months, they will have been fourteen years on the road. There was much hugging, kissing and back slapping as they parted and a few tears. Jude and Liz booked in for one night at the agreeable Hotel Titanic to plan their next move and they count their blessings that they did not get any more involved with Juan Javier Hernandez.

DAY FIVE

HANNA and BARBARA

I'm woken by Liz, getting out of bed at 6-30 to walk the dogs, she feels the mattress movement and stands up from the bed a fraction of a second before I lunge in her direction.

"You're getting old and slowing down."

"Come back in here." I say pulling her side of the covers back.

"Too late I'm up."

"So am I." I say, and pull back the quilt further to reveal my aroused condition. She laughs and leaves the room.

"You love those dogs more than me."

"Yep."

I shower and dress, knock the girls bedroom doors to wake them and being unable to resist its magnetic pull arrive at the kitchen, for coffee, toast and the morning offerings from the national press. Normally Liz collects the papers from the bin by the gate and puts them on the kitchen table, but today the weather must be bad, they are on the dinning room radiator drying off.

As always I pick up the Mirror first, and today is a good day for curious news. Two tourist who saved a drowning pony at St Just in Cornwall, had to be rescued themselves after it kicked a hole in their boat. I'm beginning to appreciate why my father bought this particular daily, also former president Jimmy Carter has accused the sitting president George Bush of being a disaster for the United States, here I feel they should have included the phrase the kettle calling the pot black. News from Scotland, more than 3000 chickens were released onto the A80 after a lorry jack-knifed, apparently not many chickens were successful in crossing the road! And finally a mother has used her four week old child as a club and swung the infant by its feet to hit her boyfriend with it. The child suffered a broken skull, the mother has gone to jail.

It is time to refresh my coffee and wake up the girls, again. It's a big day for Clare today, it's her driving test.

Now for the Times, again here it's a rich day for curious news, Britons have caused more than three hundred and fifty million pounds worth of damage to their own homes, attempting to copy things they have seen on DIY television shows. Plenty of work here for Richard (I can do that), or perhaps he is responsible for some or most of the damage. Off to Mexico City next, an aspiring horror novelist has been arrested after police discovered his girlfriend's torso in his closet, a leg in the refrigerator and several bones in a cereal box. Jose' Luis Calva admitted that he had boiled some of his girlfriends flesh, but that he had not actually eaten any of it. So yes, he was a depraved murderer and a tasteless cook, but he was not a cannibal. Staying on to the subject of limbs, a distraught mother has clashed with the MOD after discovering that the body of her son, a British soldier was returned from Iraq with the wrong limbs, unbelievable. David Cameron is openly declaring to all who will listen that he is the future of Britain and that Gordon Brown our encumbered Prime Minister should 'make way'. There is news from the McCartney divorce, it seems that 50 million pounds may not be sufficient to silence what will be his ex wife after their legal separation, what a troubled world we live in. And finally from the paper today there is an amusing item on the letters page, a gentleman writes that when he was recently randomly called by his bank he asked the caller to prove his authenticity by giving him the second letter of his password and his mother's maiden name. The caller said that he did not have access to that information, the gentleman then said that in that case he must conclude that he was not his bank! How sweet to turn the tables so swiftly.

Clare is keen to drive for what she hopes will be the last time as a learner. I drop her at the Hardye School as her test is at eleven o'clock from the college. I wish her luck and tell her to forget about dolphins and bungee jumps and concentrate on the Highway Code, dads can be so boring.

Today is wet, the Hardy statue is glistening. By the time I arrive in the courthouse my feet are also far from dry. Everyone seems to have put yesterday's unpleasantness behind them, it is perhaps only Joyce (matching accessories) who still looks a little pale, but as today's ensemble is based on cream and lilac, she is looking rather pale from head to foot. The lilac scarf, belt and shoes, are nicely offset by the cream blouse, cardigan and pencil skirt. The cardigan open at the front to reveal a hint of ample bosom cradled in a laced edged lilac bra. My less than honourable intentions towards her are interrupted by Hanna's all to obvious and poorly concealed silicone assets. Would it be too rude to suggest that she take some tips on the delicate art of concealment from Joyce? Hanna has obviously comforted herself overnight under a sun lamp, possible the entire night. She has a complexion that I think the French would put between appoint and bien cre, that being medium to well done. As is usually the case with Hanna the skirt is lacking in length and the war paint is a little too much in evidence. At sixty paces this woman is a head turner, at three paces she is not. We commence a conversation that somehow drifts onto cars, she says she has a superb, top of the range Audi TT, it is convertible and in racing red, why am I not surprised? I idly ask her where she bought it from, telling her that Liz and I are going into Yeovil to test drive an Audi in the morning. She lights up like a Christmas bauble.

"Oh you must talk to my husband Geoff, he's a salesman for Audi in Yeovil, tell him I sent you in please, he'll look after you."

"Thank you I will." I make a mental note of the name. She is a pleasant woman to talk to, with lovely eyes, it is a shame they look out from a face suitable camouflaged to perform in a circus, this is an expensive and high maintenance woman.

I break free from Hanna and notice that Lynda (menswear) is giving the two sport enthusiast Terry and Tim an ear bashing on the irrelevance of national sport, good luck to her. With pivotal games for both teams this weekend she might as well be pissing into the wind, or flogging a dead horse perhaps more appropriate, it was the male attire that confused me. The only empty seat as is often the case is next to Barry (Chaplain), who like myself has his copy of 'Far from the Madding Crowd' to hand, of all the printed material there is in the world how is it that he and I chose identical novels? Barry has many 'post it' notes sticking out of his copy of Hardy's novel, each one is highlighting a phrase, paragraph, or an old disused term he had marked for us to discuss, we deal with many of them whilst we are waiting to be called into court.

As a body of jurors we were sharing John (foreman's) more serious poem than was his norm, which described yesterdays rather traumatic events, when the rather lovely Dawn (white linen) called us into court. She brought with her such a pleasant aroma and now that we did not have Alice (fake fur's) dominant and inexpensive odour to compete with Dawns, it could be fully appreciated, and as Andy (body odour) was as yet conspicuous by his absence Dawn's fragrance had no competition and could be singularly enjoyed.

Once settled into court under the ever-watchful Hawkeye of judge (perverse) the prosecution outlined its case at length, again repeating the charges to the satisfaction of Hawkeye. The prosecution barrister, a stout man of perhaps fifty-five years and the owner of a bulbous whiskey nose and curiously an artificial leg, which appeared to hinder him not a jot consumed over an hour of the courts time. He tackled the charges from many different angles, listing his witnesses and his methods and approach to every aspect of the case. He informed us that as the victim Holly Banks was under age at the time of the alleged offence, she could and had chosen to give her evidence by video link from an alternative room from inside the courthouse. Even though she was now, as were her two friends and witnesses, Sophie Green and Lucy Cambridge of age, being over sixteen. But that due to the intimidating nature of the courtroom, all its paraphernalia and the obvious stress involved in sharing a room with the accused she had been offered this option and had expressed a preference for it, as had her two friends.

It was an immediate and palpable relief to us the jurors, that the victim was not a very young child and was in fact now sixteen, we recognised that this was now more a case of a question of consent or regret and perhaps less so one of brutal rape, as we had feared. Did the alleged offences take place before or after Holly Banks was sixteen and did this occur with a degree of consent or not. The gravity of the situation that faced us had eased a degree, to the considerable comfort of all of us who sat in the jury, this did not lessen the serious nature of the charges, merely the way we viewed them.

My thoughts went to Clare who was at this moment on her driving test, I was disappointed in myself for I had brought my mobile phone into the jury room for the first time to send her a last minute text of good luck. I now realised that the phone was still in my pocket and turned on, worse still it had a loud and obscure ring tone, which Clare had installed into it, which would without doubt halt court proceedings should it sound. I tried to put it to the back of my mind but it refused to be diminished. Indeed the phone seemed to grow larger and larger in my pocket, until it made me feel lopsided and weighed down. At the completion of the prosecutions opening statement and just prior to the commencement of that for the defence, I requested a comfort break that Hawkeye reluctantly agreed to, it was just after twelve o'clock, as I left the courtroom and an instant before the door closed behind me, my mobile received a message. I could hear one or two sniggers behind me, I headed for the toilets to silence my loud and obtrusive phone. It was a text from Clare, the message was full of smiley faces and exclamation marks, she had passed. Now we would begin to share in the eternal parental nightmare whenever she was out on her own. Is she safe? Is she being careful? Has she broken down? Is she upside down in a ditch somewhere? What time is she getting home? She is a sensible kid but I could imagine the scenario, it's eleven o'clock in the evening, she's out in her car, I'm tired, I want to go to bed, I've got to drive to Manchester in the morning, getting up at four o'clock to give myself a chance of getting through the obstacle that is Birmingham before eight, and Clare or Emma aren't back yet. Do I go to bed and lie there awake waiting for the sound of the car, or do I absorb some drivel on the television to distract me, and then it's midnight I have to sleep or it will affect my ability to perform at my normal level the next day, my only comfort in these thoughts is in my hand as I stand in the immaculate surroundings of the county court toilets, my mobile phone. We made the girls wait until they were fifteen until they had mobiles, but they could now prove to be a great source of comfort to us both.

I switch off my phone, make use of the facility and quickly return to my hard bench in the court. The judge explains to us that a doubt has arisen with regards the eligibility of certain evidence and that the court needs to debate whether it is appropriate for this evidence to be put before the jury. Whilst this debate is to proceed, we the jury are to be excluded from the court, so that Hawkeye and the two legal teams can concur as to the worthiness of the testimony in question. So it is an early lunch for us all.

I do not linger in the jury room, not wishing to debate the weather, numerical oddities, and the advantage of nylon rope over the traditional jute or flax, or the progress or lack of our national teams. My first impression of the day as I exit the courthouse from the discrete side door, exclusively for the use of the jury members and court officials, is one of pleasure. The rain has ceased and the cloud all but disappeared east towards Hampshire, eventually to unburden itself over our great capital. As I walk across the small and discriminatingly restrictive car park, used only by Hawkeye and the barristers, I hear my name hailed loudly by a female voice. The intensity of my pleasure with the day slips a rung, it is the voice of Hanna, I turn toward the sound only to experience both her ample silicone assets at close quarters and a business card is thrust into my face.

"Let me give you one Geoff's cards, I've had these tucked behind the sun visor since I've had the car, he'll be pleased I've given one out."

"Thank you, but it's not strictly necessary as I've already got an appointment for tomorrow, but thanks anyway."

"Oh don't be a killjoy, if you turn up with one of his cards I've given you, I'll be in his good books, I might just get that new kitchen I'm after."

I don't imagine this woman would have much use for a kitchen, perhaps somewhere to apply nail varnish in a hurry, pluck her eyebrows over the sink, perform fellatio at the breakfast bar, or perhaps in an emergency to shove a TV dinner in the oven. She then asks,

"Where do you go for lunch?" I very quickly consider all the possible answers and come up with the most likely answer to repel her,

"Oh I'm going down Cornwall Road after I've bought a roll for lunch, down to the main cemetery, I'm a bit of a morbid bugger, I wander places of internment and sometimes just sit and read." I hold up my copy of Hardy's novel, to add weight to my deception.

"Oh super, Geoff's mother is pushing up daisies in there, could you just wait for me to get some flowers on the way and I can score another point towards my kitchen." I didn't see that coming, my actual plan now that we had a two hour lunch was to go to Clare's car and pick up Jayne's book. I'd last left it with Jacqueline Forbes-Brewer in a odd situation. With Hanna now to be an attachment for today's lunch break, the despairing Miss Forbes-Brewer would have to wait for a day or two for her due restitution.

"You're welcome of course, but you will never make it in those heels."

"Oh that's no problem, my car is very close, I've got my ugg boots in the back, I can change into those in a moment." She links her arm through mine and leads me towards her car. I cannot recall feeling this uncomfortable in a long time, I am walking arm in arm with a woman whose apparel would suit a twenty year old in a nightclub and whose war paint would not be out of place in a circus ring. I instinctively look around to my left and right to ascertain if I'm being observed by anyone with functioning cerebral matter. I do not notice Joyce (accessories) ardently in attendance. We reach her car and whilst she is changing her footwear, I infuse the one high point of this extraordinarily presented woman, her perfume, it is Chanel, Allure and is delightful. Until she then re-administers the fragrance, using sufficient to drown a small rodent!

We walk together towards the town centre and pause for her to buy the least expensive bunch of flowers available and for me to buy lunch, she doesn't purchase any to eat stating,

"I haven't kept this figure by eating lunch." She lights a cigarette, the smoke from which is both revolting in its close proximity to myself and adds further fuel to the unattractiveness of her persona. I find that even naturally beautiful women become repulsive with a cigarette between their lips, there are women who are gorgeous in both looks and figure, who also have a gifted sense of what to wear to enhance their image, who can then light a cigarette and plummet off my scale of attractiveness deep into the pit of unsightly, nay, ugly oblivion, Hanna was doing her best in this regard.

"Do you smoke?"

"Thank you no." Is my short reply and I add, "I must pause for a moment to text and congratulate my daughter who has this morning passed her driving test" Whilst I am texting she ask me about my offspring, I give her brief details of ages, sex and college courses. She adds that she and Geoff have no children, just a pair of small Yorkie dogs, called Lady and Tramp after her favourite Disney DVD. She says that,

"We never really got to the bottom of why we never had kids, I think I'm ok and the problem is with Geoff, he had a brush with prostate cancer a few years back, which he got over completely, but now he's so big that side of our marriage is a bit of a problem. Looking at her figure I envisage she is no more than seven and a half stone, perhaps a hundred pounds, so menstruation would I imagine have been irregular at best and none existent at worst.

Clare text me back she is a very happy seventeen year old. We walk through Cornhill and observe that the George Café makes several claims on its façade, among them that 'Our pleasure is great service and great food is our pleasure' but more curiously, it boast a spurious claim that 'Even Thomas Hardy would be delighted', it would be interesting to put that claim to the test. What indeed would Hardy think of a pizza, a panini or a cappuccino, today's international cuisine being unrecognisable to that of the nineteenth century. I notice that many people are hurrying in all directions whilst consuming their various mobile lunches, I think this hurried behaviour even more than the continental diverse fare on offer would be a great and abhorrent revelation to someone born in the eighteen hundreds. We arrive at the aptly named Junction public house, which uncommonly sits at the union of no less than six roads, clearly this has been a focal point in the towns long historical past.

Opposite The Eldridge Pope building, which is part of the enormous and historical Dorchester brewery, is H Y Duke and sons auctioneers in Dorset since 1823, further evidence of the towns stability since Hardy's time, much has changed dramatically, but much also has not, is this the very auction rooms where Hardy's mother both bought and sold items of furniture? Passing the police station and ancient Maumbury Rings, which I promise myself to return to at a later opportunity we cross the railway line, its banks now overgrown with Buddleia, Ash, Hazel and Sycamore, the same railway used by Hardy for his maiden journey with his mother in 1849.

On reaching the cemetery we wander aimlessly pointing out one curiosity after another, to the backdrop of the railway. Hanna still attached to my left arm points out that Elsebeth, wife of James William Latch isn't dead at all, she was merely called to rest as was he later. I point out that Nancy Hordley fell asleep in1913 and her husband Henry had 'I will never leave or forsake thee' inscribed on her memorial, but that oddly it goes on to state he did just that. He simply died in 1945 and was interred at Loxwood cemetery in west Sussex. Hanna notices that Robert Alexander Departed this life where as Sergeant F.E.Dawson of the rifle brigade simply died. My next choice is Thomas Warner who accidentally drowned in 1919 aged 33, on his tomb is a poem 'Death to him short warning gave, and quickly called him to his grave, then haste to Christ make no delay, for no one knows their dying day'. Hanna speculates as to whether there is any form of drowning other than accidental. Andrew James Curtis son of the above was killed at sea aged just seventeen 'when thou passes through the waters I will be with thee'. Hanna notices that Raymond John Tuck was killed in action aged twenty-one, where as his wife Fanny was at the age of seventy-one suddenly called home. Hanna is now in full flow,

"Look George E Cuppy entered into rest, Luke Green was suddenly called to rest and Emma Gladys Marsh is to be envied for she passed peacefully away." I notice a Cherry Florence Ashfield who was born Oxford, Jamaica and who died a very long way from home.

We eventually pass by the grave of her husband's mother, which is how she refers to her and not with the more usual term of mother-in–law, this I soon learn is because she never met the woman, she had died a year before she met Geoff. She drops the bunch of chrysanthemums, complete with cellophane and price tag on the grave, she makes no attempt to present them or put them in the vase and having done that duty with a degree of detachment, she mentally clicks up an advantage point towards her new kitchen.

We sit on a bench amongst others, the timber seat now both dried and warmed by the midday sun. I eat my lunch, Hanna goes uncharacteristically quite, she is observing in detail other people who have decided, as we have to enjoy a short outdoor break, during this window of fine autumnal weather. I notice a middle aged gent who has plainly positioned himself on a corresponding bench directly opposite us, for what is becoming abundantly clear is the express purpose of gaining a prime view of Hanna's legs as they eventually disappear under her now alarmingly short skirt, which as she is sitting has risen up just short of her arse. I remark,

"You might want to pull your skirt down a tad, I think the gent opposite is both in danger of glimpsing your navel and occupying the newly dug grave we passed earlier."

"Good luck to him."

"You're not concerned that this man will go home and abuse himself with your image on his mind, or may have sex with his overweight, beige, soap opera loving wife tonight, whilst sucking a Werther's Original, thinking of you."

"No, like I said good luck to him and if it gives her a rare orgasm good luck to her too." I didn't feel at all surprised by her reply, in fact it was stimulating to converse with someone with such a relaxed and open attitude. She added,

"Geoff and I often sit in a public situation where we can watch the effects my skirts and bust have on people, its just a bit of fun, no harm done, its Geoff who really gets off on it, I've got used to wearing this garb, and these." She lifts her silicone assets slightly with her palms as she says this. At this juncture I believe the gent in his early sixties opposite, is both wishing himself to be a younger man and me to simply evaporate.

"These are his idea not mine, he insisted, its not that we consider I'm a trophy wife, Geoff just likes to think he's got what other men want and can't have."

"And is that true."

"Oh Christ yes, I wouldn't dare get involved, I wouldn't even touch another man and neither would Geoff cheat on me, not in a month of Sundays, I love him to bits and him me, but we both

285

get a bit of a lift out of other men and occasionally other women mentally undressing me, and if they go off and abuse themselves to use your rather posh term for a hand job, so what."

"You touched me earlier, in fact you walked arm in arm with me all the way from the high street."

"That's 'cause your safe to be with, I can tell, I've watched more men than you've had hot dinners, you're the sort who likes to look, not stare, just look and move on and if I'm on your arm others to will just look and not stop and engage me, I wouldn't be here now if it wasn't for you. The way I dress is a bit of a handicap to me when I'm on my own, which isn't often." She's beginning to make a very different impression on me from the way she looks, she continues,

"It's a bit like something Geoff does, he doesn't drink at all due to his lucky brush with cancer, but if he's at a wedding or in a pub with a lot of friends or family, the first thing he does is to buy everybody a drink, including a pint for himself, which he leaves in front of him all night, so when people pester him or keep asking him if he wants a drink, he points to the pint and says I'm ok thanks and they leave him be." "Towards the end of the evening he gives the pint away, so people think one way and they leave you alone, it's the same with me, when I'm walking close to or arm in arm with a man, I'm like a dressed dummy in a shop window, they can look but they can't touch and anyway with those corduroy trousers, those shoes and that shirt you've got safety written all over you, you might as well be wearing a hard hat and a hi-viz vest." I laugh audibly and realise that once again I am guilty of judging a book by its cover. There is a woman of quality and sensitivity beneath the absurdity of Hanna's apparel, and I feel some degree of guilt that I have had some fun with her image, but I am glad that it has not been to her cost. My instinct now is to pull her skirt down six inches, to protect her from the views of others, but then that's because I just don't get the game she is playing. She is right in that she is doing no harm to anyone, other than her reputation in the eyes of complete strangers, whom she is never going to engage with, in fact to a few she is giving a short term treat, as a nursery teacher might hand out a sweet to a child, a short term harmless fix. Our conversation drifts through varied and diverse subjects and eventually it is time to make our

286

way back to the courthouse, I stand, hold out my arm for Hanna to lock onto and with a pleasant smile she does just that. As we begin a slow return to court, Hanna notices a grave of a Hanna Beatrice, which is cursorily also her middle name, this one lived 97 years, she touches the grave in consolidation of her namesake. I believe in the vain hope that her longevity will rub off.

To my disappointment most of the more interesting, larger, older, upright or listing stones are illegible. A century or more of corrosive wind and rain has eroded the written memorial tributes and the facts celebrating the lives of those who lie beneath, long since forgotten. The huge graveyard itself is now deathly quite for a moment, the background sounds of the railway to the east and the traffic to the south-west, which are normally a reminder to all visitors that time stands still for no man, have temporarily abated. We pause to take in our surroundings, Hanna's thoughts are for a moment private, I look to the south to view the hills that separate Dorchester from Weymouth and the coast.

I then imagined the sun setting to the west, casting ever lengthening shadows from the tombstones, until Harold Arthur Platt is leaning on George Dennis, who is in turn leaning on Jonathan Henry Dalton and eventually all is darkness, almost as dark above ground as it is below. A time for the nightshift of hungry bats, toads, hedgehogs and all manner of night loving insects to occupy their cemetery, It is a time for the hunted to eat quickly before they are themselves consumed, a time for murder and copulation. I notice a lonely stand of Cyprus and yew trees, which would at night take on sinister, black forms, sentinels standing over the long since departed.

Hanna jerks my arm, breaking my dream like state.

"Look at these," she says "Fanny Doris May entered into rest suddenly, Elizabeth Lockwood was called to higher service and Muriel Kitty Collinson was called to a fuller life, there's a lot of dishonesty here, it seems that most of these people aren't dead at all."

"It's simply a way of softening the blow to the bereaved, look this ones interesting." I read out the inscription. "A youngest and beloved son, one Leonard William Tattershall, died in 1918 of disease contracted whilst on active service in Salonika." I remark that I have never heard of Salonica, Hanna agrees, I vow to get one of my girls to look it up on the accursed but increasingly useful internet later. One or two of the stones have themselves fallen to rest long since grown tired of their task and who I wonder will resurrect them to recommence their tireless and thankless duty? As we emerge from behind a clump of yew Hanna jerks me back, she has noticed an elderly man, perhaps in his nineties who clearly believes himself to be unobserved. He is urinating upon a grave, without ceremony or gestures, a very matter of fact act. After he leaves we note that the modest and unobtrusive stone is in loving memorial to one Stanley Arthur Thompson, born 20th January 1903 – died 7th of June 1967, was the man a parent, an uncle, a brother or an acquaintance? It was clearly not the first time that this form of weed killer had been utilised, was this the settling of a grudge perhaps? Or has Hanna speculated perhaps Stanley was a rival for the affections of another, she was intrigued. The grave was otherwise unadorned and it was clear that Stanley Thompson had few sympathisers in the living world. Whatever degree of comfort or satisfaction the old gentleman extracted from his act was undecipherable. It would be a secret that we felt he would take with him to his grave. Oddly, just before we left the cemetery Hanna noticed the grave of a Julian Cannon Wilkes, he simply died, he was not called to higher service or any such thing, and he was a parish priest of Dorchester.

Curiously both of the churches, or chapels in the cemetery have their doors firmly shut and padlocked, a solid barrier against all who would visit, or shelter from adverse weather or acts of god. We leave the cemetery and head back towards the town. It takes us twenty minutes to reach the courthouse, during this time I am engaged in playing Hanna's game, I am paying particular attention to all the male members of the public who are walking in the opposite direction, to notice how many of them glance or stare at her semi-exposed hemispheres and fully exposed legs, to my amazement it is almost everyone. I could also get a feel for which men would turn their heads to gaze at her rear view once they are past. Just for twenty minutes of my life I am intrigued by Hanna's recreational pastime, I am also staggered by the shallowness of ninety percent plus of my fellow man. A half-kilogram of well presented silicon and a high hemline and half the population of the planet are sidetracked, if only for a moment.

As we approach the court building Hanna releases my arm and walks a couple of metres from me, so as not to raise eyebrows with our fellow jurors, she is an expert at this game, knows exactly where the offside line is and will never require a referee to blow a whistle to issue a red card.

I am met in the jury room by Terry (rugby) and Tim (football) it's Terry who opens the conversation.

"So Jude, what do you think of our chances at the weekend"?

"I think we will beat the French, we are their bogey team, just like New Zealand are for us, but with the French taking out New Zealand last week and us taking out the Australians on the same day, this world cup has turned on its head, the French fear us, its all that business about the hundred years war, Agincourt and Waterloo, they expect to lose to us as we do to New Zealand."

"So you've got us in the final then, against South Africa, who gave us a good hiding two weeks ago."

"Yes I think we will make the final and it will be a very different game this time, Johnny Wilkinson will find his kicking boots for sure."

"And what about my boys?" says Tim, "What do you reckon?"

"As I understand it you have to beat Estonia at Wembley at the weekend and then go to Russia on Wednesday and win to qualify for the European tournament, is that right?"

"That's about it."

"I imagine Wednesday might be a bit of a problem for your boys."

"Oh no not you as well, Terry here has got me on the edge of my seat."

"Your boys are done for." Says Thomas (the numbers man) but thankfully he doesn't back it up with statistical analysis.

"Oh come on you lot where's your national pride, what about the three lions and all that." Says Tim. I reply for the three of us.

"We've got plenty of national pride, we don't need three lions, just three points from Johnny Wilkinson's boot in the last minute, that's how you win a world cup and let's get this in proportion, your boys are struggling to qualify for a European competition, our lads have to just to step over the French and we are in the world cup final, for the third time in the last five tournaments, no contest." This is received with a loud,

"Here here." From both Terry and Thomas, I'll have egg on my face next week if the results go in Tim's favour.

Back in court things are beginning to gather momentum, we hear from the police officers that dealt with the original complaint, which was made two days after the alleged event took place, due we are told to fear and apprehension of the resulting pandemonium once the whistle was blown. So for this reason no DNA evidence was available. The offence allegedly occurred at a Wayside Inn on the outskirts of Bournemouth one week short of Holly Bank's sixteenth birthday. The receptionist from the Hotel and the car park attendant both identified Michael and his distinctive car being at the lodge on the night in question, but the CCTV footage was inconclusive as to exactly who his three young female companions were. Character witnesses were both questioned and cross-examined, during which time they presented near perfect reputations for the three girls involved, these include school teachers, dance instructors, and the owner of the local livery stable frequented by the girls.

It was refreshing to listen to adults, apparently telling the truth and not a penis, tongue bar or clitoris was mentioned, much I imagine to the disappointment of Hawkeye, but in general an undeniable weight of opinion was building in favour of the girls and against Michael. The afternoon session went by quickly, all the witnesses called to the court were on the periphery of the case, none were very close to the victim and none spoke for the accused. Indeed no character witnesses were ever called by the defence, which the judge drew to our attention at the close of play and as it was Friday and Hawkeye himself had a train to catch, we were dismissed early at three thirty.

I sat in the car reading 'Far From the Madding Crowd' and failed to realise sleep had overtaken me. Had I not turned on my mobile phone prior to picking up the book I may have been even later than the half hour which Clare spent waiting for me. She tore the learner plates from the car the moment it stopped and went immediately to the driver's door.

"I can't believe I can drive this home now on my own, that feels so good."

"You can if you want to, drop me at the station."

"Can I really?"

"Yep, but you'll have to come to Sherborne, Salisbury or Southampton later to pick me up and remember your paying for the fuel from now on and its now up to eighty pence a litre, it's up to you."

"It's tempting but I'm working tonight, come on lets go."

"So how'd it go? Any majors, any minors?"

"No majors no, just two minors, I got one of the new road signs wrong and I got a bit too close to a lorry, but it generally felt good and the examiner was a nice bloke."

"How nice?" I say with raised eyebrows and in a slow seductive voice.

"Daaaaaad, he was I think as you would describe, about thirty, poorly dressed and wearing the wrong shoes, a bit of a saddo, with an out of date flattop haircut and a girly earring in his left ear."

"Good girl, now I can picture him, he probably lives in a nineteen sixties tired old bungalow with his ageing mother, two ginger cats and a budgerigar called Joey, he takes the Daily Star, Private Eye and thinks putting a red nose on the front of his Fiat Uno for comic relief is being risky."

"Dad you're horrible, though he did have a bit of a stale smell about him and I can picture the beige bungalow."

"He's probable cut up his mother and put her in the freezer, hacks off bits to feed the cats, that's the smell."

"Oh shut up and were not stopping to pick up road kill tonight, I'm already late, why were you so long in court today?"

"I wasn't, I was asleep in the car when you rang me, we were dismissed by the perverted, Hawkeye of a judge at three thirty."

"Judge sounds nice." Her driving on the way home was fine, I did point to a particularly healthy looking dead hen pheasant but a loud no from Clare was her only response. We arrived home north of Buckland Newton to our village that Hardy had re-named Nuttlebury with just the aforementioned pheasant and a healthy looking but dead tabby cat to add to the years tally.

It was Friday night, there was no post worth a mention and Emma was at the door, car keys in hand in her waitress's uniform. As I was late, she had changed, presumable so that I can drop her at the pub at the end of her lesson. She is happy and chatty, things have gone well for her at college today, she drives well and expresses a great conviction to equal Clare's achievement on Tuesday. A few miles short of the pub where she works the damn car begins to overheat again. I take over the driving, this was a problem I had discussed albeit briefly with Richard (I can do that) earlier in a break from court proceedings. Apart from stating the obvious, that he could sort the problem out for me, he had advised that a sure way to clear an air lock is to drop the gearbox down a couple of gears to boost the revs whilst your driving at about sixty miles an hour in top gear, he said it would definitely kill or cure. As the car had only cost me fifty quid I took his advice, the engine revs went from around two thousand to seven thousand as I changed from fifth gear down to second, the noise was deafening, Emma put her fingers in her ears, I crossed mine. The poor old car only suffered around ninety seconds of this treatment and Richard was right. We abandoned the car with its seized up engine and walked the last half mile to the pub, The Green Man, where Emma worked. She was a little upset when I told her that Clio had expired.

"But why can't you put a new engine in it."

"Listen it's just not worth it, I'll find you another one."

"But if I pass on Tuesday I want to use it straight away."

"I know you do, Clare's got a decent working car, so I'll get you one, I was always planning to change Clio for another, it was living on borrowed time, but as you liked it I let it go."

"But what's going to happen to Clio?"

"I'll take her home, take off the tyres, the windscreen wipers and a few bits and pieces and then she will go to the great scrap metal yard in the sky."

Emma went very quite and I'm sure she was a little upset, which I understand, it was her first car, there is always an attachment to your first car, mine was a Morris Minor, old, bits were falling off but I loved it. I sympathised with her and reassured her that I would find her something soon.

"Look I'm going out car hunting with your mum tomorrow, I'll have a look for another Clio for you."

"OK, thanks Dad." Was all she could manage as she blinked back tears, she opened the pub door and went inside to start her shift. I too went inside and ordered a pint while I rang home to get Liz or Clare out with my tow rope. An hour later Clio was in the drive and I was in the bath with 'The Madding Crowd' and a large glass of Rioja Reserver 2000, heaven. With Emma working and Clare off in her car somewhere, Liz and I spent a lovely quiet evening, with a bottle or two of red catching up on each other's week by the open fire with the dogs hogging the warmest spot. Liz had taken a class in the morning and gone shopping in the afternoon, she was ready to unwind with a good wine. We ended up watching two episodes of Sherlock Homes on DVD, something we did occasionally, something we both enjoy, its easy watching and I believe that never was a man more disposed to adopt the personality of the fictitious detective than Jeremy Brett. I imagine if Sir Arthur Conan Doyle had met Brett he would have adopted him as the perfect embodiment of his fictional character.

Thankfully both girls arrive home in reasonable time and we are able to go to bed, a little drunk but not too late, as I pass Emma's room she is searching the wonderful World Wide Web for a replacement for Clio. She shouts through our bedroom door just before midnight.

"There's a really good green one with a years MOT and six months tax for nine hundred and ninety five."

"Where is it?"

"Newcastle."

"Good, best place for it."

"Where's Newcastle."

"Go to Scotland, turn right and stop when you hit the sea, goodnight."

"But Dad."

"Goodnight."

"I'd really like a green one."

"Goodnight."

"Night Mum, night Dad." Says Emma with resignation.

Clare adds "Night John Boy."

Emma "Night Grandma."

Liz "Night Mary Ellen."

Clare "Night Jim Bob."

Jude "Shut up and goodnight to everyone."

Emma, "What about the dogs?"

Clare "Night Itchy, night Scratchy."

Eight o'clock the next morning found me in a surprising position, on the fast catamaran ferry out of Weymouth bound for St Malo, France. Our phone rang at four thirty in the morning, it was my sister Barbara calling from France, she was both frantic and fighting back panic attacks. Her husband Jean Pierre was dead. He had died in his sleep during the night, she had left him to sleep in another room because his snoring was particularly bad, she had woken at five am feeling cold and alone, when she went back to him, he too was cold and not breathing, efforts to revive him failed. Barbara is distraught beyond description. Liz booked my ferry passage on her computer, whilst I tried to placate Barbara, she was off the scale with shock and grief, I believe that if I can spend tonight and part of tomorrow with her, then perhaps I can be a shoulder to cry on, help get her through her first night without her soul mate.

So it's a croissant with my coffee for breakfast today. Thankfully the English Channel is calm, and the crossing is to be a smooth one, for me it is a familiar one, we have taken this route several times during the past two decades. My choices of papers today are Le Monde, La Liberation and Le Figaro, not being an artistic professional or a lefty socialist I choose the latter and glean what I can from the many rugby pages, covering today's game between our two nations for a place in the world cup final. The game was to be my afternoon's entertainment, after I had taken Liz into town to find a replacement for her ageing car. Emma will go in with her now, which may prove expensive, with Emma's encouragement Liz may just push the boundaries of financial reason to breaking point.

Liz also now has to take Clare, her friend Kate, Kate's mother Page and her lezzie friend George to Heathrow on Sunday, which was going to be my task. Apparently Kate's mother has this week been banned from driving and her live in George has never driven. So it was a quick goodbye to Clare at six o'clock this morning, a nag to be very careful and to text me every day, I stuffed forty quid in her favourite trainers, which I knew she wouldn't leave behind. I left the house at six thirty, got to the Weymouth ferry terminal at seven fifteen, boarded with my Mercedes van at seven thirty and as I was last but one on we departed immediately, so it was French papers only for me, all the English being already taken.

I have never heard anyone so distraught as Barbara was on the telephone at four thirty our time this morning, five thirty for her, I don't think I've heard a person that distressed before, it was a very hurried decision to go to her, in fact it was Liz's decision, in an emergency she certainly proves herself fit to handle one, just like Hardy's Miss Everdene. Liz had very quickly prioritised all that really mattered. Barbara needed support, she needed my support, hence the call. She established that there was a Brittany ferry Condor out of Weymouth which would land me in St Malo at one o'clock lunchtime, a five hour drive and I could be with Barbara by six pm. I could leave my sister twenty four hours later. Sail from St Malo at midnight, sleep on the ferry and arrive back in Weymouth at eight am Monday morning. Giving me half an hour to disembark, drive to Dorchester and I would have a further half an hour for breakfast before I was required in court. Liz would go into town with Emma to look for cars and she would take Clare plus the others to the airport on Sunday, all of this she got across to me as she put my wallet, phone and van keys in my pockets and shoved me out the door with a very loving,

"Take care, look after Barbara and come back in one piece."

I was appalled with myself as I added my first ever badger to my road kill total, on the Downs south of Buckland Newton, a case of driving a bit too fast and being a tad pre-occupied, none of that being of any comfort to a very fit looking young badger, the magpies and crows will eat well today.

The Condor ferry is full to capacity, I was clearly fortunate to get on, I look around my fellow passengers, it looks to me to be a fairly even split between elderly couples going back to their second homes, from a visit to the grandchildren in England, or returning to their French bolt holes after medical treatment for that worrying mole, that new set of dentures, or that stress relieving or condemning M.I.R. scan. Now they can return to their verandas, empty bottles of Cote du Rhone and Vins de Pay and await their pensions from blighty and the other half of the passengers are white van man.

On the lower decks surrounding my silver Mercedes were all manner of sign written vans, 'Plastering by Steve and Dave', 'Taylor and sons Bricklayers', 'Bespoke kitchens by South West kitchens Ltd', 'Kenny the Plumber', 'North Dorset Roofing' and many more. All of these builders were here to earn monies from the aforementioned passengers. Half the ferry customers providing a service for the other half, thereby ensuring that the pensions, isa's, premium bond and equity release payments that are being pumped abroad down the cross channel financial umbilical cord to the elderly are being redistributed to the next generation, brought back to UK and turned into beer, cigarettes, tools, diesel and family holidays. Of course after the French ferry company has had their cut from both groups, France two, England nil, not a good omen for today's rugby, which I will now miss.

Thankfully the crossing is a smooth one, a quick stop off at Guernsey, another at Jersey and we are in sight of the French coast. The two conversations I am unable to avoid confirm my earlier suspicions; a gang of three in their twenties are expecting to make a killing plastering a farmhouse and barn in the Val de Loire for a Welsh couple in their seventies. Also an elderly English couple, complete with new spectacles and flu jabs, can't wait to get back to their farmhouse and gite near Berjerac, to see how the work they are having done is progressing. Being almost last on, I am inevitably last off, I leave the beautiful old port and historic walled city of St Malo at one thirty French time and head south at ten kilometres over the speed limit towards the city of Rennes. The drive is for me a familiar one, I've not visited Barbara for two years, but I've driven this route half a dozen times in the last twenty years and I find once I've driven to a place I can find it by instinct, so no maps or sat-navs are necessary.

The ordinary countryside of northern France gives way to the beauty of the Val de Loire and later to the Vendee, I pass by Rennes and take the périphérique around Nantes and push on towards Niort, here I leave the peage, the toll roads and head deep into the French countryside of the department of the Poiteau Charentes. I pass through many charming and seemingly abandoned villages, such as Mêlée, Chef-Boutonne, Villefagan, St Angeau, St Mary and Chasseneuil-sur-Bonnieure. With just one short pit-stop in the Vendee I arrive at the medieval looking hamlet of Chez Thoma, which sits on the borders of the Charente and the Limousin, quite exquisite countryside, stocked with healthy looking Limousin cattle, walnut, oak and chestnut trees. There are no grapes and sunflowers here, they have been left behind to the south of the Val de Loire.

I pull off the road onto the lightly gritted area under a huge walnut tree, where we have often played boules, Jean Pierre usually being unbeatable, until the red wine had dulled his aim. Barbara hears my van pull up and comes out of the vine clad, beautiful, rambling old farm house and focuses on me like a heat seeking missile, she hits her target and clings on as if her life depends on it. Not before I catch a glimpse of her eyes, they are deep, empty pools of misery, holes cut into raw meat. We stand entwined as one for several minutes on a lovely October afternoon, surrounded by the full range of autumnal colours, Barbara sobbing into my chest. Eventually her grip on me is released and we walk into the house, she has aged since I saw her last, just two years ago, she has grey in her hair, or perhaps it has been there for a while, but that she does not have the effort to conceal it at present, we enter her vast, welcoming farmhouse kitchen.

"Thank you so much for coming, what am I going to do? Jean Pierre was retiring next month, we were going to travel all over, why did I leave him? His breathing was terrible, I shouldn't have left him, I could have helped him, I could have done something, I let him down, I shouldn't have left him."

"Did he have any health issues? Anything you haven't mentioned to us?"

"Yes he was waiting for a minor heart operation, he had a lazy valve that needed surgery, but it was described as nothing more serious than a tooth extraction."

"Clearly it was more serious, was he OK in himself? Happy with where he was in life?"

"No he wasn't, he was becoming very bitter and resentful with his forced retirement at sixty, he felt his work with the children was unfinished, some of the kids he is....., was working with he had been seeing for up to ten years, he was becoming more and more angry at not being able to see them through to maturity".

" He was always very involved in his work, perhaps this anger or stress you describe, along with his heart problem was too much for him." She paused to wipe her face and to regain control.

"I can look back and see so many signs now that I should have reacted to, so many small things, normally he never drank wine during the week, but lately he started drinking every night, not bottles only a couple of glasses and his temperament had changed, he was quick to anger, he would overreact to tiny problems, which was unlike him, I thought it would all improve once he retired. He had just six weeks to go, but I think now that he couldn't see past those six weeks, it was a barrier looming ever larger on his horizon, Oh Jude what am I going to do? I've never imagined life without him, we've been together over thirty years."

"I know I can't seem to remember a time before Jean Pierre for you."

"He was my past, he was my future, he was everything, I cannot imagine sleeping in this house without him, I've never slept here without him, how can I wake up and he not be there?"

"I know that's why I'm here."

"How did you get here so quickly? I only rang you this morning, I can't believe that your here already, I'm so sorry if I woke everybody at home."

"Don't be, we all needed an early start, I got the fast cat' out of Weymouth to St Malo."

"How long can you stay?"

"I have to be back home by Monday morning I'm due in court at Dorchester at nine am."

"In court, what have you done?"

"No no don't panic, it's nothing like that, I'm in the middle of two weeks jury service, looks like I've got to send some pervert to jail for interfering with under aged girls."

"Oh Jude you shouldn't be here, I'm so sorry to burden you."

"No I should be here, tonight is going to be a huge obstacle for you, you know it, I know it, if I can help at all I'm glad I'm here."

"Thank you, thank you so much, how is everyone at home?"

"Oh Liz is fine, you know what she's like, takes everything in her stride, she had me out of the door and booked onto the ferry ten minutes after you rang, I think she's a little bothered by the hospital, they seem to have mucked up her latest mammogram results, so she's got to go in on Monday for another, but she doesn't show it, she just gets on with everything. The girls are fine, Clare has just passed her driving test and is off to Cuba with a friend tomorrow, and Emma, well Emma is Emma, ever demanding ever watchful of me should I make the tiniest mistake and wham she pounces like a lion, that girl has a very sharp brain and an even sharper tongue to go with it, she takes her test on Tuesday, I really hope she passes, or she will feel inferior and get all down about it, other than that life's OK, Mums OK and so is Anne and all her brood."

"I've always looked at Anne and thought how can she cope with all those kids, all those boyfriends and girlfriends, now all those grandchildren arriving, seems to be one every spring, I guess Jean Pierre and I were selfish, we only needed each other, but now look at me, Anne is right, if she lost Derek she would be surrounded by her family."

"There is no right or wrong, we do what we do because it is the best option for us at the time, look at me when I lost Jayne I thought the world had ended, but I was wrong, you too have many years in front of you, I know you don't want to and can't look forward at the moment, but you have another life to live now, you're what, forty-nine? I know you've had thirty years with Jean Pierre, but you could now have another thirty years . . . . ."

I nearly said without him, I just managed to prevent the words escaping my lips, but Barbara heard them anyway, all my efforts at conversation had been lost, she too was lost again in grief. I managed to settle her down and pour us both a glass of wine and I asked her if there is anything I can do, unusually and understandable the house was looking a little untidy. I found my mobile phone and switched it on, it reacts immediately with a message from Liz, with a question, can I pick my other sister Anne up from Limoges airport tomorrow at four pm? And drop her off at Barbara's before I leave, she will stay with Barbara for a week, that's good, that will make the impossible task of leaving, just about possible. I text her back confirming that I have arrived and that her request is no problem, I tell Barbara that Anne is coming over tomorrow for a week with her daughter Karen, I'm unable to discern if she is pleased or annoyed, I guess its relief, any company is good company at the moment. The two of them have never got on well, since Barbara met and fell in love with Jean Pierre, when she was just nineteen and on a student exchange visit to Paris, Jean Pierre was thirty and he was one of the lecturers at the University where Barbara was visiting as a guest with a friend. Our father had declared Barbara virtually one of the enemy, his opinion of French men was positively prehistoric, his mind closed with bitter resentment, so caustic had he been towards her for three decades that she had not attended our fathers funeral recently. She had written a long letter of reconciliation to our mother Faye and was awaiting a reply, I believe and hope for both their sakes that they will now communicate again.

My phone signals to me that another message has been received, a big thank you and a smiley face from Clare for the forty pounds and another still from Emma 'Mum loves the A3, and the garage has an old Clio that came in on a trade in yesterday, it's got 9 months MOT and 6 months tax, its only a thousand and its GREEN, please please PLEASE!!! xXx'. Barbara is curled up on the sofa with a cover over her, though the temperature doesn't demand it, she has her eyes closed for the moment, I respond to Emma, milking the situation, 'what about telling me I'm the best Dad in the world!!! X'.

'I don't need to tell you that, you're always telling me so it must be true!!! xXx'.

'Ok I'll look at it Monday after court, to see if it's worth it xx''.

'Look out for the salesman he's a grossly overweight creep ☺ xXx'.

I empty and refill my glass, Barbara pats the sofa next to her, I join her and she leans on my left side and gives me a sisterly kiss, she settles her head against my neck, says several soft thank yous, and she gently and surprisingly sobs herself to sleep and manages to escape her grief and desperation for an hour. When Liz pushed me out the door telling me Barbara would need a shoulder to cry on I hadn't envisaged it being literally. I exchange one handed text messages with Liz, as my left arm is buried under Barbara, we catch up with each other's day. Then when I think I might sleep myself, I notice that the television is switched onto standby and the remote is just within reach of my right hand, I press the necessary buttons to see the last half hour of the world cup semi-final between England and France in silence. Terry will be delighted, France has once again capitulated, one more to add to the list with Agincourt and Waterloo. I switch off the TV and do manage a few minutes of sleep before I felt Barbara once again sobbing on my left side, after I calm her down we go through a repeat of the conversation to that which we experienced earlier, with no differing conclusions.

Eventually Barbara goes into the kitchen, half-heartedly motivated to prepare some food for me, I join her, recognising her lack of enthusiasm but let her go through the motions of cooking, believing that its better that she does something rather than nothing, but within minutes she exclaims,

"I 'm sorry I can't do this." I help her back to the sofa and make her comfortable.

I cook us a simple meal of tagliatelle pasta with a basil, parmesan and tomato sauce, throwing in a couple of handfuls of frozen prawns, I give my very unhappy sister a half bowl full but she doesn't touch it, it is now nine pm French time and as I haven't eaten since the service station in the region of the Vendee, I eat both my hot bowl full and Barbara's cool half bowl, she does continue to sip wine but eats nothing that I know of.

The night that follows is the most difficult that I have ever experience, Barbara cried herself to exhaustion but never went to sleep, three times I had to talk her out of full blown panic attacks, by shouting at her to breath normally. I gave her cold, wet flannels to help with her hot panicky sweats, I gave her very sweet tea to lift her blood sugar levels twice after she had come round from passing out. She was frightening to watch during the panic attacks, all I could do was to hold her, sympathise and be there, somehow we got through the night, we both eventually slept for a couple of hours around dawn. When Barbara got up to shower at around eight o'clock, I don't think I had ever seen a more wretched and miserable human being, but she had got through the night somehow, constantly blaming herself for abandoning her husband, Jean Pierre at his hour of most need. She was suffering extreme survivor guilt and punishing herself for her selfishness. I could only hope for her sake that her next night would be a little easier, hopefully she will be so exhausted that her body will sleep, she will have our sister Anne with her, a trained nurse, I both hope and believe that she will be able to cope better than I did.

I shower after Barbara and we share breakfast together, in that we share the room and the table but it is only I who eats. The telephone rings a little after ten o'clock, Barbara conducts a long and protracted conversation in her near perfect French, I am able to ascertain that it is a medical report on Jean Pierre, when the conversation is over she clings to the telephone as though it is Jean Pierre himself, she is reluctant to let go, it is as though she is letting go of him for the last time, eventually the receiver is released, she takes a deep breath and sighs, it is the sigh of a thousand life times.

"It was his heart, the valve became blocked, causing a massive heart attack, they say he would have died even before he knew he was in trouble."

"You must take a small degree of comfort in that, had you been there with him, there is every chance that you would not have noticed and clearly there would have been nothing you could have done for him, I know that it is terrible that you have lost him, believe me I know what that is, but try to get rid of the guilt, had he had a doctor with him, it would have made no difference."

"I think I know that now, but I miss him so much, I….." She never finished her sentence, when she had calmed down I said,

"Come on, let's get out of here, take me on your favourite walk around the lanes, this beautiful autumnal weather won't last forever."

"Ok, but give me a couple of minutes."

We spent the morning walking and talking, mainly about Jean Pierre, his childhood and his love of his work as a child psychologist attached to many of the schools in the region. Barbara said that one of the reasons that he had not wanted his own children was that he had witnessed so much misery, heartache and abuse in others, that he did not want to bring more children into such an imperfect world. Barbara said she was always happy to go along with his wishes, because she had him, he was all she needed. After a very light lunch she did fall asleep on the sofa for a couple of hours, I sat outside on the veranda and took pleasure in the many birds and late flying butterflies that were on the wing enjoying an unusually warm mid October day in France.

I left her asleep and drove away from the house just after three o'clock, so as to be at Limoges airport by four to collect Anne and her daughter Karen, who had had a very straight forward flight from Southampton in just over an hour, we were back at the house before five. I had fully briefed my elder sister on the state of mind of our younger sister, I think Anne had reached a mindset that there was going to be no nonsense, and that Barbara would have to pull herself together, I caught an upward movement of Karen's eyebrows and an intake of breath which indicated that she was bracing herself for a difficult few days. They were staying until the next weekend, so I thought that perhaps I'd come back out again in another week. I told Barbara this and told her I would call her in a few days as I left the house shortly after five pm, I had no time to waste as my place aboard the fast cat' to Weymouth had not been confirmed. If I was to avoid incurring the wrath of Hawkeye I had to get to Caen by eleven o'clock to get into Poole by seven thirty, which was to be a tight schedule if I was to sit in court by nine am tomorrow

Barbara clung onto me like a child about to be fostered as I tried to leave, eventually she extracted a promise from me that I would be back as soon as I could and we would all be with her for Jean Pierre's funeral, and that I would stay for much longer next time. It was only after she had gained this promise that she reluctantly released her grip on me and I drove away, to leave her in the very capably but rather unloving care of our sister.

The long drive north was uneventful other than the bulk of it was accompanied by heavy rain, how is it that France seems to have little or no road kill, I reasoned with myself that it was because they have many more thousands of kilometres of road than we have, so incidents are fewer and father between and that they had killed and eaten most birds and mammals, leaving few to chance.

I boarded the huge Mont Saint-Michael ferry at eleven thirty pm and joined thousands of others, whilst having a very late dinner and a pleasant glass or two of Cellier Des Dauphins, a red from the Cotes du Rhone. Before retiring to my cabin, I observed a coach load of nine to ten year olds poorly supervised by seven adults, clearly it was half term in England, hence the crowded nature of the ferry and the disproportionate number of juveniles on board. All sixty three of the children in front of me, Thomas, the numbers man would be proud of me, queued up to buy a plate of chips, or French-fries, I've always thought what a ridiculous name it is to give to one of our most popular gastronomic catastrophes, it is as if we are blaming the French. Not one of the sixty three children had the courage to be individual, to be different and to order any thing other than a plate of fried chips for supper,and not one of the supervising teachers had the guts to try to prevent it.

The crossing was neither smooth nor rough, I slept ok which was a necessary requirement after the events of the previous night, if I was to be of any use to the British judicial system tomorrow, I hoped with all my heart that Barbara had had a better night.

DAY SIX

A VEILED PRISON

I breakfasted on the ferry, enjoying a full English as described by the chef, the inclusion of garlic sausage was to my liking, but I doubted that it would be to most from our Isles, I also witnessed the purchase of sixty three cans of coke-cola and a similar number of chocolate yoghurts, how many of these children will need the services of a dedicated professional like the late Jean Pierre in their forthcoming years?

I departed the ferry at seven fifty, stopped to buy The Times and The Mirror and drove to Dorchester with a half hour to spare, I text Liz my congratulations on her travel arrangements, wish her well for her hospital appointment and confirmed that we will go into town tonight together to do the deal on her choice of car, just as soon as I get back from court. I spend my spare half hour with a decent coffee from the car park café at the top of town and as a light drizzle begins to gently fall on Hardy's Casterbridge I perused today's papers, though my thoughts were back in Chez Thoma with my distraught sister.

After a weekend off its back to the nationals for the news, I have rather missed my early morning half hour with the unorthodox and bizarre items that were deemed worthy of the nation's attention. The Mirror, apparently you can now vote on line with your preference as to whether you would prefer England's football team to qualify for Euro 2008 or England's rugby team to win the world cup. I wondered if any one other than Tim or Terry would bother, and I speculated that those living north and west of the border would rather vote for a pay cut! The Mirror also reproduces a famous quote from Oscar Wilde that catches my eye, claiming him to be the king of wits, whilst on his death bed he is quoted as saying 'Either those curtains go or I do' on a more joyous note Britain's youngest ever heart transplant recipient is celebrating surviving twenty years since receiving her new heart at the tender age of just sixteen weeks, and she thanked her donors family from the bottom of her heart. I also note that the eleven who are sitting on the Princess Diana inquest were whittled down from an original total of 227, the jury selection process must have been extremely rigorous and painstaking.

A sip of coffee and I'm on to The Times, in which I find it a rich day for items of interest, civil servants have proposed that Britons stop using fresh milk and use long-life as an alternative, to save on green house gas emissions caused by refrigeration, how odd that these civil servants have only milk in their fridges, sad lonely buggers. Also that Middlesbrough has come out top of a poll of the worst place to live in Britain, I speculate that they should be bottom of the poll. Bakers in Harare, Zimbabwe have with   government advise increased the price of a loaf of bread to one hundred thousand Zimbabwe dollars, as a counter measure to help with the shortage of flour, this measure would seem to assume that if no one can afford a loaf of bread no one will want one. And England has beaten France in the world conker championships, a good omen? My final item of curious note is a number of quotations attributed to some of Britons most popular characters, obviously it is a day for quotations. The comic genius that was Spike Milligan is quoted as saying 'All I ask is the chance to prove that money won't make me happy' and from Sir Winston Churchill 'A politician needs the ability to foretell what is going to happen, next week, next month, next year, and to have the ability afterwards to explain why it didn't', Paul Merton is quoted as having said 'I'm always amazed to hear of air crash victims so badly mutilated that they have to be identified by their dental records, if they don't know who you are how the hell do they know who your dentist is?' Noel Coward is quoted, 'People are wrong when they say opera is not what it used to be. It is what it used to be. That is what's wrong with it', and finally one from Shakespeare, 'Maids want nothing but husbands, and when they get them, they want everything'. Enough of this it's time to go to court.

I hurry in the drizzle past the damp Hardy statue into the court building, it is no surprise that Terry (rugby) is my first encounter,

"What did you think of that? It's so good to stuff it to the French, it was a classic."

"I only caught the last half an hour, looked like a game of attrition to me, something along the lines of a rock and a hard place, and it was a very close result."

"You didn't see the whole game, whatever were you doing man, we shoved 'em back a hundred years."

"I was busy, but it's good that we're through."

"Busy, busy, Christ how busy can you be? What do you reckon Tim? I think it's the world cup for us again, good old Johnny and that boot of his, the French must hate him." Fortunately Tim (football) and Terry moved off towards what looks like a new coffee machine, something I must try later. Hanna (silicon valley) walks past me, giving me a very subtle wink, which I hope is unnoticed by anyone else and a half twirl, today's ensemble is black hot pants over black leggings and Ugg boots, below an orange and black blouse which is only partially concealing a black lace trimmed bra whose vivacious contents are competing to escape first. I remember as a child, I would see young girls who had raided Mums wardrobe and would dress up in clothes of a different generation, here we have the same in reverse, whereas Lynda (menswear) has made not the slightest effort to appear female.

John (Foreman) reminds us all of today's word challenge, it is asperity, I forgot to look this up, or barely had a chance at the weekend, so I quickly text Liz to both let her know that I've made it back OK and I ask her to check its meaning, I've half an idea but want to be sure. She replies quickly, she must be sat at her laptop, it means harshness, roughness, ruggedness or acrimony, this one shouldn't be too difficult and the real challenge will be to upstage the very sharp Lynda.

Barry (Chaplain) collars me for an update from Hardy's novel, I am forced to admit that I am fully a hundred pages behind him and ensure him that I will get up to speed tonight, he doesn't conceal his disappointment, he has I imagined anticipated the encounter all weekend. A weekend in which the emotional vacillations of the lead female character were not to the fore of my thoughts, I have also left Jacqueline Forbes-Brewer in a difficult situation, I have much to catch up on. I hope it was a weekend in which Barry's long suffering wife had been able to disappear into something outrageously salacious, before being obliged to return to his approved reading list next week.

I catch a glimpse of Joyce (matching accessories) she clearly has been busy at the weekend, shopping, she is superbly turned out in a jade green trouser suit, with a lace edged cream blouse, cream shoes, handbag and scarf, the trousers fit her rear perfectly, to a man we will all want to follow her into court, the exception perhaps being Barry who would I think not notice should she be wearing no trousers at all. I engage in a quick conversation with Thomas (the numbers man) it is a conversation in which I inform him of the sixty three children I met on the ferry with a uniformly poor diet, he is indifferent, unimpressed almost disbelieving of numbers quoted to him by others, he then delves into his experience for a story with a larger number, I have not noticed this shallow aspect of his character before, he is a competitive numbers man.

I try the new coffee machine, the coffee is surprisingly good, I comment to this effect to anyone close enough to hear me, it is Richard (I can do that) who picks up on my comment, he turns me back to the machine and taps his finger on a card adhered to the top right hand corner, which reads 'Supplied by Richard Barnett, Telephone ......' I congratulate him on his success with the supply of what I am sure will be a popular development and I inform him that his advice with regard my daughters car, kill or cure, resulted in the former.

It is Andy (body odour) who ushers us into court today, not only has he lost his natural odour, which has been replaced by what I imagine is the entire contents of a ten year old, out of date bottle of Brut, can we please have a window open here, he is paying close attention to Elizabeth (chain smoker) and she to him. If she is the reason for the improvement in his general redolence, then I speculate that perhaps he can be of some influence with regard her problem, which leaves her also bearing an unpleasant scent. I am not feeling fresh myself today, I did mange an early morning shower on the ferry, in a cubicle who's dimensions left a lot to be desired, I feel that I have retained a generally crumpled appearance.

In court today the general level of questioning and giving of evidence is ratcheted up a notch, the witnesses are more central to the plot, the girl who is deemed to have been abused and her two friends all give evidence by video link and are cross examined by use of the same technology. The three girls all now sixteen are convincing when questioned by the prosecution barrister, but a little less so when cross examined by the younger, female defence council, this is the first time we have heard anything of substance from the defence barrister, her line of questioning is surprisingly aggressive, even acrimonious, the young girl on the stand, Sophie Green becomes very upset when the truthfulness of her testimony is called into question and at this point her delivery becomes much less coherent. I seize my opportunity, I write a question and pass it to John who in turn passes it via Andy, now (unpleasant fragrance) to the judge. Now judge (Hawkeye) is no fool, but this one he allows passed him, he addresses the defence barrister.

"A member of the jury wishes to state that he or she is aware of a certain asperity that exist between yourself and the prosecution witness which has caused some distress and could you please ask the last question again for the clarification of the jury." It is my first success, I receive a curt nod from John.

The entire case seems to revolve around one night in February, in a Wayside Inn near Bournemouth, when it is stated by the prosecution and the three girls that the three criminal offences took place. Holly Banks claims that she was the victim and her two friends, Sophie Green and Lucy Cambridge claim to have witnessed the events. All three request and are granted breaks in proceedings during the difficult cross examination, I suspect there is a degree of premeditation to this, to both break and frustrate the momentum of the defence's interrogation, but once a break is requested, due to their tender age Hawkeye is obliged to comply, this is obviously very frustrating for the barrister in question, but on reconvening she is swift to regain her degree of asperity.

Lunch is taken during one of these distress breaks, the drizzle which had consolidated into steady rain has passed, so I collect yet another Cornish pasty and amble in a new direction. I wander

309

off of the high street into North Square, I am determined to use what time I have to explore as much of Dorchester as I can.

After just a short walk I am met on my left hand side by a five-meter high brick wall, surrounded on its south side by delightful and quaint cottages and cottage gardens. I continue to walk with the huge wall to my left, it is built in the form of a huge fortification. I am intrigued as to its purpose, I am, a little further on greeted by an equally high razor wired, gated entrance. Eventually a sign is evident, H.M.Prison Dorchester. Its huge main gate and arched entrance are massively imposing, above its high walls a vast collection of ornate Victorian chimneys stand erect and defiant. I am surprised by both the prisons close proximity to the town centre and a complete lack of signage on its approach. The grandees of the town have achieved a remarkable degree of invisibility, barely credible. Walking this area of the town, visiting the nearby library, town hall and court buildings, the close proximity of the huge and imposing prison is something few people would be aware of. I look again at the small town map that I collected recently from the tourist information office, the prison is absent from the town guide, an oversight? This hidden Victorian structure is remarkably close to many domestic dwellings, as I approach the immense and unwieldy prison doors, I can hear loudly and clearly in my mind familiar words, in a deep, echoing tone, 'Norman Stanley Fletcher, you are a habitual criminal' which is the opening line of the memorable TV series, Porridge, set in the imaginary Slade prison. My musings at the front door are interrupted by the appearance of a prison governor, who along with a colleague has been observing my meanderings on CCTV. I am required to explain my presence before being asked to move on and not to linger, I take heed.

Leaving the prison behind I follow steps down to the River Frome, to walk along a river after a night and morning of heavy rain is a pleasure, the air is fresh with a profusion of natural aromas. The many loud plops as droplets fall from trees and buildings left over from the deluge are a constant distraction, each one could be a bird, fish or frog. The abundance of mallard ducks are today subdued and scant few birds are to be seen, a pair of wrens and a very damp, unhappy looking heron are all that show themselves this day. The sky appears still to be heavy with moisture, this all too brief respite is to be no more than a punctuation in the day's downpour. I reach the allotments on my left, which are full of all manner of plants with heads bowed by the weight of water, beaten into submission by twelve or more hours of relentless rain. The few remaining blooms are both sodden and crestfallen in defeat, only the last few colourful heads of the tall delphiniums are struggling to defy the rain and gravities remorseless pull. Some of the sycamore boughs heavily laden with huge clusters of autumnal seeds are dipping in and out of the rivers surface, all too soon the constant dripping from the trees increases again, as more moisture is added from above. I turn my back on the river and quickly ascend the steps of Clyde Path Road, I return early to the courthouse and use what time is left to gain some ground on Barry (Chaplain) with 'The Madding Crowd'.

The afternoon session continues exactly where the morning one left off, questions, upsets, delay, questions, upsets, delay, it is as if the entire court procedure is hamstrung by its own rules protecting the giving of evidence by minors. The questioning becomes more specific towards the three girls. The two witnesses to the charges, Sophie Green and Lucy Cambridge did not cope well emotionally with the questioning. Whether it was due to a degree of embarrassment at being asked such questions in an adult situation, or whether they had indeed not had a good view of the alleged assaults was for us and us alone to decide. It was only the victim Holly Banks who gave clear and positive answers, why did she not protest and struggle, she replied that she was afraid to, why did she go to the room with the accused? She replied 'just for a bit of fun' she stated that she thought she would be safe with her two friends, she was afraid to go through with what Michael wanted and she was afraid to stop him. Throughout the whole day Michael Merryweather was passive, unmoved and as always he wore the same ill-fitting suit that he had worn on the first day. Clearly something had transpired between the four of them, but to what extent and with whose consent was unclear. To sum up the girls evidence, there was no doubt that they were all singing from the same hymn sheet, they all say that they witnessed the offences taking place. When asked repeatedly from many angles and view points as to why no significant protestations had taken place and why they had not run screaming from the hotel room in protest, they had answered uniformly. Perhaps a little too uniformly, that they had feared reprisals from the defendant and that he had threatened them with exposure to their parents, for all the times they had missed school, sampled alcohol, marijuana and ecstasy, in short they feared him, he had a hold over them. Also that he had promised that they were meeting friends at the hotel, it was only when they had entered the room and Michael had quickly stripped off his clothes, revealing his considerable erect appendage, that they had realised the gravity of the situation that confronted them and that they were paralysed with fear, and yes perhaps just the slightest hint of curiosity, but that did not change the date on their birth certificates. Holly Banks was fifteen at the time, so were her two friends

We were dismissed at four pm, the highlight of the day was to follow the delightfully well clad rear of Joyce (accessories) from the court building toward the car park, whilst she was in conversation with David (The weather man) about what I could only speculate. By this time the steady rain had fallen back to drizzle, which continued throughout my journey home and into the evening. I paused once on the way home to collect an unusual meal, a very tidy looking drake mallard duck, still warm and fit for the kitchen.

It was good to be home again after the busy weekend and good also to receive my first text from Clare in Cuba, she had arrived safely, the hotel was OK, not great but OK and tomorrow it was to be skydiving strapped to an instructor, out of the plane at twelve thousand feet, free fall for ten seconds and then parachute down onto the beach, nothing to it, don't worry Dad! I felt my guts turn over on reading the text.

"Hi love, any post and how did it go in hospital today?"

"Oh it was just a routine mammogram, they screwed up the results of my last one, this was on the brand new half million pound machine, I think they've decommissioned the old one, too many problems and there's no post to worry about."

"Ok great."

"Tell me about Barbara, how is she?" Over a quick snack I give her a full description of my French trip and Barbara's state of mind, we were then on our way into Yeovil with cars to the fore of our thoughts. We go straight to the Audi outlet and I finally get to meet Geoff Preston, husband of Hanna (Silicone Valley), he's a sleazy sort of guy, Emma as usual is spot on. He's genuine enough in his knowledge of the product and his attention to detail, if you overlook his sales patter, but he's got two roving eyes and struggles to look Liz in the eye when talking to her, He is grossly obese and has a damp urine stain on his trousers just below his crutch where he has leaked after visiting the gents, which of course is obscured to his view by his colossal stomach. I run through a checklist of a few things we need in a car, I mention that Liz needs a back support and I ask,

"Does the car have one as standard." His reply is,

"Oh yes, you're lucky your wife only needs a back support my wife needs financial support." When I ask him to show me the boot open, as we need to get two dogs in the back, he again uses Hanna as the butt of his joke.

"There's plenty of room for a dog in the boot, but I've never tried to get my wife in there." All this is nonsense and bravado and is easy to dismiss as such, he does have all the right answers when it comes to the car and the price is acceptable, so we agree to take an ex-demonstrator, just four months old, Liz is delighted.

"Now," I say, "Show me the Renault Clio my daughter is hankering for."

"Oh yes the Clio, we've had it thoroughly cleaned today and as you've taken the A3 I can let you have it for seven fifty." I check the car over quickly and take it out for a quick drive and after trying unsuccessfully to knock his price, I agree to the sale. We take Liz's car home and return for the Clio, all in all a satisfactory day. I get the Clio in the garage and check it over, apart from a leaky brake cylinder it seems to be a good buy. I promise myself to get the car checked out by Eric, our local man, but fail to see how its got a new MOT with a brake problem, but then I guess it had to happen some when. I tell Liz not to let Emma drive it until it's been checked over by Eric, not a problem today as she is staying with friends for the night.

I telephone Barbara for an update, but I am told by Anne that she is OK and not to be disturbed. Liz and I have a good catching up session mentally over dinner and a very physical and intense catching up session later in bed. After which Liz turns out her bedside lamp and rapidly goes to sleep, I remember my promise to Barry (Chaplin) and dutifully slip into the pages of 'The Madding Crowd'.

After reading four chapters of the Hardy novel, I look up our word for tomorrow, which is inimical, which I discover is to be injurious or detrimental.

Sleep still eludes me, so I delve once again into the world of Jacqueline Forbes-Brewer.

JHIRO de MONTAYA de VALE de CABRERRA

"Yes Jhiro is two years in England, one at university of Bath and one at London Business School, paid for by Jhiro's father, the great, Luis De Montaya, this is where Jhiro develop his love for blonde women." "So you had me kidnapped, you killed my father and put me through all manner of horrors because of the colour of my hair!" She is about to explode. Jhiro too raises his voice,

"No, no, no, Jhiro he never kill, this is nothing of Jhiro's doing, Jhiro he pay monies to rescue you from Garcia Brothers, how they come by you he does not know, but please you must believe if you are one more day with the Garcia Brothers You do not live." "Please can I go home?" "It is not possible." "Why not?" "Because your life is here now, Jhiro he buy you." "You can't just buy people." "Jhiro can and he buy you, to help you, you English you import people from all over the world, you imprison them in slavish task, on low pay, they cannot go free." "They are free to leave we do not import them." "Yes you do and if they try to leave your so called employment, where can they go, how is it you say 'out of pan into fire' no they are trapped in low paid work, they are less like servants and more like slaves, and they hate you upper class as much as you think you hate Jhiro, Jhiro has heard them in London, they speak freely among other foreigners, they do not hide their contempt for your upper class."

Jackie thought of the many eastern Europeans, Jamaicans and Portuguese that worked in the kitchens, the laundry and in the gardens at St Georges. Probably she thought all of them on a minimal wage, barely able to support themselves, probably unable to better themselves as they are caught in a net of low wages and accommodation provided, making it impossible for them to buy or rent a property, or to get one foot on the ladder of prosperity, she shook the uncomfortable thought from her mind.

"No matter what argument you purport how can you defend your actions? You imprison me here against my will, you are a criminal."

"A criminal yes perhaps from a long line of criminals perhaps, but you are not imprisoned here you are free to leave and remember Jhiro he rescue you." "Free to leave that is nonsense, that jungle is impenetrable you know it, and the road is guarded." "It is not safe for you to venture from the estate you would not survive, the men who watch the road have many duties, one of them is to protect you from harming yourself." "Did you order me to be kidnapped and my father killed?" "No, no, no, no, no, Jhiro did not do this, Jhiro is sorry your father is killed, Jhiro's father is also gone, it is a very bad thing to lose the man who is making you who you is."

"I was kidnapped from the Olympic Games in Los Angeles, I was an Equestrian competitor do you understand?" "Yes Jhiro knows what this means, Jhiro is sorry for your losses, he is informed by a local man who is, what you will call a dealer, that a beautiful natural blonde English woman is in the hands of the Garcia Brothers, so Jhiro make it known he is in the market for such a purchase and it must be very quickly, before the Garcia's can spoil the goods, so you are brought here and you have time to recover, had you been raped or made with child by them you will have stayed with them, believe Jhiro you would not be alive today, so you see, Jhiro he rescue you, he did not kidnap you."

"Phrase it how you like, I'm a prisoner here." "You can phrase it how you like, you are free to leave, the forest yes it is impenetrable and the road is not for you, you must believe there are more evils down the road than in the jungle as you call it and the Garcia brothers and many others like them are in waiting for a bonus such as yourself."

"If you do decide to leave Jhiro advise you to choose the jungle, here you will only be eaten, a much worse fate awaits you on the road." "Thank you for what is useless advice." "Now that we are in conversation can Jhiro order a bottle of champagne to celebrate?" "Order what you like, I don't much feel like celebrating." She hands him the phone saying,

"Here, you seem to be able to order anything you like on this, perhaps you could order me a taxi to the airport and a single

316

ticket to Heathrow." He laughs and orders the bottle in Spanish. The bottle arrives and he pours two glasses, she accepts one, and then repeats to him,

"But you are the criminal here, you have broken the laws of reason and humanity," she continues "you are a disgraceful and dishonourable person guilty up to your neck." He stands proud and says,

"We are a long established honourable family, for many hundreds of years we grow coffee, some of the finest in the world. We have not forsaken coffee for cocaine or coca like many estates, we are still sixty percent coffee and only thirty percent coca leaf, the United States has an unquenchable appetite for cocaine. It is a case of how do you say? Supply and demand, they demand, so we supply." "But you are a criminal surely is it a crime to grow cocaine in Colombia?" "No it is a crime to sell to the ever demanding Americans, Jhiro does not sell to them, he sells coca leaf to Colombians, they are criminals not Jhiro, it is a crime to make cocaine, not to grow coca leaf." "If some one steals fruit from Jhiro's tree and sells it to you because you are hungry and you have money who is the criminal? Not Jhiro for growing the fruit, the thief yes and you for to receiving the stolen fruit."

"Jhiro is the innocent people here. The money from the coca leaf feeds and supports many of the people in our country, now that the whole world is growing coffee which steals from us our traditional monies. So Jhiro De Montaya he fights back, he is growing grapes to steal monies from other peoples, so tell Jhiro who is the criminals here and who is not?" Jackie looks into his face, amazed at what she is hearing but more amazed she is hearing it in English. He continues,

"So now we start to grow vines, Jhiro want to make wine, but we have problem with the humidness of our country, the vines grow too much and make not enough grapes So we have to be always cutting the vines three of four times in the season, to make more black grapes, So now Jhiro buys some hills that face east, they are dryer better for the grapes, we want to make a good wine in ten years and a very good wine in twenty." Jackie lifts her champagne which she notices is an extremely good vintage and says to him,

317

"So who are you?" He is still standing, he lifts his head and draws a deep breath,

"Don Jhiro De Montaya De Vale De Cabrerra the twelve, our family own land around here for many kilometres, if you walk from here in any direction it will take you two weeks to stand on soil not owned by the De Montaya family, my family."

"And you would be eaten by the jungle in the process." "Ah yes of course, Jhiro is proud to be at the head of this family, it is a great responsibility and honour, Jhiro have a duty to over two thousand peoples who look to him always for their provisions, for their work, for their money, for food, schools and medicine, if he fails they fail and they are hungry. This is why we stay with growing coffee, it does not pay like the monies we get from the coca leaf, but coffee is here for ever, and we grow some of the best in the world, who knows how long we can grow Coca, the Americans are already destroying many of the coca plants in the north of our country."

"Also Jhiro hopes the wine will be another long term investment for our family who knows one day, Chateau De Montaya might be international selling, so we produce three of the world's most powerful and most popular drugs, caffeine, coca and alcohol, who is the criminal, the man that grows it, the man that sells it, or the man that poisons himself with it, the whole world knows that these drugs are all harmful to the body, but it is the educated so called western and developed world that has an insatiable appetite for these drugs, it is the man that consumes who is the criminal. He knows what he is doing is wrong, another glass of champagne perhaps? I am Jhiro what does he call you?" "Prisoner 23-11-57." "OK so you is born in fifty seven, your twenty seven now, any children?" "No." "You want children?" "I wanted children with my husband to be, Richard, Richard Brewer we were going to be married this year, can you tell me what date it is?" "It is October twenty one."

"We were to be married last week, I will have that champagne, I don't understand why he hasn't come for me." "Nobody can come for you here, we are in remote place only accessible by helicopter, everything our people need comes in on the return flights from the cocaine and coffee drops." "Even a blonde English woman."

318

"Yes even blonde English woman." "But somebody could land a plane or helicopter here if they knew I was here." "Nobody knows you're here and nobody but our own planes can land, our planes have numbered codes under the wings if someone else tried to land our super missiles would blow them to, what is your English phrases, ah yes, blow them come to kingdom , where ever that is." "You have missiles?" "Oh yes American made, very good, we have a practice day once a year releasing and exploding large balloons, the operators are very accurate so you see no one can drop in for you and Jhiro's is the only helicopter allowed to land on the roof, anyone else tries, same result, boom, Americans will sell weapons to the man with the most monies. And all but one hidden road have been destroyed by our people to prevent American law enforcement getting to us, if they try we have so much notice that all but the crop is moved, so you see we are all but impregnable, sometimes they spray the crop with plant killer but our missiles are good and they know it, they leave us alone now and concentrate on the border, they are a joke, all Americans have their price, even the president, Jhiro is sure, America wants to be the police of the world, but they are the most corrupt people in the world, show me an American Jhiro show you a hypocrite, they say one thing and do another."

"But how is it possible that you can buy America missiles to use against their own people." "It is not difficult, just very expensive, they go first to Africa and then Brazil but eventually we get them, they cost big monies, but they help our people to sleep in our beds." Jackie throws in a random question to change the subject, this man's argument on criminality is well rehearsed.

"How is it that you do not have a wife?" "Jhiro he had a wife years ago, a local girl, we went to school together she was Jhiro's how you say, soul mate but unfortunately she and our first child die in childbirth, she had blood that did not clot, we did not know, she lost so much blood giving birth to our child she die, the child also." He touches the two rings that hang suspended by a thin gold chain around his neck.

"Jhiro is on his own for ten years after that." "Eventually he buy a blonde woman from the bad brothers as you call them she was from somewhere called Sweden, Jhiro does not know it, she was a little like you, but she was very unhappy, you are angry,

319

she was unhappy, eventually she came to Jhiro's bed it was almost a year before she did, she seemed to be OK, more happy, then after she was having a child, she changed, she was how do you say, she go inside herself."

"Withdrawn." "Yes withdrawn, she is always asking Jhiro to take her in helicopter, always she ask and ask, so one day he say ok, why not, perhaps it make her happy, Jhiro is desperate for her to be happy, Jhiro like her very much and she is with child, we are in helicopter just for two minutes, we are over what you call jungle and she opens door and steps out, it was very difficult time, that was two years ago now is new situation. You are here perhaps it is too late for Jhiro with children who knows, but you do not go in helicopter. So Jhiro he drink too much, he talk too much, tell Jhiro your life."

Jackie does exactly that, after refilling her glass. Jhiro orders more champagne. He listens intently to her tale, only occasionally interrupting to clarify a point or to ask for the meaning of a word, He listens for two hours, a time that takes her from a very privileged childhood in the green shires of England to her present situation, by which time the second bottle of champagne has gone the way of the first. Both of them are to put it simply, drunk. It is two am Jhiro offers his bed, Jackie accepts. There is no physical experience in a sexual sense, Jhiro lays on top of his vast bed, Jackie along side him her head on his chest, she gently sobs herself to sleep thinking of all the times she had led in a similar position as a young girl with her father, she is overwhelmed by close, comforting physical contact.

Jackie wakes alone with a heavy head, all of the previous nights events flood back into her mind, she is fully dressed in the red blouse and black pleated knee length skirt she was wearing last night, she can feel that she is still wearing knickers but is unable to stop herself lifting her skirt to instinctively confirm what she already knew, she is intact, she scans the huge room for Jefe or Jhiro what ever is his name, she is unaccompanied. She begins to chastise herself and to deal with the disappointment she feels in herself for succumbing to his advances, after just a few moments of mentally berating herself she comes to a snap decision. I'll play this mans game, I'll share his wine, his food, even his bed but I will never accept this situation, I will always

320

be on the lookout for any tiny advantage that will give me an opportunity to escape this confinement, I won't give in, I won't be defeated and I won't take my own life.

She sees a blank sheet of A4 in her mind, top left corner, 1) I will let him think I'm comfortable here, 2) I need a supply of English magazines, 3) I must find out where I am, exactly where I am, and 4) I must get word out of this place to the outside world, her page was half full, the first two she felt she could accomplish in the first month, numbers three and four she knew were beyond her at present, she got up, made his bed and showered, wandered into the kitchen area to make breakfast, this room was not well equipped, all the meals she had eaten had been prepared elsewhere in a huge well supplied kitchen staffed by local girls, Jackie made coffee and ate fresh bread, both were delicious and both were produced on site, she had to admit that the fresh local coffee was a new and delightful experience, it was indeed the best she had ever tasted, also the bread which was made fresh every morning and left in the kitchen for her was much to her liking.

She decided that being unhappy and crying often was never going to illicit sympathy from her captor, he was convinced that he was her rescuer, he had paid a handsome price for her and wanted a return for his investment. She saw the logic of his argument, had she stayed with the bad brothers she knew that she would not be in a healthy state physically and mentally, if alive at all. She believed that he was not party to the conspiracy that had put her in the hands of such evil men, but she had two great dilemma's constantly churning over in her mind, who was responsible for her being in her present situation? And had killed her father? And the second equation to solve was how could she work her way out of this place? Or could she earn her way out? She refilled her coffee and moved onto the veranda which overlooked the whole De Montaya estate of buildings, the kitchens, the bread house, the school, garages, missile houses etc, etc, she sat on an old wicker chair made for both comfort and elegance, the veranda was beautifully draped with cascading bougainvillea and traditional flowers of many kinds, some with exotic scents which attracted the spectacular butterflies and humming birds.

She sat drinking the finest coffee and contemplated her two points of anguish. She could think of no one other than Louise to put in the frame for the first dilemma. Louise had shown herself to be deceitful and cunning just prior to Jackie's departure for the Olympics. Could she have paid someone to destroy her life? With her father and herself gone Louise would inherit both St Georges Hall and her father's enormous wealth. Originally she had assumed herself a kidnap victim and her father shot by mistake but if that was the case, why had she been abandoned, cast into the wilderness like an item of jetsam or was it flotsam she had never learnt the distinction between the two. If she was a kidnap victim she reasoned that Louise would do little or nothing to expiate her return, her last exchange with Louise was both confrontational and had carried threats from Jackie to have her 'cast from this house', so Louise was not top of the list of people who would buy her back. If it was not a kidnap, but an attempt to eradicate both her father and herself then it was Louise and perhaps Gould who were to gain the most. Either way she had decided Louise was the person who most deserved her spite and venom. She couldn't understand where Richard fitted into any conspiracy he seemed to be superfluous to any plot. She recalled his overreaction to the news she had given him of Jonathan's plans to replace her on the British Equestrian team, it was extreme, she also remembered the death of poor Troy and what she thought was idle comment by the two men who came to collect the stricken carcass of her beloved reserve horse. She had overheard one of them saying to the other, 'That's a terrible leg break, one of the worst I ever seen, but very odd little or no blood, looks to me like this poor bugger was shot first and had its leg broken afterwards, what do you think.' His colleague had replied, 'Come on we got a job to do, don't get mixed up in the whys and wherefores of these rich folk, but I fancy you're right." She agonised over these comments, those people had no reason to invent strange opinions, if they were right and Richard had shot Troy and then broken his leg, why would he do such a thing, surely not just to remove the threat of Jonathan, what was Jonathan threatening? To prevent her going to the Games, so she surmised that she had to go to the Games at all cost, why? To be abducted and her father killed? No surely not Richard and

Louise, not possible, but Richard was very odd and distant over the last six weeks they were together, he was reluctant to experience physical contact, he was avoiding sex with her, no, he was avoiding all physical contact with her. If he was her loving and devoted husband to be where is he? Why hasn't he shown up to rescue his damsel in distress? In her mind she was beginning more and more to doubt Richard. Though Louise she had decided was to blame for all the horrors and discomfort she had experienced since being pulled from her fathers car in Los Angeles.

Little did she know that written proof of everything she suspected had been recorded onto paper by Richard Brewer after the second unsuccessful attempt on his life, which had taken place whilst he lay prone in his Los Angeles hospital bed, after the first attempt. Richard had decided that Louise had dealt him out of the equation, he now knew he had become a target. He wrote a letter to his English solicitors confessing all, with strict instructions that the letter should not be opened for twelve months from its receipt, this provision was in case he was incorrect in his summations and he would live to return to England and retrieve the letter himself, whereupon he could destroy it, but should he not return the inner letter was to be passed to Arnold Elliot, Sir Johns right hand man. Richard knew Arnold would be horrified at the letters content, but he would also see that justice was metered out upon those who deserved it most. Without the knowledge of this sleeping letter, Jackie was on her own to decide or surmise as she saw fit, again little did she know that she was beginning to hit upon the truth.

She asked herself what did she know?, she now felt reasonable sure that Jhiro was guilty only of rescuing her, and that he was fundamentally a good man who cared for his people and his families reputation. He did not see it as a crime not to help her return home, she would work on him, she would think of him as her father would often describe a project that had not reached its conclusion, he would be a work in progress. He was an intelligent, articulate, handsome and humorous man, she would delve into his psyche and discover if he had a conscience. So this day she felt that she had made some progress in her mind, Jhiro was not the enemy, he was just a quite pleasant jailer,

Louise was the enemy and there were serious doubts regarding Richard. She had spent the whole morning in deep thought, her mental vacillations were interrupted by the sound of an incoming helicopter, it is of course Jhiro's Sikorsky C76, Jackie looks up to see the black sleek looking machine and clearly notices the huge white lettering of J-H-I-R-O on its underside, the five letters protect its occupant from the constantly armed and readied missiles.

She realised that if anyone if ever going to drop in to this place to rescue her it will have to be in Jhiro's helicopter, no one else will stand a thread of a chance, she dismisses the seemingly impossible obstruction to her potential escape and awaits Jhiro's return.

The helicopter lands as always on the flat fortified concrete roof of the huge villa and a fresh looking Jhiro wearing an almost boyish grin joins her on the veranda with a coffee

"Good morning how is you?" He asks.

"OK a little heavy in the head but this coffee is as good as you say it is, a perfect cure for a hangover, where have you been?" "Ah yes Jhiro is sorry he is not there when you wake, Jhiro is needed to look at a problem to the north, there is problem with transporting some of the many thousands of new grape vines up to the slopes where they are needed for planting so we use the black bird it is perfect for the work."

"The vines are your priority at the moment?" "Sorry Jhiro no understand." "The vines they are more important than coffee and cocaine at the moment?" "Yes, yes always it is the vines for Jhiro the coffee is long established and takes care of itself, Jhiro's youngest brother looks after the coffee his other two brothers look after the coca, we call it coca leaf, it is not cocaine until much later, but Jhiro he is always busy with the vines, the vines are the future, Jhiro want to stop producing coca and produce only coffee and wine." "So you think you can just make a great wine?"

"No no, now you are mocking Jhiro, he thinks we can produce a wine, but it takes many years, first he buys an expert from France, Thierry Le Blanc he is an expert with the husbanding? of the vines." "Husbandry." "Thank you, he test the soil in many places, we plant only where he agrees and then we wait five years

324

for the vines, ah what is the word the part which is in the ground." "Roots." "Yes the roots we must wait five years until the roots go below the, the…..urg." "The topsoil." "Yes the topsoil, after five years the roots will be below the topsoil and into the acidic soil which is good for the flavour, so next year we can pick the grapes and see how the flavour is, for the last three years and this year we do not pick the grapes we have only one important thing that is the health of the vines." "OK you are a patient man, so next year what do you hope for?" "Next year we will pick the grapes for the first time, then we use the juice from the grapes to make a wine, an experimental wine, I have another expert wine man from France, Jean Michael Pluyaud. He is the man with the good nose, we have build a small factory under his instruction but it is for him to show us the way, these Frenchmen they are very clever but very expensive, Jhiro wonders should he have used Spanish persons, they are easy for me to understand, but Jhiro knows that the wine from France is the best, better I think than the wine from Spanish peoples, so Jhiro is trying to learn a little French, it is very different from Spanish language." "Yes I know French, perhaps I can help you." "That would be good." "Yes I can help but you must pay me." "Jhiro can pay you yes but money is no good to you here." "Oh I don't want money." "Then how can he pay you?" "With a helicopter ride to an international airport." "Ha ha you smarter than most women, come on lets eat, then we can go to Jhiro's bed." "Slow down Casanova, first we must establish some ground rules, you are an educated man, we both know I am a prisoner here." "No, no you will grow to like it more, maybe even love it." "Listen to me I have a life in England and I will never give that life up, I will always look for a way to leave here, but in the meantime I will share your beautiful house, your food, your wine, your coffee and perhaps your bed and there are things you will do for me."

"Yes, yes Jhiro he will do things." "Listen to me, is your name Jhiro or Jefe?"

"Both, the people here call me Jefe it means boss man, the chief but my name for you is Jhiro" "OK Jhiro, you will bring to me a regular supply of English literature, magazines and books, also you will bring back the tall maid I had some time ago, the one who always wears a red flower." "Ah yes Catalina De

Francisco why you want her?" "Because I believe she speaks a little English and she was very polite and pleasant to me."

"All the girls are polite and pleasant." "Yes I am sure, but I liked her and you will allow me to organise meals, to order what I prefer and I will explore your wine cellar, my father taught me a great deal about wine, I have my likes and dislikes." "You can do as you will please in Jhiro's kitchen and with his wines, the cellar needs someone with some knowledge, Jhiro was going to ask Jean Michael, the man with the nose, because it is not been organised for many years, it is Jhiro's fathers passion, he was an expert, he wish he is here today to see Jhiro's vines, he will be very happy." "OK and lastly you will when I request it take me on your trips in your Sikorsky and I will do two things for you, I will help you with your French and I will not step out of the helicopter, do we have a deal?" "Yes as you say we have a deal, you make Jhiro a very happy man, Jhiro will do these things, the English literature will take some time to organise, but it is possible he is sure, Jhiro will be nervous with you in his flying machine, but first you teach Jhiro the French."

"I have to teach you French before I can fly?"

"Yes, Jhiro he thinks it is so." Jackie believes that getting into the helicopter will be fundamental to her discovering her whereabouts, she remembers a little trick her French tutor played on her whole class to boost their confidence.

"OK, so how about after I have taught you, say, one thousand words then I can go with you in your flying machine, is that a deal?"

"Yes, Jhiro will be very happy man if can say one thousand words in French".

"OK, say after me, information, confirmation and conversation"

"Now?"

"Yes."

"OK, information, confirmation, conversation."

"Good, now can you say, informass'eon, confirmass'eon and conversass'eon"

"Of course it is very much like Spanish."

"Go on, say them."

"Informa'cion, confirma'cion, conversa'cion."

"That's very good, there are more than one thousand words that end in 'cion, in fact there are over twelve hundred and there are only three exceptions which will be your next lesson, so now you can speak more than one thousand French words, I can go up in your big black bird, would you like your second lesson today or tomorrow?" For a moment Jhiro is speechless, he stares at Jackie and wonders if he paid too much or too little for her, when he does find his tongue it is to say, through a wry smile,

"OK, today you are too clever for Jhiro, he will take you in the blackbird but he will have extra device fitted to the door, but he don't think you are like Olga she was a very troubled person." "I wonder why?" "Oh Jhiro think it is because…" "Its OK you don't need to explain, it was my English sense of humour." "You make joke of tragic death of Olga?" "No, no I do not make joke. There are some things you do not understand, some English expressions." "Jhiro English is not good." "No its very good, apart from the fact you are mostly stuck in the present tense, which is not a big problem, but if you are to learn French it would be a problem, I will make sure it doesn't happen, if I am here long enough to help you with it." "Oh Jhiro think so, you can make this your home, Jhiro very happy, now for lunch yes?" "Yes but don't forget our deal." "No Jhiro not forget, he ask Juan Pablo the pilot of our plane, our beautiful Piper Aztec to collect the English literature when Jhiro see him next." "OK, so let's eat." Jhiro is in a mood to celebrate he orders a local delicacy of River Clams, Almejas De Rio and champagne for lunch, after which the two of them explore each others bodies in what is for Jacqueline the most intimate and breathtaking physical encounter of her life, Jhiro shows himself to be a very considerate and passionate lover, he is fascinated by her natural blonde hair and her petit features, which are in contrast to the dark hair and voluptuous characteristics of the local women. He is masterful in the use of his tongue on her most private quarters and she is responsive to his touch, eventually they lay on his bed naked and exhausted under the huge ornamental ceiling fan, which cools their perspiring bodies, Jackie finds this particularly refreshing as her thighs and abdomen are tingling with prickly heat. It is Jhiro, who sparks conversation,

"You are everything Jhiro have always wanted, he is a very happy man." "Slow down Casanova, prisoner 23-11-57 is only here for as long as it takes me to escape." "Ha ha now Jhiro know you make joke, this name you call Jhiro, Casanova what is it?" "It is a name we use in England to describe someone who is a great lover, or sometimes someone who thinks he is a great lover." "And which is Jhiro." "Yesterday I thought you were someone who thought he was a great lover, but today you are a great lover." "Today Jhiro is very happy and now you make him double happy, so if he is Casanova what do I call you?" "Prisoner 23-11-57."

"Jhiro cannot call you that, no what do you prefer to be called?" "My name is Jacqueline but I prefer Prisoner 23-11-57." "OK Jhiro call you Jzzacouleen but sometimes as joke only, prisoner 23-11-57." "OK so now let's take off in your black bird to look at the jungle and your vines." "OK Jhiro ring his pilot, Carlos Alberto Cavalia and see if its OK, but you promise not to jump." "I promise, I want to live long enough to telephone you from England to ask how the great Casanova is?" "OK now you make joke, listen Jhiro speak to Carlos." He picks up the telephone and is informed by his pilot that the helicopter will be ready in one hour.

She remarks,

"Your people have such lovely names, why do you always use the full name, like Carlos Alberto Cavalia and your maid Catalina De Francisco."

"It is our history it is who we are, you are talking to Jhiro Luis Eduardo Rene De Montaya De Val De Cabrerra" "Why do you have such long names?" "We have four first names, our name, our fathers, grandfathers and great grandfathers the women have three names their own, their mothers and the grandmothers, so that when you speak to someone using their full names you are speaking to three or four generations or their family, it is a reminder to them who they represent and honour by their actions or who they dishonour by their actions, you will hear women who wish to chastise their children use the child's full name, indeed if Jhiro's mothers called him Jhiro Luis Eduardo Rene, Jhiro knows he is in trouble, and his father his grandfather and his great grandfather are angry with him, often the use of a full name is enough to bring a bad child back to be a good child. It is not the same in the cities, they have abandoned tradition and use only two names, their mothers first and then the fathers. But here in the country we stay with what we know. Jhiro's son if he will have one will be Rene, Jhiro, Luis, Eduardo, his son will be Eduardo, Rene, Jhiro, Luis and so on." "If Jhiro have a daughter she will be Angelica, Anna-Maria, Valentina, Jhiro's mother was Anna-Maria, Valentine, Angelica and so it goes on through the generations." "And if you have a second or third son or daughter?" "We are free to choose the first name always but the rest are traditional, so a second son could be Philippe then Jhiro, Luis, Eduardo it has always been so and will never change, not as long as the sun wakes in the east and sleeps in the west".

"Your names are beautiful like your house." "Thank you, the house was much smaller than this in Jhiro's fathers time, but when we have to change to using the helicopters it was necessary to make the house much bigger and stronger, it is all because of the Americans, it is not safe to use roads, so we have to fly, Jhiro like to fly, Carlos Alberto is teaching Jhiro to fly the Sikorsky, so eventually he is good to fly on his own." "But not today." "No not today, come with Jhiro he show you his fathers wine collection, it will be a surprise for sure." They dress, leave the main house and descend several flights of crude steps cut into the natural rock, each flight is of around ten steps and twisting to the left, only occasionally is there any hand rail, Jackie finds it unnerving being so close to a drop of between five and twenty meters, eventually they arrive at a door in the rock face, Jhiro opens the door and turns on a light which exposes a dimly illuminated corridor cut into the solid rock, the corridor is six meters in length with a small channel cut in the centre of the floor for drainage, at the other end is a wooden door that speaks loudly of age, it looks to Jackie to have come from an Aztec building many centuries before. Jhiro opens the second door and switches on another light. Jackie is more than surprised, she is astonished, what confronts her it is a revelation. She is in a vast natural cavern, complete with stalagmites, stalactites, beautiful natural rock formations and an uncountable quantity of wooden bottle racks. In all she estimates she is looking at ten thousand bottles, in truth it is in excess of eleven thousand, over nine thousand red wine and just short of two thousand champagne and a few hundred white wines. A very small amount of water is dripping through the natural stone roof of the chamber in several places, this water is gathered into channels and runs out of the cavernous cellar via the door and corridor, the building is naturally cool. Jackie is gobsmacked by both the vastness of the room and the sheer quantity of bottles. She remembers her father's cellar, much smaller and containing less than one thousand bottles and bone dry, she asks,

"Isn't this water a problem too much moisture on the corks and the wine will spoil." "Immediately Jhiro can see you know wine, yes if we did not take precautions the wine will spoil, the moisture will get into the wine, but every bottle here is sealed with wax, before any bottle comes into this chamber the neck is dipped in hot wax and then into cold water, but no new wine has been bought for several years now, Jhiro is trying to use this wine for his table, but as you see there is too much for one person." "I can help you there." "Do you have a list of what is here?" "The list died with Jhiro's father, it is in his head, he knew this chamber very well, he was passionate about red wine and champagne, the white wine was for guest only, he never touched it." "Where has it all come from?" "The red it is mostly French from Bordeaux and Bourgogne, there is a little Spanish and Italian but very little, all the champagne is from the Champagne Region naturally, the white Jhiro doesn't know, like his father Jhiro doesn't touch it." "White wine can be very good." "Sure but it is not for Jhiro, only the champagne and the red. You are welcome to explore this cellar and bring whatever you think is best to Jhiro's table." "OK, I might do that, is it always so cool in here?" "Yes the temperature is always eleven degrees, apparently perfect for wine, the cavern was already here and known to the local people but the only way in was to crawl on your belly through the wet, Jhiro's father had it opened up and cured most of the wet problem, the temperature is always the same, it is naturally so, come on pick up a bottle or two and lets get out into the air this place makes Jhiro feel strange." Jackie spends just a few minutes looking through the reds and can't believe what she finds. There are wines which could grace the tables of any European aristocrat perhaps even royalty.

Jackie had been at the home of Jhiro De Montaya for three months, but was just beginning to feel she was getting to know her surroundings, she had for a long time been looking inward, now she was both physically and mentally exploring her prison and her captor, she decided that she would try to learn as much as she could about both and eventually one day use that knowledge to her advantage.

She had put a voluntary end to her self-denial and solitude, with what Jhiro believed was co-operative subordination, but in Jackie's mind it was calculated cooperation and the start of a fact-finding exercise.

When they returned to the main house, Jackie is carrying two bottles of red, a 1976 Chateau Mouton Rothschild and in her eyes quite unbelievable a 1972 Petrus, two of the finest wines in the known world.

After climbing the precarious steps back to the house she puts down the wine and says to Jhiro, on calling for his full attention,

"Look Jhiro what we did today was very careless on my part, we cannot do any such thing again until I am taking contraceptive pills," and after a short pause she adds "do you understand?"

"Yes, yes Jhiro he understands. You wait one moment." He picks up the telephone in the modest dining room cum lounge area they have shared and he rapidly gives an order to someone in his medical centre. Before they finished their coffee Jackie is in possession of a twenty eight day blister pack of familiar small blue tablets, she asks Jhiro which day it is, he replies

"Lunes." For Monday, she locates the word on her blister pack, pops out a tablet and it is swallowed.

Then she says,

"How is it possible that you can do that so quickly?" He slightly boasting replies,

"Jhiro de Montaya he can do any thing with a telephone, order tablets, order food and order his flying machine." She injects,

"Order a blonde English woman?" "No, no, Jhiro he did not order, the telephone it speak to him, it tells him beautiful English laaaydeeee, is with problem, big problem, Jhiro he rescue beautiful woman." "Ok let's not get into that debate again, I'll

331

just put these into my bedroom." Holding aloft the blister pack of pills.

"Then perhaps we can go up in your flying machine and I promise you I will not jump out." "No, no Jhiro believe you do not do this terrible thing, but you can put those in Jhiro's....... our bedroom, if you wish."

"Slow down Casanova, one swallow doesn't make a summer!" She grins to herself knowing he will never understand the double entendre.

He is a little nonplussed but replies,

"Ok we fly now."

She drops the pack of pills in a small bedside drawer, but before she does she kisses them and whispers to herself 'thank god for modern medicine'. It is the clear familiarity of the tablets and their monthly format that causes Jackie to make a tumultuous mistake. She does not read any of the lettering on the recognisable every day packet, mainly because it is in Spanish, but she trusts their appearance. Jhiro requested contraceptive pills, but a meddlesome girl at the compounds own medical centre with only the best of intentions, substituted his request for birth control tablets with similar looking but strong anti depressants. Her motivation was to make her boss, the Jefe, a happy man, she knew as everyone did in the compound that his new wife was very unhappy, so she thought she would kill two birds with one stone. Make his new wife happy and give Jefe the child he had always wanted, bringing joy to his life. If he was happy everyone was happy, what possible harm could she be doing?

CELESTIAL NAVIGATION

They take the two flights of steps leading to the roof of Jhiro's hacienda, on passing the top floor of the building Jackie points to it and asks,

"What goes on in this floor?" Her reply is, "Jhiro he show you later." On reaching the roof, on what is a clear but hot and humid day Jackie pauses to take in the vista, it is simply breathtaking, the top story of the building and the roof stand above the tree canopy, the views all around are stunning. She stands and slowly turns a full circle, for mile upon mile in every direction there are endless green forested hills that eventually become the horizon, far away to the east the hills become mountains some of them showing their permanent white caps, as her gaze moves to the west between two hills, she glimpsed a sparkle of light, she asks,

"What is that shimmer of light on the horizon?" Pointing almost due west,

"It is the great Pacific Ocean but from here it is just a twinkle like a day time star, don't worry it will never be a danger to us here." She estimated, almost correctly that the flicker of light that was the immense power of the late afternoon sun reflecting off the largest feature on the planet was approximately twenty miles away, this was her first piece of information to be compartmentalised for the day, she now knew she was roughly twenty miles east of the west coast of Colombia, she felt she had already achieved much on her first day of her new plan. In her mind she saw a large globe and she now had a vague line running from top to bottom, just off the coast of this lush green country, she needed to sharpen the line, focus it more clearly, to within pin point accuracy and then add another line running left to right around the globe, where the two lines crossed would be her current residence, or as she now told herself, her temporary residence. She was feeling good about herself for the first time in months, in addition to her improved disposition the tablet she had swallowed was about to enter her bloodstream. She was eager to get into the air to add to her geographical knowledge.

The roof was not only painted green but was covered in camouflage netting, as was the body of the helicopter, which was now being stripped away. Whilst they wait just a minute or two, Jackie looks over the rest of the compound, from her newly elevated position she has a commanding view. She notices that all the buildings have camouflage netting draped over their green painted roofs and she ask Jhiro,

"Is all this netting and disguise necessary?" "It is a precaution against the Americans, but you are not to worry we are safe here, this is just to stop the American eye in the sky from finding us and hurting my people." "They would do that?" "They would if we did not have protection, our real protection is in our government in Bogota. Jhiro's fathers' younger brother is high in the government, he protects all of Jhiro's people and coca leaf fields, and we look after all of his family, who live in the north, it is where our mother lives now with Jhiro's ...." "Uncle." "Yes my unkel, he is a good man, he is our real shield against our enemies." "Are they your enemies?" "Yes they would destroy the coca plants if they could find them and perhaps Jhiro's house, but some people in our government are working for our people, they give the Americans small successes and after, with the money the Americans are paying our government the people affected are paid to rebuild their homes and plants in another place." "Really?" "Oh yes people in our capital they gave the information to the US Forces but first they warn the local people, unless it is a cocaine trafficker who is becoming a big problem to our government then they don't give a warning and everyone is killed, and the Americans believe they are clever, they have only remove a problem for our politicians." "Why exactly do the Americans do this?" "They are crazy, we grow coca because it grows very well in our soil, it makes good profit, but because it eventually arrived in the United states in a form that they cannot resist, they come after us, they are crazy, their problem is at home not here," he continues passionately "tell me do you have alcoholics in your country?" "Yes of course we are no different to any other country, we are not exempt from life's addictions." "Yes but your government does not send your soldiers to France to destroy the grape vines there and to kill the people who grew them, they grow them because they grow well

334

and they made good monies to feed the people who work there, you understand?" "Yes I understand you, but your comparison is unrealistic, the entire cocaine trade is illegal, but it is not illegal to drink wine" "And it is not illegal to grow coca leaf in my country." "Perhaps it will one day." "Yes you may be right perhaps it will, if the United States pays our government enough money to pay all our people not to work! And this is the reason Jhiro want to grow grapes for the wine, to be one step in front of all the corrupt politicians in our country and in America." "I understand your reasoning but is this a place the United States would really like to destroy?" "Yes it is a possibility but they do not know we are here, so we are safe, we are protected by these nets, by our missiles and in our capital, so we have many layers of protection, come now the machine is ready." As the sleek black Sikorsky became airborne the surroundings became even more impressive, she experienced a three-hundred and sixty degree panoramic spectacular, she looked down and back for a moment, the compound and all its buildings were like a bucket of water in an ocean, as they gained altitude it simply disappeared into a sea of similar green, she was able to appreciate and fully understand some of Jhiro's comments. Conversation was difficult because of the engine and rotor blade noise, but as they flew along a wide stretch of river ten minutes into the flight she pointed to the long expanse of muddy coloured water and Jhiro said loudly.

"The San Juan." She smiled to herself and for the second time that day compartmentalised information, the compound she now knew was east of the river and to their left was the now expansive pacific ocean. She was not able to gain any more geographical facts during the short half hour flight but she did gain an awareness of how simply vast the area of rain forest was in which she was now a resident and a perception of how difficult her task would be to pinpoint her position, but she knew she had made progress, it had been a positive day.

On returning to a miniscule green dot in a plethora of green, this message was driven home to her again. Back at the house they descended the stairway and Jhiro took her into the top floor of the building.

335

Not for the first time this day she was astounded. The entire top floor was one room. Jacqueline Forbes-Brewer had grown up in one of England's stately homes, but had not seen a room of such proportion. It was forty meters square with a four-meter high ceiling. Its dimensional facts were a woefully inadequate description. The centrepiece of the vast room was a huge ornate dining table and twenty-four matching high backed chairs, all placed on the biggest oriental style rug she had ever seen. Set back from this midpoint of focus were four decorative timber clad, steel columns, doubtless their unenviable task in life was to provide support to the large flat roof. It was both the scale and quality of the ornamentation, which stupefied Jackie, all four outside walls were more than fifty percent glass, allowing natural light to filter into the very heart of the room, those parts of the walls that were not transparent held a dazzling display of fabulous art. Some showing typically Colombian or Spanish scenes, but as she slowly circumnavigated the room she identified works by Picasso, Gauguin and Van Gogh, she presumed not original. The most extraordinary element of the spell binding room was its widely spread collection of furniture and artefacts.

There was a Steinway grand piano, a Wurlitzer jukebox, a huge globe and a two hundred year old ostentatious billiard table. As she continued to slowly peruse the more than generous expanse Jhiro watched her in amusement, he had done the very same thing with many people, family, politicians and associates, he never tired of gauging their wonder when he first introduced a person to his inner chamber, his hopes were that one day Jackie would view what he knew to be a remarkable space, as part of her own home. Everyone who had ever seen the fourth floor of his home had fallen in love with it, he hoped that she would do so also and perhaps one-day fall in love with him.

He stood stock still in admiration of both her slender beautiful form and her blonde hair, also what little he had learnt of her inner determination and resourcefulness had impressed him. Jackie continued her pedestrian circumnavigation of the room. There were exquisite baroque European pieces, stunningly ornamented works from closer to home and amazingly rare and elaborate effects from the orient, all these were blended in the same vast space with remarkable care and attention to detail, amongst the furnishings were many exotic plants, brought into the room for the purpose of absorbing moisture backed up by an extremely efficient air-conditioning and extraction system which was engaged twenty four hours a day to protect the effects and the art from Colombia's humidity. On completion of her circle of the vast chamber Jackie said to Jhiro,

"This is remarkable, simply remarkable." "Thank you, this room represents the history of our family and its journey in the world." "You must be very satisfied to own so much beauty." "No, no you do not understand, Jhiro does not own all this, Jhiro does not see it as his, Jhiro is its keeper, no that is not the word he is wanting to say, ah yes, he has it, he is its caretaker, all of this is in Jhiro's care until he passes the responsibility to another, to Jhiro's son or to his brothers son." "It is not Jhiro's, it is our families, no, it is our family, some of the wooden pieces my great grandfather had made for his beautiful wife, others were buyed by my great uncles when they toured to Europe, to sell our coffee, many years ago. What you see here is the history of our coffee production for three hundred years, Jhiro's always aware of his responsibility here, fortunately the monies from the coca leaf make it possible that he can protect it all here under one roof, many many dollars have been spend to protect and preserve our history, this is one of the reasons, no a big reason why Jhiro want to make a success of the grapes, so that we as a family can stop to growing the coca leaf and the eye in the sky, that is America will no longer be looking for us, and all of this will be safe." Jackie draws another deep breath, looks around her, exhales then ask,

"Tell me those works of art, the European ones they are prints, copies yes?" "Jhiro cannot tell you that, in this room there are two by Picasso, one by Van Gogh and one Gauguin, my father when he went to Europe to sell coffee to the French, the Italians and Spanish, would usually arrive back home with a present to himself, plus he buy many, many cases of fine wine and always a gift for my mother, often beautiful rolls of material which she used, to have many nice things made, my father had an eye for quality, Jhiro is very sorry he is not here today to see all of this brought together for the first time." Jhiro becomes a little impassioned at this point and feigns a mild obstruction in his throat but his clumsy deception is clear for Jackie to view. She can feel that he is a passionate man with entrenched views on criminality and morality, however warped by worldly affairs. Clearly he is a man of integrity, a principled man with a deep love and sense of responsibility for his family and their history.

She leaves him alone for a moment and moves to the centre piece of the room, the huge ornate table, not at the present time set for a meal, but she doubtless believes that amongst the furnishings is a fine collection of porcelain and silver or gold cutlery, currently atop the table is a glass case with a truly complicated looking, but modest sized ornament proudly occupying centre stage, she recognised it but is not able to name it, of all the staggering and valuable works of art on display, she estimates that the four European originals to be worth in excess of twenty million pounds, this basic brass tool for ships to find their way at sea takes pride of place. Jhiro joins her, Jackie points to the instrument and says,

"Tell me its history." "Jhiro doesn't know its name, but many years ago when Jhiro's grandfather was a young man on a sailing boat coming back from Spain with my great grandfather, a storm put them way off of their route, they were lost at sea and they were in big troubles. Fortunately on the ship was a very clever man, when after a week the storm is finished, this clever man is able to use this thing to look at the stars to know where he is, and eventually everyone is safe, Jhiro's great grandfather is so happy that he and his son are safe he paid big money to bring this thing home with him. It is like everything in this room, it is part of our history, without this small thing we will have lost a part of our family and Jhiro would not be made today, so it sits at the middle of the family table when we are not eating. My grandfather says to Jhiro when he is a small boy, if Jhiro is ever lost and must make a big decision in his life he should sit by and touch this thing, it will help Jhiro chose the right path, it will steer Jhiro in the right direction." "You believe this?" "Jhiro cannot be able to say no, he comes to sit here when he is asked to decide about you, before he makes decision and call back." She recalls a portable radio phone ringing when the young jungle boy was pissing on her, perhaps Jhiro's phone call via the slimy agent was the reason her head was pulled out of the bucket of water, the alternative with its violent and cruel connotations makes her shudder and helps her to think of Jhiro as her warder and not her ensnarer.

"And what did this thing say to you?" "Jhiro sit here in silence, thinking of his first wife Juliana Cristina Maria and of Olga, Jhiro knows some of my people believe he is disloyal to the women of Colombia, but they are not able to say this to Jhiro, no, he knows who he is and what he wants in his life and most of all it is someone like you, someone beautiful, intelligent and resourceful. So this machine it says to Jhiro follow your heart not your head."

They left the room in silence but as she is about to close the door Jackie looks back one more time to confirm she is not in a dream. He asks if she wants to eat dinner later in the room they have just left, she replied,

"No, not tonight it's too grand for a lunes night." "OK I'll tell Sofia Estefany that we eat in the small place." "And will I have Catalina De Francisco back tomorrow."

"Yes, yes Jhiro sorry he forget, but he also tells Juan Pablo that he must come back tomorrow with American book and magazines."

"Not American, English, she spells it out to him E.N.G.L.I.S.H."

"OK again Jhiro is sorry but first you will get American then later E.N.G.L.I.S.H."

"OK I'm going to shower in my room now and think about a few things I'll join you later for dinner." He says "Eight o'clock." She replies with a simple,

"Yes." Once in her room her buoyant mood of the day is eclipsed by a heady dose of reality, she comes down to earth with a bump. She now realises exactly what she has done by opening up to this man, an almost total stranger and she is embarrassed at the thought of just how intimate they were earlier. She is pleased that she has made some progress as to her whereabouts, but is impatient to learn more. Jhiro, the helicopter ride and what it revealed of her position, the fourth floor and the wine cavern were all a bit too much for one day.

Following a quiet dinner she feigns tiredness and after just two glasses of the Petrus, the finest wine she has ever tasted, she goes back to her own room and leaves a thoughtful Jhiro to do likewise.

During the night the tiny but powerful antidepressant cruising through her veins has a profound effect, both it and the wine she had consumed combine to have a compelling influence on her.

She awakens at five o'clock feeling lonely and without considering the consequences leaves her room, she enters Jhiro's bedroom and slips into his bed beside him. He, almost disbelieving thinks that maybe she is sleep walking and does not react, but when after a few moments she reaches between his legs he is unable to prevent a very natural response. They make love, Jackie taking the lead, after which they both fall back to sleep, Jackie cuddled up against him, his incredulity vaporises to be replaced with fulfilment.

After a breakfast of coffee, bread and cold meats Jhiro reluctantly flies out for two days, he has people to meet in the north, Jackie almost casually replies to his information with,

"Ok see you when you get back," and jokingly adds, "If I'm still here." They share a smile as Jhiro departs.

She continued to work on her life story on the veranda and took delight in the many humming birds and exotic butterflies that visited the diverse and colourful flowers that surround her, eventually the afternoon humidity forced her inside. She visits the fourth floor to look closer at the huge globe that occupies one corner, she finds Colombia and in her mind draws a vertical line a little to the right of the Pacific Ocean it is between 76 and 78 degrees longitude, with regard the horizontal lines she knows she is north of the Equator which runs through the Ecuadorian Capital of Quito, but she has no idea between which two lines of latitude she is, but is determined to find out. She is surprised to see that half of Colombia drains into the Pacific Ocean and half into the Caribbean, but then she remembers that the reflection they saw from the water yesterday was the Pacific, this knowledge narrows her possible search area down, she finds the scale of the globe and using the first joint of her thumb to its tip calculates that there is approximately one thousand kilometres of Pacific coastline and she knows she is roughly twenty miles from it. She is content for the moment with this limited knowledge, but knows it will not satisfy her for long. She looks around the cavernous room and focuses on Jhiro's historic machine that sits centrally on the table and thinks to herself, he may have this thing to talk to and guide him but I have the globe which I can consult, which will talk back to me and eventually tell me where I am. Before she leaves she wanders the room taking in the art and is staggered to realise that such valuable pieces are hidden deep in a South American rain forest, to be appreciated by almost no one. Also the fact that they are unsecured she finds stupefying, the knowledge that she or anyone in the compound could just walk in and remove one or worse destroy one or all of them sits uneasy with her. She realises that it is a reflection of the elevated position and total respect that Jhiro commands, that such valuables are left undefended.

Jackie is pleased to have her favourite maid back, but the girl is nervous and unsure when Jackie tries to find out the depth of her English speaking. After many days of trying it is an almost unnoticeable nod of the head from Jhiro that relaxes the girl and she opens up a little to Jackie, her English is very basic and was taught to her by an uncle who travelled widely. On the next occasion that Jhiro is away for two days Jackie ask the girl a carefully thought out question. She enquires of her,

"Did you always live here at the home of Jefe?" Which is the only word she is comfortable with to describe her boss, Jackie has noticed she is very uncomfortable with the name Jhiro. She replies,

"No I come from Buenaventura." Jackie points to left and right and asks,

"From where?" "It is big town." She points to the south. Jackie asks,

"It is many kilometres?" "No it is trienta kilometres in this way," again pointing south, she adds, "It is in the way of San Isidro" Jackie shrugs, the girl holds up her fingers three on the left hand a zero with the right. Jackie quickly changes the subject and asks the girl to come with her to the wine cellar to help her bring wine to the house. Later in the afternoon she visits her confidante, the Globe, or as it is in her mind the Orb of knowledge. She eventually locates Buenaventura, much farther to the south than she assumed, near a large city that is unknown to her, Cali. She cannot locate the other name of San Isidro she now knows she needs a more detailed map. She looks again at the globe and now sees her two circular, slightly out of focus lines crossing just to the north of the town of Buenaventura she now needs to define these two lines more clearly. She is once again pleased with her progress.

She is buoyant on Jhiro's return for he has a box full of English books and another full of magazines he says,

"You see, Jhiro he keep his promise, these came from America yesterday, Jhiro he is good to you, yes?" She thanks him and says,

"If you are feeling generous perhaps you can take me to the airport." He laughs and replies,

"No it is not possible." Her reply of,

"OK, but we both know that it is." Goes unanswered.

She quickly discovers that all the literature is American and tells him,

"This is a good thing that you do for me but I ask for English books and magazines, these were printed in the United States, can you please get me some English?" "OK Jhiro he try, it will take much time, he ask the people he knows who go to Madrid to ask people there, but it will take much time." She replies,

"How much time do I have?" He laughs, and adds,

"Sometimes you too clever for Jhiro." She spends the next two days catching up on celebratory divorces, sex scandals and new film and book releases, she knows its gossip and tittle tattle but it is so good to absorb the familiar text.

Her days are spent reading American based romantic novels, perusing magazines and adding to her life story. In which she has now reached her university years at Bath, she finds it odd to think that Jhiro also attended her same lecture rooms more than a decade prior to herself. The late evenings after her second shower of the day are spent with Jhiro at the modest dining room cum lounge between their two bedrooms, she now uses her room when he is absent and their room when he is present. On her second helicopter ride she ask Jhiro what is the small town to the south that they passed over, he is concentrating on the mechanics of flying and does not appreciate the reason for her request,

"It is San Isidro, I have many grapes there, please Jhiro's trying to learn to fly this crazy machine" Three weeks later on a trip to the north to visit another area of vines they pass over a small town Jackie points down and knowingly makes the mistake of calling the town San Isidro, Jhiro replies no it is Cucurrupi". She spends two hours in the Sikorsky as it is used to lift huge bundles of new vines from the nearest access point to the high east facing slopes that have been cleared by cutting all that grows and by later burning to make way for planting. She speculates that incalculable amounts of wildlife and plants were destroyed to make way for the new vines.

She is careful to calculate the distance they travel back to the compound after they fly over the small settlement of Cucurrupi, she estimated that Jhiro's home is halfway between this small town and the next one to the south, San Isidro, she now cannot make any more progress with her orb of knowledge or with flights in the helicopter she must think long and hard to more clearly define her imaginary vertical and horizontal lines that circle the globe and which cross in the rural south west of her adopted country.

The days, which rapidly turn into weeks, are now collecting into months, it is three months since Jackie's calendar began, which was the day Jhiro admitted he could speak English.

She had been waiting for the end of one of her blister packs of pills to coincide with Jhiro's absence so that she might take a bold step and pick up the telephone, on the pretence that she is in a panic because her tablets have run out. She was given by Jhiro an American/English- to Spanish speaking dictionary so that she might learn the rudiments of his language, to help her communicate with the staff. She has put it to good use and has learnt the necessary vocabulary for the conversation she has in mind. She is hoping that when she picks up the telephone in their modest lounge to be able to hear a dialling tone, but knows in her heart it cannot be so, as the phone itself has no numbers to dial with, it must be an extension. She is as expected disappointed, immediately on lifting the phone she hears a young woman's voice, asking if she is ok, she explains her tablets have all gone and pretends to be a little distraught and ask for the Centro Medical. The girl pacifies her and says it is not a problem. Jackie puts down the phone. Her suspicions confirmed, the internal telephone system is not for her.

Later that day when Jhiro hands her another twenty-eight day blister pack of 'contraceptives' he tells her not to worry and it is best if she doesn't use the phone, it will confuse the staff. She nods in co-operative subordination. She is becoming very frustrated that she has made no more progress on the exact location of the compound and a method to use to transmit information. The following week the most event-filled since she was taken from her father's car in Los Angeles, changes everything. On the Monday she received another box of American gossip magazines and on flicking through the front covers recognises what is to her the most familiar face in the world, her own.

Sitting down on the veranda to the backdrop of quarrelsome monkeys, toucans and macaws she reads the latest news in the Forbes-Brewer affair. It felt extraordinary to see pictures of herself, her father and Richard and read the sub-text. She learns of Richard's death and how police are baffled by two facts. One that there has never been a follow up ransom demand for the missing now presumed dead heiress and why three attempts were made on Richard's life, until the last was successful. Jackie is shocked by Richard's death but not devastated as she felt she should be, the reasons for this were two fold, firstly deep down she now suspected Richard of being complicit in her current situation or at least duplicitous, and her arteries were continuously pumping a powerful anti depressant through her body that was responsible for her general buoyant mood. She read the text over and over again until she knew it verbatim. She concealed the magazine in her room and remarkable quickly absorbed the news of the death of her fiancé and moved on

Her second but smaller revelation of the week came about by chance. In the morning they were awake but not out of bed, when a telephone rang in a side room off of Jhiro's bedroom, he unlocks the door and goes into this room which Jackie had not concerned herself with because the door is a perfect match to the wardrobes in his room, she was not aware it was a room at all. Whilst he is in there she can hear him quite angry on the phone, after the conversation dies he stays in the room in silence.

She suddenly realises that it is on or around the twenty third of November and shouts to him

"Jhiro what day is it today?"

He replies "Miercoles." Which she knew to be Wednesday,

"No what date is it?" "23rd November, por que?" He has taken to using simple Spanish to help her become familiar with his language.

"It is my birthday." He flies from the room leaving it open, kisses her and says you wait,

"Jhiro he get the best champagne." He leaves the room in his dressing gown, she knows he has to go to the cellar because there is none in the kitchen area. She takes the opportunity to enter the previously well-disguised room. It is an Aladdin's cave of walls maps, all four walls are covered in extremely detailed charts and maps, the room has no windows, which has facilitated its concealment. She stands in awe for just a few seconds and seizes the opportunity. On one of the larger scale maps she finds the town or Buenaventura, north from there she locates San Isidro she follows the San Juan River north until she reaches the tiny town of Cucurrupi looking for the location of the compound, she was wasting her time, it is clearly marked on the map between the two towns around five kilometres east of the river, this does not tell her anything new, but confirms everything she had learnt. She has now confirmed to almost a square kilometre where she is in the world, birthday present enough, she feels she has achieved much but it has taken three months, she steps back from the map and is stood innocently in the centre of the room when Jhiro returns.

He finds her there and says "Come out of Jhiro's headache room, lets drink to your birthday is it twenty eight?" "Yes, yes but tell me what is this room?" "You really want to know?" "Yes, yes I do someone has worked long and hard in this room, is it you?" He sighs and puts down the champagne and commences a lengthy monologue,

"This room is Jhiro's headache room, the wall behind you is all the plans showing where we grow coffee, every place to a half kilometre squares, this wall here is the same information but it is where we grow coca leaf, and this wall to my right is where Jhiro grows his grapes, that one in front is plans of all Colombia and our neighbours." "So why is this a headache room?" "Because there is always more and more pushing to make Jhiro do what he not want to do, Jhiro want to grow coffee and grapes, but everyone want Jhiro to grow coca, always coca, coca, coca, we grow for the Medellin, Jhiro think you call it Cartel, but always Medellin want more coca, now the Cali cartel are at war with Medellin, they want Jhiro to stop selling to Medellin and to sell to Cali. It is big problem for Colombia now that Cali is fighting a war with Medellin, this is biggest problem for Jhiro also, not the Americans with their guns and bombs and not our government with politicians who take monies to give the Americans the position of farms who grown coca leaf." "So why don't you stop growing coca?" "If Jhiro say he grow no more coca, Jhiro balls is cut off and Jhiro falls from helicopter, if Jhiro stop selling to Medellin same thing, if Jhiro do not sell to Cali soon same thing, if Jhiro do sell to Cali same thing, and if Jhiro goes, all the grapes go and the coffee will go, it will be coca, coca, coca, from here to America, that would be a very bad thing for Jhiro, why is it America not grow its own drugs?" At this point he walks around the room and slaps his hand on all the maps. He is now in tears.

"This is a betrayal of Jhiro's family, of our father the great Luis Eduardo Rene Jhiro de Montaya De Vale De Cabrerra and his father our grandfather and all our fathers but this will never happen if Jhiro is alive, we are honourable family we grow best coffee for three hundred years, now we want to grow good wine, Jhiro want to stop the coca but everybody hates Jhiro." He is openly crying as he is ranting "Jhiro cannot let down the coffee co-operative, we belong to it for many, many years, hundreds of years, Jhiro cannot let down his people and Jhiro will not pull up his grapes, this is why he buys new land to plant grapes, he cannot plant grapes here and here." As he delivered his rant he slaps his hand on the coffee and coca maps.

"But it is your land you can do as you wish." "Oh no not if you is dealing with Medellin and Cali, and government and Americans, and co-operative oh no, Jhiro is a monkey stuck in his own tree." "Can your brothers not help?" "They are weak, they would vote to stop the grapes and cut the coffee but Jhiro he carry the family name alone, he is true family, he has the name

346

Jhiro Luis Eduardo Rene de Montaya de Val de Cabrerra, not the brothers."

"What will happen Jhiro?" "Jhiro must buy more land in the south to grow coca to sell to Cali, but not in Jhiro's name and he must buy more land in the north to sell more to Medellin, but Jhiro he just wants to grow grapes, it is like every time Jhiro comes home there is an extra mistress, now there is six mistresses soon it will be seven when we start to make wine, enough for today Jhiro has headache again, we can close this door and it can be your birthday." They leave the room which currently represents Jhiro's long running family torment, the nature of the pressure on him is becoming ever more menacing. After just one glass of champagne Jackie is sick but soon recovers, Jhiro asks her what she wants to do on her birthday she replies,

"Ride a horse." "OK it will take an hour to organise." "We can?" "Of course, Jhiro has horses." "Where?" "Not far, we go in truck, the flying machine it upsets the horses, but you are ok now?" "Yes I think it was too early for me to drink champagne, let's have breakfast." After breakfast they drive in what feels to Jackie to be an armoured four by four. A huge and heavy American made vehicle, she jests to Jhiro,

"The Americans make something good then." Slapping the dashboard,

"Oh yes the Americans made many good things, trucks, burgers, movies, music, weapons but best of all wars." "That's a bit unfair." "Is it? The Americans are happy when they have a war a long way from home, they don't like a war at home, Pearl Harbour still hurts them now, but they give hurt around the world and go back home to their safe chairs on their porches, and their movies, and their burgers and blueberry pies." Jackie gives up on conversation as clearly Jhiro is in poor humour. They arrive after just twenty minutes at a small field that could be a sports field, with a stable block at one end. Staff are on hand and soon two horses are made ready, Jackie rejects her mare which she claims is too old, too small and too pedestrian, she chooses a much larger stallion to Jhiro's dismay and protestations. They are soon trotting along a dirt road under an almost total canopy of green, where the fierce mid morning sun manages to break through the umbrella of leaves a radiant shaft of light hits the floor. After approximately two kilometres they arrive at a thin belt of pastureland that Jackie had not noticed from the air, it was just fifty meters wide and almost a kilometre in length. The grass was not too long, Jackie looked at Jhiro and said,

"Let's give the horses some freedom." With that she kicks her mount and is in full gallop before Jhiro can react. He decides not to respond to her challenge and watches her use her skill and daring to cover the kilometre of unused airstrip in a fraction of the time he had ever done himself, or had seen anyone else achieve. He feels pride in her achievement. He trots his mount to meet her half way back but she is once again in full flight, this time as she passes him with a sideways grin he attempts to match her speed, but is simply not in the same league as Jackie when it comes to horsemanship. Eventually when they come back together he asks her,

"How is it you learn to ride with so much skill and no fear?" "I was born on a pony and have been riding ever since, you forget I was a competitor for Great Britain in the Olympic Games, or rather I should have been." "You have great skill, can you teach Jhiro some of that skill?" "A little perhaps, it comes down to what you just said, a lack of fear, if the horse feels good and you feel good with him, we say you give him his head, let him go, this horse wants to go." "No one has ever ride him like that." "He's starting to sweat up now in this heat, lets get him back under the tree cover, do you want me to give yours a run, I enjoyed that." "No its OK Jhiro manage, he does not think he wants his people saying that you had to work his horse." With that he completes a gently gallop around the airstrip, Jackie watches and thinks that if he's trying to impress her with his finest command of a mount then there is little she can do to achieve an improvement, he is too stiff, he looks as though he is bracing himself for a fall at any moment, she can tell that he did not ride as a boy. When he returns she says,

"I have to be honest, if that's your best then its better you stay in the helicopter I don't think we could make a jockey out of you, in the time you have left, how old are you?" "Now you make joke of Jhiro, he starts to ride after Juliana Cristina died and we do not have Olympic teacher here." "OK point taken, come let's get out of this heat."

As they walk their mounts back to the stable, she looks left and right down various tracks thinking it might be possible to take a horse and bolt down one of them to a town or village, but then she remembers the map, nothing for miles and miles to the east and then mountains, she asks Jhiro,

"Where do these paths lead?" "All of these on the east side go to coca plants." She dismisses the thought from her mind.

Each day she wakes she asks herself what can I do today to increase my knowledge, already today has been a good day, for apart from confirmation of her position on the wall maps in Jhiro's headache room, she had noticed that the phone in there had a dialling pad and is possible a direct line to the outside world.

That evening she drinks a little more champagne than she should have, Jhiro thinks it is to celebrate her birthday, but in truth it's to help forget all the others.

In the morning she is sick, soon after she wakes. Jhiro sleeps through her nausea. She is fearful that the cause of the sickness is something more than the champagne, as she feels no other ill effects. She goes back to her own room and checks that she has not missed any tablets, once she has confirmed this, she examines the packet more thoroughly than at any time before and is soon aware of the probable cause of her sickness. She experiences a rage of proportion unknown to her. She brings with her the blister pack of pills, a sharp knife from the kitchen and she unties the belt of her silk dressing gown, as she enters Jhiro's room he is still asleep, she also slips the silk belt from the loops of his dressing gown which is led on the floor at the foot of the bed. She now has exactly what she needs, the evidence, a form of physical restraint and a long bladed sharp knife. As she gets back into bed she gently rolls Jhiro onto his front, he half wakes. She kisses his ear and whispers to him,

"Give me your hands I'm going to tie them so that we can celebrate my birthday properly." He obliges, his hands are soon tied behind his back, she then ties his ankles and rolls him on to his back, he is already aroused in anticipation.

She holds the knife to the base of his penis and grins at him. He is now awake and confused, and says, "What are you doing?" She throws the packet of pills at him and shouts,

"Read those you bastard, you substituted anti-depressants for contraceptives pills, so instead of me taking those to prevent me getting pregnant I'm taking happy pills to make sure I do and now I am. You bastard, I'm going to cut this off, what have you got to say?" He realises she is deadly serious, all pretence vanishes with his erection, his penis now being the size of a child's.

"No, no Jhiro he did not do this, he would not do this thing." "Liar, say something pretty damn good or say goodbye to little mister floppy here." She has it in one hand, the knife in the other, poised at its base.

"No, no, no Jhiro he promises he did not do this thing, he will find out who did and drop them from his flying machine." "Is that what really happened to Olga, she would not play your game, so you dropped her out of the sky?" "No, no Jhiro swear, he swear on his father and his grandfather and all his family." Then a realisation hits him, he calms down looks her in the eye and placidly says to her,

"Jhiro swear on the life of his unborn child, Jhiro did not do this thing, but if that is not enough for you, you go ahead and cut Jhiro, without you and the child that grows in you, this thing that you hold is no good to me, it is too late for Jhiro to start again, he does not have the strength. So go ahead and cut Jhiro, cut his balls, cut his throat, but do not cut his unborn child." She stared at him still gripping his limp appendage, she knows he is sincere, she releases her hold and throws the knife to the floor adding,

"Please don't throw anyone from your helicopter, I don't want another life ruined." He relaxes and takes a deep breath, he knew he was very close to partial mutilation by the degree of anger in Jackie's eyes, he responds,

"OK, but Jhiro find out who do this thing and they never work for the De Montaya family again, now please Jhiro's hands." "If I release you now you'll probably kill me." He shouts loudly, and he is clearly and visible upset,

"No, no, no, no, no, Jhiro never kill, Medellin they kill, Cali they kill, our politicians they kill, the police kill, the Americans kill, but Jhiro he does not kill, he never kills, Jhiro does not kill, Jhiro grows wine." She cuts the silk cord to his hands and awaits the storm of consequences. Jhiro frees his feet quickly, he dresses and leaves the room without a word.

In his silk dressing gown without a tie cord he walks to the compounds own medical centre, kicks open the door and rages at the two young female assistants and one doctor who hand out prescription drugs, treat small wounds and care for the elderly. They are shocked at his outburst, he barks out the nature of his complaint against them, the male doctor hold up his hands in submissive disbelief, one of the two young girls stares at the head of the family in shock, the other looks to the floor and starts to cry.

She is physically pulled from the room and marched back up to the main house, she is dragged into Jhiro's bedroom and ordered to kneel, she is crying loudly. Jackie yells at him,

"Jhiro what is this, what is going on?" "This girl is the one who did the terrible thing to you, Jhiro will find out why." He drills the sobbing girl until she coughs out the truth amid tears and mucus, the threat of being dropped over the jungle from his helicopter proving persuasive.

Jhiro then explains to Jackie that the girl thought that you were unhappy and Jhiro wanted a child more than anything in the world, so she tried to make everybody happy, now everybody is not happy." He forces the girl to apologise to Jackie and then he ask her,

"What do we do with her? Drop her in the ocean, feed her to the snakes?" Jackie says,

"I suppose she has a family who need her wages." Jhiro establishes her home situation and replies she has no father, she and her mother support three other children. Jackie then ask,

"What is the worst job on the estate?"

"That one is easy to answer, it's the place where they wash the clothes." "The laundry." "Yes that is it, the laundry, it's so hot in there it is always the last job anyone wants." "Ok let her work in the laundry for three months, only three months and she is to keep her same monies and then have her job back, I don't want her treated horribly, but what she did was very wrong, if she messes with other pills she could make someone very ill, she did after all have very good intentions, she just tried to make everyone happy."

351

Jhiro delivers Jackie's verdict to the girl, who immediately stands up and puts her arms around Jackie in gratitude, she leaves repeatedly saying 'arrepentido, arrepentido', she is expressing deep repentance.

After she leaves Jackie says to Jhiro,

"Is that what your life is here? Making decisions that affect other people." "Always, always, people fight, Jhiro make judging, people steal, people sleep with the wrong woman, or with a girl who is to young, always Jhiro make judging, in a place like this the Jefe is the law but if someone kills, Jhiro call in the soldiers and they take someone away." "What happens to them?" "Jhiro doesn't ask but they do not come back." "Do they simply shoot them or do they go to prison?" "If they are very bad people from their shoes to their heads I think they lose them in the jungle along the way, but if they are decent people that lose control, they have to work on big government works, making roads, bridges or tunnels watched always by the soldiers." Jackie shakes her head in disbelief and asks,

"And you have had to do this?" "Two times, I think one was lost on the road, the other is working for ten years." Jackie shaking her head changes the subject,

"I now want a pregnancy test, do you think you have someone who can find such a thing, or will I get a hearing aid instead."

Jhiro does what he always does when a request is made of him, he reaches for the telephone.

An hour later, it is confirmed Jackie is carrying a minute extra life.

For the first time since hearing her name four months ago Jackie has genuine sympathy with someone she had never met, Olga. She asks Jhiro to show her the young woman's grave, she laid two flowers upon it.

Over the next few days Jackie sorts out her priorities.

Her secondary considerations are to continue with her own life story, ride the stallion occasionally, which she found tremendously therapeutic, request a small plot in the family graveyard for her father and Richard, she wants to see their names in stone, she wants a quiet place to sit and remember them, but as she has doubts regarding Richard she wants them set apart, not on one stone. This request is again something Jhiro deals with

352

quickly, with his oh so versatile telephone. Her two primary concerns are how to make progress in her search for the exact location of the compound and the small innocent life that is growing, hour by hour within her. Should she terminate the process? If she could find someone to support that decision and assist her, certainly she believed Jhiro would not be the person and without his backing little or nothing seems to be achieved here. Should she have the child? The thought of having the child here in the vast rain forest appalled her. She would want a complete team of medical experts with all the background support that entailed. She would want as a minimum high standard her own British NHS, people she could trust. She smiled a wry smile to herself at the thought of telling her father she was pregnant, he would do a Jhiro. Pick up the telephone and put all sorts of experts on standby.

She then compared her father and Jhiro, they are, were, both responsible for thousands of people and they both cared deeply for these people, and she realised that her father would have to make many disciplinary decisions sitting on his many boards. He would decide which areas of the business to put funds into, which areas to withdraw support from or terminate his group's connection with, or to sell or buy assets and just like Jhiro he could achieve all of this and more by reaching for a telephone. She remembered that if ever she had a problem with a pony, whatever the nature of the difficulty he would pick up the telephone and someone else would erase her dilemma, even if sadly as was the case with her second pony Arabella, the problem was catastrophic, it was the telephone he reached for to have the stricken animal removed.

Both men too she thought had a conscience and their own set of standards, which although applied to very differing circumstances made them both in her mind appear to be very resourceful individuals, but always whatever she thought sympathetically towards Jhiro she would remind herself that he is basically her gaoler, and that he is involved in illegal activity, both of these things would appal her father.

She knew deep within herself that she could not stop the process that was the creation of a new life, she could use the threat of it against Jhiro as a bargaining chip, but she could no more bring to an end the defenceless tiny life inside her than she could deny her love for her father.

Apart from the pregnancy she had her two perpetual dilemmas, exactly where was she and how could she get the information out, if and when she knew it. Within a week she would make significant progress on both issues.

One morning Jhiro had to answer the telephone in his headache room, he had left the door open whilst he spoke very firmly to his caller. Jackie listened very carefully, once he had ended the incoming call, she then heard his fingers tap out a number and he began his next conversation directly to a man called Ramos. He did not ask to be connected or pause for an instant. She was now reasonably confident that she could pick up that telephone and dial to England, she knew to call home she would need to dial 00-44 and then the number, dropping the first zero, she had done this several times from Los Angeles.

It excited her greatly to think that she could simply walk into Jhiro's office pick up the phone and it would ring in her fathers' study. Then she berated herself she couldn't ring St Georges, but what other numbers did she know by heart? She had to admit that she knew none, all the regular numbers she used were on a keypad, which self dialled the number when she pressed a code. She knew number eleven was Arnold Elliot, number twelve the farrier etc etc. She actually knew only the British Emergency number, nine nine nine, which she could fall back on if all else failed. Though she felt trying to explain who she was, her exact dilemma and where she was would take an age, she could hear the reply to her explanation 'So is that, ambulance, fire brigade or police' in a high pitched patronising voice.

Her second and most significant breakthrough to date came in the third delivery of books from the United States. There were a number of large reference books, it appeared to Jackie that someone had either died or had a good clear out, there were titles such as 'The Wild West, An Illustrated History', 'The Slave Trade, A History', 'The American Civil War', 'The History of the Buccaneers of America' and so on, at the bottom of the second box was a huge reference volume titled 'The History of Astronomy through the Ages'. Though dismissed by her at first, the book was to be her most appreciable breakthrough in her search for the answer to her biggest quandary, where was she, exactly?

The volume sat un-viewed by her for three days, eventually she flicked through it, for no other reason than she had disciplined herself to miss nothing, leave no stone unturned. At the bottom of page two hundred and six, in a section covering the history of Celestial Navigation, there was a diagram of a device used by ships navigators in Centuries past that Jackie wrongly assumed had long since become obsolete, it was a Sextant. In truth by maritime law it is a requirement today that all ships carry such a device and a person versed in its use. The book went on to boast the accuracy of the device, its original principle first invented by Sir Isaac Newton who curiously never published a paper on its usage. It was two other men who independently developed the device to its full capacity. They were John Hadley an English mathematician and Thomas Godfrey a Glazier from Philadelphia. Jackie would perpetually be grateful to all three of them. The significance of this device was immeasurable to Jackie, for two reasons, firstly the page boasted that with a sextant and an accompanying chronometer it was possible to pinpoint, both the operators exact position of latitude and longitude and secondly Jackie knew where she could get her hands on such a contrivance, there was one sitting under a glass cage in the centre of the large dining table in Jhiro's enormous fourth floor room.

The next twenty pages of the book gave full instructions for the use of such an implement and all relevant mathematical tables for calculations, Jackie hugged the book, she felt she had now got through her foothills, had successfully scaled her lower slopes and could now view her summit, there was still a significant climb ahead, but she had a visible target at which to pit herself against. Had it not been for the discovery in the volume, 'The History of Astronomy' Jackie would have fallen into a dark place mentally, the shock of her pregnancy and her discontinuing to take her 'happy pills' would have resulted in her being overcome by overwhelming circumstances, but fortunately for her the realisation that in the room above where she slept, there was her possible salvation kept her true to her course, kept her focused and made her feel in control of her own destiny, albeit by a narrow thread, but it was a tangible thread.

Over the next few days she added to her life story and she rode the strong stallion once more, she also read other material, but her focus was on the use of the sextant. When alone she visited the device to confirm it was in fact exactly what she had thought. She checked also that it was not fixed to the table or locked in its glass cage and that the hugely necessary chronometer was with it, she was not disappointed on any point. She now not only believed that the instrument could show her her way forward, but that it would. She knew she had much to learn and that a high degree of precision would be required.

Whenever Jhiro was around she read other topics, but when she was alone she absorbed all the information at hand, until she knew how to use the device without question. She knew she needed a great number of clear night skies, she took to regularly viewing the stars after they had dined, feigning an interest in the many hundreds of twinkling night lights, she learnt constellations, she could locate planets, she often saw satellites slowly passing over, what Jhiro called 'The Americans eye in the sky' and many dramatic shooting stars. Jhiro began to share this interest with her and took her onto the roof of the main house when the entire night sky was visible to them.

He had become extremely considerate toward her, since they had confirmed she was expecting a child, his child, he was always considerate but he had taken it to another level. She knew he loved her, she was becoming fond of him, but if he asked her if she needed anything she would reply, 'Prisoner 23-11-57 would like a ticket to Heathrow' and he would laugh it off. She felt that if she allowed herself to give in to grief and circumstances and fall into a slough of despondency, cried constantly and withdrew into a state of listlessness, then she might achieve something by drawing on her gaoler's sympathies, but this was not in her, she was competitive by nature. If there was a distant prize, which in this case was literally on the horizon, it was to be won not handed to her in woeful piteousness.

Their nightly star gazing was producing dividends, she was not only able to identify numerous individual stars, constellations and planets, but various staff would come to know that it was the norm for Jhiro and his new wife to be on the roof after dark, she would need a degree of complacency of their part, if she was to achieve her goal.

The next two occasions that Jhiro was away, the afternoon rains persisted long into the night, she knew she should not be on the roof at three or four am after the rain cleared it would arouse suspicion. Jhiro was also away less often now that she was pregnant, he was protective of her, but his business dealings with Medellin in particular would not release their hold upon him and it was often the case that he would not be able to fly back before nightfall. This was a watershed, the reason being that the Americans had persuaded the Colombian Government to impose a curfew on night flights in the Medellin and Cali areas, to enable them to gather intelligence and information on day flights, where they were landing, most common used routes etc, and Jhiro feared his helicopter lights and engine heat might attract missiles if he gambled and flew after dark. This information made Jackie feel unsafe in general, but safe to experiment with the sextant if Jhiro had not returned an hour after dusk.

On many evenings on those occasions when the humid, tropical afternoon rain had cleared Jackie would have to be content with sitting on the west veranda and enjoying a spectacular sunset. Small areas of trees that were on higher ground than their neighbours would form islands in the vast expanse of shadows. The sky was often a blaze of yellow fading to orange through red to pink, and always there was a distant sparkle from the Pacific Ocean and the backdrop of monkeys, tropical birds and fruit bats.

Eventually her opportunity came a month after she had discovered exactly what a sextant was capable of.

Which was a few days after Christmas, a time when Jhiro had bought together many members of his family to celebrate his new joy, her pregnancy, Jackie had feigned illness for the three days, which had left Jhiro mortally embarrassed. She spent Christmas day in her room extremely hungry, studying the use of a sextant. She had no desire to meet and greet his wider family, she sympathised with him, he was a handsome well presented, kind man, but she did not want to meet the brothers and the cousins, and be looked down upon by their buxom, colourful, loud wives, she was now single minded in her plan and wanted no artificial friendships and superficial conversations. She felt she was in training as if for an Olympic event, distractions were a disadvantage, a weakness and she would not allow anything to side line her. She did not want to become part of the Colombian equivalent of the Morning Coffee set or the Afternoon Tea brigade.

Jhiro was not pleased with her and was quiet for two days but he could no more deny her than he could deny his birthright, he had grown to love and admire her, he was becoming very pliable in her hands, on all daily and domestic issues. Jhiro left for Medellin on the twenty ninth of December. During the day just before noon she took the instrument from its case and took it to the roof unseen for it was necessary for her to take a reading of the angle between the sun and horizon with the sun at its highest point. Later a little after midnight in the first few minutes of the thirtieth of December, Jackie had with her her new found knowledge of the heavens, a slice of common sense and a fairly complex set of calculations, with which she established her exact position of latitude, to four degrees, twenty two minutes and eighteen seconds north of the Equator. She did the calculation over and over and always came up with exactly the same result, she was overjoyed that she had now defined her line that circled the globe east-west, in her case just above the Equator to a precise clarity.

She felt she had all but booked her ticket home. She knew from the book that was guiding her, that to establish her position of longitude was far more difficult, but the encouragement she received from her success with her first calculation was a huge boost, she was ecstatic with her progress. She had taught herself to use an ancient instrument that had so quickly been sidelined by the modern satellite-dependant global positioning system, the GPS. She promised herself that if she ever, no she corrected herself, when she got back to St Georges she too would have such a device in her home. She corrected herself again in her father's study, her study. She had originally viewed or attempted to view progress on a daily basis, then weekly, it was now monthly and in the next month she made none at all.

The main cause being, that she woke early one morning in extreme pain, which quickly worsened to literally produce howls of discomfort from her. Jhiro was extremely agitated and worried for her, he screamed down the telephone to his doctor to come at once. He had watched his first love die and with her his child, he had seen his second love falling from the sky carrying his child, on both occasions he had felt totally impotent. Those heartbreaking visions flashed across his consciousness, he simply would not let it happen again. The ten minutes wait for Jhiro's own doctor were silently as agonising for him as they were audible agonising for Jackie.

He would look at her and try to comfort her, to no avail. He made himself a false promise that if he lost two more people he loved excruciatingly, he would deny god and destroy all the so called precious art in the floor above him, what good he told himself is a god that punishes decent people again and again, and what good is all the monies in the world. Amidst Jackie's groaning the doctor arrived, as it is four am he is looking a little dishevelled himself. Through Jhiro he asks basic questions, what had she eaten last night? Had she had any alcohol? When was her last bowel movement and when did the pain start? Is there any additional pain when she urinates? He then exposes her abdomen and prods her in various places causing an extreme reaction from Jackie. He then rolls her on her side, again this produces yells of pain. He puts on a medical glove, which he lubricates and inserts his middle finger deep into her anus to confirm that constipation is not the cause of her discomfort, producing a cry of pain from his patient, hitherto unheard. Jhiro looks at the man and imagines holding his hand over an open fire until he mimics the sound. After laying his hand several times on her abdomen and suddenly releasing it, again causing Jackie to scream, he is satisfied that his examination is complete. Jackie is both crying and howling in pain, Jhiro is crying with his mental pain.

The doctor suggests two possibilities, either it is appendicitis or he thinks more likely it is an ectopic pregnancy, a pregnancy which is stuck in the fallopian tube and had not reached the womb, both are life threatening, she must go to hospital now. Jhiro panics and does what he does when he panics, he picks up the telephone. The wife of his helicopter pilot answers the phone eventually to remind Jhiro that Carlos Alberto has two days off work to celebrate the wedding of his daughter and that he is asleep and as drunk as a pig in a barrel of tequila. Jhiro screams as he puts down the telephone, and he makes a monumental decision.

He asks the doctor to inject Jackie with a painkiller. This he does but as the pain is deep in her abdomen this has little effect, the two of them then struggle to get Jackie out of bed, they wrap her in a sheet and somehow carry her up the stairs to the roof and into the helicopter, with Jackie howling all the while. Jhiro then sits in the right hand side in front of the prime set of controls for the first time. He is frightened. He has often taken over the controls in flight and he had taken off and landed a few times but always with the backup of Carlos. This is a new experience and it is dark and there is a curfew. He fires up the engine, checks he has fuel and transfers power to the main rota blade, he can feel the machine twitching, it wants to be airborne. He engages the smaller tail rota, increases power and they are airborne. He applies too much power and they swing ninety degrees to the right Jackie falls against the door and squeals in pain. He steadies the craft and blindly flies north into the darkness. He reaches a reasonable altitude and applies almost full power to hasten his journey. He starts to pray, he prays it is light when he arrives at the Medellin Underground Laboratory that has the best equip medical centre in the entire district. He prays that the Americans and their missiles are asleep. He repeatedly says out loud in Spanish,

"Please God let us live, let Jhiro do this thing, Please God, Please God hold Jhiro's hands, please God, please God let me do this thing."

Jackie is aware that she is airborne but believes Jhiro is talking to the pilot, after two hours of flying due north which Jhiro manages by compass flying, it begins to get light. He cannot radio ahead because all the helicopters and light aircraft never use radios as they can and will be intercepted by the Americans, so they all fly in complete radio silence. If he were to attempt to use radio communication he would put himself at further risk by both alien and allied forces, as he would be breaking a code of silence, he himself would become a target for both Americans and Colombians. As it begins to get light, he gets his bearings, Jackie has gone quiet, he doesn't know if she's dead or has responded to the dose of morphine.

Ten minutes later he finds his target-landing site and is relieved that the American missiles did not find theirs. He flies two circles anti clockwise which is the signal to those below that he is genuine and is not being coerced by passengers and tries to land, he is descending too fast in his haste to get Jackie the treatment she needs. The ground is coming up to him far too quickly, he attempts to halt his rate of decline, unsuccessfully. The craft slams into the ground, crumbling its undercarriage skids, fortunately for Jhiro and his passenger he hits the ground level, both skids collapse simultaneously which keeps the helicopter upright, had it turned to one side or the other the main rotor would have made contact with terra firma, making disaster their only possibility.

The force of the impact, shuts off the power, breaks two of Jackie's ribs and shatters both Jhiro ankles.

They are removed from the wrecked Sikorsky, Jhiro is released after having to cut away much of the front of the machine, destroying electrics, cables and hydraulics, they are then taken into the labyrinth that is the largest laboratory in Colombia. Jhiro refuses medication or treatment until he is satisfied that Jackie has the care she needs, she is examined and scanned which produces a fairly conclusive result that she has an acute inflamed appendix and two broken ribs. She is taken into theatre for the necessary and corrective operation and finally Jhiro is released from his pain, made unconscious and his ankles are reset.

During the following night Jackie awakes first and is alarmed on many levels, firstly she has pain throughout her rib cage but the terrible pain of the previous day is gone. Secondly she is clearly in a hospital of some sort, but not one in her experience, the dimly lit room affords her little vision, but she can see that the ceiling is curved, resembling an aircraft hanger, painted a dull white. She lifts her head, which causes her a degree of pain, but nothing like the pain she remembers.

361

She looks to her right the bed is empty, she slowly looks to her left and as her eyes acclimatise to the dim light she focuses on the person in the bed in her view, it is Jhiro, on his back with both legs in plaster and lifted a little off the horizontal. She is confused, very confused, she remembers waking with horrible pain and a doctor examining her who she wanted to kill, but nothing more. Suffering a lot of pain she sits up in bed slowly and carefully slides to her left and to her feet, she moves to Jhiro's bed. She puts her hand to the side of his face, he is warm, he is ok, but why is he in this position? Her confusion is paramount. Why are his legs damaged? The discomfort in her ribs causes her to jerk her hand, which wakes him.

He opens his eyes, she waits for two seconds for his consciousness to catch up with his vision.

She whispers,

"Jhiro why are we here?" He is overwhelmed with joy, he puts his arms around her and sobs with relief, he only releases her after almost a minute because she wrenches with pain. He continues to cry openly and inconsolably. Eventually when his breathing is semi-normal she repeats the question,

"Jhiro why are we here?" He is still sobbing and griping her hands, he replies,

"You have big problem with baby, Jhiro he fly you to this place, but he is not good enough man, he broke his flying machine, but it is not important you are alive, it is everything to Jhiro." "Have I lost the baby?" "Jhiro doesn't know, Jhiro has been asleep, he hurt his legs." "What has happened to your legs?" "They are like the flying machine, broken." "How did this happen?" "Jhiro not good enough, he broke everything." He starts to sob again,

"Jhiro how did you break everything?" "You are sick, Jhiro have to fly the machine, he is no good." "You flew the helicopter, why?" He looks her in the eyes and gives her the only answer he can,

"Because Jhiro loves, he loves more than before, more than ever, he loves you." The full implications of what he has said hits home, he has flown the helicopter for the first time alone, in the dark and he doesn't know if she has lost the child or not, but still he is weeping because she is alive. Half of her heart goes out

362

to him, she embraces him and they cry together, Jhiro through shear relief and Jackie because.......... She is not prepared to admit to the because. They maintain their tearful embrace for several minutes until Jackie's discomfort forces her to stand upright, they are left gazing into each others eyes, it is clear that Jhiro has crossed his Rubicon, Jackie has one foot on either bank.

In the morning everything is explained, Jackie has had an appendectomy, the pregnancy is untroubled, but she has two broken ribs, Jhiro has badly broken his ankles, they are shattered, both of them will need to remain where they are for seven days. It is seven days they use to get to know each other, better than over the previous five months. They talk sincerely of their past and their hopes for the unborn child. After hearing the full story of her night flight she is in awe of Jhiro's potential self sacrifice and the many risks that he took on her behalf, both the number of risk and their potential repercussions cause Jackie great consternation and emotional confusion. Whilst in the hospital Jackie asks Jhiro,

"Since I came to you have you been totally honest with me, about your past, your first wife and Olga and everything else?" He hesitates and says,

" There is just one thing that Jhiro has not said right, the four paintings from Europe that are in the family room, they are not the families, they are belonging to Medellin, it is their way to hide monies and to make Jhiro be trapped with them, they are fifty million dollars US, Jhiro is just the keeper, he is ashamed he does not tell the truth."

When Jackie is able to move around with less discomfort she attempts to leave the room, which apart from herself and Jhiro contains seven other men, all are suffering broken limbs, or stab wounds, she never inquired as to the cause of their injuries. She is restricted in her movements and only allowed to the latrines. She ask Jhiro why this is the case.

"This place is the biggest laboratory in the country, in here coca leaf from Peru, Ecuador and our country is processed into cocaine for the Americans." "So how big is it?" "Five years ago our politicians gave hundreds of millions of dollars to build a huge tunnel two kilometres through these mountains to make it faster to travel from Cali to Medellin. It was to be for a road tunnel." "The Medellin people decided it was a good idea, so they paid the contractors a similar amount to build two tunnels, there is only one tunnel at each end but for over one kilometre inside there is two tunnels. The trucks from all Peru and everywhere turn into the second tunnel after they are inside the first one. It's very clever, there are empty trucks at the out end, so when a full truck comes into the in end, after one minute an empty one comes out of the out end, so if the Americans eye in the sky is watching they don't see anything wrong." "So what happens in here?" "Everything, coca leaf is processed into cocaine, hundreds of tons of it a year, it is taking your breath away. There are scientist in here that can turn cocaine into almost anything, they turn it into a water, then it is soaked into wood and clothes, it is mixed into wine and other drinks, made into plastics, into glass fibre into anything, then it is used to make many, many things, boats, bits of cars, trucks, seats for aeroplanes, these scientist, they can make cocaine disappear and appear again in United States, Spain anywhere." "Why did you bring me here?" "It is best doctors near to Jhiro's home, in here they have best thing in world for seeing into your body." "X-ray?" "No no much better than x-ray." "They have M.R.I scanners in here?" "Yes that is it, scanner it can see inside, Jhiro brings you here, here there are better machines than in Medellin hospital." "Why do they have scanners?" "To make sure new products will get into America, go through the airport machines and they have special dogs with clever noses to make sure there is not problem at airport." "You mean these people have state of the art scanners, they own sniffer dogs and highly skilled scientist" "Oh yes, nothing too good in here, always one step in front of Americans, if they find cocaine in shoes they stop making cocaine shoes and make something else, they even have people who fly every week to America to have treatment on missing legs." Jhiro laughs, "But new leg is made of cocaine plastic and they come back with wood leg, the wood legs are burn on fire to cook food in kitchens. People they make so much money they are asking to have a good leg cut off, these people will do it in here." Jackie holds her hands to her mouth in disbelief. Jhiro half laughs,

"Even their wheel chairs are made of it, the seats, the tyres, all the tubing is full up of it, then the whole thing is put in a tank of resin, that the dogs cannot smell through, but the resin is fifty per cent cocaine, and the stupid Americans are so proud to help man or woman with one leg to get on airplane." "Women as well?" "Yes, more women than men, the monies will take all children to best schools and university in our cities." "Jhiro are you telling me there are qualified doctors in here that will amputate a woman's leg that is perfectly healthy?" "Yes there are doctors in here who would take off their mother's leg for half a million US, their own leg if they could." "Just how much money is coming back from the United States?" "Try to think of as much monies as you can, then by one hundred times more, there is monies hide everywhere, it is buried, it is driving around our country in trucks, because no one knows where to put it. Medellin are buy land to build many houses for their work peoples, hidden in the walls is billions of dollars, there are houses worth almost nothing, with pictures worth millions of dollars on the walls, there is monies everywhere. There is a school in Medellin with a half billion dollars under the floor and a church also, it is crazy," he jokes, "soon we will burn money to stay warm in the mountains in the winter." "Jhiro where will it end?" "It will never end, peoples will take drugs, always there are new young peoples to take drugs, it will go on and on and on and on, always new peoples, always more drugs." "But the people of Colombia don't use cocaine they know it is not good for them, they use cocaine to pay for school, medicine, new house, American cars." He laughs and continues, "Everyone wants American car so we are giving them their money back to have their cars, you know even the light and all the power in this place, are come from the road tunnel next to it, Jhiro thinks that is funny, our government are paying for the power to turn coca leaf into cocaine."

"Jhiro how many people work in here." "Two thousand." "Two thousand." she exclaims,

"Yes that is why they have small but good hospital, people cannot leave in daytime so if they have problem they come here."

"It sounds very organised." "Oh yes everything take care of in here, Jhiro is lucky to get you here. Because the family sell many thousands of tons of coca leaf, Jhiro is allowed to bring you in, but we must leave soon it's not good to be your colour and be in here, they trust Jhiro so they trust you, but still we must leave soon."

They do just that as soon as they are able. They are taken back to Jhiro's home after a week, flown in a Medellin helicopter, an identical replacement for Jhiro's is ordered, it will be delivered in three months. In the intervening period he is grounded both because of his legs and his lack of a flying machine. After a month he has joint usage of a similar model Sikorsky to his own, which is an agreement with a Medellin cartel member, which furthers nails his colours to the Medellin mask and additionally alienates himself from the ever strengthening Cali cartel.

It is a month in which they spend a great deal of time together and Jackie's pregnancy is becoming evident. Jhiro has several irate phone calls defending his decision to take Jackie into the tunnel, one or two senior figures in the Medellin organisation are zealous in their criticism of him.

Jackie is unable to make any progress with the sextant and has to bide her time. The hospital experience and the full knowledge of the risks Jhiro took to protect her has shifted her position towards him, she is aware that she is touching him more often and when she goes to the wine cellar she finds herself choosing one of the Margaux vintages, Chateau Marquis de Terme or indeed Chateau Margaux itself, these being Jhiro's most preferred wines, but she still allows her fingers to slide across what she is sure are the finest wines in the world, Chateau Latour, Laffite- Rothschild and Petrus. Some mornings she picks out the clothes she prefers him to wear and leaves them on the bed for him, he always comes out of the bedroom with them on. She is denying her feelings towards him but is beginning to fully understand the difficulty that her man is struggling with, the constant and building pressures from the two big warring drug cartels, the coffee growers co-operative, the politicians, the eye in the sky and the weakness of his brothers, which heaps more and more pressure on him.

She begins to experience a new emotion, which is a degree of guilt when she thinks about her next opportunity to use the sextant. Her newfound emotion bleeds into disloyalty for Jhiro

366

but she compresses these feelings, she is driven, she has a cause, right is on her side. In a periodical debate with herself she turns her driven task more from that of a compelling force to that of a dare, she is now repeatedly goading herself to overcome the last two hurdles of her challenge. Which are to establish her exact position of longitude and to somehow get that information back to England. Though her motivation is changing, she does not lack for mental strength.

Her inducement to succeed is stimulated further by a visit to the two small graves stones that Jhiro has had erected for her, she now visits daily the stones that carry her fathers and Richards names. It is at the stone of Sir John Forbes-Brewer that she lays the finest flower stems, Richard Brewer must settle for second best. Her determination to succeed receives a gargantuan shot in the arm with her first consignment of genuinely British magazines and books. More than seven months has passed since she saw her father killed and in the cosy shires of England, things have moved on, there was much to absorb.

SUMMER 1989

EAST AUSTRALIA

Jude and Liz prepare to leave Colombia reluctantly, they have grown fond of the people and the scenery, they know that they do not need to go home yet. Jude has no plans other than to finish the book, Liz is free also. They have the money from Blenheim Cottage and Liz's grandmother's house, so there is no pressure on them. Liz says,

"Let's have one of those holiday experiences of a lifetime."

"OK but where shall we go?" Jude replies,

"Why don't we write down our favourite three ideas each and drop them in a pot or something and draw one out?" They are sitting on the vast rooftop veranda of the Hotel Titanic, they do exactly as Liz suggest, each record their ideas which takes half an hour and the bulk of a decent bottle of local red, to decide upon. Once written down the proposals are neatly folded and put into one of Jude's boots, which he gives a good shake and hands to Liz.

"OK I'll draw out the first one."

"The first one, we only need one."

"Yea but we want to look at them all don't we?" She grins empties her glass and removes a small folded piece of paper from the boot.

"OK this is one of mine, Drive around Australia."

"That'll do for me." Says Jude but adds, "I'm not sure we have the time to drive around the whole country, you've got photographic commitments in the autumn."

"Go on you pick one out, I can't wait to see the others."

"But the first one is the one, right?"

"That depends if you've come up with something better." Jude draws out and unfolds the second suggestion.

"This is another one of yours and it sounds great to me, Alaska."

"It's another place like Australia that I've wanted to visit for a long time, I imagine the photographic opportunities would be fantastic."

"Go on it's your turn." Handing her the boot, she picks another,

"Blimey this ones starting to curl at the edges, must be your smelly feet! Now this ones different, one of yours 'Train journey from St Petersburg to Vladivostok', I know where St Petersburg is, where the hells Vladivostok?"

"At the most eastern side of Russia, over near China. The journey is I think eleven thousand kilometres."

"Eleven thousand k's on a train don't think I could stand that."

"It was just a suggestion it's an ambition of mine."

"Go on you pick another." Jude drew again it is the last of Liz's ideas,

"Now this sounds fun, Sail around the Mediterranean and Greek Islands, do you have any experience of sailing?"

"Nope, just fancy it."

"No, neither do I, but how hard can it be?" Liz picks the penultimate piece of paper from the boot

"You big softy, 'Marry you, have a family, live happy ever after, that's not a holiday idea, that's a lifestyle choice,' She leans toward him and kisses him full on the lips. She folds the last one back up and puts it in her pocket saying,

"I'll keep that one for later and anyway was that a proposal? If it was it was done on the cheap, go on pick the last one out."

"This last one will be the one, I know it."

"How can you know it, when we said we would accept the first one out?"

"Because it's the same as the first one, well almost," he reads the note, "drive across Australia"

"Wow, that's incredible and your right it's decisive, I wrote 'drive around Australia' and you've written 'drive across Australia', Australia it is." She throws her arms around him and embraces him

"I can't believe we're going to Oz, when shall we go?"

"As soon as we can book it, I don't know if we need any special paperwork or visas do you?"

"Haven't a clue, lets pack up tomorrow, get ourselves to Bogota Airport and get a flight to where, Sydney?"

"I suppose so, I don't know my geography that well, but Australia is something like twenty one thousand miles around the outside, so I think that's going to take too long, we would need a year, but we could do Sydney to Perth, or Perth to Sydney, something like that."

"OK let's get over there, buy a map and go for it." This was how the decision was made to fly half way around the world and drive across what is almost a continent.

They were as good as their promise to each other, after spending a pleasant last evening eating under the stars at the Hotelotel Titanic, where one or the other of them would often mention Dirk and Anna, they slept for their penultimate time under South American skies, packed their backpacks, said their goodbyes and left the town of Buenaventura for the last time. A short taxi ride, three uneventful bus rides and a train journey saw them arrive at Bogota late evening, exhausted. They showered, ate and collapsed onto the bed of a small, second rate hotel near the airport, they were too fatigued to telephone the airport to enquire as to any possible flight times out the next day and also too fatigued too attend to each others personal needs.

They woke only partially refreshed the next morning, the lack of air conditioning and the constant squeak from the ceiling fan made it difficult to achieve a satisfying sleep. They showered again and ate fresh bread and drank coffee in the street outside the hotel, the owner Miguel Caliero was very obliging, he accepted their tip gracefully and hailed them a taxi. At the airport there was much to debate, they could fly out at two pm, which was a four hour wait, to Los Angeles, wait half a day for a connecting flight to Sydney via Auckland, New Zealand or leave at twelve noon fly to Madrid, Spain, then onto Paris, Hong Kong and Perth. Jude stated that he would rather drive with the sun at his back as he felt they were more likely to do most of their driving in the mornings. Liz looked at him as though he were from another planet.

"What are you talking about?"

"Look if we start at Perth we will be driving east, not only is the sun in your face but we will be losing time as we cross the

370

time zones, but if we start at Sydney we will have the sun behind us, better for driving and photography and we will gain time as we cross the time zones and not lose time, so its LA and Auckland for me."

"I haven't got a clue what you're talking about but I hope you're right and actually Paris is a bit too close to England, we might be tempted to go home, what am I saying? We don't have a home, ok let's go to LA, what time was it?"

"Two pm we have four hours to kill."

"OK lets book it then we know what we're doing." They did exactly that.

Jude was able to sit and enjoy the anticipation of the journey to come and to allow the muscular fatigue of the work he had done over the last few weeks to slowly evaporate from his body. Liz was up and down like a yoyo, buying drinks, buying food, looking through shops and book racks, until with just an hour to board she settled against Jude's right shoulder and dozed.

Los Angeles came and went, they slept in an airport hotel, this time the air conditioning was a little to efficient, they enjoyed the warmth from each others' post coital glow. Another hotel breakfast and they were airborne again bound for Auckland, they spent just two hours in the transit lounge at the North Island Airport before once again flying a thirty three thousand feet courtesy of an international airline. Their arrival in Sydney was at eight pm local time, although they were both disorientated with jet lag, another meal, a shower and a good night's sleep left them feeling able to deal with the paperwork nightmare that confronted them. They had to report back to immigration control at 8am the next morning or risk arrest and deportation.

In the morning they persuaded the airport authorities that they were not terrorist or aliens, they were given a six month visitor visa, on the condition that they book a return flight on the spot, Jude guessed at a likely return date from Perth and gave themselves twelve weeks to travel the three and half thousand miles from eastern Australia to the west coast. With the home flight booked they were allowed temporary entry into Australia. They were both overjoyed and relieved to have entered the country legitimately less than forty-eight hours after they had scribbled their ideas for a unique experience onto scraps of paper back at the rooftop terrace at the Hotel Titanic. To achieve such a longstanding ambition so quickly after its genesis as a practicable notion, left them feeling almost surreal, they were pinching themselves, and grinning to each other often, they were almost walking on air, despite the disorientation of jet lag.

They spent a week in a medium quality hotel in central Sydney, they enjoyed the usual tourist attractions in the city, which included a trip on the Manly Ferry, a walk across the famous Harbour Bridge and an evening attendance at a classical music concert in the Opera House. They also filled their stomachs on more than one occasion at the awesome fish market, they experienced both pleasure and guilt at the vast array of fish on offer. The weather varied between very warm and genuinely hot, they were pleased to be near the coast. Sydney had surprised them in only one respect, which was the number of Asian peoples in the city, not just as tourist but as owners. The huge and international recognised fish market and all its restaurants appeared to be owned and run by the Chinese, for the Chinese, large residential areas of Sydney were owned and occupied by Chinese and Japanese peoples, add to these many Malaysian and Singaporean visitors and residents, this international combination gave Sydney a veritable cosmopolitan make up. A genuine revelation of Sydney too was the myriad of enormous and colourful day flying fruit bats that had made home in the Royal Botanical Gardens, to enjoy an al-fresco lunch below their bickering antics was a unique experience, there was much other bird and animal life to view amongst the profusion of exotic plants, but it was the brightly coloured quarrelsome bats with their metre wide wingspan that left an indelible print on the memory of all visitors.

Jude and Liz were both keen to be on the road, they had each stayed in the city for a week partly for the sake of the other, feeling that it was the decent thing to do. Once they were in their hired camper van they were in their element, it had cost them dearly due to it being a short notice booking, and they had had to pay an additional thousand dollars to leave the van in Perth, some six thousand kilometres from their pick up point. The touristy stuff as they termed it they found fascinating, but they both felt that the atmosphere which had developed between them had become a little too organized, now they were travelling they felt like teenagers with total freedom. They had freedom to choose direction and when and where to stop.

They stopped for their first night in the Camper van at Goulburn, it was here that the clear southern sky first impressed them, the light pollution in and around Sydney made star gazing prohibitive but out in the semi bush the night sky was spectacular. This coupled with the warm temperature and the vans pull-out built in barbeque left Liz and Jude feeling as though they had truly arrived in Australia. Sydney, its unique attractions and its hotels had been a pleasure, but to be free to roam and stop as they wished to eat and star gaze, had no equal. The pair of them felt like children whose parents had left them alone without a sitter for the first time, the joint sense of freedom was unparalleled in their experience.

They arrived at Canberra, Australia's capital mid morning and took the lift to the top of the Telstra Tower from which the view was awesome, during the next week they drove through the Kosciuszko Mountain Range and the Alpine National Park, they were surprised to view many ski runs complete with ski lifts and Alpine style lodges. Their arrival at the extreme South Eastern tip of the mainland at Wilson's Promontory Point coincided with three unseasonal days of heavy rain and thunder during which they caught up on laundry, letters home and sleep.

When the weather cleared they were treated to two days of unprecedented wildlife viewing. They had parked the van by the waters' edge, at the western end of a stretch of coastline known as Ninety Mile Beach. It was the first time they had seen kangaroos on the shore and to see four of the female grey kangaroos supporting Joey's was a joy, in addition to which a large pod of adult and juvenile dolphins were surfing in the huge waves which are a feature of the area. Moreover amongst the small number of camper vans enjoying the spectacular scenery, weather and wildlife were two giant two meter long lizards, plodding amongst the tourists looking for titbits, and to boot four huge white tailed sea eagles were cruising the beach at a low altitude scanning for a free meal. This gave Liz forty-eight hours of peerless photographic opportunities. In Jude's experience, he found that as was usually the case when life seemed spectacularly sweet, there was a sour note around the next bend. For Jude this was during their second day of ecstasy at the Port Albert Campsite, He and Liz had heard other people's excitement, due to a small pod of giant black rays at the very edge of the surf. On joining the small number of animated people at the waters' edge they were bowled over by the sight of seven two meter wide black rays in water just ankle deep, a local fisherman was filleting a bucket of Tommy Ruffs, a small strong tasting Australian herring and he was tossing the heads and bones into the water for the rays. He informed those watching that it was a daily occurrence which the rays had learnt to respond to. Jude and the other visitors waded into the shallow water amongst the eye catching creatures after being assured that as long as the barbed tail was avoided no harm would come to anyone, the rays would brush past their ankles and were comfortable with being handled, one in particular was heading straight towards Jude's legs, he instinctively stepped a few paces backwards as the lustrous huge black creature moved slowly and gracefully towards him. As he continued to step away his right ankle brushed something unfelt and unseen in the sandy water kicked up by human activity, it was the tentacles of an extremely venomous jelly fish. The pain that shot through his right leg and into his nervous system was of such severity and immediate nature that Jude screamed and went into shock, Liz dropped her camera and covered the short distance between them in time to arrest his fall.

The local fisherman took control of the situation, dragging the screaming Jude from the waters' edge, he looked at the minor wound on Jude's ankle and ran to use the emergency phone at the Beach Head, he told a panicking Liz to make sure she kept bathing his leg in salt water for no other reason than to give her something constructive to do, Jude went into a frighteningly convulsive fit, his nervous system was overwhelmed with pain. Jude believed he was dying, Liz believed he was dying, the local fisherman who had seen this before was unsure, fortunately for Jude Australia is geared up for such an occurrence, after just sixteen minutes of utter agony a small rescue helicopter landed fifty meters away from the now new scene on the beach, the rays were long forgotten. The first paramedic to arrive to Jude's now

374

prostrate and shaking carcass injected him with a mixture of morphine and antidote to jelly fish venom, Jude passed out and was air-lifted to Melbourne Memorial Hospital.

Liz was left stupefied by the experience and when those who had been present to witness the incident took leave of the beach, she was also left alone. She asked the last person who was present, the elderly fisherman, of whom she was unaware had saved Jude's life with his swift response, how far it was to Melbourne. He replied,

"It'll take you a good three hours, but you'll be no good to him today, he'll be out of it for twenty four hours at least."

"He is going to be OK though right?"

"Sure he'll come to in a day or two with nothing left but a terrible memory." Was his reply but he couldn't quite conceal a small amount of doubt in his voice. Liz thanked him for all he had done, did not hear his reply of 'No worries.' She returned to the van. A three ton camper which to date she had not driven. She packed everything into drive mode, got behind the wheel and looked at the map, it was quite a drive and as it was now late afternoon she considered her options, if she arrived at the hospital at say nine pm assuming she could find it, where would she park? Then she reheard the elderly fisherman's last words 'You'll be no good to him, he'll be out of it for twenty four hours'.

She decided to stay put and leave early in the morning that way she would have all day to find a suitable parking spot in the city. She and Jude felt uncomfortable stopping overnight in built up areas since their first 'hoon' experience had been in a town, several young hooligans had bounced on their rear bumper at one o'clock in the morning, waking them up with a shock, it felt to Liz that the van was moving, not just being shook. Jude had become irate with the culprits, she had stayed awake for the rest of the night. After two consecutive nights of such deliberate inconvenience they had always stopped at lonely, or even desolate spots, which did produce both a degree of security in that there was no one to interfere with them, but she also felt insecure in a more sinister way, in that if someone decided to target them they had no camaraderie with other campers, who were always friendly and generous to help with any problems.

Liz decided to stay put, as she was one of four vans on the beach-front site, she converted the van back into night mode. As was the norm, the sun very quickly set into total Australian bush darkness, her feelings of insecurity increased, as by nine pm she was the only camper left. She now felt extremely vulnerable, she chided herself for her weakness, surely she who had travelled extensively throughout Europe and North America alone could deal with one night out in the bush, the sound of the ocean gently lapping onto the shore was a soothing comfort, but as time ticked by she felt less and less comfortable. She locked the doors, closed the curtains which surrounded the sleeping section and surprised herself for not venturing out of the van to use the bar-b-que, she ate cold food inside, she earnestly berated herself because of her frailty and timidity.

All her fears were realised when she was shocked into consciousness at just before midnight with the roaring sound of two high performance cars, which she assumed were driven by what Australia calls hoons and Britain call yobs. The cars were skidding at speed in a broadside motion around and around her van with both horns blaring, she was terrified. Each car did three trips around her van, when both vehicles stopped her sense of fear became an overwhelming sense of dread. Many thoughts raced through her mind, including thoughts of defence, the only weapon to hand was the camper's fire extinguisher which she tore from the wall, breaking its brackets. She stood poised by the door awaiting her fate, her mouth parched dry, her heart beating at an unsustainable two hundred beats a minute, and a slight trickle of urine leaking from her body. She stood in that pose for almost two minutes. They were two of the longest and most terrifying of her life, save that which happened to Jude earlier in the day. One thought kept repeating itself, what are they waiting for?

The four teenagers with the two powerful cars were intent on being a terror and a total nuisance, but nothing more, having stopped to light cigarettes they did one more lap of Liz's van, blasted their horns and disappeared into the darkness from whence they came. Liz was left in shock and total silence, with a fire extinguisher still in her hands, which were sore due to the tightness with which she had gripped it.

She knew sleep would be impossible for the rest of the night, she rapidly once again re-organised the camper back into day mode and drove away from what had been a charming location, its memory now sullied by a few thoughtless, immature idiots. She paid little attention to the direction in which she drove, her sense of relief was paramount when she steered the van off of the two-kilometre dirt track that lead to the beach and onto sealed tarmac road. She drove for a further twenty minutes where the road then offered her a choice, to go left was to head toward Melbourne and Jude who were two hundred and sixty kilometres hence, to go right was to aim for Sydney six hundred and twenty kilometres. She bought the van up to her comfortable maximum speed, which for Liz was eighty kilometres per hour and tried to relax. She found the next four hours inordinately tiring, she was relieved to view many and regular signs to the hospital whose car park she pulled into at four thirty five am. Without speaking to anyone she stepped into the rear of the van and slept on the sofa in day mode, nothing like as comfortable as night mode, she was simply too tired to bother.

At eight o'clock there was a state trooper banging on the door of the van, she opened the door bleary eyed to be given a ticket for illegal parking, she accepted the ticket and paid the instant fine without fuss, she left the parking lot to use the hospitals toilet and washing facilities and to ascertain Jude's condition.

She discovered he was on the third floor, he was not in any danger but not yet conscious and could not be visited until two pm, as she past the reception desk on her way back to the van, she noticed a small stack of familiar blue disabled parking plaques, without compunction she removed one, put it into the front of the camper, once again transformed the rear into night mode and slept for four hours without a movement.

On waking she showered in the camper, ate another cold meal and presented herself at reception at exactly one fifty-nine pm, she was allowed up to the third floor where she found Jude conscious and still suffering a measure of pain, which was now confined to his right leg only. He was delighted to see her, they embraced passionately, Liz was greatly relieved to see him comfortable. Their embrace was both lasting and intense, eventually it was Jude who broke their silence.

377

"Hi how'd you get here?"

"I drove of course, I quite enjoyed it, Think I might do a bit now and then."

"If we're going anywhere in the next week you'll have to drive, they tell me this right leg may and probably will suffer spasms for up to seven days. So I'm sorry I can't drive."

"OK so I'm the driver, where we going Darwin, Brisbane?"

"Well now we've reached Melbourne, though I don't recall much of the last two hundred kilometres we will head gently north west through Bendigo and catch up with and follow the Murray River, it's in flood apparently which is unusual, should be fun."

"Jude stop, can we go back a bit, you could have lost your life there you know."

"I know that now, I was a bit excited being in the shallows with the rays forgot all about the bloody jelly fish."

"Did they say it was a bad one?" "Yep, if no helicopter was available or if it had been out on another call and you had driven me I could have been a goner."

"Christ Jude don't be so flippant, I was scared to death." "Me to, that's not something I want to repeat, ever." "When can you get out of here?" "Now, I was waiting for you, did you just get here?" "No, no I've been in the car park since four am I'll explain why later, come on then get up lazy bones."

Jude needed help and a crutch to get to the hospital reception desk where he was signed out, given drugs to take for the next week and charged twenty bucks for the crutch, and almost as a afterthought Liz was asked to return the disabled plague she had borrowed, she replied,

"Of course and thanks for your help." The hospital receptionist replied with what had become the standard Australian reply to any kind of thank you or appreciation, which was,

"No worries."

Liz helped Jude into the passenger seat and fired up the van, she pulled into traffic and aimed north for Bendigo. They reached their target in late afternoon, Liz subsequently took over all of Jude's normal duties and they ate a barbequed meal and relaxed with a bottle of red, after first checking his medication for approval.

Over the next three days they followed the Murray River, swollen with floodwater from Queensland which had fallen a month previous, the area they were driving through was baked and dry, it was a novelty for locals to view the river in flood, the last such occasion had been more than twenty years prior. At Mildura they took a guided river trip, the water birds were fascinating and they glimpsed a very rare bird, a Crested Royal Spoonbill, but this trip was to be remembered for a different reason, the increase in water had greatly boosted the usual number of birds and fish into the area, but had also caused an explosion in the mosquito population. Both of them had omitted to use insect repellent and were subsequently feasted upon, for the next forty eight hours they were extremely uncomfortable, sleeping was particularly difficult, the van was hot which aggravated the hundreds of bites plus Jude's right leg would often shoot out in a painful spasm requiring them to change sides in the vans' bed. There was no physical activity between them. They reached Adelaide in another four days but did not linger, they drove the Yorke Peninsular and the area known as the Copper or Cornish Triangle, where to their amazement they were able to buy Cornish pasties.

A week after Adelaide they were in the Flinders Range National Park, a hilly area that they both delighted in, as Jude was now fully fit they were able to walk extensively in this alluring combination of high ground, huge gums and waterfalls, it was teaming with wildlife, they lingered in the Flinders Range for four days before setting off south for Port Augusta. They were disappointed with the city, which sits at the crossroads of Australia, with roads south to Adelaide, west to Perth north to Darwin and east to Sydney, it was a busy industrial city, they drove on a little way south to their perpetual benefit and pulled into a delightful camp site situated literally on the shoreline, with no barrier and a five meter plummet to the beach, Jude teased Liz and stopped the van with its front bumper overhanging the drop.

It was an enchanting evening, the combination of the gentle surf lapping onto the white sand and the last of an engaging sunset was sufficient to gladden any heart. Jude left the van poised at the very margin that separate terra firma from ocean to Liz's not so well disguised irritation. As he walked behind the van to look for the campsite's facilities he was brought to a halt by a comment issued in a broad Aussie tone,

"It's a camper van mate, not a fucking boat." The comment had come from one of two men seated under a canopy around a table adjacent to two caravans, Jude decided that the comment was an Aussie "hello", he rose to the bait. He joined the two men, both of whom were in their sixties and both of whom had consumed a quantity of wine, as Jude sat between them he raised an empty glass and asked,

"Is this one mine?" The simultaneous answer of,

"No worries mate." Put him at his ease and rapidly the guy to his left introduced himself as Peter McKinley, he filled Jude's glass with a quite superb red and introduced his college as Gary Francou, so began an agreeable twenty year association that only the eventual demise of those persons present would terminate.

Jude could not recall an occasion when he had been put at ease by people who were new to his acquaintance so swiftly, later when they were joined by Liz and the two wives Helen and Trish, the six of them enjoyed an exceptionally convivial evening. The two couples were third generation Australians and proud of it, as they were travelling in the opposite direction to Jude and Liz they were able to give each other tips on places not to miss and hints of places to avoid. It was after two o'clock in the morning when Liz put her head on the vans' pillow next to Jude's and said,

"What lovely people."

In the morning home addresses were exchanged and a genuine expressions all-round of let's make the effort and meet again, either in England or back here, was declared by all. As Jude drove west and Peter and Gary drove east, they all doubted their own sincerity but they all aspired to be true to their word. Within a year the four agreeable Australians were guest of Jude and Liz in England.

They were crossing the Eire Peninsula, a region of over three hundred kilometres across, which is a precursor or foretaste to the great Null'abor Plain, a drive which Peter and Gary had declared was only surpassed by the road from Port Augusta to Darwin, a road which bisects Australia north – south. They were also told to respect the drive, fill up the tank at every opportunity, and carry plenty of water and food. The Null'abor Plain is an area of semi-arid natural bush of over a thousand kilometres that demanded respect.

In mid afternoon they drove through a infestation of locust, Jude slowed the van but could not believe the intense rattle emanating from the front of the vehicle as he drove through the dense swarm, Liz insisted he stop so she could leave the van to use her camera, she declared it an opportunity not to be missed.

Jude stayed inside and was staggered to witness such an immense multitude of insects, this was a biblical plague, as far as he could see the air was thick with the large winged insects and his windscreen was splattered with yellow daubs, so too was Liz when she almost in a panic opened and quickly slammed the passenger door. Jude took one look at her, held his nose and pointed to the rear of the van and said "Shower now!" She was covered in foul smelling yellow dabs of locust excrement, they had witnessed an unusually large host of the infamously ravenous insects.

SUMMER 1989

SOUTH AUSTRALIA

That evening they made for the coast at an attractively named but disappointed halt called Streaky Bay, they felt lazy, unusually for them they bought take-a-ways, which was a mistake on Liz's part as she spent the night vomiting and suffering extreme bouts of diarrhoea, they came to the conclusion that had she eaten the 'roo burger that Jude had and not the sea food curry she would have been OK. She wanted to take the Imodium tablets that they had in their first aid kit, to suspend the diarrhoea but she knew Jude's advice that she should take nothing but water until the bug had been evacuated from her body was sound advice. She felt wretched and useless and voiced on several occasions that they had only so many days in Australia and she hated to waste even one of them. She had had an extremely uncomfortable and sleepless night. Jude sympathised and tried to insist that they stay put and wait it out. Eventually she persuaded him to drive on, Jude drove with Liz lying in the back of the camper, which has been left in night mode to accommodate her. Assuring Liz that if the scenery should turn unusually dramatic or if a unique wildlife viewing opportunity should present itself he would offer her the chance to view or photograph it. He drove slower than was his norm, for the comfort of his prostrate passenger, as oncoming traffic was no more than one vehicle per hour, Jude assessed the additional danger to Liz to be minimal. They paused for lunch for Jude and for Liz to make use of road house facilities. Jude drove all afternoon through repetitive but fascinating landscape, the Null'abor Plain was aptly named 'Null' meaning none and 'abor' meaning trees, it was an area of semi desert, frequented by eagles and dingoes. Both of which Jude disturbed Liz to view but it was clear to him that she was both very weak and very tired.

When he pulled in to refuel the van in late afternoon he put his head through the curtain that Liz had closed between the cab and the sleeper compartment to ask Liz if she needed anything. Her reply was,

"No nothing, just sleep, keep driving though. The drone of the engine is hypnotic, leave me to sleep and drive as long as you like." This left him to decide on their day's progress. The pull-in was typical of many in outback Australia and also in the American mid west, it consisted on one wooden constructed building with a wrap around veranda and it had fly screens to every door and window. The range of goods on offer from this one room shack was staggering, there was fuel, beer and food, camping and hunting equipment, clothes, postage stamps, magazines and flower seeds. If anyone had ever walked in the door and asked for something Jude imagined the proprietor had the next day ordered six of them to make sure he had every request covered. Customers could also have a shower, a bath and a haircut, play pool, watch TV and rent a bed for the night. Jude imagined an Alfred Hitchcock horror movie being filmed there, which was unkind, as the man who ran the service station at the one horse town called Yumbarra, which was toward the eastern side of the Null'abor Plain was very accommodating and sympathetic when Jude mentioned the discomfort of his travelling companion. Jude chatted to him for a couple of minutes, with regard his best options as to where to stop should he decide to drive on during the evening. His advice was to stop at Eucla, at the sight of the ruined Telegraph Station, it was he said both historic and a likely spot from which to observe whales in the Southern Ocean if there were any to be seen.

Jude strode out to the van purposefully, his body language advertising that he had come to a decision. He opened the drivers' door and started the engine, just before pulling away he shouted to Liz, "The chap in there's just recommended a good pull in for later, so I'll drive on for a bit see how I feel, you shout me if you want me to stop."

He steered the camper off of the dusty forecourt of the single building pull in, the van went through its gear box, Jude settled both the vehicle and himself into automatic pilot and focused far ahead into the west, with just the first hint of a weakening sun now in his front windshield, he put on his sun glasses and let his mind wander. He wandered back to Colombia and its enormous contrast to his new host country, he thought that if Australia could benefit from the same climate as Colombia it could be the richest producing country in the world. He thought of Dirk and Anna and wondered exactly where they were and what they were doing, he thought of Jacqueline Forbes-Brewer and her problems, a solution to which was beginning to ferment in his mind. Finally his thoughts went back to Dorchester, he wondered where they would live on their return to Dorset, would it be Mrs Naylands, or would they rent somewhere longer term. Throughout the long drive he allowed his mind to roam where it would, undisciplined and liberated.

He hoped that the weather and the scenery would be as accommodating the next day as they had been this day and hoped with all his will that Liz would be able to enjoy it. He didn't want to admit to himself but it was one of the most pleasant drives of the tour to date. The road was straight for hundreds of kilometres and there was almost no traffic, no more than a solitary truck or car once or twice an hour, as the sun began to set in front of Jude so the landscape was transformed into a red shadowy scene. The hollows in the terrain became black holes and the ridges, red escarpments, topped off with silhouettes of shrubs, cactus and kangaroos. To view the outback at sunset without town or car light pollution was a moving experience, he turned off his headlights to increase the sensation, flicking them on if a vehicle was visible in the distance. Shadows lengthened, stars began to appear and Jude began to feel he was the only person on earth enjoying the moment. He was pleased also that Liz was catching up on lost sleep. He decided he would drive until the last rays of the sun were invisible to him beyond the curve of the earth or until he reached his target destination, as he was travelling due west at a hundred kilometres an hour he was prolonging the sunset and was playing mind games with the dashboard clock and the setting sun in an attempt to estimate the time of the last flicker of red light. His moment of anticipation coincided with a road sign declaring one hundred and two kilometres to Eucla, this distance he knew he could travel in an hour, it was nine o'clock, he wasn't hungry and Liz was still quiet. He decided it was a target he could achieve and as he hadn't yet driven in total darkness he enjoyed the prospect.

He saw numerous examples of Australian wildlife, sadly fifty per cent of his sightings were road kill, he saw kangaroo, wallaby, wombat, rabbit, fox, dingo and wedge tailed eagle all were either victims of road kill or feeding off road kill. He estimated that he had seen as many dead kangaroo as live ones during the day.

The sun was now high over the Indian Ocean a thousand miles ahead of him, at the very moment he began to think he'd had enough, a road sign informed him that he had six kilometres to travel, within minutes he pulled up outside the Eucla caravan and recreational vehicle campsite. He shouted to Liz they had arrived and he would cook them some dinner and that she could take it or leave it, but that she must keep drinking water.

He parked the van, stretched his arms, rubbed his eyes and pulled out the on board barbeque, ignited it with the in-built pilot light and went in search of the toilets, as it was after hours he merely had to deposit ten dollars with his registration number written on the bill in pen and he was free to set up and use the facilities, he inspected the showers for locust, moths and other wildlife, they were clean except for a foot long lizard that scarpered quickly on seeing him. He decided to shower later before bed.

On returning to the van he took a small roo steak and two large potatoes from the fridge behind his seat cut them up and dropped them onto the hot plate, instantly the aroma of the searing surface of the meat stimulated Jude's appetite, he poured himself a large glass of what was becoming his favourite South Australian red wine, Banrock Station. He slid open the side door of the van knowing that if Liz wasn't awake, the noise of the door would wake her, he thought it best that she wake for an hour or two, before she slept again for the night. On opening the door he shouted to her,

"Wake up my sleeping beauty we've pulled in for the night." He put his hands onto the bed to touch her legs, odd she appeared to have no legs, he reached further into the dark interior of the camper, she appeared to have no torso either, he reached for the pillows, openly calling her name,

"Liz, Liz," again he shouts much louder "Liz." She wasn't there, in disbelief he shouted louder still, "Liz, Liz." His mind was scrambled, she simply wasn't there.

It wasn't possible that she'd got out of the van whilst he visited the toilet block, it was only a few paces away he would have heard the door, he turned on the rear interior light, a crime during the hours of darkness because the van would suck in mosquitoes like a sponge would suck in water. The bed was empty, he pulled back the duvet and put his hands on the exposed surface, there was no warmth, no body heat, she had not been in the back for hours, he ran round the van, checked the cab, under the van, he ran around it again calling her name, he used the flashlight to search the immediate area, no footprints, no Liz, nothing. He felt sick, his pulse was now so fast he felt lightheaded, he was hyperventilating, he knew it was counterproductive, he couldn't stop it. He threw the food off of the barbeque onto the dirt floor, to the later benefit of a Giant Monitor Lizard, he tossed away the glass of wine and slammed the side door shut. He revved the van turned it around and drove as fast as he dare in the direction from which had had just come. He assumed she must have got out of the van when he last filled the tank at Yumbarra, he couldn't believe he had left her behind, five hours behind, he searched his consciousness for an alternative but knew there wasn't one.

He checked the dashboard information, he had travelled just over five hundred kilometres since he last filled the tank, he knew this as he had by almost force of habit zeroed his trip odometer each time he fuelled the van's tank, trying with each tank full to drive more economically and beat his previous distance travelled, and he had approximately half a tank of fuel left, enough to get back to Yumbarra? He didn't know, he could only guess and chance his luck. He looked at the speedometer, in his panic he was driving at over one hundred and fifty kilometres per hour, he knew this was madness both in its inherent dangerousness should he hit a kangaroo or even a camel which was possible if the warning signs were to be believed. In addition he knew that such a high speed was uneconomical he would use more fuel than he used on the westward journey and would be stranded in the middle of the bush, no fuel, no Liz, frustratingly he dropped his speed to ninety kilometres per hour and switched in the cruise control.

He was angry with himself, he rebuked himself, he went over his actions back at the service station earlier in the day, she must have needed the toilet and walked in behind him whilst he was talking to the owner, he was chastising himself out loud,

"You idiot, you idiot, how could you have done that?" He knew it was late, he knew it was dark and out in the semi desert the nights rapidly close down, he hoped she was ok. He then remembered that she was wearing an old t-shirt of his and some jogging bottoms as pyjamas, as neither of them actually owned any. Also she had no money and possibly no shoes, she was always walking around bare foot or at best in flip flops, he kept checking the vans speed and fuel gauge, the first wouldn't increase and the second would only decrease.

The westward journey had been one of the most pleasant he could remember, driving into a beautiful, almost mesmerising unnaturally slowly setting sun, the return eastward journey was and would always remain one of the worst of his life. He repeatedly told himself that Liz was at the refill station at Yumbarra and that the guy there seemed ok, but he also recalled the Hitchcock Horror moment he had experienced at the one building pull in, which made him shudder. The five hour plus return journey seemed to last forever, Jude's anxiety level increased proportionately as the fuel gauge register decreased. His frustration at travelling slower than the van could travel built up in him, he became more and more tired, frustrated and angry, he avoided colliding with the first two kangaroos that were in his path but greatly out of character made no attempt to miss the third, killing the animal out of sheer spite, he loathed himself for his lack of avoiding action, for the rest of his life if ever the word kangaroo was spoken in his presence he would squirm internally, he castigated himself more than a thousand times for his moment of insanity.

Other than his abandoning of Liz his greatest concern was the fuel gauge, it seemed to be working against him, cursing him to a night alone in the bush, with no knowledge of Liz's whereabouts. He dropped his speed to eighty kilometres per hour in an attempt to economise his rapidly emptying fuel tank. He was hungry, tired and so worried about Liz's dilemma he couldn't focus on any other thought.

At three o'clock in the morning he saw a road sign Yumbarra one hundred kilometres it was like a blood transfusion from an Olympic athlete on banned drugs, it boosted him, he knew if the fuel would last he would be back with Liz in one and a quarter hours if only he had enough fuel. Liz had suggested they carry a spare ten-litre tank with them but when Jude learnt that their fuel tank would carry them an estimated thousand kilometres he told her it wasn't necessary, again he felt stupid and inadequate, for he had known better at the time and she had deferred to his knowledge.

Thirty kilometres from Yumbarra the low level fuel warning light came on, he turned on the internal light reached for the handbook from the glove box and eventually found the right page, his studying of the manual twice caused him to drift off the road onto the dirt verge, the second time he unknowingly killed an echidna, but he did discover that the vans fuel warning light would come on with approximately thirty kilometres worth of fuel left. He threw the book behind him, turned off the light just in time to avoid a wombat.

To his great relief he reached the Yumbarra filling station at four fifteen am, what he would never know was that he had just six kilometres of fuel left. He jumped from the van, ran to the mesh fly screen door and hammered on it until his hands were sore. There was no response. There were no lights on in the building, he circumnavigated the wooden structure spooking a family of Possums and a Wombat who were actively involved in emptying the two dustbins at the rear and consuming its contents. He banged on the door again. He drove the van almost up to the door, blasted the vehicle's horn many times and put his headlights on to illuminate the front wall. Again there was no response, the place was as dead as a churchyard, it had only now occurred to Jude that he had not seen a single vehicle on his return trip, the remoteness of his location hit him like a train, the desperation of Liz's plight was a second hit, the nausea he had been suppressing since his sickening realisation at Ecula welled up inside him again. He banged on the door again, tried the windows then he noticed a note pinned to the side of the door frame.

'Gone to Best Western Hotel, One Hundred K south east of here at Wudinna, due to the kindness of others, got no money please come quickly Liz x'.

He was flooded with relief and frustration, she was ok but in a bit of a fix, he couldn't go to her as he had no fuel, he searched the notices around the door for opening hours, eight to eight Monday to Saturday. "Shit, shit, shit, shit, shit," he exclaimed. He was already four and a half hours into Sunday. His hands were tied, what could he do?

He knew his only option was to leave the van and hitchhike east but how long would it be until a vehicle of any description came by, he knew too that local and indigenous people would know that less fuel was available on Sundays making the huge gaps between fill ups even greater and any traffic less likely, he surmised his only hope was a truck or a road train but he hadn't seen one for hours, he parked the camper around the back of the fuel station, once again annoying the feeding possums.

He packed all their valuables including passports, visiting visas, money, maps, Liz's camera, his Colombia notes and many other irreplaceable items into a large backpack, added a changes of clothes for Liz, ate half a dozen apples and two bananas, locked the camper and went to the roadside, sitting on his backpack awaiting any vehicle travelling east, his head dizzy with lack of sleep. After half an hour of unprecedented darkness and silence he moved his backpack two hundred meter east of the service station, dropped it in front of a telegraph wire pole, sat back on it and rested his head against the pole so that he could doze. He stayed in this position until after it became light, around eight o'clock.

The first vehicle on the road was just before ten am, a truck with triple trailers Jude assumed it to be carrying cattle by its stench, it was of no use to him as it was travelling west and at speed, it did not slow as it passed Jude, the all enveloping cloud of dust left him looking and feeling like a depiction of a victim of the eruption at Pompeii, ashen grey with dust. He returned to the camper to clean off the dust and grab a packet of biscuits.

Dusted off he returned to the roadside, at eleven ten am he saw and heard the second truck travelling west long before it covered him, he took evasive action, eventually at one twenty pm he saw a small cloud of dust in the west it took a minute or two to establish if it was a truck or a local phenomena called a Willie Willie, a miniature tornado like dust storm that forms and dissolves constantly in the arid bush. This was no Willie Willie to Jude's relief it was a truck, he stood up shouldered his backpack and started to walk east with his thumb held out as far as he could stretch it. As the truck approached him it began to slow to Jude's overwhelming relief, as it passed him he was coated in dust once again, with a grinding of gears screeching of brakes and burning of tyres, the one hundred and forty ton combination of a enormous Kenwood Tractor unit and three forty foot, four tier trailers loaded with over eight hundred urine soaked stinking sheep came to a halt a half mile past Jude. He ran as best as he could with the heavy backpack in the direction of the truck which he couldn't see because of the dust, the slight breeze was heading east-west blowing the dust and the overpowering stench of sheep wool, soaked in urine and shit toward him, as he approached the tail end of the vehicle he saw that the driver was walking towards him. Jude took a breath to express his thanks but never got to say it, the driver, Mac' was a sixty four year old dust covered redneck dressed in cowboy boots, faded denim jeans and no shirt, opened with a verbal volley in a very coarse Australian accent.

"What the fuck are you doing out here, you stupid bastard, if you knew how fucking dangerous it is to be out here on foot you wouldn't fucking be here. You silly fucker, you haven't got a clue its just cost me around a hundred bucks in brake linings, fuel and tyre tread to stop for you so whatever it is you want start off by putting your hand in your pocket and get a hundred bucks out of it, you daft fucker what the fuck are you doing out here?" Jude overwhelmed by the verbal assault first apologised and then tried to tell his story.

"Might have know it, a fucking pom, just give me the bills and get in the cab I ought to kick your arse from here to Tennents Creek."

He took the money from Jude, walked back to his side of the truck, climbed the five steps into the cab as did Jude, the driver then slipped a gear released the hand break and kicked the throttle, the truck barely moved, he continued to select gears, double dip his clutch and kicking the throttle for several minutes until he had traversed the trucks thirty two gears, and the combination of truck, loaded trailers and passenger were travelling at one hundred and twenty kilometres per hour.

Jude took in his surroundings, the stench of sheep fleece was all encompassing, the inside of the cab was covered in dust, the questionable human that was in control of the road-train was silent, he was staring ahead into the distance with total concentration as if he was looking for something miles ahead.

After a half hour of silence Jude asked him what he was looking for as it was obvious his level of concentration was above the level normally required to drive,

"What am I looking for, trains the same as me you daft fucker, the winds taking the dust from left to right so if I cross with another train I'll be on the dirty side won't be able to see a fucking thing for miles, could run off the road or hit a second train in the cloud, and if I stop the next train coming up my arse could knock me into the next world, if I can see another train early enough I flash my lights and swap over to the other side of the track, then I can pass 'im on the clean side, at least then I can see what I'm gonna hit." "Is that usual?"

"Yep been doing it since me granpappy's time, only thing what fucks it up is if you get a pom or a slope in a car in the middle then you got yourself a heap of trouble." "I know I'm a pom what's a slope?" "What's a slope? What's a fucking slope, how long you been out here fella?" "A couple of weeks." "That's just the blink of an eye in aussie time."

"How long you been here?" "Me I'm a rare animal a fourth generation aussie, it was my great granpappy who got sent out here because 'e was up to no good, you asked me what a slope is well we got slopes and we got boongs, you must'a seen the boongs, the black fella's they hang around the liquor shops like fly's hang around shit." "You mean the aboriginals?" "Yea if you like, abo's we call 'em boongs."

"Why?" "Boong, that's the sound they make when they bounce off the aluminium bull bar on the front of the truck." "You're joking." "Don't try me." "And the slopes?" "Oh the slopes are the slitty eyes, the Asians, they are the real dangerous fuckers. We call 'em slopes cause of the shape of their eyes." Jude could not believe his ears, this abhorrent creature sat in condemnation of other races of people, he himself was a fucking useless Pom, the indigenous peoples of Australia one of the oldest races on earth were boongs, no better than flies, and all the Asian peoples of the world were dangerous fuckers, and slitty eyes, this was the most detestable man he had ever met.

"We got problems with all of em, the boongs we bent over backwards to accommodate." He said the last word with as posh an English accent as he could manage.

"We've built 'em houses, hundreds of 'em, schools and hospitals you name it and we've built it for 'em, give 'em jobs and education and what do they do? They rip out the furniture to burn on their camp fire, then the doors and windows and finally the timber holding the place up, so there's fuck all left, our state governments spent ten of millions of dollars on the useless fuckers and for what, nothing. We've spent money sending 'em to university and what comes of it, as soon as you try to educate a Boong he turns round and stabs you in the back by trying to claim land, no we did it wrong here on the mainland, we should have dun what Tassie did, clear 'em out." "Tassie?" "Tasmania, Christ you haven't picked up much in two weeks 'ave you." "And how did Tasmania clear 'em out?"

"They shot the fuckers in Tassie, every last one of 'em", except the last few, they fed them bread laced with strychnine, 'cause they ran out of ammo'." "They shot and poisoned all the aboriginals in Tasmania?" Jude expressed with utter amazement.

"Sure we should have dun' the same here only we had some liberal lefty do gooders laying down state legislature back in the eighteen hundreds, biggest mistake we ever made." He corrected himself

"No no, the biggest mistake was letting that crazy fuck of an English man bring out two dozen rabbits 'cause he was bored with shooting roos, that was the biggest mistake, now we got three hundred million of the little fuckers."

"Are you being straight with me, all the aboriginals were simply shot in Tasmania to get rid of them?"

"For sure in my great granpappys time you could shoot 'em on the mainland to feed to your dogs, we just didn't do enough of it, now we have to say sorry to them in Parliament, makes me wanna' puke."

"OK enough horror stories tell me about the slopes?"

"The slopes now they are the real dangerous fuckers cause they've got money, big money, they've got enough dollars to get our parliament sucking up to 'em, my family that's gone before me would be spitting in their graves. The problem is we're selling the whole damn country to em, all the iron ore, the tin, copper, zinc you name it we've sold it, they're now buying vast tracks of bush across the south for a pittance, turning it into grapes to send millions of litres of wine back home, none of its for the 'oz market. You mark my words after I'm gone the slopes will form a political party, then all vote for each other and take this hard but beautiful bitch of a country away from us, they already own half of Sydney, I hope I don't live to see it. My dad's two brothers died in the barbed wire at Tripoli defending the free world, turns out the world isn't free at all, everything's for sale, if you've got the bucks or the Yen, you can have anything you want. British intelligence must have been in the boozer the day they sent thousands of Anzacs to die in that barbed wire, we never even got the bodies back, probably eaten by the sharks, good hard working men wasted, now guess what, we got foreigners turning up in Sydney with bucket loads of Yen and buying whatever they see." Jude felt like a liberal lefty do-gooder, he replied with,

"You have a very low opinion of immigrants and how to deal with them." "Fucking right, makes you laugh don't it and we wouldn't play rugger and cricket with the South Africans cause of the way they been knocking their blacks about, good on em I say." If Jude had not been desperate to catch up with Liz he would have demanded the guy stop and let him out, he had no idea that such abhorrent individuals existed, but realised he didn't have another hundred dollars to pay him. It was his companion who to Jude's relief changed the subject.

"Tell me how come you was out there on foot, and I don't suppose you had any water with you, you got to respect this

393

country or she will kill you just as soon as look at you." Jude recounted his tale of his last twenty-four hours.

"OK you got a fair reason for being there, forgive me for tearing you off a strip but it plays hell on the rig when you have to pull up quick."

"I appreciate you stopping for me but you didn't have to." "Now your showing yourself to be a silly fucking pom again, of course I had to, your white and I could of been the last train through Yumbarra today, I didn't know you had a fitted out camper behind the store, you could have been fried to the road like a roo shit tomorrow."

"I appreciate you stopping thank you." "No worries, so I gotta pull in at Wudinna, that'll be about an hour." "Is that going to cost me another hundred?" "Naa that's only for a quick stop, about three K short of Wudinna I'll knock her into neutral and let her coast to a stop. Saves brake linings, fuel and tyres." His driver went quiet for the next half hour as he had two road-trains opposing him, Jude found it unnerving to witness the truck crossing to the wrong side of the road so that he and his companion could pass the oncoming vehicles on their clean side, he appreciated the reason for the manoeuvre as the dense cloud of dust to their left after passing both head on trains was all encompassing and lasted for several kilometres.

Jude was beginning to enjoy the panoramic view from the windshield and was allowing his mind to wander to Liz's current predicament when he felt the truck relax and the engines revs drop to an inaudible level, he looked to John McLaren the driver,

"This is your stop mate." It took the truck three minutes to stop by which time they were in a small town, Jude opened the door pulled his backpack behind him and said a loud genuine,

"Thank you." Mac replied,

"No worries." Just as Jude closed the truck door he added, "You forgot this." He threw a ball of paper out at Jude, before engaging the first of his many gears. Jude picked up the tightly screwed ball of paper, he unfurled it to discover it was his hundred dollars, he concluded that Mac whose name he had never asked, was not as hard a man as he would liked others to think he was, and he hoped that a great deal of his racism was just bravado.

After the dust from the train had settled Jude looked for the Best Western Hotel, which was thirty yards back off the road directly in front of him. All of his feelings of guilt and panic were evaporating from his body as if they were dew in the morning sun. He opened the Hotel door triumphantly, bid the guy behind the desk g'day in a mild Australian accent and asks which room Elizabeth Reece was in. The semi smartly dressed man behind the desk coloured red asked Jude to wait a moment and swiftly exited stage left.

It was a full two minutes before a much better dressed weasel of a man with the badge of Hotel Manager on his lapel arrived behind the desk and asked Jude,

"Can I help?" "Yes you can, can you tell me which room Elizabeth Reese is in please?" "And you are?" "I'm Jude Saunders her travelling companion." "Ah Mr Saunders, actually Miss Reese is no longer here, she was here, but she left early this morning with a police officer." "She left with a police officer, why was that?" "That was due to non payment of a bill." Jude quickly put two and two together, his voice lifted a ratchet

"You had her arrested for not paying for one room, for one person, for one night?" "Please be calm it's not as straightforward as it seems, she had no money, she promised that someone would arrive to settle the bill, no one arrived so it is company policy to inform the local law enforcement in such a circumstance." "Who owns the hotel?" "That would be........I do."

"So it's your policy to have a young woman who is the victim of unfortunate circumstance arrested?" "Well please don't…" "How much does she owe you?" "I beg your pardon?" "How much does she owe you?" "That would be thirty dollars." "And how much is a room here for the night?" "The same, thirty dollars." "So she had no food here, no drinks, no dinner, no breakfast." "I believe not." "And why was that?" "Because she had no money." "She promised you I was coming to pay her bill and you wouldn't let her eat or drink a thing and then you had her arrested. Is that right? Have I read the situation correctly?" "Please Mr Saunders you must understand the Hotels position." "Oh I understand your position and for the moment it is a standing position, here take your thirty dollars and shove 'em up

395

your arse, I hope that one day I meet you at a disadvantage and believe me I will do my best to worsen your position, now if you want to remain in a standing position tell me where the police have taken her." "That will be Kimba, forty kilometres east on the main highway." "When I find her I hope for your sake she's well and I hope your hotel burns down, you inconsiderate arsehole."

With that as his parting exchange Jude walked back into the street, he shouldered his weighty backpack and began to walk, in the full heat of the day he knew he couldn't walk the forty kilometres, in fact he was sure he wouldn't manage four, but he knew he had to put distance between him and the smarmy weasel behind the desk of the Best Western Hotel. He tried to recall the last time he had offered physical violence to anyone, it was he thought over thirty years previous at junior school when his best friend Tim Evans was getting an undeserved kicking from the school bully Alan King, they were names he hadn't remembered since. He needed to calm down so he just kept walking, walking and dehydrating. He had just managed two kilometres, when he was prevented from doing himself any serious harm as a car pulled up alongside him, the electric window smoothly opened and a woman of around forty, well dressed but wearing a skirt too short for her years and looking remarkable cool on such a hot day spoke to him,

"You're going to Kimba I know, but if you walk all the way you won't be any use to anyone when you get there, if you get there at all." "How do you know?" "Just get in the temperatures shooting up in here with the window open, it's screwing with the air-con." Jude got into the classy looking estate Oldsmobile after putting his backpack in the rear, he closed the car door and found himself in a silent air conditioned, very desirable world, he again asked,

"How do you know?"

"I overheard your exchange with the arsehole back at the Hotel."

"You're right, he's a bloody arsehole, he had my girlfriend arrested 'cause he wouldn't wait for me to show up and pay her bill."

"You're a good judge of character for someone who's only met him once, believe me I know he's an arsehole, I'm married to 'im."

"I don't know what to say now"

"You don't have to pull your punches just because he's my husband." "Okay then he's an arsehole." "You can open the window and shout it out loud if you like. No, on second thoughts don't, you've raised the temperature in here six degrees by just getting in, were you really going to walk to Kimba on a day like today?" "I don't know what I was doing, I just had to put distance between me and.... well you know me and the hotel." "I understand. You think a lot of your girl?" "She's absolutely everything to me, I've got to get to her as soon as I can, to check she's ok." "I understand, well I think I do, can't say as I've ever felt quite like that about anybody. You wouldn't have half an hour to pull over and enjoy this cars cool air on your naked butt then." She delivered her last sentence without batting an eyelid and lifted her skirt as high as it would go. Jude was shocked for probably the sixth or seventh time in the last twenty-four hours. He looked her in the eye and replied,

"Look please don't take this the wrong way I'm flattered, really I'm flattered, but I am and always have been a one girl man, please understand." "Oh I do, all the best guys are, still no harm in asking." With that she dropped her skirt back on to her thighs and drove on. They covered the distance in less than half an hour, conversation between them had been pleasant but shallow for the rest of the journey. She dropped Jude directly outside the police station in Kimba and wished him well and added, with a grin,

"Say hi to Sergeant Roger Jackman for me." Jude was sure her parting comment was genuine, he thanked her and never thought of her again, his mind was pre-occupied. He took the four steps up to the veranda of the Kimba Police Station in two jumps, opened the door and said,

"Hi I'm Jude Saunders, I'm looking for Elizabeth Reece." "No worries mate, you'll be looking for prisoner 22-01-89." "You've imprisoned her?" "Na, I told her she could wait for you out here, but she wanted to lie down, the cell doors are wide open, she's done in mate, she needs somebody looking out for her."

He winked at Jude, "I offered but she's got her heart set on you, can't think why."

Jude drew a breath to fire back,

"Don't get thooey with me mate just pulling your leg. Look if you take my advice I'd go get her and get out of here, she supposed to be up in front of the magistrate in a couple of days, but as you've paid the outstanding bill, the Hotel have confirmed that, there's no case to answer, go get her and get as far away from Kimba as you can, get across the Null'abor into W A, we won't post any warrant posters out that far."

He smiled and raised his hands as if in submission on recognising Jude's lack of humour

"You need to loosen up mate, that's a pretty girl back there you left adrift, I'd take more care if I were you."

Jude had had enough of Australian humour, he fired back at the desk sergeant with everything he had, giving him the full story of his and Liz's parting. When he eventually paused to draw breathe the officer in front of him merely raised his eyebrows, smiled and pointed toward the cells. Jude ceased his tirade and walked to the rear of the building, through an open door that led to the cells. All six doors were open, he looked into the first cell on his left, curled into a foetal position on the cell mattress was Liz, asleep. Her face belied her emotional condition, she looked peaceful, even serene. Jude stooped to blow gently onto her face, her eyes blinked twice and opened. At the moment she focused on Jude's face, the recognition betrayed itself with such emotion he felt that it would have registered on the seismological Richter scale, she flung her arms around his neck and pulled him to her with all the force she had left in her.

Neither of them spoke, words were superfluous they hugged for some time. Eventually her grip on him relaxed, Jude looked into her eyes and said,

"Request permission to take prisoner twenty-two, oh-one, eighty-nine home." Liz smiled and said,

"I'm so sorry."

"Me too, let's not do that again." "How far did you get before you realised?" "Half way across Australia." "Oh Jude I'm sorry, it was my fault, I kept hearing my last sentence to you, just let me sleep, drive as long as you like" "Don't be sorry its nobody's fault, it's shocking that we were over five hundred kilometres apart and heading in opposite directions." "Five hundred kilometres, oh god."

"It's over six if you count the bit you did backwards."

"Come on we can laugh about it later, we've still got some travelling to do, the van's back at Yumbarra." They kissed and hugged again. As they walked past the desk sergeant Jude asked what chance the officer thought there was of them hitchhiking back to their van today. His reply surprised him greatly.

"None at all mate, but we haven't sent a patrol out west yet today so you and missy here do yourself a favour and go two doors up and kill an hour in Sally's Dinner and I'll have one of my officers come by and shout you when he's ready, you take care now." Jude offered his hand and said a loud clear slow,

"Thank you." Which Liz repeated. "No worries, you two look after yourselves now." They did as the sergeant suggested, sitting at their table in the empty diner with a drink and a sandwich they looked into each other's eyes and smiled, Liz said,

"Let's promise we won't do that again." "That's easy, that's a promise." Liz finally let go of Jude for the first time in several minutes to raise her cup to her lips. Jude took a drink of his coffee, put down his glass and was first to speak.

"I think I'm beginning to work out the outback sense of humour I've just been abused by a couple of characters, firstly they kick you in the guts verbally, then when you're down they soften up and put out their hand to help you back up."

"I think you need to explain that a bit more." Jude described the exchanges he had had with Mac the road-train driver and the desk sergeant, which both ended in uncommon kindness. Liz replied,

"Perhaps it's in their psyche, get on top of you mentally and then offer the hand of friendship."

"I really don't think any of the insults are heartfelt, it's just their way of demonstrating familiarity."

They caught up with each other's stories over the next forty-five minutes. Liz was staggered that Jude had travelled so far west only to have to repeat the journey in the opposite direction. Jude's amazement was reserved for the hotel back at Wundinna, he couldn't accept that the manager there had had her arrested and wanted to go back there to remonstrate with the guy concerned. Liz interjected,

"Oh no, I'm not going back there." Soon a uniformed officer came into the small diner where Liz and Jude were the only customers.

"Hi I'm your ride back out west, you must be the two dummies who lost track of each other."

"That's us, thanks." Said Jude and he whispered to Liz as he got up, "That's the first kick, there'll be more to come."

The journey back to the camper was much quicker and smoother than Jude had experienced earlier. On passing the Best Western at Wudinna Jude exclaimed to the officer that in his opinion the hotel manager was a total arsehole. He replied,

"In his case mate its part of his job description." Little else was said between them, both Liz and Jude fell asleep in the rear of the patrol car.

It was late afternoon on another hot dry day when eventually they pulled up beside their camper van at the Yumbarra road house, Jude thanked the officer who merely replied,

"No worries." He then sped off to re-drive the two hundred kilometres back to Kimba. They both knew that this hadn't been a patrol, but an exceptional kindness by the desk sergeant, allowing them the use of a patrol officer and a car for four hours.

Jude unpacked everything from his backpack, Liz had a shower and was delighted to put on fresh clothes, as was Jude. They ate a small meal and both fell asleep mid evening, Jude had parked the van behind the road house in the shade, consequently heat was not a problem for a change, they both slept so well that the sound of quarrelling possums on the roof of the van and a wombat searching the remnants of the dustbin for food failed to wake them.

SUMMER 1989

WEST AUSTRALIA

Early morning Jude barbequed a breakfast and they were parked by the fuel pumps ready to fill up and head west at eight o'clock, when the owner arrived to commence his Monday shift. Liz now fully recovered was sat up front with Jude as they cruised the five hundred kilometres to Eucla, they arrived mid afternoon after twice stopping along the way for photographic opportunities, firstly for a pack of Dingo's at unusually close range and secondly for their first and only view of a small cluster of wild camels. Jude paid again to spend the night at the campsite, Liz spoke with utter incredulity of her surprise at just how far Jude had travelled alone two days previous.

They viewed the ruins of the old original Telegraph Station and walked to the cliff head in a hope of sighting whales, with no luck. After a quiet night Liz wandered back to the high cliff top viewing point whilst Jude once again barbequed their breakfast, after just a few minutes apart she came running, breathless back to their camper.

"Jude forget breakfast there are whales, quick." He did as ordered, they reached the cliff edge in time to view a pod of six Southern Right whales that put on a show for them for the next half hour, it was to be the only time in their lives they would see free swimming whales. They had no idea how fortunate they were to experience the viewing, as it was an unseasonable occurrence. For the rest of the day and the following day they were effervescent, often recalling the encounter with the whales.

Their crossing of the Null'abor Plain was completed in two days.

The next four weeks were consumed in agreeable meanderings along the coastal southwest. Points of note were the exceptional shoreline between Esperance and Denmark. Liz in particular was besotted with two small coves, one of which bore the unattractive name of Cole Mine Bay and the other was Wilson Inlet, retrospectively she attributed her attraction to these particular features because they were pocket sized and more proportional to the coastal peculiarities in the south west of England. This realisation made her experience a pang of homesickness for the first time in her life.

At the second of the small bays near the town of Denmark, they decided to stay put for a few days. The area was as Jude was fond of saying soft on the eye, they parked the van in a small sheltered park just thirty paces from the shoreline, next to their van was a much smaller vehicle, a Nissan Urvan which had been parked long enough to have a washing line attached to a convenient tree. The occupiers of the van were a sixty seven year old lady called Amelia and her poodle/terrier cross, Teddy.

On their first evening the conversation between them was no more than exchanged greetings and satisfaction toward the weather, though the lack of rain was becoming a serious concern to all Western Australians. On their second night at the site the three of them got together for a barbeque. Jude did the cooking on their van pull out, Liz and Amelia chatted whilst preparing salad and opening wine. The two women had become extremely comfortable with each other very quickly. Amelia swiftly became the mother Liz never had and Liz the absent daughter in Amelia's life. At the moment the food was presented to the outdoor table three powerful cars tore into the site, circled their two vans blasting their horns and skidding up a cloud of dust which enveloped the three of them, their camper vans, their abundant washing hanging to dry and their food was sheathed in red dust and grit. Before the dust had settled the cars had left the site and sped away toward the forest, both the speed of the incident and the thick cloud of dust made it impossible to record a registration number, indeed after the event the three of them could not agree if it had been two or three vehicles or even what colour they had been. Jude raged in anger, Liz was screaming in frustration and annoyance, Amelia sat motionless with her flat palm over her wine glass. When the dust had settled and the cars engines were but an unpleasant memory, she lifted her glass to her mouth saying,

"You two still have a lot to learn." Liz just managed a smile and asked,

"What was that about?" She replied,

"That was what we call hoons, idiotic young men with too much money, fast cars and alcohol are their vices, you and I are their victims, we do have a problem with young white men in this country that the government doesn't seem to want to find an answer for, if they had been young black men they would be stopped and their cars taken away and crushed." Liz asked why the difference?

"Oh these white boys are the overpaid sons of wealthy farmers, politicians and police officers, their daddies are members of the same shooting, hunting, racist, drinking club, their sons are untouchable." Liz added,

"That's disgusting and it's not the first time I've encountered them."

"It sure is and so is all this food." She scraped the food into a waste bin as Jude reloaded the barbeque, this time with sausages and burgers as all the steak and chicken was now trash. Liz and Amelia cut up new salad and both women were resigned to re-washing their clothes in the morning.

On their third evening they got together around the outdoor table, the wine and conversation flowed, Amelia felt relaxed and comfortable in her new neighbours company, subsequently she told her story.

She said that she was more than half way around her fourth circumnavigation of one of the largest countries on the planet, both Liz and Jude filled their cheeks and exhaled in amazement at that one fact. She liked to travel alone with Teddy, she occasionally stopped for a calendar month in one of her favourite spots and Wilson Inlet was one such place. She said it was a fascination to stay in one place and observe those who pulled up either side of her, she made a point of not engaging neighbours on the first night as most people only stayed for a single night, she described herself as occasionally social, by waiting for the second or subsequent night she could preserve her conservative nature. On this particular evening, which was the anniversary of the death of her first husband, and partially because the pitches either side of her had been empty for a week, she opened up in a rare and complete exposé of her past, she was aided by the seductive conviviality of the amicable company of her new neighbours and a bottomless bottle of soft red wine from the Franklyn River region of western Australia.

Throughout her narrative Liz and Jude only commented when required to do so and only moved to refill their glasses when required. Amelia had been brought up in a succession of children's homes in the Camden town district of London, by a multiplicity of carers, many of them she had fond memories of, but there were a few she said who knew no limits of indecency, who, she hoped would get their recompense in the next world. She was, she said, very fortunate to be in the right place at the right time to be given the opportunity of a lifetime, she had reached her eighteenth year in 1941. She was sent with two other girls by her current children's home, in which they had stayed on after the normal kicking out age at sixteen to help in the laundry and kitchen, to the forces recruiting office in Ealing, North London.

Immediately prior to the girls' arrival the officer in charge had received a telephone call from the R.A.F. requesting six young women to train as Radar Spotters. Amelia and her two friends were enlisted into the Royal Air Force to perform a task they knew absolutely nothing about. After training they transferred to Malta, Cyprus the Middle East and Singapore, spending all their workings days or nights studying radar screens and communicating with pilots, informing them of imminent approaching danger or of clear skies. The work she found tedious but the rapport the girls developed with the pilots was their delight of the day. Most of the pilots were just happy to hear a female voice and would play up to the girls asking them out on unachievable and imaginary dates. She confessed to having many liaisons with pilots and remarked a little regretfully that perhaps she was a little too friendly with some of the cheeky ones, but then she added, blushing slightly that for many of the pilots she knew she was the last girl they ever kissed. At this point she retrieved a photograph of herself aged twenty-two. She was still an attractive woman at sixty-seven, but it was abundantly clear to both Jude and Liz even in a torn and tattered black and white picture fading to yellow, that as a young woman she had been exceptionally beautiful. As Amelia looked at her own faded image her eyes glassed over with moisture in what was interpreted by her companions as a regret of the aging process, but Amelia wasn't regretting that her looks had changed she was regretting that her life had changed.

She expressed her opinion that the second world war had been a horrific and terrible time for millions upon millions of people, but for her it had been the time of her life, she was plucked from obscurity out of an ocean of domestic chores with no hope of escape and propelled into a world of pilots, travel, entertainment and short term love, it was for her a world of riches beyond her comprehension, she expressed that she felt guilty that she did not feel guilt towards her wartime experience. The end of the war coincided with her meeting again one of her cheeky pilots, despite him being almost twice her age she was bowled over by someone who wanted to be with her on more than one occasion, her upbringing in the children's home in North London had taught her that only brutes and priests were likely to come back, and that their affection was to Amelia incomprehensible in its brutality and subsequent physical and mental pain. At this point in her reflections she went into a fixed stare at a point that neither Jude nor Liz could focus on, she paused, dried her eyes, seemingly overwhelmed. Liz put her hand on Amelia's arm, as Jude refilled her glass and said,

"Amelia you don't have to do this to yourself." She replied,

"Oh now I've got this far I'm going all the way, I want somebody to know my story, why shouldn't it be you, you're two of the most honest people I've met in a long time and I can feel that you two have a solid core, a shared dynamo that is working with the same purpose." She continued. The war ended, she married Charles her Australian pilot despite him being old enough to be her parent, they lived in a small town in Queensland and had just four happy years together by which time Charles had succumbed to a long history of chest infections, pleurisy and emphysema. After Charles death Amelia said that she discovered his flight log, she told her two keen eared listeners that the information it contained was simply staggering. She gave one or two for examples.

She said that he might be taking off from Dar-es-Salaam in a Baltimore bomber, one of perhaps sixty, seventy or even ninety bombers with hurricane and spitfire escort, he would drop six two hundred and fifty pound bombs on what was always listed as a M/T this she assumed was a military target but she knew from Charles that all pilots were always informed that their target was a military one, for example a German tank division or an armoured munitions convoy, but Charles had told her that a factory making tank or military vehicle parts employing perhaps two thousand civilian workers would be listed as a military target. In his blacker moments which Amelia said came to him more and more as his illness weakened him, he would say that during his one thousand two hundred flying hours, all in bombers he must have been responsible for the deaths of enough people to fill a soccer stadium. His log she said also recorded information like Plane holed, or rear gunner killed on return leg, or as was the case twice, plane destroyed on belly flop landing as undercarriage failed, she said she was astonished at the lives the pilots led. They were facing dangers on a daily basis that were unimaginable to the millions in civilian life.

On a less serious note she said his log contained a page of misdemeanours such as Malta May 1942 wing torn off Bristol Bomber whilst taxiing, pilot error, and Cyprus September 1942 misjudged length of runway Baltimore bomber abandoned in olive grove, plane written off, pilot error. She smiled a wry smile at these confessions and added that Charles would grin a naughty boy grin whenever he recalled his pilot errors.

She moved on quickly admitting that she married the first man she met who reminded her of Charles and confessed too that she knew little of her second husband, they had a son, Philip who was now thirty six and living with his boyfriend in New Zealand. She simply shrugged her shoulders at this confession. After twenty ordinary years of domesticity she said that her second husband whose name she never once used found God. He rewrote his history and qualified as a minister of the local branch of The Pentecostal Church. She disclosed that he had always been a bit of an arse but that when he discovered God he took it to a new and unimagined level. She was she said very frustrated that the community took to him so readily, they adored him, she rebelled, she wore short skirts, low cut blouses and acquired a discrete but visible tattoo, they began to dislike her, she said that she couldn't help but aggravate them, for she knew that their new priest had a history of pornography and a tendency toward buggery. She could not simply stand by and watch this man prostitute himself in public in the name of God, without registering her discomfort. He confessed one day, 'that touching her made him feel dirty', she openly cried at this disclosure. She then filed for divorce, banked her half of the revenue from the house sale, bought a camper van and simply drove away with her only friend in the world, Teddy, her dog. She had now been on the road for over four years and had many regrets but being a modern day 'grey nomad' was not one of them.

Conversation between the three of them moved to more general subjects and road stories, of which Amelia had many more than her companions, one of which Liz would recall from time to time in later life. Amelia had been driving through rough country in the Northern Territories between Tennents Creek and the infamous Fitzroy Crossing, an area normally dust dry but liable to occasional elephantine bouts of flood water coming from the Kimberly Mountain Range. After one such flood her camper had become stuck in a rut washed out of the dirt road by flood water, she had been stuck there for a day and a half before help arrived in the form of four forty to fifty year old men, who were on a hunting trip in a huge recreational vehicle, she revealed that she felt extremely vulnerable being in such a remote place with four men, and she felt that either before or after they had freed her vehicle they would take advantage of her, but to her shock they released her van from its disposition and when she laid on the bunk of her van and said 'please don't hurt me' the four of them simple replied, 'No worries' and drove off. This was for Amelia a eureka moment, in that moment a lifelong burden was lifted from her, the burden of her prepossessing looks, perhaps now she thought at last she would be able to engage in conversation with the opposite sex without automatically calculating the cost, or as she put it to Jude, maybe her four hero's batted for the other side, checking that she had phrased it correctly, Jude nodded, She continued to describe her thoughts after her rescue. She was she said mildly disappointed that her looks had faded to such a point that she was no longer desirable to men, but she was overwhelmingly relieved that her looks had faded to the point that she was no longer desirable to men. The three of them laughed at this latest admission of Amelia's past, the rest of the evening was consumed in many incidental road stories. Sleep when it came was sweet and undisturbed, courtesy of three bottles of good quality red.

In the morning they gave Amelia Mrs Nayland's address and conversation was back to the weather and their immediate plans, at around ten thirty Jude manoeuvred their camper onto the highway as Amelia was walking back to the campsite with Teddy. Jude slowed the van to a crawl wound down his window and sang to her in a clear voice,

"We'll meet again, don't know where don't know when, but I know we'll meet again some sunny day."

He blew Amelia a kiss and drove on leaving her opened mouthed and wiping a tear from her eye.

From Wilson Inlet they motored inland where Jude was smitten by the previously unimagined colossal red gums of the Franklyn River Area, he commented to Liz that he felt the magnificent oaks and elms of England were as sticks of rhubarb in comparison, he also relished the experience of the underwater observatory at the termination of the Busselton Jetty. He revelled in the Sub aquatic Building giving the unique experience of being able to witness millennia of ocean species in their normal environment, to be inside the Aquarium and to be observed and not to be the observer.

Liz's greatest pleasure of the sub continent was to view the late evening landscape, at these times she took her most satisfying photographs, the day landscapes, shoreline and animal shots were a pleasure but she felt like an opportunist snapping at a subject that fortunately presented itself, but in the fading light of evening with the red setting sun glorifying the interior ancient landscape she was in her medium, she felt that she had a degree of interpretation, that she could construe the resulting frame. She often wandered short distances from their vehicle relishing in the selfish indulgence of solitude with her camera, the pinkish red dusty soil of the outback and the last low rays of the sun playing with the contours of the unique landscape produced astonishing colours, if she timed it perfectly each few seconds would produce new shadows some lengthening to enhance a particular feature, others all but linking up to highlight a previously unnoticed aspect or facet of the unrivalled vista. On these occasions time was her enemy and friend, each minute would both rob her of a great subject and reveal another, time would pass too quickly for her, and often she would be returning the short distance to the camper van feeling both frustrated and satisfied. She knew it was a dangerous occupation being off the road in poor light due to the venomous nature of their host countries wildlife, but she found the appeal of perusing the ever reshaping, reforming and shifting shadows enticing. With the heat of the day reduced to comfortable warmth and the first stars appearing this was her time of day, she would ultimately be as delighted and proud of her photographic results on these short excursions as any of her life's work.

They knew that they had enjoyed a fabulous and memorable episode. They knew too that time was running low with a little more than a week to their departure date. They headed north along the shoreline towards Western Australia's capital city and the beginning of the end of their encounter with the largest of Britain's former colonial possessions.

They arrived at Perth with mixed emotions, the sense of achievement was paramount but it was underscored with an end of term feeling, they were all too aware that arrival in Perth spelled almost the end of what had been an enlightening, frightening and memorable experience. They still had a week before their departure date, but they knew that the adventure was all but over. Soon the pair of them would be back in Dorchester, which is where they had decided to make their home and Liz would after six more weeks be flying north with her camera and Jude would be writing.

They had shied away from Australian cities such as Melbourne and Adelaide because they longed for the open road and the genuine bush but they took to Perth and felt a degree of camaraderie with the modern mainly white occupied Australian city. Its limited number of skyscrapers was impressive but not overbearing. In particular they were both impressed with the elevated area known as Kings Park, an area of hundreds of acres that overlooks the city centre and is partly ornamental parkland with cafes and restaurants, it also had a huge acreage of natural bush, due to the foresight of one or more cities elders this area had been preserved in its natural state, despite it occupying a central site in a modern city.

They both felt that the financial and development pressure on this zone of preserved natural bush must be tremendous and hoped that it would survive such pressures, it occurred to both Liz and Jude that the parcel of land must be almost unique, it occupied a central city location and it was possible to a great deal of naturally occurring wildlife. The formal area of the park also impressed Jude, all the vegetation from grasses to trees were indigenous species, some of the gum trees were magnificent and often rang out with the squabbling laughter of the resident Kookaburras, to witness or recall the song of this iconic bird would for both Jude and Liz bring back floods of memories of the whole Australian experience.

Whilst Jude was collecting refreshments for them both from the restaurant/cafeteria that overlooked downtown Perth, he stood for a moment to witness a young couple getting married in the open air on a purposely built, ornamental wrought iron and stone arch, which was draped in magnificent flowers and commanded a panoramic view of the city and the Swan River estuary, he envied them their moment of licensed ecstasy and a seed germinated in his mind.

Liz decided to walk one more time around the park with her camera and was surprised to hear from Jude that he would prefer to sit, relax and people watch, and enjoy the ambivalence of Kings Park. Secretly she was pleased to be alone with her camera. Also secretly Jude was inspired to make a monumental decision. As soon as Liz was out of sight Jude went to speak to the person who appeared to be in overall supervision of the enviable outdoor ceremonies. He was a typical Australian with a typical European name, Barry Fitzgerald, although helping in a supervisory capacity he was as were most Australians dressed in shorts, albeit smart shorts. Once he was able to gain the undivided attention of Mr Fitzgerald, Jude asked him if there was an opportunity for a couple to marry at short notice, and what would be the cost. Mr Fitzgerald replied,

410

"You'd be lucky mate, every weekend and holiday weekend is booked up six months in advance and anyway it'll set you back six hundred bucks."

"And if someone wanted to marry during the week?"

"Then you'd either be a freak or desperate, we could do you tomorrow."

"Really."

"Yes really, only freaks and desperado's marry in the week, which are you?"

"Well I'm not desperate so I must be a freak, can you do two freaks next Wednesday?"

"Sure you got the six hundred?" "Yes when do you need it?" "When you book it." "OK I'm booking it."

"OK I need it." "Come with me to that crappy little kiosk that doubles up as my office and its booked, do you have ID for both persons?" "Actually I do I've got both our passports in the camper, can you wait just two minutes?" "No worries." Jude ran to their van quickly grabbed their passports and ran back to Mr Fitzgerald who seemed to him to be just a little bit too much down to earth to be real. Passports were inspected, the fee paid and one of two signatures recorded, the second to follow next Wednesday at twelve noon. Jude was issued with a provisional marriage licence, subject to the second signature in six days time. Jude shook hands with Barry a man who had surprised him with his degree of pragmatic realism and downright sense of if there's a job to be done, let's get on with it.

So he had paid six hundred bucks to be married next Wednesday at twelve noon. He just needed a bride. Was it the most reckless thing he had ever done? No, he thought leaving Dorchester and flying to Los Angeles on impulse two years ago on Liz's prompting had been and would always be in his mind the most reckless thing he would ever do, temporarily forgetting his experience with the jelly fish, this was just gambling six hundred Australian dollars, win or lose he was still a happy man.

No sooner had he put their passports back in the secret compartment of their camper and returned to the table with a cold beer when Liz came back excited that she had photographed a pair of day roosting tawny frog mouthed owls at close range. She picked up Jude's beer and downed it without pause, dropped the empty bottle onto the table and said,

"Thanks." She flopped into a chair opposite Jude. He looked into her mesmerising and inviting eyes, smiled a wry smile and retraced his steps to the cafeteria for two cold beers, as he returned to their table he instinctively knew he was under the scrutiny of a telephoto lens, he tried to suppress a grin but failed,

"What are you looking so smug about?" Liz injected,

"I can't believe I'm in one of the nicest places in the world with the loveliest girl in the world." Liz laughed and put two fingers down her throat as if to induce nausea, he thought many private thoughts, none of which surfaced. They spent two more hours just lazily enjoying the ambiance of Kings Park whilst making plans for the last six days down under.

They hired a two berth cabin cruiser and spent three days on the Swan River, three days they would always cherish, they motored inland as far as the river would allow, spent two nights on the boat and slowly motored back, the wildlife and photographic opportunities were exemplary, the weather in Western Australia seemed always to be convivial. The three days were reminiscent of their river trip on the Murray but this trip was thankfully devoid of mosquitoes. They handed back the cruiser and re-occupied their camper on Monday night, they had very little of their trip of a lifetime left. They quizzed each other as to any last request they may have as they were flying out of Perth International Airport on Thursday morning they had just two days to spend. Jude said that he would like to lunch in Kings Park on their last day a request Liz readily agreed with and Liz wanted to use their last unallocated day tomorrow to enjoy the coast of Western Australia just one more time. They drove the two hours to the coast in the evening so they could wake with the sea in the back window the following morning.

They enjoyed a superb sunset over the Indian Ocean off the coast of Western Australia, witnessing the sun setting over the sea was a treat that very few Australians enjoyed regularly, as the bulk of the population lived in the Eastern States of Queensland, New South Wales and Victoria and even those who occupied cities such as Adelaide, Darwin and Perth were still out of sight of the ocean, Jude and Liz had fallen in love with Frazer Range to the western end of the Great Nullabor Plain and the Franklyn and Margaret River areas of the western state, but at the moment that the sun finally dipped below the horizon they both felt if they were to ever seriously consider settling in this vast country, it would have to be somewhere on the west coast. To reinforce this feeling they were treated once again to a small group of friendly black rays enjoying the warm shallow surf at the waters' edge, and a large flight of pink and grey Galah Cockatoos, and they were delighted that a pair of laughing kookaburras serenaded them as they walked along the warm waters edge.

They strolled for more than two hours along the increasingly quiet and desolate beach, it was clearly noticeable that as human activity diminished wildlife activity increased, by the time they were back at their camper van they were surrounded by grey kangaroos, red flanked wallabies, two huge monitor lizards and innumerable rabbits, added to those were a rare and beautiful night heron, a large flock of evening bats, and a pair of tawny frog mouth owls. They were mesmerised by the night shift occupation of the beach and its backdrop, so much so that neither of them had given a thought to food. As the stores were closed, they shared a takeaway pizza and a bottle of local red in the open air on a gloriously warm evening under a canopy of celestial lights. Conversation between them had tailed off, both of them were experiencing a slight sickening feeling that this was all about to end, as they knew it must, there were commitments that both of them had undertaken at home, Liz leaned on Jude's shoulder and took from her pocket one of the six crumpled scraps of paper they had written their travel idea's on, back at the hotel Titanic in Colombia. She unfurled and placed it in front of him, putting her wine glass over one end to prevent the strengthening breeze from lifting it skyward. There were ten words written on the small fragment of paper in Jude's handwriting 'Marry you, have a family and live happily ever after'. They both stared at the simple note. Just for a moment it seemed as if the world stood still, even the cacophony of evening bird song appeared to draw a breath.

As Jude said nothing, Liz thought that she had misjudged their relationship and put Jude on a spot, for just a moment she hated herself, her confidence dissolved into doubt, how could she have got things so wrong? She misinterpreted Jude's discomfort. She was now torn between regret and disappointment, regretting her action and disappointment at receiving no response, and unusually for her, not knowing how to start their next conversation. There was a huge 'elephant in the room'.

Jude was both overjoyed that he felt Liz was waiting for him to propose but also not wishing to give away his surprise. He was juggling ecstasy and a very different kind of disappointment, the moment was over, it had lasted to long, Liz took back the notice and screwed it back up, placing it into the pocket from where it had come, saying,

"Come on we need to get the camper into night mode."

"Wait, wait, please, please put your head back on my shoulder and the note back on the table." There was another silent moment, Jude reinforced his request with an additional,

"Please." Liz did as she was asked but felt that her fireworks were now a little damp and would struggle to re-ignite. Jude read out the notice,

"One, marry you, two have a family and three live happily ever after, please forgive my silence I was considering how greedy I was to make three requests on one small note of paper and I was thinking how long it would take to achieve all three."
"Surely a life time?" Liz stated,

"The third one yes, but the other two, who knows?" He continued, "Have a family perhaps between two and ten years, but marry you, if you could find the right person you could probably achieve that tomorrow."

She elbowed him in the ribs, Jude laughing said,

"So if I decided to ask you to marry me tomorrow, would you say yes?" "Do you mean if you were to ask me to marry you, comma tomorrow, or if you were to ask me to marry you tomorrow, no comma?"

"Either."

"Not good enough, which do you mean?" Jude felt he was on the edge of a cliff on tiptoe with an offshore wind pushing him over the edge, he had minimal control of his emotions. He said,

"Can we sleep on it and I'll ask you tomorrow." "Ask me what tomorrow? Version a or b?"

"That's what I want to sleep on, I promise I'll ask you one version tomorrow."

"What time tomorrow?"

"Twelve noon." "OK deal." With that Liz carefully folded the small note and put it in her pocket.

The note eventually was to be put behind glass in a small frame and would occupy pride of place in their family home.

They converted the camper into night mode, had some fun in the deserted camp site shower block and spent the night with all the windows open to enjoy their last warm night by the sea. Dismissing the jelly fish incident they had had a fabulous experience which they knew must end, they fell asleep with differing degrees of anticipation for the following day. Other than a possum scampering across the roof of their van they enjoyed an undisturbed and refreshing sleep.

After a barbequed breakfast of bacon and sausage they tidied the camper and drove the two hours back to Perth City Centre. It was almost eleven thirty when Jude parked the van in Kings Park with a view toward the city skyscrapers and the Swan Estuary, through the decorative wedding arch. Liz noticed that preparations were under way for a ceremony, she like Jude had done just a few days previous envied the couple who were about to be married in such magnificent surroundings on such a beautiful day. She looked across the cab of their van into Jude's eyes for a spark of similar recognition, and said to him,

"Just look at that gorgeous scene what does it make you think?" Jude seemingly completely oblivious to her mood replied,

"It makes me think I want one of those super coffees from the café over there," pointing to their left away from Liz's gaze "You want one?" "Oh I don't know," said Liz, she almost betrayed her thoughts by saying, "Surprise me, get me something I haven't had before." Jude left Liz in dream land and closed the van door with a loud crash which still did not bring Liz back to earth, she felt like a five year old who wanted her daddy to work magic, cover the world in pixie dust and wave his wand. When out of Liz's sight Jude ducked into the souvenir shop and quickly went to the seashell jewellery, he picked a necklace made up of worn rings of broken hermit crab shells which he bought for just four dollars, the shell rings were quite small at the ends of the necklace and increase in size toward the centre, he found one which was comfortable on his little finger and snapped it off, putting the necklace in his left pocket and the single ring of shell in his right.

He then bought himself one of his favourite coffees and Liz a coffee mocha something he's never heard of and didn't know what it was, but realised after purchasing it that the clue for the content was in the name.

Back at the van he handed Liz her something special and notices she is still focused on a different year to the one he is in, it is now ten minutes to twelve, Jude is struggling to contain his emotions.

Liz is feeling excited, elated, disappointed and deflated all at once, she knows in her mind that Jude is going to propose to her and that he wanted to wait until he was in his favourite spot at the Highpoint in Kings Park, but she is wishing for more, she is craving for so much more. She is wishing that they had just one more day to fulfil her starry eyed dream, she wipes a tear from her eye which contrary to her belief does not go unnoticed by Jude, who is sitting in silence apparently selfishly enjoying his coffee.

At five to twelve he puts down his coffee puts his hand out toward Liz and says,

"Please come with me." They step out of the van and into an awkward silence, Liz takes Jude's left hand, Jude's right hand is fingering the shell ring putting it on and off of his little finger repeatedly.

As they are walking toward the unoccupied alter it occurs to Jude for the first time that they did not dress for an occasion, he is wearing faded denim jeans and a white short sleeved shirt, he says to Liz

"Hold on just a sec." He runs back to the camper and grabs his favourite t-shirt which he puts on replacing the buttoned shirt, it is the buff coloured t-shirt that Liz gave him at Heathrow over two years before, it is a little worn and worse for wear but now he has 'forget me not' across his chest. Liz laughs and they continue to walk toward the arch. Standing by the ornate alter is the presiding registrar who is to marry them and the Clerk of works as Jude has nicknamed him Mr Barry Fitzgerald, he gives Jude a nod of recognition as Jude approaches the arch, Liz pulls back,

"Jude we can't get any closer they are waiting to marry someone."

"I know they are, just come with me." Jude shakes hands with Mr Fitzgerald and Mr McKinnon the Registrar and climbs the three steps onto the elevated platform under the stunning floral arch, and just for a moment he takes in the all round panoramic view, it is breathtaking, he then puts out his hand to a bewildered Liz who looks towards both officials and who both nod approval in her direction.

She is flabbergasted that Jude has borrowed the outdoor arch for his moment, she looks into Jude's welcoming eyes and more than slightly embarrassed steps up to be level with him. Jude takes her hands in his, drops to one knee and asks,

"Will you please marry me, not next year, not next week or tomorrow, will you marry me today, here, now?" "What, are you for real?"

"Don't doubt or question me, I'm for real." Jude is smiling, Liz is welling up, tears are rising to the surface of her flushed face, she looks to the presiding officials, they are both smiling and nodding to her, she looks back at Jude who now has the small ring in one hand and an expression on his face she will never forget.

"Can we, can we do it now?" "All booked and paid for." "How, when?" "That doesn't matter, will you marry me please? Now." "Stand up, you idiot." Jude does as he is commanded and holds out the tiny shell ring.

"If it doesn't fit I've got a whole load more." He says as he holds the necklace in front of her face.

"You silly bugger, of course I'll marry you."

"Now?" "Yes now." She puts her arms around his neck, pulls him in close and kisses him. A small round of applause is audible from close range. Jude looks to the small crowd of less than ten persons and ask an elderly couple if they would be their witnesses, they smile and agree in a moment. Barry asks if they are ready to commence the ceremony, they both reply,

417

"Yes." Liz asks, "Where do I sign?" He replies, "All in good time." Mr McKinnon now steps forward, some formalities are read out, vows are exchanged, certificates are signed and witnessed and in a short time, Liz Reece becomes Mrs Saunders, dressed in flip flops, denim shorts and a bright ref kaftan top, she is both overwhelmed and overjoyed. She kisses Jude and says, "How the hell did you fix that?" He replies,

"I'll tell you later, come on let's get a bottle of something bubbly and go for a walk in the park, you only have half a day left of your honeymoon."

They thanked the witnesses and the two officials and walked to the restaurant for a bottle and two glasses.

Once seated at a distant table Jude asked,

"How does your ring fit?" She kisses him again and says,

" It's hopelessly too big, but I'm not swopping it for anything in the world." "I can't believe I'm married, how did you do that?" "You're not married, we're married, it was simple, a few days ago I watched a couple getting spliced when you were off with your camera so I went along with our passports paid six hundred bucks and bobs your uncle we're married." "What if I'd said no?" "Until last night I wasn't sure of your answer. It would have been six hundred down the drain but when you brought out that note I was pretty confident." "I nearly pissed on your fireworks there didn't I?" "Yep, not sure how I kept stum." "Jude, I love you." "So do I." "So do you what?" "I love me too." They laughed, drank their champagne and spent the afternoon, their last afternoon in Australia in and around the surroundings of Kings Park, Liz bought a couple of corny souvenirs of the Park, their wedding venue, to take home. They spent their wedding night in the camper van in the Park and consummated their wedding vows to the sound of squabbling kookaburras, a sound that would forever be to both of them evocative with their back to front honeymoon and wedding trip.

In the morning they had breakfast in the Park, Liz took a few last photographs and Jude drove them to the van hire company where they said good bye to their mobile home. They then took a taxi to Perth International Airport where they spent three hours in the airport lounge with little conversation between them. Jude was blending thoughts of the last ten weeks with thoughts of

Jayne's unfinished book and the dilemma of Jacqueline Forbes-Brewer, Imprisoned in a Colombian rain forest.

Liz was on cloud nine.

WINTER 1989

DUAL SUPRISE

She was sitting in the airport lounge living and reliving the events of the last week leading up to her stepping onto the memorable, floral decorated celebration arch and she was also people watching, inventing real life situations as to why they were travelling, why they were happy, melancholy or tearful. She zoomed in on a well dressed, well tanned Middle Eastern looking man of perhaps fifty five or sixty, he was greying at the temples, his companion was a twentyish year old girl, almost bedraggled. She was poorly dressed in torn jeans, holed shoes, a torn and unwashed top and hair to suit. Liz decided they were not companions, not father and daughter, possibly grandfather and granddaughter, but when the smartly dressed man whom she gave the name of Lawrence, as in Lawrence of Arabia got up to buy food for himself only, she dismissed her last notion. The girl who Liz had labelled Pollyanna watched him eat, she couldn't understand the relationship between them. Looking out from the girls unkempt hair was a stunningly beautiful face and eyes of the brightest sapphire blue Liz had ever seen, she longed to capture that face in close up and was rehearsing an acceptable sentence with which to approach the girl. The lack of conversation or any degree of familiarity between them rendered her thoughts inappropriate, when Lawrence had finished his food he disposed of the empty cartons in a convenient waste bin and cleaned his hands on a disposable pre packed napkin, he appeared well satisfied with himself. He spoke briefly to the girl, handcuffed her to her chair and left her alone to visit the toilets. Pollyanna, as Liz had now named her looked so forlorn Liz approached her saying,

"Please don't be offended but may I offer you ten dollars to buy yourself some lunch." The girl smiled a wry smile and looked into Liz's face, she said in a strange accent,

"No, no thank you, please go, please." Her accent was middle-eastern, her eyes were saying something quite different, 'Thank you, thank you so much for caring, how did you notice, how can you know?' Liz crumpled a ten dollar bill into a tiny ball and dropped it into the girls lap, smiled into her dazzlingly blue eyes and quickly returned to her seat. She sat down just in time to see the girl drop the bill into the nearby rubbish bin. She wanted to ask the girl so many questions. Shortly after the gentleman's return, a flight to Abu Dhabi was called for boarding, Lawrence and Pollyanna immediately stood up, they clasped their possessions and walked away, as Liz watched them depart the girl put her right hand behind her back with the thumb clearly pointing upwards in a signal to Liz. Jude said,

"What was that about? Those two seemed as well matched as chalk and cheese." "I know I've been trying for some time to pigeon hole them but I just can't."

"I reckon she's a runaway from a rich Middle Eastern family and he's a hired bounty hunter."

"Rubbish he wouldn't have left her along to go to the loo if that's right."

"Sure he would, he's probably got her passport in his pocket not to mention the hand gun, come on he did handcuff her to her seat."

"No you're being over dramatic." "OK so you try to put the pieces of two different puzzles together." "I can't I've been trying to do that for half an hour." "How much did you give her?" "Only ten dollars, should I have given her more?" "She looked like she could do with a thousand." "Jude she threw the money in the waste bin, her eyes were the clearest sapphire blue I've ever seen. I wish I could have photographed her close up, she had a face that could have launched a thousand ships." "And clothes that look like they have been worn a thousand days." "Come on let's forget about her." "Can you?" "Yes let's get some lunch." "I thinks she's a runaway princess. To her ten bucks was nothing and now she's going back to her arranged marriage." "OK I'll go along with that for now until I can sort it out. Come on I'm hungry." They enjoyed a plateaux de Fruits de Mer pour deux in the French restaurant and a half bottle of bubbles.

Soon they were sitting beside each other on a Boeing 747, Liz by the window. It was early afternoon Western Australian time, they had a seven hour flight, a four hour plane change in Hong Kong, an eight hour flight, a two hour refuelling stop in Bahrain and then a further eight hour flight to Heathrow in front of them. In all twenty nine hours travelling or waiting, they were dreading it, by gaining eight hours crossing the equivalent number of time zones they would land exhausted and jet lagged twenty one hours after they had taken off. Liz had a job getting her head around the time zone issue. Because she had once had an eleven-hour flight to Johannesburg, South Africa, and she was a little confused because she had landed with no adjustment required to her watch. During the flight at a time when they were both awake and alert, which was seldom, Jude asked her to imagine an orange with the peel off that had exactly twenty-four segments. Jude explained that each segment represented perfectly the way the world was divided into time zones, so that if you travelled from the North Pole to the South Pole, from the top to the bottom of the orange, within the same segment you were in the same time zone, but if you travelled around the middle of the orange, each segment represented approximately a thousand miles and one hours gain or loss.

"OK I can see that, but what's the time at the poles at the top and bottom of your orange world?" "There is no time at the poles, time isn't measurable because all twenty four time zones come together."

She thought for a moment and replied,

"You should have been a teacher, I wish my geography teacher had explained it that simply, so travel North-South or South-North is in the same time or same segment of the orange, travel East-West or West-East is either with or against time." "Exactly."

"So this journey is lasting twenty nine hours, but as we're crossing eight orange segments clockwise, we have to take the eight segments off the twenty nine making the journey only twenty one hours." "Again, exactly." "Jude your giving me a headache, can I go back to sleep now? And will there be a bump when we jump from one segment to the next?" She laughs,

"I'll tell you what I'll poke you in the ribs each time we cross an international date line." "And I'll stuff your orange where the sun doesn't shine, I tell you what, would you get me a glass of orange juice just so I can imagine somebody squashing your little world and if I'm asleep when you get back, you can have it, now run along teacher, ouch what was that for?" "We just jumped across a segment."

"Go squash an orange." The plane change in Hong Kong went without a hitch but the two hour refuelling in Bahrain took in all three and a half hours due to an elderly gent in first class suffering a mild heart attack, finding his luggage took most of the extra time.

Arrival in Heathrow was late afternoon on a damp drizzly April day. They had not slept well during the flight and the relatively short train journey to Dorchester via Basingstoke and Southampton seemed to be double its actual length. Mrs Nayland was glad to see them and she was pleased that she had their favourite stable room available for them, she was also delighted that they had married during their long absence. After two days of little more than sleeping, eating and making love they put a plan together, which rapidly gained momentum.

Jude had long ago decided not to return to work with Jack Mortimer, the horror of Kris's death had made that decision for him. He would spend the summer sorting out long-term accommodation and tackling Jayne's book, he planned to look for employment in the autumn. They bought a vehicle, the first either of them had owned for a long time, it was a Volkswagen camper van, they had loved having a camper at their disposal in Australia and felt they would make good use of one in England, as and when they were both available, Jude's only disappointment was that it was an automatic, Liz had just five weeks before her new photographic commitment kicked in, this time it was the largest of her commitments, twenty weeks in northern Europe.

They needed a home, after viewing more than a dozen places they decided that what they wanted exactly wasn't available, they started to look for a suitable plot of land with permission to build and during the evenings they would design their own home, this gave them great pleasure. Jude cut out a handful of squares of paper each no bigger than the size of a human hand, each square he said represented a twelve foot by twelve foot room and they had fun moving them relative to each other, they decided that one would be the kitchen, another next to it the utility, two would be the lounge and four the central day room of the house. Each room was to be connected to the day room, plus one for an office/study and one more square was cut in half, half for a entrance hallway and the remaining half for a toilet shower.

Many times one of them would return to Mrs Nayland's stable room to find that the other one had moved a room, often the kitchen and utility would swop or the study and hall would do likewise.

One evening just a few days before Liz was due to depart they got serious, the rooms were cellotaped together, an upstairs of a bathroom and four bedrooms also added, and Jude gave Liz a red pen and said to her,

"Here use this pen and trace a line representing a days movement for yourself, I mean pedestrian movement from the moment you come down the stairs in the morning, until you go back up them at night, everything you would do if you're in our imaginary house for a day. Trips to the kitchen for food, to the toilet, etc etc, literally everything, every movement you would make in a whole day and I'll do the same with a green pen." "What's this about?" "Well by doing this we can see where the doors should be, which way they should be hinged and where the light switches need to be." "OK you pour a glass and I'll have a go." Once they had both done this it was clear that major adjustments were needed to the floor plan, rooms were nudged this way and that to reduce unnecessary pedestrian traffic, on the second version of the house this reduction had been accomplished and they were able to decide on which side the internal doors were to hang and where to place the light switches and power sockets. They repeated this process with different coloured pens on two more imaginary days, made minor changes and felt happy with their design. Mrs Nayland and another elderly long term guest were given blue and black pens and asked to perform the same task, to provide a foot print of an imaginary day, after they grasped the idea and concluded their days, it became necessary to move the downstairs toilet closer to the back door, Mrs Nayland explained,

"When your my age laddie you spend a lot of time drinking tea in the garden and you often need to spend a penny. That's why you got a blue line back and forth across your middle room." Mrs Parks agreed,

"You've got a young persons' house here my lad, when you're our age a loo just inside the door means you don't have to keep on bending to take your wet shoes off." This point was noted and an adjustment was made, also the stairs was changed from a straight flight to a half flight with a turn of one hundred and eighty degrees and another half flight, to accommodate an internal window between study and day room to allow more light into the central part of the house.

Once they were happy with their paper house they search the market place for a site on which to build it.

Nothing suitable was available in and around Dorchester, the sites overlooking the sea to the south were prohibitive in price, the sale of Blenheim Cottage and Liz's grandmother's house had dictated a budget that excluded an ocean view. They started to look North of Dorchester into an area known as the Blackmore Vale and immediately felt at home with the nature of the countryside, this was part of what had also been referred to as Hardy's Wessex. A number of small villages and hamlets scattered across North Dorset's countryside were very soft on the eye. There were no great sways of corn or oil seed rape, but plenty of pastureland, grazing sheep, cattle and woodland, just two days before Liz was due to depart with her camera they stumbled across a derelict farm yard for sale with planning permission, which also had stunning views across the Blackmore Vale toward Duncliffe Hill (exactly the view described by Thomas Hardy which was enjoyed by Sue Brideshead and Phillotson in 'Jude the Obscure') it was on the extreme North West outskirts of Hazelbury Bryan, a village visited in the novels of Thomas Hardy, though he had renamed it Nuttlebury.

Jude explained to Liz that his mother had named him after one of Hardy's characters and that to live in one of Hardy's villages would in part give him a feeling of coming home. They both loved the plot, none of the existing buildings were sufficiently well built to retain so a new structure was envisaged, they paced out the plot, which to their delight was comfortably sufficient to absorb their design. A fee was agreed with the farmer, a curiously named Mr Butterber, hands were shaken and they drove home in celebratory mood.

The very next day Jude employed a local man to convert their design into presentable drawings which were then in turn presented to the local council for approval, as the farm yard already had permission for a new structure Jude did not have to wait until the next planning meeting for approval, the drawings were passed with minor changes to the roof design by delegated powers, and as the farm had for over a hundred years been named Nuttlebury Farm, Jude and Liz were delighted to adopt the name Nuttlebury Farm Cottage for their new home.

Before the drawings had reached North Dorset District Council, Liz had departed with her beloved Camera to Northern Europe. Jude knew her departure would tear him in half for they had been together every day for months, together day and night, through Colombia, Australia and in Dorchester, but it was Liz who was most surprised at her own feelings. As the date of her exodus drew near she became withdrawn and began to suffer poor nights sleep and a loss of appetite. Jude began to wonder if she was ill or pregnant, but she knew the cause of her malaise, she was beginning to feel home sick, even before she had left, she had never been so totally in love with anyone or anything before, the thought of not seeing Jude was pulling her apart, she did not give voice to her emotions until Jude was driving her to the airport, he was full of ideas for the house and for the book, both of which he knew would keep him occupied for the entire summer. It was not until Jude turned conversation to the point where he declared his regret at her parting and how much he would miss her that she began to lose control. He said,

"I've decided I'm not going to stay at Mrs Nayland's, I'll miss you too much there, I'm going to live in the camper on site up at Hazelbury, or shall we call it Nuttlebury, yes why not, and if I'm on site I can keep an eye on things and do a bit of physical work when it needs doing, clearing up, unloading lorry's, loading skips that sort of stuff, I can sit in the van and write when the weathers bad, what do you think?" Liz hadn't heard a word after

Jude had said I'll miss you, she was choking on her tears, and looking away from Jude out of the passenger window. After a few minutes silence he asked,

"You ok?" She looked at him with tears falling down her cheeks, the first tears Jude has seen from her, indeed they were the first tears she had cried in a very long time. The degree to which she was going to miss Jude had surprised her, she had thought herself an island in an impregnable fortress since she had lost her parents in a boating accident as a girl, but this man, this optimistic, fun to be with hard working, ordinary man had knocked down the doors of her fortress, swam across to her island and invaded her, body and soul. At this moment she could understand Anthony and Cleopatra, Romeo and Juliet, Liz Taylor and Richard Burton, she had never imagined such momentous love for another person was possible.

After a brief moment she replied,

"No, I'm far from ok. I'm missing you already, I don't want to go, I don't ever want to travel again without you. I'll tell them during the summer that this is my last assignment, I'll find something else to do with you, you promise me you'll be waiting for me and I'll promise I'll be back as soon as I can." "That's easy, I promise." He replied starting to well up.

"Look what you've done to me, I'm babbling like a soppy teenager, I'm Liz Reese, Paul Simon's Song I am a rock, I am an island, was written for me."

"No your not Liz Reese, your Liz Saunders now and I'll miss you like hell too, but don't throw in the towel yet, it might be something we can do together, or you might be able to get someone to do it for you, sub it out, keep the contract and make some money by staying at home, don't make too quick a decision."

She dried her eyes and clasped his left hand in her right,

"I love you but I don't love what you've turned me into." "I love me to." He replied, for which he received a punch in the ribs.

"Listen we'll sort out a new life for ourselves in the Autumn, we've both got a busy summer, I'll finish the book and get the house started, you do what you do best, you'll be ok as soon as you get there and start working. By the time you get back we will

427

have run out of money, so we will have to make some decisions about work, enjoy your last period of freedom, I don't want you to feel tied down or restricted because of me, and I love you too."

The rest of the journey was spent talking of practicalities and Liz insisting that Jude not change the room arrangements for the new house. The goodbyes at the airport were brief. Liz settled into her seat, Jude had sown a seed in her mind with regard the possibility of sub contracting her brochure work, she also had the beginnings of an idea of her own, she had began to think she would like to hold photographic classes, perhaps at a local college, she knew she would have to put aside her trusted single lens reflex camera and fully embrace the digital age, she had much to ponder on her four hour flight.

Jude returned from London to Dorchester intent on moving out of Mrs Nayland's immediately. He paid her for one more week, packed his bags into the camper van and headed North across the downs through Buckland Newton to 'Nuttlebury', the day following Liz's departure. Mr Butterbur was very accommodating, allowing him the use of an outside toilet and a power point for lighting and heating in the van, should he need it, for a fee of course, he was after all an ex-farmer.

Once he was on his own Jude made things happen very swiftly, he hand collected and delivered all correspondence between solicitors, banks, Mr Butterber and the local council, and was soon the owner of the plot now known as Nuttlebury Farm Cottage with local authority permission to build their home.

When he wasn't driving between offices, groundwork and brickwork contractors and shopping for himself, he was engrossed in writing. Whenever he wasn't occupied with details of the house build he was mentally engaged with one or more aspects of the book, he enjoyed the feeling of power he had over the events and characters in Jayne's Book, the book, his Book.

He had constructed a basic skeleton of the remainder of the novel whilst he was in Colombia, the major events, plot twist and an ending were on paper, and in his mind he now needed to knit them together, the most difficult aspect of the book for Jude was dialogue, he would write and rewrite the conversation between his characters and he would of course draw heavily on his experiences in Colombia, backed up by Liz's many pictures. He was able to vividly recall faces, voices, accents and many expressions of the local people who had been so accommodating and hospitable to both him and Liz, and then of course there were the few occasions when they had experienced genuine menace and felt threatened, these memories too were replayed, analysed and reproduced in a format that would lend itself to the discomfort of Jacqueline Forbes-Brewer. He was convinced that Jayne had stored all the emotion necessary to formulate each and every turn or twist of her plot in her mind, this did not work for him. He needed a foundation, a backbone to work towards, Jude had listed each chapter and its title, and would work on a single chapter at a time, knowing its beginning and where he wanted it to conclude. He found problem in the detail, he was forever grateful to Liz who inspired him to get off his arse and fly to South America, he knew it would not have been possible to seriously attempt to finish the novel sitting at home. The two trips to Colombia had been invaluable, he also had maps, his trusty guide book and reference books on the economy, culture, flora and fauna of the country, as well as a few novels written by Colombian celebrities and those associated with the drug cartels. With this wealth of information, the notes he had made on his visits, Liz's pictures and his previous experiences he felt equipped to do the book justice .Though he felt that anyone who read the book would perceive a change in style between Jayne's writing to his.

When he was lacking passion or inspiration he would try to use the character of other people he had met in his life, his family, various people he had worked with, he would imagine how they would react in the situation he was creating. This pursuit kept Jude busy half the days and all of the evenings, with no television and only the camper van radio which he would listen to last thing at night, he listened to Book at Bedtime on Radio Four at 10.45pm sometimes he would plagiarise a sentence, a phrase or a word from the author, he followed this with news from the BBC world service as he converted the camper into night mode. Another favourite radio programme was Desert Island Disc.

He was able to park the van inside the large two storey stone barn which fronted the property, the ground floor had once been for the exclusive use of wintering dairy cattle and their calves. Jude had swept out the building and opened up the huge two-hundred year old double doors and reversed the van in. This protecting him from the rain and the summer sun, the barn had strong stonewalls which insulated Jude and his vehicle from the heat. This barn doubled as a store for building material keeping it both safe from theft and the weather.

The new building made slow progress at first, but once the foundations had been dug out, back filled with concrete and the superstructure was commenced, progress was impressive. Jude employed only local people, most of whom were suggested by the affable Mr Butterber, he paid cash and encouraged all the traders to work seven days a week, he also laboured for some of the tradesman during the day, to both speed up their process and reduce their price, most trades were paid on a day rate, so the more work Jude did, the quicker the job was done and the lower the price. The exception to this was the electrician and the plumber who were working to a price so Jude left them to it, he laboured with ground workers, bricklayers, carpenters, and roof tillers all of which were glad of the free help, none of which put two and two together and realised the cost of the free help.

Liz had sent him several letters care of The van in the barn, Nuttlebury Farm Cottage, Hazelbury Bryan, Dorset. Jude would sometimes wake to find a letter under the windscreen wiper of the camper, he found it a little unnerving that someone could get so close to him early in the morning on a regular basis without him knowing, so he bought himself an alarm from a nearby rescue centre. His alarm was a two year old English Setter who came without a name, Jude couldn't bring himself to call the bitch Alarm, he looked the word up in his Thesaurus which sat on the dashboard of the camper, the choice was Siren, bell, alert, tocsin, danger signal or warning sound, he chose the first, Siren, which the dog soon reacted to, she slept outside the van but inside the barn. Jude's alarm was soon effective, but never did the postman any harm.

During the day it was as if the dog was connected by a short length of rope to Jude, he enjoyed the camaraderie of the animal and it was clear that Siren had adopted Jude as pack leader from day one. Jude hoped Liz would take to the dog as quickly as they had taken to each other. During the night Siren was happy to sleep next to the van, if any person, fox or badger visited, the dog would live up to its new name.

Jude slipped into a comfortable routine, he would wake at around six thirty, make use of Mr Butterburs' outside facility, in what was a small dairy parlour. Next to the toilet Jude had rigged up a temporary shower, it consisted of a hose pipe with a watering can rose forced into the end of the pipe, this he looped over a timber beam for a cold shower, the small room already had a drainage channel across the concrete floor to allow any surplus water to drain under the door. During many years the room had been used to chill milk in churns and butter, the farm had been famous for many generations for the production of local butter, hence the farmers' name which had been given to the present incumbents great, great, grandfather. Jude never made the connection. This was the only time of day that Siren was a little shy of Jude, the dog was not a water lover.

After a cold shower Jude would brew tea and cook himself eggs on toast, the eggs were sold to him by Mr Butterbur's wife, he cooked them on his makeshift kitchen top, which was nothing more than two scaffold boards propped up on old milk churns, he also had a fridge and washing machine in the barn, all this was powered by the extension lead from the retired farmer which Jude was paying five pounds a week for.

He would then walk Siren for an hour, close by the property was a huge area of common land, called Dead man's Heath, its title given away nothing of its nature, it consisted of several hundred acres of heath, some wooded some covered in gorse, blackthorn and hawthorn, this area was crisscrossed with foot paths that were rarely used by people but often by animals, most mornings it was possible to see roe and monk jack deer, foxes, rabbits, pheasants, squirrels and all manor of wild birds, Siren would love to chase everything she saw, so that Jude usually only glimpsed the fleeing rear of most mammals, early morning along with the dog, Dead man's Heath was a delight.

On returning to the site, Jude would brew a coffee for himself and whichever trades had turned up for the day, he would quickly ascertain if his labours would make a significant difference. If not he would convert the camper into day mode and write, most afternoons he would find an outlet for physical excursion on the site, stacking bricks, moving timber, clearing up, he would spend hours wheel-barrowing rubble from all over the site into a huge pit that had been uncovered by the digger on the first week, the digger had in fact fallen through the thin roof of the pit, it had been a huge urine tank used when the farmyard had regularly milked almost a hundred cattle twice a day. It was when full, pumped onto one of the fields, the capturing of the urine had prevented contamination of the farms' only well. Jude was using the pit to save money on builders skips, the price of each was over a hundred pounds. He estimated that the old urine tank would save him around two thousand pounds, such was the value of a relatively small hole in the ground.

Lunch was usually cold food eaten outside if the weather permitted, dinner was always something hot cooked in the barn on a Webber bar-b-que, Siren was fed just before Jude sat down to his evening meal, At this time of day Jude would normally be reflective on the days accomplishments and usually he would enjoy a huge sense of achievement. The building was progressing well, the super structure was complete in six weeks, it being a chalet style building most of the walls were single storey, excepting the three gable ends which had risen to support the roof, the wall construction he had chosen was to Jude's knowledge unique, with both the inside and outside wall being built of a lightweight thermal block, it was both fast and easy to build with tremendous insulating properties, the outside would need to be rendered and painted later.

Jude's evenings were all spent in the camper writing, he felt he was making good progress with both the house and the book, he couldn't wait for Liz's return. Some evenings he would walk Siren for another hour while he waited for his arms and hands to recover from the punishment they received wheel-barrowing, he would spend the whole afternoon barrowing blocks onto the site and rubble off the site, his tendons in his forearms were constantly being stretched.

He would always finish his day with radio four's Book at Bedtime and the world service news, he would then settle down Siren with a biscuit and convert the camper into night mode. On warm nights, he would now sleep with the camper open, completely trusting in his canine alarm.

The letters from Liz were a great treat, her assignments were going according to plan, she would ask question after question regarding the house, Jude made use of one of Liz's old cameras and sent her pictures of the progress of the house, of his sleeping arrangements, the 'kitchen' and of course Siren, she would sometimes give a forwarding address if she was confident of being at a particular location at a specific time, but if this failed the tour company would usually forward her mail. Her replies became more and more excited regarding the house build and she longed to meet Siren, but heavily criticised his choice of name, 'What was he thinking of, poor bloody dog', she said she was homesick, for a home she had never seen and what stage would it be at when she returned.? Jude replied that he hoped the roof and chimney would be complete leaving all the internal works to finish, much of which he planned to do himself. It was the roof that both gave Jude great pleasure and caused him great pain. There were no local roofers available so Jude got a price for all the materials from merchants and a labour only price from a national roofing company who had depots throughout the country. They were the fixing arm of a national roof tile manufacture, their local depot was in Yeovil which he later learned, covered the whole of the West Country.

Having employed a very local scaffolder, his yard being just two miles away, Jude telephoned the roofing company, it was his first call on his own phone, he was now very glad of his own telephone which had been connected into the barn temporary, the local call box had been a pain, in that he could not receive calls, he had waited by the phone box a few times to speak to Liz, but he like Liz found that actually speaking made them miss each other more, they reverted to letters.

The following week the four roof tilers arrived to start work, Jude was impressed, they were fast and tidy workers, he tried to keep up with them but was woefully slow in comparison, he decided to stand back and watch. They had to install six roof light windows in addition to their tiling work. After their third days work the whole roof was felted and half battened ready for tiling, the weather had been dry for three weeks, the building was dry

433

inside and now any future rain could do it no harm, Jude was delighted. He went up on the roof early evening to garner satisfaction from the works to date, he walked up the battens to inspect the lead work around the chimney, he was walking on the battens which were well spaced out to prevent the felt from lifting in the wind, the battens would be in-filled the next day prior to tiling. He was cock-a-hoop with the progress. What Jude did not know was that the tillers had cut out spaces for three of the roof lights and had temporarily covered them with felt and a single narrow batten to protect the building from any possible rain, as Jude pushed off with his left foot to climb further up the roof his weight snapped the batten and he was through the roof. He broke his left wrist as he put out his arms instinctively to save himself. He broke his left leg above the knee as he hit the ceiling joist ten feet below the roof level, and he snagged and left behind his left little finger on two skew driven nails as he fell between the joists on his gravity fuelled journey to the concrete floor. His head had been undamaged on its downward journey, but as his body was twisted on its decent by the loss of the finger his head struck the concrete floor, he lay motionless.

There was no-one on the site except himself and Siren, the dog lived up to its name, she barked at the temporary door to the half built house relentlessly. It was Mr Butterbers' wife, an elderly lady of some sixty-nine years who had on occasion slipped Jude a fruitcake for himself, unbeknown to her husband who would have been quite likely to charge Jude for the pleasure, who eventually found Jude. She had heard the dog barking continuously and had after ten minutes come to investigate, in all it was forty minutes before skilled help was at hand, by which time Jude was conscious but unable to move. Siren was eventually pacified and Jude injected with painkillers and hospitalised.

Mrs Butterber looked after Siren for forty-eight hours until Jude's return. His head had been badly bruised and he had suffered concussion, both his left leg and left forearm were in plaster. The ambulance men who dropped him off could not believe his living conditions, he assured them he was ok and that his wife was out shopping and she would join him later in the day.

Jude sat on the doorstep of the van with his crutches fussing Siren with his good hand knowing exactly why he had lied to the ambulance crew. He wanted to be on the site, it was his home, their home. He felt he could cope, perhaps having a shower would be difficult but he could do the rest. All he could do in a day was to feed himself and the dog, Mrs Butterber helped him with shopping for a consideration towards the cars petrol, he knew this was a Mr Butterber suggestion. He did manage, it was very good that he had only three weeks until Liz would return. He had a hell of a surprise for her and little did he know, she had one for him.

The pain in his wrist and leg were of the low but persistent variety, not too difficult to mask with painkillers, but the pain of the missing finger was of a far sharper more immediate nature, and would not be dulled by drugs. The day after his return to the Nuttlebury Site, Tim Rowbotham, the contracts manager for the roofing company, visited him. He came, he said, to inquire as to Jude's condition but in truth he came to ascertain if Jude held any degree of blame towards his company. He did not, he knew that he should not have stepped onto an unfinished roof, Jude knew the blame was his alone. Jude questioned Tim as to the full nature of his work. Tim explained that he was responsible for pricing work, and getting several gangs of tilers and material on site, on time and ensuring the job was completed satisfactorily and on budget, invoicing the job and chasing the money, he was in fact almost a franchise, the company supplied him with a car, a wage and a continual supply of drawings to price, also he could buy materials at a discount rate from the company, which gave them an advantage in the market place. Jude asked,

"How much knowledge do you need of the roofing industry?"

"Only the basics really that the felt goes on the timber, the batten on the felt and the tiles on to the batten, each gang of tilers has an old hand who knows the crack and a bunch of young labour to do the graft, why do you ask?" "Well once I'm fit again and this project is finished I'm looking for work, I think it would suit me, I've been involved in contracting in both the Forestry and Agricultural industries, you looking for anybody?" "Not right now, but each satellite office has two contracts managers, my mate Andrew is moving up to London at the end of the year, in about six months, I'll put a word in for you, it's the least I can do, I feel a tad responsible for the mess you're in." "Nonsense, my fault entirely, do me a favour and put the kettle on for me will you, we need to talk some more." They did exactly that, Tim spent another hour with Jude, by which time they both felt a degree of comfort with each other, Jude felt that it was rare to develop such a good rapport with someone so quickly, Tim felt the same.

At the end of the week the roof was completely finished, Jude also felt very satisfied with the additional material he had added to the book, he was feeling better about his situation but his movements were very restricted and painful, the missing finger continued to give him more grief than the two breaks. Tim visited early the following week to sign off and invoice the work, after making sure that Jude was happy with the job. He called on Jude at a bad time, Jude was extremely frustrated that his work, the tidying up and general labouring was behind, Siren was badgering him for a walk and he was fed up with his physical restrictions and fed up eating out of tins.

Tim recognised that Jude's anger was misplaced and stayed with him long enough to see him into a more positive frame of mind, he took Jude to a local pub for lunch, which he claimed he could book to expenses, the truth was that he paid for the lunch himself. He had observed in Jude a man he liked, a man he could work with, he knew he was in a slough and wanted to help, he informed Jude that in around two months his work partner Andrew would be applying for his transfer to London as they both knew one of the Ealing managers was leaving and Andrew would not be permitted to move until they had found a replacement, so Tim would then recommend Jude,

"What you've got to do," he said "is get your body fixed and get yourself in a positive frame of mind." Jude thanked him for his concern and his time and assured him that two months were more than enough to get him back on his feet. Tim left promising to keep in touch, Jude did not doubt his word.

He was so pleased that the house was now watertight, but also frustrated that he was unfit to work, though he took great satisfaction in that the book was well on the way to completion.

He knew he needed Liz back more than he had ever needed anything in his life, since the loss of Jayne. He had two more weeks to endure, would he be able to drive to the airport? He would have to practise, his one criticism of the camper had been that it had an automatic gear box, this was now heavily in his favour.

In the last two weeks he did little else but write and drive short journeys. He was OK with the steering, accelerating and braking, it was the signalling that was causing him a problem but he found by placing his left wrist cast on the knee of his left leg cast and by lifting his foot up to tiptoe the knee would nudge the wrist that would in turn nudge the indicator, turning right was no problem. Turning left he would have to do without signalling, he dismissed this problem as he felt it was not as dangerous as turning right, he was content with his driving, he was a little slow to react, but he was happy that it was possible to drive and not be a danger to others, Liz could drive home.

The cast would come off in four more weeks, two weeks after Liz's return, then he could get on with the house, he was disappointed that all the monies he had saved labouring and making sure all materials were well looked after and cutting out waste was now being used to employ a gang to plasterboard and insulate the entire inside of the house. Which was work he had planned to do himself, but he was delighted that the house was now dry, they could work on regardless of the weather. As the plaster boarding was being completed room by room, Jude was chasing the electricians to complete first fix, the plumber was also back to fit the oil fired heating. In the last week before Liz's arrival Jude employed six plasterers to turn the site into a house, they also rendered the outside of the building, and on the very last day before Jude had to drive to Gatwick Airport he had the scaffolding dropped and cleared, it now looked like a house, he still had much to do inside to turn it into a home and the outside to paint but fortunately there were still funds available, but only just.

Jude stood and admired the grey rendered walls, contrasting sharply with the dark wood UPVC windows and doors, all under a red tiled roof, topped off with an ornate terracotta chimney, inside it was far from finished, there was no kitchen, no joinery, flooring, light fittings or sanitary ware, but he felt as he hobbled to the van that much had been achieved in twenty weeks. His last action on leaving Nuttlebury Farm Cottage was to whistle to Siren who readily jumped into the back of the camper anticipating some kind of treat. He had said nothing of his mishap either in writing or on the telephone to Liz, he simply couldn't wait to be with her again, he had he felt a few surprises for her and one shock.

He left the site at ten am to collect Liz from Gatwick at two pm, the drive was for the main uneventful, he was astonished at the number of people who could just stand in the hot midday sun and stare at the stones of Stonehenge, to Jude the ancient monument meant little more than a delay on the otherwise unobstructed A303, yes he believed they were two thousand years or so older than the pyramids of Luxor, and some of the smaller stones he knew had been cut and transported from Wales, but he had sat in traffic jams so often within sight of the famous stones that to Jude they were a sideshow that had over the years cost him dearly in time and patience. He hoped that the next public enquiry in a long list of enquiries would solve the problem, either build a new road or take the stones back from whence they came! On this day, the often slated motorway system of England performed its task smoothly, Jude arrived at the airport with a half hour to spare, he parked the camper, gave Siren a very short walk and a biscuit to settle her down and hobbled on his crutches to arrivals, he was grateful to the airport authorities because of the many adaptions which had been made to entrances, lift and stairways to accommodate the disabled, a category which Jude knew that he belonged to, if only temporary.

He reached arrivals a just ten minutes before Liz was due in. He watched those arriving from the bowels of the airport and scanned the mass of assembled people who had come to meet them, there were those who were overcome with emotion at seeing a loved one, huge smiles of ecstasy and tears of joy, excited grandchildren who were released from their parents grasp at the last moment who would leap into granddads arms, or wrap themselves in grandma's skirts, there were lovers who had missed each other dearly, the half smile hid something much deeper that only the glassy eyes hinted at, tonight, passions

438

would be unleashed that had been denied for an indeterminate period. There were also those who would acknowledge their contact with no more than a curt nod of the head, deliberately emotionless, wishing not to give away any degree of comfort or familiarity and there were those who stood open mouthed in disbelief that their contact had not made it in time to meet them, they would scan the mass of assembled persons desperate for recognition, not knowing what to do next or where to go without their missing companion. And there were of course the loners, the ten or perhaps twenty percent of people who knew in advance that there would be no one to greet them, because there was no one to greet them, there never was, they would hurry through arrivals deliberately failing to focus on anyone or anything least they accidentally share someone else's moment of pleasure, and have to blot it out or erase the moment from memory, this was, Jude felt a sub-conscious protection mechanism 'If I don't see happiness in human companionship then I can continue to deny its existence' and then there were the kind of people who looked like Liz, it is Liz, Christ she's fat, how could she ......? Liz stood in front of Jude, they pointed at each other and both said,

"What the hell?" Liz followed this with,

"You first." "No, no, no, you first." "Jude I insist, you first." "OK I fell through the roof and broke a few things." He waved his left hand showing his lack of a digit, he continued almost accusingly,

"You're pregnant." She winced on seeing his missing finger.

"I am and guess who the father is." She said with a beaming smile, they embraced each other and kissed, pain shot through Jude's left arm from his wrist trapped between them. Liz recoiled,

"I'm sorry."

"It's nothing." He put his right hand on her considerably swollen abdomen,

"Why didn't you say anything?" She pointed to his plastered leg and said,

"Ditto." He replied,

"I didn't want to worry you." "Ditto." "How long have you known?" "I suspected when I left but I've known for sure for three months I'm overdue a scan so it's something I need to sort out quickly, how the hell did you manage to do all this?" Pointing at his cast,

"Never mind that, you're pregnant." "I am, are we going to stand here all day with you accusing me of being pregnant or shall we go home?"

"I've bought home with me, it's in the car park. Yes, come on let's go, there's someone in the van who's dying to meet you."

WINTER 1989

HOME

"I've missed you so much, and I can't believe you're pregnant."
"I can't believe you're a cripple and I've missed me too."

They laughed, Liz looped her left hand through Jude's right arm and they moved slowly toward the camper, Liz pulling her wheeled bag behind her. She asked,

"I hope you didn't damage the roof?"

"Oh no, no problem there, but I haven't yet found my finger."
"Yuk grizzly, I hope I don't find it." "I think probably Siren found it and ate it." "Great, we've got a man eating dog, any more surprises?" "Oh you'll love her, she's good company and I don't think my surprises are in the same league as yours, have you been ill at all, any problems with it." "By it, do you mean our child?" "No, it is the pregnancy, he or she is the child, do you know or have any idea which it is?" "No I don't, I need a scan or ultra sound or whatever it's called, an old woman in Finland last week put her hands on me and told me it was twins, but she was a bit of a witch doctor so I'm taking that with a pinch of salt, and no, other than the normal sickness I've been ok, if I had even a slight problem or worry I'd have come home immediately and even the sickness has eased in the last couple of weeks."

"But you've grown so big in the abdomen how can it not be causing you problems?" "That's not the only part of me that's grown big, you wait till I take my top off you won't believe your eyes."

"I think it will have to wait till we get home, not much room in the van for a cripple, a pregnant woman and a dog, what am I saying the van is our home, until I finish the house, I'm sorry but we're going to be a bit cramped for a while." "A while?" "Well perhaps a long while, I'll get on with the house as soon as I can."
"I can do some now I'm back." "No way, you can't work, your

441

pregnant." "Don't start that over protective fatherly crap with me, it won't wash, I'll decide what I can and can't do with it."

"OK, but stay off the roof." "Shame you didn't listen to your own advice." "I was just checking that the work was up to scratch." "Who was with you at the time?" "Nobody, it was early evening Mrs Butterbur found me unconscious 'cause Siren had been living up to her name." "Christ you idiot you could have been killed." "Don't start that motherly over protective stuff on me it won't wash." He got a dig in the ribs for his reply

"Here we are, welcome home." At the sound of Jude's voice Siren was up on her hind legs and clawing at the side window, Jude opened the van and the dog enveloped them with love.

"Oh Jude she's lovely, she's adorable, but Siren, what were you thinking?" "It's ok she's used to it, you'll get used to it." "I'm sure I will, she's really lovely, now come on let's get back there's something I want you to do, to me." "Then do you mind driving we'll get back quicker if you drive." "Christ that's a good point, how the hell did you get here?" "Carefully, Siren was giving hand signals, I managed the rest." On the drive home, they caught up with each others' stories, Liz had many tales of her adventures and Jude many points of progress and interruptions on the house build, Liz was desperate to view Nuttlebury Farm Cottage, or what there was of it to see. Traffic was slow, to start with it was rush hour time on the M25 which now seemed to last from six am to ten pm, but once they had swung left onto the M3 and past junctions four and five the road seemed to give a sigh of relief, they slipped off the M3 onto the A303 heading west, there were still a few lingerers at the stones but now the sheep outnumbered the 'sheep' as Jude loved to say. They arrived at Nuttlebury Farm at a little after eight thirty pm having stopped briefly for a meal in the services at Andover.

Liz backed the van into the barn as instructed by Jude, Siren was released and immediately ran around in circles barking at anything and everything, Jude fed her which did the trick, she was pacified. He put the kettle on for no reason, just habit, checked that the fridge in the barn was still cool something he did often as the weather was hot and dry and had been for some weeks, he was dependant on it for fresh food and cool drinks, he pulled a bottle of bubbly from the fridge, opened it, poured two glasses and hobbled to the van.

Liz was right he couldn't believe his eyes, she had converted the camper to night mode, opened the sliding side door and was sat facing him, naked, legs open, provocative in extremis. He didn't know where to focus, her breasts were huge and taught as was her abdomen, her labia were glistening, he felt an immediate rising of his ardour and his manhood, he moved toward her handing her a glass of champagne which she drank one mouthful from and poured the rest over her breasts, the cool evanescent liquid further engorging her nipples, Jude downed his glass in one. He set his focus on her eyes, she likewise kept her gaze set to his, he moved forward so that his thighs were between hers, she grabbed for him, exposed him and pulled him onto and into her. The passion that followed was only eclipsed by one previous occasion some two years before at Mrs Nayland's lodgings the first time that they had been naked together. This was remarkable considering Jude's restrictions. They enjoyed a post coital hug and kissed until their pulse rates had recovered to something resembling normality. Liz was first to speak,

"Now you can show me our house, but first I need a shower." "Ah well that's one of our problems." "Jude, tell me we have a shower." "We have a shower." Jude winced, adding, "and tell me it's OK, to make love when in your present state." "Bit late to ask that now lover boy." She could see that it was a serious question that needed a sober reply.

"Yes Jude it's OK, I'll let you know if it's a problem, please just treat me as normal until I tell you I need help or consideration."

"OK."

"Now please can we have a shower." "OK but can I wash the twins?" "Like I said I don't believe it is twins." "Not that, these." He said holding her swollen breast

"OK if you must, I didn't bring you a present I though these would suffice." "Why are they so big so early, you've got what four months to go." "Something like that, I think it must be mother nature stocking up the larder early." "You're not kidding stocking up, they're unbelievable." "Make the most of them they're only yours to play with for three or four months then

443

you're second fiddle, literally." It dawned on Jude at that instant he would be just that in the queue for Liz's attention, perhaps never again would he have her to himself quite as he did now, he chided himself, too late for that now, it was he who had wrote the note, 'Marry you, have a family, live happily ever after' and it was he who had caused the pregnancy, but he felt in that moment that he had lost something, not something that you put in a box or buy from a shop but something was lessened. He looked into her eyes and saw and felt love at a depth he had not previously experienced, it coursed through his body and almost by mistake exposed itself as a regaining of his erection.

"I love you so much." He said, She smiled replying,

"I can see that but just at the moment I'd love a shower even more." "A cold shower." "Any kind of shower lead the way." She said holding out her hands. He was still standing as he had been throughout their passionate physical encounter, his left leg was becoming increasingly uncomfortable as he pulled on Liz's hands to help raise her from the vans' bed he received sharp pains in both his left arm and leg, which was a reminder that his injuries still had some distance to go before he was fit again. Liz registered the pain and said,

"Perhaps I should shower on my own, I think you've been on your feet long enough."

"Nonsense I wouldn't miss washing the twins for anything, I've just got to tie a bin bag over my leg and a plastic bag on my arm, no problem." "Jude how the hell have you managed on your own? You should have called me back." "I didn't want to muck up or shorten what I thought might be your last trip on your own."

"What made you think it might be my last trip?" "Last trip on your own, not last trip, if you're going again I'm coming with you, it was horrible being without you even with a house to build and a book to write, I wouldn't want to try it without such massive distractions." "That's odd 'cause I've already decided it was my last trip accompanied or alone, I know what I want to do I'll go through it with you later but now, that shower." They wrapped towelling robes around themselves, pacified Siren and walked across the courtyard that separated the barn from the house, kicked off their shoes outside the shower and went inside. Jude had cleaned it as best he could and given the un-plastered brickwork of the small room two coats of white emulsion paint, but there was no disguising the fact that the old dairy parlour was nothing less than a very crude attempt at a shower. They hung their gowns on two nails in the tiny alcove that had once housed a stone sink and Jude released the flow of water by undoing a stopcock that he had installed into the run of hosepipe. Liz shrieked, the water was direct from the mains and stone cold, she continued to shriek and grabbed for Jude, they hugged each other and allowed the cold water to wash over them.

"Bloody hell that's cold." "Sorry it was the best I could do, another month and we'll have warm water in the house." "Christ this is enough to bring on premature labour, here grab some soap and warm me up." They washed each other, Jude was amazed at the hardness of her breast and nipples and the tautness of her abdomen and she surprised at his ability to maintain an erection under the onslaught of the very cold water. After they had both had enough of the cold Jude turned off the stopcock, Liz put on her robe, looked around and said,

"There's going to be some changes around here and this showers going to be the first of them." "Can't see what we can do to it really, Paul, the Plumber is back tomorrow, he'll be working in the house another few weeks and we'll have a hot water shower available."

"I don't need hot water, just warm, he won't be working in the house, he'll be fixing up a black plastic water tank on the roof of this crappy little building, that will at least absorb some of the warmth of the day and take the chill off the water, by late afternoon we will be able to have a luke warm shower, get him on it first thing in the morning, now let's get dressed I want to see our house."

"That's a bloody good idea why didn't I think of it."

"Cause you've been sitting here writing a book feeling sorry for yourself." "OK I'll get him on it tomorrow, first thing." "Good we can have a warm shower tomorrow, if the suns out." As they walked back into the barn to the camper Jude asked,

"Tell me about your plans that will free you from your photographic duties?" As they dried and dressed Liz gave a comprehensive reply,

445

"Well firstly we are having a child, so I'm going to be busy during the day, so I want to run some evening classes and I've already writing to Kingston Maurward College down in Dorchester and I'm on a short list of one to run their future Photography classes, starting in the autumn. Maybe one day class and two evenings a week, then I'm pinching one of your ideas. I'll hopefully find a capable student who can do my brochure work and I can earn a bit of money off the top of that, but don't worry I'm never going to be an absent mother. Kingston Maurward have got a crèche for the one day a week and I have a very capable and reliable babysitter for the evenings, you. So hopefully within a few months I'll be able to bring in my share of the finance, plus I'll continue to sell my own work as and when, perhaps some time in the future I'll exhibit, still working that one out, what do you think? And what are you going to do when the house and book are finished, and probably the cash from Gran's house and your cottage have expired?" "I'm impressed, pregnancy is obviously good for you, all of that sounds great you've obviously spent a long time pondering your future, our future whilst you've been away." "Jude I hated being away, I believe I've done some of my best work, but I hated it, ever since I knew I was pregnant it made me more determined to do a professional job, make the best use of my time, I'm not just working for my pocket money anymore I'm working for the three of us, it makes earning money a necessity and a pleasure, and don't give me that bollocks about I don't need to work, you can keep us, I don't want to be kept, I believe I have a talent and I want to use it, enjoy it and pass it on." "I understand that and you have my full support. I've got a possible opening as a contracts manager for a national roofing company, they want a manager in Yeovil in a couple of months."

"Roofing, Christ you've got a bad track record there, what do you know about roofs except how to fall through them." "Its simple really, felt, batten and tiles, in that order and don't walk where you shouldn't, but I won't need to get on many roofs, I'll need to organise the guys and the materials how difficult can that be?" "Well that depends on how reliable the guys and the suppliers are, is the job in the bag?" "Not yet no, I've got to get rid of these casts and get fit, but the job if I get it comes with a car and a mobile phone, both of which would be a bonus."

"A mobile phone you said you'd never have one, what did you call them? An unnecessary and expensive modern accessory."

"If it comes with the job, I'll take it." "Hypocrite." "And it'll be good for keeping in touch with you in the later stages of your pregnancy." "Oh I'm already convinced of their usefulness. When I establish an income I'll get one myself, come on show me our house it looks lovely from the outside." Liz was astonished at the progress, she was amazed that the house was dry and delighted with the view from the rooms at the back of the house, the kitchen, lounge and main bedroom,

"Oh Jude it's fabulous and it's nearly finished."

"I'm glad you think so but there's still a bit to do." "It's only the kitchen, electrics, plumbing and decorative stuff, how long do you think?" "A couple of months I guess, six weeks if I could start work tomorrow." "Well I can, what should I do?" "Painting if that's OK with you." "No problem. This is going to be such a lovely place to bring up kids, all that space out there and that view, will you be the sort of Dad who builds swings and a tree house?" "You bet 'cha but I'll finish this house first, do you want to move in now, put a couple of mattresses on the floor?" "No let's stay in the van until it's finished I quite like the cosiness of the van, it is safe here? Any problems?" "Nothing yet, but it's the reason I got us an alarm." "You've put in an alarm?" "Yes she's called Siren and she works. The postman used to be able to put your letters under the windscreen wipers of the van without me waking up, not anymore." "The ridiculous name makes a little bit of sense now." "She great" he adds jokingly "But I hope she hasn't connected her finger treat with me." "Jude this place is just superb, how did you get so much done so quickly and shall I just paint everything a cream colour for now then we can think about each room individually when we're living in it?" "Good idea, as for getting so much done, most of it has been a pleasure to work on, had a few long days but once all the paperwork was complete it's been a labour of love." "I can see that, I've got a few ideas for the kitchen and the outside we'll talk them over tomorrow, come on let's make a fuss of ......Siren, I think I can get use to that and how's the book coming on?" "Nearly there, you take Siren for a quick walk, she's missed out in the last weeks and I'll pour us another glass." "OK deal." Liz collected the dog and strode purposely out of the yard, it occurred to Jude that she had no idea where she was going. He couldn't quite put his finger on it but he recognised a change in Liz. She appeared to have gained in both confidence and maturity, he felt that she now knew exactly what she wanted out of her life and that most of it was within her grasp. She had always been a confident person, knew her own mind, Jude felt that now she knew his mind as well as or if not better than he did. He liked the new Liz, he liked the old Liz, but this one he knew he could rely on like only one person he had known before, what had made the difference? The pregnancy, the marriage, the security of the house, or was it himself? He thought that it was perhaps a realisation that the combination of all these new elements in her life had brought her a degree of stability that had been missing, not missed but missing. She seemed to have an air of consummate fulfilment about her, Jude felt that he could hand over any amount of responsibility to his new Liz, should he need to with complete confidence.

He poured himself a glass of champagne and picked up his book, and did as he often did, which was to read the last twenty of thirty pages he had written, on reading these pages something occurred to him, something was wrong with his main character, he went back two chapters and read forward again, this was sufficient to confirm his new suspicion he would ask Liz's opinion, he wrote a short note on the back of his last written page. When Liz returned with a still lively dog Jude handed her a glass of bubbles which she partly drank and then kissed him full on the lips with a soft, lingering wetness which was to Jude both surprising in its intensity and sensuality.

"Mmm, what was that for?" "I love everything you've done here, I love the house, the dog, our cosy little home in the barn and I love you." "Me too, will you do me a favour, while I tidy up our makeshift kitchen and sort a few things out in the van, will you read these last two chapters? I think I've identified a problem, I'd like your opinion." "OK but after that its bed, I'm all in and you must be." Liz settled down in the passenger seat of the camper, her back to the door and her legs bridged over the handbrake and onto the drivers' seat, Jude put Liz's washing in their machine in the barn, made tidy that which he felt was necessary, topped up Liz's glass from the bottle and wandered the site, refilling his mind with tomorrows questions and instructions for the plumber and electrician. He returned to the camper just over an hour later, Liz was asleep in the back he had forgotten how quickly she could read. He saw the two chapters face down on the passenger seat, on the back page under where he had written 'Main character too weak?' Liz had added,

'You're absolutely right, where did you get the idea that all women were feeble minded and compliant, go back and give her some balls!' He knew she was right, they were both right, his Jacqueline Forbes-Brewer needed an injection of Liz's blood. He would go back to the point where he became responsible for her character and base her a lot more on Liz and a lot less on..... Jayne? He wasn't sure where the essence of Jackie had come from, perhaps that was the problem when he thought of Jackie. He thought only of her as an imaginary character, all the other individuals in the book he could identify with, they were based on people he knew, people he had met, Liz had confirmed his suspicion, he needed someone strong to base his heroine on. He looked into the back of the van and focused on the new Jacqueline Forbes-Brewer, he undressed and got into bed with his fictional character.

They were disturbed during the night by two barn owls under the roof of the barn directly above them, whether they were quarrelling or mating they could not distinguish, the owls set off Siren who needed to be subdued. The rest of the night passed peacefully until at six thirty Siren again greeted the postman with a volley of barks. After another hour Liz climbed over Jude to get out of the camper bed she said,

"Did I say I liked dogs?" After she made them coffee she bought one cup to Jude and dropped a magazine on the bed next to him,

"What's this."

"Have a look at the page with the corner turned down." Jude picked up the magazine he guessed that it was written in Arabic. He opened it to the page indicated it was a very glossy and lavish picture celebrating the wedding of Crown Prince Ali Abdul Akbar Mohamid El Salik to his beautiful bride, Jahidar Aleenah Aidhar. "What am I looking at?"

"Look again." Jude looked at the groom dressed in full ceremonial costume complete with sabre, he looked very regal and satisfied and Jude thought very rich, immensely rich. Then he looked at the young woman in plain white with a headdress covering most of her face, only her eyes were clearly visibly, the rest of her face was slightly obscured by the veil, and what eyes they were, they were of the purest sapphire blue he had ever seen, as beautiful as the girl in Perth Airport whom Liz had wanted to photograph. Jude looked into those eyes again, they were unmistakable.

"Yes I think your right, it is the same girl, where did you get the magazine?" "It was in the lobby of one of the hotels I stayed in, had it not been open on this page I would have never seen it, it is her isn't it?" "Yes I think so." "You were right Jude she is obviously a Princess." "Yes and I guess she was a runaway, I can see now why she didn't need your ten bucks," he continued "would you have loved a lavish wedding like that?" "My wedding was better than that, at my wedding both the bride and the groom wanted to be there."

"It was good wasn't it?"

"It was perfect, now get up you lazy bugger and sort out the plumber so we can have a warm shower tonight." "Ok, thanks for the coffee, are you walking Siren?" "Yep I'll do that at least until your un-crippled."

Jude looked again at the girl's eyes before he put down the magazine, they were so beautiful and so deeply damaged with sadness, he felt that he would never forget them.

The day passed much as planned, Liz disappeared in the van to request a hospital ultra sound scan and buy a dozen gallons of cream paint and Jude hovered over the plumber and electrician for a while. Liz's shower was simple and complete by ten o'clock, as it was promising to be another fine sunny day she would get her warm shower. Jude returned to his writing with more enthusiasm than he had had for a few weeks. The ink seemed to him to be released by his pen at a swifter pace than ever before, and his thoughts were becoming more and more positive, there were far fewer pauses than usual, his hand and his mind were in unison. By the end of the afternoon he had neglected both the dog and his body's need for food and he had completely forgotten about Liz's visit to the hospital.

When eventually he did pause to use the toilet he checked the time, she had been gone seven hours, he was feeling both concerned and guilty for his earlier lack of concern, now he couldn't write, he couldn't sit still he paced the site half heartedly checking the days progress, all seemed satisfactory. In truth either tradesman could have made an alarmingly obvious error, Jude would not have focused on it, he was becoming very concerned about Liz's absence. He realised just how valuable the newly available mobile phone could be to them, and made a decision to correct the omission as soon as was financially realistic.

A half-hour later Liz returned she could read the relief on his face,

"I'm sorry, the hospital said that I was six weeks overdue for a scan and that if I waited I could have one today, it was far more important than I thought."

"I'm just glad to have you back, I think we need to look at the cost of mobile phones, I've been tearing my hair out worrying about you two." As he said this he put his hand through the open window of the van and patting her abdomen

"You're wrong to worry about us two." She said. As Jude opened his mouth to reply she added,

"It's us three, it is twins, the old witch lady was right."

"Wow you're not going out of my sight for a few days I don't think I can take anymore of your homecoming surprises, bloody hell, twins." "I know and I don't want to be out of your sight for a long time to come, all this paint in the back of the van should keep me busy for a month or two, how'd it go here today?" "OK I've been writing like never before, my hand couldn't keep up with my brain, it was the most satisfying days writing I've ever had." "That's great, but I meant the site, did I get my shower?" "Of course, let's go try it." "Can we eat first I'm famished, have you eaten?" "No I forgot to eat, I forgot we had a dog, I forgot I had a wife." "That's good, well most of it anyway, I'd love to read today's fertile production." She finished the sentence with raised eyebrows.

"That's a good word to describe it fertile, talking fertile it's you who's the fertile one, twins, I can't believe it." "Yea, how about that a family in one attempt."

"Is there any twin history in your family?" "None, yours?" "No none, we must have done something right." Jude added. After a make shift dinner of sausages and pasta they had a lot of fun in the shower. The water was surprisingly warm and they were both in a playful mood. In fact that crude shower in the old dairy parlour was to be remembered by them both as a short but very exhilarating and stimulating period of their relationship. They joked that Mrs Butterbers' surprisingly colourful hair would turn white if she'd known everything they did in her old butter parlour. They would mimic her tone,

'Shocking it wuz and e wuz a crippled u no, an she wuz with child' 'the fings 'ay got up to, me old Dad would a whipped the pair of 'em'. They laughed knowing no harm had been done, they thought of her and treated her like a dearly loved grandmother. The next few weeks seemed to pass in a moment, Liz was kept busy walking Siren, painting the house inside and out, a task she enjoyed. Jude was engrossed in his writing, he would break for lunch and dinner, which he prepared. Neither of them tired of their task, toward the end of the month everything changed, the fine summers weather they had experienced broke, and the heavens opened up, the electricians and plumbing were finished and Jude finally was relieved of his casts.

They enjoyed one last frolic for old times' sake in the parlour shower but it had been a dull overcast day, the water was not warm enough to be pleasant, they had pushed their luck once too often, their last memory of their play room was not a pleasant one, indeed they went into the house to have a genuine hot shower, immediately afterwards, they never used the parlour again. The next day they celebrated by buying a bed and moving into the house, Nuttlebury Farm Cottage, it was to be their home for many years to come. Within a week of the removal of Jude's cast he finished the book, he was more than pleased with his efforts, he was positively euphoric, it was a task he had decided to undertake three years before and he was delighted with the result. Liz too was happy that he had got the monkey off his back, she asked,

"What now, send it to a publisher or let if gather dust?" Jude replied,

"A little dust wouldn't do it any harm, I've got other fish to fry for a while." He hoped that Jayne would have approved of his work and made himself a promise that he would offer the manuscript to a publishing company in the not too distant future.

His left wrist was now back to normal, but his leg was still a little painful at times, it was the stump of his missing finger that caused him more pain that the two breaks put together, for many months to come whenever he stubbed the exposed remnant of his former digit the pain was both excruciating and lasting. He set too, to finish the interior of the house, he fitted wainscoting board, architrave, doors and laid timber floors, and Liz stained and varnished them behind him, the contrast of the oak timber against the cream walls was, they both agreed predictable and a little corny in its design, but beautiful and satisfying in its application. Now that Liz had thumbed through many brochures and decided her colour scheme for the kitchen Jude could go ahead and purchase and fit the final room, which in all took him another two weeks but they were both pleased with the result.

Liz's pregnancy started to slow her down, she would tire early and wake later in the mornings, the timing of this was convenient for now Jude was gaining in strength by the day, it was as if her life force was being transferred into him.

Liz received confirmation that she would be required to start photographic courses for one whole day and two evenings a week, but not this autumn. The take up on the course had not been sufficient to warrant its inclusion in this autumns' curriculum, but they felt sure that given a whole year's promotion next year it would not fail, it was a blow to them financially. On top of that Tim Rowbotham from the Yeovil based roofing company called in one day to inform Jude that he was sorry, but head office had overruled him and given him a replacement for his colleague, who had indeed jumped ship to Ealing branch, he left saying he would keep in touch.

The atmosphere between them was less than celebratory the day the kitchen was finally complete. Liz's opinion was that he must offer the book for publishing and did not completely understand his reluctance.

Jude did not fully comprehend his recalcitrance either but agreed if things did not improve he would do anything to keep the house, their house, he would not put it at risk. They were fortunate that they had no finance on the house, no mortgage, the monies from Blenheim and Liz's Gran's house had given them all they needed, a new home, trips to Colombia and Australia, and a camper, but it was all but gone and Jude was determined not to borrow from banks.

Jude took a job as a heavy goods driver, delivering milk and cider in aluminium tankers from the West Country to all over Middle England. Most of the milk went up to London, and the cider to Birmingham. He found the work repetitive and spent most of the day on his own in the cab, he used the dead time driving to brush up on his French, his aim was to visit Barbara at least once a year, she had been so pleased that Jude had married again but disappointed that she had not yet met his wife.

The final financial bombshell was an unexpected bill for four thousand pounds from the local Water Authority to allow them to connect their new home into the mains sewage system, the money was needed as a contribution to possible future cost toward sewage farm re-development. Jude fought it but lost, the comment from the local belligerent planning officer the ever-unfriendly Mr Palmer, was that Jude would put in a septic tank 'over my dead body' meant they had to connect into the mains and pay the bill, which wiped them out of funds. Mr Palmer and the local water authority were forever hate figures in the Nuttlebury Farm Cottage household. The result of losing the aforementioned battle meant there would be no furniture, curtains, carpets, light fittings, lampshades and worst of all in Jude's eyes, no mobile phones.

Jude made some makeshift furniture from spare planks and left over floorboards that amounted to a crude table, bookshelves and bedside cabinets, his attempts to make chairs all ended in firewood, at least they would have something to burn in the winter, they also collected the few pieces Liz had stored from her Gran's house. They did buy two white plastic patio chairs, apart from food it was the only purchase they made in several months.

Liz's pregnancy continued without major incident, the morning sickness came back with a vengeance in month seven and lasted into month eight, before it again abated and she then became anaemic which was controlled by iron tablets, Jude was forever amazed at the size and tautness of her abdomen, joint showers or playtime as they both referred to it was eventually curtailed and moved to a more conventional setting, the bedroom. Liz was less active and the lack of monies meant no further works could be done to the house or garden. She was both physically and financially restricted, she was very frustrated that she couldn't plant trees, shrubs and flowers in the garden, which was now a meter deep in weeds, Jude assured her that as soon as funds were available he would hire in a digger and the garden would be transformed, but it was depressing looking out onto a quarter acre of dandelions stinging nettles and brambles.

Jude spent most of his day looking at the vehicle in front, he was driving a heavy goods vehicle governed to approximately fifty six miles an hour, which meant that he spent his day behind or beside another such vehicle. The aspect of tanker driving that he found most odd was what happened to the product if it did not come up to scratch, if he had to take twenty six tons of cider from Somerset to Birmingham to be bottled and labelled as their local brew, the cider had to be lab tested before it was sucked out of the trailer, the test was to ensure its alcoholic content was up to scratch, which was typically six percent. If the result was low the whole load was rejected and delivered to a pig farm on the outskirts of the city, the cider was pumped into a huge length of trough, the pigs would gorge themselves on the liquid, its apple content being irresistible to them until they were so intoxicated they would lay in their own filth and suffer flatulence on a scale he would not have believed possible had he not been there witness to it. Jude thought it strange that the pigs were never sick as humans would be, they would just lay where they collapsed and fart endlessly, most of the rejected loads were milk, it was only rarely that cider of hooch was rejected because of the cost of losing a full load, it was the job of the brewers chemist to ensure that it was a rare event.

After two months of tanker driving and two months of Liz looking out the window at the ever growing weeds they both knew something had to give. They had talked about borrowing from the bank and were ready to offer Jayne and Jude's books for publication. Neither of them wanted the twins born into an empty house, it wasn't yet a home, it required many finishing touches.

They were beginning to despair when the tide turned. Liz had offered some of her photographs she had taken in Colombia to the National Geographic magazine, they were interested in several landscape's, industrial landscapes and portraits she had taken for a major article on Colombia, which was planned for early in the new year. A figure was negotiated and a cheque was received which all but replaced the funds that the local water authority had blackmailed them into paying, they had their first bottle of bubbles for months. They set about the house, light fittings, lampshades, curtains and a nursery bedroom were all fitted out, Jude hired in a digger and the garden was transformed, turf was laid, shrubs and trees were planted, the gloom of a few months of being on their uppers was lifted. In the middle of this euphoria Tim Rowbotham turned up one day whilst Jude was on the M5 to request of Liz that Jude contact him. His colleague Andrew's replacement had not come up to the mark and had been dismissed, Tim needed a fellow contracts manager ASAP.

The next day Jude pulled a sicky, put on his only suit and called in to see Tim at Yeovil, a hasty interview was arranged with Tim's director at which Jude repeated almost to the word a short speech he remembered that Tim had given him when he said that he did not know the roofing industry well. When Jude was asked what he know of roofing he replied,

"I know the basics, that the tiles or slates go onto the battens which in turn go onto the felt, which in turn go onto the rafters, but I don't need to know everything, I need to get the right men and the correct materials on site, on time, to do a competent job within budget, get the site cleared up, the job invoiced as soon as possible and chase the money when its due." He added that he had done this in the forestry industry and in agricultural contracting and that other than technical expertise, where he would learn quickly from Tim, he saw contracting in the building trade as little difference from the agricultural trade, he repeated.

"Get the job done on time within budget get the money in and move on to the next contract."

He had made a solid impression, the job was his, the salary was three times what he was earning as a tanker driver and the job came with a car and a mobile phone, he was cock-a-hoop when he returned home only to find a note that Liz had been taken by ambulance to hospital as she was losing blood, this was as much information as Mrs Butterber was able to give Jude. He rapidly fed Siren and drove over the Downs to Dorchester Hospital where he found Liz resting on a ward, she was OK, the twins were OK, but she was staying in overnight as a precaution, she had lost quite a lot of blood but the pregnancy was safe, they wanted to observe her for twenty four hours. Should the blood loss continue she would have an emergency caesarean as she was into her ninth month, but this was a last option.

Jude was both upset at finding her in hospital and delighted to tell her that he now had a proper job, a car and at last he would get the thing he had sworn never to have, a mobile phone. As he was driving the tankers through an Agency he stopped immediately to both care for Liz in her last month of pregnancy and work on finishing the house, both task he felt he achieved with distinction, in time for their first Christmas in their new home.

The twins Clare and Emma were born either side of midnight on 20-01-90 and 21-01-90 given them separate birth days which they felt was appropriate, as they were not identical twins, they were a double conception as opposed to a divided cell. The birth had been long and difficult, in all twenty six hours, Jude felt for a time ashamed that he had caused Liz's anguish, pain and discomfort, and felt guilt that he could not share her problems, eventually after much gas and air and an epidural the births were natural, the girls were healthy and Liz was in no danger. They both felt so fortunate and overjoyed that the babies were robust, for some time to come all other considerations were secondary. Liz and the twins returned home after forty-eight hours by which time Jude had dressed up the house and nursery in celebration.

From the point when the babies came home they felt as though previously they had been living in slow motion, everything was now in real time, the twins demands were always of an immediate nature and were around the clock, they had visitors from Jude's family, his sister Barbara and husband Jean Pierre arrived from France, not able to wait any longer to see Jude's new family, his mother Faye and father Bob came with Anne his eldest sister, all at a time when sleep was their most important and rarest resource.

After two weeks Liz had got herself and the girls into something resembling a routine and Jude was able to start work, he took delivery of his car and phone and immediately bought a mobile phone for Liz, he was determined to have the ability to contact her at all times.

He took to the work like a duck to water, he was once again travelling throughout the West Country, this time in a car wearing a collar and tie, not in a tractor wearing overalls. His responsibilities were as he had quoted them at the interview. Get the men and materials on site, get the job done, invoice it and chase the payments, all were within his capabilities. Some of the tilers he got on with very well, others, the more experienced ones resented him for they were aware that they knew far more about the industry than he did, he could live with their resentment and he was a quick learner.

Liz and the twins thrived, days turned into weeks and weeks into months, the girls were already showing the beginning of differing characters, spring arrived, the garden began to bloom, as did the girls.

The next two years sped by, apart from the twins continued development and Jude's settling into a comfort zone in his work, this period was punctuated by one horrendous event, Liz required emergency surgery to remove a life threatening ectopic pregnancy. An abnormal pregnancy, which had formed in the fallopian tube as opposed to the womb, the subsequent surgery left her unable to bear further children. She and Jude were pragmatic, they had their own health and two healthy daughters, it was time to count their blessings.

Liz had started to work for Kingston Maurward College and had been delighted to find Sally Tucker a sharp witted and very capable student who took over Liz's brochure work, the twenty two year old graduate could not believe her luck. The fledgling Saunders family of Nuttlebury Farm Cottage had reached a point of relative comfort, the girls were at a local nursery school, Liz had transformed the cottage into a very comfortable home and had begun to grow vegetables and was now keeping both chickens for eggs and for the table, and ducks for eggs and pleasure, money was not a worry, it seemed that domestic bliss was within their grasp.

Jude came home one day in a quandary. A Company in Peterborough called Fast to Last Buildings who provided timber framed ready-made buildings mainly for schools but also for universities and hospitals, were making demands of him. They were well established in the market of supplying flat roof units for classrooms, but wanted to offer a pitched roof option nationally. Their first units had been in the West Country, several schools in and around Exeter had contracted to have their prototype units and were delighted with the results. Jude had supervised the roofing of the first buildings with satisfactory results all round. The company's next two projects were in Essex and Greater Manchester both had gone badly there was water leaking into the buildings and the company was unable to get the roof tilers back to complete the work. They had telephoned Jude in a plea for help, they had a number of orders to satisfy but could not afford any more problems, in short they wanted Jude to supervise all their work nationally and Jude's tilers to do the work. Jude had explained that working within the boundaries of his existing company he could only be responsible for their work in the West Country. This led to a dilemma, the managing director of Fast to Last Building a Mr Brian Peterson was persistent, he wanted Jude and his men and had asked Jude to meet him at their factory unit in Peterborough as soon as he could. After explaining all this to Liz she said,
"OK, spell it out, I'm not stupid but I want to hear exactly what this man wants from you." Jude looked into her troubled eyes, could he do this to her? she had not long recovered from the horrendous ectopic surgery and they were now in a comfort zone, which could see them well into the future, their incomes were as secure as was reasonable to expect and their life was good, but he did fear middle aged mediocrity, selfishly he dived in at the deep end.

459

"In short I think the guy wants me to start my own national roofing company, a small one man operation, he wants to talk to the same person to solve all his roofing requirements throughout the British Isles."

"Shit, I thought you were going to say he wanted you to work for him." "He does but I don't think he wants the commitment of employing me and my tilers, he wants us as sub contractors, I don't think he wants to take the risk of employing us."

"But he wants us to take the risk." "Let me go and talk to him I'll see what his offer is." "Jude I think your scaring me." "I'm scaring me too, I'll talk to him no harm in that." "I know you, you've been thinking about this for sometime, how well do you know this guy, how good are his company at paying their bills? How reliable are your tilers?" As was usual Liz had come straight to the crux of the issue and the last question Jude couldn't answer.

"Look around us Jude, Look at what we've got now, it seems only five minutes ago we were living in a camper van, a cripple a pregnant woman and a mad dog, and having cold showers in the old butter parlour, then we had no furniture, no light fittings only bare bulbs and no nothing for months, please don't lose it, it's not just you and me now it's the girls future to." "I know I know, I'll go and talk to the guy and then we can talk." "You bet 'cha." Three days later Jude visited Brian Peterson in Peterborough and returned with his mind a soup of fear and ambition.

Jude had seen the companies order book, the success of the school buildings in Exeter had swiftly flashed through the local authority network, the buildings were erected so fast by crane that from groundwork's to completion would take no more than six weeks, it would minimise disruption in schools, some schools would have new classrooms appear as if by magic during the school holidays, hence their order book was full for the next three summers. Jude had received payment guarantees but he knew in truth these were only valid if the local authorities were paying the company on time. It was a huge risk, he would have to employ his own men, he felt confident that his best and most reliable tiler Paul Flanagan would come with him and bring his team. He would also have to buy his own materials and invoice

460

his own contracts, initial cash flow was obviously the stumbling block. He explained all his fears and ambitions to Liz who listened diligently and she sensibly wouldn't allow either of them a glass of wine before the discussion was at an end.

"You've seen the company order book?" "Yes they have work lined up for three years not continuous but they can fill the gaps, success brings success." "How can they build a classroom in six weeks, it sounds impossible?" "The units are finished in the factory, all the electrics, windows, flooring and decoration are already done, they crane the forty foot by eighty foot units next to each other, seal the joints and I put a roof on 'em and Bobs your uncle, hey presto a classroom." "Sounds incredible." "It is, it's an exciting concept, the guy who's designed and developed the ideal is a genius."

"What about payments?" "Thirty days after I invoice, guaranteed." "Guaranteed?" "Well that's what Robert Peterson the MD has told me." "Only as long as he's got money to pay you." "Agreed." "What's he going to do if you walk away?" "Find someone else to do the work, advertise nationally for a sub contracting company who will appoint one person to oversee all his jobs." "Why doesn't he employ you?" "He doesn't just want me he wants a roofing company." "What's your gut feeling?" "I think it's a fantastic opportunity it could be the making of us." "Jude getting married, building this house and having the twins was the making of us." "But this will be the icing on the cake, this could give us financial security." "When does he want an answer?" "I've given him my answer." Liz stood up poured the open bottle of wine down the sink and took Siren for a long walk. She was back in time to collect the twins from school but did not speak to Jude. After dinner which Jude cooked and after the girls had had their bedtime story from Jude it was Liz who first spoke. In a tone Jude did not recognise.

"Right, here are the ground rules, you're going for it I know you are, don't even try to deny it I can see it's a fantastic opportunity but I can also see pitfalls, your main problem is going to be cash flow, you will have to pay tilers and pay for materials, fuel and lodgings before you get paid, so you will need to borrow money, no bank is going to lend a new business money without security, the only security you have is our house, I will

461

agree for you to borrow up to fifty per cent of the value of the house, your half, not our half, meaning me and the girls, you should not have gambled with our future. But now you have, make it work, if you work your arse off I'll back you all the way up to fifty per cent of the house, after that you're on your own, and the half of the house that's left belongs to me and the girls if we have to sell it you walk away with nothing, agreed."

"Look Liz I'm sorry......." "Agreed." She wasn't to be pacified, Jude replied in a sober quiet tone,

"Agreed." He knew his unilateral decision had been unfair, he knew he had betrayed his family, it was the first time that either of them had been so inconsiderate of the other. Nothing more was said that night or in the morning, Jude swiftly cracked, he simply couldn't stand it, conversation had never been strained to the point of silence between them before.

On his drive to work he telephoned Robert Peterson to reverse his decision, apologising and explaining the risk was too much for his young family. Robert regretfully understood. The following day Jude received two notable phone calls, one from Head Office asking both him and Tim to visit the following day for a meeting, the other was from Robert Peterson informing Jude that 'Fast to Last' would be advertising for the right man and that Jude could still get him to pull the ad by once again changing his mind, Jude wished him well.

The following day Jude and Tim drove together to the Birmingham head office and were surprised to find all sixty-eight of the company contracts managers were present. No sooner were they assembled than they were given the bombshell that the company was undergoing a restructuring programme and in short they were reducing from thirty-four satellite depots to twenty-six, Jude guessed the rest. As the Yeovil depot was one of the ones to close and as he was last in he would be first out, Tim would move to Bristol which would house three contracts managers in one of the new super depots, it was all about reducing cost, remaining competitive in an ever increasingly difficult market, bla bla bla, Jude didn't need to hear any more, he stood up, handed in his phone and car keys and left the room. He walked to the railway station in a daze.

The following day he sat down with Liz, bought her up to date with his rejection of Robert Peterson's offer and his current lack of employment. This time they jointly decided to take the risk, Jude apologised for his earlier error of judgement and Liz apologised for her harsh ground rules and wasting a very good bottle of wine. They opened another bottle, drank it and went to bed to resolve their differences. Jude telephoned Robert to cancel the advert and agreed to form his own company to look after all 'Fast to Last' contracts, Robert was delighted that he had got his man. Jude was very excited about his future, but also a little sorry that he would no longer be working with Tim, he had proved to be a very reliable and trustworthy colleague.

Jude phoned an accountant who agreed to take him on board, who in turn contacted Companies House and 'West of England Roofing Contractors Limited' was formed, with two equal Directors, with one ordinary share each, Liz and Jude. Things moved very swiftly from this juncture, Jude borrowed just twenty thousand pounds, bought a car and a mobile phone, he spoke to Paul Flanagan his most reliable tiler who was delighted at the prospect of travel and school work as opposed to site work and after another visit to Peterborough to solidify the relationship with Robert, work commenced. The first half dozen jobs came swiftly one after the other, there were two in Kent, one in the Midlands, two more in Leicester, and one at the University of Portsmouth. Jude couldn't believe how well it was going, the work was relatively simple but the vital factor was the building programme. Jude usually had just three of four days allocated to him to start and complete the works so he had to chase tilers and suppliers and keep them to a tight deadline. He was making ten times the money he had been whilst employed. After six months he had paid off the loan and had a similar amount in the company account, cash flow was now no problem, Jude was happy, Liz was wary.

Then came a change of government, the new administration accused the outgoing one of deceiving the country as to the true state of the nations finances, they had been recklessly borrowing and spending money the country didn't have, billions upon billions were being wasted in interest payments to the international monetary fund and to those of the population who held government bonds. Belts would have to be tightened, ministry and local authority budgets would have to be slashed, police, nurses, and soldiers would be made redundant, it was an all too familiar picture of government sponsored boom and bust.

In short many hundreds of school projects were shelved, 'Fast to Last' buildings order book dried up and Jude had perhaps one job every two months it was another dip on life's rollercoaster. Jude was soon back on the motorways of England in the cab of a tanker full of Cider bound for the Midlands, and was reminded that cider gave pigs terrible flatulence.

It was almost three years before the country fully recovered from the austerity measures instigated by the change of government. Three years in which Jude and Liz kept their heads above water with a combination of Liz's photograph classes and Liz taking a little money off the top of the holiday brochure contract, which came to an abrupt end when her student Sally Tucker formed her own business and disappeared with the contract. Jude continued to drive tankers for a local agency part time until eventually the school contracts built up to the point where he could again make it his sole form of income, he hoped he had driven his last tanker.

The twins were now seven and becoming very interesting, demanding and humorous young ladies.

A decade seemed to simply fly by. Liz continued her photographic classes more as a hobby than a necessity, as Jude's business had recorded ten very good years, each one more profitable than the last, for purposes of reliability Jude eventually joined in with his most dependable gang of tilers and worked with them, this kept cost and waste down and wages to a minimum, they travelled the country together staying in lodges, working hard and playing hard, they would often go ten pin bowling or play pool in the evenings much as Jude had done many years before with Kris and Nick, whilst working for Jack Mortimer. He also stood in from time to time for a friend who supplied furniture to the events industry, it was very occasional work and was paid in cash, which proved to be useful pocket money for the whole family.

Their greatest pleasure was to enjoy the mental development of Claire and Emma, they were both bright students who had finished senior school with a fantastic set of GCSE's, they had both developed a terrific sense of humour which Liz and Jude found deeply satisfying, they had also developed a competitive streak, not with the rest of the world but with each other. Which continued to frustrate and annoy their parents, but as Liz would often point out to Jude during one of his bouts of frustration with them, they were bright, attractive and intelligent girls who knew right from wrong, they had a lot to be thankful for.

The four of them had enjoyed good health for the greater part of the last decade and a half, they all had their scars and stitch marks but none of them had any underlying health issues..

Siren had passed away when the girls were twelve, after a short interval Liz brought two Dalmatian puppies home one day, one each for the girls, which quickly dissolved their distress caused by the loss of siren. They all thought that Siren was a bit of a mad dog but 'Itchy and Scratchy' as the twins had named their new canine friends after two characters on the Simpsons TV cartoon show, were completely without a sense of discipline. Only Liz could get anything resembling a proper response from them, they were now five years old and still as 'crazy as a bag of howler monkeys', as Jude often referred to them.

DAY SEVEN

MICHAEL

I enjoy a quite breakfast, Clare and Emma are away and Liz as usual is out with the dogs. Today's Mirror reports that the health minister has taken action in the debate over the shortage of NHS dentists, by telling patients not to pull out their own teeth, is this a decisive minister who actually wants to solve a problem? Sir Paul McCartney is still having legal problems, and has quoted another knight of the realm, Sir Winston Churchill, he quipped, 'If you're going through hell, keep going.' Also a judge has agreed with Zoran Kostic's opinion of his father, who he claimed was insane to leave his £8.3 million fortune to the Tory party 'he would not have left his fortune to the party if he had been of sound mind.' Was this a moral judgement or a political one? Boris Johnson, on the popular news quiz Have I Got News For You, has stated that as he has had his bicycle stolen seven times he should be Mayor of London, Mr Merton replied 'If you can't look after your bike how can you look after London.' In the 'wasteland' that is the second half of the paper there are reasons given why chocolate is better than sex, apparently chocolate cannot make you pregnant, it is not terrified of the word commitment, and never disappoints.

I move quickly on to the Times, it appears that Menzies Campbell has gone as head of the Liberal Democrats, crude oil has again risen to a record price, once again a British solider has been killed by 'friendly fire' in Iraq, what a comfort that must be to his or her family. I further read that researchers have found by repeatedly disturbing fish by use of electric shocks during the night, that said fish who have suffered a disturbed nights sleep will catch up on their sleep at the first opportunity in the morning, surely had they done this to themselves in their spare time they would have reached a similar conclusion, at no expense to the taxpayer. My final curiosity from the Times is that, research suggests that, men who suffer fertility problems because of low sperm quality may be able to improve their chances of fatherhood if they have sex every day! What odds I ponder would I get with the local bookie that it was an all male research team.

I send Emma a text wishing her well on her driving test and tell her that I'll sort her new car out for her as soon as I can. The rain has abated today and the landscape is blessed with the first real frost of the year, the skies are clear and there is a beautiful sunrise, and no new road kill to mar the journey. Whilst crossing the downs south of Buckland, I am often tempted to turn off the main route, to follow the enticing signs, which have such appealing names, I am invited to follow the road to Middlemarsh, Charlton Down, Charminster, Piddletrenthide and Cerne Abbas, the latter boasting a giant cut into a chalk hill which itself boast a thirty meter erection. It is a day today to notice signs that have hitherto eluded me, one is at the entrance to a farm yard and warns of 'Danger, due to free range children and animals', another is advertising 'Casterbridge Boarding Kennels', this one keeping Hardy's memory alive. On reaching the town there is a sign for 'Pre-owned' cars that momentarily holds my attention, I assume that to be second-hand is no longer in vogue.

Today the Hardy statue is dry with just a hint of frost to his bald pate.

Most of the jurors have beaten me to it and are enjoying the fruits of the new coffee machine, which is becoming evermore popular, even with the ushers. The delightfully soft on the eye Dawn (White Linen) is on duty today and as is often the case informs us of a delayed start to proceedings, I take this opportunity to get up to date with Barry (Chaplain) with regard our shared experience of reading Hardy's novel. I then engage with Joyce (matching accessories) with regard the case, we have not as a body discussed the case privately with each other to any degree. She states that she is puzzled as to the authenticity of the girl's claims, she is unable as she puts it, 'To see through the fog.' She is voicing the opinion of most or all of us. I reply that,

"Perhaps today when Michael takes the stand things will become clearer." Joyce has dressed down today in a heavy beige cardigan and full length navy, corduroy skirt, she is not presented to her usual standard, this perhaps reflecting her mood. There is no such conservatism with Hanna (silicone valley) who is cock-a-hoop in a multi-coloured array of skimpy garments, as soon as I'm free she descends on me to thank me for making Geoff, her husband so happy that last night he promised her, her new kitchen and a face lift thrown in for a bonus.

"It's botox here I come." She is a most delightful but vain individual, or is it him?

After an unusually protracted chat with David (the weather man) during which, once we had covered his pet subject, he was eager to learn which species of butterfly I had seen on the wing in France at the weekend, this being his other interest. We were finally ushered into court and without further delay Michael Merryweather was put on the stand.

His appearance has not altered a jot since we first saw him enter the court, last week, the same crumpled brown suit, at least one size to small, the same tightly knotted tie, grey collared unwashed white shirt and stained socks, he has also maintained an un-groomed growth of facial stubble, what my mother would describe as a five o'clock shadow. Michael is clearly very anxious as he leaves his glass cage to take the stand, the trembling in his left leg unmistakable, his hands too are not the steady hands of a young man as he is asked to swear on the bible. I doubt that he has much regard or respect for the Bible, but the extent to which he is shaking is evidence that he at least fears the court and its procedure, if not actually respects it. I believe at this point, despite Michael's nervous state, that he has twelve members of the jury against him, the testimony of the girls was very emotional and fairly convincing, it was not disputed that this twenty-eight year old man was in a hotel room with three fifteen year old girls, and one of them at least, was naked. Perhaps they were promiscuous? Perhaps they led him on? Maybe they were willing participants in a sexual act? But they were under age and he was old enough to know right from wrong, all irrefutable facts.

He is asked to state his name and confirm his address, this he does in a very timid and unselfconfident manner, he is then asked simple, warming up questions. Does he own a certain car? Does he know Holly Banks, Sophie Green and Lucy Cambridge? Did he book into a certain hotel on February sixteenth this year. His

468

replies are simple, quiet answers, this is obviously a prepared and rehearsed, question and answer session from his own team. His female defence council is both treating him and questioning him as if he was a child and his replies are childlike. The questioning is slowly and carefully increased in its intensity, and its seriousness, until he is eventually asked about the physical activities that took place in the hotel room of the night in question. He is now becoming visibly upset, his council continues in a very calm and controlled manner to put questions to him.

"Did you undress Holly Banks?"

"No she did it herself."

"Liar." Is shouted from the public gallery which the judge quickly addresses.

"Did you have intercourse with her?"

"What? I don't understand."

"Did you put your penis inside her?"

"No I didn't want to."

"You didn't want to, Michael there is a naked, young girl in front of you and you didn't want to have sex with her, please explain."

"I didn't want everything to change, we were friends, it always changes if you have sex, it always goes wrong." Michael's answers were artless, they were the responses of a simple mind, each and every member of the jury was having to make mental adjustments, clearly he was not the monster that we had been expecting. His council continued,

"What do you mean by we were friends."

"I use to pick them up after school, they liked my car and they liked my cigarettes, and I would buy them vodka ices, they couldn't buy them, they were too young."

"That's exactly the problem Michael, they were too young, why were they your friends, why do you not have friends of your own age?"

"People my age don't like me, they won't talk to me and they laugh at me."

"Why is that Michael?"

469

"I don't know, it's always been like it, when I was at school I used to hide in one of the cupboards until they had all gone home."

"Why did you like being with the girls Michael?"

"They would talk to me, they liked my car and they liked the things I bought them."

Michael was clearly a very simple undeveloped person mentally, and this was no longer a straightforward case of one party forcing themselves on another. We had all forgotten our word play for the day, there was much to digest here.

Michael's barrister continued to ask him about his relationship with the girls, how they met, when they met, she had calmed him back down. It was as though he were a temperamental musical instrument and she a truly skilled musician, she was able to caress the instrument to produce a tranquil response, or to play more vigorously should she chose to induce a mild storm, but she was always in complete control. As lunch approached she skilfully reduced Michael's level of agitation, but her final words to him were to ask him to prepare himself during the lunch break to be questioned by the prosecution barrister. Just one glance towards him did much to reverse her skilful work of the last half hour. One fleeting look towards him from us confirmed our suspicions, he resembled an un-sprung tiger that could not wait to pounce on his prey.

Hawkeye explained that it was a little early for lunch, but that he did not like unavoidable interruptions in a defendants testimony, so we were free to go, but were to be back sharp at two pm. It was only twelve o'clock so we had time to kill.

After a brief conversation with Thomas (the numbers man) during which I inform him of my road kill tallies for the year, and I compare this years figures with my totals for the past decade, I leave him clearly believing I am just a tad unhinged, he did not recognise the mirror image of himself I had portrayed.

I left the courthouse and wandered down the high street, I passed by the impressive entrance to The Kings Arm's Hotel, which is now I notice one of many in the Best Western chain. I drift into the Tom Browns public house, order a sandwich for lunch and peruse the unusual array of beers on sale, there is Old Rosie Cloudy Scrumpy, Old Growler, Essex Boarder, Tom

Browns itself and Flashman Clout. As tempted as I am, I know I must retain a clear head for the afternoon session. I allow caution to prevail and order a ginger beer, which I drink slowly whilst regretting my choice and I promise myself that I will one day return for a Flashman Clout. The pub is itself adorned with bushels of hops and a husky voiced, dark haired, brown eyed, attentive young barmaid, who I am sure, causes most that are served by her to speculate on her physicality, two portions of which are on display. The pubs clientele give off the impression that they are resident, all seem to know each other, and are all to clearly aware of a new species which has just entered their watering hole and ordered a non alcoholic drink, despite the impressive array of beers available. There are seven males ranging from thirty to fifty, they each join in conversation in turn as if scripted, the subject matter is tedious, but the enthusiasm of those present appears to be genuine. On leaving Tom Browns I enter the Dorchester County Museum on little more than impulse, I pay scant regard to the detailed exhibitions of the county's Jurassic past and the buildings wonderful Victorian structure, my legs know exactly where my mind wants to be. The building is a labyrinth of archways and stairs, but within two minutes of entering its portal I am standing at the entrance to Thomas Hardy's study. I am prevented from entering his study by a huge piece of plate glass, but in front of me, literally just in front of me is the great man's study. Not a replica or a representation, but a reconstruction. There is his desk and chair, his carpet, fireplace, mantle, ornaments, pictures, musical instruments and chess set, there too are the original hand written, bound manuscripts of 'The Mayor of Casterbridge', 'The Woodlanders' and 'Under the Greenwood Tree', plus an original first edition of 'Far from the Madding Crowd', it is an Aladdin's cave to the literary world. I stand in front of a plethora of literary treasures transfixed, inviting some kind of epiphany, I am awaiting the manifestation of a great realisation, or moment of truth. In truth the moment passes silently without occurrence or event, I leave both Hardy's study and the museum as swiftly as I had entered.

As the day is both warm and dry I decide to try the river walk again, on this occasion commencing from the reverse direction to my previous excursion, beginning at the bottom of the high street. After the recent heavy and prolonged rain the water is both fast moving and clear, the river is often punctuated by narrow pedestrian bridges, complete with ornamental wrought iron railings. There are a large number of mallard ducks on the water today, many of them animated, some comically washing in the clear waters of the Frome. There are long, beautiful tresses of red and yellow Virginia creeper hanging to the surface of the water from sycamore trees still green in leaf, allowing the colours of the vine to be sharply highlighted by their variance. On the left bank there are a variety of town houses and cottages, in total contrast to the right there is open countryside and garden allotments. I hear the short, shrill, familiar high-pitched piping of a moorhen and witness at close quarters a majestic mute swan. A pair of domestic looking ducks follow me in a forlorn hope of nourishment, they appear to be part khaki-Campbell and part Muscovy, and are most peculiar in appearance. The allotments are now festooned with the last of the red flowers of the many regimental rows of runner beans, awaiting the first and decapitating severe frost, nasturtiums and late flowering sun flowers are the colour of the day, their heads now lifted upwards to the sky to catch the suns precious rays. Jackdaws are squawking overhead and a pair of magpies are doing exactly what they are best known to do, quarrelling. I am surprised by the appearance of a family of very late season, juvenile moorhens, with little or no chance of surviving the coming winter, it is a reflection of the abundance of food which must have been available this summer for such young chicks to be abroad in early October, I imagine that only artificial feeding from the nearby domestic dwellings will grant these fledglings survival into the next season. The shallow, stony bottomed, clear waters of the southern arm of the Frome is a natural barrier to human occupation, on one side, literally to its bank there is a mixture of aged and modern housing. Some sporting many original features, such as ornate chimneys, occupied dormers, decorative cornice's, mouldings and bays. Others are displaying poor, economical imitations, and pseudo reproductions of these features.

In sharp contrast, to the north side of this swiftly flowing, narrow river is open farmland, grazing sheep, with herons stalking the fields, overseen by crows and buzzards, competing for the same airspace. The Frome is guardian to this landscape and long may it endure. A gust of wind rattles loose a number of dry sycamore leaves, which fall noisily to the tarmac pedestrian way, a number of which are airborne once again temporarily by a speeding, passing cyclist. I cross the water utilising a timeless triple arched stoned bridge, as two quarrelling male mallards speed underneath, the argument is postponed by an elderly woman, who whilst passing discards several handfuls of bread crust. A domestic cat sits by the waterside tantalised by a few small minnows in the shallows, unable to overcome his fear of the water, he is alarmed by my approach and rapidly moves away.

The background noise to the river, is the constant murmeration and whistling of the many mallard ducks, only occasionally does one burst into classical and comical quacking laughter. Curiously a pair of pure white call ducks, partially come into view, they stay almost completely hidden and do not interact with the more animated mallards. The very last of the summers swallows and house martins are skimming low across the fields, gorging themselves on a plethora of recently hatched mosquitoes, in a resolute effort to fatten themselves for the long and arduous flight ahead. A moment before I turn my back on the river to ascend the many steps towards the courthouse I see a grass snake, silently and swiftly with a minimum of effort it slides across the surface of the water. As I still have half an hour before I'm due in court and I do not feel I am prepared for a conversation with Barry (chaplain), Tim (football) of Terry (rugby) I call into the library and study a map of the river Frome, and I find a description of the Rivers local course, eloquent as it is, it is not attributed to an individual.

It reads as follows; The River Frome curiously divides into two on its approach to Dorchester from the more remote northwest. The northern arm of the river steadfastly refuses to interact with the town, acting in a manner betraying shyness of human activity and development, none of which can be said for its southern arm, which both flirts with and defines much of the

473

boundary of the historic town. It first meanders through long abandoned settlements of the Roman town of Durnovaria, after which it prevents the further spread of modern industrial estates by its existence, it slides silently beneath the approach road to the town from the wilder, less occupied north of the county. The river then executes an acute deviation at the weir, only to turn sharply again to recover its original course at Hangman's cottage, it delineates town and country as it passes quietly by the townsfolk underneath majestic, shapely sycamore trees, the clear waters of the Frome provide a perfect habitat for bird, butterfly and reptile alike. Sliding under the eastern end of the ancient high street the river rejoins its timed half and together they leave the town meandering eastward in union. It is not long before the two arms again chose to run separate paths, before finally settling their differences and in harmony they join that great body of water which is known to the wide world as the earth's supplementary greatest natural harbour, Poole harbour, a sheltered watery playground to many, many thousands, be they clad in scales, fur, feathers or cloth, the harbour is and has been a nautical link to the world beyond, since before mankind put pen to paper.

It is refreshing to know that there are people in our midst with Hardy's eloquence, even though they may be similar in nature to their own depiction of the northern arm of the river, modest, hence the aforementioned description goes un-attributed.

I return to the courthouse with no time to spare, John (foreman) still feels it is possible to bring our word of the day into play, he reminds me it is inimical, my dictionary has informed me this means to be, harmful, injurious, or hostile. It is now not difficult to predict an opening, but who will seize the opportunity.

We are all present except Elizabeth (chain smoker) and more seriously Andy (body odour) the court usher, these two are five minutes late and return almost together, unbeknown to us all they have in fact indulged in the pleasures of the flesh in a local hostelry, but there is little or no visible appearance that any such thing has occurred. Other than a slightly flushed completion on the part of Elizabeth and Andy is not wearing socks. It is I believe only Joyce, Hanna and myself who take note of these minor observations, a fleeting glimpse of recognition flashes between us, unnoticed by our colleges. There will be no case to answer for Elizabeth, but for Andy to be late by just one minute, could result in serious repercussions, any such repeat would be terminal for his employ.

We are once again seated facing the open court and all the players are present. Hawkeye gives a warning to the public gallery to remain quiet throughout the proceedings, or risk expulsion. Michael is again led to the stand for further examination. The prosecution barrister rises to his feet, or rather his foot, his artificial limb seemingly no impediment, he tucks his thumbs behind the lapels of his court gown in classical pose, he gives the impression of a man of supreme confidence, who is about to relish a fine victory. He opens with a few gently delivered questions regarding Michael's background, but clearly Michael has been primed by his team, he is agitated and tense, his answers are monosyllabic and are bordering on hostile. His inquisitor cannot restrain his natural instincts, his ratchets up his line of questioning, intimidating Michael with his intensity, verbosity and volume.

"Mr Merryweather you have lied to us all, is it not the case that the three girls did not go willingly with you to the hotel room, you persuaded them, you bribed them with alcohol and cigarettes."

"No."

"It was your idea all along, you lured them into your trap, as a spider does a fly."

"No."

"It was you who paid for the hotel, it was you who set the tone and the agenda, and it was you who pulled the strings."

"No, it wasn't, they had no money, they liked me when I had money."

"It was you who undressed Holly Banks, it was you who removed her clothes for the purpose of having sex with her."

"No is was her."

"You bloody liar." Is broadcast loudly and clearly from the public gallery and to the frustration of the prosecuting barrister proceedings are halted whilst the pin-stripped suited gentleman who issued forth the utterance is forcibly evicted from the court. It was Holly's father, Viscount Alistair Banks, a well educated, and well connected individual of considerable wealth, who has struggled to deal with the ramifications of the charges, and the knowledge of his daughters association with 'pond life' such as Michael.

Michael's inquisitor attempts to regain his command of the situation, he repeats his last question, having set his tone a notch or two up on the aggression scale from where he left off.

"It was you who undressed Holly Banks with the express purpose of having sex with her."

"No it was her." Michael is struggling to remain in control.

"It was you who forced yourself on Holly Banks."

"No."

"It was you who put your erect penis in her mouth."

"No."

"It was you who put your penis inside her, in her vagina."

"No." The barrister's delivery becomes even louder and does not disguise his contempt for Michael.

"It was you who used your tongue on her, it was you who had sex with her and it was you who forced yourself onto her and inside her."

"No no no no no no no no." Michael crying now and his legs are shaking "No, no I just wanted to be friends."

"Michael you're lying, do yourself justice and this courtroom justice and admit the truth, you forced holly Banks into having sex."

"No, no, no." At this point Michael semi-collapses and puts his hands to his chest and throat, his breathing becomes erratic and irregular, he is having a panic attack. The judge raises his hand to prevent further questioning and he request an usher and a police officer to assist the defendant. Michael manages to remain conscious, just, but does not manage to stay on his feet, he slides from our view to the floor of the witness stand. He both needs and receives help, he is taken from the court to allow him to recover. The judge asks all who are present to be patient, whilst the defendant is allowed time to compose himself.

Lynda (menswear) ever sharp and not one to miss an opportunity, slips a note via Dawn (White linen) to the judge, which to Lynda's satisfaction the judge duly reads out to the barrister for the prosecution.

"The jury member wishes forgiveness for the question, but asks if it is necessary to be quite so inimical within your line of questioning." There is a glare from the barrister to Lynda and to follow up a raised eyebrow from Hawkeye also in Lynda's direction, and a congratulatory nod from myself, Thomas, David and John. The delay is no more than twenty minutes and Michael is led back to the witness box, we all brace ourselves for the next round. Michael does not appear to be fully composed, but replies positively to the judge when questioned as to his state of preparedness. The prosecution barrister continues in the exact same fashion from the point where he was interrupted. He appears to believe that to bully Michael is his best strategy.

"Mr Merryweather I want you to admit to yourself and to this court, that you had intercourse with Holly Banks on February the sixteenth of this year at the Wayside Inn in question."

"No."

"Admit it now and all this nonsense can be over with, you just have to admit it and you can be free of this horror."

"Objection."

"Sustained, Mr Fellows please keep your line of questioning to direct questions, do not load your interrogation with veiled threats or false promises."

"Mr Merryweather, have you ever had sex with Holly Banks."

"Yes, once after she was sixteen."

"Where did this take place?"

"In the car, she insisted because I wouldn't do it at the hotel."

"Michael you're lying, we have already heard Holly and her two friends confirm you had sex with her at the hotel, on the night in question."

"No they are lying." Once again up comes the volume and the intensity,

"Mr Merryweather you're lying, you're trying to tell the truth by admitting that you had sex with Holly Banks, but you're lying regarding the occasion, I want you to admit the truth now and tell this court that you put your erect penis into Holly Banks on February the sixteenth."

"No it's you that's lying, I came in here and had to swear to tell the truth." He is in tears again, his breathing erratic, he continues,

"But its you whose lying, why don't you have to tell the truth, why can you say whatever you like?" Struggling to stay composed, to stay on his feet, he looks toward the judge,

"Make him tell the truth, why can he say what he wants, why is he allowed to lie?" Hawkeye ask him to be quiet, he demands he be quiet, he bangs his gavel several times, but Michael is way out of his comfort zone.

"He's a liar, your all liars, you all think I'm stupid, you're all liars."

At this point Michael becomes less coherent, he is using his sleeve to wipe mucus from his face, he is in floods of tears and he then goes into a huge rant about his father, his school friends, his teachers and just about anyone who has ever felt was judgemental of him in his entire life. The repetitive use of Hawkeye's gavel renders the bulk of his comments inaudible to the jury. Michael is removed from the court by two police officers, he is both struggling to be free of his escorts and on the verge of a convulsion. He is for the moment a wretched, untidy individual, seemingly without a friend in the world.

Hawkeye, to his obvious satisfaction with the aid of his gavel regains control of his court. He informs everyone present that Michael Merryweather will in his opinion require a medical assessment to ascertain his suitability to continue with his trial and that he will ensure that the assessment is carried out swiftly, and that there will be no further need of us, the jury today. We should turn up tomorrow not as usual at nine am, but at the later time of ten am. He then thanked us for our attention and we were dismissed at three pm, another early day.

Many of us linger in the jury room, the general consensus is that Michael's anger and frustration were genuine and that every time he is accused of using force, coercion or persuasion he erupts. Yet everyone feels that it is significant that he has now admitted intercourse with Holly Banks, and that she was at the very least naked in front of him whilst she was still fifteen, in a hotel he had paid for with two witnesses, and he twenty-eight.

478

All are inescapably facts and all very detrimental to Michael's defence.

We all drift from the court in two's and three's, all of us seemingly reluctant to depart, with the one exception of Richard (I can do that) who has no doubt shot off somewhere to 'do that' for someone. I am ambling towards the car park with David (the weather man) and Thomas (the numbers man) refreshingly neither of them are engaged in their almost obsessive subjects, but both are voicing for the first time an element of doubt as to Michael's guilt. They are hoping for further conclusive testimony from one side or the other, which I think sums up the feeling of the bulk of the jury.

I know my mind and the way it's leaning, I believe John too is firming his opinion, but I also believe that at least two of the women, Elizabeth (chain smoker, lunch time shagger) and Joyce (matching accessories) are in the opposite camp. I'm not a hundred percent sure of this, but from comments made in the jury room it is not difficult to discern a bias, or a leaning one way or the other, our deliberation to find a verdict will not be so straightforward this time. I part company with my two fellow jurors, with a warning from David to expect the first real frost of the year overnight, and an addendum from Thomas to expect minus four in the rural north of the county, where as the town should escape with no more than a healthy minus two. I make a mental note to never get into a lift with either of these two guys, without at least one swift form of suicide, should it occur that the elevator malfunction.

I pick up two slightly messy cock pheasants on my homeward journey, both for the buzzard feeder, obviously the two male pheasants were so preoccupied with a territorial dispute, they were oblivious to their imminent destruction, and I note a weasel for my annual road kill tally. It is an unusual species to be hit, but sadly the rare occasions when I do see stoats, mink and weasel's are almost always after they have experienced a rather one sided encounter with messrs Goodyear, Michelin or Pirelli.

"No there isn't any post, yes I have heard from Clare, she's fine, she absolutely loved the skydiving and the dolphin swim, go look on the computer screen, she's e-mailed a couple of pictures and yes I have had a shit day."

479

"Go on, tell me."

"I've had to take Itchy to the vets, something stuck in her throat, that was a hundred and twenty quid, and I've just finished cleaning dog sick out of the back of the new car."

"Why did you put her in the back seats, what's wrong with the boot?" As I said this I knew it was coming straight back to me.

"Because there is a heavy gas bottle and two heavy sacks of dog food in there that I'd asked you to take out last night, remember, I picked them up on the way home yesterday."

"I thought it would be my fault."

"It is your fault."

"I said I thought it would be my fault, its comforting to be right even though I'm in the wrong."

"Arsehole."

"I love you too." We come together in a hug.

"Oh it was horrible, she'd puked into the seatbelt sockets and all over the back seats, she must have been shaking her head as she threw up, can dogs do that?"

"She probably sat back in it, I'm sorry, what can I do to help?"

"You can go and get that stuff out of the boot, tell me you love again and get Emma off my back, she wants to drive her new car, poor kid you know she's on half term, she's over the moon at passing her test today, and she doesn't appreciate that your tied up this week and can't, won't help her."

"OK I'll ring Eric."

"She's been out there most of the day cleaning it out and putting her stuff in it, she loves it already and hasn't driven it yet, go talk to her, I'll make you a cup of tea."

"OK thanks I will." I go out into the yard, having not noticed Emma when I drove in, even though both car doors and rear hatch are wide open.

"Hi well done on your test today, any problems with it?"

"Not with the driving or the car, but the examiner was a total creep."

"In what way?"

"Well he was like, totally looking at me all the time, kept like, looking at my legs and boobs, instead of my driving, he was a total slime bag and he like, stunk of garlic, I bet he's a perv'."

"Were you wearing what your wearing now."

"No, I had my new denim mini on, and that red top that you keep telling me I'm falling out of."

"Christ what do you expect, you torment the poor sod and expect him to ignore you."

"Well I didn't want him to like totally ignore me, I wanted to pass, but this creep was just like, staring at me."

"Why didn't you wear something a tad more conservative?"

"Oh its just a bit of a game, we've all done it, my mate Beth' had her test first and she failed, she was like wearing jeans and a high neck top, so the rest of us have worn next to nothing, that's Sophie the other two Emma's, Wendy and me, and we all passed, coincidence? We don't think so."

"You little minx! How can you complain then, when the guy notices you?"

"Look we did it so that the creeps wouldn't take too much notice of our driving, but this creep was like, his eyes were totally coming out of his head, I reckon he was like, imagining taking me back to his punishment basement, have you seen that film 'kiss the Girls'?"

"No and I don't think I want to either, anyway bloody well done, let's forget the creep, how's it going with the new car?"

"I really like, like it, thanks so much, but when can I drive it?"

"I'll ring Eric now, you stay here and you can listen."

I ring Eric Mathews, our local car man, who usually seems to be able to fit in my problems at very short notice, he looks after, services and MOT's all our vehicles, which I guess I do use a bit in conversation with him.

"Hi, Eric its Jude, I've got another one for you, it's a ten year old Clio, for my youngest, to replace the one that had the airlock, its got a leaky brake cylinder, should I bring it to you, what do you think?" I put my phone on to speaker, just as Liz arrives with my tea, it's good for us all to hear Eric's reply.

"No don't drive it, if you need to do an emergency stop the seal could fail and the fluid escape, leaving you with no pressure on your brake pedal and your straight into the arse end of whatever is in front of you, I can't pick it up today, how's tomorrow morning?"

"Hang on I'll ask Emma, Emma?"

481

"I've still like got some bits and pieces to do on it, can he pick it up tomorrow afternoon? I'll be done by then and I'll be over at Sophie's."

"OK, did you get that Eric?"

"Yep, kids ay who'd 'av 'em, OK you text me when she's done and I'll pick it up."

"Cheers mate, and thanks for the quick response."

"That's what you rang me for, see y'a, and make sure you leave the keys in it Emma."

"OK, will do."

With that settled I give Emma forty quid for her first tank of fuel, she just says thanks and takes it without question, for me it's a balancing act to even out the forty I gave Clare, as extra backup pocket money for her Cuba trip. We have always done this with our kids, I know my sister does the same, the kids never ask if their siblings have had the same, they just receive it gratefully. Thinking of my sister I ring Barbara, and again speak to Anne, who assures me that our sister is ok, I get the feeling that Barbara is under house arrest, with her unloving sister as gaoler, I return to the house.

"Liz, I get the impression that Barbara is in detention with Anne, I think I should go out there next week, how are you fixed?"

"I can only come for a day or two, do you know when Jean Pierre's funeral is?"

"No, not yet, I'll call again on Friday, that'll give 'em a couple more days to get some answers and this jury business will be out the way by then."

"How's that going?"

"You know I can't discuss it, but I think it's in the balance, not like the first case which was cut 'n' dry."

"Is all the evidence and testimony done with?"

"Almost, it's mainly the summing up and deliberation left, if tomorrow goes well without delays, we just might get Friday off."

"That will be good, I'm free Friday because its half term, we can go out for the day, we've got a busy weekend, one of us is up to Heathrow on Saturday to collect Clare, Kate and the two oddballs, and Sunday we've got a lovely surprise."

"How can it be a surprise if you know about it?"

"I can't keep it from you any longer, last Saturday just as I was leaving for the airport, Dirk and Anna turned up."

"Wow, how are they?"

"Fine I think, I couldn't talk to them long, I explained that you were in France, they were surprised to meet our babies, they went off down west for a week, but they are coming back on Sunday and staying the night, it was so nice to see them."

"How did they find us?"

"That was the only question I asked them, apparently they did just as you suggested, they traced us via the electoral register."

"That was nearly twenty years ago, how did they remember that?"

"I don't know, but it will be so good to spend some time with them and catch up on all that's happened since we parted company in San Isidro."

"You bet, I can't wait."

"Now come back down to earth for a moment, what shall we do with Friday?"

"OK well lets hope tomorrow goes well, we haven't visited the Eden Project for about three years, how about going there?"

"Actually I fancy Llanhydrock House, which is not a million miles away from the Eden Project, so if we get an early start we could do both."

"OK you're on, I've got to decide weather or not to hang a pervert first, actually a hundred years ago or so in Hardy's era when hanging was common place, his crime would not have been a crime at all, such liaisons were common place."

"What's he supposed to have done then?"

"Good try, I'll talk to you at the weekend, can you have a look at ferry times and opportunities next week?"

"You'll be lucky it's still half term, I think you'll have to drive through the tunnel and if I can I'll fly out to join you, have you thought about if and how your going to get your mother out there?"

"No and I don't want to at the moment, I need to discuss that with Barbara without Anne being around."

"And don't forget you've got your exam down in Liskeard on Monday, so you will need to swot up for that on Sunday night."

"Christ I'd forgotten that, Sunday night I'll be getting pissed with Dirk, it's so good that they found us, and what with Jayne's book, Hardy's novel and biography, and jury service, I've sort of got enough on my plate this week."

"Well you can't neglect that, with the roofing slowing down and you're not getting any younger, that could be the future."

"I tell you what, put a tea towel between my teeth and shove a broom up my arse and I'll look after the house at the same time."

"OK, brush end first? Oh and please don't let Emma down, she's spent all day on that car."

"All day on the inside I'll grant you and piss arseing about with the CD player, and making it look and smell pretty, I bet she hasn't got a clue if there's any oil in the engine, any water in the radiator, or what the tyre pressures are." From Emma behind me comes,

"No and I never will, that's your department, Mum have you got any of those double sided sticky pads, I want to stick some bits and bobs in the back window."

"What sort of bits and bobs? You can't obscure the back window with rubbish, you need to see through it you know."

"Keep your hair on old man, just stuff, anyway you taught me to reverse using the wing mirrors, you said woman like Mum who can only reverse looking backwards shouldn't be on the road."

"Thanks Emma, I owe you one, you couldn't lend me forty quid could you?"

"Nope, I'm skint."

I pour two glasses of red and I then disappear in search of a hot bath, with Thomas Hardy.

DAY EIGHT

EMMA

We had a couple of text from Clare overnight, she is having a whale of a time, or perhaps that should be a dolphin of a time, having now swam with four of them, she's been scuba diving and sky diving, both with instructors, we just have the jet-skiing and the bungee jump to overcome! I feel sympathy for Jean Pierre and wonder how it is that my heart is still functioning normally.

I look up John's word for the day, it is maladroit, which is a new one to me, I wonder if he gets them from his memory or his dictionary, I suspect the former. My thesaurus informs me that maladroit is to be awkward, tactless or ham-fisted, I can't immediately see an opening for this one today, it would be a shame, we haven't missed one yet, I believe Hawkeye is on to us, but as yet he has played along if he is, I believe also that Lynda (menswear) is home and dry if anyone's keeping a score. What am I thinking, of course someone is keeping a score we have Thomas (the numbers man) in our midst. Liz asks me why the Thesaurus is among the breakfast things, I fill her in on our little bit of amusement, she leaves the room with the two dogs leaping all over her as she has the two leads in her hand, muttering something about adults behaving as children and should know better.

The papers today, as with most days have a wide ranging collection of nonsense, I have decided to knock The Mirror on the head after this week, as my father was sadly lacking a deep sense of humour, I'm beginning to think that the elements I'm finding amusing in his paper were perhaps articles which caused him not to pause at all. That being the case, there seems to be little left but overblown, sensational headlines, tittle tattle and an unacceptable bias towards football and celebrity gossip, but for today and two more days at least, I will scrutinise it's offerings, on Wednesday the seventeenth of October 2007, The Mirror claims that Romsey Council in Hampshire is under fire for spending over £58,000 entertaining the Queen for a three hour visit, which included, and there are several complainants, that £5,000 was spent on a new toilet, which she never used, are Her Majesty's toilet habits now of national concern? Also firemen are engaged in using twenty-eight stone/four-hundred pound dummy persons during practice rescues, as it is becoming more and more frequent that they are having problems rescuing the morbidly obese. Odder still, two couples who's babies were accidentally swapped at birth have been told by the hospitals psychologist to 'put gravestone's in their gardens and pretend their original child is deceased', what a simple and thoughtful solution. Moving on, Durex have launched a new range of condom called the performa, which has a mild anaesthetic in its tip, its effect is to prolong ejaculation and has been a great success with the ladies, and a great commercial success, boosting sales by some twenty-four million pounds. A final offering from today's Mirror is a report that a staggering million plus people have now resorted to paying their mortgages by credit card, and financial institutions are now offering one hundred and twenty percent mortgages! Just how low will the banks allow us all to sink in the quagmire of inescapable debt before they talk to us, all these billions of unsecured lending, which is now a fashion, must surely have its day of reckoning?

To the Times, there is much about Ming Campbell and age concern. In New Delhi, health and sanitation experts have informed the seventh World Toilet Summit that they must find ways to provide lavatories for the two point six billion people who do not have access to one, this on the same day Romsey Council have spent five thousand pounds on just one, which proved to be superfluous. There is embarrassment all round at British Airport Authorities annual senior management conference, when someone, opinions differ as to whom, hired a comedienne who's stage name was Pan Am. She dressed provocatively as an air-stewardess, and had a reputation for telling joke's who's subjects include, plane crashes, terrorism and demonstrating lewd uses for duty free lipsticks, and alcoholic bottles. Curiously a restaurant in Cumbria is the first in the country to offer squirrel pancakes, and Wokingham in

Berkshire is said to be the best place to live in England, I'm sure the people of Middlesbrough, which was recently judged the worst place to live would disagree, and London traffic is now the slowest in Europe. And amusingly, Parliamentary under secretaries have turned the tables on their political masters, by overtaking a commons committee that was to recommend MP's be allowed to queue jump all other commons staff in the line up for commons restaurants, post offices, telephone kiosk, photo copiers and all other facilities. Further to this there was a moment of levity, when Lembit Opic, the Liberal Democrat MP who had joined the campaign to overturn the motion, was forced to apologise for using his right of priority to jump the queue to gain access to the crowed room to vote against the proposal. Finally my eye is drawn to an amusing entry in the letters page, a gentleman has observed with alarm that a survey has stated that drinking between seven and seventeen large glasses of wine a week puts him in the 'hazardous' range, but that he is comforted in that if he increases his consumption by just three glasses a week he will lift himself out of danger!

As we have a late start in court today, I finish 'Far from the Madding Crowd' which will be much to the annoyance of Barry (Chaplin) as his ambition was that we would read the novel simultaneously, but I'm sorry to admit, even to myself, that there is a small part of me that likes to wreck other peoples plans, it's not a nice part, not something I'm proud of, but it's there. I don't do such things with malice aforethought, but more I believe to be a little smug, like I said, not a nice part.

With the novel read, I can mentally tick off one of the week's challenges, I glance to the clock, and it is time to be on the road. It is a gorgeous frosty start to the day, on leaving Buckland Newton and climbing uphill towards the Dorchester road, the ever seeing and piercing eye of the early morning sun has failed in its bid to thaw the entire landscape, and has left behind pockets of north facing hoare frost, surely one of natures most handsome and captivating natural features. Huge bushes of blackthorn, hawthorn and elderberry are disguised with a mantle of the purest, white, wintry tines. My imagination, conditioned as it is by my upbringing, with its subconscious Walt Disney influence, fills in the absent details. I see the frighteningly beautiful and terrifying ice queen, the white hart and the frozen magical fountain of life. I am brought sharply out of my imaginings, by a woman in the road in front of me dragging a deer carcass towards her land rover, I stop to lend a hand to swing the lifeless animals body into the rear of the motor, and curse my luck at being just one vehicle too late for a considerable bonus of venison. I quickly ascertain that it is a three-year-old roe stag, and that it was in prime condition.

I continue across the downs, mentally going through the discipline of butchering the carcass, two large shoulders, two superb loins, chops, breast and two substantial haunches, plus fresh kidney, liver and heart, so deep am I in my thoughts of dissection I almost add another roe to this years tally. There are three hinds, clearly confused and panicky in the road, I stop the car and usher them through a gap in the hedge into a recently ploughed field. They are, I imagine, the hinds that belonged to the deceased stag, I see them safely on their way and continue my journey to Dorchester without further disruption. We are an hour later today, Hardy's statue is free from frost.

We assemble in the now all too familiar jury room, Dawn (White linen) is on duty, and Tim (football) is the first to collar me,

"I know your boys have made the final, but it's like a final for us tonight in Russia, its win or we're out of the tournament."

"Oh I think they'll be OK." I say with no intimate knowledge of his subject.

"Terry thinks were done for."

"He's just winding you up, what will be, will be, regardless of what Terry thinks."

"Yea, but it's a bit dodgy, don't you think?"

"They will probably be three up at half-time and then you can relax."

"Christ I hope so." We are interrupted by Richard (I can do that), who is prominently displaying his right hand, which is encased in bandaging and a splint, half way to his elbow.

"Come on then, what you been up to." I say.

"Went to help a couple of lads I know move a piano, for a woman who's husband died, she was selling it and needed to get it into the garage."

488

"So how did this happen."

"I didn't know the bloody thing was upstairs, she wanted rid of it, 'cause it was a constant reminder of him, we got it almost to the bottom of the stairs and it got away from us, wrecked the piano and just caught my hand, pinned it to the banister, apparently I've broken my scafoid bone, I've never heard of it."

"We've all got one apparently." Says Tim jokingly.

"Two actually." Says Thomas (the numbers man), I add,

"How was it left with the woman and the piano?"

"Well I stayed to supervise it, we got it into the garage, by then the woman is in tears, she is all upset at the damage to the plaster down the staircase, and the broken balustrade and banister, but I said don't worry love, I can do that, I gave her my card and Bob's your uncle, every cloud and all that."

"You jammy bugger." Adds Tim.

"Well she will have to wait a couple of weeks, 'cause of this, but it should be a nice little earner, about four hundred quid, which actually was the amount she would have got for the piano." I ask,

"So what happens to the piano now?"

"Oh I told her I could get rid of it for fifty quid."

"You bloody rogue!"

"Yea good 'en it."

My attention is caught by Joyce (accessories), who is back to her usual form today, in snug but not to tight fitting black trousers, floral blouse and a full range of matching ornamentation, the endless hours this woman spends shopping and embellishing herself are not wasted, the overall effect of her clothes and trimmings are quite delightful. At the opposite end of the scale is Lynda (menswear) who has opted once again for brogue shoes, men's grey socks, moleskin trousers that may have belonged to her grandfather, a farmers check shirt and a plain navy v-necked pullover. She would not look out of place at the Dorchester cattle market. I approached Barry and he raises a flat hand in a stop sign gesture, his hand is held aloft for some thirty seconds, he then drops both his outstretched arm and the book he is reading, in what is clearly a definitive action, he too has completed the Hardy novel. I sit next to him and we compare thoughts. Later I serve myself with what is now a quite decent coffee and sit with John (foreman) who is sitting alone and is quietly pensive.

"A penny for your thoughts John."

"Oh hello Jude."

"Sorry if I brought you back to earth there, you were I think miles away."

"Actually I was years away, I was back with my Emily, its been nine years to the day I lost her, sometimes it seems like nine weeks, sometimes its like she was never really there."

"I'm sorry if I interrupted your private thoughts."

"Oh no don't apologise, you merely adjusted the mental wanderings of a silly old man."

"An old man you might be John, but you're not silly, how'd your crossword go today?"

"Oh just stuck on one, I'll catch up with it later." There is something subtly different about him today, same blazer, similar shirt and slacks, but his demeanour is adrift of his norm. He is distant, he is almost in a place that is above and beyond all earthy cares and woes, he seems to be at peace, as though he has solved the great mystery of life.

"You ok John?"

"I am yes, I'm very much OK, Emily came to me in my dreams, more vivid and vibrant than at any time since she died, the dream was so intense I was sorry to wake up, the dream has put all this nonsense that we are here to adjudicate on into perspective, it is just so much froth," he continued "I enjoy the camaraderie of you fellow jurors, and I enjoy the court procedure, but as for the quality of the witnesses and defendants in both cases, really they are woeful people, whose education and parenting have left them high and dry, barely able to converse in the adult world, their dismal command of the English language is matched only by their appalling lack of intelligence."

"John I'm afraid you're sounding like a dinosaur, someone whose time has passed, I'm sorry if that sounds………"

"No, no, don't apologise, you're right, I can remember a time when much of court procedure was conducted in Latin, the process was enriched by such phrases as 'Ignorantia juris neminem excusat' ignorance of the law is no excuse, and 'Res-ipas loquitor, the thing speaks for itself."

490

"Ah your referring to a time long since departed."

"Oh not that long ago, and there was a great one my father heard a few times in his days as a court official, 'Suspendatur per collum, let him be hanged by the neck."

"Now your wandering back to Thomas Hardy's times, I've been swotting up on him these past two weeks."

"Yes I've overheard you and Barry with the yellow streak, discussing 'Far from the Madding Crowd' I saw the book as a not so subtle comedy, extremely descriptive, like all his work, but a little thin on plot, he was a failed architect did you know, only turned his hand to writing because he was unable to take the step from being an assistant to a designer, what a great thing that was for all of us who followed after him, hell of a writer don't you think? Have you read them all?"

"No not all, my favourite is 'The Woodlanders', so descriptive."

"Yes I like it very much, but I'm a romantic at heart, for me it's 'Jude the Obscure 'and 'Tess of the D'Urbervilles'."

"I've read 'Tess 'but not had the pleasure of 'Jude the Obscure' despite being named after the lead character."

"Oh you'll enjoy it I'm sure."

"Changing the subject what do you make of things here today?"

"I don't think the boy's fit to take any more questions, those little trollops have used him, wrung him out to dry, and set all this up as a way of proportioning blame away from themselves, but it's going to be hard work to deliberate, I bet all the woman want to see him 'Suspendatur per collum." I say that,

"I think David and Thomas are leaning that way too."

"I doubt that Hawkeye as you call him will accept anything less than eleven- to- one this time, so I can see a split decision, which is no decision, and then a dismissal or a retrial, another half million pounds down the preverbal drain, when as far as I can see this case is summed up by the phrase 'Flagrante delicto', when the wrong is blatant." He continued "I wish you luck with your deliberation."

"You wish me luck, where will you be?" He laughs and says,

"If I have another dream tonight like last night, I hope I'll be with my Emily, it was quite the most extraordinary occurrence, I could touch her, I could hear her voice, I could smell her, it wasn't just a dream it was a physical experience, I know I'm starting to sound like a cracked pot now, I don't believe in ghost, mediums and séances, but last night was an unprecedented occasion in my lifetime, as criminal as it sounds, I am wishing the rest of the day away, I simply cannot wait to be asleep tonight, should there be a recurrence of the encounter."

"John I wish with all my heart that this coming night does not disappoint you."

"Me too, I can't see much happening here today, if the judge wants a physical and psychological profile on the lad, we could be hanging around all day."

I leave John to use the latrine and refresh my coffee, on my return he is into what looks like an advanced sudoko, so I sit across the room from him between Hanna (silicone valley) and David (the weather man). Hanna is by her extraordinary standards, dressed rather conservatively today, the hemline is almost in sight of her knees and her silicone asset's are less than fifty percent on display, David is leaving a healthy gap between them, least he should get sucked into a life of promiscuity and immorality. I have no such unease and fill the gap between them, in doing so raising Hanna's skirt by my action of sitting down to its normal level, just short of her arse, and there it stays, I'm not going to gawp at her exposed upper thigh, I'm not going to be caught in her net. I'm a fool, of course I am, I do, I believe if John opposite were inclined, he could discern as to the sharpness of her lady shave. It is David who commences a conversation.

"Jude, I think the two butterflies you saw on the wing in France at the weekend, were a very late flying swallowtail, and a monarch, your description was very good, I'd say one-hundred-percent the swallowtail, not completely sure on the other one, dam good sightings though for October." I add that,

"It was quite warm and sunny for a couple of hours, after midday." Hanna jumps in,

"You were in France at the weekend that must have been a tighter fit to get a weekend over there than this bench is." Looking down at her exposed legs, I shift my weight and pull down her skirt, winking in her direction.

"Oh it was just a quick visit, my sister who lives there had a problem, she needed a shoulder."

"Good for you, family and all that." I'm interrupted by a text from Emma, 'U can tell ur man he can have the car anytime, and thanks 4 the money xxx'. I'm pleased that my kids don't do text language to the extreme. We then start a three way conversation, on the pro's and con's of all things French, reaching the conclusion that their bread, wine, and cheese can't be beaten, but that their warmongering and their personal hygiene leave something to be desired.

We are eventually ushered into court, at eleven o'clock to be told by Hawkeye that the defendant has been medically and psychologically examined and deemed fit to attend the court, but deemed not fit to undergo further questioning. He then informs us that in the afternoon session we will hear the summing up for the prosecution, as he the judge has concluded that the members of the jury have heard sufficient testimony, in his opinion to reach a decision. We are then released once again for a long lunch, to give the prosecution adequate time to prepare their final statement.

Once again I find myself with time to kill in Dorchester (or Casterbridge) as I am increasingly becoming to know it as. I wander into town, drift into a fashionable store and purchase a sweat top in an unusual colour for me, the label describes it as crushed strawberry, Emma will think I've 'come out', which I believe is the term in vogue. I then make a spur of the moment decision, I still have almost two hours before I'm needed in court.

I drive the eight miles to Weymouth in twelve minutes and park at the old boat yard, along side a large fishing boat curiously called 'Boy Michael' whose ID initials were CK, which singled it out from all the other boats which were clearly Weymouth based, as they sport the initials WH, being the first and last letters of the towns name. I tried to guess the boats homeport, Cannock I know is land-locked, my best guess is Crannock, which I may have just invented, but it sounds genuine, and Scottish. Other nearby smaller fishing vessels are intriguingly named, Playaway, Lady Helen, Forever Amber and Life of RileyII. On leaving my vehicle the primary sensation is one of smell, there are more than a hundred lobster pots stacked four high along the dockside, their aroma is pungent, several have herring gulls picking at them for scraps of old bait. I stand on the side of the dock and listen, apart from the argumentative gulls the audible backdrop of the dock area is one of angle grinders and welding plants, a number of the boats are receiving much needed repair after an arduous season at sea.

Leaving all things nautical behind me, I walk away from the now empty cross channel ferry terminal, a daily link to the Channel Islands and St Malo, France, It is here I sailed from last Saturday. Today's passengers have long since departed, many hundreds of croissants and full English breakfast will have been devoured. I now have full view of the panoramic sweeping curved bay, with its extensive row of painted, three and four storey guest houses and hotels, the exceptions being the one Georgian, gable ended building and the dominate, twin domed, five story Royal Hotel, doubtlessly named due to Queen Victoria's association with the town. Legend has it that a nearby town lost its name because of Victoria, and her Victorian values, the small town that was for centuries known as Piddletown, due to it sitting along side the Piddle river and at the foot of the Piddle valley, had its name changed fictionally by Thomas Hardy to Weatherby, and more seriously it's name was permanently altered to Puddletown, as it remains today. This was due to the word piddle, which meant clear water in Saxon times being adopted commonly to mean, to urinate, take a leak, or have a piss. This was deemed to risqué for a visiting monarch, so it is believed locally, though it is difficult to corroborate with evidence that the town's name was altered to avoid any possible embarrassment.

As I wander along the front I feel that the town is a little tired, it is in need of a coat of paint and a little TLC, which the towns people will be expecting to be delivered in the not to distant future, now that it has been announced that Weymouth will host the sailing events for the twenty-twelve Olympic Games. There will be much expectation of refurbishment and renewal, a whole new road system is anticipated, and much besides.

Looking out from the terrace of welcoming hotels, food outlets and less attractive souvenir shops and coin gobbling machine arcades towards the open sea, no one can fail to focus

494

on the stark, white chalk cliffs of Chaldon Down, which conceals the famous landmarks of Durdle Door and Lulworth Cove. Apart from two cargo boats way out in the bay, awaiting a favourable tide to silently slide in to unload, the only other visible vessel is a huge tug boat, one of a small number stationed around the British Isles in anticipation of a maritime disaster, or a large vessel with engine failure, which could in turn lead to a calamity. I think of it as a vulture patiently awaiting a stricken carcass for it to feed off. Today the sea is flat calm, the future Olympic sailors will anticipate far more challenging conditions. My wanderings bring me to the base of the elaborately decorated, centrally positioned, gold topped clock, which stands several meters high to commemorate the long reign of Queen Victoria. Slowly ambling, I retrace my steps back along Gloucester Row.

I arrive at Hope Street, where Liz and I rented a small property behind Mutiny House, after Liz had sold her Grandmothers place. I walk with a painted, terraced row of houses to my right, their second story bay windows being a particularly attractive feature. To my left is the harbour which today is fully occupied with boats of diverse shape, colour and size. The myriad of brass ornamental door knockers on the buildings catch my attention, they each nave a nautical theme, there are anchors, lobsters, dolphins, mermaids and ships amongst others. It is a comfort to walk such familiar streets, I am aware that Thomas Hardy himself rented accommodation at West Parade, Weymouth, I keep this in the back of my mind, should I stumble across a commemorative plaque. I notice Terry's (rugby) rope and sail shop, it has an impressive range of goods on offer.

Looking for lunch I walk through the popular area of Brewer's Quay, which today resonates to the sound of filled aluminium beer barrels being unloaded and their empty counterparts being re-loaded. I leave the Quay looking for a quieter spot. Ignoring the temptation to go into the King's Head, the Sailors Return or the trendy Quay Bar, I buy a takeaway lunch and take it into the Nothe Gardens, I am surrounded by memories of being here during my first winter on the south coast, looking for inspiration with Jayne's book, which was before I met Liz and was shoved onto a American Airlines jumbo jet bound for Los Angeles. After my lunch on the move I stroll past the posh marina which is packed full of sleek, modern, powerful boats, these half-million pound plus toys boast far more pretentious names than their lowly fishing cousins, such as Titan and Conqueror, and there are many names suggesting speed and power, Swift'n'Sure, Speed King, White Water and Speed 'a' Way, to mention but a few. Five more minutes walking and all the black windows, polished chrome, and aerodynamic fibreglass of the powerboats gives way to the Radipole Lake RSPB Bird Sanctuary. I had just fifteen minutes to walk into the vast reed bed and much coveted conservation area, which is heartening to see that right here in the town there is a genuine concern for wildlife. In a small way I am reminded of King's Park in Perth, Western Australia. In the very short time I was there I was thrilled to see, swans, mallard, tufted and shell duck, as well as cormorants, shags and terns. I knew that I was now tight for time, as I had watched the antics of the ducks and tern's squabbling for food longer than I should have. After pulling the parking ticket off the windshield wiper, I missed the sign that informed me I had only one hours free parking (unless I was disabled) I drove almost blinkered back to Dorchester, arriving in the jury room with just a few minutes to spare.

The afternoon session commences sharply at two o'clock, Mr Fellows the prosecution barrister stands directly in front of the jury benches, and he delivers his long, long, closing statement. Had he delivered this speech from some distance, I think he may have lost one or two jury members to sleep, but he is so close to us, and is constantly raising and lowering the pitch and tone of his voice, it is both possible to detect that his lunch contained an element of onion, and it is occasionally possible to receive a smattering of spittle, at each and every one of his crescendos. He is not a pleasant man and this performance endears him to no one. The summery of his summary is predictable and concentrates on the events of the night of February sixteenth earlier this year, and two facts. One that Holly Banks and her two friends Sophie Green and Lucy Cambridge say that Michael Merryweather had penetrative sex with Holly banks, and two that Michael Merryweather himself admits to having penetrative sex with Holly Banks. He arrives at these two conclusions from

496

many different directions, but arrive there he does, again, and again, and again, despite his unpleasantness, he is both professional and convincing. He consumes an hour and three-quarters of court time, I believe he deliberately does not leave sufficient time for the opposition to commence and conclude their summing up, so that we are dismissed with his words on our minds. Predictably Hawkeye states that as there is inadequate court time left today for the defence to complete their closing statement, this will be heard first thing in the morning, tomorrow, followed by his own summing up, and then we the jury, would have the opportunity to initiate our deliberations, which he foresaw would hopefully terminate sometime on Friday.

Liz will be as disappointed as I am, there goes our only chance of an away day on our own for some time, perhaps I can persuade her to skip a couple of her photographic classes and come to France for three or four days, who am I kidding she won't let her students down, just for personal reasons.

By the time we are once again briefed not to discuss that which has taken place here today with anyone other than each other, it is a quarter to four, and we are then dismissed for the day.

I join a three-way conversation in the jury room between Elizabeth (chain smoker, lunch time shagger), Joyce (accessories) and Tim (football), all of them are clearly undecided and pull me into their dialogue, Tim addressing me directly,

"Here's Jude, he's a man of the world, which way are you leaning on this one Jude?"

"I think it's a little premature for me to be voicing an opinion that might influence you, we need to hear the summing up of the defence, but I will say this, if I were you I'd concentrate on the testimony of the girls and Michael, remember exactly what they said, don't give to much credence to the script that is being put to us by the barristers, they were not there at the time, they actually don't know any more than we do, they are professional performers, they have the stage, we are the audience, it is for us to sift through their words and reject those we are uncomfortable with."

"Wow that was all rather profound." Replies Tim.

497

"It was a little, sorry I don't know where that lot came from." I replied.

"No, no you're right," said Elizabeth, "and thank you."

"Yes," agreed Joyce, "He's right the legal teams don't actually know any more of the truth than we do, they are merely being paid well to appear decisive for our sake, if the two barristers swapped sides they would be equally convincing, thank you Jude."

"Can I go now?"

"Yes of course, and thank you again." Replied Joyce, with just a hint of extra sparkle in her beautiful green eyes. I was glad to have been of some use, and believed what I had just said, we have to see through the smoke and mirrors of the legal teams, who actually deep down may not be convinced they are on the right or moral side, but we must remember that they are consummate persuaders of public opinion.

I reach the van and turn on my mobile, which immediately reacts, receiving a message from Claire 'Everything great the bungee jump was awesome ☺, jet skiing tomorrow lul xxx' and another from Emma 'When will car b ready?'

OH bugger, I chastise myself, I haven't text Eric, I correct the omission straight away and text to my car man, 'You can take the car any time you like' I then send a very disappointing message to Liz 'Sorry this case is going into Friday, some other time soon please, any post ? xx' I then turn my phone off to conserve its low battery, so I don't receive this further short message from Emma, which would have confused me a little, 'thanks your one of my favourite parents xxx'. This message is stored in my dead phone for my later perusal.

It is unusual to see two magpies lifeless in the road, near a badger carcass on my journey home, I imaging the quarrelsome birds had been too intent on feuding over the remains of the deceased animal, to be sufficiently aware of an approaching vehicle, a magpie was a rare item of road kill, a pair was unique in my experience. A black-headed gull is the only other item to add to my tally today, clearly it is a day for extremely uncommon perished, creatures to adorn the road. I did not retrieve any items this day, my mind was split between, Claire in Cuba, Barbara in France, and the disappointment I felt at having to make an appearance in court on Friday, and ultimately the disenchantment I would recognise in Liz's eyes. She would hide it, she would disguise it well, I might not see it but I would feel it.

I arrived home a little before five pm and I was pleased to see Emma's little green Clio was absent, Eric had moved quickly, hopefully it would be back tomorrow sometime, which would put Emma on a high for the near future, life can be so rewarding for a parent! I walk into the house feeling good, and walk almost into Liz,

"Hi how's you?" I ask,

"Oh OK, its been a shitty day, Itchy is still not right, the washing machine is on the blink and I haven't had time to go shopping, so it's a takeaway tonight, but at least Emma's happy, the problem was obviously a minor one, good old Eric."

"I'm sorry, I don't understand, I text Eric just an hour ago to tell him he could take the car."

"No you text Emma an hour ago to say she could take the car."

"I text Eric, look." I switch on my phone, and whilst it's waking up I add,

"Are you telling me Emma's got the car, she's driving it?"

"Yes, why is that a problem?"

"Yes it's a problem, Eric should have it, not Emma, where's she gone."

"Only over to Sophie's to show it off, she rang a couple of minutes ago to say she was on her way back, Jude, what's the problem?"

"Eric hasn't touched the car yet, the brakes aren't fixed."

"Shit, how did this happen?"

"I don't know, you ring her now, stop her I'll ring Eric."

"Screw Eric, if she's out in that car, she's not safe, ring her, do it now."

"She won't answer me, I've made her promise she won't use the phone when she's driving, she'll think I'm testing her."

"Do it." I call and predictably get no reply, our level of panic and anxiety is increasing, notch-by-notch.

"Jude, how has this happened?" I look at my outgoing text messages, instead of sending 'You can take the car any time you like' to Eric, I've sent it to Eric and Emma, and I now receive the stored message 'Thanks your one of my favourite parents xxx'.

"Oh Christ I've sent the message to Emma and Eric."

"How can you do that, how fucking careless is that?"

"Its careless yes, but easy to do, Eric's company name as on my phone is E M Mathews, so the E M MA of E M Mathews is next to Emma on the key pad."

Another stored message comes in, this one is from E M Mathews, it simply says 'thanks for fucking me about, I'll stick an hour on your next bill'.

"Look Eric came in a while ago to get the car, which way does she use to get to Sophie's?"

"I don't know there's two ways."

"You keep trying to get her to answer the phone, and stop her, I'll go out in the van and hope I get lucky." I add "She should be OK if she doesn't hit the brakes hard."

"And if she does?" Liz's statement goes unanswered, it's not something I want to dwell on. At that moment two large, battered transit vans block the exit from our drive and the neighbour's drive, they are the slating gang, who have been re-furbishing the roof of the large farmhouse next door, for the arsehole of an architect who lives there. As they walk away from their vehicles and turn to lock them, I call out to them.

"You can't park there I need to get out." My reply comes from a man who is like me, climbing a ladder towards mental darkness.

"I'm not fucking moving for anyone until I get paid."

"I told you he was a bad payer before you started, I warned you, now move the van."

"Yea you fucking knew alright, I understand you're a roofer, how come it's not you chasing the bastard for money?"

"'Cause he's an arsehole, I told you he was an arsehole, you shouldn't have taken the job."

"We needed the work."

"You'd be better of shovelling shit for nothing, than working for a wanker like Alex Nash."

"Don't I know it."

"Now move the van."

"Fuck off, I'm going to sort this cunt out first." He along with his three mates disappeared into Nash's house. At this juncture I am fit to burst, my teeth and fist are clenched, if I had the power in my small van I would happily force this clowns vehicle out of the way. I turn towards the house, Liz is running towards me, a mobile phone in one hand and an expression I've never seen on her face, she holds out her mobile to me,

"Talk to Emma, she's rolled the car, I don't know how she is or where she is."

"Emma, Emma where are you?" Between sobs and chocking sounds, she replies as best she can,

"In a f...field, down the.............road from home."

"Are you bleeding?"

"I don't know, I'm sorry."

"Don't be, it's my fault, are you in the car?"

"Yes, I'm sorry."

"Get out, it might burn, can you get out?"

"I don't know, help me please."

"I'm coming, which field?"

"By the old m.......mill, Dad please be quick the c........cows are c........coming, I'm scared." I run to my van, no good can't get out of the drive, she's only half a mile away, I shout at Liz to get that arsehole to move his van and follow me to the old mill in her car. There doesn't seem to be enough time to do ordinary things, my pulse is racing, I have never felt so utterly useless and impotent in my life, I quickly size up my options and run out of the driveway, still talking to Emma,

"I'm coming love, hang on, can you get out of the car?"

"I don't know I'll try."

Are you bleeding?"

"I don't know I'm afraid to look, I'm sorry, I think I've wrecked the car."

"Emma if your backs ok try to get out of the car, it could burn."

"I'm frightened dad please come now, I can't o......open the d....door."

"Try the window, can you open the window?"

"There aren't any windows."

"Christ what has happened?"

501

"I don't know."

"Emma I'm running to you 'cause I can't get my van out, can I put the phone down for a minute, so I can run quicker."

"No, no, no please don't stop talking to me, I have to talk to someone, dad I'm scared, I can't be on my own."

"OK." I gasp, I haven't run at full pelt for a long time, my lungs are hurting, I've started at a pace I cannot maintain, talking is now very difficult, I have simply and very quickly run out of oxygen, run out of power.

"Emma try to get out of the window."

"I can't the cow's are everywhere."

"Emma you've got to try if you can, the car might burn."

"OK but please be here now."

"I'm trying, I'm trying." I pause for breath, my useless body bends forward in a compulsory movement, my hands go to my knees, from my throat to my abdomen my body is in pain, burning pain, I cannot seem to get any useful breath into my lungs, I can cycle thirty miles in two hours, I do it regularly, but it seems I cannot run a half mile. I am distraught, I throw up, my daughter could be dying, bleeding, burning and I am unable to help, she's just a little girl, she was never meant to experience such a thing without me there to hold her hand, how could she suffer such a horror? Without my help, my assurance, my guidance. My throat seizes up, the tears overwhelm me, I have images of Emma burning in the car, burning to death on her own, I recall Kris burning in his combine, these imaginations are too much for me, I know I'm going into shock, my legs refuse to obey my command. I take a few breaths and somehow propel myself forward.

"Dad you OK?"

"Yes I'm just throwing up."

"Dad please hurry."

"I'm trying love, are you out of the car?"

"I'm half out the window, where are you?"

"Just at the bottom of the hill, I'll be two minutes." Then I hear a terrifying scream from Emma, and the phone is dead.

"Emma, Emma, Emma answer me." Nothing, "Emma, Emma, Emma."

502

I force myself on, I can't do this, I can't run half a mile, I feel worthless, I have no value, my child could be dying and I am gasping for air because I have lost my youthful fitness. I turn right at the bottom of the hill and start on the last few hundred yards, Emma and the car are not yet in sight as the mill is in a dip, I can see the buildings roof which spurs me on, I keep screaming her name down the phone but there is no reply. My only consolation is that I can see no smoke rising from where I believe she should be, this is just too much like the death of Kris for me to deal with. There is just two hundred yards more to go, I am receiving pain from most of my body, my lungs and my throat are struggling for air, and I am chocking back tears and mucus, my calves are fighting the pain of oncoming cramp, I am reduced to a fraction of my normal capacity to function, and I am repeating in time to my feet pounding on the road, please, please, please let her live, please, please, please let her live, please, please, please let her live, nothing in my fifty years of living on this planet has prepared me for this.

I give up on the phone and swing both arms as I run, which helps my lungs a little, but does nothing for the deepening pain in my calves, somehow I run through cramp, I didn't know it was possible, I crest a small rise, I am a pathetic figure of a human being, struggling to run, struggling to breath and giving in to the chocking flood of tears that is obscuring my sight. I can now see on my right hand side a destroyed section of hedgerow and a large group of black and white cows, most of them in a clump in the field, four of them on the road. I am forced to give in to the cramp in my calves, I slow down as I approached the damaged hedgerow. I see a Renault hubcap on the ground, but where is she, I force my way between the cattle on the road and the mangled stumps of hawthorn and elder, there is a black car bumper in the field, she is here somewhere. I hear another scream, a repeat of what I hoped wasn't the last ever sound that I would hear from Emma, I shout,

"Emma where are you?"

"Here Dad I'm here." I still can't see her, but I can see forty or more Holsteins Friesian cattle in a group, they are almost forty meters from the road, well into the field, I charge into them shouting and waving my arms, to make myself as intimidating as possible, I notice huge gouges in the field, and a snapped off wheel half buried in the soil, her car had clearly flipped more than once. The cattle split like the Red Sea before Moses, and there in the centre of them is a completely wrecked, windowless Renault Clio, with my little girl on its disfigured roof. I take a deep breath, attempt some degree of composure and go to her. She clings onto my neck, her tears mingling with mine. We maintain an intense embrace for a half-minute; we are clinging to each other in desperate mutual relief, the vehemence of our emotions equal to that of a couple who are embracing in the ruins of their home after a hurricane has ripped their lives apart.

"Emma are you OK?"

"I don't know, I'm sorry dad."

"Don't worry, focus your eyes on my finger."

"What?"

"Just do it." As I move my finger from side to side and up and down she follows it, I conclude that she is not badly concussed.

"Give me your hands." She does as I ask, "Wiggle your fingers." She does this,

"Now wiggle your toes." Which I can see she does, as she is bare foot, bare of shoes but her feet are caked in wet, fresh cow shit.

"OK, your brain, arms and legs are still attached and working, where are you bleeding?"

"Just my elbows and knees I think."

"Are you sure that's all?"

"I think so but everything hurts, oh Dad look at my lovely new car."

"Screw the car, why did you scream?"

"One of the cows nudged me and I dropped the phone in the mud and shit."

I look at her face again, apart from a slight cut on her forehead she looks OK, but her eyes aren't right, her focus is drifting from me, it's going through me, she is not focusing on anything, I hope this is shock and nothing more serious. It is a cold day and Emma is not sufficiently dressed in t-shirt, jeans and bare feet, I give her my jacket as Liz arrives in the car, she walks through the cattle like they don't exist, takes stock of the situation in a split second and picks Emma up from the roof of the Clio, something I would not have thought possible and carries her to her car, announcing to me.

"We're going to hospital are you coming?"

"I don't know I............" Emma interrupts,

"I don't want to go to hospital."

"That's not a choice I'm giving you, Jude are you coming?"

"I don't know I haven't got my breath back yet."

"OK, keep your phone on." With that Emma is put in the back seat, plus a kilogram or two of fresh cow shit, which should tone down the smell of dog sick, Liz gets in the car and they are gone. I lean on the destroyed car, recover my breath and the tears of relief wholly consume me.

Liz is a champion, her priorities exactly where they should be, she was matter of fact, no histrionics or blame, she will be concerned as to whether Emma has any broken ribs or internal bleeding, something we cannot asses. I begin to recover, and look around me, the cattle have lost interest in today's event and have moved to the west side of the field, apart from the four in the road, who are heading in the direction of the Green Man pub. I start from the destroyed section of hedge and retrace the flight of Emma's car. After smashing through the dense hedge of thorns, it obviously flipped end over end loosing its bumper as it took off, it must have landed hard on to the rear of the roof, it is then not difficult to ascertain that it flipped over side to side twice more, discarding both wing mirrors, one wheel and the windscreen, which sits intact on the grass, it finally came to rest on the remaining three wheels, all the windows either smashed or out, all body panels are crumpled, the only part of the roof that is semi-intact is where Emma's head was. Had she not been wearing a seat belt there is no doubt that she would have been maimed or killed, and had another person been in the vehicle they could not have survived. This realisation that we could so easily have lost one or both of our daughters, because I miss sent a text message overwhelms me, I throw up again, even though my stomach is empty, and I cannot control my tears.

Emma sends me a reassuring text on Liz's phone, 'I'm OK Dad, but my ribs are starting to hurt when I breath, so I think mums right, I probably need an x-ray ☹ xxx can you mend the car?'

I telephoned the local scrap yard, their number being recently familiar to me, as Emma's last Clio had been collected by them just a few days previous, he said he would be no more than an hour. I then telephoned a good friend, Steve, he works for me sometimes when he is slack, he says he will come straight away to repair the fence as there was an hour's daylight left, and he will bring his two able bodied sons , who had been school friends of Emma.

I then set about the task of putting all the debris from the car, back into the car, after recovering Emma's handbag, shoes and CD's. The bumper, the windshield, the wing mirrors and the snapped off wheel all went inside the now destroyed and reshaped Clio, it is testament to the strength of the cars body that Emma got out of the car alive. I eventually found a very muddy and shit covered mobile phone that she had dropped when she screamed, it had been trampled by cattle and was of no further use, it then occurred to me that as Emma had, with our approval taken out third party insurance only, the value of the written off car would not be reimbursed, effectively her new car was gone, no more than scrap metal. How long would it be I wonder before she asked me to find her another one? She was blameless for this catastrophe, so I should get on to it, but it would be a sorry day for Liz and I when Emma or Claire next drove away from the house. Poor kid, she only passed her test yesterday and she has already had a far worse accident than anything I've experienced in thirty-five years of driving.

The thought of her flipping from end to end and side to side waiting for the next impact, the one that might switch her off, blacken her world, kept repeating itself in my mind. I was submerged in feelings of guilt and impotence, the knowledge that I was not there to protect her from what I hoped would be the worst horror to ever visit her life was too much for me. I lean on the ruin of the car and experience a few moments of total mental breakdown, a complete collapse of normality, which washes over me like a tide. Leaving me feeling wrung out and utterly spent, I cannot say how long I dwelt in that state.

I was jerked out of my suspension by Steve and his two strapping sons, Andy and Rob, in less than an hour they have put the wandering cows back in the field and secured posts and wire across the damaged hedgerow. During this hour I clear up every minute piece of debris, and Jim Smyth the scrappy turns up with his crane lorry and a suitable length of chain, he drags the disabled car across the field to the hedge, and in the failing light of early evening lifts it onto the truck. As he is doing this Liz and Emma pull up on their way back from Sherborne hospital, it is now two hours since the accident, Emma is calm but still not in focus, Liz is still on auto-pilot. I shake hands with Mr Smyth and tip him twenty quid, I put my arm around Steve in thanks and make him promise to send me the bill, for himself, his boys and the post and wire. It is a promise he never intends to keep, our kids have grown up together, they are simply pleased to help us in a crisis, damn good reliable people.

Emma has a few tears as she sees the disfigured and crippled Clio winched onto the truck, she was so happy with that car yesterday, how is it possible that such joy could be transformed into such despair in twenty-four hours? Liz pulls into our driveway, I get out of the car and walk back along the short drive to close the gate, not something I do often, subconsciously it was probably a defensive act, I was shutting the world out. As I approached the gate the loathsome figure of Alex Nash, the neighbour approached me, instinctively and with a degree of calculation that I would not have credited myself with, I put out my wrong hand, my left, to shake his, he is spouting a muffled and insincere apology. As he puts out his right hand, he recognises that the two hands are like two negative magnets, it gives me the half second I need, I draw my right arm back, fist clenched, he then looks up, my timing is perfect.

Two hours later with my right hand in a splint, curiously identical to that worn by Richard, (I can do that) I once again walk the short length of the driveway to close the gate, after a pleasant interlude and chat with two nurses in the local A & E hospital department. Oddly the same one's that ex-rayed Emma to establish that she had three cracked ribs, I think we will get her something with airbags and ABS breaking next time.

Eventually the three of us are closeted indoors with a good wine by the wood burner, and the full tale of miss sent text messages, a deer in front of the Clio, an attempted emergency stop, a huge swerve at around fifty miles an hour, a loss of control and a roller coaster ride into a field are told.

The three of us are tearful, we are emotional and physical wrecks, but somehow despite such a comprehensive chunk of bad luck, we all voice thanks for our good fortune. Liz adds that an e-mail has come in from Clare, there has been a jet-ski accident, George is in hospital with a broken shoulder and collar bone, Clare was thrown off the back into the water as George hit part of the pier, Kate's mum has been arrested for drunken behaviour, but is now released, they are all ok and are having a couple of quiet days sunbathing by the pool before they return at the week end. After what we have just been through the news is received along the lines that there is no bread to go with dinner, which was for us fish and chips, which I collected on my way back from hospital after receiving treatment for my broken hand, worth the discomfort as my neighbour has a broken nose. I'm not proud of myself, it is the first time since junior school that I have aggressively struck another person, not proud, but immensely satisfied, Emma could have burnt to death in that car wreck, because the arsehole next door is just that, an arsehole.

The three of us are completely spent and all go to bed early, my last comment to Liz is,

"Emma must be more shock up than we realise, she hasn't mentioned a replacement car."

"Oh she did, when you disappeared to sort your hand out, after your little stunt with Nashy."

"She did? What did you say?"

"Not good timing Emma, leave it for your Dad to mention, he's feeling worse than you right now, so just leave it." Both Liz and Emma had terrible nights, horrendous nightmares, bouts of crying and self-torment, it was a very disturbed and unhappy household. Several times during the night we sat with Emma, her nightmares were consuming her, the night was not dissimilar to the one I had spent recently with Barbara in France, both were nights I would love to be able to forget, but unfortunately they would live long in the memory.

508

I gave up all pretence of sleep in the early hours of the morning and instead took myself into the troubled world of Jacqueline Forbes-Brewer and that of her intriguing gaoler, Jhiro de Montaya.

ARREPENTIDO PADRE

Jackie reads that a female friend of hers had become engaged to a minor royal, and as is usual there is talk of a spring election, also the perennial swell of opinion amongst West Country beef farmers, contrary to the population at large, is once again gathering a momentum for a mass extermination of badgers. She is surprised to learn of a number of celebrity deaths. She had known that the ever popular television comedian Eric Morecome had died a short time before she left England, she had at the time wondered, would Christmas ever be quite the same without him, she now learnt that the actor Richard Burton had died of a cerebral haemorrhage at far too young an age. He was a man who's distinctive voice reminded her of her own grandfathers, who's father had been Welsh, bringing the Brewer half of the family name with him, she recalled her grandfathers speech, he had that same gravely mixture of dialect and classical tones. She was also appalled to learn that the Indian Prime Minister Indra Ghandi had been shot dead by her own bodyguards. Her anguish of her exploration of her priceless several months old British magazines continued, a favourite actor of her fathers, Michael Redgrave had apparently succumbed to Parkinson's disease, he was a man Jackie had once met at a function, she recalled his outstanding performance in 'Goodbye Mr Chips', and also Wilfred Bramble the much loved creator of the much despised character of old man Steptoe in Steptoe and Son had passed away. She had had enough of the woe of the obituaries. She flicked casually through many pages of advertising, it was comforting to see such familiar products, including several iconic British names. She also realises that these magazines are full of telephone numbers, they are for companies selling their wares, they are contemporary British telephone numbers, she has taken another small step. She was sitting on the east-facing veranda, enjoying late afternoon shade listening to the spider monkeys an hour before the onset of the early evening rain. She picked up another publication and took a giant leap.

There on page forty-two is a picture of Louise and Peter Gould, she on his arm smiling to the camera, with her home, St' Georges as its backdrop. She can see in the frame part of the ancient Cedar of Lebanon tree, it is to the right of the picture, in her mind she sees the other half of the tree which is out of shot, it contains the remnants of her childhood swing. Above the cosy, offending photograph is the heading, 'New joy comes to house of sorrow', Jackie reads on. 'The engagement is announced of Louise Forbes-Brewer and Peter Charles Gould, the newly appointed chair of the Forbes-Brewer group. Ms Forbes-Brewer describes herself to have been extraordinarily fortunate, to enjoy the support of Peter Gould, to help her overcome the grief of loosing her devoted husband, Sir John and her wonderful stepdaughter Jacqueline. Ms Forbes-Brewer goes on to say', ' with so much going on at the hall at the moment it is a welcome distraction'. The article continues, 'The distraction to which Ms Forbes-Brewer refers, is of course the use of St' Georges hall, the Forbes-Brewer family seat, by a well known television production company to film the fourth and latest series of the ever popular, mercurial, upstairs-downstairs style television drama, 'Marsden Manor'. The decision to switch production to St' George's hall at the eleventh hour was forced on the production company, due to the extensive fire damage suffered at the drama's resident country estate, Middleton Park. Ironically responsibility for the damage to Middleton Park, the countryseat of member of the upper chamber, Lord Matthews of Aylesbury has been put firmly at the door of the very production company, Viscount Productions, that have themselves elevated Middleton Park, 'Manser Manor' to the nations attention. We understand there is ongoing dialog between, electrical sub-contractors, Viscount Productions and representatives of Lord Mathews, one for the lawyers to get their teeth into!' Jackie is pulsing with rage, anyone within ten meters could have heard her say,

"That silly bitch has allowed the world and his dog into our home, my home."

The article continues with the disclosure that as the TV drama is sponsored by a well known company that markets quick snack products, part of the deal is to produce all future television advertisements at the hall, further exposing the previously very private, former home of the late Sir John Forbes-Brewer to the nations attention. The article finishes with a quote from Louise, 'I am extremely fortunate, after all I have suffered to have the devotion of such a caring man as Peter, to find love again, when it was not sought at my time of life, is indeed an unexpected pleasure, and not one I prompted, let it be a ray of light for all those who find themselves in a dark place.'

Jackie is beyond livid, she again speaks her mind, "I I I I I I I have suffered, she doesn't know what suffering is, but she will if I have my way!" There is a footnote to the article, which reads; 'The recently ousted Chairman of the immense Forbes-Brewer Industrial Group, a man decorated in the New Years Honours List, the now Sir Arnold Elliot, wishes it to be known that he still burns a candle for the missing presumed deceased, Jacqueline Forbes-Brewer, Sir Arnold was godfather to Miss Forbes-Brewer. He has announced his intention to continue to make the sum of one million pounds sterling available for anyone coming forward with conclusive information as to the whereabouts of Miss Forbes-Brewer, and he has set up a dedicated telephone line for this express purpose (the number is then quoted with a variation for use outside the United Kingdom).' We are informed that there is a twenty-four hour answering service connected to this number. Similar announcements have been made in journals in the United States'.

Jackie is completely nonplussed by all that she has read, her thoughts and emotions are scrambled. She says to herself, good for you Arnold, stick it to them, they have kicked you out and softened the blow with a Knighthood, the bastards, she is now continually focusing back to the article and its main picture, her family home, and that smug witch in the foreground. She thinks again of Arnold, God bless him, he has given her the missing piece of her puzzle, a telephone number, and one dedicated to her, bless him, bless him, bless him. She now believes she can achieve her dare, she can get back to England. She thinks of Jhiro, she knows he is a good man, she has pangs of guilt for him, looking at the picture of St' Georges Hall, helps her to fully realise exactly what Jhiro's family home and all its history, possessions and memories means to him, it is his St' Georges.

She makes herself a promise that if, no when she gets back to England, the first thing she will do is to invite him to dinner, at her table, in her house, and he can drink her wine and they can talk as equals. The thought of showing him the full extent of her ancestral home excites her. She corrects herself, the second thing she will do is to call Jhiro, the first of course will be to see Louise 'thrown from this house', her former words come back to her with a vengeance.

She now feels more content with her current situation, for she views it as temporary, the magazine article has more than replaced the anti-depressants, missing from her bloodstream. She continues to become more considerate of Jhiro, more often she orders his preferred meals, more often they make love.

She wonders how a man who has relatively little sexual experience, has taught himself to be such a considerate and skilful lover. Now that her pregnancy is clearly showing he is even more considerate of her, she is realising more and more that he is simply a very decent person, caught between a rock and a hard place. She fantasises that when she is home, that perhaps Jhiro could live with her at St' Georges, but knows realistically that he is as welded to his family history as she is to hers, all such fantasies end in confusion.

Once Jhiro is flying again, Jackie, slightly guiltily pursues the use of the sextant. To establish her exact position of longitude is far more complex than her previous calculation. Apart from the sextant it involves the use of a chronometer, an extremely accurate clock, which must be accurate to within three tenths of a second per day, and its rate of gain or loss must be consistent. She has three attempts and produces three differing results, always she is grateful for her constant, the small patch of Pacific Ocean that is her horizon. She is content with her celestial knowledge, but is making mistakes with the heavyweight and confusing calculations, despite her astronomical volume having all the necessary tables in black and white print in front of her. She risks one more clear night whilst Jhiro is away. Always she has to wait until the night sky is just right, if the afternoon rain lingers too long the sky is opaque, if there is a full moon, some of her known stars are absent, if there is no moon she cannot get a fix on her horizon, that oh so valuable clear flat patch out to the west. She needs very little or no cloud, a quarter moon and Jhiro to be away, which since he broke his legs, and now that her pregnancy is acutely obvious, is becoming less and less often.

Eventually on her fourth occasion of trying, which had consumed the greater part of two months, she is happy that her position of longitude is 76 degrees, 53 minutes and 48 seconds west of the prime meridian. Her readings from the sextant were accurate and constant which gave her confidence to continue, but she had been reversing one calculation and inserting a decimal point incorrectly, the two mistakes had compounded to confuse her, and had cost her six weeks.

As she now viewed her occupation of Jhiro's home as temporary, she was significantly more comfortably in her surroundings. She knew that if she could get the right information to Arnold, that she was dropping an immense and extremely dangerous task at his feet, but she knew too that aside from her deceased father he was to her the most trustworthy person on earth.

Her relationship with Jhiro went through a stable, almost playful period, he would choose the evening meal one night and her challenge was to select the most suitable wine, these roles would be reversed the following evening. They both very much enjoyed local river clams, and a small local type of crayfish that Jhiro called, Cahgrejos de Rio, with these meals they would enjoy some of France's finest champagne. Jackie doubted that in the vast underground system of champagne caves at Epernay in northern France, one of the few places she had visited with both her mother and father, there was a better vintage.

The closer Jackie got to making her phone call, the more excitement and guilt she had to suppress. Eventually the day came when Jhiro was away again, she knew she was armed with all the knowledge she needed, she had rehearsed her message so many times, she knew it faithfully, but still she had it written down in the form of a half page, should nerves overcome her. Access to Jhiro's headache room was now a given, as she had learnt where he kept the key, it was on the top rail of a work of art adjacent to the door.

Jhiro had left after breakfast, saying that he would try to come back late afternoon, but that,

"Because everyone wants to cut Jhiro's balls off and feed them to the monkeys, he will probably be back tomorrow." Apart from all the other pressures he was under he was now receiving additional harassment because of his decision to take a non-Colombian into the tunnel. There were growing calls for him to hand his new woman over to Medellin after the birth of his child. It was only a deep-seated respect for Jhiro and his father that prevented an immediate and terminating intervention to his relationship with Jackie. Everyone at the table at Medellin knew his unfortunate history with regard to his attempts to produce an heir, but few or none sympathised with his preference for European women, for this they blamed his father, whom they all held in high regard, for indulging him as a young man. After Jhiro had left the table, his peers would say such things as, 'what is wrong with the man, he is surrounded by beautiful fertile women, every one knows that the women of our district are the most beautiful in all Colombia'.

It had become the general consensus at the table that his new wife would have to be dealt with after the child is born, the current fashion for dealing with people was to tie their hands and feet and run them over with a coca leaf truck, leaving their mutilated corpse to be consumed in the jungle, but fashions change. Next year they may return to last year's most popular form, which was forcing people to skydive over the jungle, without a parachute.

Jhiro knew that pressure was building against him, he was aware of the risk, but knew also that he had breathing space until his child was born. Whilst Jhiro is defending his position on Jackie, coffee, and grapes, the latter item becoming increasingly difficult to protect, Jackie lifts the headache room key from the top of the picture frame that surrounds a print of a Van Gough self portrait, not all art in Jhiro's home is genuine. She inserts the key into the lock, her heart rate doubles as she turns the key and opens the door. She looks around herself nervously, although she knows no one would ever enter Jhiro's bedroom, without his permission, when they do so it is to change the bedding or to clean the room, chores which have specifically allotted times.

She moves to his desk and stands in front of the phone, she rehearses her short oration. She picks up the telephone, which does have, as she anticipated an audibly dialling tone, she dials the number carefully, it rings four times, and she then hears an English voice, Arnolds, it is a massive comfort to her, she draws a deep breath to speak, and drops the telephone in response to an incredibly loud shriek from a nearby howler monkey, her heart rate hits two hundred beats a minute, unsustainable for any human being. Jackie recovers her composure, picks the phone up from the desk in time to hear, '- message after the tone' She draws a fresh breath, waits for the tone and speaks into the mouthpiece,

"Jacqueline Forbes-Brewer is at; longitude, 76 degrees 53 minutes and 48 seconds west of the Prime Meridian, and latitude 4 degrees 22 minutes and 18 seconds north of the equator, the place is heavily defended with missiles and armed guards, you must have a black Sikorsky C76 helicopter with the letters J-H-I-R-O written in white underneath, the lettering must be six hundred millimetres high and sixty millimetres wide or you will be blasted from the sky. Arnold please help me if you can to come home. For the avoidance of doubt, my mother's maiden name was Charlton, I had a white pony called Pollyanna for my eight birthday, and your pet name for me when I was little was Poppy, you are my only hope, but please, please, please take great care." She then pauses, somehow holds on to her emotions and ads,

"If I am beyond your reach, you are not to worry, send my love to everyone, oh and you cannot call back, you must not call back." She is physically upset and exhausted when she drops the receiver back on to its mount. As she does so she sees a number of lights flick on and off on a grey box on the wall to her right, she panics and imagines the box has recorded the number she dialled. Small lights continue to flash after she has put down the phone. Jackie knows that she has to destroy the box, but does not know how to do it without attracting the blame. She notices it has four screws holding the front panel in place, from the kitchen she retrieves a knife, and is able to loosen the screws, once she can see inside the shoebox sized unit, she sees a thick black cable entering the box from the left, which she assumes is mains power, this cable goes into an American made black cube which has 12V under its US labelling, she knows this to be a transformer, or power reducer, from this many smaller and coloured wires go into the body of the grey unit, which has the flashing lights. This part she knows is her enemy. She has little or no knowledge of electronics, but sufficient to know that electricity and water are not the best of bedfellows. She gets a small jug of water from the kitchen, and with it she slowly drips a little water unto the small grey unit and onto the transformer. The three different coloured lights all flash on and off in protest, and there is a small but audible crackle. To Jackie's delight the lights go out and there appears a thin vapour of white electrical smoke from the box. She waits until the smoke thickens and hurriedly tightens the four screws. She pauses before she leaves the room to give the electronic unit time to reach a ruinous condition, as she shuts the door the first tiny flame is visible. She replaces the key above Van Goughs ever watchful eyes, as she looks into his sad blue eyes she puts her finger to her lips. She takes great care to replace the key so that its fob faces the same way it had prior to her intervention, the knife and jug are returned to their usual situation. She counts to one hundred, picks up the telephone and in an alarmed voice declares,

"Fuego, fuego, rapido rapido." Jackie was feeling deeply satisfied, she had made her phone call to England, destroyed the spy box and made use of her limited Spanish to raise the alarm.

It was the enormous man she had seen on her first day who came to her rescue. Jackie pointed to Jhiro's headache room and said in Spanish that she could smell smoke, words she had looked up in the intervening two minutes that it took for the colossal man to arrive, he disappeared and quickly reappeared with a huge bunch of keys, after trying several he opened the door, the room was now filling with thick white smoke, flames were licking up the wall and had just caught the first of Jhiro's maps. Peru and Ecuador were ablaze, Colombia and Central America were in its path. Jackie's rescuer was able to douse the flames before the Panama Canal dematerialised, he took off his huge top, which he used to smother the flaming electrical unit, the smell of burning lingered in the room for many weeks.

On Jhiro's return the incident barely merited a mention, Jhiro's only comment being, American rubbish when referring to the cause of the fire, he was very grateful to Jackie, for saving his family home, which added just a little more guilt to her accumulation. Jackie's satisfaction at achieving her call back to England was short lived, the following day alone on the veranda she was going over the text of her message in her mind, to make double sure she had removed all ambiguity, she heard herself describe the helicopter as a black Sikorsky C76, her mouth dropped open in amazement at her own idiocy, she berated herself, speaking audibly,

"You imbecile, you dull witted ass how could you be so crass, so gormless." She now realised that she had put the lives of others in even greater danger than she at first thought, Jhiro did not currently have his own flying machine he was using a different model, which was also a different colour. She was horrified at her own stupidity, had she realised the full devastating consequences of her inter-continental telephone message, she would not have been able to live with the enormity of the burden.

The excitement of achieving the list of targets that she had set herself months before dulled as post-call days turned into weeks, which in turn turned into months. It was her pregnancy, now in its final weeks that was her daily drudgery, after the cessation of the morning sickness, she had blossomed in mid-pregnancy as a percentage of women do, but the later stages had left her greatly fatigued each day by mid-afternoon. The humidity of March into April had been oppressive, even to the locals, but to a heavily expectant European woman it was totally debilitating and stifling. She would, late afternoon often simply lie on their bed and enjoy the breeze from the lazily turning ceiling fan on her naked, bulging abdomen. Jackie became less and less comfortable with her own body, and increasingly anxious with regard the birth of her first child, Jhiro was constantly reassuring her that he would fly her to the best medical care, but she knew he was becoming ever more troubled at what he felt was a no-win situation, that he was being forced into by others, far more powerful than himself. Jackie's discomfort had caused her to abandon her life story to date, it had reached the point where she discovered she was pregnant, she had smiled to herself throughout her recollection of threatening to sever Jhiro's penis, but the volume had caused her many more tears than it had given her smiles. Jhiro was disappointed for her that she had not completed it, he had sometimes joked that it might be a best seller one day, and a Hollywood Movie, and then he said the world would know the name of Jhiro de Montaya.

The pressures on him had reached a conclusive maturity, he is called to Medellin for a meeting of all the cartel members, and he feels it will be decisive. He kisses Jackie on the lips and on her extended abdomen prior to leaving for the meeting, his parting comment is,

"Keep Jhiro's child safe in there until he comes back." She smiles but does not watch him leave the room, she is lying on their bed reading her own handwriting, reliving her early childhood, she replies,

"Don't be too long it's any day now," and adds "Now that you have got your blackbird, flying machine back, will you be the pilot?"

"No, not today, Jhiro has big headache today, but also he thinks he might have a big answer to make big headache go away, adios." It is late morning she is left alone with her story, in their bedroom. She dozes for a short while, but is woken by the surprising sound of Jhiro's helicopter landing back on the roof, he has obviously forgotten something. She rises from the bed to meet him, allowing her huge maternity dress to cover her equally huge abdomen. She casually gathers up her scattered pages from the bed, which she tidies and then walks into the kitchen and almost literally into a Lieutenant Colonel in the British Special Air Services, his all black commando style clothing, full helmet and weapon shock her, she squeals in fright. The all black figure raises its visor and speaks clearly to her in the Queens English,

"Are you Jacqueline Forbes-Brewer?"

"Yes."

"Come with me now, Sir Arnold Elliot invites you home." Jackie is overwhelmed, all she can say is,

"But what, how, how did you?"

"Miss it has to be now, we are leaving now."

"But I have to......Give me ten seconds." She turns the last page of her story face down on the dinning room table, and writes on it,

'Don't worry
I'll call you
I…'

"Miss it has to be now." Is the forceful command that is repeated to her. She glances around the room, picks up Jhiro's favourite drinking vessel, his taza, and leaves, still clutching the many pages of her own handwriting. She is airborne and flying west at almost two hundred miles an hour, within ninety seconds. There was much hand slapping and all round congratulations among the helicopter crew. They had executed a difficult and dangerous job perfectly, without loss of life, and just as importantly to the crew without raising the alarm. When the two men with her remove their helmets she could appreciate the release of tension, it was palpable, as was the perspiration dripping from their heads, these were extremely courageous, and expertly trained men. One of them introduced himself,

"Lieutenant Colonel James Wiltshire at your service mam." He then relaxed and added,"That's a hell of a bruise you've got there." Referring to her extended abdomen, and more seriously, "Do you have any ongoing medical issues we should be aware of?" Jackie, absolutely stunned by events, was sitting on the floor of the Sikorsky, as all seating and everything that could be removed had been to make room for extra bodies and equipment, she held out her right hand and replied,

"Jacqueline Forbes-Brewer, it is very good to make your acquaintance, and no this lump is my only ongoing medical concern." She then added through a wry smile, "I'm afraid I've either wet myself due to the excitement of meeting you, or my waters have just broken, do you fully understand what that means?" A colleague of the Lieutenant Colonel leans over his shoulder and interjects with,

"Yes mam, we understand exactly what that means, though James here will be disappointed not to be the cause, him being our pin up boy, I'll radio ahead immediately for the appropriate backup." Jackie relaxes as much as it was possible, and thought thank God I'm in British hands, and thank God for the British sense of humour. She asked,

"Where are we going?"

"To a British naval vessel eight miles off shore, we shall be there in another four minutes." Was her reply, "Then you are going on to RAF Brize Norton, Oxfordshire, we have further operations." As James Wiltshire had predicted the Sikorsky landed on H.M.S.Venture promptly, there were no more introductions, with swift military precision Jackie was lifted from the Sikorsky and into a huge Chinook helicopter, which had been fully fitted out as a mobile medical theatre, everything and everybody needed to perform all but the most complicated medical procedures was on board. It was one of four such units available to the Ministry of defence. As the huge rear door of the Chinook was closing, Jackie looked out just in time to see the letters J-H-I-R-O lifting into the sky for the last time, she was submerged in mixed and confusing emotions. She was put onto a centrally positioned hospital bed and given a mixture of anaesthetic gas and oxygen, which relived her of her early labour pains and a portion of the anxiety which was building within her. She released her grip on the two hundred A4 pages of her story to date, but held on tight to Jhiro's taza, his favourite cup.

Jhiro completely oblivious of these events was touching down his blackbird two hours north of his home, for what he knew was a crisis meeting. He entered a room in one of the many farmhouses owned by the cartel, in which were eight cartel members and two domesticated politicians. After customary greetings everyone sat to the table, at the head opposite Jhiro is the richest and most powerful man in the criminal world, everyone present knows it, it does not need to be announced or acknowledge, even the two members of Colombia's government are in awe of this man. He is The Jefe, he nods to the man on his left, who then addresses Jhiro. He is told that he must abandon grapes, he must cut his coffee production by half, and one day after his child is born he must hand over his woman to the cartel. Because she has seen too much, she is a risk they cannot live with, and until she is handed to them she must remain at his home. Jhiro stood to make his protestations, The Jefe raised his hand to indicate that Jhiro should sit, Jhiro dropped back into his seat. The man who had been speaking, Rockero Jimenez, 'the rock', continued to make his point. He reminded Jhiro that not only did the woman know of the location of the tunnel but that she had also seen the thousands of drums of ether and other chemicals stockpiled there. Drums that were vital to turn the raw coca leaf paste into the finished product, and that the drums all had visible labels on them, declaring the name of the American company that supplied them, if this woman blew the whistle on both the tunnel and their supplier of ether it could suspend production for a year, costing billions of dollars, and that there was no doubt that he, Jhiro had been foolish, he had allowed his love for this woman to blind him. Jhiro tried to protest, but was not given the opportunity to speak, out of respect for his family name he is given twenty-four hours to consider his response, he must come back to the table with an agreeable reply at the same time tomorrow, no other outcome is acceptable, everyone present knows this, Jhiro is one of few people who would qualify for this concession. He is dismissed with a half-hearted gesture, a wave of the hand from The Jefe.

There is a short debate in his absence, the men of Medellin want and need his land, which runs into hundreds of thousands of hectares. There is general consensus that he must cut back on coffee, and cast aside his two loves, his woman and his grapes, and they must buy more weapons to station at the De Montaya compound, they must be ready for a bloody battle with Cali over the de Montaya land holdings in the south. With Jhiro in non-attendance there is a vote, it is unanimous, Jhiro has run out of friends. Before the meeting is dispersed, the question is asked,

"What about the art he is holding?" The Jefe responds,

"Leave them with him, as long as they are there he will feel safe, his woman could cost us billions, their value can be recovered on one return flight." With a wave of his hand, four near priceless works of art are dammed.

Jhiro flies home a very troubled man, he lands on the roof and does not at first go to Jackie, he goes into his family room, stands by the device in the centre of the table and looks to it for answers. He knows that he must decide between everything that has made him and his family what they are, and his love for Jackie. He also knows that if he stays with the land, all his power and his ability to make decisions will be taken away from him, he is to be a puppet to the cartel, he knows too that the cartel gave him twenty-four hours to decide out of respect for his father and his name. The more these thoughts go around and around in his mind the more physically and mentally exhausted he becomes. Deep within him his instincts tell him what he must do, there is only one acceptable option, he is experiencing thoughts more radical than he would have felt capable of just a few weeks before. He openly says,

"Arrepentido Padre, Arrepentido Padre." Sorry papa, sorry papa, this he repeats many times as he removes the four extremely valuable paintings from the walls and puts them together just inside the door. There is only one thing he can do, leave Colombia, taking with him his woman and his love for her, his child and the four works of art, the proceeds from the sale of which will support them wherever they go. As he shuts the door to the fourth floor, he repeats,

"Arrepentido Padre." He enters their lounge area looking for Jackie, finds the page on the table, and reads;

'Don't worry
I'll call you
I . . . . .'

DAY NINE

JOHN & JOYCE

Both Liz and Emma were asleep when I leave our bed in the morning, I did my utmost to creep around in the Kitchen, not one of my best skills.

I felt an emotional emptiness, and a sensation akin to having been put through a proverbial mangle, and having had all the goodness wrung out of me. I wonder, for how long will Emma's car wreck dominate the house? Two strong coffees do not help, even the two dogs do not pester me to be let out or to go for a walk, it is as though they sense a melancholy or gloom had descended upon the house. I let them out when I retrieved the papers from the gate, they take their despondency with them into the garden.

The Mirror today has much about the England football team who seem to be disgraced after losing to Russia after a 'moment of Rooney madness', poor Tim, bad day for him today. Plus the fire brigade have said it may charge for moving obese people, as crews were called out eight times in the last year to lift people over thirty stones, or four–hundred pounds, obviously the obese dummy training did not go well. Inflation is now at an annual rate of 8,000 percent in Zimbabwe, two pounds of beef now cost a million Zimbabwe dollars, and still the world does nothing. Also teenage pregnancy in Britain is now the highest in Europe, and a study has shown that Britain is only the nineteenth safest place in the world to give birth, worst for example than Cuba, clearly more of those anaesthetic condoms are needed. A last offering from today's edition is that the most popular funeral rite requested, is for people to be cremated along with the ashes of their favourite pet.

In the Times, apparently the UK house market is heading for a crash, all those people who paid their mortgages with credit cards, are about to find that the caring banks have allowed them to paint themselves into a corner. It is no surprise that a Nobel Prize winning geneticist who has claimed that black people are less intelligent than whites, has had to cancel the London dates of his promotional speaking tour. A man in a Hong Kong hospital with an injured toe, has been arrested and jailed for theft, after he drank two vials of blood whilst in the hospital, he claimed to have been extremely thirsty, and the first black presidential hopeful, Barack Obama is polling at just twenty-one percent, for the democratic nomination way behind the first female hopeful, Hillary Clinton at forty-seven percent. Finally the heroic return to Pakistan of exiled former Prime Minister Benazir Bhutto is expected to rally hundreds of thousands of supporters in Karachi today, possibly as many as a million, Ms Bhutto's pledge is 'I will never give in to tyranny'.

I leave the house as quiet as possible, but have to do an emergency stop on the gravel at the end of the short drive, some idiot has closed the gate, fortunately I drive an automatic, so the inconvenience of driving with two broken knuckles in my right hand is minimal. It is another clear bright morning with only a hint of frost today, no terrifying ice-queen or hoare frost, road kill wise, there is one hedgehog and two rabbits to note. There are many deer in the valley to the left of the road, I estimate that perhaps there are as many as thirty, I hope for their sakes they are able to stay clear of the road, I have a passion for all things free and wild and would prefer all of our mammals and birds to stay that way, but once they are deceased they are meat, either for miscellaneous carnivores or for individuals such as myself.

The Hardy statue never actually alters a jot from one year to the next, it is my mood and perception that changes with the weather, subsequently I transfer a combination of an element of my melancholy and the disposition of the weather of the day onto the great man, so that today Thomas Hardy seems to me to be a little downcast and preoccupied in distant thought upon his plinth. My timing has become consistent so that I am one of the last to arrive in the jury room. Terry (rugby) greets me and loudly expresses,

"What the hell have you done to your hand?" For the benefit of all who are assembled, with an equally loud response I reply,

525

"Well I was helping this chap move a piano ......" The by-product of the resulting burst of laughter is that Andy (body odour) rapidly enters our room to request a degree of propriety, we had apparently over stepped an invisible line of etiquette, a lack of decorum was the actual term Andy had used. Since his chastisement, which had resulted from his lunchtime physical liaisons with Elizabeth (chain smoker) he has lacked any degree of pleasantry, he has become humourless, but regrettably not odourless. I chat to Hanna (silicon valley) for a while, she curiously had the lower half of her body concealed from public gaze today, in black trousers, though her artificial breast were doing their best to commandeer the attention of all who should pass within a visible radius. Indeed pinkie and perky were giving the impression that they were competing to be the first to pop out. Andy returned, we assume it is to usher us into court, but to our surprise he informs us that as we are one short, in our number, there will be a half hour delay, to establish the whereabouts of the missing person.

We all look to each other to ascertain the identity of the person who is absent. It is John (foreman), the realisation that it is John who is the non-attendant strikes me like a blow to the solar plexus. The hairs are up on the back of my neck, I recall our conversation of yesterday, 'I wish you well in your deliberations' and more significantly I recollect his mood, his aloof disposition, he was a man who had been elevated, he was above all earthly cares and woes. Most of us take the opportunity to pour ourselves a coffee, from the now very popular vender, Lynda (menswear) and Elizabeth (chain smoker) leave the room in a predictable pursuit. I both imagine and hope for Elizabeth's sake that the permanent taste and smell of nicotine in her throat and nostrils would have protected her from the worst of the excessive waft of body odour emanating from Andy our usher, as he reached the peak of his physical exertions with her.

Richard (I can do that) grabs me with his good arm,

"Come on lets have a better answer to Terry's question, how is it that we have matching hands?" He says this holding aloft his damaged limb.

"Oh it's a long story, I've broken two knuckles."

"Go on I've got time."

I then give him a fairly comprehensive account of the trauma, it's upsetting to recall it, but also comforting to use the past tense to describe the horror, in such terms as, it had been, and it was, this puts a little distance between me and the emotional damage of yesterdays catastrophe. As I recall my tale I am clearly hitting a personal note with Richard, he is welling up and blinking at an increased rate. I wind up my story by actually winding it down, I take it away from the danger to Emma's life and focus on the problem of the car, to deliberately depersonalise the conversation, finishing with the sentence,

"Of course, that now leaves me for the second time in a week looking for a car, for Emma." Richard puts his good arm out and clasp my good arm,

"I think I can help you there." I take a deep breath and brace myself, assuming he is going to go into one of his, I can do that routines and he is going to try and make himself a bit of money. But as is often the case, the book is of a differing quality to the cover, he continues,

"We've got an six year old Ford Fiesta in the garage, it hasn't been used for over a year, air-bags, central locking, power steering, ABS brakes the lot, and has hardly been used in the last four years, I bought it for our daughter Penny, when she was at university, I paid six thousand for it, but I think its only worth two at best now."

"How come it's had so little use?" Not for the first time or I imagine the last time, my mouth was too quick for my brain to control, I instantly wished I could swallow the words I had just spoken. Richard takes a deep breath, and I think because I had been so open with him and trusted him with what was a very personal confession, he released the air from his lungs slowly, and decided to match my intimate disclosure, with a revelation of his own.

"Well, when Penny started at uni', I bought the car and told her that it was a six-thousand pound loan, but that each year she successfully completed her studies, she would reduce the loan by two-thousand, so effectively if she graduated after year three the car was hers."

"A great idea, what did she study?"

527

"English literature, it was very intense, I've seen that Hardy book that you've been dragging around the place before, believe me, and a lot of others besides."

"How'd she get on?"

"First year great, she got a bit bogged down in her second year, and I know she felt like quitting, I did my damnedest to persuade her to complete the course, and of course the on loan car was another incentive."

"I didn't want her to start something and not see it through, all her mates were off on gap-years, trips to Oz' and New Zealand, or Cambodia and Vietnam, I told her I would help her travel but she must graduate first."

"Sounds like good advice."

"Well it wasn't" he starts to well up and choke on his words, "She didn't see any of the world in her short life because of me, and she didn't graduate either." He is talking to me calmly but tears are falling across his cheeks, he takes hold of my arm and continues.

"She contracted meningitis, just a week into her third year, everybody thought it was flu and then pneumonia and it was left undetected for too long, she was dying in hospital as all her closest friends were surfing, sailing and seeing the world, if I'd let her go travelling we would probably still have her now. I would cut off an arm if I could go back and not bully her, what difference would it have made in the long run? She was a good kid, she knew right from wrong, I saw the gap year as a danger, so she stayed at home and died because of me." He is now openly crying, we have moved into the corridor for a degree of privacy.

"God I'm sorry, there's me bending your ear on a near miss, but you shouldn't blame yourself, she could have contracted the meningitis at any time."

"I do blame myself and so does my wife, we've been living like strangers ever since, in fact its killed our relationship, its only a matter of time until she moves in with her widowed sister, she's always threatening to do it, I wish she would. You see all twelve of her mates that went travelling came back in one piece, I knew she could have gone and been eaten by a shark, stung by a jelly fish, or experienced any one of hundreds of other

528

problems, some of them fatal, but she didn't go, she didn't see any of the world in her short life, her mates did go, they had the holiday of a lifetime, and my lovely Penny died because I stopped her enjoying herself." At this point he is no longer able to speak, he walks into the toilets to calm and compose himself. I stay alone in the corridor blinking back tears, one rung below him on life's emotional ladder. When he returns it is obvious that he has been upset, but his voice has returned to its normal pitch.

"Anyway, the point is we have this car, it's in near perfect nick, you interested?"

"Are you sure you want to sell it, is it not a memento that you and your wife want to keep?"

"Oh Christ no, my wife has been after me to get rid of it for a year now, it's a hateful reminder for her, as she puts it, 'its one of the weapons I used to blackmail Penny into not travelling'."

"Well I have to be honest two grand is a lot more than I was looking to pay, I'm not wishing to knock you down or strike a bargain, it sounds a good car at a good price, but I've just spent a grand this week already, and ended up with nothing."

"Oh I don't want any money for it, you can if your up for it do me a favour for the car."

"Go on."

"Well I got a large chimney that needs a bit of re-pointing and a bit of new lead work, is that your sort of thing?"

"Yea sure that's bread and butter work for me and my boys."

"OK then if you're happy to do that for me the car is yours, or rather it's your daughters."

"I can do it yes, but surly so can you, 'no job to big, no job to small, if you want it done, I can do it." I quote him his own business card.

"Ah yes, but now were talking heights, I can only get about six runs up a ladder and I shit myself, don't know how you do what you do."

"OK then, that's a deal." I hold out my left hand to shake his, he considers this for a moment, leans as far back as he can and shakes my left with his, and says,

"I'm not fooling for that one, don't want my nose all over my face." The moment of levity between us returns all our previous emotional conversation to a normal level, he puts his good arm around my shoulder and leads me back into the jury room. In front of us in conversation, are the ever contrasting Joyce and Hanna, with these two standing together in profile, the difference between them becomes a chasm. Joyce is poised and carries herself with immaculate, subtle flirtatiousness, each item of her apparel very carefully chosen to conceal, but yet hinting at its content, and there's Hanna, far more casually and provocatively dressed leaving less to the imagination and more to the eye. They are both genuine, caring, thoughtful people, little to chose between them in depth of character. It is these musings of mine that are interrupted by Andy, who is on duty today, he asks us all to assemble in the jury room, he needs to communicate with us. We wait for Elizabeth and Lynda to join us from the smoking room, and we are then told that a police officer was dispatched to John's address to ascertain the reason for his delay. I had forgotten about John's absence and the reason for it. Andy continues,

"The uniformed officer had to force entry into John's house, where it was then discovered that John had passed away in his sleep." After a brief pause to allow us to absorb this knowledge he continued,

"Today's court session will carry on as normal, the judge has been informed, and has stated that he will accept a decision from the remaining eleven of you, can you in a few moments appoint another of you to take over as foreman, I will return to escort you into court in thirty minutes." He then manages to add "I am sorry to be the conveyor of bad news." No one fills the void which he leaves hanging in the air, as he vacates the room.

It is Thomas (numbers) who first speaks,

"That's unbelievable he was here yesterday, as large as life." Joyce adds a little chocked,

"Wow he delivered that message without the dressing, don't you think?" David (weatherman) adds,

"I can't believe it, he was a super chap, full of whit and intelligence." Most of us chip in with a comment or two, many clichés bounce around the room, 'fit as a fiddle', 'bright as a button' and from Tim, "That puts everything in perspective, here's me making a fuss about England's footballers having a disastrous night in Russia last night, and poor John is dead, what a super chap he was."

I sit in quiet contemplation, I hang on John's thoughtful words of yesterday, 'all this is just so much froth' and 'I can't wait to go to sleep tonight, should there be a re-occurrence of the encounter with Emily'. I hope with body and soul that John got his wish, he was on the surface an ordinary man, but as with most of us he was a complex character. He also had a deep knowledge of chemistry, and was able I'm sure with simplicity to induce in himself any level of sleep he chose, with the aid of available drugs. I don't doubt that he could have and may have self induced a state of hallucinatory sleep, very deep sleep, coma or death. I doubt his death was from completely natural causes. I made a mental note to look out for the conclusion of his inquest, if there was to be one. I know he wanted to share another night with his Emily, more than he wanted his life to span into old age and an uncertain future, in short he loved his lost wife more than he loved life itself.

This had been an extremely emotional few days, when this jury business is behind me, I must make an allowance for Liz, she needs now more than ever, to have some respite from the daily grind. I think it was John Lennon who came up with the line that 'Life is what happens to you whilst your making other plans' never did a celebrity quote feel more appropriate, and his quote was never more appropriate, ironically than when applied to his own demise. I decided to keep my conversation with John yesterday private, but I did enter the current debate regarding him by saying,

"If no one else wants to take over from John Foreman as foreman, I'm happy to try to fill his shoes." This was greeted with relief by most persons present, and was agreed unanimously and swiftly.

After much kind reflection on John's life and the little we knew of him, we were called to attention by Andy and ushered into court. I felt as I'm sure we all did, that John's passing was not marked by any significance, there had not been a cessation of activity for a period of solemnity, I wanted the world to desist for a moment, to stop, whilst a bell was rung to his worthiness and his wordiness, give us all a pause to honour his existence.

531

Yet this world of ours would not hold its breath for an instant. People would go about their daily business without so much as a missed heart beat, children would be born, have fun, suffer and die, the good and the evil in the world would continue to struggle against each other, lovers would fall in and out of love, and this court would continue in its theatrical charade, without John Foreman (foreman).

Everyone but me sat in their usual seats, I sat as instructed nearest the judge, from this close up view he more markedly resembled my comic image of himself, a sharp Hawkeyed decrepit body of a man, he was physically diminished, but he had eyes of such piercing intensity. He spoke all too briefly regarding John's absence, thanked me for stepping up to the plate and signalled to the defence team that they may proceed. The court, our miniscule part of the world had not paused for a second. The defence barrister stood to face us, she was a consummate performer, we were ready for an hour or two of her wordiness, her command of our language was polished, her slow and careful delivery mesmerising, she was almost too good for her own good, it was sometimes possible to concentrate on the grace and eloquence of her delivery, more so than its content. I made a mental note that should I ever be on the wrong side of the law, it would be her with her poise and fluency that I'd prefer to sit between myself and a prison sentence.

She opened with a simple greeting.

"Good morning members of the jury, please accept my commiseration at the untimely loss of your foreman, would you all like to pause for one minutes silence in reflective thought, would that be acceptable your honour?" How could he refuse, she was a professional. After a minutes silence, during which I confess I was unable to discipline my mind, I nagged myself to remember to contact Barbara and Claire at lunch time, and debated whether to go for a pasty or a sandwich, the barrister for the defence continued. "You have heard at length my erstwhile and learned college spout forth." As she said this she moved her right hand from under her chin forwards as if to eject a projectile, showing us with this action and the most discrete and subtle of grins, that she understood the spittle problem of yesterday.

"And spout forth at length he did, with admirable loquacity on the singular subject of Mr Merryweather's guilt, I have just two things to say to you."

"Firstly on the subject of Michael's guilt, or lack of, I believe with all my being that he is not guilty." Allowing a long pause after the words not guilty, this quickly became the norm.

"I believe he is not guilty........ of the charges he is accused of, if I did not believe in his innocence........I could not and would not be standing here before you today. It is not my intention to take a considerable fee from the tax payer........yes Michael is receiving legal aid for his defence as he has no private means, it is not my intention to take a considerable fee from you the tax payer, regardless of my personal conviction in this case."

"It is not my intention to leave this court, richer for the experience in both knowledge and finance, and allow a man who may or may not be innocent........ To walk our streets, it is my intention to leave this court with an innocent man........free to carry on with his life, free to enjoy his liberty as is his right."

"If I had a modicum of doubt over Michael's innocence........I could not defend him, I like all of you am a principled person, I like all of you have a conscience, and I like all of you want to leave this place having seen and experienced justice at first hand, I want you to reach a verdict of not guilty........so that you too can leave here doubt free, your conscience clear."

"Secondly you may have noticed that Michael is a simple person, this is not said as an insult or meant as a derogatory term, but said as a matter of fact, Michael is not a multifaceted, complex individual, his mind does not operate on more than one level, or concentrate on more than one subject at a time. He does not possess cunning, he cannot practice deceit, he cannot take advantage of other people, he would not disagree with anything I have said, but being simple he can be taken advantage of, he can be used, steered and abused by the cunning of others."

"This is a source of great frustration to Michael, he judges other people as either good or bad, he is looking at the eleven of you now hoping that you are good people, but fearing that you are not, he cannot read body language, or make considered judgements, but he is hoping that you can, he has no middle ground, it is black or white for Michael, he has no understanding of deceit, or of duplicity, he does not recognise underhandedness or insincerity in others until it is far too late."

"In short he does not have the ability to lie and get away with it, please don't misunderstand me, of course he has the ability to lie, just as you and I do, he is not unique in that he has a medical deficiency in that he cannot lie, but where Michael differs from most of us is that he does not have the capacity to recall a set of lies accurately, should he need to repeat them. He does not have the ability to remember a complicated web of deceit, indeed he does not have the ability to remember a complicated sentence."

"Let me give you an example of Michael's capacity to remember, to recall, his capacity to comprehend, on the night of Michael's arrest, which was for Michael the single most frightening day of his life, until today. You have seen Michael under pressure, under intense pressure, from my learned college, he does not respond well, this is because he feels his inquisitors hate him, and he does not understand why someone he has not previously meet would hate him, indeed it was one of your number who asked why it was necessary for Michael's questioning to be quite so inimical, if I recall correctly."

"Back to the night of Michael's arrest, his speech became incoherent, he was so upset he was unable to put a sentence together, so police sergeant Peter Fuller put to Michael a set of simple questions to ascertain his mental state, not a full psychological profile, just a simple set of questions, which are sometimes used by the police to help decide how inebriated people are, with regard to alcoholic consumption, or drug abuse."

"Now Michael's answers are no secret, police sergeant Fullers notes are a matter of public record, for the avoidance of doubt I have verified these notes with Sergeant Fuller. Sergeant Fuller asked Michael just six questions, once Michael had been given time to calm down, Michael has stated to me that he thought it was a test, so he did his best to try to pass the test, believing if he did that police Sergeant Fuller would allow him to go home, remember these are Sergeant Fuller's notes not mine."

"Objection."

"Overruled."

534

"Question one was, who is the president of the United States? Answer I don't know', question two, what significant event took place in New York on September eleven two thousand and one? Answer 'I'm sorry I don't know', question three, who is the Prime Minister, Answer 'I don't know', question four, what is the national speed limit? Answer 'I don't understand', question five, what type of animal is an Alsatian, answer 'I don't know what you mean' and question six, what type of trees does wood come from? Same answer, 'I don't know what you mean', now Michael believes he was incarcerated that night, in the police cells because he failed the test."

"This is all I have to say to you, you are I am certain decent people who know right from wrong, you have seen Michael perform in this court, and I leave you now to put the pieces of the jigsaw together, to make sense of what you have heard in this court in the last week. To use your judgement and considerable experience to good effect, I urge you to find Michael Merryweather not guilty......... of the charges set before him."

Her summing up took less than twenty minutes, Hawkeye was very surprised, so much so he had not crossed the t's and dotted the i's on his own summing up, he expected as we all did that the defence summing up would occupy the morning session. He immediately called for a suspension until lunch, to as he put it, 'allow time for the proper court protocol to take place', he was not at all amused at being left unprepared, and his hawkish glare to the defence council bench was with evil intent. The defence barrister had, I believe achieved exactly what she wanted, we now had three hours to consider her words, three hours for her message to sink in, to resonate in our minds, very skilful.

Consequently, much quicker than expected we find ourselves back in familiar surroundings, our jury room, this free time would give me an opportunity to catch up with Barbara and Claire. Most of my fellow jurors leave quite quickly, only three others and myself linger. I take out my mobile phone, switch it on and receive a stored message from Claire instantly. 'All ok here, George in plaster, Kate's mum sober, Kate and I just chilling on beach, lul xxx, PS see you Sunday, who's coming to get us?' I reply 'Me, take care love u2 xx'. I notice we have Tim and Terry left plus Joyce, the two men are as always in light-hearted competition, with our national football team in disgrace, and our rugby team in the world cup final on Saturday, it was I am sure a one sided conversation. As I dial France to speak to Barbara, Tim and Terry leave the room, which leaves just Joyce, she is loitering, reminiscent of a student who wishes to talk to sir after class. Barbara answers,

"Barbara Lefe'vre."

"Hello Barbara, big brother here, how are you?"

"Well I'm allowed to answer the phone now so I suppose I'm doing ok."

"How's the house arrest going?"

"That's exactly what it feels like, it's claustrophobic."

"How come you're talking so freely?"

"Oh Anne's taken Karen to get a bit of shopping, Karen's a lovely girl, she speaks a good bit of French too, where are you? You're talking as though you're in a library."

"I'm in the jury room, we've just been dismissed for an early lunch, anything decided about next week?" Her voice slumps,

"Yes, Jean Pierre's funeral is on Thursday, is that OK for you?"

"Any day is OK for me, as the girls are on half term I think we will all come, if that's OK with you?"

"Yes please bring them, and please come over as soon as you can, I've got to send Anne back home she's....... well she's Anne."

"I think I'll come over Monday or Tuesday with probably one of the girls, and Liz will fly over say, Wednesday with the other, is it OK if we stay until Saturday?"

"Of course, stay as long as you like, I'm dreading the funeral, but dreading even more everybody leaving me afterwards."

"You know you can come back with us, for as long as you like, that's no problem."

"Thanks but......well let's talk about that next week, I can't think past Thursday at the moment."

"OK I understand, how are you really?"

"Can we talk about that next week too, Jude I'm sorry I can't keep this normality up any longer and I've got to go now the Gestapo are back."

"Hang on what about mum?"

"She's coming out just for the day, with Anne."

"OK bye sis, see you in a few days."

"Bye, please come soon." I put the phone down knowing that Barbara is in tears, Joyce then looks up into my face, now she can talk to teacher.

"Jude, have you got a few minutes, can we talk?"

"Sure here or shall we go into the real world?"

"Oh not here, do you fancy a coffee or something?"

"Yes OK, let's go down to the arcade, we should be able to find a quite spot there at this time of day, plus a decent snack." We leave the court building on what is a dry but cold day in mid-October. I say,

"Are you leaning one way or the other in this case?"

"Oh I was sure when I listened to the girls, I was solidly with them, I wanted to see him locked up and the keys thrown away, but then when he took the stand he wasn't the evil manipulative figure I'd imagined, I felt sorry for him, and now the two barristers have pulled me left and right and I don't know where I am, what do you think?"

"I think we need to listen to the judges summing up, he may give us some direction."

"But he's a bit of an oddball himself, don't you think?"

"I do yes but he's got command of that court room, or rather he did have until just now, I think he got caught out by the short delivery of the last summing up, hence we now have a three hour break, I think he's not yet put the seal on his own summing up."

"Do you think so? I never considered that, I just thought that......well I don't know what I thought really, the truth is I didn't think about it at all, I'm just following orders like a sheep."

"No no, now your being self-deprecating, you are I'm sure as bright as the next man, or rather woman."

"I'm really not Jude, I don't think I'm very good at body language and all that, reading between the lines stuff, that's partly why I want to talk to you."

"I'm intrigued." I say light heartedly with a grin, and a short laugh.

"See, I don't know if you're making a joke or laughing at me."

"I assure you I'm not mocking you, you seem a little troubled, are you OK?"

"No I'm not, but let's stick to the case until we reach the café."

"OK where were we?"

"You were saying we need to hear from the judge."

"Yes I've not been on a jury before, but I believe the last word always goes to the judge, because he's the wise old owl, he's impartial, and because we may have heard something which he believes will have unbalanced our opinions one way or the other, he may wish to influence us in some way to redress the balance, I hope by this afternoon we will all have a sense of direction, or perhaps I've seen to many films or cop shows."

"No I think your right I need someone to clear the fog that's in front of me, you could do it, if you've made your mind up, please tell me why you think the way you do, and that would be OK for me, I'll go along with you."

"I can't do that, it's too much responsibility, that's for the judge to do, that's part of his remit." My obligation as the jury foreman just hit me like a hammer blow to the head, could I if I wanted to sway several people to my way of thinking. I quickly ran through the nine remaining jury members, how many of them would be open to persuasion, Barry, Terry, Tim, Thomas, Lynda, David, Elizabeth, Richard and Hanna, I decided that all of them with the exception of Lynda could probably be manipulated, and that John had been the only other one, that I think was his own man. He had come out with his viewpoint, he had voiced his opinion clearly to me. Had he been manipulating me? Did he massage my thoughts, there was no doubt that John was a step above all of us in intelligence. Did he recognise something in me? Did he plant a seed in me to influence the others, this would need to be slept on, to be sorted out. I am now feeling a little like Joyce, am I a blind sheep prepared to do Johns biding? I remind myself never to go into politics. After a moment's thought Joyce replies,

"Well I hope the judge does give us some direction, as you put it, I feel like I'm driving a car with no steering wheel."

"Is that what you wanted to ask me? For help with the case."

"No it's unrelated to the case, here we are lets get across this road and get comfortable in the café." As its only eleven-thirty the place is almost empty, we are in a delightfully converted stables, which has retained the wooden panels which acted as separators to the original occupants, who's names are now the table names, Prince, Beauty, Polly and Lady to name but a few. We are spoilt for choice, I defer to Joyce, she chooses Polly, it's in the corner and has a table and just two chairs, Polly must have been a pony, or a Shetland, the space is cosy, too small for a working horse. We sit, order coffee's and a light snack, and I look into Joyce's gorgeous green eyes, as I formulate my sentence, I try to recall, have I ever seen such a vivid green in human eyes before, my conclusion is no, I have not.

"So put me out of my misery, why are we here?"

"Oh I hope I'm not making you miserable."

"No, no, it was just a stupid figure of speech, please carry on." I now know I'm going to have to tread carefully here, she is either being very thick, or very sensitive, I decide it's the latter.

"Hang on the coffee is coming." The cups are put in front of us, we thank the waitress, a pretty, fresh faced girl of about twenty, lovely complexion, beautiful brown eyes, but what is it about body piercing that revolts me, she has a silver stud in the side of her nose and a black lip ring, almost as ugly as smoking. Once the waitress is gone we are left with a classic pregnant pause. I am waiting for Joyce to open the conversation, what she is waiting for I have no knowledge of. Actually it's me who is not doing so well with body language today, for it is, in reality, Dutch courage that Joyce is attempting to summon up.

"Jude, I don't know how to start this, so I will just say something and see what happens."

"Good idea, I'm all ears."

"I'm in a very unhappy situation at home, I live with a man ten years older than me, I'm forty nine and he's almost sixty, I know that's not a crime and its not that unusual, but we've got absolutely nothing in common, not any more, when we got together fifteen years ago I was just thirty four, I'd been mucked about by a married man for twelve years, that sod wasted my chance of children. I hoped it would happen with my current partner, but he proved to be no better than his predecessor, he didn't want children, in fact he didn't really want any thing other than, clean clothes, a plate of food and a place to lay his head at night, he doesn't even want sex, and I've only recently found out by poking my nose into his medical records that the bastard had a vasectomy before we met, he doesn't know I know that."

"Joyce these are intimate details of your life, are you sure you want to do this?"

"Oh yes, I want to carry on, now I've started, I've wanted to have this conversation with someone for ten years, there's no stopping me now, so the first lying bugger ruined my chances of having children, this one has just ruined my life." She starts to well up a little, she is blinking more frequently, she finds the fortitude she needs to carry on.

"When we first met, he used to come to classical and jazz concerts with me, he used to read similar books to me, and he used to notice me, want me, but gradually he has stopped doing anything that interest me, he was I think paying lip service to my hobbies, my pastimes, he just wanted a housekeeper, a cook and a nurse, he's had the best of me for fifteen years, I'm worn out, I'm ignored, I'm defeated, and I can never forgive him for the cruel deception."

"You paint a grim and lonely picture of your home life, what are your options?"

"It is a very unhappy situation, and I haven't been able to see a way out, I feel guilty even thinking about myself on a day like today, when that lovely man John has just died, but if I don't think about myself nobody else is going to, I'm trying to overcome so many emotions here, selfishness, loneliness and desperation in just talking to you." She pauses to dry her eyes with a napkin.

"Do you see? My life just hasn't worked out the way I hoped it would, I feel that someone, somewhere is out there living my life, someone is happy with their life, they have loving children, Christmas's that smell of log fires and spices, they have worn out trampolines, remnants of old tree houses and a dent in the lawn where the swings used to be. They share good music, wine and most of all intelligent conversation with their partners, they watch and enjoy the same films, they sleep touching each other, and they share wonderful intimacy. I've given my life to two selfish, inconsiderate men, sometimes I hate my imaginary double who's living my real life, sometimes I wish her well, I look for her in the street and in the super market, I look into her shopping trolley to see what she is buying for my family, all those pizza's and yoghurts, I look for her on the TV and in books, but mostly I simply feel defeated, crushed by my own inadequacy, by my own short comings." I open my mouth to respond, but before I can conjugate a sentence, Joyce is once more fluent.

"I've never been in the company of a man who not only notices what I'm wearing, but notices so much more, my jewellery, my perfume, my eyes, Jude you have given me hope, hope that my life isn't a futile waste of time." Ding, ding, ding, ding, ding is that the cafeteria's fire alarm, shit no it's an alarm bell in my head, Jude you dick, how did you get here?

"Oh Joyce, I'm so sorry that your situation is an unhappy one, I'm not your answer, can't you leave? Kick him out? Start again?"

"No I haven't got the guts, I haven't got the strength, physically or mentally, I've never been any good on my own, I am one of life's also rans, if I was in acting I'd be an extra, if I was a performer I'd be a perpetual understudy, always in the shadows, never in the sun."

"But you have such a talent for fashion, every day has been a revelation, to greet you in the morning has been such a pleasure, you have brought light into the room."

"That's what I mean, you notice everything, perhaps it would be better if I were more like Hanna."

"You could no more dress like Hanna than you could like Lynda." She laughs, her face is lovely when she smiles.

"I was devastated when I saw you leave the court room arm in arm with Hanna, but it did happen only once I think."

"Yes she just wanted an escort to get her down the high street, she is uncomfortable on her own, all the ridiculous skirts and tops are just nonsense of her husband's doing, it's actually a handicap to her."

"Jude I see you don't wear a wedding ring, I want to ask you what your situation is at home, I have to know."

"Happily married I'm afraid, no that's the wrong word, I'm very happily married, with seventeen year old twin girls." I look into her alluring green eyes, they are now very blue, and overflowing with longing, longing for emotional fulfilment, and also they carry the pain of doleful, cheerlessness and sorrow.

"I'm sorry Joyce it's not going to happen, please, please don't take this as a rejection of you it isn't, I've got everything I want at home." She puts her hand on top of mine.

"She's a lucky lady."

"No I'm a lucky man, I don't know if she's got everything she wants and needs, do we ever know, but I know I have in her." She is clearly a little overwhelmed, she isn't upset and she is holding everything together, just. She stands up as do I, she steps towards me, puts her hands on my chest and kisses me full on the lips, it is a soft, sensuous, lingering kiss. She breaks off from the embrace, pushes me back into my seat and leaves the cafeteria. Leaving me one last glimpse of her strikingly beautiful eyes, which are now overflowing with defeat. She heads back towards the high street. I stay put, drink my coffee in contemplative thought. Eventually I head towards my vehicle, but before I leave the café I send Liz a text. 'Get me a wedding ring when your in town next, I'll explain later xxx'.

I arrive at my van and decide it is too good a day to sit inside the confined space of a vehicle and read for two hours, I walk toward the Hardy statue, which I now notice stands out boldly against the white rendered wall that is its backdrop. I pause at its base, as I have done often during the past two weeks, I notice Hardy is developing an increasingly greenish complexion, it is time perhaps for a wash and brush up. Crossing the roundabout at the top of town, I walk into the borough gardens, in which stands proudly, the huge, decorative clock tower which proclaims on all four sides, that it was presented to the borough of Dorchester by Charles Hanford Esq. In AD 1905, another local celebrity who would have, I don't doubt been known to Hardy. The timeless atmosphere of the gardens is further enhanced by the decorative, Victorian, wrought iron, lead roofed bandstand. It is occupied by a few less well intentioned skate boarders, wearing their trousers in that most uncomfortable and peculiar of fashions, below they're arses, how odd that so many young people copy a trend that causes themselves to walk in such an awkward and clearly irritating way, perhaps it is even painful, just to send out a message to us, the uneducated and wooden headed masses, a message which is clearly not being received. This handful of individuals, discarding their cigarette butts and their special brew tins are in flagrant contradiction to their surroundings, which are otherwise tranquil and colourfully autumnal. The bright low flowering red fuchsias, white alyssum and red begonias, are also in sharp contrast to the yellowing silver birches and red Acer's. Magnificent too are the huge copper beech trees which provide a screen from both traffic and dwellings. I saunter down Cornwall Road, I am now determined to reach Maumbury Rings, which I by-passed the day Hanna and I visited the main cemetery.

Cornwall Road itself has an impressive and large terrace of three and four storey decorative, Victorian homes. There is so much impressive Victorian architecture in the town, during the reign of our longest serving monarch, the town must have been transformed beyond recognition, and all these structures have endured, a testament to their workmanship and design. I take a short cut through the vast, empty cattle market and eventually reach my target, Maumbury Rings.

I enter the impressive structure, which I had wrongly assumed had always been a Roman Amphitheatre, I am informed by a nearby plaque, that its origins were as a Neolithic Henge, dating back to two thousand five hundred years BC. I am looking at a structure which was conceived as an extraordinary site more than four and a half thousand years ago, when the world as we know it today was not even in its infancy. It was the Romans, who much later in the first century AD converted the site into an amphitheatre, one of the largest in the country. It is impossible to imagine exactly what took place here, but it is easily possible to believe in its scale. To walk the top of the embankment, looking down into the arena, one can, with just a little imagination conjure the image of a huge audience, thousands either in approval or disapproval of central proceedings. Today my cup is half full, I hold out my arm and raise my thumb. The rings were remodelled into an artillery fort in 1642 to protect the southern edge of the town during the English civil war, and are

543

used today, for plays, choirs, live bands and firework displays, what a treasure the rings are, but today the arena is deserted. In stark contrast, to the very busy concrete skateboard and BMX Park juxtaposition to the rings, is it because their trousers are around their knees that they keep tumbling off their boards.

There is an interesting footnote, which catches my attention as I take my leave of the arena, oddly it was the celebrated Victorians, in the form of the London and South-west Railway who wanted to destroy the historic rings, to facilitate further railway development. Much of Dorchester stands as a tribute to the glory of Victoriana, but the rings stand in defiance of that period.

I take Monmouth Road and wander through the Fordington area of town, an area which is described in Hardy's biography as suffering from a cholera outbreak, with raw sewage running in the streets, unusually for me I do not take in my surroundings, I am preoccupied with thoughts of Joyce, Barbara, Liz and Emma, almost without knowing how I got there I find myself in sight of the courthouse, a little early by my standards, but I'm sure a cup of coffee, and a numerical discussion of the weather and England's chances of winning the world cup at the weekend will fill what time there is left.

I only spend a few minutes in the jury room, Joyce is almost the same Joyce she always is, her shoulders are perhaps held a little lower than is the norm, and there is not a single outward sign that she has had her hopes of a different life shattered. The afternoon session begins at two o'clock, the judge commences his summing up by very slowly and deliberately reading out the charges, savouring every last dirty word. He does not point us in any particular direction, he emphasises the importance of the testimony given from both sides, and stresses that we must pay attention to the events of the evening of February the sixteenth, we must give credence to one side or the other, we must judge for ourselves the reliability of the witnesses who have spoken before us. That is our task, we must give value, merit, significance to the disposition of either Mr Merryweather or Holly Banks and her two friends, he finishes his address to the eleven of us by saying;

"It is you eleven persons and you alone who now has the task of deciding whether Mr Merryweather is guilty or innocent of the three charges put before him, please now retire to consider your verdict, and I want you to return with a verdict to which you all agree, go into your deliberation room now for an hour today, and come back refreshed tomorrow, and remember discuss this case with no one but yourselves, I believe you have heard sufficient testimony to reach a unanimous decision, as to whether Mr Merryweather is innocent or guilty of." He then once again went through the three charges, not missing a penis, clitoris or vagina.

As we walked from the court into the deliberation room, I said to Elizabeth,

"Was that just a dirty old man getting pleasure from reading out naughty words?"

"Yes without a doubt." Is her reply. As Dawn (white linen) closed the door behind us, Hanna said out loud, "What is it with that creepy old man and words like, penis, vagina and clitoris, he's a bit sick." Sounds of approval came from, Joyce, Elizabeth, Lynda and a couple of the guys.

Coffee, tea and biscuits were passed around the table, I instinctively sat at random in the nearest seat, and looked for John to speak, Terry shouted,

"Oi." He clicked his fingers and pointed to me and to the head of the table, I moved to my new position. I noticed Joyce had already seated herself next to the head of the table, I sat next to her, briefly looking into her eyes, there was a deep sadness about her, she looked like a woman who had had one defeat to many, she appeared to be punch drunk with life itself. It was then an idea germinated in my little grey cells, perhaps, just perhaps, all was not doom and gloom with her future, there may be a way that I can bring light into her shadowy existence.

I started procedure much as John had done the previous week, declaring,

"If John were here he would say to us, let us for the moment not declare our position with regard this case, let each and every one of us pass comment first, let's start to my left with you Tim."

"Well I was impressed with the barristers, particularly the lady one, with her it was definitely a case of less is more, she

545

seemed to hit home with me, more in her fifteen minutes or so, than the other guy did in half a day."

"Terry?" He always sits next to Tim, despite their competitiveness regarding sport, I think these two have become friends, Terry answers,

"I'm a bit concerned about the girls, I think a lot of pressure was brought on them to get this thing into court, I would have liked to have seen them in open court, it wasn't so easy to read between the lines with the video link, which after all is what our job is all about, if we believe both sides then we're never going to sort it out, we know what Michael is made of, we know his limitations, but we didn't really get to grips with the girls, I just don't know whether to believe them or not." A general murmur of agreement went around the room supporting his comment. Next I bring Elizabeth into the debate,

"Well I think they are a bunch of unreliable little bitches, and I wanted to go and give Michael a cuddle." A general silence meets her comment, she adds, "I'm sorry I've rather declared my hand, I just think they set him up."

"David?"

"I don't agree, I think they did ever so well, to go through what must have been a frightening ordeal for them, probably with the father pulling the strings, all the police interviews and what not, it must have been hell, and remember they were only fifteen at the time, can we remember being that age, how well would we have coped with it?" I reply,

"A good point David," and again there is a general murmur of support. "Thomas, see if you can do this without putting any numbers in it." There is a general good-natured laugh, Thomas himself joins in.

"Well I think I've got in sorted out in my mind, it's a case of three against one, and who do you believe?" There is another laugh from the rest of us, this time Thomas did not join in, he genuinely not realising his gaff.

"Hanna?"

"Well I've changed my mind more times this week than I've changed my underwear, I need to hear what the rest of you think."

"Barry?"

"I'm on the fence, I've got a natural trusting instinct, I like to believe everyone, and I like to think there is good in everyone, this is the very reason why I asked not to be on the jury, I'm afraid I've got to find the bad here in one side or the other, there is no grey, one side is lying, I hate to admit it but there it is, and the utter conviction of the legal teams I find disturbing, one of them is talking nonsense, but which one?" Another murmur of support, clearly this is going to be quite a task. Just three to go, I bring Richard into the debate,

"I'm like Thomas, I think I've got it sorted out in my mind, but I want to hear what you've all got to say first, before I declare my opinion."

"Lynda?"

"Well its do you believe the three little pigs, or do you believe the big bad wolf, either way someone has built their house of straw and its coming down, I'm a little surprised this has come to court, there isn't any corroborating evidence to help us, its simply a matter of whose lying."

"Joyce?"

"I just don't know, I need some direction from somebody, we didn't get it from the judge, Jude you're the foreman now, what do you think, and do you know what John thought?" Thanks Joyce. I consider my reply.

"I like your analogy Lynda, your right someone has built a house of straw here, and we are going to blow it away, I can't emphasise enough the importance of our decision, either Michael goes to jail for a considerable term, and is on the sex offenders register for the rest of his life, or the girls and their families are devastated, reputations shattered and possibly a guilty man is freed to do it again. I think we have to take our time on this, we will all benefit from a nights sleep, and some private thought, but remember it must be private, none of our friends or families have heard a word of the testimony, so they cannot help us, in fact their opinions are dangerous, discuss this only with each other." Joyce interrupts,

"I just need some direction, what is your opinion?"

"I'll keep that to myself for now, and John's, he spoke to me Wednesday and declared his hand, I think he had some kind of epiphany, or out of body experience, he didn't expect to be in

547

today, I hope he is now reunited with his wife, it was all he hoped for. Lets first have another cup of this super coffee, well done Richard that old machine was well past its sell by date, then I suggest we have a secret ballot, so as we know where we are with this thing, we might be closer to a decision than we realise, that might give us a little direction, a nudge one way or the other, Joyce can you hand round to everybody a piece from this note pad whilst I refresh my coffee, every one take a blank page, don't put your name on it, just write privately, guilty, not guilty or don't know, and fold them in two and pass them this way, all agreed?" A general mumble of agreement was forthcoming. I refilled my cup and sat down, Joyce gave me a blank sheet of notepaper, which I left unused, I knew she would be scrutinising my every move, I now knew where my mind lay on this issue, I had I believe got Johns comments in perspective. I received the ten folded notes, opened and then closed them individually and calculated the result, tore the notes into shreds and binned them. I realised that just for a moment I could now exert a huge influence on my fellow jurors, I could declare it eight or nine to one, one way or the other, I did not, I added in my vote and declared we were split, four guilty, three in the middle and four not guilty. Once that had sunk in I asked the rest of them for any further comments, starting once again on my left with Tim.

"Well I'm not one of the don't knows, I believe I've got it straight in my head, but it's a bit disturbing that four of you think the opposite from me."

"Terry?"

"Same as that."

"Elizabeth?"

"Well I declared my hand the last time around, obviously I'm a not guilty, I don't believe a word the girls said."

"David?"

"I'm as decided as you are, but I don't agree with you."

"Hanna?"

"I envy you both, I just don't see how you can be so sure, look we've asked Jude to be our foreman, he's kindly agreed and if he's asked us to not yet declare our hand I think we should do as he ask, or perhaps others would like to be foreman."

"Thank you Hanna, Thomas?"

"I'm like Tim, I think I've decided but I find it odd that four of you disagree."

"Barry?"

"I think you all know I'm a don't know, and I'm not looking forward to the rest of the debate."

"Richard?"

"Having heard you all I'm less sure than I was, but I did vote decisively just now."

"Lynda?"

"I think that the big bad wolf is huffing and puffing on the little pig's house, I think."

"Joyce?"

"I don't know, I don't think I'm smart enough to fathom this out, and we are split right down the middle here, so how are we going to sort this out?" I respond,

"Actually we are not split down the middle, the three don't knows belong with the not guilty, remember the golden rule if your not sure, if you're a don't know, then your in the not guilty camp, you cannot convict a man of anything if your not sure, remember the quote, 'beyond reasonable doubt', if you have doubt then its not guilty, so at the moment we are seven not guilty and four guilty. If one or two not guilty slip into the don't know camp then its nine to two, but if two guilty and a couple of don't knows go the other way then it's the opposite, so remember you have to be sure, convinced that Michael is guilty or innocent."

"Shall we throw it out to open debate, or ask his lordship if we can go home to sleep on it, let's see if we can agree on that, a show of hands please if you've had enough for today?"

"Unanimous, you see we can agree, lets go home, Thomas can you ring that bell behind you please?"

This was quite acceptable to Hawkeye.

It was a relief that nobody wanted to discuss the case in the jury room, which soon emptied, I felt an obligation to be the last out, should any body want to talk over a problem, but most left with sport, numbers and weather to the fore. Joyce was waiting for me outside the building, I believe I hid my disappointment, I didn't have the mental energy to go deeper into her life, I wanted to be home. All she said to me was,

"Please tell me which way to vote, please tell me your decision." I pitied her for just a moment, I shouldn't have I know, but I gave her my opinion, she immediately relaxed, a little of the sparkle came back into her eyes, I think sharing a little secret with me, was enough for her to carry on with her misfortunate existence for the moment.

It was with Joyce in mind that I then strode down the high street, I went into the White Hart Hotel and booked a discreet table for two, for tomorrow night, Friday. I looked at the menu, quickly calculated the price of two meals, added starters and desert, a medium priced bottle of wine, I then paid this amount plus thirty for a bottle of champagne, which I requested to be placed on table twelve at eight o'clock the next evening. I then asked for two of the hotels cards, on the back of each I wrote 'table twelve eight o'clock, Friday the nineteenth', and put the cards in my wallet. I paid a hundred pounds at the Hotel desk, giving the very helpful, well presented, softly spoken young man who was in attendance, and who's eye shadow had been skilfully applied, my mobile number to ring should the bill be in excess of that which I'd paid, and informed him if it was not, the Hotel was to retain the balance as a tip.

Feeling a little smug and on a high, I wandered back up the high street, paused at a jewellers, and on impulse, no more than a caprice, I went in and purchased a pair of matching wedding rings. A half hour later I left the shop, the rings were in their velvet boxes in my pocket, I was feeling pretty damn pleased with myself, sometimes a man's got to do what a man's got to do, regardless of the expense. The effervescence did not have long to linger on my consciousness, soon after I left the jewellers I stepped into a considerable heap of dog shite, whilst stepping back against a shop front to allow a wheelchair user to enjoy the mainstream of the pavement. So covered in shite was my shoe, and as always so spotlessly clean was my van, that I scraped the shoe off of my foot, by putting my heel on to a municipal waste bin, and dragging my foot backwards so that the offending shoe, not one of my best, fell into the bin, where it remained. A thought occurred to me, where is Liz when I need her to rescue something from a bin.

I put the matching white and yellow gold banded, slightly decorative wedding rings in the small secret compartment I had built into the van, originally to conceal cash, should I obtain any from roofing customers, but as all of my work has been local authority work, it has all been invoiced, there never was any cash. The only use I have had for my little hide-e-hole has been to conceal my favourite sweets, American hard gums, from my family. It's a pleasure to put something of value in it for once, it was a lot of work to construct, so it gives me satisfaction to use it for its intended purpose. With the table booked for two, the meal paid for, and the two rings tucked away, I was once again feeling self-satisfied, nay almost conceited, but then my wet, cold left foot reminded me of my failings.

I did not stop to pick up the healthy looking dead cock pheasant on the way home, as it was by now raining fairly hard, and my left foot had come back from the cold to rejoin the rest of me. I got home a little after five thirty and managed to get in my signature greeting of,

"Any post?" Before Liz had noticed my arrival.

"Hi, yes you've got some drawings to price, doesn't look like your sort of work."

"Where is it?"

"Central London, and its slate, you won't want to do it, but you could sub it out to Tim, and perhaps earn enough to take me away."

"That reminds me, did you do any thing about a possible skiing trip at Christmas?"

"I've been looking today, there isn't much left, but we can go to Finland on Boxing Day for a week, and the monies not bad."

"Finland, great lets do it, perhaps we could catch up with Kris's family."

"From what I remember there wasn't many of his family left, what a sad tale that was."

"Absolutely, still on a brighter note, we've got the pleasure of Dirk and Anna on Sunday, it will be so good to catch up with them, oh and can you book me and one or both of the girls out by ferry if possible on Monday, I spoke to Barbara today, she's just about holding things together, but Anne and Karen come back at the weekend, she's not ready to be on her own yet."

551

"Will she ever be?"

"Good question, you want a glass of red or a tea?"

"Its Thursday Jude, I've got my evening class in Yeovil, remember, so its tea for me."

"OK, that's one tea one red."

"Jude you need to watch what you're drinking, it's getting a bit too regular."

"OK will do, I'll just get this jury thing out of the way then I'll look at it."

"I'll just get this out the way, I'll just get that out the way first, beginning to sound like a stuck record, I'll just get this jury service out the way, I'll just get Christmas out the way, I'll just get the rugby season out the way, I'll just get the girls grown up and out of the way!"

"Very good, very droll, nice to see you've got Emma's crash out of the way."

"Jude, we will never get that one out of the way, it's not just me and Emma that's having nightmares you know," She adds, "Not only are you sleeping badly your dressing like a tramp, anything you want to tell me about your other shoe?"

"Not just now."

We do catch up on each others day over a cup and a glass, Liz is right as always, I am putting away too much red wine, it was always that we would share a bottle on weekend nights, now I'm opening and sometimes finding the bottom of a bottle most nights of the week, without help from Liz, I'll just get Jean Pierre underground then I'll tackle it.

We eat together, Emma is working, but still very quiet, withdrawn, we think its beginning to sink in that she could so easily have died. Liz goes out and Emma comes back early.

"They have told me to go home and get some TLC, apparently I'm not concentrating."

"You'll be OK in a few days, you've had your first big shock in your life, these things affect us all differently."

"How do you mean?"

"Its classed as trauma, look it up on your computer, its what causes our lads who are coming back from Afghanistan to crack up weeks or months later, in their case they have seen or witnessed too much too quick."

552

"Yea one of my classmates has a brother out there, she like said he came home last Christmas and totally forgot to like bring his head back with him, and sometimes he comes back with like someone else's head. Talking of computers can we go to the scrap yard and see if the cars still there, I've lost my memory stick and its like got a load of my course work on it, how much have you had to drink?"

"Oh I'm OK, only half a glass, we can go there now, I'll ring Jim Smyth and see if he's about."

"Are you sure? It's a bit late, its half past six."

"He lives in a bungalow on site, he'll be OK, he's a good old boy, are you sure you want to go? the cars not very pretty." Privately I thought it might be a good idea for her to see the car again, it might reinforce the message of just what can happen if you loose concentration for a moment, or drive a car badly maintained, or get a text from your stupid father that wasn't meant for you.

"Yes, I need to find my memory stick."

"OK I'll ring Jim." Which I do and I receive a positive answer, so in a few moments we are in my van and on a short five mile journey, to one of those out in the middle of nowhere scrap yards. This one probably started as a breakers yard or a dumping ground for machinery and vehicles during the Second World War, it is now a sprawling mass of twisted metal and shattered cars, covering some five acres of Dorset's handsome countryside, and in an area of outstanding natural beauty, but as it was there before the area was designated as such, there it will remain. As we turn off the road and pull into an area that is either a mass of mud or dust, today its mud, Jim is there to meet us.

"This the young 'un what was driving it?" We both nod, he puts his arm around Emma, "Yous is a very luckee young gel, I can show 'e a number of moters 'ere, don't look anyfing near as bed as yourn, an' people died in 'em." Emma is horrified that a seventy year old tramp, as she would refer to him, dressed in the dirtiest clothes she has ever seen, this side of a third world documentary, has his arm around her, and worse, is looking unlikely to release her any time soon, Jim continues,

"Look at that white B M dubbaya, not a winda' broke in it, 'e died, and that there litta' blue vaux'all wouldn't need a lot to put that back on the road, she was a goner too."

"Well Jim I don't want to keep you all evening, can you show us my daughters car?"

"Yep there 'e is under them two fiesta's, I'll just fire up me slew and whip 'em off." To Emma's relief Jim releases her from his grasp, she cannot help but look at her shoulder and side, to ascertain the degree of contamination. She'll never see the likes of Jim for what he really is, a good old boy, and the salt of the earth, do anything for you if there's a note involved, a note with the picture of the Queen on it.

Very quickly Jim fires up a huge machine, which to most of the country is a twenty-ton excavator, but to this part of the world it's a slew, to others still it's a three-sixty. A cloud of black, diesel exhaust fumes drifts off toward the local beauty spot, the viewing point from which one can see four counties on a good day, Emma looks at the black cloud, and I know she is thinking, global warming, and carbon footprint, stuff she is covering at college at present.

We eventually gain access to the mangled wreck of her Cleo, Emma quickly finds the missing memory stick, not on the floor but in the head lining, it must have got rammed into a crevice on one of the cars bounces. I thank Jim, slip him a twenty for his trouble, and walk through the mud to my van, thinking I might just as well have contaminated it with dog shite earlier. I look behind me, Emma is not with me, she is stood stock still, staring at her car. She has that stare crazy look about her, that we all get from time to time when we walk the beach, often one can see a family, mum, dad, kids and the dog frolicking on the beach, when suddenly one of them becomes motionless, as if pole-axed by an idea, and they stare out to sea, lost in a dream, they are the ancient mariner, Christopher Columbus, or Captain Kirk on the USS Enterprise. Emma was transfixed on what remained of her car, I called to her and got no response, I walk back to her and speak to her softly,

"Em you ok?" Still no response, I nudge her arm, "Come on 'Em." That nudge was like the boy pulling his finger out of the dyke. She turned to me with tears in her eyes, took one step and

554

buried her head in my chest, she put her arms around my waist, held on tight, and simply burst. The floodgates opened and she sobbed, she sobbed until I could feel her tears through my shirt. She cried like I have never known her cry before, I think she cried not just for the loss of her lovely car, but because it had come home to her just how close she had been to losing her life. I believe she wept for the loss of her Grandfather, which she had taken in her stride at the time, and for the loss of her uncle, Jean Pierre, who had been a favourite of both the girls for as long as we could remember. Finally I think she wept because of a deep realisation that it is not a perfect world that we live in. The magic that is childhood, the indestructibility that is your parental guidance, can come off the rails, it can let you down, things can and do go horribly wrong. It was the moment Emma said goodbye to her childhood, and realised that to survive and prosper in the adult world, she would have to look out for herself, it was a pivotal moment for both of us. I knew that when she let go of me, she wasn't just letting go of me physically, but mentally also, I had showed her that I can be seriously flawed, something she had never considered before, I had made a careless mistake that could so easily have ended her life, I'm sure that she now realised that one day she would have to face life's problems without me and her mother. I would never be the best dad in the world again. It was a life changing and deeply painful moment for both of us, which when she eventually stopped crying, we shrugged off with a hug and me saying something shallow, and totally disproportional,

"Come on 'Em, let's get you home away from this shitty place."

Emma never spoke on the way home, but when we got home she asked when her Uncle Jean Pierre's funeral was, I told her it was exactly in a week, next Thursday. She then asked if she could come, and apologised to me for not attending my father's funeral just two weeks before. We never compelled her to come, Emma invented a reason why she was to busy, we knew that at the time, she couldn't face it, she wasn't ready to step into our world. She was in it now, up to her neck, I mourned for the loss of her innocence. I imagined that in Emma's new world, Pinocchio didn't just have a funny nose, he was a liar, and Cruella Deville

555

wasn't just a weird old lady who chased puppies, she was a murderer.

I then told Emma about the Ford Fiesta that Richard (I can do that) had said I could have, I explained it would be about four weeks as I had to do some work to earn the car, and as my hand was out of action, was it OK if she waited. The new adult Emma just shrugged her shoulders and said,

"C'est la vie." And gave me a big hug, I think I could get to appreciate the new Emma, just as much as I'd loved the old one. I changed the subject,

"Talking about my hand, do you know why Nashy hasn't had me arrested?"

"Oh he came round after I'd come back from the hospital and while you were still there, he told mum he'd rung the police and reported you for assault, but after mum filled him in with the full details of my accident, and explained that you had to run to get to me, 'cause he was blocking our drive, and I think he saw me looking a bit iffy, he said he would phone the police back and drop the complaint, but you should have seen him, he looked like a panda." We had a good laugh, Emma went in to clean the mud off her memory stick, while I cleaned the mud out of my van.

On returning to the house, I see Emma is on her computer, and I ask her if she will do a little research for me.

"OK, what do you want to know?"

"I saw a grave that interested me the other day down in Dorchester, is it possible that you can ask your computer to look into the British forces campaign in a place called Salonika in 1918?"

"Sure." I wanted to discover more, of exactly what had been expected of Private Leonard William Tattershall, I knew something of the militarily disastrous campaigns on the western front during the First World War, indeed my maternal Grandmother had lost her first husband on the catastrophic first day of the battle of the Somme. Salonika was unknown to me, I thought it might be a challenge to Emma's laptop. I was astounded by the instantaneous and detailed response, within mere moments I had several pages to read, Emma had printed them out as I watched, I was more than surprised with the computers swift and detailed comeback, which I voiced to Emma when I thanked her.

"That's nothing that was easy, you can ask the search engine anything you like, literally anything."

"Search engine?"

"Sorry its just a term it means...............it means..................well it's a sort of electronic vehicle, you can use it to go anywhere in an instant, go on ask me a random question." I sigh, then say,

"OK, how much concrete is there in the Hoover Dam?"

"Blimey, well I did say random, here goes."

"Six million six hundred thousand tons, go on give me another one."

"How many species of butterfly are there in Colombia?"

"3273 confirmed, it is estimated that there is a possible maximum of around 3800."

"OK in what year was the Telstra Tower built in Canberra, Australia?"

"Piece of cake, 1980."

"Bloody hell is there nothing that thing doesn't know, here's one for you, is Michael Merryweather guilty or innocent, no sorry that's not fair, ok ask it this, what are the ten most common questions it has been asked?"

"Wow that is really random, do you want me to print them?"

"Yea, why not." I walk away with several pieces of A4 paper in my hand, the top one is amusing, interesting and an indictment of modern society, it appears that the inquisitiveness of our nation is random at best, if not downright obscure, I was though very impressed with my introduction into the World Wide Web, I read the list as I wander through to the kitchen in search of my unfinished glass of red,

1 What is the meaning of life?
2 Is there a God?
3 Will I get laid tonight?
4 How many credits do I need to get a degree?
5 Is there life on other planets?
6 How much oil do I put in a chocolate fountain?
7 Do I really have a soul mate?

557

8 What is bilingualism?
9 Do blondes really have more fun?
10 Why is my computer so slow?

I discard the nonsense, collect my refilled glass, and learn that Salonica has now changed its name to Thessalonica, and is in northern Greece. So breathtaking is the information which Emma printed out for me, I read it twice.

Liz and I never really caught up later in the evening, she came back late from her evening class, a trifle hot and bothered, something had obviously not gone according to plan, and I found the bottom of a rather lovely bottle of nineteen ninety eight Pomerol, anything from that Saint-Emillion region is to my liking. I never told her that I was now foreman, and that I'd found a new car for Emma, and she never asked me to explain my text re a wedding ring, she was unusually preoccupied, but I did manage to bring her up to date with Emma's outburst, to which she replied,

"Good I knew it would come."

DAY TEN

DECISION

Friday the nineteenth of October, my last day in court, my last day of enduring my Dads paper, events are a little more normal today. Its seven am and Liz is out with the dogs, Emma is asleep, it was a better night for us all. We still have a long way to go, particularly with Emma, twice in the night she was calling out for help in her sleep, I hope she wasn't in a burning car, but just surrounded by cattle. Liz has already said that if it continues for more than two weeks, she will ask around her network, to see if anyone can recommend some help for her, someone professional, out of the family she can talk to. Liz is off to Dorchester today to Kingston Maurwood College, but just for the morning so there is no gain in going in one vehicle, for the first time is strikes me as significant that Liz is working in a building that the Hardy family helped to construct. It is a real connection with our local history. I must remember to mention this to Hardy's statue when our paths cross a little later. Liz still has an air of preoccupation about her, it's probably Emma's near miss, I'll see what I can do with a couple of bottles of red tonight and a broad shoulder. I pour myself a coffee but admit to myself that our coffee at home is not up to the standard of the new machine in the jury room, I must have to talk to Richard (I can do that).

The Daily Mirror today is full of promise of world cup victory for our rugby team and full of woe for the disgraced footballers, despite this I'm sure Terry and Tim will be side by side today. This thought makes me realise just how successful the jury system has been for us, we came together only ten days ago, as total strangers, ten days we have all put to good use. The two sports enthusiast seem to have struck up a genuine friendship, four of the jury members, Joyce, Hanna, Richard and John all felt they had got to know me well enough to trust me with intimate details of their troubled lives, remarkable in such a short time.

Clearly Elizabeth and Andy the usher have taken this intimacy to another level, I believe that most of us feel that we have gotten to know each other well, conversation flows between the twelve of us; we have become comfortable with each other. The exception is probably Barry, he much more than anyone else has struggled with the whole process. I'm not sure he is capable of finding anyone guilty of anything, thinking back to our removal of Alice (fake fur) on day three, John would have been equally justified in removing Barry for the same reason. I know that if Michael is found guilty today, that it will have to be on a ten-to-one decision. I've thought long and hard about what John had told me, there is no doubt that he was a step above us all in intelligence, I believe also that it is beyond doubt that he knew he would not see this case through, and his confession to me of his opinion with regard Michael Merryweather's guilt or innocence was to get me on board. I believe he saw me as a likely stand-in foreman, and he wanted to influence the verdict through me. I've now got this in proportion in my mind, and I will not do John's bidding, other than to rescue the floundering Joyce I am determined not to influence the jury today.

I pour myself a second coffee, and find just three minor points of interest in today's Mirror; The Welsh town of Caerphilly, is to scrap over one thousand road signs as it is believed they are causing accidents, and two teenagers have been jailed for torturing and beating an innocent man to death, in the process they extracted his PIN numbers from him, to enable them to later empty his bank accounts after his death, one account contained seven pence, the other six. And finally a teenager in Poole, Dorset has paid to have 'mum' tattooed across her back in Chinese letters, her father joked that it said 'chicken chow main', she was horrified to discover that a real translation was in fact 'friend from hell'.

The Times has much about the two suicide bomb attacks on the bus carrying the returning, previously exiled, former Pakistan Prime Minister, Benazir Bhutto, who escaped this time, just. Transport strikes in Paris are threatening to bring chaos to the travel plans of thousands of English rugby fans in the capital for the world cup final, would these strikes have been allowed to go ahead, had the French beaten England into tomorrow's final?

560

Nick Clegg is now favourite to succeed Ming Campbell as Liberal Democrat leader, though it is thought that Chris Huhne will push him close. Huhne has launched his leadership campaign saying his position could be summed up in nine words, 'A fairer and greener society where we put people in charge', a charming sentiment, although eleven words, let's hope he doesn't work in the treasury, the paper speculates, 'what sort of leader would he be?' A rather witty letter caught my eye, it was with regard to a debate running in the letters column about alcohol consumption, a chap writes today the 19th October 2007, that earlier in the year he realised that drinking an excessive amount of beer was likely to be bad for him in the long term, and he therefore resolved to limit his intake to a pint a day, and he is proud to say that he has stuck to his resolution, and further he has now drunk his way into the future, he has reached April 20th 2009 with no ill effects. Pupils at a school in Chelmsford are to be given time out cards, which they can hold up in class when they feel they are about to lose their temper, and this time out card gives them the right to walk out of any lesson whenever they choose, quite bizarre. As is the comment on page thirty-eight that one in four Germans believes that the Nazis had their good side!

The weather is clear bright and sunny today, with four degrees of frost, nothing new on the road to mention, perhaps the intermittent black-ice has slowed traffic just enough to allow the wildlife to cross the road, no such luck for a black BMW, or as Jim Smyth would say a B M Dubbaya. This vehicle has lost control on a bend and done an Emma, nobody is with the car, and there is brightly coloured police tape around it, so I do not pause, there is no need for a good Samaritan.

I park at the top of town as usual, I have enjoyed visiting Hardy's main town of Casterbridge over the last two weeks, we, the town and I have become more familiar, I now feel a new affinity with the town, which I hope will stay with me. I cross the top of town roundabout, which as usual brings me to the foot of the plinth upon which Thomas Hardy is looking a little more optimistic today, gone is his long face of yesterday. I stand for a few moments and look at this small framed individual, and recall the last instalment which I read of his biography last night whilst waiting for Liz to return.

I nip into the Library to return my copy of Hardy's novel and also to take out a copy of 'Jude the Obscure' as I was named by my mother after one of Hardy's central characters, I think it is finally time I read the book, I've purposely avoided reading it up it now, I've not wanted to delve into the personality of Hardy's creation, not wanted to draw comparisons, look for fault, but having now read a good portion of Hardy's excellently informative biography, I am now interested to learn what events and what characters led to the creation of his Jude, perhaps I'll take it to France with me next week.

We are held only very briefly in the jury room this morning, there is just time for a few cursory good mornings, we are soon settled in our customary positions in the deliberation room, which is accessed only from the main courtroom. Hawkeye is keen for us to recommence our cogitation, I imagine this is another judge with another train to catch. After a few introductory comments and preliminaries, I request another secret ballot, which is swiftly conducted, resulting in a considerable altering of opinions.

The resulting figures show a seven-two-two result, over night five of our number have shifted in their viewpoint, either from one extreme to the other, or from off of, or on to the fence. We then at my suggestion, all in turn declare exactly what our decision is and provide as full a reason as possible, as to why we have reached the position we have. This declaration of our viewpoint takes two full turns around the table, and more than two hours to complete. We then have an open vote and we have moved to nine-two-nil, we are almost there, this is mainly due to some very well expressed opinions around the table, several of our number, both male and female have spoken eloquently and with conviction. We pause for a snack, which today is provided by the court, or rather by us the taxpayer, and Elizabeth serves coffee all round. One or two people at the table have surprised me, in the nature and power of their debate, Elizabeth is one of them, she has today been both forceful and astute in her comments, so two has been Hanna. In fact along with Lynda, those three women have contributed much to the discussion, and they may well have carried the day, and three of the male jury members along with them, they would be the wet's, Barry

562

(Chaplain), Thomas (numbers) and David (the weather man). Joyce offered little to the debate, perhaps I have misjudged her, in that she does not have the mental depth to match her fashion sense and considerable good looks, I think from the moment last night, my moment of weakness, when I wrongly declared my hand to her, she has been treading water, waiting for the vote.

After the drinks break we do another circuit of the table, and have a free for all question and answer session, a second pause for coffee and another open vote, we are ten-one-nil, this process has been a little easier than I expected, it has still been a long and arduous procedure, but I feel that from our position of last night when we were four-three-four, people have altered their positions remarkable quickly. This I believe all boils down to a matter of confidence. If one perceives that intelligent and articulate people around you, are of firm opinion and are confident in their persuasion, it chips away at your own assuredness, you become less positive, less sure of your own point of view. I watched this process unfold in front of me this day, it was an education, and it was perhaps just one or two percentage points an indicator of politics, at high table. It is not knowledge that wins the day, but perception of knowledge that is spoken with assured confidence. We were now stuck at ten-one-nil, we had one person on the fence, I set the other nine to ware down the doubter, and oddly it was Thomas, whose name is forever linked with doubt. He eventually stated that,

"I respect all of you, and I have listened intently to your argument, I feel there has to be something lacking in me, that I cannot see and hear what you can, so I will join you in the belief that you cannot all be wrong." For the avoidance of doubt, I check with him that his vote is now with the majority, he replies with a firm,

"Yes." I check the clock, it is two-fifty-five, perhaps Hawkeye would catch his train yet.

"OK, Thomas please ring the bell and lets put this thing to bed."

As we all stand to leave the room, that had become our cell for the day, I slipped one of the two cards from The King's Arms Hotel in front of Joyce, she picked it up and read the front, I then turned it to reveal my own writing on the back, 'Table twelve,

Eight o'clock, Friday 19th'. We looked into each others eyes, mine giving away nothing, hers had fireworks going off deep inside them, fireworks and disbelief, I put my hand on top of hers for just a moment, the gesture was not missed by Hanna, who misread it, caught my eye and winked, very subtly. I smiled in return.

We filed out of the deliberation room, escorted by the beautiful aroma of white linen, for the penultimate time. As the door is opened to the main courtroom, it is not the courtroom we have been accustomed to, the court is occupied to capacity, there are many more people present than at any time during the last two weeks. I doubt that I will ever walk into another room in my life with so many people looking toward me. If this is what Andy Warhol had in mind when he termed that we should, each and every one of us have our fifteen minutes of fame, I would happily abstain from mine. I feel deeply uncomfortable, almost naked under the gaze of so many, for two weeks the courtrooms attention has been on others, it is now towards me, my mouth and throat are as dry as chaff, the hairs on back of my neck are up. Not only are the public gallery and the press area full, but every member of the defence and prosecution teams are present, as are the attendant court ushers, all the witnesses and police officers involved in the case are also in attendance for the decision, our decision. We the jury return in file on to our all too familiar hard benches. One quick glance from all of us to the glass cage in the centre of the room is all that is necessary to bring home to us the importance of the moment, there is a stark realisation that Michael's moment has arrived, he is for the first time standing. He is trying unsuccessfully to control himself, his legs are trembling and he is sobbing, he is unable to find a resting place for his hands. He holds his head, he wipes his face, he puts his hands to his sides, he holds his legs attempting to control them. He is shaking slightly from head to foot, Michael is out of control with the terror of the moment, he watches us take our seats, he is soon to discover whether we are good or bad people, whether we hate him or like him.

The jury all sit with the exception of myself, I take up position one, as instructed by Dawn, and remain standing. We are all transfixed by the trembling figure of Michael, I try not to look at him, and look into the Hawkish eyes of the judge, the room is absolutely quiet, apart from Michael's sobbing, guttural noises, which are exaggerated by the vast, hollow, silent building.

The rest of the jury and all other persons present cannot move their gaze from the distraught, shaking frame of the defendant. I am compelled to follow their stare. An image passes through my mind of a man awaiting execution, as I have so recently read of in Hardy's past, how is it possible, that when faced with a man reduced by terror into the state I see before me, to have the presence of mind and resolve to flick a switch to deliver an electric current, or to draw back a bolt to release a trapdoor on a scaffold, or indeed to pull a trigger to dispatch such a suffering man from this world. Hardy himself had witnessed two such events, and found them to be profound. Michael is showing tremendous guts and bravery, to stay on his feet as best he can, and await the decision of eleven complete strangers, it must take an equal and opposite fortitude to carry out a death sentence.

Somehow during the first World War in appalling and in humane conditions, like those I read about last night, Allied soldiers who themselves were terrified, were able to shoot at point blank range a number of their fellow men, who had not through weakness, but through terror, succumbed to the constant fear, and refused to face the enemy. They had subsequently been labelled as cowards and put to death by their colleagues. That thought struck me at this moment to be an impossible situation for any ordinary man such as myself to deal with. The boys we sent out to defend France and the free world, were just that, ordinary lads, what had they seen? What had they experienced? That the country presumed would make them able to do what was required for King and Country.

Looking at Michael now almost convulsing, there appears a dark stain on his inner left thigh, which quickly reaches to his knee, before he somehow regains control of his bladder, I cannot swallow, I feel now that it is possible to read out only one verdict. Several members of the jury are struggling to breath regularly, at least three of the females are in tears, and visibly upset, those being Joyce, Hanna and Elizabeth, Lynda is unmoved, several of the men are having to work hard to remain composed, it is very

565

difficult to witness a fellow man so reduced by fright and fear, to the point of petrifaction.

The judge address's me,

"Have you reached a verdict on which you are all agreed?"

"We have." A loud cheer goes up from the public gallery, the supporters of the girls clearly sense victory, Michael takes this as a blow, his knees wobble, but he somehow remains standing.

"With regard indictment one, how do you find the defendant?" The dark stain on the inside of Michael's left leg reaches his shin.

"Not guilty." There are loud groans from the public gallery.

"Is that the decision of you all?"

"It is."

"How do you find the defendant with regard indictment two?" Michael is unchanged.

"Not guilty."

"Is that the decision of you all?"

"It is."

"How do you find the defendant with regard indictment three?" Still Michael is unchanged.

"Not guilty."

"Is that the decision of you all?"

"It is." I watch every moment on Michaels face, and I glimpse a split second, a split second of disbelief, when his horror turned to relief, his legs finally buckle. To his credit he is able to re-stand, he wipes his face, his sobs of terror are now sobs of release, but none the less diminished. There is a half-minute during which every decent person present shares Michael's solace. Hawkeye breaks the moment.

"Thank you foreman, thank you jury, Mr Merryweather you are free to go." We file from the court, following the trail of white linen for the last time, we are all shaken but relieved, I hope that we all believe we got it right.

In the jury room we say our goodbyes, a peck on the cheek from Hanna, a last glimpse into her bottomless silicone valley, awkward handshakes with my left hand to all the male members, there was some thanks for my foremanly duties and it was goodbye. I keep my last handshake for Richard (I can do that) with him its left hand to left hand so its more comfortable, and in my hand is the other card from The King's Arms Hotel, he looks at the card, both sides and looks back to me, I give him a firm and very deliberate nod and a sideways look towards Joyce, who has today for the last time in my experience, made a superb effort. She looks matchless amongst her peers, indeed in these limited surroundings as regard her sense of dress she is peerless. Richard immediately catches on, his eyes widen and eyebrows lift, again I nod, nothing is needed to be said, he mouths thank you silently. I say,

"Your welcome, don't squander the opportunity, and I'll be in touch regarding the car, I've got your card and address, I don't suppose my daughter, Emma will be able to contain herself, I will eventually give in to her demands, and call in one day, to let the dog see the rabbit, it won't be next week, I've got a funeral to attend in France, I'll give you a call in a couple of weeks."

"I understand, whenever." He then holds up the hotel card and says,

"Thanks again." With Richard leaving, I am just able to shout good luck to Terry (rugby) for tomorrow's world cup final, he shouts back,

"Thanks I'm watching it with Tim, thought I might educate him, as the football team has now been disbanded."

"Good luck with that too." They leave the room together, I didn't hear Tim's reply, but I'm sure it was equal to Terry's jibe. Now it's just Joyce with all her matching accessories and myself, she asks,

"Can I walk with you to your car?"

"Of course, come on take my arm, let's get out of this place." This time, as we are no longer jury members we are able to take the short cut directly across the main door of the courthouse, this had previously been out of bounds to us, to make certain that we had no interaction between us and the main cast. As we stroll past the glass double doors, Michael appears, a free man, he stops abruptly in front of me, still sporting one leg a shade darker than the other. I put my left hand out to meet his, he meets it with both his hands, shaking my hand with his left and gripping my wrist tightly with his right, he looks me in the eye and attempts to say thank you. He tries several times to mouth this one simple phrase, but speech is beyond him, not a sound is forth coming, I look him in the eyes and say a short sentence that I hope stays with him for a very long time,

"Michael, make good use of the rest of your life, and choose your friends with care." He nods and through his tears he manages a faint, almost inaudible,

"Thank you." We leave the courthouse for the last time, and as I take my final leave of Thomas Hardy, I introduce Joyce to him, and tell her,

"This man has greatly added to the whole experience of the last two weeks, he has educated me into the ways of Dorchester in the nineteenth century, through his remarkable writing I have learnt a great deal, in the future when I visit this town it will be with only one eye in today's world, the other will forever search out and find that which is left from his era, I will drive to Dorchester but I will wander and explore the streets of Casterbridge." She replies,

"You're quite eloquent, have you ever thought of writing?"

"Me, write, look at my hand I can't even hold a pen, come on." We cross the road and I pause under a plane tree, to look into Joyce's face, she opens the conversation,

"So come on what's this about?" Holding aloft the hotel card,

"It's about a chance for you to have a future."

"Tell me more."

"No I won't tell you much more, if you turn up you will I'm sure have a pleasant meal, in pleasant company, not my company, but the company of a man who I know admires you, he's a sensitive man who has had problems of his own, and is in a much similar position to yourself, stuck in a loveless marriage that like yours is doomed to fail, go beneath the bravado, get to the soft underbelly and I think you will be pleasantly surprised, oh and the meal is on me and my wife Liz."

"I don't know what to say."

"Don't say anything, just turn up with an open mind."

"Thank you Jude, you're very kind, and that was such a kind thing to say to Michael, I hope he takes your advice."

"Me too, he's a young man, he can start again, but he must be careful how he chooses his friends."

"Yes he must, and I would like to count you as one of mine."

"Of course, now off you go and enjoy your evening, don't try too hard, go with the flow."

"Thank you Jude, thank you for everything, I trust you and maybe you've given me hope."

"I'd like to think so, who knows, if you, no, when you turn up tonight, go with a blank page, without loaded expectation, suck it and see." I put my arm out and she responds, and we share a hug of intensity and familiarity.

"I've never had a big brother, but you've made me feel what it would have been like to have one, to have someone looking out for me."

"Good luck and take this chance, make good use of the rest of your life." We part company, her smile is genuine, I hope I haven't misjudged Richard.

Before I drive home from the court for the last time, I sit in my vehicle and take in the last of the work that Jayne and I put together, independently, almost twenty years ago.

I . . . . .'

RESOLUTION

Jackie's four-hour flight in the Chinook has resulted in the birth of a healthy girl. The giant helicopter lands for a brief pause to refuel on the humongous, United States aircraft carrier, The U S S Roosevelt, in the Caribbean. During its pause, a twenty-eight year old exhausted and apprehensive young mother, and her daughter of just one hour are moved to a more comfortable position.

The Chinook, refuelled lifts off again and flies a further hour, upon its next contact with terrafirma Jackie is transferred to a luxury twelve seat Lear jet, on a small private runway on the Caribbean island of Barbados. She is fully trusting of everyone in the hugely complicated chain of logistics, as at each and every interruption of her long and exhausting journey, she is reminded of the original greeting she received at Jhiro's home, 'Sir Arnold Elliot invites you home'. Each time Jackie hears those words she is deeply comforted, and is able to concentrate all of her devotion to where it is most needed, towards the comfort, care and nutritional needs of her newly born daughter. Who has come into the world in extraordinary circumstances, in good health, albeit she is a little jaundiced and quite small at just over five and a half pounds.

In the mind of the father of the dark haired, brown eyed new arrival, the full implication of the short, six word message, 'Don't worry, I'll call you, I', takes time to sink in. He does what he does in any crisis, he picks up the telephone. He questions everyone he can find, no one has seen her today. He talks to his armed guards who patrol the only entrance-exit road, and is assured that no-one has passed that way today. He searches the house, he has many people look into every possible space that a human being could occupy outside the house, but every one draws a blank. It is only very late in the day that a young man who works in his garage-come security building, tells him that when he came back in his Sikorsky this morning, he thought it must have been to collect Jackie, he thought that the baby was arriving, that Jhiro first learns the truth. So his pretty blond lovebird had somehow flown the nest, he questioned the men who's job it is to defend his hacienda, they confirmed that he took off at 12-04 pm, landed at 12-31 pm and lifted off again at 12-34 pm.

How had she done this? He loathed that both Jackie and his child were out of his reach, at first he suspected is was Medellin, but dismissed the thought as quickly as it had arrived, they would not take his child, he would have to be very careful with them tomorrow. A moment of pure clarity came to him, it was a moment of realisation, everything he now had to do became transparent, he could see through the fog, he could now not escape with her, but he could still protect Jackie and his child, he knew the cost to himself would be high.

He went back into the house, picked up the telephone and announced that he had found her, she had passed out on the fourth floor, but that now both Jackie and the child were fine, she would need rest and quite, so no-one was to visit their rooms. He stayed up throughout the night, he could not consider sleep. He paced his rooms waiting for the telephone to ring.

The Lear jet landed at R A F Brize Norton in Oxfordshire, allowing for a gain of six hours, it touched down at shortly before six am, Greenwich Mean Time, Sir Arnold Elliot and Simon, Jackie's long standing and loyal groom were waiting by the side of the runway, in Arnold's Rolls-Royce. Jackie and the child had a brief medical check, and were told by the base's commanding officer that they would very much appreciate her making herself available for a de-briefing session in the very near future. As they believed that she may possess information vital to the American effort against drug trafficking. An image of the tunnel laboratory flashed through her mind, she knew that one word from her and more than two thousand people could lose their lives, and just as many family's would be missing their income, she dismissed the thought from her mind, this was something she would have to grapple with another day, that much responsibility was a staggering burden, but instinctively she knew that she could not be responsible for thousands of children losing one or more parent and their school funding. Arnold, who came in the room as the request for the de-briefing session was made, said,

"Never mind all that now, let me get a good look at her." Their greeting was a genuine, warm and long one, he was greatly surprised to see her with such a young child in her arms. Jackie said to Arnold,

"Can we do all the thanks and catching up in just a while, I've never been so exhausted, but before I collapse into your care, I have to make a phone call." She had been existing on adrenalin, and prescription drugs given to her by the skilled and caring staff of the Chinook, and was all but completely drained. She felt that if she could make just the one call which she knew she had to do, she could then pass the child into someone else's care, and she could sleep the sleep of a thousand years. She is shown into the commander's office and given a clear line. She knows the number by memory.

Jhiro is involved in a deep an emotional debate with himself, when, just after midnight, the phone rings in his headache room, he runs to it and answers,

"Hola, hola."

"Hi Casanova, how are you?"

"Where are you? How is you and Jhiro's child?"

"We are fine, we are in England."

"England, how is that possible?" She gave him a brief resume', including his great uncles sextant, a little celestial navigation, a telephone message to England, and a second, identical black Sikorsky C76 landing to collect her, with the help of some very brave and clever people.

"Jhiro cannot believe you do all this on your own."

"We English can be very resourceful, and of course I had a great deal of help."

"Yes yes you surprise Jhiro very much, you always too clever for Jhiro, what happen to us now, will you come back?"

"Jhiro listen to me, I must tell you, you have a beautiful daughter, she has your lovely brown eyes."

"Jhiro has child, what is her name?"

"Angelica, Anna-Maria, Valentina." Jhiro is silent, he thinks of his mother, his Grandmother, he tries to speak, but cannot,

"Jhiro listen, I'm very concerned at what you do…" He butts in,

"Jhiro he concerned too."

572

"Jhiro when I saw that underground laboratory I realised that you are a big part of the illegal drugs trade." He tries to interrupt, she continues,

"I know it is not illegal to grow coca leaf in your country, but you are the first link in a huge operation that supplies the United States with drugs."

"No no you don't understand…" She interrupts him,

"Jhiro if I am making huge monies because I am making gas for the Nazi's in the second world war, and I know that my gas, which is not illegal to make is being used to destroy the lives of many thousands of people, can I just pretend that I am making gas?"

"Ok, sometimes you are too clever for Jhiro, are you coming back?"

"I can't answer that right now, but I do want you to come here, so we can talk, on equal terms."

"Ok, Jhiro he comes, he needs a few days to make things good here, then he comes." She didn't doubt his sincerity, but thought that it would be dangerous for him to travel.

"Jhiro I fear for my safety if I return, and I fear for yours if you come to me, what can we do?"

"Jhiro he comes, there is nothing left for Jhiro here, he thought to fix all his problems was to buy more and more land, to make everyone happy, but now he knows it was wrong, Jhiro has to sell all his land, then no ones can push push push, but Jhiro's father and grandfather would not understand him, Jhiro he has had enough of push push push. He want to sit on the veranda with his beautiful woman and his daughter, Angelica Anna-Maria Valentina, Jhiro loves you both." With thousands of miles between them, Jackie is able to complete the third and last line of her note that she left for him, she tells him for the first time,

"I love you too Jhiro." He laughs.

"You make Jhiro very happy, Jhiro can go to his grave a happy man now."

"Jhiro, what do you mean?"

"Casanova means he is a happy man." It's now Jackie's turn to laugh.

"Goodbye for now Jhiro, I will call you again in a day or two."

"Yes goodbye for now, adios, Kiss my Angelica for me." He puts down the phone, he now feels that he is a contented, but condemned man.

Jackie finally gives in to her jaded and fatigued body, she hands Angelica to Simon, who gets a belated hug, slips into the back of Arnold's car, and quickly falls into a well deserved sleep. The car journey is another hours travelling to reach Arnold's Wiltshire home. The time passes for Jackie in a moment, both she and her tiny child are asleep for the hour. On arrival at the Elliot household Angelica requires immediate attention, once she is pacified the four of them come together in Arnold's study, behind closed curtains for a briefing. Jackie fires the first volley of what is to be an enlightening conversation for them all. After she has respectfully thanked her white knights in shining armour, she says,

"Thank you so much again, but did it have to be such a panic, it must have been an organisational nightmare, did I see both British and American troops?" Arnold responds,

"Indeed you did, and indeed it was," He continues, "There have been two aspects to this whole undertaking, first and foremost was your safe return, and secondly the need for swiftness and secrecy, you will need to brace yourself my dear for some sorry and sordid revelations." Jackie looked into the half squinted, tired, seventy year old watery eyes, of the man who had been her fathers confidant, she realised now that her cry for help had put this aged, kind gentleman under great strain. Arnold asked,

"Which would you prefer for entrée my dear, the logistics or the betrayal?"

"Well I've experienced much of what was a bold and daring feat of co-ordination, let's have the treachery, some of which I believe I've worked out for myself, how have you come by such knowledge?"

"Richard, your ex-fiancé put a letter together whilst he laid prone and apparently an easy target in the Los Angeles Hospital, he had been completely ensnared, beguiled, corrupted what have you, by your step mother Louise, it loathes me to use her name in your company or in this house." Jackie interrupts,

"I'd guessed that she was at the root of everything, let's call her the witch from now on shall we?"

"Very good my dear, she had seduced your Richard utterly, I'll show you his letter."

"Thank you, no, carry on Arnold."

"Well as you say the witch was at the root of everything, to remove both your dear father and yourself from the face of the earth, something obviously went awry with their plans in your case, the evidence of which thankfully sits before me now, you are alive and I never believed otherwise."

"Thank you Arnold, I think you were the only person who had not given up on me, I believe the reason I am alive is this." She held up a handful of her now less than glossy blond hair.

"It was this I think that made me more valuable alive, but when did this letter surface, and from who?"

"I received it just a week ago, a year to the date that Richard had penned it, he wrote it whilst he was in Los Angeles fearing that he had been betrayed by Lou…. by the witch, and he gave instructions to his solicitor that I should receive it exactly a year after its receipt, and it completely incriminates Louise, sorry the witch, can't quite get used to that, I must say your taking the corruption of Richard far more calmly than I imagined."

"I'd more or less figured his part out for myself, with hindsight a lot of things did not add up, I've had a great deal of time to ponder over the last year, that he was led astray for want of another term, is not a complete surprise."

"Led astray, is rather a soft term, the bastard sold you down the river."

"You don't know just how close you are to the truth."

"Anyway the police have a copy of the letter and as it also detailed the financial, or shall we say the pay off for a job completed, which is something the police informed me yesterday they have traced and confirmed, they are now ready to arrest both the witch and, this one I can easily get used to, the warlock. That bastard Gould initiated a boardroom move against me at the first opportunity."

"So when are they going to move against them?"

"It was agreed to do nothing until you were home and safe, until that letter arrived this was a rescue mission, but everything

575

changed when it became a criminal investigation, I must say the police have been marvellous. We have had a complete press blackout on the latest and might I say the most remarkably satisfactory twist in what they like to call the Forbes-Brewer Affair."

"How did you manage that?"

"Oh that's been the police's orchestration, like I said they have been exemplary, they went to the high-court and obtained an injunction on any further reference to Forbes-Brewer, they did not want their, or rather the Ministry of Defences' strategic planning, or tactics all across the tabloids. Are you OK to hear all this my dear, you do look a trifle worn out, wouldn't you rather sleep it all off first?"

"No please carry on, as long as my little precious here is quite, I'm OK, I will have a shower if I may in a while, but I'll catch up on my sleep when I get home, do you know when that will be?"

"Tomorrow, I asked the detective inspector to give you a day's grace, though no-one expected you to be with a child, born in a Chinook I understand?"

"Yes, that team were brilliant, whoever put them together left nothing to chance or speculation, I want to thank them."

"We are getting ahead of ourselves, the police could not afford to run the risk of the press blowing the whistle as this may endanger your rescue, by alerting the guilty two, who now have enormous resources at their disposal, so we've also got the press to thank in a way, I'm afraid you can't thank the team that brought you out, they were all S A S, Special Air Services, anonymous, all of them. They absorb hazards and risk, fearless bravery is all in a days work for those chaps."

"Of course I've just made the connection, you were one of those perilous daredevils a long time ago."

"Can't confirm or deny it, you know the drill."

"Come on Arnold, I know you have worked behind the scenes, pulling strings in all directions, I don't doubt."

"Lets say I have utilised some long established, and senior contacts in the defence ministry, who, once we had had an initial discussion bought into the idea, lock, stock and barrel, they very soon put together a management team to oversee the venture. The entire enterprise didn't require any degree of selling to the operational boys, they couldn't wait to get their teeth into it, took to it like a duck to water, splendid chaps. It was a co-operation with the U S, their satellite observations were invaluable, the place was being watched daily from a week after you left that wonderfully exciting and incredibly accurate, and informative message, bloody well done my dear, seems to me it wasn't just our lads who have been daring and resourceful."

"Flattery will get you everywhere, when do I get my million pounds?"

"Million pounds?"

"Yes, the magazine article I read, from which I used your dedicated number mentioned a million pounds."

"Good to see you have brought your sense of humour back with you, in fact you have saved me a million pounds, bless you girl, another reason to celebrate." They both laughed.

"I think I've had enough now Arnold, is there someone who can look after little Angelica for me, whilst I have a shower, and can I borrow some clothes from someone in your house, has your daughter Kimberly left anything here, she is about my size."

"Of course, not a problem my dear, I'll ask Mary to come up from the kitchen, she's had a hat full of offspring, she will be only too delighted to man the breach." He then did what all powerful men do when they require a solution, he picked up the nearest telephone. By the time Jackie had handed over Angelica, showered, chosen some slightly ill fitting clothes, breast fed the child, eaten a meal and fallen into a deep satisfying sleep, Jhiro was preparing to face his nemesis.

He had received a telephone call from one of his brothers, who spoke for the three of them, urging him to abandon his grapes, his folly. He was nauseated that even his brothers had abandoned him, he told himself they were weak and did not deserve to bear the name De Montaya De Val De Cabrera. Their family had owned the Vale de Cabrera for hundreds of years, he knew that he was the only one left with pride in the name and a sense of history, a sense of duty. He was in control of the Sikorsky as he flew to his meeting with the Medellin cartel, but little else. He would have been proud of his new blackbird had he not been preoccupied with the challenges ahead, he knew he would be outnumbered nine-to-one at the table, the cartel wanted control over his land, he had become superfluous. He sat when commanded to do so by The Jefe, without preliminaries he is asked again if he will tear up his vines, cut coffee production drastically and hand over the European woman once the child is born. He feels he has the upper hand in only one respect, everyone else in the room believes Jackie still to be pregnant and still to be at his family home. He pauses for a moment, and looks into every face in the room, there are people there he has known for many years, for decades, people his father knew, but it is clear to him that greed has left him without an ally. He knows what he must do, he must draw their fire towards himself to protect Jackie and Angelica. He slowly and carefully replies,

"No, no, no, no, my woman stays with me at my home, but you can buy my land, you can buy all my land." It was his last desperate bid to rid himself of his burdens, but he knew even this would not solve the problem of Jackie. His answer came from The Jefe.

"Jhiro we do not need to buy your land." Nine words that sealed his fate, they all knew it, he knew it. Jhiro stood up shook hands with everyone present, and left the room.

It was late afternoon when Jhiro flew himself back home, he flew with Carlos, his pilot, along a stretch of the Pacific shoreline, and the full length of the Vale de Cabrera. He ate his favourite meal of river clams and champagne, which he drank two bottles of. Behind him at Medellin a convoluted debate ensued as to their next and decisive course of action. They could not believe their good fortune when news came from one of their tame politicians who held a central governmental role that the United States Special Delta force had obtained coordinates as to the whereabouts of a jungle hideout, of what was believed to be a big player in the drug trafficking business. Did The Jefe want to use his power to protect or sacrifice, a decision was hastily taken, the meeting was over.

Jhiro's uncle, himself a member of the government, was taken to one side, he and his entire family were threatened with excoriation and mutilation, which was rapidly becoming the fashion of the day, this ensured that no protest or warnings were to come from his direction.

Jhiro spent the rest of the evening and night, for he did not sleep at all, sat with two bottles of Jackie's preferred wine, on the east-facing veranda, with him was the sextant that had betrayed him. When he saw the very first hint of daylight he stood up and threw the ancient implement from the terrace into the plants below. As the darkness of the night reseeded with the first rays of a new day, and the primary sounds began to filter from the trees, he sat facing eastward looking directly towards the early rising sun.

Jhiro knew they would come from the east. Jhiro knew they would come at dawn. Jhiro knew.

Jackie woke feeling fresher, but it had been a long evening and night, Angelica would not settle, and she was having trouble with breast feeding, she wasn't able to satisfy the ever hungry child, and her breast were extremely sore. Mary came to her aid at four o'clock in the morning, with a warm bottle of baby milk, as Jackie watched the child greedily suck on the bottle she felt pangs of jealousy that another woman could so easily make comfortable her own child, but thankfully sleep soon overcame her and all such thoughts vaporised. She showered again in the morning, and took an early breakfast in Arnold's comfortable old farmhouse kitchen. It was a cool late spring day in the west of England, she was ready for whatever the day would demand of her.

It was an hour's drive from Arnold's large Wiltshire home to St' Georges Hall, a rendezvous had been arranged with the police for eight am, two miles from St' Georges, the house had been under surveillance all night, and as yet Louise Forbes-Brewer had not been seen. Peter Gould had been arrested shortly after six am as he left the house, but he had been unable to communicate with the house post his arrest for conspiracy to commit murder, financial irregularities, and perverting the course of justice. He had said nothing and was waiting in a Devizes police cell, for the appearance of his lawyer, who contrary to Gould's belief had not yet been informed of his arrest, as the trap on operation resolution had not been fully sprung. Sir Arnold Elliot met with the detective Inspector in charge of the operation, who was himself delighted to meet Jackie, but somewhat surprised to see her cradling a very young infant. It was agreed that Jackie could walk the quarter mile curved driveway in front of the police cars, and also she could be present at the arrest, but could not say one word. It was pointed out to her that her request was highly irregular, it was agreed also, that so too were her circumstances. The cars halted at the two huge opposing stone pillars at the entrance to St' Georges Hall. On stepping out of the car Jackie asked,

"Who are all those people on the front lawns?"

"They are the television production crew, who are making that programme, you know, Marsden Manor, I believe it's called." Replied Detective Inspector Lewenden. Jackie responded,

"Sorry, no I don't, I haven't caught much television lately." A polite laughter went through their company. As she walked the all too familiar driveway, which was now once again resplendent with early rhododendron blossom, just as it had been the day she left for America, the anger that had fuelled her whilst the Hall had passed through four full seasons subsided, her overwhelming emotions were those of protection for her fragile daughter, now asleep in her arms, and sadness that the first of the next generation of the family would never know her patient and caring grandparents. Thoughts of her mother and father, and Jhiro were both uncontrollable and overpowering. She stood stock still for a moment and from somewhere deep in her psyche she gained the fortitude necessary to put one foot in front of the other. She turned the last of the long sweeping left hand bend in the drive, the full façade of the familiar white stonework of her family home came into view, her joy at seeing the magnificent structure was tempered with resentment for both its occupier and the two dozen or so people and all their paraphernalia, who were milling around the front lawn. She thought to herself she would have to look closely at their contract, for what had become one of her fathers preferred terms, a loophole, it was to become the first of many task on her to do list. She approached the door with four marked police cars behind her, and Arnold's Rolls-Royce to the rear, which were all contributing to a background noise of crunching gravel that had a furious director shouting,

"Cut, cut, cut who the hell is…….." He cut his exasperation short, when he saw such a collection of police, he was an intelligent man who had made a very comfortable living being guided by his instincts, he indicated to both his camera and rifle mike operators that they should keep running and aim at the front door of the hall, there was a potential situation here that could prove to be interesting and possible profitable.

Just short of the door Jackie paused and was overtaken by three police officers, two male, and one female. The main bell in the hallway sounded its familiar tone, within moments Roddy, the butler opened the door he was both surprised to see the doorway filled with uniformed officers and shocked and delighted to see Jacqueline standing to the right. He nodded and smiled openly in her direction, he was overjoyed, but remained in control, he quickly responded to the request from the police to fetch Mrs Louise Forbes-Brewer to the door. Louise came after just a few moments saying,

"What is it now, are you all part of the filming, it really is too much, all these interruptions." Police sergeant Nicholas West said the following words; (which were later broadcast on all television news bulletins as their prime item, until the middle of the next day when a bomb went off in the Lebanon killing one hundred and sixty two people, relegating police sergeant West to second spot),

"Louise Forbes-Brewer I am arresting you for conspiracy to commit murder, financial irregularities and perverting the course of justice, you are not obliged to say anything, but any thing you do say may be taking down and used in evidence against you in a court of law, have you anything to say before we handcuff you and put you in a police vehicle?" Louise opened her mouth to speak, still thinking that this was a theatrical stunt by the film crew, she then glanced to her right and focused on Jacqueline and her small child, Jackie was looking directly into her eyes with a deep contempt and loathing, with tears running down her cheeks, she knew this evil woman was responsible for the horrendous murder of her father. Louise's world was instantaneously and consummately shattered. Her mouth closed, she knew the game was up, she had finally met her equal, she said nothing and left the house handcuffed and flanked by two uniformed officers. The director of the film crew would be content with his bonus.

581

Jackie walked into the doorway of her home, hugged Roddy and said to him,

"Roddy I want you to meet the first of the next generation of Forbes-Brewers. Angelica Anna-Maria Valentina, she, like her mother has come home to stay, things will be rapidly going back to normal here Roddy, and it is so good to see you and this house."

"Miss Jacqueline I am as delighted to see you as I am sure you are to be home, can I get you anything?"

"Yes please Roddy a cup of good old fashioned English tea, oh and the contract that St' Georges signed with those people on the front lawn."

"I'd be delighted to do both, Miss Jacqueline."

"Oh and Roddy, the door to my right is it still my fathers study?"

"Indeed Miss, indeed it is." She opened the study door, this room had always been the Halls inner sanctum, the very embodiment of her father and all that he was. She was horrified to see that not only was there a television in the room but that it was turned on, showing a news item from the Middle-East. She put Jhiro's favourite taza on her father's desk and picked up the remote control, to kill the image. As she aims the device toward the television the news coverage switches to another item, she hears; 'there has been a big success against the Medellin drug cartel in Colombia. We hand over to our U S studio and CBS News, she turns the volume up instead of off. She hears a woman's voice talking over a picture of a burning building, and to the top left of the screen, is an out of date police mug shot picture of the father of her child.

"Our reporter Dan Jackson is in Colombia and has just filled this report;"

"In the early hours of this morning U S Delta Force troops using Apache helicopter gun ships carried out operation gunpoint, they are claiming that they have hit at the very heart of the Medellin drug cartel, you can see now on the screen pictures shot at four am eastern seaboard time, of the burning compound that U S intelligence is telling us is the former fortress style home of Jhiro de Montaya, one of the powerful leaders of the Medellin cartel."

Jackie is dumbstruck, she stares at the screen open mouthed. The television is showing many burning buildings, Jackie recognises the school and medi-center, the camera then swings left to reveal the main house, which is half destroyed. Part of the fourth floor is left precariously hanging in the air, she then gasps as she witnesses a huge slab of the flat roof fall, the chunk of concrete is then followed by the Steinway piano and Jhiro's helicopter. The picture then changes to a colossal pile of burning rubble and the commentary continues,

"You are now viewing live footage, the site has now been declared safe by special US forces. What you are seeing is the remains of the four-storey building that was believed to be the home of one of Colombia's most senior drug barons. In fact the delta Force unit that carried out this dangerous operation, lost one Apache helicopter and its compliment of four crew in the raid, shot down by what is believed to be Russian ground to air missiles. It is they say conclusive proof, if proof were needed that this heavily armed compound was indeed at the very centre of the billion dollar cocaine trafficking business." Holding one ear piece he continues, "And I can now add that it has just been confirmed by US Special Forces that the body of Jhiro de Montaya, a very dangerous and powerful man, and one of the notorious Medellin cartels leaders, has been recovered. So in all a very successful and bloody day in the long battle to keep illegal drugs off the streets of America, but lets not forget those four brave young men who gave their lives to make the world a safer place for us all to live in, and to wrap up this report it is believed that US intelligence gained knowledge of the whereabouts of this hidden jungle compound through its vast and ongoing surveillance operation and help from its closest allies, the British. This is Dan Jackson, reporting for CBS News from Bogotá, Colombia."

The screen then switches to homespun news, Jackie silences the TV, and collapses into her father's chair. Tears flow for her former gaoler whom she grew to love, they flow freely and combine with those for her parents. She cries for Jhiro, for his family, his history and the many people who relied upon him, who are now dead, injured or homeless, she cries for the wines, the art, the sextant, and Jhiro's vines. She picks up Jhiro's taza and holds it to her face, she cannot accept that everything he was is gone, she weeps for an undeclared love that is lost, she weeps for the father of her child, who is lost.

Angelica Anna-Maria Valentina stirs and demands her attention.

CESE TEMPORAL

DAY TEN (CONTINUED)

LIZ

I close the volume in reflective mood and recall a very different time in my life and for just a moment Jayne is with me again.

The last drive home is a quiet one, there is very little traffic, I am able to reflect on our decision in court today, do I have any doubt that we got it right, just one or two percent. Even if Michael did have sex with Holly a week before she was sixteen, I'm still happy with our decision, a week later he could have done it without repercussion, he is not a malicious person or a sexual predator, just a very simple one, I wish him good luck, as do I Joyce and Richard tonight. I pick up two rabbits on the journey home, one for the pot and one for the feeder, its about time the flush of red kites up country started to show themselves here on a regular basis, though I suspect that we still have an entrenched ignorant few in the game keeping fraternity, who are intent on their destruction and who selfishly deny a great deal of pleasure to thousands of others.

Its time to transfer my thoughts and energies back home, I tuck the two wedding rings in my pockets, I can't wait to see Liz's face, I grin all the way home, I never wanted a ring before, always thought them a bit effeminate and dangerous on site. I know its always been a bit of a disappointment to Liz that I don't wear one, she still has the shell one that I bought from the souvenir shop in Kings Park, Western Australia, so I plan to put it right this weekend, take her out for dinner tomorrow, I'll pull the rings out of the bag at the table, do it in style, like they do in the movies.

As I pull in the driveway I'm feeling relaxed and satisfied, smug even, to use one of my favourite terms, I turn on my phone, a stored message lights up, its from Claire, 'Hi just keeping my promise, thanks again 4 the 40 quid, I needed it, c u Sunday, lul xxx'. As I walk to the house I make myself mental notes, must phone Barbara, I must phone my mother to talk about France, I must ring Richard tomorrow to find out how he gets on tonight. I approach the door feeling good about the world around me, so smug am I that I have forgotten what the world does to me when I'm feeling this good. I open the door, Liz is in the kitchen with her back to me, still a sight for sore eyes,

"Hi, how's things, we let him go free." My hands are in my pockets each one fingering a small velvet box. Emma is nowhere to be seen, or heard, without looking at me Liz replies,

"Hi, you let who go?"

"Oh the guy on trial, I'll tell you about it one day, but now I want to talk about us, I want us to have a bit of what the modern world calls quality time, let's put the Emma near miss behind us, get Claire back, get Jean Pierre underground, and chill out, book this skiing trip at Christmas, my hand will be good by then." Slowly she turns to face me, her eyes are beginning to well up, to fill with tears, I move toward her, and put my arms out to hug her, let her have her cry. She backs off, and puts her hands out flat toward me, but keeps her eyes focused on mine. She is blinking fast, there's something more here, more than just a shit day, more than Jean Pierre, more even than Emma's car wreck, there is something terrible, something that is going to take us deeper than we've ever been before. The look in her eyes is frightening me, I cannot hold her gaze.

"Jude, look at me." I focus on one of the dogs to deny the situation, my hands go back into my pockets to gain solace, to buy me an instant of comfort, by gripping the two boxed rings.

"Jude look at me." Eventually I do, she has the look of a condemned person, I look into her eyes but I feel I may be seeing her for the last time, this feeling is dreadful, it is all consuming. She says slowly and deliberately,

"Jude you haven't asked me if there's any post." We are staring into each others eyes, both of us with tears falling down our cheeks, I can hardly speak, I feel like Michael must have felt earlier, I squeak,

"Any post?"

"Yes, one came yesterday, I had to see an oncologist today." I open my mouth to speak, but for the first time in my life it is not engaged to my brain, I produce no sound, we hold each others gaze for perhaps a half minute, tears flow freely. It is Liz who breaks the silence.

"Jude I'm so sorry, I have breast cancer."

THE END

The Author lives in the far South West of Cornwall with his wife, Kim, and their cairn terrier, Maisie.

He is a volunteer Coast Watch Officer at Cape Cornwall for the National Coastwatch Institution www.nci.org.uk and a member of the much loved Cape Cornwall Singers www.capecornwallsingers.co.uk

If you have a comment on this book, please send to hughthomas.redumbrella@gmail.com

.